STEPHEN

KING'S

THE

DARK TOWER

A CONCORDANCE

VOLUME II

Robin Furth

SCRIBNER

New York   London   Toronto   Sydney

SCRIBNER
1230 Avenue of the Americas
New York, NY 10020

Copyright © 2005 by Robin Furth

SCRIBNER and design are trademarks of Macmillan Library Reference USA, Inc.,
used under license by Simon & Schuster, the publisher of this work.

For information about special discounts for bulk purchases,
please contact Simon & Schuster Special Sales:
1-800-465-6798 or business@simonandschuster.com

DESIGNED BY ERICH HOBBING

Text set in Sabon

Manufactured in the United States of America

1   3   5   7   9   10   8   6   4   2

Library of Congress Control Number: 2003054272

ISBN 0-7432-5208-X

FOR MARK

FOR STEVE

FOR ROLAND

Commala-come-come,
Here's the twin of Volume I!

ACKNOWLEDGMENTS

It takes many people to transform a manuscript into a book. I would like to thank the talented and hardworking people whose time, labor, and dedication helped to make this *Concordance* a reality. Here's a heartfelt thanks to Ralph Vicinanza, my agent; Eben Weiss and the people at Ralph Vicinanza Ltd.; Brant Rumble (my U.S. editor) and all the folks at Scribner; Philippa Pride (my U.K. editor) and all the folks at Hodder and Stoughton; Marsha DeFilippo and Julie Eugley, for years of help and support; my husband, Mark, for living with me through all of this; and Burt Hatlen, who believed in me enough to recommend me for my job as Stephen King's research assistant. Finally, I'd like to give an extrahearty thanks to Stephen King, who had faith in a struggling writer living in a secondhand trailer in the Maine woods.

CONTENTS

ABBREVIATIONS AND TEXT GUIDE

ABBREVIATIONS USED FOR PRIMARY TEXTS BY STEPHEN KING

I: *The Gunslinger.* 1982. New York: Plume-Penguin, 1988.

IR: *The Gunslinger.* 2003 (revised edition). New York: Plume-Penguin, 2003.

II: *The Drawing of the Three.* 1987. New York: Plume-Penguin, 1989.

III: *The Waste Lands.* 1991. New York: Plume-Penguin, 1993.

IV: *Wizard and Glass.* New York: Plume-Penguin, 1997.

V: *Wolves of the Calla.* New Hampshire: Donald M. Grant in association with Scribner, 2003.

VI: *Song of Susannah.* New Hampshire: Donald M. Grant in association with Scribner, 2004.

VII: *The Dark Tower.* New Hampshire: Donald M. Grant in association with Scribner, 2004.

E: "The Little Sisters of Eluria." *Everything's Eventual: 14 Dark Tales.* New York: Scribner, 2002.

SECONDARY TEXTS BY STEPHEN KING

Bag of Bones. New York: Scribner, 1998.

Desperation. New York: Viking-Penguin, 1996.

"Everything's Eventual." *Everything's Eventual: 14 Dark Tales.* New York: Scribner, 2002.

The Eyes of the Dragon. New York: Viking-Penguin, 1984.

Insomnia. New York: Viking-Penguin, 1994.

It. New York: Viking-Penguin, 1986.

"Low Men in Yellow Coats." *Hearts in Atlantis.* New York: Scribner, 1999.

"The Mist." *Skeleton Crew.* New York: Putnam, 1985.

The Regulators (Stephen King as Richard Bachman). New York: Viking-Penguin, 1996.

'Salem's Lot. New York: Doubleday, 1975.

The Stand. New York: Doubleday, 1978.

SECONDARY TEXTS BY STEPHEN KING AND PETER STRAUB

Black House. New York: Random House, 2001.
The Talisman. New York: Viking-Penguin, 1984.

PLEASE NOTE

1. Page references are as follows:
   V:199
   (volume):(page number)
2. Although Mid-World was the name of a specific historical kingdom, Stephen King also uses this term when he needs to refer (in general terms) to Roland's version of earth. I have followed this practice.
3. In volume I of this *Concordance,* I often capitalized the term *Our World.* In the last three books of the series, we find out that there are many, many versions of our world, so I no longer use capitals. However, when I refer specifically to the world in which Stephen King writes his novels (and where I'm fairly certain you and I are reading them), I use the term *Keystone Earth.*

Commala, come-come,
Journey's almost done . . .

NORTH CENTRAL POSITRONICS LTD.

MAXIMUM SECURITY

verbal entry code required

COMMALA

(THE RICE SONG)

Song and Dance in Honor of Lady Oriza, Lady of the Rice

SINGER/DANCER: Do I not give you joy from my joy, and the water I
carried with the strength of my arm and my heart?
CHORUS: Give you to eat of the green-crop.
SINGER/DANCER: Give you joy of the rice.
CHORUS: Come! . . . Come! . . . Come!

*Come-come-commala
Rice come a-falla
I-sisser 'ay-a-bralla
Dey come a-folla
Down come-a rivva
Or-i-za we kivva
Rice be a green-o
See what we seen-o
Seen-o the green-o
Come-come-commala!*

*Come-come-commala
Rice come a-falla
Deep inna walla
Grass come-commala
Under the sky-o
Grass green n high-o
Girl n her fella
Lie down togetha
They slippy 'ay slide-o
Under 'ay sky-o
Come-come-commala
Rice come a-falla!*

CHORUS: COMMALA!

A CONCORDANCE

VOLUME II

INTRODUCTION:
FOUR CHARACTERS
(AND A BUMBLER) IN SEARCH OF
AN AUTHOR: OR, A FEW REFLECTIONS
ON THE SIMILARITIES BETWEEN
FICTION AND REALITY

Spoiler's Warning: This Concordance *keeps no secrets. Read it only after you have finished all seven of the Dark Tower books.*

For those of us who have traveled with Roland Deschain from the wastes of the Mohaine Desert to the Castle of the Crimson King and then beyond, to the farthest reaches of End-World, the journey has been a long one, say thankya. For many Constant Readers, it has taken over twenty years; for sai King, the travels have spanned more than thirty. And for Roland, who is able to leap over whole generations in pursuit of his quarry and his quest, the pilgrimage has lasted more than three hundred.[1] Yet as Eddie Dean points out at the beginning of *Wolves of the Calla,* time is elastic. Despite what we've been told about the accuracy of clocks, no two sixty-second periods are ever identical. Although a minute may move like dried mud while we're waiting or when we're bored, it speeds to the point of invisibility when we're in the throes of change. And what is a novel but a tale of transformation and discovery?

Over the course of the Dark Tower series, we witness tremendous transformation, both in our characters' natures and in the parameters of their quest. What began, in *The Gunslinger,* as the story of one man's obsessive pursuit of a goal becomes, in the final three books of our story, a tale of personal, and universal, redemption. By the time we reach the final page of our saga, we have witnessed so much. Roland, once a lone traveler willing to sacrifice anything and anyone to the achievement of his end, has drawn three companions to him[2] and has trained

---

1. For an explanation, see my time line, listed in Appendix II.

2. The three companions are Eddie, Susannah, and Jake. Roland's fourth companion is the billy-bumbler Oy. Although Oy doesn't train to be a gunslinger, he is an important member of Roland's ka-tet.

them to be gunslingers. With his new tet-mates, Roland discovers the Bear-Turtle Beam and follows it to the haunted regions of End-World, where the Dark Tower sits. Along the Path of the Beam, the bonds of khef, which unite his new ka-tet, are tested and prove to be strong. And Roland, always an emotionally reticent man, rediscovers his ability to trust and to love. With this newfound knowledge, he can finally admit, and repent of, all of his previous betrayals.

In many ways, the Dark Tower series falls into two parts: the adventures that Roland and his companions have in Mid-World (all of which were written before Stephen King's accident in 1999) and those that take place in the borderlands and End-World, which were penned after King began to recover from the accident that almost claimed his life. The adventures our tet have in both halves of their tale are dramatic, but the nature of the changes they undergo as a result are quite different. In the first four Tower books, the transformations our tet experiences are, in large part, personal.[3] As well as bonding as a group, united in their vision of one day reaching the Dark Tower, each member has to battle his or her own demons. Eddie overcomes heroin addiction. Susannah's dual personalities of Detta and Odetta merge into a unified whole. Jake abandons his lonely life in New York to join his adopted father's quest, and Roland, who up until this point has been a self-obsessed loner, learns to value his tet as highly as he values his search for the linchpin of existence.[4]

Yet if the first four Dark Tower books are about the khef[5] that binds self to ka-tet, in the final three novels, the responsibilities of khef ripple outward, encompassing not just the debt the individual owes to his tet-mates but the responsibilities each of us has to the greater world—or, in the case of the Dark Tower series, to the multiple worlds.

In the final three books of the Dark Tower series, Roland and his friends extend the scope of their quest. While keeping their ultimate goal in mind, they set out to accomplish a number of specific tasks that, when taken together, simultaneously halt the erosion of the Beams, frustrate the apocalyptic plans of the Crimson King, and work for the common good. In *Wolves of the Calla*, they destroy the robotic, green-cloaked horsemen who have been stealing children

---

3. For a more detailed discussion about the first four books of the Dark Tower series, see *Stephen King's The Dark Tower: A Concordance, Volume I*.

4. As Constant Readers will remember, in *The Gunslinger*, Roland allowed Jake to tumble into the abyss below the Cyclopean Mountains so that he could pursue the Man in Black. However, by the time he reaches the city of Lud in *The Waste Lands*, Roland puts his own life in danger to save Jake from the child-hungry gang of Grays.

5. The High Speech word *khef* means many different things, including water, birth, and life force. It implies all that is essential to existence. Khef is both individual and collective; it is the web that binds a ka-tet. Those who share khef share thoughts. Their destinies are linked, as are their life forces. Behind the multiple meanings of this term lies a philosophy of interconnectedness, a sense that all individuals, all events, are part of a greater pattern or plan. Our fates, for good or dis, are a result of both our own and our shared khef.

from Mid-World's borderlands for more than six generations.[6] By doing so, they not only liberate the people of the Callas but undermine the efficiency of the Breakers—those prisoners of the Crimson King who have been forced to erode the Beams with the equivalent of psychic battery acid. In *Song of Susannah,* Jake and Callahan manage to put Black Thirteen, the most evil of Maerlyn's magic balls, out of commission. With the help of John Cullum (their Stoneham, Maine, *dan-tete*), Roland and Eddie begin to lay plans for the Tet Corporation, a company created to undermine the powers of the evil Sombra Corporation and to protect both the wild Rose, found in New York City's Vacant Lot, and our kas-ka Gan, Stephen King, creator of our tale.[7]

By accomplishing these tasks, our tet remains true to the Way of Eld, which demands that gunslingers protect the weak and vulnerable from those who would oppress or exploit them. Yet in defending the White against the ever-encroaching tide of the Outer Dark, our tet (like our author) comes under the shadow of ka-shume, the shadow of death.[8] In *The Dark Tower,* Roland and his friends destroy the Devar-Toi, or Breaker prison, and free the Breakers.[9] They halt the erosion of the Beams (which we are assured will regenerate), but Eddie Dean pays for this victory with his life. Not long after, when Roland and Jake travel to the year 1999 so that they can save their maker, Stephen King, from his predetermined collision with a Dodge minivan, Jake Chambers heaves his last breath. It seems that ka demands a life for a life, and though Stephen King survives his terrible accident, Jake does not.

And it is here, on Slab City Hill in Lovell, Maine, by the prostrate and profoundly injured body of our kas-ka Gan, and by the side of our gunslinger Roland, who grieves over the corpse of his adopted son, that I would like to pause. It is not a comfortable place to be—either for sai King, who lies bleeding in a ditch, or for us, who are unable to help—but it is an important place. Like Detta Walker's *Drawers,* this little patch of road in the year 1999 (when the ka of our world and the ka of Roland's world are united) is a place of power. It is a doorway between the rational and irrational worlds, a place where the veil is at its thinnest. And it is in this place where life and death meet that Roland accomplishes something worth discussing. By sacrificing what he loves above all else in order to save the life of the man who created his universe—a man who must live if the story of the Dark Tower is to exist in any world—Roland does what we assume is impossible. He stops the wheel of ka and alters its path.

6. The Wolves steal one of every pair of prepubescent twins born in the Callas so that their masters in Thunderclap can extract the chemical that causes twin-telepathy. This chemical is then fed—in pill form—to the Breakers. (It increases their psychic abilities.) Unfortunately, once this chemical is removed from a child's brain, the child is roont, or ruined.

7. As Constant Readers all know, on Keystone Earth, the Dark Tower takes the form of a magical wild rose.

8. Ka-shume is the price one pays for altering ka, or the course of destiny.

9. Unfortunately, many of the Breakers don't appreciate this newfound freedom.

Throughout the final three books of the Dark Tower series, we are told that, in the Keystone World we inhabit, there are no do-overs. Once an event has taken place, it cannot be changed. Yet it seems that this "truth" is not necessarily true. At the end of *Song of Susannah*, we are given Stephen King's obituary—ostensibly taken from the *Portland Sunday Telegram*—which states that King died at 6:02 PM on Saturday, June 20, at Northern Cumberland Memorial Hospital in Bridgton, Maine. Yet King didn't die. As we all know, he survived (albeit with terrible injuries) and returned to his computer keyboard to finish the last three books of his Dark Tower saga. On one level of the Tower, King's life was saved by paramedics and doctors, and that most fickle of mistresses, Lady Luck. But on another level, the one that we all inhabit when our rational minds switch off and our imaginations wake up, Stephen King was saved by his characters.

When I was nineteen, I read a play by the Italian playwright Luigi Pirandello. The play was called *Six Characters in Search of an Author*. In it, six characters—all of whom have been abandoned by their original creator—go in search of a new person to pen their story. The person they turn to is a theater manager, already in the process of staging a different play. At first, the theater manager thinks these characters are either mad or joking, but as their traumatic story begins to unfold, he finds himself drawn into it. But no matter how the new playwright (for that is what he becomes) tries to bend the plot or alter the characters' temperaments, he can't. You see, the story already exists, from beginning to end, and the characters who live within its unwritten pages stubbornly hold on to their unique identities. What they want, and what they demand, is a writer who is willing to stand and be true—a person able to *facilitate* their tale and give it life, tragic as that tale turns out to be.

A number of years ago, in a writers' magazine, I read a firsthand account of an author's experience creating a character, and that, too, has remained with me. The author of the article (who was writing for an audience of apprentice authors) told of her experience with a character she called Bird. And though I lost the article long ago (which, like so many things in my life, I put in a place that at the time I had deemed "safe"), I still remember Bird. You see, Bird saved his author's life.

The story began when the author in question received a grant to finish her novel. She and her husband went to a remote cottage where the isolation and quiet would be perfect for the task at hand. However, it was winter, the cottage was old and cold, and the journey had been long. The woman and her husband shut the door and windows, turned on the stove, and decided to take a nap.

What felt like hours later, the writer was roused by Bird shaking her. Groggily, she opened her eyes and there was her character, standing by the bed. Bird put his hands by his throat. "I can't breathe!" he said. And then suddenly, the author realized what had happened. The old cottage was much less drafty than it had originally seemed, and the fire had eaten almost all of the oxygen. She and her husband, unconscious beside her, were asphyxiating.

Almost unable to move, the writer rolled onto the floor, crawled to the door, and managed to push it open. Fresh winter air wafted into the room, and both she and her husband survived. But only because of Bird. The explanation this author gave for her paranormal experience was this—she hadn't finished telling Bird's story yet, and Bird couldn't survive without the umbilical cord of thought which connected them. In order to live, Bird needed *her* to live, and Bird was determined to exist in the world. Self-serving heroism? Perhaps. But does that lessen the act's importance? Definitely not. Especially as far as the author is concerned.

I once read an article about the early-twentieth-century French explorer, Alexandra David-Neel. Evidently, while she studied with monks in Tibet, she learned how to create thought-forms by focused concentration. These thought-forms, which spring from the imagination of the creator, eventually gain an independent existence and can even (if they are especially powerful) become visible to other people. For me, characters are a kind of thought-form. An author creates them (or facilitates their passage into our world), but then the characters exist in the minds of many. They can live well beyond the lifespan of their creators; they can even exist independently of the book or story they originally inhabited. Think of Hamlet or Heathcliff or Dracula. Or of Roland Deschain.

There are some Dark Tower fans out there (including some very close to my heart), who like it when Stephen King appears in his films, but who are not comfortable with him entering his fiction. The reason? When King enters his own stories and his characters are shown to be just characters, it breaks the spell. When you think about it, such a reaction—even among devoted Tower junkies—isn't so surprising. Given the world we are expected to live in, where fact is supposed to be fact and fiction is supposed to be fiction, the two of them as separate as our waking lives and our dreaming lives, the events that take place in the final two books of the Dark Tower cycle are bound to confound us. The traditional *suspension of disbelief,* which we put on like a thinking cap whenever we sit down to read a fantasy adventure of any kind, isn't enough anymore. We have to allow the magic of *that* world—the world of the book—into *our* world, where we must earn a living, pay rent, eat, argue, and worry. In other words, those barriers we erect for our self-protection—barriers which separate our imaginative lives from our mundane ones—begin to break down. And if we're not careful, the guardrails of the rationalist, no-nonsense universe begin to snake out of control. And if those rails disappear, then we can free-fall into todash space, that no-place between worlds where monsters lurk.

As normal, functioning adults, we can't believe in surreal experiences any more than we can maintain that clapping our hands will bring Tinkerbell back to life. After all, we left all that behind us in grade school. Or did we?

For me, the scenes where Stephen King's characters enter his life, *and change it,* are very powerful. They are powerful because they express the secret relationship King has with his creations. As every writer knows, writing is a two-way street. We may give birth to our characters, but our characters also change us. When Steve King writes about Eddie and Roland visiting him in Bridgton and then, many years later, Roland and Jake coming to him in his hour of deepest need, he is spinning a yarn, but he is also sharing with us the secret story that, in some deep part of his mind, he is telling himself. For the members of Roland's ka-tet, saving Stephen King is essential. But for Stephen King, his characters call him back from the void. Their need explains his survival. Some people have guardian angels. Authors have characters. This may be a strange thing to say, but all of you out there who write know it's true.

I suppose I have always believed that reality is a subjective affair. Of course, there are always events outside ourselves that are concrete and real, and that—small as we are—we cannot change. Yet in the back of our heads, there is a voice that takes our experience in the world and weaves a story from it, for good or dis. And I suppose that it is this doorway, the doorway of the imagination, that is the ultimate Door to Anywhere. It gives us hope when there seems to be no hope, and it allows us to enter worlds that our rationalist culture tells us are unreal. I don't know about you, but I'm certainly glad the rationalists are wrong.

And so, my fellow Constant Readers, on this note, I will leave you. During my 1,396 days living and working in Mid-World,[10] I, too, have changed. But that's the nature of both life and fiction, isn't it? Ka turns, and the world moves on. If we're lucky, we move on with it.

Cam-a-cam-mal,
Pria-toi,
Gan delah.
(White Over Red,
Thus Gan Wills Ever.)

I wish you well.

Robin of the Calvins
January 26, 2005
Tell Gan Thankya.

---

10. 1+3+9+6=19. Are you surprised?

CHARACTERS,[1] MAGICAL OBJECTS, MAGICAL FORCES

There's only three boxes to a man. . . . Best and highest is the head, with all the head's ideas and dreams. Next is the heart, with all our feelings of love and sadness and joy and happiness. . . . In the last box is all what we'd call low-commala: have a fuck, take a shit, maybe want to do someone a meanness for no reason . . .

V:630–31

A

AARON JAFFORDS
See JAFFORDS, AARON

ABAGAIL, MOTHER
In the alternative version of KANSAS which our tet traveled through in *Wizard and Glass,* JAKE CHAMBERS found a note tucked under a camper windshield. The note read, "The old woman from the dreams is in Nebraska. Her name is Abagail." Although our tet never meets this 108-year-old black woman, her path is nevertheless linked to Roland's. In STEPHEN KING's novel *The Stand,* this daughter of a former slave is a Warrior of the WHITE, and her archenemy is the evil RANDALL FLAGG.

In *Song of Susannah,* we discover that Mother Abagail's world is definitely linked to Roland's. Both the Red Death (the plague which devastated the END-WORLD town of FEDIC) and the superflu (the disease which wiped out 99 percent of the people in Abagail's version of earth) are both physical manifestations of a metaphysical illness. As the GREAT OLD ONES' technology fails and the mechanical BEAMS collapse, such viruses and plagues are breaking out on many levels of the TOWER.
VI:405

---

1. As all Constant Readers know, the Dark Tower books contain many references to political and cultural figures from our world. Unless these figures play a central part in the narrative, they have been relegated to Appendix V.

ABRAHAM, DAUGHTER OF
See TASSENBAUM, IRENE

ADAMS, DIEGO
See CALLA BRYN STURGIS CHARACTERS: RANCHERS

ADAMS, RICHARD
See GUARDIANS OF THE BEAM: SHARDIK

ADAMS, SAREY
See ORIZA, SISTERS OF

AFFILIATION
The Affiliation was the name given to the network of political and military alliances that united MID-WORLD's baronies during Roland's youth. (See *Stephen King's The Dark Tower: A Concordance, Volume I.*) By the time Roland reached adulthood, the Affiliation was in tatters, due in large part to the bloody rebellions and terrible betrayals staged by THE GOOD MAN (JOHN FARSON) and his followers.

The Affiliation—which played such a large part in *Wizard and Glass*—does not figure directly in the final three books of the Dark Tower series. However, we can guess that the gunslingers who fought beside Roland in the final battle of JERICHO HILL were all that remained of the Affiliation's forces. *For page references, see* DEMULLET'S COLUMN.

AIDAN
See TET CORPORATION: FOUNDING FATHERS: CULLUM, JOHN

ALAIN JOHNS
See JOHNS, ALAIN

ALBRECHT
See VAMPIRES: TYPE THREE

ALEXANDER, BEN
See CAN-TOI

ALIA (NURSE)
See TAHEEN: RAT-HEADED TAHEEN

ALICE OF TULL (ALLIE)
See TULL CHARACTERS

ALLGOOD, CUTHBERT (ARTHUR HEATH)

Cuthbert Allgood was Roland's beloved—if sometimes irritating—childhood friend. (See *Stephen King's The Dark Tower: A Concordance, Volume I*.) Although possessed of an anarchic sense of humor and a deep-seated belief in human dignity, tall, dark-haired Cuthbert was every inch a gunslinger. At age eleven, he and Roland informed upon the traitorous cook HAX and then scattered bread crumbs beneath his feet as he swung upon the gallows tree. Under the name Arthur Heath, he and another gunslinger-in-training friend ALAIN JOHNS accompanied Roland on his dangerous MEJIS adventure, which figured so prominently in *Wizard and Glass*.

Long before EDDIE DEAN took the job of being Roland Deschain's wise-cracking mouthpiece, thin, dark-haired Cuthbert held that position. In fact, in *Song of Susannah* we find out that Eddie and Bert—both considered by Roland to be *ka-mais,* or ka's fools—are actually twins. The two of them appeared to seven-year-old STEPHEN KING, who was on punishment duty in his uncle's barn. They saved him from the CRIMSON KING (who appeared in the form of tiny red spiders) and won him over to the cause of the WHITE.

Roland once predicted that Bert would die laughing, and so he did, on the battlefield of JERICHO HILL. Still holding the HORN OF ELD, the horn of Roland's fathers, a laughing but badly wounded Bert accompanied his friend in a final, suicidal charge against the legions of GRISSOM'S MEN. Unlucky Cuthbert was shot through the eye by RUDIN FILARO (another manifestation of Roland's longtime nemesis, WALTER) and entered the clearing at the end of the path at the much too young age of twenty-four. The Horn of Eld tumbled into the dust and Roland, perhaps out of grief, did not bother to retrieve it, a decision which he regrets greatly by the time he reaches the TOWER.

V:59, V:78, V:79, V:84, V:85, V:164, V:170–72, V:182, V:218, V:240, V:347 *(Jericho Hill),* V:400 *(indirect),* V:410, V:590, VI:16 *(experienced a beamquake),* VI:132 *(and Eddie),* VI:292, VI:293, VII:118, VII:174 *(killed by an arrow through his eye, shot by Rudin Filaro),* VII:219 *(Arthur Heath),* VII:220, VII:270, VII:404, VII:465, VII:497, VII:552, VII:585, VII:695, VII:758, VII:762, VII:801, VII:819, VII:825, VII:829
ALLGOOD, ROBERT (CUTHBERT'S FATHER): V:85 *(father),* V:590 *(indirect)*
ROOK'S SKULL: V:170

ALLGOOD, ROBERT
See ALLGOOD, CUTHBERT

AM
See PRIM

ANDERSON, DELBERT
See DEAN, SUSANNAH: ODETTA HOLMES AND THE CIVIL RIGHTS MOVEMENT: ODETTA'S "MOVEMENT" ASSOCIATES

ANDERSON, JUSTINE
See MAINE CHARACTERS: TOOTHAKER, ELVIRA

ANDOLINI, CLAUDIO
See BALAZAR, ENRICO: BALAZAR'S MEN

ANDOLINI, JACK
See BALAZAR, ENRICO: BALAZAR'S MEN

ANDREW (ANDREW FEENY)
See DEAN, SUSANNAH: ODETTA HOLMES'S ASSOCIATES

ANDREW (LOW MAN IN TUX)
See CAN-TOI

ANDRUS, CORTLAND
See CORT

ANDY
See NORTH CENTRAL POSITRONICS

ANGSTROM, JUNIOR
See MAINE CHARACTERS

ANSELM, HUGH
See CALLA BRYN STURGIS CHARACTERS: FARMERS (SMALLHOLD)

ANTASSI, OFFICER PAUL
See GUTTENBERG, FURTH, AND PATEL: DAMASCUS, TRUDY

APON
See GODS OF MID-WORLD: OLD STAR

ARMITAGE, FRANK
See WARRIORS OF THE SCARLET EYE: DEVAR-TOI CHARACTERS: HUMANS

ARRA
See MANNI: CANTAB; *see also* CALLA BRYN STURGIS CHARACTERS: FARMERS (SMALLHOLD)

ARTHUR, KING

King Arthur (also known as King Arthur of the Round Table) is the hero of the Arthurian legends. He is also the manifestation of ARTHUR ELD found on our level of the TOWER. When pregnant MIA searches SUSANNAH DEAN's memory banks for a name for her CHAP, she settles on MORDRED, Arthur's betraying son-nephew who was born to Arthur's sister after their incestuous coupling.

V:111 *(Tales of Arthur)*, VI:107 *(indirect)*

ARTHUR ELD

See ELD, ARTHUR

ATWOOD, TIM

See BREAKERS: BRAUTIGAN, TED

AUNT MOLLY

See BREAKERS: BRAUTIGAN, TED

AUNT TALITHA

See RIVER CROSSING CHARACTERS

AVEN KAL

See APPENDIX I; *see also* BEAMS, PATH OF THE, *in* PORTALS

AVERY, BONNIE

See PIPER SCHOOL CHARACTERS

B

BABY MICHAEL

See MIA: MIA'S ASSOCIATES

BACHMAN, CLAUDIA Y INEZ

See CHARLIE THE CHOO-CHOO

BACHMAN, RICHARD

Richard Bachman began life as one of STEPHEN KING's pseudonyms, but as often happens with fictional characters, he soon assumed his own identity and made a break for freedom by taking up residence on one of the other levels of the TOWER. During his lifetime, Bachman published five novels. These were *Rage, The Long Walk, Roadwork, The Running Man,* and *Thinner.* Although

Bachman, a survivor of adult-onset leukemia, died of cancer of the pseudonym in 1985, additional manuscripts (including *The Regulators*) were discovered by his widow, CLAUDIA INEZ BACHMAN (now Claudia Inez Eschelman) as late as 1994. This raises the inevitable question—did all of the Richard Bachmans, on all levels of the Tower, actually reach the clearing at the end of the path? Or is it possible that at least one Bachman still lives on? If so, we will see more of his books mysteriously appearing in our world.

VI:288, VI:392

BADMOUTH KING
See WARRIORS OF THE SCARLET EYE: CASSE ROI RUSSE: HUMANS: FEEMALO/FIMALO/FUMALO

BAEZ, VAN GOGH
See CAN-TOI

BAJ
See BREAKERS

BALAZAR, ENRICO (IL ROCHE)
We first met the drug-smuggling, house-of-cards-building mafioso kingpin Enrico Balazar in *The Drawing of the Three.* (See *Stephen King's The Dark Tower: A Concordance, Volume I.*) For a short while, EDDIE DEAN worked for him as a drug runner, although that profession was cut short by the appearance of Roland Deschain inside Eddie's brain during a flight from NASSAU to JFK, and Eddie's short trip to the LOBSTROSITY-infested beach of the WESTERN SEA. (In retrospect, Eddie was damn lucky that Roland kidnapped him and forced him to dump his stash on the bleak stretches of that beach, since otherwise he would have been caught with some rather large bags of cocaine strapped to his armpits.) Eddie's loss of Balazar's property (not to mention the part he played in the destruction of Balazar's offices and the death of Balazar himself) left some mighty bad ka between Eddie and this short, chubby, but murderous second-generation Sicilian, a ka destined to replay between Eddie and all of the Balazars on all levels of the DARK TOWER.

At the beginning of *Wolves of the Calla,* Eddie Dean and JAKE CHAMBERS return to a TODASH version of NEW YORK and witness a much younger Balazar and two of his men harassing CALVIN TOWER, owner of the MAN-HATTAN RESTAURANT OF THE MIND. It turns out that Balazar has been hired by the SOMBRA CORPORATION (one of the many companies serving the CRIMSON KING) to "persuade" Tower to sell them the Vacant LOT, home of the ROSE. Caught in the invisible (or *dim*) todash state, neither Jake nor Eddie can intervene on Tower's behalf. However, they do get a good look at the document which Tower signed almost a year previously, promising not to sell the lot for twelve months but giving Sombra first right of purchase after that time.

Deciding that the Rose must be kept safe from the WOLVES of New York every bit as much as the children of CALLA BRYN STURGIS must be kept safe from the Wolves of THUNDERCLAP, Eddie returns to New York (this time via the UNFOUND DOOR) to persuade Tower to sell the lot to him rather than to Sombra. However, when he arrives at Tower's bookshop, he finds two of Balazar's gentlemen—namely JACK ANDOLINI and GEORGE BIONDI—leaning over Tower in his office, threatening to burn his precious books unless he agrees to sell the lot. With a skillful use of Roland's gun (both the firing end and the sandalwood butt) Eddie sends a double message to Balazar, courtesy of his two thugs. First, Tower isn't selling the lot to Sombra because he has already decided to sell to the TET CORPORATION. Second, Calvin Tower is now under the protection of people who make Balazar and his cohorts look like hippies attending WOODSTOCK.

Not surprisingly, Balazar doesn't listen. Acting on a tip given to the agents of the Crimson King by MIA, SUSANNAH DEAN's demon-possessor, he sends his gunmen to EAST STONEHAM, MAINE, both to flush Tower out of hiding and to give Eddie and Roland (destined to enter our world here through the Unfound Door) an unpleasantly warm welcome. Thanks to Roland and Eddie's amazing gunslinger reflexes, they survive Balazar's ambush. They even manage to persuade an anally retentive Tower to sell them his lot.

V:60, V:61, V:62–68, V:91, V:93, V:96, V:104, V:164, V:167, V:178, V:180, V:393, V:396, V:453, V:504, V:519, V:522, V:525, V:527 *(Il Roche)*, V:528, V:535–37, V:542, V:544, V:550, V:627–28, V:705, VI:28, VI:128, VI:139, VI:140, VI:142, VI:144, VI:146, VI:189, VI:277, VI:334

> **BALAZAR'S MEN:** For additional information, see *Stephen King's The Dark Tower: A Concordance, Volume I.* V:91, V:393, V:519, V:520, V:525 *(tet)*, V:535, V:542 *(goons)*, V:550, V:705, VI:129–48, VI:154 *(indirect)*, VI:162 *(indirect)*, VI:185, VI:194, VI:215
>
> **ANDOLINI, CLAUDIO:** JACK ANDOLINI's brother. He is also one of Balazar's bodyguards. For more information, see *Stephen King's The Dark Tower: A Concordance, Volume I.* V:528
>
> **ANDOLINI, JACK (OLD DOUBLE-UGLY):** Old Double-Ugly is Balazar's trusted field marshal and is the man the big boss puts in charge of working over CALVIN TOWER and then ambushing EDDIE and Roland in EAST STONEHAM, MAINE. Although he looks Cro-Magnon, Andolini is actually both intelligent and sly. During the battle at the EAST STONEHAM GENERAL STORE, Andolini takes to calling Eddie "Slick." However, his sticks and stones break no one's bones, and at the end of the day, Andolini—a New York big shot—ends up sitting in a Maine county jail. Humiliating as Andolini might find this particular fate, it's better than the one that awaits one of his other selves on the *Drawing of the Three* level of the DARK TOWER. In that particular where and when, he dies blind and faceless beneath the tearing claws of a LOBSTROSITY. V:61, V:62–68, V:169, V:518–28, V:529, V:530 *(hoodlum)*, V:531, V:535, V:536, V:544,

V:548, V:550, V:623, VI:130–48 *(present from 129; calls Eddie "Slick")*, VI:150, VI:154 *(indirect)*, VI:162, VI:164, VI:166, VI:168, VI:183, VI:184, VI:185, VI:189, VI:191, VI:192, VI:193, VI:194, VI:196, VI:211, VI:215, VII:40, VII:118, VII:396, VII:418, VII:426, VII:495

    ANDOLINI FAMILY: V:527, V:582

BERNIE (OF BERNIE'S BARBER SHOP): EDDIE DEAN briefly considers holding up Bernie's Barber Shop (home of Balazar's weekend poker games) in order to scrape funds together so that CALVIN TOWER can leave NEW YORK CITY and escape the serious maiming that Balazar is sending his way. Instead, Tower borrows money from his old friend AARON DEEPNEAU and the two of them flee to MAINE. V:537

BIONDI, GEORGE (BIG NOSE): George "Big Nose" Biondi isn't as intelligent as his gunbunny workmate, JACK ANDOLINI. When EDDIE sees this particular piece of pond scum during the battle at the EAST STONEHAM GENERAL STORE, he's still blue from the bruises Eddie gave him in the backroom office of CALVIN TOWER's bookshop. Biondi doesn't have to worry about his looks for long, though. Eddie uses Roland's gun to (literally) blow the bruises away. (And the rest of his face as well.) V:61, V:62–68, V:93 *(Big Nose)*, V:98, V:518–28, V:530 *(hoodlum)*, V:535, V:536, V:548, VI:140 *(present from 129; Eddie blows his face off)*, VI:143, VI:166, VII:397, VII:495

    MOTHER: VI:140

BLAKE, KEVIN: In *The Drawing of the Three*, Kevin Blake hurled HENRY DEAN's head at EDDIE in order to flush Eddie and Roland into the open. V:61, V:544

DRETTO, CARLOCIMI ('CIMI): One of Balazar's personal bodyguards. V:528, V:544

POSTINO, TRICKS: One of Balazar's thugs. V:528, V:536, VI:134 *(present from 129; dies this section)*, VI:135

BALAZAR'S NASSAU CONNECTION:

    SALLOW BRITISH MAN: While working as Balazar's cocaine mule in NASSAU, EDDIE DEAN has to have dealings with this unsavory and untrustworthy character. (See *Stephen King's The Dark Tower: A Concordance, Volume I.*) V:453 *(sallow thing)*

'BAMA
    See CHAMBERS, JAKE

BAMBRY, JOHN
    See DEAN, SUSANNAH: ODETTA HOLMES AND THE CIVIL RIGHTS MOVEMENT: ODETTA'S "MOVEMENT" ASSOCIATES

BAMBRY, LESTER
See DEAN, SUSANNAH: ODETTA HOLMES AND THE CIVIL RIGHTS MOVEMENT: ODETTA'S "MOVEMENT" ASSOCIATES

BANDY BROOKS
See CALLAHAN, FATHER DONALD FRANK: CALLAHAN'S HIDDEN HIGHWAYS ASSOCIATES

BANGO SKANK
See SKANK, BANGO

BARBARIANS WITH BLUE FACES
See FARSON, JOHN: FARSON'S MEN

BARKER, JUNIOR
See MAINE CHARACTERS

BARLOW, KURT
See VAMPIRES: TYPE ONE

BEAM BOY
In the final book of the Dark Tower series, SHEEMIE RUIZ (now a BREAKER in THUNDERCLAP) meets this human incarnation of the BEAM. To Sheemie, the Beam Boy looks like Jake, only his face is covered with blood, one of his eyes has been poked out, and he limps. Although this dream-creature was beautiful when he arose from the PRIM, by the time Sheemie sees him he is near collapse. Despite the torture he has undergone, the Beam Boy still loves the world. If our tet can save him, he promises to bring magic back to the multiverse.

VII:333–36, VII:338, VII:378 *(Beam says thankya)*, VII:389 *(Beam says thankya)*, VII:391 *(Beam speaks to Sheemie)*, VII:400

BEAM BREAKERS
See BREAKERS

BEAMS
See entry in PORTALS

BEAMS, GUARDIANS OF THE
See GUARDIANS OF THE BEAM

BEAR GUARDIAN
See GUARDIANS OF THE BEAM

BEASLEY, JESSICA
See DEAN, SUSANNAH: ODETTA HOLMES'S ASSOCIATES

BEAST, THE
See GUARDIANS OF THE BEAM

BECKHARDT, DICK
See MAINE CHARACTERS

BEEMAN
See CAN-TOI

BEEMER, CHARLIE
See MAINE CHARACTERS

BEEMER, RHODA
See MAINE CHARACTERS

BEEMER, RUTH
See MAINE CHARACTERS

BENDS O' THE RAINBOW
See MAERLYN'S RAINBOW

BENZYCK, OFFICER (BENZYCK O' THE WATCH)
Benzyck is a rather chubby officer of the law. Each day he gives a ticket to REVEREND EARL HARRIGAN (CHURCH OF THE HOLY GOD-BOMB) for parking illegally on the corner of SECOND AVENUE.
VI:258–59, VI:260 *(Benzyck o' the Watch)*, VI:313, VI:316, VI:319, VI:320

BERNARDO
See CALLA BRYN STURGIS CHARACTERS: OTHER CHARACTERS

BERNIE'S BARBER SHOP
See BALAZAR, ENRICO: BALAZAR'S MEN

BERNSTEIN, MRS.
See DEAN, EDDIE: EDDIE'S PAST ASSOCIATES

BERTOLLO, DORA
See DEAN, EDDIE: EDDIE'S PAST ASSOCIATES

BESSA
See GODS OF MID-WORLD

BESSIE
See DANDELO

BIG COFFIN HUNTERS

The Big Coffin Hunters (also known as REGULATORS) were the nasty harriers that Roland and his childhood friends CUTHBERT ALLGOOD and ALAIN JOHNS were forced to fight in HAMBRY. (See *Stephen King's The Dark Tower: A Concordance, Volume I.*) Their name came from the blue coffin-shaped tattoos located on the webbing between right thumb and forefinger. In *Wolves of the Calla,* we find out that many of PERE CALLAHAN's LOW MEN bear similar coffin tattoos. Evidently, this sinister insignia is a sigul of the CRIMSON KING. EDDIE DEAN believes that BALAZAR and his associates are our world's version of Big Coffin Hunters.

V:100, V:104, V:291, V:469, V:516

DEPAPE, ROY: Spiteful, twenty-five-year-old Roy Depape was one of ELDRED JONAS's sidekicks back in MEJIS. He wore gold-rimmed glasses and laughed like a braying donkey. In *Wizard and Glass,* CUTHBERT ALLGOOD saved SHEEMIE from an outburst of Roy's murderous temper. (Roy was angry because his fifteen-year-old prostitute girlfriend was out working the ranches.) For more information, see *Stephen King's The Dark Tower: A Concordance, Volume I.* V:187, VI:242, VII:220

> **DEPAPE, AMOS:** Brother of ROY DEPAPE. Roland thought he was stung to death by a snake. Actually, he was fucked to death by SUSANNAH DEAN's demon-possessor, MIA, who (while still a wraith) functioned as a kind of sexual VAMPIRE. VI:242

JONAS, ELDRED: Eldred Jonas of the long, silky white hair and mustache was the leader of HAMBRY's Big Coffin Hunters. In *Wizard and Glass* he was often referred to as a white-haired wolf. Jonas was lame in one leg due to an injury he'd suffered in his coming-of-age battle against CORT's father, FARDO, in GILEAD. Like all other failed gunslingers, the young Jonas had been sent west. In his bitterness, he turned his back on the WHITE and joined with FARSON, a representative of the chaotic Outer Dark. (For more information about Cort's father Fardo and about Eldred Jonas and his gunbunnies, see *Stephen King's The Dark Tower: A Concordance, Volume I.*) V:187, VI:242, VII:175, VII:297, VII:336

> **REYNOLDS, CLAY:** Clay Reynolds was another of ELDRED JONAS's gun-toting companions. Though not as clever as Jonas, he was still a brighter bulb than ROY DEPAPE. Clay was vain. For more information, see *Stephen King's The Dark Tower: A Concordance, Volume I.* V:187

BIG SKY DADDY

> *See* GODS OF MID-WORLD

BILLY-BUMBLER

> *See* OY *and* THROCKEN; *see also* APPENDIX I

BIONDI, GEORGE
See BALAZAR, ENRICO: BALAZAR'S MEN

BIRDMEN
See TAHEEN

BISHOP DUGAN
See CALLAHAN, FATHER DONALD FRANK: CALLAHAN'S OTHER
PAST ASSOCIATES

BLACKBIRD MOMMY
See DEAN, SUSANNAH

BLACK MAN IN GRAY FATIGUES
See HARRIGAN, REVEREND EARL: CROWD

BLACK MAN IN JAIL CELL
See GAN

BLACKBIRD, LADY
See DEAN, SUSANNAH

BLACK MAN WITH WALKMAN
EDDIE DEAN and JAKE CHAMBERS first see this man singing along with his
Walkman when they travel TODASH to 1977 NEW YORK. While preparing
himself to travel back to 1977 through the magical UNFOUND DOOR, Eddie
fixes the date in his mind by imagining this man walking in front of CHEW
CHEW MAMA'S.
    V:48, V:231, V:514

BLACK THIRTEEN
See MAERLYN'S RAINBOW

BLAINE
See NORTH CENTRAL POSITRONICS

BLAKE, KEVIN
See BALAZAR, ENRICO: BALAZAR'S MEN

BLEEDING LION
Even though the CRIMSON KING's followers in END-WORLD are system-
atically and purposefully eroding the final two BEAMS so that the DARK
TOWER will collapse and the macroverse will blink out of existence, they have
their own set of superstitions concerning the fearful end of the world and about

how their master's plans may yet be thwarted. Though we don't know the details of these superstitions, we do know that at least one concerns a Bleeding Lion stalking to the north. Another is about a gunslinger-man coming out of the west to save the Tower.

VII:238, VII:239

BLUE-FACED BARBARIANS
See FARSON, JOHN: FARSON'S MEN

BLUE LADY
See DEAN, SUSANNAH: ODETTA HOLMES'S ASSOCIATES: SISTER BLUE

BOOM-FLURRY
Boom-flurry is a Calla term for the fantastically misshapen organ-pipe cacti that live in the desert dividing CALLA BRYN STURGIS from THUNDERCLAP. Their thick barrel arms are covered with long, nasty needles and they smell of gin and juniper. Unlike the cacti of our world, boom-flurry are sentient, vicious, and carnivorous. Hence, they make remarkably good sentries. JAKE and OY encounter some boom-flurry on their way to the CALLA DOGAN. Luckily, the salivating plant-monsters don't manage to pierce them with any of their spikes, but they are plenty fashed by the time ANDY the Messenger Robot and the treacherous BEN SLIGHTMAN come upon them.

V:561, V:562, V:567–68, V:571, V:577

BOSCO BOB
See DEAN, EDDIE: EDDIE'S PAST ASSOCIATES: OFFICER BOSCONI

BRANNI BOB
See MANNI

BRANNIGAN, SKIPPER
See DEAN, HENRY: HENRY DEAN'S KA-TET

BRASS
See WARRIORS OF THE SCARLET EYE: CASSE ROI RUSSE: HUMANS: FEEMALO/FIMALO/FUMALO: FEEMALO

BRAUTIGAN, TED
See BREAKERS

BRAWNY MAN
See CALLAHAN, FATHER DONALD FRANK: CALLAHAN'S HIDDEN HIGHWAYS ASSOCIATES

BREAKERS (BEAM BREAKERS)

The Breakers of THUNDERCLAP are both the prisoners and the servants of the CRIMSON KING. Imprisoned in the DEVAR-TOI, located in the poisoned land of END-WORLD, they use their psychic abilities to weaken the BEAMS, which hold the DARK TOWER in place. Although few (if any) of the Breakers willingly undertook the job of destroying the macroverse (most were tricked into accepting *an offer-of-a-lifetime*—an offer which really *did* turn out to be for a lifetime since most of the MECHANICAL DOORS leading into Thunderclap are one-way only), almost none of them complain once they experience the diverse pleasures available beneath the Devar's artificial sun.

"To break is divine," or so we are told. The Devar's 307 Breakers make use of their so-called wild talents in the STUDY, a room which looks like a richly endowed library in a nineteenth-century gentlemen's club. They work in shifts of thirty-three individuals, each sitting in his or her accustomed place, seemingly reading magazines or contemplating pictures, while actually their minds are rising, reaching the Beams, searching out cracks and crevices, and expanding those fault lines as much as they possibly can. Although the damage done by this activity is almost incomprehensible, the act of Breaking is intensely pleasurable, both for the Breakers who are doing it and for the balcony guards who relax in the "good mind" vibe which rises from below.

Even if an individual doggedly ignores the moral (or perhaps I should say immoral) implications of Breaking, this act has another very human cost. To keep their skills at top form, the Breakers are regularly fed pills which contain a chemical culled from the brains of prepubescent twins, a chemical which causes "twin-telepathy" and which, once removed, leaves the culled child ROONT, or ruined. Although few Breakers know exactly what they are being fed, many have their suspicions but choose to ignore their consciences. Why worry when the accommodation is classy, the food is great, and the *sim* sex is almost as good as the real thing? As the Breaker saying goes, "Enjoy the cruise, turn on the fan, there's nothing to lose, so work on your tan."

According to TED BRAUTIGAN, most of the Breakers are able to turn off guilt at will because they are *morks* (a term taken from the 1970s sitcom *Mork & Mindy*) and so don't readily form deep attachments to other people. It's not that morks are antisocial—in fact many of them are very sociable—it's just that their "friendships" are based on convenience rather than emotional compatibility. For example, if you have a pack of cigarettes in your pocket, a mork who is jonesing for a smoke will suddenly be your greatest buddy. Although this emotional coldness is disturbing to contemplate, it serves a protective purpose. Most of the Breakers spent their KEYSTONE EARTH lives (and most of them are from Keystone Earth) as the butt of jokes. Their talents have forced them to be perennial outsiders, freaks, and they have always been treated (as DINKY EARNSHAW so aptly puts it) like "Carrie at the fuckin prom." Hence, emotional distance from their fellow humans has been a matter of survival. It's not surprising, then, that for most Breakers, existence in the Devar is preferable to life on ordinary earth. (That is, once they get used to the eczema, acne, and multiple illnesses which come from inhabiting a poisoned land.)

In the final book of the Dark Tower series, Roland's ka-tet arrives in Thunderclap and—with the help of a number of rebel Breakers—puts an end to the abominable practices of the Devar-Toi. Although they slaughter most of the Devar's CAN-TOI, TAHEEN, and hume (or human) guards, they do not harm the Breakers themselves, but tell them to make their way to the CALLAS and beg the *folken*'s forgiveness. (Their only other option is to stay in the ruins of the Devar.) Needless to say, most of the mork Breakers are incensed at such a suggestion, claiming that they had no idea what they were *really* doing in the Study. Rather than taking responsibility for their past actions, they choose to blame Roland's ka-tet as well as those Breakers who joined forces with the "enemy."

We never find out what happens to the majority of Breakers, but those who aided our ka-tet in their time of need decide to go to CALLA BRYN STURGIS. Once there, they hope to pass through the UNFOUND DOOR and back to America-side. We can only hope that the Calla *folken* help them achieve their goal.

V:659–60, VI:16, VI:18, VI:110, VI:111, VI:114, VI:115, VI:245, VI:246, VI:255, VI:378, VII:58, VII:121, VII:148, VII:150, VII:152, VII:153, VII:178, VII:180, VII:187, VII:211, VII:212–13, VII:214 *(indirect),* VII:230, VII:232, VII:234, VII:235, VII:236–37, VII:238, VII:239, VII:241–45 *(study),* VII:251, VII:256, VII:262, VII:288–89 *(rhyme),* VII:291, VII:292, VII:293, VII:294, VII:295, VII:296, VII:307, VII:311, VII:312, VII:326–27, VII:332, VII:338, VII:343, VII:344, VII:349, VII:356–85 *(Devar-Toi battle),* VII:388–90, VII:391–93, VII:394–95 *(accusing Roland),* VII:399, VII:406, VII:407, VII:408, VII:411–14, VII:416, VII:505, VII:507, VII:510, VII:532, VII:563, VII:577, VII:595

ADDICTS: Addiction of any kind is not tolerated in the DEVAR, since addiction can interfere with Breaking. Those Breakers who arrive at the Devar hooked on drugs or booze are quickly detoxed. However, those who can't seem to give up their habits simply disappear. VII:211

BAJ: Like SEJ, gentle little Baj is a hydrocephalic savant. In other words, he is a person who has hydrocephalus (enlargement of the head due to water collecting in the brain) but who is amazingly gifted. Baj has no arms, and so has no way to protect himself from the dangers of falling. During the DEVAR's final battle, eleven-year-old DANI ROSTOV tries to save both Baj and Sej from choking to death in the smoke of DAMLI HOUSE. However, while she is pulling them on wagons, Baj tumbles out and falls on his head. He doesn't survive. VII:212 *(indirect),* VII:375–76 *(dies),* VII:377

BANKERLY LOOKING BREAKER NUMBER ONE: *See* WORTHINGTON, FRED, *listed below*

BANKERLY LOOKING BREAKER NUMBER TWO: Despite holding our ka-tet personally responsible for destroying his life in the DEVAR-

TOI, this morose, gray-haired gentleman has a certain amount of courage. Acting as a group spokesman, he confronts Roland with the ruination of the Breakers' lives. Roland reminds him what terrible crimes he and the other Breakers have been committing and tells him that he and his friends should travel to the CALLAS and beg the *folken*'s forgiveness. VII:412

BRAUTIGAN, TED STEVENS: To STEPHEN KING's CONSTANT READERS, the *totally eventual* Ted Brautigan is a familiar, well-loved character. We first met Ted in "Low Men in Yellow Coats," the opening story of *Hearts in Atlantis*. In that tale, Ted was a powerful psychic who could pass his talent on to others when he touched them. Because of this unusual ability, he was pursued by the CAN-TOI (referred to in the context of the story as the LOW MEN) who wanted to force him to use his skill for evil ends. Trying to remain unseen, a fugitive Ted moved into a CONNECTICUT boardinghouse already occupied by a young boy named BOBBY GARFIELD and his young but bitter widowed mother, LIZ. Thanks to their shared love of books, Ted and Bobby became friends. Bobby agreed to work for Ted, ostensibly to read the paper to him each day, but actually to act as a spotter for the garishly dressed low men and for the lost-pet posters and strange, occult designs which they used to hunt for their prey.

At the end of "Low Men in Yellow Coats," Ted was betrayed by Bobby's mother, Liz, who wanted to collect the low men's reward money. The last distressing glimpse Bobby had of Ted was of him sitting in the backseat of a huge DeSoto, surrounded by low men. He was on his way back to END-WORLD and a job he despised. However, he agreed to do his job willingly, as long as the low men left Bobby and his other young friends alone.

When we meet up with Ted again in *The Dark Tower*, he is imprisoned once more in the DEVAR-TOI in End-World. We also learn that he has not kept his promise to his captors. Although he appears to Break willingly enough, he and two of his fellow inmates—DINKY EARNSHAW and STANLEY RUIZ (otherwise known as SHEEMIE)—are preparing for the arrival of Roland Deschain, the savior-gunslinger whose appearance he predicted at the end of "Low Men in Yellow Coats."

In *The Dark Tower*, we find out that although Ted isn't from KEY-STONE EARTH, he is much more than a run-of-the-mill Breaker. He is a *facilitator*, or a psychic whose special skill is his ability to increase the power of other psychics. This, we learn, is why the servants of the Red King were so determined to bring Ted back to the Devar, and why he was not severely punished for his "little vacation" in Connecticut. While the other Breakers work shifts in the STUDY, Ted comes and goes as he pleases. But whenever he arrives, the number of *darks* generated by the Breakers increases exponentially. Much to his chagrin, Ted's special skill has taken years off the Red King's work, and by the time our tet arrives in THUNDERCLAP, only two of the BEAMS are still intact.

Like his twin, FATHER CALLAHAN, Ted Stevens Brautigan becomes a temporary member of Roland's ka-tet. He, Dinky, and Sheemie help our tet destroy the Devar and begin the healing of the Beams. Not only does Ted use his psychic abilities to help confuse both guards and Breakers during our tet's attack, but he also employs his deadly mind-spear to kill the can-toi guard TRAMPAS. When we finally take leave of Ted in the twisting corridors beneath the FEDIC DOGAN, he, Dinky, FRED WORTHINGTON, and DANI ROSTOV are on their way to the CALLAS. From there they hope to pass through the UNFOUND DOOR to one of the many ALTERNATIVE AMERICAS.

VI:407, VI:408, VII:197–220, VII:233, VII:234, VII:238, VII:243–45, VII:247, VII:249, VII:261, VII:265–302 *(twin of Pere Callahan)*, VII:304, VII:306, VII:307, VII:315, VII:318–24, VII:326, VII:327–36, VII:337–42, VII:349, VII:356–58, VI:359, VII:366, VII:370, VII:372, VII:374–75, VII:376–77, VII:380, VII:382, VI:384, VII:388–90, VII:391, VII:392, VII:393, VII:394, VII:400–401, VII:404–8, VII:409, VII:411–17, VII:532, VII:535, VII:536–37, VII:538, VII:539, VII:540–41, VII:560, VII:563, VII:802

ATWOOD, TIM: Tim Atwood was Ted's wealthy, childless uncle. He paid for Ted's education, hoping that Ted would take over his furniture business. Needless to say, Ted didn't. VII:273, VII:276

AUNT MOLLY: Ted's Aunt Molly and Uncle Jim lived in BRIDGE-PORT, CONNECTICUT. VII:415

DALE, MR.: A butcher. VII:277

DOCTOR NUMBER ONE (SAM): This doctor gave Ted a 4F when he tried to enlist as a soldier during the First World War. He was deeply disturbed by Ted's psychic abilities. VII:274–75, VII:280

   GUY: Doc Number One's brother. VII:275

DOCTOR NUMBER TWO: This doctor consciously undermined Ted's "proof" of his psychic ability. VII:274–75, VII:277, VII:280, VII:286

GARFIELD, BOBBY: Redheaded Bobby Garfield was Ted's eleven-year-old CONNECTICUT friend, and the main character of the story "Low Men in Yellow Coats." Despite the difference in hair color, he and JAKE CHAMBERS are practically identical twins. PIMLI PRENTISS, the Devar Master, and FINLI O'TEGO, his security chief, have both made it clear to Ted that if he tries to run away again, Bobby will be put to death. VI:407, VI:408, VII:197, VII:199, VII:207, VII:215 *(indirect)*, VII:218, VII:234, VII:288, VII:298

   GARFIELD, LIZ: Bobby's young but bitter mother. She never forgave Bobby's dad for dying of a heart attack at age thirty-six. She turned Ted in to the LOW MEN for the reward money they offered. VII:218

GERBER, CAROL: Carol Gerber was BOBBY GARFIELD's friend/girl-friend in "Low Men in Yellow Coats," the first story in *Hearts in Atlantis*. Carol also appears in "Why We're in Vietnam," "Heavenly Shades of Night Are Falling," and the book's title story, "Hearts in Atlantis." Like Bobby, Carol would have been killed by the LOW MEN had Ted attempted to escape from the DEVAR-TOI. VII:234, VII:298

   MOTHER: VII:298

KIDS PLAYING KICK-THE-CAN: These kids in AKRON, OHIO, witnessed the first throw of Ted's deadly mind-spear. VII:277, VII:278

MUGGER: Directly after attacking Ted, this fleeing mugger dropped dead. The reason? Ted had arrowed a thought in his direction. This event changed Ted's life and made him fear his psychic ability. VII:277–78, VII:279, VII:376

SERGEANT AT ARMS: This sergeant at arms threw Ted out of a First World War recruiting station. VII:275–76

SOUTH AMERICAN SEABEES: *Listed separately*

SULLIVAN, JOHN (SULLY JOHN): Sully John was friends with both BOBBY GARFIELD and CAROL GERBER. He and Carol became a couple after Bobby left town, but Carol later abandoned the relationship. In the story "Why We're in Vietnam," found in STEPHEN KING's novel *Hearts in Atlantis*, we learn that Sully John had one of his testicles shot off in VIETNAM. VI:407, VII:288, VII:298

UNCLE JIM: Ted's Aunt Molly and Uncle Jim lived in BRIDGEPORT, CONNECTICUT. VII:415

DICK: We never learn Dick's last name, even though he arrived at the DEVAR on the same day as TED BRAUTIGAN. Dick died six months after entering THUNDERCLAP. HUMMA O'TEGO insisted he died of pneumonia, but Ted thinks he committed suicide. VII:283 *(not yet named)*, VII:286–90

EARNSHAW, DINKY: CONSTANT READERS know Dinky Earnshaw (born Richard Earnshaw) from "Everything's Eventual," the autobiographical tale he narrated in STEPHEN KING's book of the same name. At the time "Everything's Eventual" was written, Dinky worked for a POSITRONICS subsidiary as a psychic assassin. His method of attack was a personalized letter (either posted or sent via computer) which contained strange shapes and designs, the meanings of which not even Dinky seemed to know. Dinky's death-magic was incredibly powerful, and his employers rewarded him well for his services. Dinky's only problem was that he wasn't a full mork. When he began to admit to himself what he was doing—and when he started to learn about the people he was employed to kill—he decided to cut and run. Dinky sent one final personalized death-letter (this time to his control, the sinister MR. SHARPTON) before trying to retire in obscurity. However, to the WARRIORS OF THE SCARLET EYE, psychics stand out like blazing fires. He was recaptured and sent to the DEVAR-TOI, where his skills were used to help destroy the BEAMS.

Like many of the other Breakers, Dinky is a precog. However, since the future is always a multi-forked path, Dinky cannot always tell which particular future will manifest. Despite this uncertainty, he joins forces with TED BRAUTIGAN, SHEEMIE RUIZ, and Roland's ka-tet to end the horrors of the Devar. After the future of the Beams is assured, he, Ted, FRED WORTHINGTON, and DANI ROSTOV set off for CALLA BRYN STUR-

GIS. Once there, they hope to pass through the UNFOUND DOOR to one of the ALTERNATIVE AMERICAS. VII:197–220, VII:228, VII:231–32, VII:247, VII:267–70, VII:271, VII:272, VII:273, VII:276, VII:279, VII:285, VII:288, VII:290, VII:291, VII:292, VII:293, VII:296, VII:300, VII:318–36, VII:337–42, VII:356–57, VII:359–61, VII:363, VII:364–65, VII:371, VII:374, VII:375–77, VII:380, VII:384, VII:388–90, VII:392, VII:395, VII:396, VII:397–99, VII:400–401, VII:405–8, VII:409, VII:411–17, VII:532, VII:535, VII:536–37, VII:538, VII:539, VII:540 *(indirect)*, VII:541 *(indirect)*, VII:560, VII:561, VII:563, VII:802

J.J. THE BLUE JAY: VII:325

SHARPTON, MR.: Mr. Sharpton was a talent scout for a NORTH CENTRAL POSITRONICS subsidiary. His specialty was recruiting psychic assassins. Before going *alleyo*, Dinky sent Mr. Sharpton a death-letter. He personalized it with the word EXCALIBUR—the magical sword which was printed on Mr. Sharpton's ties. VII:232, VII:398

ITTAWAY, DAVE: Dave Ittaway was recruited to be a Breaker at the same time as TED BRAUTIGAN. VII:283 *(not yet named)*, VII:286–90

LEEDS, TANYA (TANYA LEEDS RASTOSOVICH): Like DAVE ITTAWAY, JACE McGOVERN, and DICK of the unknown last name, Tanya Leeds of BRYCE, COLORADO, was recruited to be a Breaker at the same time as TED BRAUTIGAN. Tanya is a tough young woman, but though she may once have been willing to join forces with Roland, by the time our ka-tet arrives in THUNDERCLAP she is newly married and wants only to snuggle with her fella, JOEY RASTOSOVICH. Unfortunately, during the DEVAR's battle chaos, Joey is run over by a robotic fire truck. VII:230–31, VII:283 *(Bryce, Colorado)*, VII:286–90, VII:293, VII:295, VII:337–38, VII:373, VII:393 *(indirect)*

McCANN, BIRDIE: Birdie is an ex-carpenter with a receding hairline. VII:370–71

McGOVERN, JACE: Jace entered the service of the CRIMSON KING at the same time as TED BRAUTIGAN. VII:283 *(not yet named)*, VII:286–90

RAPED BREAKER: This unnamed Breaker was raped by a LOW MAN called CAMERON, who said that the act was required of him by the CRIMSON KING and that it was part of his process of *becoming* (or becoming human). The DEVAR MASTER sentenced Cameron to death, and the Breakers were invited to watch. VII:326–27

RASTOSOVICH, JOSEPH: Joseph Rastosovich (never Joey, at least to his face) married TANYA LEEDS in the DEVAR-TOI. Although the Devar Master PIMLI PRENTISS performed the official ceremony, the couple asked TED BRAUTIGAN to marry them in secret, since Ted's blessing meant a lot more to them. During the chaos of the final Devar battle, Joseph is run over by a robotic fire truck. VII:230–31, VII:295, VII:337–38, VII:356, VII:371, VII:373

ROSTOV, DANEEKA (DANI): As far as we know, eleven-year-old

Daneeka Rostov is the youngest of the Breakers. She is also Russian, which sets her apart from most of the others we've met. Unlike the selfish mork Breakers, Dani has a good heart. During the DEVAR's final battle, she tries to save BAJ and SEJ from the smoking wreck of DAMLI HOUSE. After EDDIE DEAN's death, she also helps TED BRAUTIGAN, DINKY EARNSHAW, SHEEMIE RUIZ, and FRED WORTHINGTON send Roland and JAKE back to NEW YORK. (At this time, she gives Jake his first and only romantic kiss.) Like her Breaker friends, Dani hopes to travel to CALLA BRYN STURGIS so that she can enter one of the ALTERNA-TIVE AMERICAS via the UNFOUND DOOR. VII:243, VII:375–77, VII:393, VII:404–8, VII:415–17, VII:536–37, VII:538, VII:539, VII:540 (indirect), VII:541 (indirect), VII:560, VII:563

RUIZ, STANLEY (SHEEMIE): Sheemie Ruiz, one of the most powerful Breakers in THUNDERCLAP, is none other than the mildly mentally hand-icapped tavern boy whose life was saved by CUTHBERT ALLGOOD in MEJIS. (See *Stephen King's The Dark Tower: A Concordance, Volume I.*) When we meet Sheemie in the final volume of the Dark Tower series, he appears to be about thirty-five years old and mute. However, the arrival of Roland (good old WILL-DEARBORN-that-was) cures Sheemie of his mute-ness. Once Sheemie's voice returns, he confesses his love for SUSAN DEL-GADO and the terrible guilt he feels about her death.

Sheemie possesses the one wild talent which is absolutely forbidden in the DEVAR-TOI—the ability to teleport. With the help of his friends TED BRAUTIGAN and DINKY EARNSHAW, he uses this skill to transport our ka-tet from THUNDERCLAP STATION to the relative safety of STEEK-TETE, located several miles from the Devar-Toi. Unfortunately, teleporta-tion has its own risks. When Sheemie teleports himself, Ted, and Dinky to Steek-Tete to see how Roland and his friends are progressing with their war plans, he suffers a mild stroke. It turns out that Sheemie has had four such strokes already, the first of which hit him when he helped Ted escape to 1960 CONNECTICUT. (The tale of Ted's Connecticut adventure is told in the short story "Low Men in Yellow Coats," found in STEPHEN KING's book *Hearts in Atlantis.*) However, Sheemie's teleportation skill is not his only unusual psychic talent. Unlike any other person in the Devar, Sheemie can make fistulas in time, or balconies on the edifice of the DARK TOWER. The fistula which Sheemie creates for his friends Ted and Dinky looks like a GINGERBREAD HOUSE out of a child's fairy tale.

Although Sheemie survives the Devar's final battle, during the resulting chaos he steps on a tainted piece of glass. Sheemie dies on a train heading for FEDIC. Roland never gets to say good-bye to him. VII:84, VII:197–220, VII:228, VII:233, VII:234, VII:247, VII:256, VII:266, VII:267–71, VII:272, VII:273, VII:279, VII:290, VII:296, VII:307, VII:308, VII:318–24, VII:326–36, VII:337–42, VII:356, VI:357, VII:359, VII:366, VII:378, VII:388, VII:389, VII:391–92, VII:393, VII:400–401, VII:404–8, VII:409, VII:411–17, VII:532, VII:535, VII:538, VII:705 (idiot savant), VII:802

CAPPI: Sheemie's mule from the TRAVELLERS' REST in HAMBRY. VII:270

RUMBELOW, GRACE: Grace Rumbelow was originally from ALDER-SHOT, ENGLAND. She reminds JAKE CHAMBERS of the lifetime president of his mother's garden club. Grace is a true mork. VII:394

SEJ: Like BAJ, Sej is a hydrocephalic savant. However, unlike Baj, Sej has arms. Sej survives the DEVAR-TOI battle, although we don't know what becomes of him later. VII:375–77

SHEEMIE: See RUIZ, STANLEY, *listed above*

WAVERLY: Waverly is a fat Breaker who was a bookkeeper in his former life. VII:372

WORTHINGTON, FRED (BANKERLY LOOKING BREAKER NUMBER ONE): Fred Worthington looks like a banker, but despite his staid appearance he is willing to take risks. After the DEVAR's final battle, he helps TED BRAUTIGAN, DINKY EARNSHAW, DANI ROSTOV, and SHEEMIE RUIZ teleport Roland and JAKE to KEYSTONE EARTH so that they can save the life of STEPHEN KING. Fred hopes to eventually make his way to one of the ALTERNATIVE AMERICAS. VII:393, VII:404, VII:408, VII:538, VII:539, VII:540 *(indirect)*, VII:541 *(indirect)*, VII:560, VII:561, VII:563

YOUNG WOMAN ON MALL: JAKE sees this young woman forming what seems to be a séance circle with TED BRAUTIGAN and the other members of his Breaker ka-tet. Although we can't say for certain, it seems likely that she is actually TANYA LEEDS. See LEEDS, TANYA, *listed above*

BRICE, MR.
See TOWER, CALVIN

BROADCLOAK, MARTEN
See WALTER: WALTER'S ALIASES

BROTHER OUTFIT
See CALLAHAN, FATHER DONALD FRANK: CALLAHAN'S HIDDEN HIGHWAYS ASSOCIATES: COVAY MOVERS

BROWN
Brown was a border dweller in the desert beyond TULL. (See *Stephen King's The Dark Tower: A Concordance, Volume I.*) He had a pet raven named ZOLTAN. In *The Dark Tower,* he is mistakenly called a weed-eater.
VI:283, VII:826 *(mistakenly called a weed-eater)*

BUFFALO STAR
See GODS OF MID-WORLD

BULLET
See KING, STEPHEN: SMITH, BRYAN

BURKE, DAVID
See WARRIORS OF THE SCARLET EYE: DEVAR-TOI CHARACTERS:
HUMANS

BURKE, MATTHEW
See CALLAHAN, FATHER DONALD FRANK: 'SALEM'S LOT CHAR-
ACTERS

BUSINESSMAN (MARK CROSS BRIEFCASE)
See VAMPIRES: TYPE THREE: MARK CROSS BRIEFCASE BUSINESS-
MAN

BUSKER
See DEAN, SUSANNAH: SUSANNAH'S PRESENT ASSOCIATES

C

C3PO
See NORTH CENTRAL POSITRONICS: ANDY

CAGNEY, JAMES
See CAN-TOI

CALDERWOOD, FLOYD
See KING, STEPHEN

CALLA BRYN STURGIS CHARACTERS
Near the beginning of *Wolves of the Calla,* our ka-tet is approached by six representatives from the town of CALLA BRYN STURGIS—TIAN JAFFORDS,
ZALIA JAFFORDS, WAYNE OVERHOLSER, BEN SLIGHTMAN, BENNY
SLIGHTMAN, and PERE CALLAHAN. The Calla *folken* are in dire need of
help, and at least three of their representatives believe that our posse of gunslingers is their only hope of salvation.
    Although the Calla has been settled for more than a thousand years, over the
last six generations it has been plagued by giant, green-cloaked marauders riding out of THUNDERCLAP. These predators (called WOLVES because of the
terrible snarling masks that they wear) sweep down on the BORDERLAND
CALLAS each generation to steal one of every pair of prepubescent twins.
Although none of the Calla *folken* understand exactly what is being done to
their children, they do know that when the children are finally returned to them,
their minds and bodies are ruined, or ROONT.
    The people of the Callas realize that in most parts of the world, twins are rar-

ities and singletons are common, and that it is only in the arc of the borderlands that this natural phenomenon is reversed. It has led some among them to conclude that their children are being taken to the dark land so that a chemical which causes twin-telepathy can be culled from their brains. When our story begins, twenty-three years have passed since the last invasion. According to the town's one Messenger Robot, called ANDY, by the rise of the coming Demon Moon, the Wolves will be upon them once more.

The Calla *folken* are farmers and ranchers, not fighters. Most of the 140 men tend smallhold patches of rice near the river, and the majority of them are relatively poor. Only the wealthiest—such as the rancher VAUGHN EISENHART—have any guns at all, and everyone knows that those rusty shooting-irons are no match for the light-sticks, fire-hurling weapons, and sneetches wielded by the Greencloaks.

Although most of the Calla's attempts to stand up to the Wolves have ended in death and disaster, seventy years before Roland and his friends entered the borderlands, one of the SISTERS OF ORIZA, accompanied by a small group of friends, managed to bring a Greencloak down with one of her sharpened flying plates. The only member of that posse to survive (now an ancient old man) remembers all too well what the twitching Greencloak looked like behind its mask. According to GRAN-PERE JAFFORDS, the Wolf looked just like Andy.

By sending false battle plans to the Wolves via Andy and the traitorous BEN SLIGHTMAN, Roland, EDDIE, SUSANNAH, JAKE, and the Sisters of Oriza defeat their enemies despite being vastly outnumbered. In the battle of the EAST ROAD, MARGARET EISENHART and Jake's friend BENNY SLIGHTMAN are killed. However, their deaths are not in vain since the Calla's children are saved.

As well as the Wolf battle, many important events take place in this small town located on the lip of END-WORLD. Roland and his friends meet a final (if temporary) member of their tet, FATHER DONALD FRANK CALLAHAN, whom CONSTANT READERS know from STEPHEN KING's novel *'Salem's Lot*. It is here that Susannah Dean's haunting demon, MIA, begins to get the upper hand and finally absconds with the body they share. It is also in the Calla that our ka-tet begins to suspect just how closely their khef is tied to that of the writer Stephen King.

GENERAL REFERENCES: V:13–31 *(men in Gathering Hall)*, V:123–24, V:209, V:211–34 *(Calla fiesta)*, V:238, V:402–6, V:479, V:490, V:562, V:572, V:581, V:585, V:601–17, V:643, V:648, V:649, V:650, V:654, V:659, V:689, V:693–97 *(present)*, VI:6, VI:9, VI:10, VI:14, VI:17, VI:24, VI:131, VI:350, VII:120, VII:173, VII:207, VII:233, VII:398, VII:412, VII:473, VII:540

CHILD-MINDERS: Early on the morning that the WOLVES are due to arrive in Calla Bryn Sturgis, these characters travel with Roland's ka-tet and the SISTERS OF ORIZA to the ARROYOS northeast of the Calla. Although they initially believe that Roland plans to hide the children in the arroyos, they find out that they are actually to be hidden in LADY ORIZA's rice.

The child-minders are SAREY ADAMS, HUGH ANSELM, KRELLA ANSELM, FATHER DONALD FRANK CALLAHAN, VAUGHN EISEN-HART, JORGE ESTRADA, TIAN JAFFORDS, ANNABELLE JAVIER, BUCKY JAVIER, BEN SLIGHTMAN, and CANTAB and ARA of the MANNI. REUBEN CAVERRA was supposed to be among them, but he busted a gut the night before and could not take part. WAYNE OVERHOLSER takes his place. V:483–84 *(indirect; Roland asks Callahan for names)*, V:608, V:615, V:643, V:662–67, V:677, V:689 *(folken)*, V:693–97 *(folken)*

CHILDREN OF THE CALLA: *See also* CALLA BRYN STURGIS CHARACTERS: ROONTS, *listed below.* V:132, V:139, V:143 *(twins)*, V:150, V:151, V:152, V:206, V:211, V:214, V:217, V:220, V:222, V:225, V:341, V:362, V:508, V:575, V:584, V:585–89 *(singing)*, V:602, V:607, V:609, V:629, V:636, V:637, V:643, V:646, V:650, V:654, V:658, V:662–67, V:671, V:677, V:689 *(part of folken)*, V:693–97, VI:6, VI:80, VI:115, VI:237, VI:243 *(indirect)*, VI:247, VI:378 *(victims of the Wolves)*, VII:75, VII:142, VII:152, VII:153, VII:173, VII:206, VII:213, VII:214 *(indirect)*, VII:339, VII:412

  PUDGY BOY: V:588

  TWIN SINGERS: V:227

FARMERS (LARGE FARMS):

OVERHOLSER, WAYNE DALE: Wayne Dale Overholser, the Calla's most successful farmer and one of its most important citizens, is the owner of SEVEN MILE FARM, located just west of Calla Bryn Sturgis. His major crop is wheat. Wayne is about sixty years old, has heavy cheeks scarred with "I-want" lines, and a vast, sloping belly. Despite wearing a white Stetson like a good guy from a cowboy film, Overholser is initially dubious about the chances four gunslingers and a BILLY-BUMBLER have against more than sixty WOLVES. Obviously, he doesn't know Roland.

  Although his two grown children were both singletons, Overholser himself had a twin named WELLAND. Like so many others, Welland was taken by the Wolves and returned ROONT. Despite his initial cynicism, Overholser is eventually won over to Roland's way of seeing and even acts as one of the CHILD-MINDERS during the battle of the EAST ROAD. According to CALVIN TOWER, in our world, Wayne D. Overholser is also the name of a cowboy novelist. V:20–31 *(Town Gathering Hall; present)*, V:44 *(following ka-tet)*, V:45 *(following ka-tet)*, V:47 *(following ka-tet)*, V:57 *(Wayne D)*, V:88 *(friends)*, V:92 *(indirect)*, V:106 *(indirect)*, V:109 *(indirect)*, V:111–13, V:116, V:117–18, V:122–37, V:142–60, V:162, V:165, V:166, V:201–10 *(present—mentioned directly on 205, 206, 208–9)*, V:211–34 *(present for fiesta—mentioned directly on 212, 213–14, 216, 217, 222, 223, 224)*, V:237, V:321 *(not as shrewd as Eisenhart)*, V:329, V:340, V:404, V:488, V:497, V:509, V:557, V:572, V:576, V:601–17 *(present—mentioned directly on 604, 606)*, V:651–52, V:654, V:656, V:661, V:662–67, V:677, V:681, V:689 *(folken)*, V:693–97 *(folken)*, VI:9, VI:92, VI:303 *(the writer)*

OVERHOLSER, ALAN: Alan was the father of Wayne and

WELLAND OVERHOLSER. He died long before our story takes place. V:128, V:130 *(folks)*, V:147 *(pa)*

OVERHOLSER, MRS.: Wayne's wife. We never learn her full name. V:651

MOTHER (UNNAMED): V:130 *(folks)*, V:147 *(ma)*, V:150 *(ma)*

OVERHOLSER, WELLAND: See CALLA BRYN STURGIS CHARACTERS: ROONTS, *listed below*

FARMERS (SMALLHOLD):

ANSELM, HUGH: Hugh Anselm owns a smallhold just south of TIAN JAFFORDS's place. Tian wants to buy it. Anselm is one of the CHILD-MINDERS during the final battle with the WOLVES. V:349, V:587, V:589, V:662–67 *(not mentioned here, but we find out on 677 that he must have been present)*, V:677

> **ANSELM, KRELLA:** Krella is Hugh Anselm's wife. She also acts as a CHILD-MINDER during the final battle with the WOLVES. V:662–67 *(mentioned on 666)*, V:677, V:689 *(folken)*, V:693–97 *(folken)*

> **ANSELM TWINS:** The Anselm twins are about thirteen or fourteen years old. V:587–88

ARRA: During GRAN-PERE JAFFORDS's youth, Arra owned a smallhold patch just east of the Calla. It was near this smallhold that Granpere and the other members of the WOLF POSSE lay in ambush for their green-cloaked enemies. V:361

CAVERRA, REUBEN: Reuben Caverra is a plump man with a round, cheerful face. Later in the story he is described as a "hulk of a man" and is said to be fearless. The year the WOLVES took his twin, RUTH, he made a mark on the big pine tree in his front yard. He continued to make a mark each succeeding year. By his reckoning, the Calla had twenty-three years of peace between invasions from THUNDERCLAP. Reuben Caverra is one of the *folken* chosen to act as a CHILD-MINDER during the standoff against the Wolves. Unfortunately, Reuben busts a gut and is too ill to participate. WAYNE OVERHOLSER takes his place. *See also* CALLAHAN, FATHER DONALD FRANK: CALLAHAN'S HIDDEN HIGHWAYS ASSOCIATES: MEXICAN IMMIGRANTS (ILLEGAL). V:15–31 *(Town Gathering Hall; present)*, V:483, V:651

> **CAVERRA, DIANE:** Diane Caverra is Reuben's wife. CALLAHAN names her as another possible CHILD-MINDER. However, due to her husband's illness, she does not participate either. V:483

> **CAVERRA, RUTH:** See CALLA BRYN STURGIS CHARACTERS: ROONTS, *listed below*

ESTRADA, JORGE: Like many of the other smallhold farmers, Jorge Estrada has children young enough to be taken by the WOLVES. He acts as one of the CHILD-MINDERS during the EAST ROAD battle. *See also* CALLAHAN, FATHER DONALD FRANK: CALLAHAN'S HIDDEN HIGHWAYS ASSOCIATES: MEXICAN IMMIGRANTS (ILLEGAL).

V:16–31 *(Town Gathering Hall; present)*, V:211–34 *(present; mentioned directly on 222)*, V:488–92 *(present)*, V:656, V:662–67 *(present)*, V:677, V:689 *(folken)*, V:693–97 *(folken)*

ESTRADA, DEELIE: She is the wife of Jorge Estrada. V:488–92 *(present)*

FARADAY, NEIL: Squat, cynical Neil Faraday owns a smallhold rice patch far to the South'ards. He is a hard worker but an even harder drinker, a fact easily discerned from the dark circles under his eyes and the burst of purplish veins on his cheeks. When TIAN JAFFORDS calls a meeting to discuss fighting the WOLVES, Faraday (holding his filthy sombrero) counsels caution. Later, during the Calla meeting where Roland tells everyone to bring their children to the PAVILION on the eve of the Wolf attack, Faraday refuses. He will not allow his three children (or his wife) to take part in Roland's plan. V:18–31 *(Town Gathering Hall; present)*, V:211–34 *(present; mentioned directly on 222)*, V:601–17 *(present; mentioned directly on 611–12, 614)*

THREE CHILDREN: V:612

GEORGE: *See* CALLA BRYN STURGIS CHARACTERS: ROONTS, *listed below*

GEORGINA: Faraday's daughter. Her twin became ROONT. V:18

WIFE: V:612

HAYCOX, LOUIS: Haycox is a dark-skinned man with a black mustache. His farm is just west of TIAN JAFFORDS's, near the edge of the Calla. He has four-year-old twins. He is afraid of the WOLVES, but willing to fight for his family. V:19–31 *(Town Gathering Hall; present)*, V:211–34 *(present; mentioned directly on 222, 227)*, V:601–17 *(present; mentioned directly on 606, 608)*

TWINS: V:19

JAFFORDS FAMILY: *See* JAFFORDS FAMILY, *listed separately*

JAVIER, BUCKY: Bucky Javier has bright little blue eyes in a small head that seems to slope back from his goateed chin. Although he is not the most landed of the smallhold farmers, he is powerful. He owns eighty acres. The rest he gave to his younger sister ROBERTA as a wedding present. His ROONT twin was named BULLY. He and his wife ANNABELLE are both CHILD-MINDERS during the final battle against the WOLVES. *See also* CALLAHAN, FATHER DONALD FRANK: CALLAHAN'S HIDDEN HIGHWAYS ASSOCIATES: MEXICAN IMMIGRANTS (ILLEGAL). V:17–31 *(Town Gathering Hall; present)*, V:159 *(owns eighty acres)*, V:483, V:489–92 *(present)*, V:601–17 *(present; mentioned directly on 602)*, V:654, V:662–67 *(present)*, V:689 *(folken)*, V:693–97 *(folken)*

JAVIER, ANNABELLE: She is Bucky's wife. She and her husband are two of the CHILD-MINDERS during the final battle against the WOLVES. V:483, V:489–92 *(present)*, V:601–17 *(not yet named, but present and mentioned on 602)*, V:654, V:662–67 *(present)*, V:689 *(folken)*, V:693–97 *(folken)*

JAVIER, BULLY: See CALLA BRYN STURGIS CHARACTERS: ROONTS, *listed below*

JAVIER, ROBERTA: Roberta is Bucky's younger sister. She and her twin were only a year old when the WOLVES last invaded the Calla, so the two of them were passed over. Since his own twin died, Bucky dotes on his younger siblings. When Roberta married, Bucky gave her half of what he owned. V:159

   HUSBAND (UNNAMED): V:159

ROSARIO, FREDDY: Freddy Rosario owns the farm closest to TIAN JAFFORDS's land. He has fathered one set of twins, but since the children are still nursing, they are probably safe from the WOLVES. V:24–31 *(Town Gathering Hall; present),* V:211–34 *(present; mentioned directly on 222, 225),* V:601–17 *(present; mentioned directly on 602)*

   TWINS: V:24

STRONG, GARRETT: Garrett Strong is a smallhold farmer with the face of a pug dog. During the men's meeting at the Calla GATHERING HALL at the beginning of *Wolves of the Calla,* he is outraged by the MANNI's suggestion that the people of the Calla should kill their children and kill themselves rather than face the WOLVES. His farmhand's name is ROSSITER. V:17–31 *(Town Gathering Hall; present),* V:211–34 *(present; mentioned directly on 222),* V:486, V:601–17 *(Strongs)*

   ROSSITER: Garrett Strong's farmhand. V:20–31 *(Town Gathering Hall; present),* V:601–17 *(present; mentioned directly on 602)*

MANNI: See MANNI, *listed separately*

RANCHERS:

ADAMS, DIEGO: Diego Adams has intense black eyes. Like OVER-HOLSER and EISENHART, he is a wealthy man and so has much to lose should the WOLVES burn the town down. He does not want to fight the Wolves, though his own children are prepubescent and at risk. His wife, on the other hand, is one of the SISTERS OF ORIZA. She wants to fight alongside Roland during the EAST ROAD battle, but is not accurate enough with the plate to take part in the ambush. Instead, Roland puts her in charge of the CHILD-MINDERS and the twins they guard. V:17–31 *(Town Gathering Hall; present),* V:211–34 *(present; mentioned directly on 214, 230),* V:489–92 *(present)*

   ADAMS, SAREY: See ORIZA, SISTERS OF

EISENHART, VAUGHN: Vaughn Eisenhart is one of the most important men of the Calla. His ranch, called the ROCKING B, is located south of town. Eisenhart's foreman is BEN SLIGHTMAN, whose son, BENNY, becomes a close friend of JAKE's. Unfortunately, Slightman the elder turns out to be a traitor to his town.

   Unlike most of the other men of the BORDERLANDS, Eisenhart owns three guns, all of which have been in his family for seven generations. The best of the shooting-irons is the ancient rifle, which he brings to important meetings, such as the one TIAN JAFFORDS calls at the

GATHERING HALL at the outset of *Wolves of the Calla*. The other two are barrel-shooters, and only one of them is in good enough condition to fire.

Although Eisenhart, like the other wealthy men of the Calla, is initially skeptical about our tet's ability to best the WOLVES, he eventually has a change of heart. This change comes about because of his wife, MARGARET (originally of the MANNI clan), who is one of the SISTERS OF ORIZA. Margaret wants to stand with Roland's tet and fight the Wolves, and her husband, who knows how much she has given up for him and their six children, agrees to let her take part in the EAST ROAD battle. During the Calla's final stand against the invaders from THUNDERCLAP, Vaughn acts as one of the CHILD-MINDERS. Unfortunately, his wife does not survive the fray, but is decapitated by one of the Wolves' light-sticks. In our last glimpse of Vaughn, he is cradling his dead wife's head. V:13–31 *(Town Gathering Hall; present)*, V:153, V:158, V:169, V:205, V:211–34 *(present; mentioned directly on 219, 223, 224)*, V:234, V:244, V:294, V:302, V:313, V:318–25 *(321—shrewder than Overholser)*, V:328–42, V:345, V:404 *(countryman's sense of humor)*, V:407–8 *(heathen man)*, V:495, V:497–98, V:572, V:576, V:601–17 *(present; mentioned directly on 602, 605, 608–9, 613)*, V:655, V:662–67 *(present; mentioned directly on 666)*, V:677, V:689, V:690–94, VI:9, VI:17, VI:25 *(indirect)*

COOKIE: The cook at ROCKING B. V:553

EISENHART, MARGARET: *See* ORIZA, SISTERS OF

EISENHART, VERNA: *See* CALLA BRYN STURGIS CHARACTERS: ROONTS, *listed below*

EISENHART CHILDREN (TOM AND TESSA, SECOND SET OF TWINS, FIFTEEN-YEAR-OLD TWINS): There are six Eisenhart children. The eldest two—Tom and Tessa—were born less than a month before the last WOLF invasion. The youngest pair is fifteen. Although none of the Eisenhart children have been made ROONT, all have left the Calla in search of a place free from THUNDERCLAP's marauders. In MARGARET's opinion, she and her husband didn't lose three children to the Wolves—they lost all six. V:328–29

EISENHART'S DA: V:319

EISENHART'S GRAND-DA: V:319

RANCH COWPOKES: V:321, V:334, V:336–37, V:489, V:495, V:553 *(hands)*

SLIGHTMAN, BEN (EISENHART'S FOREMAN): Ben Slightman is the father of BENNY, also called BENNY THE KID *(listed below)*. We are told that Slightman, an earnest-looking man in spectacles and farmer's clothes, does not suffer fools lightly. In the GATHERING HALL meeting where TIAN JAFFORDS suggests that the Calla *folken* stand up to the WOLVES, Slightman counsels caution. Later we learn the true reason for Slightman's fears.

Four years before the beginning of our story, Slightman (a widower) lost Benny's twin sister to a disease called hot-lung. The child was probably infected by ANDY, but grieving Slightman didn't know this. He agreed to betray his fellow townsfolk for a pair of spectacles, a music machine which he hides in his saddlebag, and a promise that his one remaining child would be kept safe from the Greencloaks. Slightman's secret is discovered by JAKE CHAMBERS while he is hiding in the CALLA DOGAN. Jake informs Roland, who then feeds false battle information to Slightman and Andy so that the two of them will misdirect the coming Wolves. Roland's plan works, but during the EAST ROAD battle Benny is killed. A distraught Slightman (also one of the CHILD-MINDERS) blames Roland for his son's death, screaming that Roland wanted vengeance on him. Roland manages to silence him before others can hear his confession of guilt. V:19–31 *(Town Gathering Hall; present)*, V:44 *(follows ka-tet)*, V:45 *(follows ka-tet)*, V:47 *(follows ka-tet)*, V:88 *(new friends)*, V:92 *(indirect)*, V:106 *(indirect)*, V:109, V:111–13, V:116, V:122, V:142–60, V:165, V:166, V:167, V:201–10, V:211–34 *(present; mentioned directly on 211, 216, 218)*, V:234, V:294, V:302, V:313, V:323 *(da)*, V:340–42, V:384–86, V:391, V:495–96, V:533 *(indirect)*, V:534, V:551, V:552, V:553, V:554, V:555, V:558, V:559, V:561, V:567–77, V:578, V:579–80, V:581, V:585, V:586, V:590, V:601–17 *(present; mentioned directly on 602, 607, 608, 610, 611, 614–16)*, V:637, V:638, V:641, V:654, V:655–61, V:662–67, V:683, V:687, V:689, V:690–97, V:704, VI:17, VI:25, VI:67, VI:167 *(or Benny)*, VI:168 *(or Benny)*, VI:205, VII:191, VII:508

SLIGHTMAN, BENNY (BENNY THE KID): Although Benny Slightman is a few years older than JAKE CHAMBERS, Jake is the more experienced of the two boys. Hence, the pair become well-matched friends. Ben's twin sister died of hot-lung four years before our story takes place, and so no one knows if he counts as a twin or a singleton. (We find out later that Benny's twin was probably infected by ANDY.) Benny does not know that his father is a traitor, a fact which saves brave young Ben a lot of pain. During the final stand against the WOLVES, Benny, along with the TAVERY twins, hides in the fighter's ditch located on the front line of the East Road battle. After MARGARET EISENHART's death, Benny is killed by one of the Wolves' flying sneetches.

When Eddie returns to NEW YORK 1977 via BLACK THIRTEEN, he finds out that in our world, Ben Slightman Jr. (or "Benny the Kid," as Eddie tends to call him) had a namesake who grew up to be a cowboy novelist. This other Ben Slightman Jr. settled in MONTANA, but was killed during an argument with some Indians in front of a local general store. In *The Dark Tower*, we find out that this Ben Slightman also wrote science fiction under the pen name DAN HOLMES, a name shared by SUSANNAH DEAN's father. V:29, V:44 *(following ka-tet)*, V:45 *(following ka-tet)*, V:47 *(following ka-tet)*, V:88

(new friends), V:92 *(indirect)*, V:106 *(indirect)*, V:109 *(indirect)*, V:111–13, V:116, V:122–37, V:142–60, V:165, V:169, V:201–10, V:211–34 *(present; mentioned directly on 212, 216, 218, 221, 225 as Jake's friend, 227, 228, 233, 234)*, V:235, V:238, V:294, V:302, V:313, V:318–24, V:328, V:332–34 *(watches Margaret Eisenhart throw)*, V:340, V:341, V:381, V:385, V:386, V:487, V:495, V:496, V:501, V:532–34 *(namesake author; nineteen letters)*, V:552, V:553–56, V:557, V:558, V:559, V:568, V:571, V:572, V:574, V:575, V:577, V:578, V:579–80, V:586, V:601–17 *(present; mentioned directly on 602, 614, 615, 616)*, V:636–38, V:654, V:656, V:657 *(Jake's friend)*, V:658, V:660, V:661, V:662–73, V:675–76, V:679–82 *(hiding, killed on 682)*, V:683, V:687, V:688–97, V:700, V:705 *(friend)*, VI:3, VI:11, VI:24, VI:25, VI:27, VI:32, VI:167, VI:168, VI:205, VI:269, VI:340, VII:137, VII:191, VII:396, VII:398, VII:403, VII:473, VII:508

> **TWIN SISTER:** Benny's sister died of hot-lung four years before our story begins. Both she and Benny were ten at the time. At the end of *Wolves of the Calla*, we find out that she was probably purposefully infected by ANDY, who needed one vulnerable parent to become an informer for the WOLVES. V:112–13, V:204, V:385, V:495, V:554, V:580, V:660

> **SLIGHTMAN, EDNA:** Benny's aunt. V:323

TELFORD, GEORGE: George Telford, owner of BUCKHEAD RANCH, is silver-haired, tanned, weather-beaten, and handsome. (In EDDIE DEAN's opinion, he strongly resembles Pa Cartwright from the television program *Bonanza*.) Although his ranch is not as large as EISENHART's, Telford is gifted with both a silver tongue and a smooth voice, powerful weapons which he uses against TIAN JAFFORDS in the GATHERING HALL battle for hearts and minds. Like the other wealthy men of the Calla, Telford does not want the Calla *folken* to stand up against the WOLVES. He is afraid of losing his home and his land. Unlike Eisenhart, who stands with Roland in the end, Telford remains staunchly opposed to our *tet's* battle plan. After their victory, he probably has a change of heart. V:24–31 *(Town Gathering Hall; present)*, V:211–34 *(present; mentioned directly on 214, 218, 221, 223–26, 227, indirect, 230)*, V:244, V:509, V:553 *(Buckhead Ranch)*, V:601–14 *(present; mentioned directly on 602, 606–7, 608–9, 611, 612, 614)*, V:619

> **ELDEST SON:** V:601–17 *(present; mentioned directly on 608)*

> **TELFORD, MRS.:** George Telford's wife. She is described as a plump but hard-faced woman. V:601–17 *(present; mentioned directly on 602, 606)*

> **TELFORD FAMILY:** V:606

ROONTS: In Calla Bryn Sturgis, as in the other Callas of the CRESCENT, twins are the norm and singletons are rarities. However, this birthing anomaly has a hidden horror. Once a generation, the WOLVES sweep out of THUNDERCLAP and take one of every pair of prepubescent twins over the age of three. The stolen children are almost always returned (they make the journey back to the Calla upon two flatcars drawn by a train), but when they come back from Thunderclap, they are ruined (roont). No matter how clever they were before they were taken, they return intellectually devastated. Few have the ability to do physical labor and even fewer can speak. Though they grow to prodigious size (some are as tall as seven feet), they are sexually dead. Those who understand at least part of what has happened to them, or who were old enough when they were taken to comprehend some of what they have lost, suffer from terrible depression. Some even commit suicide.

At the end of *Wolves of the Calla*, we learn that the Calla's twins are taken to Thunderclap so that the chemical (or perhaps enzyme) which causes "twin-telepathy" can be extracted from their brains. The servants of the CRIMSON KING transform this substance into pills and feed it to the psychic BREAKERS who are eroding the BEAMS. Hence, it seems that ka, not random chance, has brought Roland and his friends to the BORDERLANDS.

Upon reaching their thirties, the roonts grow old with shocking rapidity. They die in terrible physical agony. V:2, V:3, V:11, V:14, V:23, V:24, V:139 *(ruined)*, V:143–47, V:152, V:220, V:319, V:589, V:609, V:630, V:658, V:660, VI:152 *(Cullum speaks of roont walk-ins)*, VI:238 *(indirect)*, VII:173, VII:206, VII:339, VII:532

CAVERRA, RUTH: Twin of REUBEN CAVERRA. V:15, V:483

DOOLIN, MINNIE: Minnie Doolin was the twin sister of MOLLY DOOLIN, the only person in the Calla ever to have killed one of the WOLVES. When Molly hurled that deadly ORIZA, she called out Minnie's name. V:361, V:363

EISENHART, VERNA: VAUGHN EISENHART's twin. V:319

FARADAY, GEORGE: Son of NEIL FARADAY, brother of GEORGINA FARADAY. V:18

HOONIK, ZALMAN: Twin of ZALIA JAFFORDS. He lives with the Jaffords family. Zalman is seven feet tall. V:10–11, V:146, V:147, V:150, V:344–46, V:349, V:351–57, V:489–92 *(present)*, V:649, V:681 *(indirect; brother)*

JAFFORDS, GRAN-PERE'S TWIN: V:11, V:362

JAFFORDS, TIA: Tia is TIAN JAFFORDS's roont twin. She is six and a half feet tall and has enormous breasts. Unlike many of the roonts, she is able to talk. Although she functions at the mental level of a young child, Tia has the uncanny ability of avoiding holes in "loose ground." She wears one of FATHER CALLAHAN's Jesus-trees. V:2–9, V:10–11, V:144, V:147, V:150, V:344–46, V:349–50, V:351–57, V:368, V:489–92 *(present)*, V:649

JAVIER, BULLY: Twin of BUCKY JAVIER. He died. V:159

OVERHOLSER, WELLAND: Twin of WAYNE OVERHOLSER. V:144, V:147, V:150

SLIDELL (POKEY SLIDELL'S SON): V:362

SLIDELL (POKEY SLIDELL'S TWIN): V:362

SISTERS OF ORIZA: *See* ORIZA, SISTERS OF, *listed separately*

WOLF POSSE: Seventy years before the beginning of our story, a small band of Calla *folken* stood up to the WOLVES of THUNDERCLAP. One of their number (a redheaded SISTER OF ORIZA named MOLLY DOOLIN) killed one of these Greencloaks, but this victory came at a great cost. JAMIE JAFFORDS was the only human survivor.

> **DOOLIN, EAMON:** Balding, mild-mannered Eamon Doolin was the husband of the fiery MOLLY DOOLIN, the only person in the Calla ever to have killed one of the invading WOLVES. He stood true, but was killed by a sneetch which exploded in his face. He was twenty-three. V:358–63
>
> **DOOLIN, MOLLY:** *See* ORIZA, SISTERS OF, *listed separately*
>
> > **MINNIE:** *See* CALLA BRYN STURGIS CHARACTERS: ROONTS, *listed above*
>
> **JAFFORDS, JAMIE:** *See* JAFFORDS FAMILY, *listed separately*
>
> **SLIDELL, POKEY:** Pokey Slidell, best friend of JAMIE JAFFORDS, was the oldest member of the Wolf Posse. Pokey had already lost a brother and a young child to the WOLVES. Like EAMON DOOLIN, Pokey was killed by a sneetch. V:358–64, V:365
>
> > **POKEY'S SON:** *See* CALLA BRYN STURGIS CHARACTERS: ROONTS, *listed above*
> >
> > **POKEY'S TWIN:** *See* CALLA BRYN STURGIS CHARACTERS: ROONTS, *listed above*

OTHER CHARACTERS:

> **ANDY THE ROBOT:** *See* NORTH CENTRAL POSITRONICS, *listed separately*
>
> **BERNARDO:** Bernardo is the town tosspot. V:601–17 *(mentioned on 602)*
>
> **CALLAHAN, FATHER:** *See* CALLAHAN, FATHER DONALD FRANK, *listed separately*
>
> **CASH, BENITO:** V:16–31 *(Town Gathering Hall; present)*, V:211–34 *(present; mentioned directly on 222)*
>
> **COWBOYS (UNNAMED):** V:601–17 *(present; named on 602)*
>
> **ECHEVERRIA:** *See also* CALLAHAN, FATHER DONALD FRANK: CALLAHAN'S HIDDEN HIGHWAYS ASSOCIATES: MEXICAN IMMIGRANTS (ILLEGAL). V:211–34 *(Town Gathering Hall; present)*
>
> **FARMWORKERS (UNNAMED):** V:402
>
> **HAGGENGOOD TWINS:** These twenty-three-year-old twins were born in the year that the WOLVES last invaded Calla Bryn Sturgis. They are incredibly ugly but are hard workers. V:601–17 *(present; mentioned directly on 603)*
>
> **HANDS FAMILY:** V:601–17 *(present; mentioned directly on 602)*
>
> **MUNOZ, ROSALITA:** *See* ORIZA, SISTERS OF, *listed separately*
>
> **POSELLA, FARREN:** A farmhand. V:22–31 *(Town Gathering Hall; present)*, V:211–34 *(present; mentioned directly on 222, 225)*, V:601–17 *(present; mentioned directly on 602)*

SPALTER: Cousin of WAYNE OVERHOLSER. V:211–34 *(present; mentioned directly on 222)*

TAVERY, FRANCINE: The talented Tavery twins draw Roland a map of the Calla and its surrounding countryside. This map proves useful when Roland plans his battle strategy. The Taverys are beautiful prepubescent children. They both have black hair, large blue eyes, clear skin, and cheeks with a smattering of freckles. If the raids from THUNDERCLAP had not been stopped, either Francine or Frank would have ended their days ROONT. V:242 *(indirect)*, V:249 *(indirect)*, V:250–51, V:294, V:310–12, V:337, V:340, V:351, V:388, V:399, V:490, V:512, V:575, V:601–17 *(present; mentioned directly on 603)*, V:649, V:662–73, V:675–76, V:677, V:679–82 *(hiding in fighters' hole; mentioned again 682)*, V:692, V:693–97 *(folken)*, VI:24 *(indirect)*, VI:27 *(indirect)*

TAVERY, FRANK: Frank and FRANCINE TAVERY draw the map which Roland uses to plan his tet's stand against the WOLVES. Like his sister, Francine, Frank is a beautiful prepubescent child. His hair is black, his eyes are blue, and his clear, smooth cheeks are covered with a smattering of freckles. Just before the battle of the EAST ROAD commences, Frank and Francine help JAKE CHAMBERS and BENNY SLIGHTMAN strew children's toys along the ARROYO path to divert the coming Wolves. However, Frank steps in a hole and breaks his ankle. After much struggle, Jake, Benny, and Francine manage to move him, but just in time. Jake's three companions are forced to hide in the gunslingers' fighting ditch with Roland, EDDIE, SUSANNAH, and the SISTERS OF ORIZA rather than in the rice with the other children. This unplanned frontline hiding place leads indirectly to Benny's death. V:242 *(indirect)*, V:249 *(indirect)*, V:250–51, V:294, V:310–12, V:337, V:340, V:351, V:399, V:490, V:512, V:575, V:601–17 *(present; mentioned directly on 603)*, V:649, V:662–73, V:675–76, V:679–82 *(hiding in fighters' hole; mentioned again 682)*, V:692, V:693–97 *(folken)*, VI:11, VI:24, VI:27, VI:205

TOOK, EBEN: Shrewd, fat Eben Took is the present owner of TOOK'S GENERAL STORE. In his high, womanish voice, he makes it clear that he does not want to stand up to the WOLVES. (He is afraid they will burn down his store and ruin his profits.) Not surprisingly, none of the Tooks have children at risk. V:18–31 *(Town Gathering Hall; present)*, V:158–59, V:205, V:294, V:388, V:400, V:401, V:402–6, V:417, V:418, V:472, V:479, V:487 *(store)*, V:497, V:601–14 *(present; mentioned directly on 604, 608, 609, 611, 612, 613, 614)*, V:695, VI:130 *(shop)*, VI:162, VII:423

TOOK FAMILY (GENERAL): The Tooks are one of the wealthiest and most important families in the Calla. They own both TOOKY'S (the Calla's general store) and the TRAVELLER'S REST (the town's boardinghouse and restaurant). They also own half interest in the LIVERY and have loan papers on most of the smallhold farms in the Calla. In the distant

past, some of the Tooks tried to hide children in their store so that the WOLVES would not find them. As punishment, the Wolves burned the store down to the ground and took the children anyway. Now, no Took will stand up to the Wolves. V:13 *(store)*, V:14 *(store)*, V:19 *(Tooky's)*, V:158–59, V:331, V:359, V:487, V:497 *(store)*, V:534 *(store)*, V:566 *(store)*, V:585, V:601–17 *(clan present; mentioned directly on 602, 606, 621)*
WINKLER: Cousin of WAYNE OVERHOLSER. V:211–34 *(present; mentioned directly on 222)*
WOMAN (UNNAMED): V:604

CALLAHAN, FATHER DONALD FRANK (PERE CALLAHAN, FATHER CALLAHAN, THE OLD FELLA, CALLAHAN O' THE ROADS)

Before the publication of *Wolves of the Calla,* many CONSTANT READERS probably assumed that Father Donald Frank Callahan was wandering the earth as cursed as Cain. Our last sight of him in the novel *'Salem's Lot* was of a broken man, abandoned by his God, waiting for the driver of his NEW YORK CITY–bound bus to return with a bottle of cheap hooch so that he could burn the terrible, damning taste of the VAMPIRE BARLOW's blood from his mouth.

Along with his companions BEN MEARS, JIM CODY, MATT BURKE, and MARK PETRIE, Callahan had dared to stand up to an ancient TYPE ONE VAMPIRE living in the town of JERUSALEM'S LOT, MAINE. But in his personal confrontation with that force of the Outer Dark, Callahan's faith had failed him. In the wreckage of the Petries' kitchen, Barlow challenged Callahan to throw down his cross, but Callahan did not have enough faith in the WHITE, that elemental force behind all religious trappings, to confront the vampire without it. But even as he hesitated, the said crucifix's blinding white fire faltered and went out. As a result, Callahan was forced to take part in Barlow's unholy communion and became unclean, both in his own eyes and in the eyes of God.

After fleeing 'Salem's Lot but before arriving in CALLA BRYN STURGIS, Pere Callahan traveled the HIGHWAYS IN HIDING, which connect the MULTIPLE AMERICAS on all levels of the DARK TOWER. Often he would "flip" between one level of the Tower and another. (For example, he would fall asleep in FORT LEE, NEW JERSEY, but wake up in one of its twinners named LEABROOK.) During his wanderings, Callahan had two brief periods of grace, first in the HOME shelter, located on FIRST AVENUE of New York City, and then in the LIGHTHOUSE SHELTER of DETROIT. However, his first hiatus ended with the death of his beloved friend LUPE DELGADO, and the second was clipped short by his own death on December 19, 1983. (He jumped out a window to save himself from RICHARD P. SAYRE, CAN-TOI servant of the CRIMSON KING, and his horde of AIDS-carrying vampires.)

When we meet Callahan in the town of Calla Bryn Sturgis, his God has taken him back into the fold, at least on a trial basis. He has been in the Calla long enough to build a church and to convert many of the townsfolk to his particular brand of Christianity. Beneath the floor of his church sleeps BLACK THIRTEEN, the most dangerous of MAERLYN'S MAGIC BALLS and the magical object which (thanks to WALTER) opened the UNFOUND DOOR in the WAY STATION between life and death and transported both Callahan, and itself, to the CAVE OF VOICES in the Calla.

Although many years have passed, the Calla's Callahan still bears the scars of his confrontation with the vampire Barlow—a burned hand from when he tried to reenter his church but was blasted away from it by the power of the White, and a disturbing ability to detect all otherworldly creatures, including both vampires and the VAGRANT DEAD. Callahan also bears a brand on his forehead (in the shape of a cross), which the people of the Calla think was self-inflicted. However, this scar was the result of mortal demons, namely the HITLER BROTHERS, who were hired by the LOW MEN to hunt Callahan down and kill him.

At the end of *Wolves of the Calla*, a shaky Callahan finds out that he is actually a character in a novel by STEPHEN KING. The name of the novel? *'Salem's Lot*. It is quite possible that rereading his own story reinforces Callahan's decision not to give in to doubt again. In *The Dark Tower*, as in *'Salem's Lot*, Callahan's faith in the White is put to the test. However, this time he triumphs. When Callahan faces down the blood-drinkers of THE DIXIE PIG with JAKE CHAMBERS, he does not lose faith. With first Susannah's SCRIMSHAW TURTLE, then his cross, and then with just the little CAN-TAH (another symbol of the White) he holds off the forces of darkness so that Jake and OY can escape. In the end, Callahan is attacked by the low men, but before the vampires can approach and feed upon him, Callahan ends his own life with Jake's Ruger. Callahan dies by his own hand, but in his final desperate hour he redeems himself in his own eyes, and in the eyes of his God.

V:2 *(Old Fella)*, V:6, V:8, V:11, V:16–31 *(on 16 enters Gathering Hall; present for action)*, V:44 *(following our ka-tet)*, V:45 *(following our ka-tet)*, V:47 *(following our ka-tet)*, V:106–16, V:117, V:118, V:119, V:122–37, V:138, V:139, V:142–60, V:165, V:175, V:176, V:180, V:196, V:201–10 *(present; mentioned on 204, 205, 206, 208)*, V:211–34 *(Calla fiesta; mentioned on 211, 212, 214, 216, 218–19, 221, 225, 227–87)*, V:234–37, V:238, V:240, V:241 *(the religious)*, V:242, V:243, V:244–45, V:248, V:249, V:250, V:252–53, V:254–309 *(Priest's tale)*, V:309–17, V:338, V:341, V:381, V:383, V:393, V:396, V:399, V:400, V:401, V:402, V:403, V:409, V:411, V:412, V:413, V:414, V:415, V:417, V:418, V:419, V:420, V:421–72 *(466; the Walking Old Fella)*, V:475, V:476–85, V:487, V:494, V:497–500, V:503, V:504, V:510, V:512, V:543 *(indirect)*, V:549, V:550–51, V:552, V:574, V:581–600, V:601–17 *(present at Calla gathering; mentioned on 601, 603, 604)*, V:618–28, V:634, V:636, V:639, V:641–44, V:647, V:653, V:654, V:655, V:662–67, V:685, V:689 *(one of folken)*, V:693–97 *(one of folken; mentioned on 693, 695)*, V:699–705, VI:3–8, VI:4, VI:11, VI:13–43, VI:80–82, VI:122, VI:123, VI:133, VI:143, VI:147, VI:168, VI:169, VI:170, VI:177–78, VI:185, VI:198, VI:200, VI:202, VI:206, VI:208, VI:210,

VI:211, VI:215, VI:216, VI:224, VI:225, VI:231, VI:245, VI:248, VI:253, VI:269, VI:271, VI:281, VI:288, VI:307–44, VI:360, VII:3–16, VII:19, VII:23, VII:24–28, VII:31–33, VII:36, VII:55, VII:70, VII:81, VII:85 *(indirect)*, VII:86, VII:90, VII:93 *(faddah)*, VII:111 *(faddah)*, VII:129, VII:134 *(indirect)*, VII:143, VII:145, VII:146, VII:147, VII:152, VII:189, VII:194, VII:259, VII:275 *(twin of Ted Brautigan)*, VII:281, VII:303–4, VII:310, VII:473, VII:503, VII:523, VII:525, VII:593, VII:689, VII:802

CALLAHAN'S PRESENT ASSOCIATES:

HIPPIE WITH ACNE/HAPPY COWBOY: *See* ROSE, *listed separately*

MUNOZ, ROSALITA (ROSITA): *See* ORIZA, SISTERS OF, *listed separately*

POSTMISTRESS IN STONEHAM, MAINE: *See* MAINE CHARACTERS, *listed separately*

SNUGGLEBUT: Callahan's cat. V:566

CALLAHAN'S HIDDEN HIGHWAYS ASSOCIATES:

BANDY BROOKS: Just as Callahan crossed the NEW YORK CITY FOOTBRIDGE, which spanned the HUDSON RIVER in his version of the Big Apple, he saw a huge vehicle on treads crossing the GEORGE WASHINGTON BRIDGE. This bizarre sight was the first indication that Callahan had entered one of the ALTERNATIVE AMERICAS. V:298

BARTENDER (AMERICANO BAR): This bartender served Callahan his first drink after LUPE DELGADO's death. Many more followed. V:285

BLACK DRIVER IN STRAW HAT: This man gave Callahan a lift in his beat-up Ford. Before dropping him off in SHADY GROVE, he gave Callahan five dollars and a spare baseball cap. V:304–5, V:445

BOY IN HARTFORD: After his terrible confrontation with the VAMPIRE BARLOW, Callahan saw this unhappy boy sitting by himself on a porch at four thirty in the morning. Callahan describes him as a silent essay in pain. V:263

BRAWNY MAN: Brawny Man was one of the day-labor companies that Callahan worked for during his years traveling the HIDDEN HIGHWAYS of America. V:292, V:444, V:467

CASTILLO, JUAN: Juan Castillo was one of the Mexican men Callahan worked with in California. V:309

CHADBOURNE: In one of the ALTERNATIVE AMERICAS, a former U.S. president named Chadbourne appears on the ten-dollar bill. V:300, V:309, V:444

CHILD SKIPPING ROPE: Callahan saw this child in FOSSIL, OREGON. It is one of the vivid, snapshotlike memories he has of his time on the roads. V:305

CHUMM, GREG (CHUMM'S TRAVELING WONDER SHOW): Greg Chumm was the greasy-haired owner of Chumm's Traveling Wonder Show. While employed by Chumm, Callahan posed as MENSO THE ESP WONDER. V:302, V:303

COVAY MOVERS (THE BROTHER OUTFIT): After the death of LUPE DELGADO, Callahan worked as a day laborer for this outfit for five straight days. (It was his soberest period that summer.) However, as soon as they offered him steady work, he went out and got drunk. He never returned to their work site. V:286–87

CRAZY MARY'S: *See* CALIFORNIA (STATE OF): SACRAMENTO: CRAZY MARY'S, *in* OUR WORLD PLACES

FORT LEE REGISTER AMERICAN: The local paper which Callahan reads while staying in FORT LEE is the *Fort Lee Register American*. On the days when he finds himself in LEABROOK, he reads the LEABROOK REGISTER. V:300

HOLLINGS, ERNEST "FRITZ": In one of the MULTIPLE AMERICAS which Callahan traveled through during his years bumming it along the HIGHWAYS IN HIDING, Ernest "Fritz" Hollings was elected president. V:305

LARS: While traveling through one of the ALTERNATIVE AMERICAS, Callahan met this little boy and fixed his radio. In thanks, Lars's mother packed Callahan a wonderful lunch that seemed to last for days. V:302

  LARS'S MOM: V:302

LEABROOK REGISTER: This is the local newspaper of LEABROOK, NEW JERSEY. Unfortunately you'll never be able to read it since Leabrook doesn't exist on our level of the DARK TOWER. V:297, V:300

MANPOWER: Manpower was another of the day-labor companies that Callahan worked for during his years traveling the HIDDEN HIGHWAYS of America. V:266, V:286, V:292, V:444, V:467

MENSO THE ESP WONDER: While working for CHUMM'S TRAVELING WONDER SHOW, Callahan played Menso the ESP Wonder. He was disconcertingly good at it. V:302, V:303

MEXICAN IMMIGRANTS (ILLEGAL): ESCOBAR, ESTRADA, JAVIER, ESTEBAN, ROSARIO, ECHEVERRIA, CAVERRA: Callahan met these men while traveling through TODASH America. Strangely, he met them again later (or, to borrow a term from *The Talisman* and *Black House*, he met their twinners later) in CALLA BRYN STURGIS. V:306, V:307, V:308

  "CAN'T DANCE" ANGLO WOMAN: This snooty woman looked down her nose at Callahan's Mexican companions. It was in her copy of the SACRAMENTO BEE that Callahan found out about ROWAN MAGRUDER's death. V:307–8

OLD GEEZER: This old geezer came across Callahan just after Pere saw his first VAGS. He tried to warn Callahan that some cops were coming, but Callahan had other things on his mind! V:284–85

  COPS IN RADIO CAR: V:284–85

PETACKI, PETE: Pete Petacki was a KENTUCKY gravedigger who had a taste for seventeen-year-old jailbait. At least one of the girls who caught his eye was a TYPE THREE VAMPIRE. Luckily for Petacki, Callahan killed her before she could sink her teeth into Pete's all-too-willing throat. Pete never found out. V:302

VAMPIRE GIRL: *See* VAMPIRES: TYPE THREE: INDIVIDUAL TYPE THREE VAMPIRES AND THEIR VICTIMS: PETE PETACKI'S VAMPIRE GIRL

POST, THE: A newspaper. V:448

ROLL CALL: This is the list of names Callahan heard while having a seizure in a TOPEKA jail cell: Nailor, Naughton, O'Connor, O'Shaugnessy, Oskowski, Osmer, Palmer, Palmgren, Peschier, Peters, Pike, Polovik, Rance, Rancourt, Ricupero, Robillard, Rossi, Ryan, Sannelli, Scher, Seavey, Sharrow, Shatzer, Sprang, Steward, Sudby. V:446–48

RUDEBACHER, DICKY: Dicky Rudebacher owned a diner in LEABROOK, NEW JERSEY. On a different level of the TOWER, another version of Dicky owned a diner in FORT LEE. Callahan worked for both of them. Like Callahan, Dicky was fond of drink. He also occasionally suffered from "itchy-foot," or the call of the roads, but unlike Callahan, he stayed put. V:300–301

RUTA: Ruta was one of the "lost pets" that the LOW MEN were after. Callahan came across a poster for her that read:

LOST! SIAMESE CAT, 2 YRS OLD
ANSWERS TO THE NAME OF RUTA
SHE IS NOISY BUT FULL OF FUN
LARGE REWARD OFFERED
$ $ $ $ $ $
DIAL 764, WAIT FOR BEEP, GIVE YOUR NUMBER
GOD BLESS YOU FOR HELPING

Callahan doesn't know who Ruta is, but he's fairly certain that she isn't a cat, and that she won't be much fun once the low men get hold of her. V:303, V:445, V:446

SACRAMENTO BEE: This newspaper carried an article about the HITLER BROTHERS and the injury they caused to Callahan's old friend ROWAN MAGRUDER. V:296, V:307–9

SLEEPY JOHN'S: *See* CALIFORNIA (STATE OF): SACRAMENTO: SLEEPY JOHN'S, *in* OUR WORLD PLACES

TEENAGE VICTIM: See VAMPIRES: TYPE THREE: INDIVIDUAL TYPE THREE VAMPIRES AND THEIR VICTIMS

CALLAHAN'S HOME SHELTER ASSOCIATES:

CHASE, FRANKIE: Frankie Chase worked at HOME. VI:332

DANCING WOMAN: V:272

DELGADO, LUPE: Although ROWAN MAGRUDER founded HOME, it was Lupe Delgado—a thirty-two-year-old former alcoholic—who invested the place with life and purpose. When Callahan first met Lupe, the younger man hadn't had a drink or drugs for five years. Although he'd been spending evenings at Home since 1974, he still kept his day job, which was working as part of the maintenance crew at the PLAZA HOTEL on FIFTH AVENUE (not to be confused with the PLAZA-PARK HYATT on FIRST AVENUE, where SUSANNAH-MIO takes refuge during *Song of Susannah*).

Like Roland's love, SUSAN DELGADO, Lupe was both honest and attractive. Callahan grew to love him, and it was a love threaded with sexual attraction, though nothing physical (besides one brotherly kiss on the cheek) ever came of it.

In March of 1976, after Callahan had been working at Home for about five and a half months, he saw the telltale dark blue glow (a little bit like electric blueberry juice) around Lupe's neck and smelled the revolting scent of burning onions mixed with hot metal. Horrified, Callahan realized that his friend had been preyed upon by a TYPE THREE VAMPIRE. By April, Lupe had become a regular hit for the vampires, and finding one actually drinking Lupe's blood made Callahan begin killing the bloodsuckers.

Although it is doubtful whether Type Three vampires can develop AIDS (they are as phantasmal as they are physical), they can carry HIV, and one such infected monster fed upon Lupe. By mid-May, Lupe was so ill that he couldn't bear the smells of the Home kitchen. By the end of June, he was dead. Lupe's death plunged Callahan into deep despair and sent him reeling along the HIDDEN HIGHWAYS of America, bottle in hand. V:267–68, V:271–83, V:285, V:293, V:304, V:423, V:424, V:428, V:429, V:445, V:456, V:464, V:591

MARK CROSS BRIEFCASE BUSINESSMAN: *See* VAMPIRES: TYPE THREE: INDIVIDUAL TYPE THREE VAMPIRES AND THEIR VICTIMS

GUY WITH D.T.'S: This man was shaking so badly that ROWAN MAGRUDER had to feed him coffee laced with whiskey. V:272

ILLITERATE (OR SEMILITERATE) MAN: V:272

JEFFY: Jeffy was one of the more psychotic residents of the HOME shelter. He used a switchblade to slit the throat of a fellow resident who was disgusted by his nose-picking habit. V:428–29

JEFFY'S VICTIM: V:428–29

LISA: Lisa was one of HOME's residents. She was attending AA. V:272

MAGRUDER, ROWAN (THE STREET ANGEL, also called GEORGE MAGRUDER): Rowan Magruder founded the HOME shelter. Along with LUPE DELGADO, he crafted its "wet" policy, which basically meant that men and women were allowed in through Home's doors whether they were drunk or sober.

As a young man, Rowan had been an aspiring writer and academic, but he gave up both potential professions for his true calling, which was to help the down-and-out. Although the nature of his work earned him the nickname The Street Angel, and though he was visited by Mother Teresa and was praised by magazines such as *Newsweek,* his sister, ROWENA MAGRUDER RAWLINGS, never forgave him for abandoning his more respectable (not to mention more potentially lucrative) interests.

Callahan worked at Home for nine months, and during that time he and Magruder became friends. In 1981, after five years on the road, Callahan hurried back to NEW YORK to see Magruder, who was critically ill in RIVERSIDE HOSPITAL. He had been attacked by the HITLER BROTHERS, whose intended prey had been Callahan himself.

Not long after Callahan's visit, Magruder died. However, the orderlies barely had time to change the sheets before Callahan landed in the same bed as yet another victim of the disgusting duo. V:267–68, V:271, V:272, V:279, V:280, V:281, V:282–83, V:288, V:292, V:293, V:308–9 *("Man of the Year"),* V:422–27, V:430, V:436, V:441, V:442, V:445, V:449, V:591 *(says George should read Rowan. Left over from earlier version of manuscript),* VI:332, VI:338, VII:281 *(George)*

RAWLINGS, ROWENA MAGRUDER: Rowena Magruder Rawlings was Rowan Magruder's twin sister. She flew to NEW YORK from CHICAGO once she found out that her brother had been attacked by the HITLER BROTHERS. Rowena thought that her brother had given up a literary career to help bums, and when she met Callahan, she slapped him across the face out of sheer spite. Rowan, who was conscious though silent during this interchange, was less than impressed by his sister's behavior. V:422–26, V:436 *(indirect),* V:442, V:445, V:465

SPINELLI, FRANK: Frank Spinelli was one of HOME's residents. He wanted Callahan to write him a letter of recommendation. V:272

CALLAHAN AND THE HITLER BROTHERS:

HITLER BROTHERS (NORTON RANDOLPH AND WILLIAM GARTON): The Hitler Brothers were a couple of racist thugs who attacked Jewish people and black people. Sometimes they did it for money, but most of the time they did it for fun. Their calling card was a swastika carved upon the forehead. While Callahan was traveling through the MULTIPLE AMERICAS, the Hitler Brothers attacked his former boss ROWAN MAGRUDER.

The Hitler Brothers' real names were Norton (Nort) Randolph and William (Bill) Garton. Because of the discrepancy in their sizes, Callahan secretly renamed them George and Lennie, after the odd-sized traveling companions in Steinbeck's novel *Of Mice and Men.* However, unlike the characters in Steinbeck's tale, it was the big Hitler Brother (six-foot-six Nort) who had all the brains. Five-foot-two Bill didn't have any brains worth mentioning. In fact, he couldn't even tell the difference between a crucifix and a swastika. Even more unpleasant, he became sexually aroused whenever he contemplated cutting someone up.

The Hitler Brothers were hired by the LOW MEN to find and kill Callahan. When they failed (thwarted by "MR. EX LIBRIS" CALVIN TOWER and his pal "MR. GAI COCKNIF EN YOM" AARON DEEPNEAU), they were assassinated. For once, the servants of the CRIMSON KING did the world a favor. V:265–66, V:308–9, V:424 *(indirect)*, V:426, V:427, V:430–42, V:443, V:447–48, V:450, VI:202, VI:269

> **MEDICAL AND LEGAL PERSONNEL:** These people had to deal with the Hitler Brothers' victims—first ROWAN MAGRUDER and then Callahan.
> > **DOCTORS:** V:308 *(Magruder)*, V:424, V:427
> > **NURSES:** V:427, V:442
> > **POLICE OFFICERS:** V:424, V:432, V:439, V:445
> **TWO YOUNG COUPLES:** These two couples witnessed the Hitler Brothers dragging a vomit-covered Callahan up SECOND AVENUE. However, they didn't realize what was really going on. V:432
> **MR. EX LIBRIS (VOICE NUMBER ONE):** *See* TOWER, CALVIN, *listed separately*
> **MR. GAI COCKNIF EN YOM (VOICE NUMBER TWO):** *See* TET CORPORATION: FOUNDING FATHERS: DEEPNEAU, AARON

CALLAHAN'S LIGHTHOUSE SHELTER ASSOCIATES:
> **HUCKMAN, WARD:** Ward Huckman and AL McCOWAN ran the LIGHTHOUSE SHELTER in DETROIT, MICHIGAN. It was while Callahan worked for them that the LOW MEN (working for the CRIMSON KING's company, the SOMBRA CORPORATION) finally tracked him down.
>
> Under the pretense of awarding a million-dollar grant to Lighthouse, Sombra's executive vice president (the evil RICHARD P. SAYRE) invited Callahan and his friends to his headquarters. Instead of awarding the money, Sayre's cohorts knocked out Huckman and McCowan. Sayre then tried to sic his HIV-infected VAMPIRES on Callahan. Pere jumped out of the window to avoid the terrible death that had claimed his friend LUPE DELGADO. He awoke in the company of Roland's nemesis, WALTER. V:450–55
> **LIGHTHOUSE CLIENTS:** V:450–51
> **McCOWAN, AL:** Al McCowan and WARD HUCKMAN ran the LIGHTHOUSE SHELTER in DETROIT, MICHIGAN, which was Callahan's final place of employment before the servants of the CRIMSON KING tracked him down. RICHARD P. SAYRE and his fellow LOW MEN tricked Callahan and his friends into visiting SOMBRA's Detroit offices. The three unsuspecting men thought that they were going to receive a million-dollar grant for Lighthouse. Instead, they were greeted by the nasty servants of the Red King. McCowan and Huckman were

knocked unconscious, and Callahan jumped out of the window to escape the clutches of Sayre's VAMPIRES. Callahan didn't exactly die; instead, he got a one-way ticket to visit WALTER in the WAY STATION, and then a transfer to CALLA BRYN STURGIS. V:450–55

> **AL'S MOTHER:** Al's mother always maintained that one should arrive five minutes early for an important appointment—no more, no less. Her son and his friends followed her advice for their meeting with SOMBRA, but it didn't do them any good. V:453

SAYRE, RICHARD P.: *See* CAN-TOI, *listed separately*

CALLAHAN'S OTHER PAST ASSOCIATES:

> **BISHOP DUGAN:** Bishop Dugan approved Father Callahan's transfer from his LOWELL, MASSACHUSETTS, parish. Little did he know it, but Callahan's restlessness was not due to urban malaise but to the malaise of the bottle. V:254

> **CALLAHAN, GRANDFATHER FRANK:** Pere Callahan's middle name came from this grandfather. V:108

> **CALLAHAN, MR.:** When Callahan was a boy, his father (Mr. Callahan) discovered some of his son's hidden *Playboy* magazines. He made Pere burn them in the incinerator, then pray by the foot of his bed. One can't help but wonder whether this influenced Callahan's decision to join the priesthood. V:254 *(indirect),* V:599

> **CALLAHAN, MRS.:** Callahan's mother bought the crucifix whose arms were broken by the VAMPIRE BARLOW. One of the reasons that Callahan finds the CAVE OF VOICES so distressing is that his mother calls to him from the pit's deep throat, asking why he let that nasty bloodsucker break her cross. V:28, V:254 *(indirect),* V:259, V:264, V:280, V:465, V:591, V:599, V:619, V:624, V:708

CROWD THAT GATHERS UPON ENTRY TO 1999 NEW YORK: *See* HARRIGAN, REVEREND EARL, *listed separately*

'SALEM'S LOT CHARACTERS:

> **BARLOW, KURT:** *See* VAMPIRES: TYPE ONE

> **BURKE, MATTHEW:** On a level of the DARK TOWER not far from ours, Matthew Burke taught high school English in the town of JERUSALEM'S LOT, MAINE, a town which (as we learned in the novel *'Salem's Lot*) became infested with VAMPIRES.
>
> Not long after becoming friends with the writer BEN MEARS, Burke invited a former student (who seemed ill) to stay overnight at his house. This student died in Matt's spare bedroom and his body was hauled away. However, not long after this, he returned for another visit, this time as a vampire. Not surprisingly, Burke suffered a massive heart attack. Until his second heart attack (which happened in his hospital bed), Matthew Burke acted as a stable contact for Ben Mears's (and Callahan's) posse of vampire hunters. V:256

> **BUS DRIVER:** After Callahan's horrific confrontation with the VAMPIRE BARLOW, Pere boarded a bus for NEW YORK. Although it was

officially against the rules to let passengers drink alcoholic beverages while riding on Greyhound, this Big Apple–bound driver bought Callahan a bottle of cheap booze. However, his motives were anything but altruistic—he earned himself a twenty-eight-dollar tip. Callahan didn't mind the driver's mercenary motives. He was desperate to get the taste of Barlow's blood out of his mouth. V:262–64

CODY, DR. JAMES (JIMMY): Jimmy Cody was the doctor who helped BEN MEARS, Donald Callahan, and MARK PETRIE stand up to the VAMPIRES of 'SALEM'S LOT, MAINE. In the end, Cody didn't succumb to the VAMPIRE BARLOW's teeth but to his treachery. He died while trying to descend stairs that led to the cellar where Barlow was hiding. Unbeknownst to him, the stairs had been sawed away by Barlow's vampire-servants, and Jimmy Cody was impaled upon knives inserted in the floor below.

On the flap of the original printing of *'Salem's Lot,* Callahan was accidentally called FATHER CODY. V:257, VI:208 *(Father Cody)*

CODY, FATHER: *See* CODY, DR. JAMES, *listed above*

COOGAN, LORETTA: Loretta Coogan worked in SPENCER'S, which was the drugstore and soda fountain of 'SALEM'S LOT. Spencer's also doubled as the town's bus station. V:262

FLIP, MR.: Mr. Flip was the name of the bogeyman that lived in Callahan's childhood closet. In the novel *'Salem's Lot,* we find out that the VAMPIRE BARLOW resembled him. V:708

FOYLE, FRANKIE: When Callahan was in the seminary, Frankie Foyle gave him a blasphemous crewelwork sampler which read, "God grant me the SERENITY to accept what I cannot change, the TENACITY to change what I may, and the GOOD LUCK not to fuck up too often." Although we learn about this gift in *'Salem's Lot,* we don't learn Frankie Foyle's name until *Wolves of the Calla.* V:708

GLICK, DANNY: Twelve-year-old Danny Glick was one of the first victims of vampirism in the town of JERUSALEM'S LOT, MAINE. (See the novel *'Salem's Lot,* by STEPHEN KING.) He was also one of the Lot's first new VAMPIRES. Danny's initial victim was the young gravedigger Mike Ryerson. On a midnight adventure several evenings later, he visited the bedroom window of his friend MARK PETRIE. Mark (well versed in horror stories) invited Danny in but then burned his cheek with a plastic crucifix from his toy graveyard. Danny's undead flesh turned to smoke. V:257, V:265, V:299

MEARS, BEN: On another level of the TOWER, Ben Mears was the author of the book *Air Dance.* Along with Father Callahan, JIM CODY, MARK PETRIE, and MATTHEW BURKE, Ben fought the VAMPIRES of 'SALEM'S LOT, MAINE. (See STEPHEN KING's novel *'Salem's Lot.*) When BARLOW (a TYPE ONE VAMPIRE) turned Ben's lover, SUSAN NORTON, into one of his own, Ben hammered a stake through her heart. (Love has many manifestations.) With the help of Mark Petrie,

Ben eventually destroyed Barlow and the two of them fled to MEXICO. Later, they returned to the still-infested Lot to burn it to the ground. V:256, V:257–58, V:291, V:469–70

NORTON, SUSAN: Pretty Susan Norton was a literary fan of BEN MEARS's before she became his girlfriend. Although lovely and wholesome, Susan did not achieve true beauty until the VAMPIRE BARLOW turned her into a vampire. At Callahan's insistence, Ben drove a stake through her heart. V:257–58

PETRIE, MARK: Twelve-year-old Mark Petrie was one of the fearless VAMPIRE hunters of *'Salem's Lot*. Although he managed to evade the toothy hunger of his friend DANNY GLICK, Mark couldn't save his parents from the TYPE ONE VAMPIRE BARLOW. While saving Mark from Barlow, Callahan was forced to take the vampire's communion. Although Callahan was devastated by this, Mark escaped. He and BEN MEARS destroyed Barlow and then, after fleeing to MEXICO, returned to the LOT ('SALEM'S LOT, not the magic LOT!) to burn its remaining vampires. Years later, Callahan traveled via TODASH to LOS ZAPATOS, Mexico. There he witnessed Ben Mears's funeral and heard Mark's eulogy for his dear friend. V:257 *(indirect)*, V:258–59, V:261 *(boy)*, V:280 *(family kitchen)*, V:469–70, VI:329, VII:11

   PARENTS: V:258, V:259, V:280 *(family kitchen)*, VI:329
STRAKER: *See* VAMPIRES: TYPE ONE: BARLOW, KURT

CALLAHAN, GRANDFATHER FRANK
See CALLAHAN, FATHER DONALD FRANK: CALLAHAN'S OTHER PAST ASSOCIATES

CALVINS
See TET CORPORATION

CAMERON
See CAN-TOI

CAN CALAH
GAN speaks through the voices of the can calah, who (in our world at least) are called angels.
   VI:318

CANARYMAN
See TAHEEN: BIRDMEN TAHEEN

CANDOR THE TALL
See DESCHAIN, GABRIELLE

CANTAB OF THE MANNI
See MANNI

CAN-TAH

CONSTANT READERS will recognize the can-tah (or little gods) from STEPHEN KING's novel *Desperation*. In that book, the can-tah (spelled without the hyphen) are ugly composite animals carved from stone. One is a coyote with a snake-tongue; yet another is a pitted gray spider with a coyote-head poking out just above its mandibles. In both novels, the can-tah can mesmerize, but there the similarity between the two types of carved creatures ends. In *Desperation,* the can-tah depict little demons, but the one SUSANNAH-MIO finds in *Song of Susannah* serves the WHITE and is in the form of the TURTLE GUARDIAN.

For page references, see GUARDIANS OF THE BEAM: TURTLE

CAN-TOI (LOW MEN)

The can-toi are none other than the LOW MEN who stalked TED BRAUTI-GAN in "Low Men in Yellow Coats," the opening story of *Hearts in Atlantis*. Although they look more or less like men (despite their outrageously loud clothes), these particular WARRIORS OF THE SCARLET EYE are actually human/TAHEEN hybrids. Like the taheen, the can-toi have hume bodies but the heads of beasts. However, while the nature of taheen heads varies (some look like birds, others like mammals), in the case of the low men, the heads are almost invariably those of louse-infested, red-haired rats with multiple rows of teeth.

The can-toi hide their rat-heads behind humanoid masks (can you blame them?), but up close, their faces are rarely that convincing. Can-toi masks are formed from a kind of living latex which cannot be manufactured but must be grown. As living things in their own right, the masks have to breathe. They do this through a red hole (which looks like a bleeding red eye) located on the forehead. These red holes usually dry up when their masters cross over to our world, which is probably a good thing. Otherwise, they'd never even begin to pass for human.

While taheen look upon humans as an inferior race, the can-toi worship the human form as divine. They even believe that they are *becoming* human, and that after the fall of the DARK TOWER, they will replace mankind. It seems that they are having at least minor success in their endeavor to become like men, since their minds can be progged (or read) by psychics. (The thoughts of true taheen sound like white noise.) At a certain point in his or her development, each low man or low woman is given a human name by their clan-fam. These names often sound absurd to actual humans. For example, one can-toi has the name VAN GOGH BAEZ. Another is called JAMES CAGNEY.

The can-toi's primary job is taking care of the psychic BREAKERS in the DEVAR-TOI, or Breaker prison, located in THUNDERCLAP. However their duties also include hunting down escapees with their duplicitous lost-pet posters and their secret pavement messages coded as moon-and-star designs. Some can-toi, such as RICHARD P. SAYRE, vice president of the SOMBRA CORPORATION, even live in our world and pass for hume much of the time.

Like the BIG COFFIN HUNTERS (or REGULATORS), who also ultimately serve the CRIMSON KING, many of the can-toi have blue coffins tattooed on their hands.

Although they occasionally get up to other nasty mischief in our world (as both PERE CALLAHAN and CALVIN TOWER can testify), when relaxing at home in ALGUL SIENTO or BLUE HEAVEN (the taheen and can-toi term for the Devar-Toi), the low men live in HEARTBREAK HOUSE. Despite their devotion to the Crimson King, the poisonous air of END-WORLD has as terrible an effect upon the low men as it does upon ordinary humes. End-World's poisons give the can-toi skin sores and nosebleeds. Even the smallest wounds they suffer can become infected and deadly.

When our ka-tet attacks the Devar-Toi, their policy is to save the Breakers but to kill the taheen and can-toi guards. The world won't miss these latter monsters much, especially since they have such a pathetic sense of humor. To a can-toi, hanging a picture of NIAGARA FALLS upside down is the height of comedy.

Like the CAN-TAH, the can-toi also appear in KING's novel *Desperation*. In that book, the can-toi are the animal servants of the demon Tak (short for Can-Tak, or big god). Unlike our can-toi, the can-toi of *Desperation* have neither human bodies nor the ability to reason or speak.

V:289 *(lost-pet posters)*, V:290–91, V:297 *(indirect)*, V:299, V:302–3 *(indirect; lost-pet posters)*, V:304, V:306, V:426–27 *(indirect)*, V:429, V:430, V:435, V:443, V:449 *(lost-pet posters)*, V:451 *(lost-pet posters)*, V:452, V:455–57, V:549, V:591, VI:64, VI:95, VI:111, VI:244–45 *(their job is the Breakers)*, VI:248, VI:278–79, VI:318, VI:320, VI:326, VI:337, VI:353, VI:364–84 *(Dixie Pig)*, VI:407, VII:5, VII:10, VII:14, VII:25 *(can-toi)*, VII:26 *(can-toi)*, VII:51 *(can-toi)*, VII:55–71 *(five in birth room)*, VII:81, VII:83 *(came through door after Jake)*, VII:85, VII:86–87, VII:88, VII:90, VII:93, VII:101, VII:104–9 *(following Jake)*, VII:111 *(posse)*, VII:133–35, VII:146, VII:209, VII:222, VII:223, VII:226, VII:230, VII:235–36, VII:237, VII:238, VII:241, VII:269, VII:272, VII:281, VII:286, VII:288, VII:292, VII:293, VII:297, VII:300, VII:326–27, VII:334, VII:337, VI:556–82 *(Devar-Toi battle)*, VII:393, VII:407, VII:448, VII:476, VII:498

INDIVIDUAL LOW MEN/CAN-TOI:

ALEXANDER, BEN: Ben Alexander is one of the guards at the DEVAR-TOI. VII:372

ALIA (NURSE): *See* TAHEEN: RAT-HEADED TAHEEN

ANDREW: When we meet him in the DIXIE PIG, just before SUSAN-NAH/MIA gives birth, this obese low man is wearing a tux with plaid lapels and a red velvet bow tie. (His jilly, TIRANA, looks equally hideous in her strapless, silver evening dress.) Andrew is shot by FATHER CALLAHAN. VI:365–71, VII:9–15.

BAEZ, VAN GOGH: One of the strange human names adopted by a can-toi. VII:294

BEEMAN: A security guard at ALGUL SIENTO. VII:235–36, VII:239–40

CAGNEY, JAMES: James Cagney (named after a famous hume actor) is a red-haired can-toi who stands five feet five inches tall and who likes Western-style shirts and boots. (He prefers footwear that makes him seem much taller.) During the final DEVAR-TOI battle, his mask rips and (at one point) he is mistaken for a TAHEEN. VII:356–57, VII:371–74, VII:379–82 *(called taheen)*

CAMERON (THE RAPIST): This can-toi raped a BREAKER. His defense was that the CRIMSON KING commanded him to do it as part of his process of "becoming" human. (*See* BECOMING, *listed in the* END-WORLD *section of* APPENDIX I.) Luckily for the other female Breakers, the former Devar Master, HUMMA O'TEGO, thought Cameron's defense was preposterous and put him to death. The Breakers were invited to watch. VII:326, VII:344, VII:385

CARLYLE, THOMAS: One of the unexpected human names adopted by a can-toi. VII:294

CONROY: A technician at the DEVAR-TOI. VII:241

DIXIE PIG GUARDS: VI:377

DOORMEN AT THE DIXIE PIG: VI:364

GANGLI, DR.: *See* TRISTUM, DR. GANGLI, *listed below*

HABER: Haber is one of the can-toi who accompanies SUSANNAH DEAN from the DIXIE PIG to the FEDIC DOGAN, where she and MIA give birth to the CHAP. Haber has a bulldoggy face, gray, luxuriant curls, and a slanted hole in his forehead. Susannah shoots him in the chaotic battle following the birth of baby MORDRED. VI:370–84, VII:55–70

LONDON, JACK: Like so many of the can-toi, Jack London took a human name (in this case, the name of a famous hume writer). London is DR. GANGLI's assistant in the third-floor infirmary of DAMLI HOUSE in ALGUL SIENTO. VII:367

RANDO HATTEN LOOK-ALIKE: VII:293–94

SAYRE, RICHARD P.: The nasty can-toi Richard Patrick Sayre is the executive vice president of SOMBRA CORPORATION, one of the many companies in our world (and our world's twinners) serving the CRIMSON KING. On July 15, 1976, he signed a contract on behalf of Sombra with CALVIN TOWER, owner of the MANHATTAN RESTAURANT OF THE MIND. Tower was paid one hundred thousand dollars in exchange for his written consent to hold on to the magic LOT for one year, and then, at the end of that time, to give Sombra first right of purchase. However, as soon as the said year began to wind down (and as soon as he knew that Tower had blown the money), Sayre began to sic BALAZAR and his hoods on the chubby bookshop owner, figuring they could bully him into selling. (Thanks to EDDIE DEAN, this tactic doesn't work.)

With the help of his VAMPIRES and LOW MEN, Sayre brought about the death of FATHER DONALD FRANK CALLAHAN in the early 1980s. He was also in charge of the sting operation which lured

MIA and an unwilling SUSANNAH DEAN to the DIXIE PIG so that Mia could give birth to her CHAP. (Susannah takes revenge by shooting him.) When we see Sayre in the Dixie Pig, he appears to be about sixty years old with white hair, a double row of teeth, and outrageously loud clothes. His humanoid mask looks lean and predatory.

Our final insight into Sayre's dirty work doesn't come from the can-toi himself, but from the bric-a-brac in his office, located below the FEDIC DOGAN. Here Roland and Susannah find files on themselves and their two dead ka-tet mates, as well as two significant oil paintings, both painted by PATRICK DANVILLE. One is of the DARK TOWER, and the other is a symbolic depiction of the Crimson King's triumph over ALL-WORLD-that-was. This second painting shows black-haired, blue-eyed MORDRED with one triumphant foot atop ARTHUR ELD's dead horse, LLAMREI. V:95, V:451, V:455–57, V:460, V:464, VI:119–24, VI:125, VI:228, VI:231, VI:234, VI:239, VI:240, VI:251, VI:254, VI:364–84, VII:8, VII:13, VII:14, VII:55–70 *(shot)*, VII:84, VII:104, VII:105, VII:106, VII:107, VII:108, VII:149, VII:240, VII:549–51 *(office)*, VII:703, VII:783

STRAW: Straw is a low man with flabby hands and many rings. Along with SAYRE and a number of other WARRIORS OF THE SCARLET EYE, he attends the birth of MORDRED, son of both the CRIMSON KING and Roland Deschain. SUSANNAH DEAN shoots him. VII:58–68, VII:71

TIRANA: When we meet this obese low woman in the DIXIE PIG, she is wearing a strapless, silver evening dress. DETTA WALKER rips off her mask and exposes the rat beneath. VI:365–71, VII:13–15, VII:25

TRAMPAS: In the final book of the Dark Tower series, we find out that all things, even eczema, can ultimately serve the BEAM. In *The Dark Tower*, we find out that Trampas, one of the few can-toi who is actually succeeding in his process of *becoming* human, has a terribly itchy scalp. Every time he lifts his beanielike thinking cap, his thoughts can be read by his BREAKER friend TED BRAUTIGAN. Although Trampas does not mean to leak the CRIMSON KING's secrets, it is while scanning Trampas's thoughts that Ted realizes just what he and his fellow psychics are doing in the DEVAR-TOI's STUDY. It is also by listening to the radiolike broadcasts of Trampas's thoughts that Ted learns what part he—a facilitator—is playing in the untimely collapse of the Beams.

Although Ted's escape from the Devar is temporary, his distressing new knowledge strengthens his resolve to oppose the Lord of Discordia's plans for the macroverse. Ted helps Roland and his friends destroy the Devar and its guards. Unfortunately, Ted also ends up killing Trampas—who ultimately obeys the orders of the enemy—with one of his deadly thought-spears. VII:292, VII:293–96, VII:298, VII:299–302, VII:306, VII:356, VII:370–71, VII:375–77, VII:407

TRELAWNEY: Security guard at ALGUL SIENTO (the DEVAR-TOI). VII:239–40, VII:325–26

TRISTUM, DR. GANGLI: The much-feared Dr. Gangli is the DEVAR's sawbones. According to the BREAKERS, the dark, squat, heavily jowled Gangli looks like John Irving after a bad face-lift. However, none of them would dare to say this to his face any more than they'd make fun of the roller skates he uses to sail through his rounds.

Dr. Gangli (who took a TAHEEN name even though he is can-toi) rules his third-floor surgery in DAMLI HOUSE with an iron fist. Because of the frequent infections that plague END-WORLD's denizens, Dr. Gangli prescribes many antibiotics. His prescriptions are losing their effectiveness, but Gangli isn't around to see them stop working completely. When the gas-pods behind the Damli House kitchens blow up during the Devar's final battle, Gangli (roller skates still spinning) is blown skyward along with all of his paperwork. For Gangli, the end of life in the macroverse comes earlier than expected. VII:223, VII:239, VII:356, VII:367–68, VII:374

    GANGLI'S ORDERLIES:
        LONDON, JACK: *listed above*
    NAMELESS ORDERLIES: VII:367

CANTORA, IRENE
    See TASSENBAUM, IRENE

CAPPI
    See BREAKERS: RUIZ, SHEEMIE

CARLINER, MARK
    See KING, STEPHEN

CARLYLE, THOMAS
    See CAN-TOI

CARVER, MARIAN ODETTA
    See TET CORPORATION

CARVER, MOSES
    See TET CORPORATION: FOUNDING FATHERS

CASH, BENITO
    See CALLA BRYN STURGIS CHARACTERS: OTHER CHARACTERS

CASTILLO, JUAN
    See CALLAHAN, FATHER DONALD FRANK: CALLAHAN'S HIDDEN HIGHWAYS ASSOCIATES

CAVERRA, DIANE
See CALLA BRYN STURGIS CHARACTERS: FARMERS (SMALL-HOLD): CAVERRA, REUBEN

CAVERRA, REUBEN
See CALLA BRYN STURGIS CHARACTERS: FARMERS (SMALLHOLD)

CAVERRA, RUTH
See CALLA BRYN STURGIS CHARACTERS: ROONTS

CHADBOURNE
See CALLAHAN, FATHER DONALD FRANK: CALLAHAN'S HIDDEN HIGHWAYS ASSOCIATES

CHAMBERS, ELMER
Elmer Chambers is the father of our dear friend JAKE CHAMBERS. He is a TV network big shot whose job is to destroy other networks, and he is uncannily good at it. (See *Stephen King's The Dark Tower: A Concordance, Volume I*.) Elmer smokes three packs of unfiltered cigarettes each day and has been known to snort cocaine until his nose bleeds. Elmer is living proof of Jake's theory that adults don't really know any better than kids do. They just pretend to.
    V:40 *(Jake's parents)*, V:46, V:104, V:155 *(father)*, V:187, V:204 *(dad)*, V:215, V:382, V:471, V:559 *(dad)*, V:561 *(father)*, V:565–66, V:567, V:577, V:590, V:617, V:637, V:656 *(father)*, V:705, VI:11, VI:32, VI:41, VI:320, VI:324, VII:7, VII:15, VII:84, VII:94, VII:95, VII:98, VII:110, VII:138 *(parents)*, VII:144, VII:191, VII:299, VII:310, VII:398, VII:399, VII:473, VII:535
    GIRL WITH BODACIOUS TA-TAS: "Bodacious ta-tas" is Elmer Chambers's term for a pair of really nice breasts. Hence, "a girl with bodacious ta-tas" is a young woman who is well stacked. The girl in the film *The Lost Continent* fits this description. VII:97, VII:99, VII:103–4

CHAMBERS, JAKE ('BAMA, KID SEVENTY-SEVEN, JOHN "JAKE" CHAMBERS, JAKE TOREN, HYPERBOREAN WANDERER)
Although Jake Chambers was eleven years old when we left him at the end of *Wizard and Glass*, by the time he reaches CALLA BRYN STURGIS in *Wolves of the Calla*, he is twelve. (See *Stephen King's The Dark Tower: A Concordance, Volume I*.) Exposure to the ROSE has made Jake strong in "the touch." In fact, his psychic abilities are so formidable that when the MANNI help Roland, Jake, EDDIE, and CALLAHAN to reactivate the UNFOUND DOOR at the beginning of *Song of Susannah*, HENCHICK (the Manni's *dinh*) places Jake directly in front of the door so that he can find its psychic "hook," or opening mechanism. In another where and when, Jake would probably have made a spectacular BREAKER.
    Jake plays an extremely important role in the Dark Tower series. In *The Gunslinger*, he is the first of Roland's ka-tet to be drawn into MID-WORLD.

(Unfortunately, Roland sacrifices him to reach his nemesis, WALTER.) Jake returns to his adopted father in *The Waste Lands,* and at the end of the series, it is Jake, not Roland, who saves the writer STEPHEN KING from death and so ensures the safety of both the BEAMS and the DARK TOWER.

Over the series, we watch Jake mature—a process filled with painful lessons. From Roland, he learns betrayal, but he also learns to forgive those he loves, and to accept that—although people make mistakes—they can change. In LUD (found in *The Waste Lands*) he discovers that adults can be sexually predatory, and that often the objects of their sadistic fantasies are vulnerable young boys. In *Wizard and Glass,* Jake gains insight into what Roland was like as a boy and begins to understand the forces which shaped the man he so loves into the obsessive being that Roland has become.

In the final three books of the Dark Tower series, Jake—now an accomplished gunslinger in his own right—continues to experience life's less savory lessons. While in Calla Bryn Sturgis, Jake witnesses another adult's betrayal (this time BEN SLIGHTMAN THE ELDER's betrayal of an entire community) and then learns to keep secrets, both from his tet and from his friend BENNY SLIGHTMAN. Although no stranger to death, Jake has the distressing misfortune of having to witness the deaths of two who are dear to him. First, he sees his friend Benny blown apart by one of the WOLVES' sneetches, and then, in *The Dark Tower,* he watches as his tet-brother EDDIE DEAN is shot in the head by PIMLI PRENTISS, the Devar Master in THUNDERCLAP.

Perhaps it is this familiarity with death, as well as his own experience of it, which makes Jake so determined to sacrifice his own life to save Stephen King rather than to witness the death of his *dinh,* Roland. On SLAB CITY HILL in LOVELL, MAINE, Jake—fresh from the horrors of the DEVAR-TOI—leaps out in front of an oncoming van, grabs King around the waist, and shields the writer with his own body. Hence it is Jake who is killed, not King, though our beloved *kas-ka Gan* suffers terrible injuries anyway.

Blond-haired, blue-eyed Jake—who was hit by a Cadillac on FIFTH AVENUE and Forty-third Street in his world and who plummeted to his death below the CYCLOPEAN MOUNTAINS in Roland's world—dies for a third time in the KEYSTONE EARTH occupied by his maker, Stephen King. Roland buries his adopted son in the Maine woods and makes IRENE TASSENBAUM promise to plant a rosebush over his grave.

Luckily for us, there are other worlds than these, and there seem to be alternative versions of Jake Chambers in almost all of them. At the end of *The Dark Tower,* a trail-frayed SUSANNAH DEAN leaves Mid-World through the ARTIST'S DOOR (another manifestation of the UNFOUND DOOR, but this time drawn by PATRICK DANVILLE) and finds both Jake and Eddie alive and well in yet another version of NEW YORK. Although it's not the Keystone Earth (here they drive Takuro Spirits and drink Nozz-A-La cola), Susannah is still delighted to find herself in this snowy twinner of CENTRAL PARK. In this where and when, Eddie and Jake are brothers from WHITE PLAINS and their last name is TOREN. It seems only a matter of time before Susannah Dean becomes Susannah Toren, and that our ka-tet, reunited as family, will find a strange-looking canine named OY to join them.

As CONSTANT READERS will recognize, Jake Chambers is another manifestation of the brave and talented prepubescent/adolescent hero who can be found in a number of King's novels. In 'Salem's Lot the boy is MARK PETRIE; in "Low Men in Yellow Coats" (the first story of Hearts in Atlantis) he's called BOBBY GARFIELD; in Desperation his name is David Carver; and in It he is the young Bill Denbrough. The boy-hero also appears in the King/Straub collaborative novel The Talisman. Although these boys have different appearances, personalities, and talents, they all prove that the adult world isn't always as wise as it thinks it is. It is the young boy (or the boy who still lives within the body of the man) who tries to remain true to his quest.

V:8 (strangers from Out-World), V:29–31 (gunslingers), V:35, V:36, V:38–47, V:48–70 (visits New York via todash), V:77, V:78, V:80, V:81, V:84, V:87, V:88–119, V:121, V:123–37, V:138, V:142–60, V:162, V:163, V:165, V:167–69, V:176–85, V:187–98, V:201–34, V:235, V:238, V:239, V:241, V:246, V:249, V:257, V:258, V:266, V:291, V:294, V:302, V:313, V:318–24, V:325, V:328, V:329, V:330, V:332–34 (watches Margaret Eisenhart throw), V:340, V:341, V:371–76 (following Mia), V:378, V:380–87, V:388–406, V:408 (indirect), V:412 (ka-tet mate), V:417–19, V:420, V:421–23, V:428–30, V:437–38, V:442–45, V:448–49, V:452–54, V:457, V:460, V:461, V:462 (indirect), V:466–72, V:476, V:479, V:480, V:485, V:487, V:488–96, V:496–505, V:506, V:511, V:514, V:519, V:534, V:552, V:553–80, V:581–90, V:592 (indirect), V:601–17, V:621, V:636–39, V:641–44, V:652–53, V:656–57, V:659, V:660, V:661, V:662–73, V:675–76, V:678, V:679–705, VI:3–8, VI:10, VI:11–43, VI:64, VI:67, VI:68, VI:71, VI:79, VI:84, VI:85, VI:107, VI:121, VI:130, VI:143, VI:147, VI:199, VI:200, VI:205, VI:210, VI:216, VI:222, VI:224–25, VI:231, VI:247, VI:268, VI:284, VI:285, VI:288, VI:290, VI:298, VI:299, VI:302, VI:303 (kid), VI:307–44, VI:360, VI:389, VI:391, VI:399, VI:400, VI:402, VII:3–11, VII:13, VII:14, VII:15, VII:19, VII:23, VII:24–28, VII:34, VII:36, VII:52, VII:59, VII:61, VII:63, VII:72, VII:78, VII:80, VII:81–104 (100 changes places with Oy!), VII:104–5, VII:106 (snot-babby), VII:107 (brat), VII:108 (snot-babby), VII:109–12, VII:114, VII:126, VII:129, VII:134 (snot-babby), VII:136–38, VII:141–59, VII:164–65, VII:168, VII:169, VII:173, VII:177, VII:186 (ka-tet), VII:187, VII:188, VII:189–220, VII:247–61, VII:262 (indirect), VII:265–73, VII:276 (indirect), VII:279–324 (279–302 listening to Ted's story), VII:325, VII:329–42, VII:350, VII:351–52, VII:362–63, VII:368–70, VII:378–85, VII:387–418, VII:421–33, VII:441–43, VII:444–45, VII:448, VII:449–67 (dies), VII:470, VII:472–75 (a rose to be planted on his grave), VII:476, VII:477, VII:478, VII:485, VII:487, VII:503, VII:509, VII:510, VII:520, VII:523, VII:525, VII:526, VII:527, VII:528, VII:532, VI:533, VII:534–35, VII:538, VII:541, VII:542–43, VII:544, VII:549, VII:554–56, VII:559, VII:585, VII:630, VII:633, VII:643, VII:645–46, VII:649, VII:657,

VII:662, VII:670, VII:697, VII:724–25, VII:727, VII:728, VII:729, VII:731, VII:733, VII:740, VII:744, VII:746, VII:747, VII:748, VII:758, VII:762, VII:769, VII:785, VII:797, VII:802, VII:809, VII:812–13, VII:818, VII:819

JAKE'S ASSOCIATES:

CHAMBERS, ELMER: *See* CHAMBERS, ELMER, *listed separately*

CHAMBERS, LAURIE: *See* CHAMBERS, LAURIE, *listed separately*

CROWD THAT GATHERS UPON ENTRY TO 1999 NEW YORK: *See* HARRIGAN, REVEREND EARL, *listed separately*

MUCCI, TIMMY: Timmy Mucci was one of Jake's friends from MID-TOWN LANES. He liked comic books. Once, when Jake bowled a 282, Timmy gave him a bowling bag that said, "Nothing but Strikes at Mid-Town Lanes." Jake picks up a version of this bag when he and our ka-tet travel via TODASH to the magic LOT in NEW YORK CITY. The only difference between the bags is that the one Jake finds in todash New York says, "Nothing but Strikes at Mid-World Lanes." V:198, V:694

NEW YORK WOMAN: When Jake and OY visit 1977 TODASH NEW YORK, this woman hitches up her straight black skirt so that she can step over Oy. Even though she can't see our travelers, she can sense them. V:49, V:57

OY: *See* OY, *listed separately*

SHAW, GRETA: Greta Shaw worked as the Chambers family house-keeper. (See *Stephen King's The Dark Tower: A Concordance, Volume I.*) In many ways, she was more of a mother to Jake than Jake's biological mother. Greta Shaw gave Jake the nickname 'BAMA, and little Jakey thought she would save him from the DEATHFLY. V:42, V:187, V:382 *(housekeeper)*, V:419, V:460, V:637, VII:89, VII:94–97, VII:381

UPS GUY: In *The Drawing of the Three*, Jake jumped over this man's dolly as he sprinted toward the Vacant LOT. While traveling via TODASH in 1977 NEW YORK, Jake recalls this incident. V:61

CHAMBERS, LAURIE (MEGAN)

We already know that JAKE's mother tended to go to bed with her sick friends. (See *Stephen King's The Dark Tower: A Concordance, Volume I.*) In *Wolves of the Calla*, we find out that she was having an affair with her masseuse as well. Jake found this affair especially depressing since the masseuse had lots of muscles but few brains.

Laurie Chambers's lullabies gave Jake the creeps. One of her favorites was "I heard a fly buzz, when I died," the upshot of which was that Jake developed a terrible fear of a monstrous creature he named the DEATHFLY.

V:40 *(Jake's parents)*, V:42 *(Jake's mother)*, V:187, V:382, VI:324, VII:94, VII:95, VII:96, VII:98, VII:111, VII:138 *(parents)*

LAURIE CHAMBERS'S MASSEUSE (BIG MUSCLES): Big muscles, no brains. V:382

CHANEY, JAMES
   See DEAN, SUSANNAH: ODETTA HOLMES AND THE CIVIL RIGHTS
MOVEMENT: VOTER REGISTRATION BOYS

CHAP, THE
   See MORDRED

CHARLIE THE CHOO-CHOO
JAKE CHAMBERS bought his copy of the children's story *Charlie the Choo-Choo* in CALVIN TOWER's bookshop, THE MANHATTAN RESTAURANT OF THE MIND. (See *Stephen King's The Dark Tower: A Concordance, Volume I.*) Charlie prefigured BLAINE the Insane Mono, whom our tet had to outriddle at the beginning of *Wizard and Glass*.
   V:54, V:55, V:57, V:91, V:104, V:118, V:152, V:167, V:600, V:709, VI:84, VI:154, VI:162, VI:168, VII:335
   BACHMAN, CLAUDIA Y INEZ: Claudia Inez Bachman was the widow of the author RICHARD BACHMAN. In the TODASH version of NEW YORK CITY, which JAKE CHAMBERS and EDDIE DEAN visit at the beginning of *Wolves of the Calla*, she was also the author of *Charlie the Choo-Choo*. On the levels of the DARK TOWER where Claudia Bachman is a published writer, her name contains a *y*, transforming her into one of the members of the tet of NINETEEN. V:57, V:59, V:92, V:93, V:94 *(nineteen letters)*, V:600 *(author)*, V:709 *(author)*, VI:84, VI:154, VI:200, VI:214, VI:288
   ENGINEER BOB: Engineer Bob was Charlie's driver and friend. (See *Stephen King's The Dark Tower: A Concordance, Volume I.*) V:91
   EVANS, BERYL: On one level of the DARK TOWER, Beryl Evans was the author of *Charlie the Choo-Choo*. (See *Stephen King's The Dark Tower: A Concordance, Volume I.*) On our level of the Tower, Beryl Evans was a victim of the 1940s British serial killer John Reginald Halliday. V:57, V:59, V:91, V:93, V:119, V:600 *(indirect, as author)*, V:709 *(indirect, as author)*, VI:84, VI:154, VI:200, VI:214–15, VI:288

CHASE, FRANKIE
   See CALLAHAN, FATHER DONALD FRANK: CALLAHAN'S HOME
SHELTER ASSOCIATES

CHASSIT
   See NINETEEN

CHEVIN OF CHAYVEN
   See MUTANTS: CHILDREN OF RODERICK

CHILDREN OF RODERICK
   See MUTANTS: CHILDREN OF RODERICK

CHIP
See MAINE CHARACTERS: McAVOY, CHIP

CHLOE
See GODS OF MID-WORLD

CHUMLEY
See NORTH CENTRAL POSITRONICS: NIGEL THE BUTLER

CHUMM, GREG
See CALLAHAN, FATHER DONALD FRANK: CALLAHAN'S HIDDEN HIGHWAYS ASSOCIATES

CHUMM'S TRAVELING WONDER SHOW
See CALLAHAN, FATHER DONALD FRANK: CALLAHAN'S HIDDEN HIGHWAYS ASSOCIATES: CHUMM, GREG

CHURCH OF THE WALK-INS
See WALK-INS *and* MAINE CHARACTERS: PETERSON, REVEREND; *see also* MAINE (STATE OF): STONEHAM: STONEHAM CORNERS: LOVELL-STONEHAM CHURCH OF THE WALK-INS, *in* OUR WORLD PLACES

CODY, DR. JAMES
See CALLAHAN, FATHER DONALD FRANK: 'SALEM'S LOT CHARACTERS

CODY, FATHER
See CALLAHAN, FATHER DONALD FRANK: 'SALEM'S LOT CHARACTERS: CODY, DR. JAMES

COLLINS, FLORA
See DANDELO

COLLINS, FRED
See DANDELO

COLLINS, HENRY
See DANDELO

COLLINS, JOE
See DANDELO

COMPSON
See WARRIORS OF THE SCARLET EYE: CASSE ROI RUSSE: HUMANS: FEEMALO/FIMALO/FUMALO: FUMALO

CONROY
 See CAN-TOI

CONSTANT READER
Stephen King's Constant Readers. This means you and me, folks!
 VI:406, VII:818

CONVEIGH, REVEREND
 See MAINE CHARACTERS

COOGAN, LORETTA
 See CALLAHAN, FATHER DONALD FRANK: 'SALEM'S LOT CHAR-
ACTERS

COOKIE
 See CALLA BRYN STURGIS CHARACTERS: RANCHERS: EISENHART,
VAUGHN

CÖOS, RHEA
 See RHEA OF THE CÖOS

CORNWELL, AUSTIN
 See WARRIORS OF THE SCARLET EYE: CASSE ROI RUSSE: HUMANS:
FEEMALO/FIMALO/FUMALO: FIMALO (RANDO THOUGHTFUL)

CORT (CORTLAND ANDRUS)
Muscular, scarred Cortland Andrus was Roland Deschain's teacher and men-
tor. (See *Stephen King's The Dark Tower: A Concordance, Volume I.*) Like his
father before him, squat, stocky Cort trained generations of gunslingers in the
art of fighting. Not only did Cort teach the apprentice gunslingers to battle with
a variety of weapons, but he also taught them to navigate by the sun and stars,
and to keep a clock ticking inside their heads. One of his sayings was "Never
speak the worst aloud." Another was "Always con yer vantage." Although Cort
was an almost legendary brawler, he (like Roland's gentle teacher VANNAY)
had a philosophical side as well. According to Roland, Cort held palaver with
the mystical MANNI.
 V:78 *(taught navigation and fighting)*, V:86, V:169, V:204, V:240, V:245,
 V:248, V:383, V:392, V:476, V:597, V:675, VI:203, VII:21, VII:34, VII:148,
 VII:247, VII:250, VII:473, VII:587, VII:589 *(saying)*, VII:778 *(always con yer
 vantage)*, VII:779, VII:801 *(Cortland Andrus)*, VII:824, VII:829

COTER, CHUGGY
 See DEAN, EDDIE: EDDIE'S PAST ASSOCIATES

COVAY MOVERS
See CALLAHAN, FATHER DONALD FRANK: CALLAHAN'S HIDDEN HIGHWAYS ASSOCIATES

CRAZY MARY'S
See CALIFORNIA (STATE OF): SACRAMENTO: CRAZY MARY'S, *in* OUR WORLD PLACES

CRIMSON KING (THE RED KING, LORD OF THE SPIDERS, LOS THE RED, LORD OF DISCORDIA)

The first time STEPHEN KING encountered Los the Red—in the form of tiny red spiders feeding on the intestines of dead chickens—King was seven years old and sawing wood in his aunt and uncle's barn. The young King was saved from the spiders (and from their deadly bites, which would have turned him into a VAMPIRE) by CUTHBERT ALLGOOD and EDDIE DEAN. Needless to say, the Crimson King never forgave Stephen King for evading his clutches, or for converting to the cause of the WHITE.

Like his half-son, MORDRED, the Crimson King is a were-spider. He is also probably the BEAST and Keeper of the Tower that WALTER spoke of in the original version of *The Gunslinger*. As the artist PATRICK DANVILLE realizes when he tries to draw him perched on a balcony of the DARK TOWER, the Red King *darkles* and *tincts* like the AGELESS STRANGER, whom Walter also mentioned during his long palaver with Roland in the GOLGOTHA. (For the AGELESS STRANGER entry, see *Stephen King's The Dark Tower: A Concordance, Volume I.*)

In his human form, the Crimson King resembles a satanic Santa Claus, with a huge hooked nose, full red lips (overhung by a single tusklike tooth), an enormous white beard, and long, snowy-white hair. Like Saint Nick, he wears a red robe, though Los's is dotted with lightning bolts and cabalistic symbols, not cuffed and trimmed with fur. Although in *Wolves of the Calla* we came to suspect that BLACK THIRTEEN, the nastiest ball of the WIZARD'S RAINBOW, was actually one of the Red King's eyes, in *The Dark Tower* we learn that it isn't. The Crimson King's eyes are as red as the roses of CAN'-KA NO REY, and when Roland sees him shouting from a balcony of the Dark Tower, he is still in possession of both of them.

Not only is the Red King ugly, but he is also completely mad. Many years before our story began, he flooded THUNDERCLAP with poison gas, darkening the land and killing everything that lived there. Although he probably originally had an hourglass-shape on his back (a sigul which Mordred still has and which is the *dan-tete*'s key to the Tower) somehow or other, the Red King managed to destroy his. Hence, he cannot enter the Tower proper without some sigul of the ELD—either his half-son's mark or Roland's guns.

Although the Red King is Roland's nemesis, he is also Roland's kinsman. According to Walter (the Crimson King's prime minister), they are both descended from ARTHUR ELD. However, whereas Roland's family branch is dedicated to the protection of the Tower, the Red King (always GAN's crazy side) is focused on its destruction. It is he, the Lord of Chaos, who enslaved the BREAKERS and who forces them to destroy the BEAMS that hold the Tower in place.

Just as the gunslingers serve the White, the WARRIORS OF THE SCARLET EYE serve the Crimson King and the cause of the Outer Dark. These servants include the WOLVES, VAMPIRES, TAHEEN, and CAN-TOI (or LOW MEN) of END-WORLD. Companies such as NORTH CENTRAL POSITRONICS, the SOMBRA CORPORATION, and LAMERK INDUSTRIES (all existing in versions of our world) also owe allegiance to the Crimson King.

When Roland and SUSANNAH journey to LE CASSE ROI RUSSE (the Red King's palace) on their way to the Dark Tower, they find out from AUSTIN CORNWELL that while they were battling the Wolves in CALLA BRYN STURGIS, the Red King foresaw their victory—both in the Calla and in the DEVAR-TOI—in one of MAERLYN's magic balls. (Six of them were in his possession at the time.) Enraged, Los forced all but three of his castle servants to eat rat poison. After watching them die from his throne of skulls, he smashed the Wizard's Rainbow and killed himself by swallowing a sharpened spoon. In his new undead form—which was safe even from Roland's guns whose barrels were made from Arthur Eld's sword EXCALIBUR—he mounted his gray horse NIS and galloped for the Tower. Although he could not enter the Tower proper, he took up a position on one of its balconies. From there, he hoped to keep his fearsome enemy Roland at bay with his huge supply of sneetches. Luckily, the Crimson King was not destined to succeed.

Although the Red King may not have foreseen it, by the time Roland reaches his life's goal, he no longer has a ka-tet but is in the company of the mute but magical artist Patrick Danville, whom the Red King was so eager to destroy in the novel *Insomnia*. Patrick's pencils can change reality, so Roland has the younger man draw the Crimson King as he stands on the balcony of the Tower, complete with nose hair and snaggletooth. Once the picture has achieved the required verisimilitude (created by dabs of red for the eyes—pigment made from the petals of Can'-Ka No Rey mixed with Roland's blood), Roland has Patrick erase his drawing, and in so doing, he erases the Red King himself. As Roland mounts the steps of the Tower, all that remains of his enemy are two enraged red eyes.

V:236, V:291, V:366 *(Red King)*, V:413 *(and the Dark Tower)*, V:452, V:456, V:463, V:465, V:468, V:470, V:539, V:549, V:550, VI:13, VI:22, VI:95, VI:102, VI:105, VI:110, VI:111, VI:120, VI:121, VI:169, VI:171, VI:199, VI:231, VI:232, VI:233, VI:238, VI:239, VI:244–55 *(Walter and the Crimson King's plans)*, VI:259 *(as Devil)*, VI:269, VI:287, VI:293 *(as Lord of Spiders; Tower-pent)*, VI:294 *(Lord of Discordia)*, VI:295, VI:296, VI:318, VI:326, VI:328–31 *(voice of Black Thirteen)*, VI:336, VI:337, VI:350, VI:374, VI:380 *(Eye)*, VI:384, VI:407, VII:13, VII:25, VII:47, VII:62, VII:70 *(King)*, VII:76 *(Big Red Daddy)*, VII:89, VII:92, VII:111, VII:127, VII:133, VII:134, VII:141, VII:149, VII:150, VII:161, VII:173,

VII:174, VII:175, VII:176, VII:177, VII:179, VII:188, VII:202, VII:210, VII:229, VII:238, VII:261, VII:262, VII:266, VII:281, VII:285, VII:298, VII:300, VII:301, VII:326–27, VII:406, VII:447, VII:498, VII:506, VII:512, VII:513, VII:514, VII:515–16, VII:539, VII:549–52 *(red goblin)*, VII:559, VII:563, VII:578, VII:580, VII:581, VII:589, VII:591 *(indirect)*, VII:593, VII:595, VII:603, VII:604 *(Los)*, VII:605 *(killed castle staff with rat poison; throne made of skulls; has six of the Wizard's Glasses)*, VII:605–10, VII:612, VII:613, VI:614, VII:615, VII:617–18, VII:619, VII:620, VII:621, VII:622, VII:623, VII:626, VII:650 *(mad guardian of the Tower)*, VII:670–71 *(six months in Tower)*, VII:703, VII:711, VII:717, VII:721, VII:724, VII:725, VII:754, VII:755, VII:757 *(indirect)*, VII:759, VII:766, VII:767–68, VII:770–71, VII:772, VII:781, VII:782–800, VII:819–20, VII:823

BANGO SKANK: *See* SKANK, BANGO, *listed separately*

NIS: Nis is the Crimson King's horse. His name comes from the land of sleep and dreams. *See also* GODS OF MID-WORLD. VII:607

CROWELL, GARY
See MAINE CHARACTERS

CUJO
See APPENDIX I

CULLUM, JOHN
See TET CORPORATION: FOUNDING FATHERS

CUTHBERT ALLGOOD
See ALLGOOD, CUTHBERT

D

DADDY MOSE
See TET CORPORATION: FOUNDING FATHERS: CARVER, MOSES

DALE, MR.
See BREAKERS: BRAUTIGAN, TED

DAMASCUS, TRUDY
See GUTTENBERG, FURTH, AND PATEL

DANDELO (JOE COLLINS, ODD JOE OF ODD LANE, ODD JOE OF ODD'S LANE, OLD MAN-MONSTER)
As he lies dying in the PROCTOR'S SUITE in the DEVAR-TOI, EDDIE

DEAN whispers a final warning to JAKE CHAMBERS. He tells his young friend that he must protect their *dinh* from Dandelo. Unfortunately, by the time Roland reaches Dandelo's den, Jake is already dead. The boy's pet BILLY-BUMBLER passes the message on to Roland telepathically, and Eddie appears in dreams to warn SUSANNAH DEAN about this particular monster, but nothing prepares the two remaining members of our ka-tet for what they are about to encounter.

When Roland and Susannah arrive at Dandelo's home on ODD LANE, located just off TOWER ROAD in the WHITE LANDS OF EMPATHICA, Dandelo is posing as Joe Collins from America-side. Odd Joe of Odd's Lane (*s* added to throw our tet off the scent) appears to be a harmless retired comedian whose only companions are his blind horse LIPPY and his cane, BESSIE. However, in the land of Empathica nothing is as it seems.

In his true form, Dandelo (an anagram of *Odd Lane*) looks like a giant insect. Like the giant spider It (found in STEPHEN KING's novel of the same name), Dandelo feeds on human emotion. But while It feeds on faith, usually the faith of children, Dandelo's favorite emotional flavors are laughter and fear. However, there is a good chance that these two monsters are (to borrow a term from the King/Straub novel *The Talisman*) twinners of each other. As Susannah kills Dandelo (clued in to his real identity by a note left for her by Stephen King), he momentarily takes the shape of a psychotic clown. As CONSTANT READERS will remember, Pennywise the Clown was one of It's favorite forms.

Dandelo grows younger as he feeds, but it seems that in the White Lands, meals don't pass by that frequently. Hence, despite his ability to sleep for long periods, Dandelo has to keep a human "cow" for nourishment. That cow is the artist PATRICK DANVILLE, whom we met as a child in the novel *Insomnia*. When Roland and Susannah free Patrick from his prison in Dandelo's basement, they discover that Patrick is mute. However, Patrick's muteness isn't congenital. Dandelo pulled out his tongue.

VII:403, VII:411, VII:520, VII:541, VII:556, VII:645, VII:653–707, VII:708, VII:709, VII:710, VII:711, VII:719, VII:723, VII:731, VII:732, VII:734, VII:736, VII:739 *(indirect)*, VII:751, VII:754 *(old man-monster)*, VII:755, VII:761, VII:774

AGENT: VII:668

BESSIE: Joe Collins's name for his walking stick. VII:657

COLLINS, FLORA: Joe Collins's mother. VII:657, VII:663 *(ma and pa)*

COLLINS, HENRY: Joe Collins's father. VII:657, VII:663 *(ma and pa)*

GRANDMOTHER: VII:674, VII:675

GRANDPA FRED: VII:674

LIPPY: This is Dandelo's demonic horse, though he is probably not a horse at all but some other kind of creature disguised by *glammer*. When MORDRED eats dead Lippy's flesh, he contracts food poisoning. VII:653–59, VII:660, VII:664, VII:667, VII:670, VII:682 *(wonder-nag)*, VII:693–94, VII:702, VII:708, VII:755 *(gave Mordred food poisoning)*

DANDO (KING DANDO)

King Dando had lots of rubies in his vault. We don't learn anything else about him.

VII:794

DAN-TETE

See MORDRED; *see also* APPENDIX I

DANVILLE, PATRICK (THE ARTIST)

We first met Patrick Danville in STEPHEN KING's novel *Insomnia*. At that time, four-year-old Patrick and his mother SONIA were attending a pro-choice rally at the DERRY Civic Center, where the feminist Susan Day was about to give a speech. Although still a child, talented little Patrick was already the focus of an assassination attempt by ED DEEPNEAU, a mad follower of the CRIMSON KING.[2] The reason? At the age of twenty-two, Patrick was destined to save the lives of two men, one of whom is key to the Purpose[3] and to the stability of the TOWER. In *The Dark Tower*, we find out that Patrick's fate is even greater. He is destined to save the life of Roland Deschain as well.

At four years old, Patrick—enveloped in an aura of pink roses—was already an accomplished artist. But by the time he reaches adulthood, his pencils are, literally, magic. Patrick has an amazing skill which sets him above even the most skilled painters and draftsmen of our world. He can transform reality by drawing it in the configurations of his choosing, then "uncreate" with his nifty little erasers. This talent alone would be enough to put him on the Crimson King's hit list, but in the end, it isn't the Red King who captures him.

By the time he is in his late teens, Patrick—himself the child of an abused mother—is the prisoner of the sadistic DANDELO, a giant, emotion-eating were-insect living in the WHITE LANDS OF EMPATHICA, not far from the red fields of CAN'-KA NO REY, which surround the Tower. After killing Dandelo, Roland, OY, and SUSANNAH DEAN rescue Patrick from a cage in Dandelo's basement. But by the time they find him, Patrick is exhausted and weak from years of being "milked" of his emotions. Thanks to Dandelo's cruelty, he is also tongueless and mentally wounded. However, despite the torture he has endured, his artistic talents are intact. In fact, he manages to "draw" the UNFOUND DOOR and bring it into END-WORLD, giving Susannah Dean an escape route from the inevitable death which seems to await all those who become ka-tet with Roland.

In the end, it is Patrick—not Oy or Susannah—who is Roland's final com-

---

2. Ed Deepneau thinks that he is destroying the "baby-killing" pro-choicers. However, he has been duped by the Crimson King into causing utter mayhem so that one four-year-old child will cease breathing.

3. In the novel *Insomnia*, two forces battle over the fate of the macroverse. These forces are the Random and the Purpose. Generally speaking, the Crimson King is aligned with the chaotic Random, while the White is aligned with the Purpose.

panion on his journey through End-World. And as it turns out, it is Patrick's magical artistic skills, and not fast guns, which ultimately defeat the Lord of Discordia.

When Roland and Patrick approach the Tower, the Red King is standing on one of its balconies. Mad as a hatter, he is determined to thwart Roland's life-long desire and prevent our gunslinger from entering that linchpin of existence. Since he is already undead (he swallowed a sharpened spoon while still resident in his palace, LE CASSE ROI RUSSE), Roland cannot shoot him. The only other option is to have Patrick draw the Red King and then erase him. By the time Roland begins to mount the first of those legendary spiral stairs, all that is left of the Crimson King is a pair of floating red eyes.

VII:514–15, VII:550–57, VII:646, VII:685, VII:695–710 *(crying before this, but Susannah/Roland thought it was the wind; 698—called Dandelo's cow)*, VII:716–24, VII:725, VII:726, VII:729–50, VII:751, VII:752 *(the Artist)*, VII:754, VII:756–65, VII:767–801, VII:802–3, VII:807

DANVILLE, SONIA: Patrick's mother. VII:514 *(mother)*, VII:709, VII:773 *(mother)*, VII:774

DANVILLE, SONIA
See DANVILLE, PATRICK

DARRYL
See DEAN, SUSANNAH: ODETTA HOLMES AND THE CIVIL RIGHTS MOVEMENT: ODETTA'S "MOVEMENT" ASSOCIATES

DAVID (HAWK)
Roland used this trained hawk as a weapon in his coming-of-age battle against his teacher CORT. In many ways, David was the first of Roland's companions to be sacrificed to his ambition. (See *Stephen King's The Dark Tower: A Concordance, Volume I.*)

V:383, V:491, V:492, VII:802, VII:824

DAVID AND GOLIATH
See MID-WORLD FOLKLORE: PERTH, LORD

DEAN, EDDIE (THE PRISONER, EDDIE TOREN)
Although he was born during the 1960s in BROOKLYN, NEW YORK, Eddie Dean reminds Roland of his two earlier ka-tet mates, CUTHBERT ALL-GOOD and ALAIN JOHNS. Like Cuthbert, Eddie's sense of humor often borders on the silly (at least in Roland's estimation), and like Alain, he has deep flashes of intuition. Although Roland sometimes thinks Eddie is weak and self-centered, he appreciates the younger man's deep reservoirs of courage and his tremendously generous heart.

A onetime heroin junkie, Eddie Dean is the maverick of Roland Deschain's ka-tet. Roland often calls him *ka-mai*, or ka's fool, and in many ways this assessment seems fairly accurate. In *The Drawing of the Three,* Eddie chose the love of ODETTA HOLMES/DETTA WALKER over caution and thus almost lost his face to a LOBSTROSITY. Yet it was Eddie's anarchic sense of humor that fried the circuits of BLAINE the Insane Mono, allowing our ka-tet to win their riddling contest and outwit this seriously suicidal machine. Each member of Roland's ka-tet has at least one special talent, and Eddie's skills go beyond making bad jokes. In *The Waste Lands,* his hidden artistic vision shone forth, and he was able both to draw a magic door to bring JAKE CHAMBERS into Roland's world, and to fashion a key to open that door.

In many ways, Eddie becomes an even more important character in the final books of the series. Of all the people we meet during our travels through IN-WORLD, MID-WORLD, THE BORDERLANDS, and END-WORLD, Eddie is the most reminiscent of the traditional Arthurian knight. By his own admission, Eddie needs to be needed. While he shares Roland's desire to reach the DARK TOWER, unlike Roland, Eddie believes that his ultimate purpose is not to serve his ka-tet, or even his wife, but to protect the ROSE, which is (on our level of the Tower at least) one of the most fundamental symbols of love.

When Roland and Eddie visit STEPHEN KING in the *when* of 1977, they learn that Eddie is actually the twin of Cuthbert Allgood, Roland's old friend from GILEAD. According to King (speaking in a deep trance state), he saw both Cuthbert and Eddie when he was seven years old. They saved him from the clutches of the CRIMSON KING, Lord of the Spiders, and turned him from the grim seductions of DISCORDIA.

Without Eddie's intuition to guide him, Roland would never have seen the formation of the TET CORPORATION, the company which protects the Rose on our level of the Tower. Nor would he have met his maker, Stephen King, in the town of BRIDGTON, MAINE. In fact, he may not even have survived the onslaught of BALAZAR'S MEN in EAST STONEHAM, if he'd made it to that town at all. However, like all ka-mais, Eddie's days are numbered. Once our tet defeats the WOLVES of CALLA BRYN STURGIS and destroys the DEVAR-TOI where the BREAKERS are eroding the BEAMS, Eddie is shot in the head by PIMLI PRENTISS, the Devar Master. As GRAN-PERE JAFFORDS predicted, for men like Eddie Dean it is always a bullet that opens the way to the clearing at the end of the path.

One of the wonderful aspects of the macroverse is that somewhere, on some other level of the Tower, another version of us always survives. This is as true for Eddie Dean as for anyone else. When Susannah Dean leaves End-World through the UNFOUND DOOR, she finds herself in an alternative version of NEW YORK CITY. Although it is not 1987 of the KEYSTONE EARTH—people here drive Takuro Spirits, drink Nozz-A-La cola, and Gary Hart is president—she is still overjoyed to be there. The reason is simple. Waiting for her in a snowy CENTRAL PARK is none other than her beloved husband, Eddie Dean.

It seems that—on some levels of the Tower at least—stories can have happy endings. In this where and when, Eddie is from WHITE PLAINS, not CO-OP

CITY. His brother isn't the bossy HENRY DEAN but his ka-tet mate Jake Chambers. In fact, the two of them aren't Eddie Dean and Jake Chambers at all, but Eddie and Jake TOREN—descendants of the family which (on our level of the Tower) are the custodians of the Vacant LOT and of the magic Rose.

V:8 *(strangers from Out-World)*, V:29–31 *(gunslingers)*, V:35–47, V:49–70 *(New York and Jake—1977)*, V:71, V:77, V:78, V:80, V:81, V:84, V:87, V:88–119, V:122, V:123–64, V:176–85, V:187–98, V:201–39, V:241, V:242, V:243, V:244, V:245–53, V:256–57 *(listening to Pere Callahan's tale)*, V:258 *(listening)*, V:260 *(listening)*, V:262 *(listening)*, V:264–71 *(listening)*, V:273–74 *(listening)*, V:275 *(listening)*, V:281 *(listening)*, V:284 *(listening)*, V:285 *(listening)*, V:290 *(listening)*, V:291–96 *(listening)*, V:301–2 *(listening)*, V:309–12, V:318, V:321, V:322, V:325, V:341, V:343–60, V:365–69, V:376–80, V:381, V:382, V:384, V:388, V:392, V:394, V:396–406, V:408, V:412 *(ka-tet mates)*, V:417–20, V:421–23, V:428–30, V:437–38, V:442–45, V:448–49, V:452–54, V:457, V:466–72, V:478, V:479, V:480, V:482, V:485–86, V:487, V:488–505, V:506–52, V:555, V:563, V:573–74 *(younger one)*, V:576, V:581–90, V:592, V:597, V:598, V:601–28 *(waiting for Callahan)*, V:629–35, V:639–40, V:641–50, V:652–53, V:654, V:658, V:662–74, V:679–705, VI:3–8, VI:10–18, VI:22, VI:24–43, VI:63, VI:64, VI:68, VI:69, VI:70, VI:71, VI:74, VI:80–82, VI:98, VI:117, VI:122, VI:123, VI:124, VI:129–216, VI:222, VI:224, VI:225, VI:230 *(indirect)*, VI:231, VI:233, VI:240, VI:246, VI:248, VI:259, VI:265–303 *(Eddie is Cuthbert's twin)*, VI:307, VI:320, VI:324, VI:348, VI:360, VI:365, VI:373, VI:374, VI:395, VI:399, VI:404, VII:1–3, VII:17–53, VII:57–58, VII:114–32, VII:134–38, VII:141–59, VII:168, VII:169, VII:173, VI:177 *(indirect)*, VII:186 *(ka-tet)*, VII:187, VII:188, VII:189–220, VII:247–61, VII:262 *(indirect)*, VII:265–73, VII:276 *(indirect)*, VII:279–309 *(297–302—listening to Ted's story)*, VII:316, VII:318–42, VII:350, VII:351–52, VII:362–63, VII:369–70, 378–85 *(Eddie is shot)*, VII:387, VII:388–90, VII:391, VII:392, VII:393, VII:394, VII:395 *(indirect)*, VII:396–97, VII:398, VII:401–4, VII:407, VII:408–10, VII:413 *(indirect)*, VII:416 *(indirect)*, VII:427, VII:428, VII:435, VII:438, VII:448, VII:453, VII:455, VII:464, VII:477, VII:485, VII:487, VII:488, VII:491, VII:495, VII:504, VII:508, VII:510, VII:518, VII:520, VII:533, VII:541, VII:549, VII:554–56, VII:559, VII:562, VII:569, VII:571, VII:601, VII:603, VII:604, VII:608, VII:629, VII:630, VII:633, VII:641, VII:642, VII:645–46, VII:662, VII:668, VII:674, VII:681, VII:683, VII:690, VII:708, VII:724–25, VII:727, VII:728, VII:729, VII:731, VII:733, VII:740, VII:744, VII:747, VII:748, VII:758, VI:762, VII:772, VII:785, VII:802, VII:807–13, VII:818, VII:819

EDDIE'S PAST ASSOCIATES:

BERNSTEIN, MISS: Miss Bernstein (we never learn her actual name) was paralyzed in a car accident. VII:103

BERNSTEIN, MRS.: Mrs. Bernstein's daughter was paralyzed in a car accident in MAMARONECK. VII:103

BERTOLLO, DORA (TITS BERTOLLO): Dora Bertollo was Eddie's mother's friend. The kids on Eddie's block called her Tits Bertollo because her breasts were the size of watermelons. V:187

COTER, CHUGGY: The Chugster was one of Eddie's old friends. While HENRY DEAN was in VIETNAM, Eddie and Chuggy went to the movies together. They liked westerns. VI:285

DEAN, WENDELL: *See* DEAN, WENDELL, *listed separately*

KENOPENSKY, MARY LOU: While Eddie was still at school, he had a crush on this girl and wrote her name all over his books. VII:144

LOONY KIDS: When Eddie was young, these kids used to run around the neighborhood shouting, "I'm the Barber of Seville-a, You must try my fucking skill-a." The comedy entitled *The Barber of Seville* was written by Pierre Beaumarchais and was produced in Paris in 1775. It later gave rise to several operas. The kids were probably actually thinking of Sweeney Todd, the demon barber, who killed his customers and had his baker-accomplice turn them into meat pies. V:631–32

LUNDGREN, DAHLIE: Dahlie Lundgren owned a shop that made great fried dough. He also sold comic books, which were fairly easy to steal. Eddie, HENRY, and their friends used to smoke cigarettes behind Dahlie's shop. We don't know whether Dahlie approved or not. V:187, V:203, V:257

MISLABURSKI, MRS.: Mrs. Mislaburski was a large-bosomed old lady from CO-OP CITY who wore pink support hose. Mrs. Mislaburski would brave the icy sidewalks of Co-Op City to attend Mass and to visit the CASTLE AVENUE MARKET. VII:102–3

MR. "FUTURE CORONARY" BUSINESSMAN: Eddie bumps into this anally retentive businessman during his first solitary sojourn into 1977 NEW YORK. The man's attitude reminds Eddie of the punch line of an old New York joke: "Pardon me, sir, can you tell me how to get to City Hall, or should I just go fuck myself?" V:516–17

MR. RELAXED WINDOW-SHOPPER: Eddie meets this guy when he travels through the UNFOUND DOOR to 1977 NEW YORK. Mr. Relaxed (but somewhat sarcastic) Window-Shopper tells Eddie the date. V:517

OFFICER BOSCONI (BOSCO BOB): ANDY, the smiling but treacherous robot of CALLA BRYN STURGIS, reminds Eddie of Bosco Bob, the cop who had the BROOKLYN AVENUE beat in Eddie's old neighborhood. When you met him casually, Bosco Bob was friendly and happy to see you. However, if he thought you'd done something wrong, he'd turn into a dangerous robot-of-the-law. V:140, V:141, V:633

PERTH OIL AND GAS: VII:324–25

SALLOW BRITISH MAN: *See* BALAZAR, ENRICO: BALAZAR'S NASSAU CONNECTION

SOBIESKI, MARY JEAN: Mary Jean Sobieski was one of Eddie's high school girlfriends. He lost his high school ring in the CONEY ISLAND sand the summer he was dating her. We can only imagine how that might have happened. V:701

TUBTHER, MR.: Mr. Tubther was Eddie's fifth-grade teacher and one of the voices-of-doom which Eddie hears in the CAVE OF VOICES. Mr. Tubther believed that Eddie's potential was ruined by his brother, HENRY DEAN. V:512

DEAN, GLORIA (SELINA)

Gloria Dean was EDDIE and HENRY DEAN's sister. She was killed by a drunk driver at the tender age of six. In *Song of Susannah*, Eddie refers to Gloria as his "little sister." Although this isn't technically correct—Eddie was two when she died—he has a point. The dead don't age. Gloria is, was, and will eternally be six years old.

VI:277

DEAN, HENRY (GREAT SAGE AND EMINENT JUNKIE)

Although we witnessed Henry Dean's death from a heroin overdose in *The Drawing of the Three* and subsequently saw his severed head lobbed at EDDIE by one of BALAZAR'S MEN in THE LEANING TOWER, the great sage and eminent junkie doesn't rest easy. (See *Stephen King's The Dark Tower: A Concordance, Volume I.*) Eddie Dean's bullying older brother continues to make cameo appearances in the final three books of the Dark Tower series, usually in the form of a nasty, nagging, or teasing voice at the back of Eddie Dean's mind. (In *Wolves of the Calla*, Henry's taunts also rise up from the noxious pit found in the DOORWAY CAVE.)

In the final book of the series, we find out that—on at least one level of the DARK TOWER—Henry Dean was never born. In that where and when, Eddie Dean is Eddie TOREN, from WHITE PLAINS, and his beloved bro is actually JAKE CHAMBERS (Jake TOREN), not Henry.

V:61, V:68, V:104 *(Eddie's brother)*, V:140 *(goodfornothin bro)*, V:152, V:163, V:183, V:187, V:203, V:216, V:221 *(indirect)*, V:284, V:292, V:349, V:509, V:510, V:512, V:514, V:524, V:618, V:619 *(indirect)*, V:704–5, VI:28, VI:80–81, VI:142, VI:157–58, VI:184, VI:204, VI:212–14, VI:277, VI:285, VII:43, VII:44 *(great sage and eminent junkie)*, VII:103, VII:118, VII:148, VII:289, VII:328, VII:336, VII:396, VII:812

GOLDOVER, SYLVIA: Sylvia Goldover was Henry Dean's great love. According to EDDIE, she was a skank *El Supremo*, complete with bad breath and smelly armpits. Eventually, she deserted Henry and went off with her old boyfriend. The only memento she left was a note tucked into Henry's wallet in place of the ninety dollars she'd stolen. The note said, "I'm sorry Henry." VI:157–58

   OLD BOYFRIEND: VI:158

HENRY DEAN'S KA-TET: For more information, see *Stephen King's The Dark Tower: A Concordance, Volume I.* V:187 *(indirect)*

BRANNIGAN, SKIPPER: V:187
DRABNIK, CSABA (THE MAD FUCKIN' HUNGARIAN): V:187, V:510
FREDERICKS, TOMMY (HALLOWEEN TOMMY): Tommy Fredericks's nickname came from his habit of making faces during stickball games. The faces weren't purposeful but were the result of overexcitement. V:187
POLINO, JIMMY (JIMMY POLIO): V:187

DEAN, MRS. (EDDIE'S MOTHER)

Mrs. Dean was EDDIE, HENRY, and poor dead GLORIA's mother. She was a single parent and so often left Eddie in Henry's care. Not a good idea. (See *Stephen King's The Dark Tower: A Concordance, Volume I.*)

V:98, V:140 *(mother)*, V:179 *(ma)*, V:182 *(mother)*, V:187 *(mother)*, V:215 *(ma)*, V:245, V:368, V:510, V:540, V:622, VI:28, VI:32, VI:137 *(exclamation)*, VI:195

DEAN, SUSANNAH (DETTA WALKER, ODETTA HOLMES, LADY OF SHADOWS, LADY BLACKBIRD, BLACKBIRD MOMMY, SUSANNAH-MIO)

In *The Drawing of the Three,* Roland used one of the magical BEACH DOORS to draw a seething DETTA WALKER from an early 1960s NEW YORK onto the LOBSTROSITY-infested shore of the WESTERN SEA. Detta, who was the sly and rather dangerous secondary personality of ODETTA HOLMES, sole heir to the HOLMES DENTAL INDUSTRIES fortune, was none too pleased about it. In fact, while Odetta was helping EDDIE DEAN maneuver her wheelchair over the many sand traps of that treacherous terrain (and simultaneously falling in love with him), sneaky, ever-suspicious Detta was trying to hatch a plan to kill her white kidnappers. Although Roland managed to unite these two warring personalities in the stronger and more vibrant third of Susannah Dean, both Odetta and Detta continue to play an important role in the final three books of the Dark Tower series, as does Susannah's susceptibility to multiple personality disorder.

At the beginning of *Wolves of the Calla,* we find out that Susannah Dean is pregnant, but within the first hundred pages we suspect (as does Roland) that the child she carries is not human at all, but the offspring of the DEMON she trapped in a sexual vise while Roland and Eddie drew JAKE CHAMBERS into the SPEAKING RING, located on the great plains of RIVER BARONY. While trying to keep his suspicions a secret, Roland follows Susannah on her nocturnal feeding prowls through the forests and bogs of the BORDERLANDS, as much to keep her safe as to try to discern the nature of her carry.

Quite soon, Roland discovers that Susannah is not the only mother of her child. Her body now contains yet another personality, that of MIA, whose name (in High Speech) means "mother." Over the course of both *Wolves of the Calla* and *Song of Susannah,* we learn that Mia (unlike Susannah's previous personalities) is not a part of Susannah's psyche at all, but an invading spirit whose sole purpose is to feed and protect the CHAP, which Susannah's body harbors. Unlike Susannah, who lost her legs from the knee down when she was pushed in front of the A train at CHRISTOPHER STREET STATION by JACK MORT, Mia can walk. Susannah can use those legs when she travels TODASH or when her psyche is completely dominated by Mia, as it is in 1999 New York. In *Song of Susannah,* we also find out that Mia is white, which does not sit too well with Detta Walker.

In many ways, this schism between Susannah and Mia propels the action of *Song of Susannah.* At the end of *Wolves,* Mia hijacks Susannah's body and travels through the UNFOUND DOOR to 1999, where SAYRE and the other WARRIORS OF THE SCARLET EYE await her and her soon-to-be-born offspring. Hoping to outsmart Susannah's ka-tet, Mia takes BLACK THIR-TEEN with her, essentially locking this magic door behind her so that no one can follow.

Not surprisingly, Mia underestimates both Susannah and her friends. With the help of the MANNI, our tet mates Jake, OY, and PERE CALLAHAN track SUSANNAH-MIO to the DIXIE PIG, which also happens to be a den of TYPE ONE VAMPIRES. Although Callahan is killed by vampires and LOW MEN, Jake and Oy follow Susannah's back trail to the FEDIC DOGAN, where Mia has just given birth to her were-spider baby, MORDRED. Although Susannah manages to kill her captors and escape to the New York/Fedic door, where she awaits the arrival of the rest of her ka-tet, she only manages to clip off one of Mordred's legs with a bullet. She is not able to save Mia, who is sucked dry by her offspring.

After the deaths of Eddie and Jake, Susannah becomes a member of a new ka-tet—one that is bound by hate as well as love. This new group consists of herself, Roland, and Mordred—the *dan-tete,* or little god, whose coming has been prophesied for generations. Wherever Susannah and Roland go, Mor-dred—child of Mia and the CRIMSON KING as much as he is the child of his "White Daddy" Roland and his "Blackbird Mommy" Susannah—is never far behind. From the wastelands of the DISCORDIA (where Susannah contracts a blood tumor above her lip) through the WHITE LANDS OF EMPATHICA, Mordred tracks his human parents, searching for a method of attack. With Susannah, he never gets the chance. Through a pair of stolen binoculars, he watches as the mute artist PATRICK DANVILLE removes Susannah's tumor and then literally draws the Unfound Door into END-WORLD so that Susannah can escape before Roland reaches his ultimate destination.

Susannah Dean is the only member of Roland's ka-tet to survive. However, ka is not always completely unkind. When Susannah passes through the Unfound Door, she finds herself in an alternative version of New York, where both Eddie and Jake are still alive (albeit under the names Eddie and Jake TOREN). Although Eddie no longer remembers his life in MID-WORLD, he has dreamed about Susannah, and he knows (as do we) that he's going to fall in love with her all over again. Susannah's gunslinging days are over. As if to symbolize this, she finds that Roland's gun (which she accidentally brought with her through the Unfound Door) seems absolutely ancient. Since it is plugged and unable to fire, Susannah throws it away.

V:8 *(strangers from Out-World)*, V:29–31 *(gunslingers)*, V:35, V:36, V:37, V:38–47, V:70, V:71–87 *(Mia hunts)*, V:87–119, V:120–37, V:139, V:140 *(Detta/Odetta)*, V:142–60, V:162, V:165, V:167–69, V:172–86 *(181— Odetta)*, V:189–91, V:193–98, V:201–39, V:241, V:242, V:243, V:244, V:245, V:246–49 *(Roland and Eddie discuss)*, V:250, V:251–53, V:257 *(listening to Pere Callahan)*, V:258 *(listening)*, V:260 *(listening)*, V:262 *(listening)*, V:266–71 *(listening)*, V:273–74 *(listening)*, V:282 *(listening)*, V:284 *(listening)*, V:285 *(listening)*, V:290 *(listening)*, V:291–96 *(listening)*, V:301–2 *(listening)*, V:309–12, V:318, V:321, V:322, V:325, V:329 *(Detta)*, V:341, V:343–46, V:351–56, V:358, V:359 *(indirect)*, V:365–66, V:368, V:369, V:376–80, V:381–82, V:383, V:386, V:388, V:390–91, V:392, V:393, V:394, V:395, V:396–406, V:408 *(indirect, "other two")*, V:412 *(ka-mates)*, V:413, V:417–20, V:421–23, V:428–30, V:437–38, V:442–45, V:448–49, V:452–54, V:457, V:466–72, V:476, V:478–83, V:485, V:487, V:488–505, V:507, V:513, V:519, V:535, V:539 *(Odetta Holmes)*, V:555, V:563, V:575 *(brownie)*, V:581–90, V:597 *(Odetta)*, V:601–17, V:620, V:628–29, V:639–40, V:641, V:652, V:654, V:658, V:659, V:662–74, V:679–91, V:695–705 *(as Mia)*, VI:3, VI:4, VI:5, VI:6, VI:7 *(indirect)*, VI:9, VI:10–11, VI:12, VI:13, VI:14, VI:16, VI:17, VI:21–22, VI:24–26, VI:32 *(indirect)*, VI:35, VI:36, VI:37, VI:43, VI:48–52, VI:53–125, VI:143, VI:147, VI:150, VI:163, VI:168, VI:171, VI:173, VI:190, VI:194, VI:200, VI:205, VI:210, VI:216, VI:219–61, VI:267 *(sweetheart)*, VI:271, VI:284, VI:287, VI:297, VI:299, VI:311, VI:316, VI:319, VI:320, VI:321, VI:322, VI:325, VI:334, VI:339, VI:340–41, VI:343, VI:347–85, VI:399, VI:400, VI:408, VII:3, VII:4 *(Susannah-Mio)*, VII:13 *(Detta)*, VII:19, VII:21–22, VII:24, VII:25, VII:27 *(indirect)*, VII:34, VII:35, VII:36 *(wife)*, VII:38 *(indirect)*, VII:47, VII:48, VII:52, VII:55–80, VII:81, VII:84 *(oops—feet!)*, VII:86, VII:87–88, VII:89, VII:91, VII:92 *(indirect)*, VII:110, VII:111, VII:112, VII:114–15, VII:120, VII:121, VII:126, VII:136–38, VII:141–59, VII:161, VII:162, VII:163, VII:168, VII:169, VII:173, VII:177 *(indirect)*, VII:182, VII:183, VII:186 *(ka-tet)*, VII:187, VII:188, VII:189–220, VII:239, VII:247–61, VII:262 *(indirect)*, VII:265–73, VII:276 *(indirect)*, VII:279–309 *(297–303— listening to Ted's story)*, VII:315, VII:316, VII:317, VII:318–24, VII:325, VII:328, VII:329–42, VII:349–51, VII:361, VII:363–67, VII:373, VII:374, VII:381–85, VII:387, VII:388–90 *(on 389 she grows feet!)*, VII:395, VII:396–97, VII:401–4, VII:407, VII:408–11, VII:413, VII:416, VII:417, VII:446, VII:448, VII:459, VII:485, VII:486–87, VII:488, VII:499, VII:502, VII:508–9, VII:513, VII:519–20, VII:531–42, VII:549–619 *(619—no feet to run!)*, VII:620, VII:621–22 *(indirect)*, VII:624–31 *(624—feet)*, VII:632–710,

VII:711, VII:715–50, VII:751, VII:754 *(Blackbird Mommy)*, VII:756, VII:757, VI:758, VI:759, VII:761, VII:768, VII:769, VII:771, VII:773, VII:774, VII:780, VII:785, VII:789, VII:801, VII:802, VII:807–13 *(gun no longer works)*, VII:818, VII:819

SUSANNAH'S OTHER SELVES:

HOLMES, ODETTA: Odetta Holmes was the birth name of Roland's ka-tet mate SUSANNAH DEAN. Odetta was the only child of the dentist/inventor DAN HOLMES and was sole heir to the HOLMES DENTAL INDUSTRIES fortune. At the age of five, Odetta was hit on the head by a brick dropped by the psychopath JACK MORT, and her personality fractured, resulting in the birth of DETTA WALKER, who shared Odetta's body if not her opinions.

Odetta Holmes was a socially conscious young woman who was active in the Civil Rights Movement of the early 1960s. However, Detta Walker had a very different way of dealing with the oppression she faced from an unjust, prejudiced society. Her angry reaction was to take personal vengeance upon white boys (whenever the opportunity arose), and at the white world, by shoplifting from stores such as Macy's.

Detta and Odetta lost their legs from the knee down in 1959, when Jack Mort once again entered their shared life. At that time, Mort pushed them in front of an A train at CHRISTOPHER STREET STATION, in NEW YORK CITY. After this tragedy, an angry Detta Walker gained more and more waking time.

For years, Detta and Odetta lived their separate lives, each unaware of the existence of the other. They were finally united by Roland, who (while occupying Jack Mort's body in our world) forced Mort to commit suicide in front of the very train which had severed Detta/Odetta's legs. Witnessing this event through one of the magical BEACH DOORS while simultaneously seeing each other reflected in Roland's borrowed gaze forced the two women to confront each other. They united to create the much stronger personality of Susannah Dean, wife of EDDIE DEAN. *For page references, see DEAN, SUSANNAH, listed above*

SUSANNAH-MIO: While traveling TODASH, our tet sees this piece of graffito written on the fence around the Vacant LOT in NEW YORK CITY: "Oh Susannah-Mio, divided girl of mine, Done parked her RIG in the DIXIE PIG, in the year of '99." Although our tet does not yet know it, Susannah-Mio refers to the combined personalities of Susannah Dean and MIA, daughter of none. *For page references, see DEAN, SUSANNAH, listed above*

WALKER, DETTA: The angry, vindictive personality of Detta Walker gained life when five-year-old ODETTA HOLMES was hit on the head by a brick dropped by the psychopath JACK MORT. She and Odetta lost their legs from the knee down in 1959, when Mort once again attacked, pushing their shared body in front of an A train at CHRISTOPHER STREET STATION in NEW YORK CITY. This second tragic event gave angry Detta more waking time than she had previously enjoyed and allowed her to do what she liked best—tempt, tease, and torture white boys as well as shoplift from white-owned businesses such as Macy's.

Although they shared a body, Detta and Odetta were completely different women. While Odetta was both wealthy and educated, streetwise Detta took pride that she "didn't go to Morehouse or *no* house." While Odetta believed in social justice and was an active participant in the Civil Rights Movement of the early 1960s, Detta had little faith in the justice meted out by white society and figured she'd be better off creating her own. This usually resulted in aggressive acts against those who angered her, or who she felt had treated her unfairly.

Although Roland succeeded in uniting Detta and Odetta at the end of *The Drawing of the Three,* creating the much more stable personality of SUSANNAH DEAN, Detta continues to make appearances throughout the last three books of the Dark Tower series. In fact, when it comes to facing the demon-spirit MIA, Detta proves to be as great an ally to Susannah and her ka-tet as she once was an enemy to Roland and EDDIE during their long travels along LOBSTROSITY beach. *For Detta's page references, see DEAN, SUSANNAH, listed above*

SUSANNAH'S PRESENT ASSOCIATES:

BELLMAN: VI:94

BUSKER: Susannah-Mio sees and hears this busker on her way to the DIXIE PIG. He is playing "Man of Constant Sorrow," a song which inundates Susannah's mind with memories of her days as ODETTA HOLMES, a Civil Rights activist. The busker's music, combined with Susannah's memories, touches MIA's heart and fortifies what good exists inside her. VI:334, VI:338–39, VI:340, VI:347–57

CABBIE (GIVES SUSANNAH/MIA A LIFT TO THE DIXIE PIG): *See* TAXI DRIVERS: TAXI DRIVER NUMBER THREE

CHAP: *See* MORDRED, *listed separately*

DAMASCUS, TRUDY: *See* GUTTENBERG, FURTH, AND PATEL: DAMASCUS, TRUDY

EXOTIC HOTEL RECEPTIONIST: *See* PLAZA-PARK HYATT CHARACTERS: RECEPTIONISTS

GIRL SCOUTS: Like MATHIESSEN VAN WYCK, these two Girl Scouts are mesmerized by SUSANNAH/MIA's SCRIMSHAW TURTLE. Susannah makes them move on, since they are not as useful to her as Mats. VI:87

JAPANESE TOURISTS AT THE PLAZA: *See* PLAZA-PARK HYATT CHARACTERS: JAPANESE TOURISTS

MIA: *See* MIA, *listed separately*

RAT, MR.: *See* MIA, *listed separately*

VAN WYCK, MATHIESSEN (MATS): Mats is the second assistant to the Swedish ambassador. He is also the first person SUSANNAH DEAN mesmerizes with her SCRIMSHAW TURTLE. Mats pays for SUSAN-

NAH-MIO's room at the PLAZA-PARK HYATT hotel. He also gives her all of his cash. In return, Susannah uses hypnotic suggestion to assure his regular bowel movements (one of Mats's problems) and to make him cease worrying about his wife's affair. VI:83–89, VI:93, VI:94 *(indirect)*, VI:256, VI:349, VII:143

> SWEDISH AMBASSADOR: VI:85, VI:88
> WIFE (UNNAMED): She is having an affair, and this causes Mats tremendous grief. VI:85, VI:88
>> HER LOVER: VI:85, VI:88
> WOMAN WITH STROLLER: VI:75

DETTA WALKER'S ASSOCIATES:
> HORNY BOYS IN ROADSIDE PARKING LOTS: VI:237

ODETTA HOLMES'S ASSOCIATES:
> BEASLEY, JESSICA: Jessica Beasley was Odetta's mother's friend. She suffered the indignity of two false pregnancies. V:121
> BLUE LADY: *See* SISTER BLUE, *listed below*
> CARVER, MOSES (POP MOSE): *See* TET CORPORATION: FOUNDING FATHERS
> FEENY, ANDREW: Odetta's chauffeur. VI:219, VII:555
> FREEMAN, NATHAN: Nathan Freeman took sixteen-year-old Odetta Holmes to the Spring Hop. VI:101
> GIRL AT COLUMBIA UNIVERSITY (STORYTELLER): At a college hen party, this girl told a story about a young woman on a long car trip who was too embarrassed to tell her friends that she needed to stop and pee. Her bladder burst and she died. VI:62
>> GIRL WHOSE BLADDER BURST: VI:62
> GRANDMOTHERS (MATERNAL AND PATERNAL): VII:643
> HOLMES, ALICE (MOTHER): *See* HOLMES, ALICE, *listed separately*
> HOLMES, DAN (FATHER): *See* HOLMES, DAN, *listed separately*
> HOLMES DENTAL: *See* HOLMES DENTAL INDUSTRIES, *listed separately*
> MURRAY, PROFESSOR: Professor Murray taught medieval history at COLUMBIA UNIVERSITY. In this class Susannah learned the story of KING ARTHUR and his betraying son/nephew, MORDRED. VI:107
> OVERMEYER, PROFESSOR: Professor Overmeyer taught Psych 1 at COLUMBIA UNIVERSITY. Odetta took his class as an undergraduate. VI:68
> PIMSY: Odetta's beloved childhood pet. VII:123–24, VII:519
> SISTER BLUE (BLUE LADY): Sister Blue (often called Blue Lady) was ODETTA HOLMES's maternal aunt. After attending Aunt Blue's wedding, Odetta was hit on the head by JACK MORT's brick, cracking her skull and giving birth to her second personality, that of nasty DETTA WALKER. As a result, Detta seemed to develop a particular abhorrence for this aunt and for the beautiful white-and-blue plates that her mother gave to Sister Blue as a wedding gift.

The Blue Lady's white-and-blue china *forspecial* plates play an important part in *Wolves of the Calla*. First, they are identical to the plates from which MIA eats in her magical BANQUETING HALL. Second, they bear an uncanny resemblance to the plates thrown by the SISTERS OF ORIZA. However, unlike Sister Blue's *forspecial* plates, the deadly weapons thrown by the Sisters are made of titanium and are honed to a murderous sharpness. While in the Calla we also find out that the delicate blue webbing found on the plates actually resembles the young rice plants called ORIZAs, after the goddess of the rice. V:76 *(Blue Lady)*, V:84 *(Blue Lady)*, VI:375

VAN RONK, DAVE: Dave Van Ronk was a white blues-shouter. ODETTA saw him perform in GREENWICH VILLAGE in the early 1960s. He must have been pretty good, since Susannah remembered some of his songs. V:168

ODETTA HOLMES AND THE CIVIL RIGHTS MOVEMENT:

FREEDOM RIDERS: In 1961, seven black and six white members of the Congress of Racial Equality (CORE) left Washington, D.C., on two public buses bound for the Deep South. They wanted to test the Supreme Court ruling which stated that segregation on interstate buses and rail stations was unconstitutional. Although they suffered terrible treatment at the hands of racists (one of their buses was burned and many of the Freedom Riders were brutalized), the protests continued. In fact, by the end of the summer, protests had spread to airports and train stations throughout the South. In November, the Interstate Commerce Commission issued rules prohibiting segregated transportation facilities. The Freedom Riders' aim—to desegregate public transportation in the South—had succeeded. VI:256

ODETTA'S "MOVEMENT" ASSOCIATES: In 1964, the Congress of Racial Equality (CORE) led a massive voter registration and desegregation campaign in MISSISSIPPI. They called it the Freedom Summer. Odetta Holmes took part in the voter registration movement. VI:351, VI:353, VI:355

  ANDERSON, DELBERT: Delbert Anderson was a guitar player involved in the voter registration movement. VI:352, VI:353
  BAIL BONDSMAN: VI:220, VI:221
  BAMBRY, JOHN: He was the pastor of the FIRST AFRO-AMERICAN METHODIST CHURCH in OXFORD, MISSISSIPPI. VI:352
  BAMBRY, LESTER: Lester Bambry was the brother of JOHN BAMBRY. He owned the BLUE MOON HOTEL, where Odetta and her friends stayed while registering black voters in MISSISSIPPI. VI:352
  DARRYL: Darryl was a white boy who became Odetta's lover during her time in the voter registration movement. VI:354–55
  OXFORD TOWN COPS: VI:220
VOTER REGISTRATION BOYS: These three young men (historical fig-

ures, every one) were killed while registering black voters in MISSISSIPPI in 1964. Their deaths mark one of the true low points of American history.

CHANEY, JAMES: James Chaney was born in May of 1943 and was a native of Meridian, MISSISSIPPI. In 1963 he joined CORE (Congress of Racial Equality) and was an active participant in the voter registration movement. On June 21, 1964, Chaney and two white activists—ANDREW GOODMAN and MICHAEL SCHWERNER— were attacked and killed by the Ku Klux Klan. VI:351, VI:352, VI:354, VI:355, VI:356, VI:357

GOODMAN, ANDREW: Andrew Goodman, from MANHATTAN, was twenty when he died on the Rock Cut Road. He had been in MISSISSIPPI for only one full day. VI:351, VI:352, VI:354, VI:355, VI:356, VI:357

SCHWERNER, MICHAEL: The rednecks of OXFORD, MISSISSIPPI, called Schwerner the "Jewboy." To the Klan members of NESHOBA COUNTY, he was known as "goatee." Schwerner was the most hated Civil Rights worker in Mississippi. His "elimination" was ordered by the Klan's imperial wizard. ANDREW GOODMAN and JAMES CHANEY died with him. VI:351, VI:352, VI:354, VI:355, VI:356, VI:357, VI:361

DEAN, WENDELL (EDDIE DEAN'S FATHER)
EDDIE DEAN's mom claimed that Eddie's father's name was Wendell. Since Eddie couldn't remember the guy, he had to take his mother's word for it.

V:215, VI:188 *(saying)*

DEARBORN, WILL
See DESCHAIN, ROLAND

DEATHFLY
This is the fly that the young JAKE CHAMBERS is certain will buzz around his corpse.

VII:95, VII:96

DECURRY, JAMIE
Jamie DeCurry was one of Roland Deschain's childhood friends. (See *Stephen King's The Dark Tower: A Concordance, Volume I.*) His favorite weapons were the bow and arrow as well as the bah (or crossbow) and bolt. In *Song of Susannah,* we learn that Jamie was one of the gunslingers who survived the fall of GILEAD. Just after this horrific defeat of the WHITE, he, Roland, CUTHBERT, and ALAIN experienced a BEAMQUAKE. Jamie died at the battle of JERICHO HILL, where he was killed by a sniper. Roland thinks that his friend was murdered by either GRISSOM or his eagle-eyed son.

V:78, V:169, V:170, V:182, V:248, VI:16, VII:497, VII:503, VII:552, VII:801

DEEPNEAU, AARON
See TET CORPORATION: FOUNDING FATHERS

DEEPNEAU, ED
Ed Deepneau was one of the major players in STEPHEN KING's novel *Insomnia*. Ed tried to crash an airplane into the DERRY Civic Center so that he could disrupt the pro-choice rally which was being held there. Ed thought his central target was the feminist Susan Day. However, Ed was just a pawn of the CRIMSON KING, whose actual goal was to assassinate four-year-old PATRICK DANVILLE. Luckily for Roland, the Crimson King failed. On the level of the DARK TOWER where the TET CORPORATION is formed, Ed Deepneau was a gentle bookkeeper who died in 1947. He was related to both AARON DEEPNEAU and NANCY DEEPNEAU.
   VII:512–13, VII:514

DEEPNEAU, NANCY REBECCA
See TET CORPORATION

DELGADO, CORDELIA
Cordelia Delgado was SUSAN DELGADO's skinny maiden aunt. She figured prominently in Roland's MEJIS adventures, described in *Wizard and Glass*. (See *Stephen King's The Dark Tower: A Concordance, Volume I*.) Cordelia wanted to sell her niece's maidenhead to Mayor Hart Thorin, but Susan chose to give it to young Roland instead. Once Susan defied her, Cordelia went mad and joined forces with the witch RHEA OF THE CÖOS. After Susan was burned on a Charyou Tree fire, Cordelia died of a stroke. (For HART THORIN entry, see *Stephen King's The Dark Tower: A Concordance, Volume I*.)
   VII:335

DELGADO, LUPE
   See CALLAHAN, FATHER DONALD FRANK: CALLAHAN'S HOME SHELTER ASSOCIATES

DELGADO, SUSAN
Susan Delgado was Roland's first (and only) true love. In the town of HAMBRY, in the BARONY OF MEJIS, Susan helped Roland and his friends CUTHBERT ALLGOOD and ALAIN JOHNS defeat the BIG COFFIN HUNTERS. (See *Stephen King's The Dark Tower: A Concordance, Volume I*.) Although Susan first met Roland and his friends under their Mejis aliases of WILL DEARBORN, ARTHUR HEATH, and RICHARD STOCKWORTH, the three young men soon took Susan into their confidence and disclosed their true identities as one gunslinger and two gunslinger apprentices from the IN-WORLD BARONY OF NEW CANAAN.
   Betrayed by her aunt, CORDELIA DELGADO, and accused of aiding and abetting traitorous murderers (all a lie), Susan was burned on a Charyou Tree

fire. Confused by the *glammer* of MAERLYN'S GRAPEFRUIT, Roland left her to her fate, though once he witnessed her terrible death in the Pink One of the WIZARD'S RAINBOW, he cursed himself for his decisions.

In *Wolves of the Calla,* we learn that PERE CALLAHAN's beloved friend and coworker at the HOME shelter was named LUPE DELGADO, an unmistakable echo of Susan's name. Like Susan, Lupe was beautiful, and like her he suffered a tragic fate. In *The Dark Tower,* the final book of our series, we reacquaint ourselves with SHEEMIE, the mildly retarded tavern boy from Mejis, who also helped Roland and his friends defeat the Big Coffin Hunters. We find out that Sheemie (now a BREAKER in THUNDERCLAP) was also in love with Susan, and that he blames himself for her death.

V:35, V:46, V:174, V:181, V:210, V:211, V:411 *(bit o' tail),* VI:234 *(indirect),* VI:269, VI:277, VI:290, VI:294, VI:391, VI:404, VII:142, VII:219, VII:220, VII:468, VII:498, VII:695, VII:762, VII:802, VII:825

DELICIOUS RAIN
See NORTH CENTRAL POSITRONICS

DEMON ELEMENTALS (DEMON ASPECTS OF THE BEAM)
According to the metaphysical map of MID-WORLD, which Roland drew in *The Waste Lands,* Mid-World is shaped like a wheel. The hub of the wheel is the DARK TOWER. Crossing at this nexus point are six BEAMS, which simultaneously hold the Tower in place and maintain the proper alignment of time, space, size, and dimension. The Beams both bind the macroverse together and separate the many worlds which spin about the great, smoky-colored linchpin of existence. The twelve termination points of the Beams are watched over by twelve animal totems known as GUARDIANS.

In *Song of Susannah,* we find out that—like the kabbalistic Tree of Life found in our world—Mid-World's metaphysical map has a darker side. Just as each Beam has two designated Guardians, each Beam is also overseen by a Demon Elemental. Although there are only six Demon Elementals, there are twelve demon *aspects,* since each demon has a male and a female self. The Guardians of the Beam watch over the mortal world, but the hermaphroditic Demon Elementals watch over the invisible world of speaking demons, ghosts, and ill-sicks—all those LESSER DEMONS OF THE PRIM, which remained in Mid-World after the magical tide of the PRIM (or GREATER DISCORDIA) withdrew from the land.

If some of the Guardians serve the WHITE, then at least some of the Demon Elementals serve the Outer Dark. In *Song of Susannah,* we find out that one such Demon Elemental tricked both Roland and SUSANNAH into helping the CRIMSON KING bring MORDRED RED-HEEL (the *dan-tete,* or little god) into being.

Posing as the ORACLE OF THE MOUNTAINS that we met in *The Gunslinger,* the demon's female aspect had sex with Roland in exchange for prophecy. Once collected, Roland's sperm was stored (probably in one of the

GREAT OLD ONES' machines) until he and his tet-mates EDDIE and Susannah Dean arrived at the SPEAKING RING near LUD, where JAKE CHAMBERS was about to be reborn into Mid-World.

As Roland and Eddie brought Jake through the magical door labeled THE BOY, Susannah kept the sex-hungry, male SPEAKING-RING DEMON busy. Though our tet didn't know it, this was no ordinary speaking-ring demon but the male aspect of the Demon Elemental who had copulated with Roland earlier in our tale.

Roland's sperm must have been defrosted beforehand, because this demon—though sterile itself—shot our gunslinger's fertile seed into Susannah, seed which was (or soon would be) mixed with that of the Crimson King.

VI:112–14, VI:117, VI:242, VI:252 *(service for the King)*

ORACLE OF THE MOUNTAINS (SUCCUBUS): This demon was actually the female aspect of a DEMON ELEMENTAL posing as a speaking-ring demon. In *The Gunslinger*, she has sexual intercourse with Roland. V:46, VI:112–13, VI:121–22, VI:241 *(indirect)*

SPEAKING-RING DEMON (JAKE'S ENTRY INTO MID-WORLD): Like the ORACLE OF THE MOUNTAINS (*listed above*), this demon wasn't a run-of-the-mill Druit Circle sexpot, but the male aspect of a DEMON ELEMENTAL. V:84, V:246, V:258, V:378, V:478, V:483, VI:106, VI:107, VI:113, VI:116

DEMONS/SPIRITS/DEVILS (LESSER DEMONS OF THE PRIM)

In the beginning there was only the PRIM, the magical soup of creation. From the Prim arose GAN, the spirit of the DARK TOWER, who spun the physical universe from his navel. When the magical tide of the Prim receded from the earth, it left behind it the Tower and the BEAMS, as well as a flotsam and jetsam of demons, elemental spirits, oracles, and succubi. Some of these intangible beings (known collectively as the Lesser Demons of the Prim) strangled in this new element, but others adapted and thrived. Among the less savory of the Prim's survivors were sexual predators such as MIA and demonic beings such as the DEMON ELEMENTALS and the TYPE ONE VAMPIRES, also known as the GRANDFATHERS.

A MID-WORLD saying states, "Ghosts always haunt the same house." This seems to be true of all Mid-World spirits. Like SPEAKING-RING DEMONS, who must remain in the confines of their Druit Stones, spirits are usually found in places where reality is "thin," and where the invisible world is already leaking through. (For more information, see *Stephen King's The Dark Tower: A Concordance, Volume I.*)

GENERAL REFERENCES:

V:2 *(bogarts, speakies)*, V:150 *(bogarts)*, V:247 *(devil)*, V:341 *(ogres)*, V:350 *(devil)*, V:394 *(demon)*, V:577, VI:36, VI:106 *(Demons of the Prim)*, VI:112 *(Speaking Demons, general)*

SPECIFIC DEMONS:

CENTIPEDE MONSTER: *See* TODASH DEMONS, *listed below*

CHAP (MIA'S CHAP): *See* MORDRED, *listed separately*

DANDELO: *See* DANDELO, *listed separately*

DEMON CHILD: *See* MORDRED, *listed separately*

DEMONS OF HOUSE: VI:112, VI:117

DEMONSTUFF, JAR OF: The people of FEDIC believed that the Red Death, the plague which wiped out their town, came from a jar of demonstuff that had been opened in CASTLE DISCORDIA. VI:244

DEVIL: VI:247, VI:259, VI:318 *(Satan),* VI:319 *(Satan),* VII:582 *(tempting),* VII:590 *(tempting)*

DEVIL GRASS: In CALLA BRYN STURGIS, removing devil grass from the fields is New Earth's first chore. This weed—which is the first growth to appear on ruined ground and the last to disappear once land is poisoned—is also narcotic. However, as we saw in *The Gunslinger,* smoking weed leads to chewing weed, and chewing leads to death. When no other fuel is available, devil grass can be burned. However, some people maintain that beckoning devils dance in the flames. (See *Stephen King's The Dark Tower: A Concordance, Volume I.*) V:3, V:403, VII:580, VII:588, VII:612, VII:829

DEVIL'S ARSE DEMONS/MONSTERS OF THE ABYSS: These telepathic demons are neither for the CRIMSON KING nor against him. However, it seems reasonable to assume that they are creatures of the Outer Dark. Although they were once contained in their crack in the earth located near the town of FEDIC, they are slowly tunneling toward the underground chambers below both the FEDIC DOGAN and CASTLE DISCORDIA. It seems likely that these creatures originated in TODASH and are the GREAT ONES which MORDRED says live in that terrible noplace between worlds. *See* TODASH DEMONS, *listed below.* VI:105, VII:539–40, VII:557, VII:567

DISCORDIA: *See* PRIM, *listed separately*

DUST-DEVILS: VI:642

GREAT ONES: *See* TODASH DEMONS, *listed below*

HOUSIES: Housies are a particularly nasty type of house-ghost. They can't hurt people but they can hurt small animals. You can often hear them whispering in the dark. VII:590

ILL-SICK DEMONS: Demons of disease. VI:112, VI:117

MANSION DEMON/DOORKEEPER (DUTCH HILL): This is the demon which JAKE CHAMBERS had to battle in the Haunted Mansion of DUTCH HILL, a story found in *The Waste Lands.* Like Druit Circle spirits, the Mansion Demon is a doorway demon and guards one of the lesser portals (or thin places) which lead out of our world and into MID-WORLD. With Roland's and EDDIE DEAN's help, Jake managed to elude this monster's clutches and join his tet along the PATH OF THE BEAM. For more information, see *Stephen King's The Dark Tower: A Concordance, Volume I.* V:50, V:68, V:93, V:258, V:478, VII:144–45, VII:249, VII:592

MIA: *See* MIA, *listed separately*

MIND-SPIRITS: These spirits knock at your mind's door, seeking entrance. If you refuse to answer, they may try to gnaw their way through. (Rather unpleasant, when you think about it.) VII:593

MORDRED: *See* MORDRED, *listed separately*

ORACLE OF THE MOUNTAINS (SUCCUBUS): *See* DEMON ELEMENTALS, *listed separately*

PRIM: *See* PRIM, *listed separately*

SAITA: *See* ELD, ARTHUR, *listed separately*

SATAN: *See* DEVIL, *listed above*

SPEAKING DEMONS (GENERAL): VI:112

SPEAKING-RING DEMON (JAKE'S ENTRY INTO MID-WORLD): *See* DEMON ELEMENTALS, *listed separately*

THINNY: *See entry in* PORTALS

TODASH DEMONS: According to MORDRED, the nastiest demons inhabiting TODASH space are known as the GREAT ONES. I imagine that todash is filled with many unpleasant "lesser ones" as well. We see some glimmers of these terrible Great Ones (and many of the lesser ones) in STEPHEN KING's story "The Mist," which can be found in *Skeleton Crew.* VI:18, VI:248–49, VII:539, VII:557, VII:559, VII:567, VII:754

> **CHEWING MONSTER:** Roland and SUSANNAH hear this monster behind an ancient ironwood door located beneath the FEDIC DOGAN. VII:560–61
>
> **THUDDING MONSTER:** The thudding monster (we never see it) is trapped behind one of the many doors found beneath CASTLE DISCORDIA and the FEDIC DOGAN. It hasn't been able to escape. (Yet.) VII:562
>
> **TUNNEL DEMON (CENTIPEDE MONSTER):** This stinking, slithering demon tries to attack Roland and SUSANNAH DEAN as they travel through the dark tunnels beneath the FEDIC DOGAN and CASTLE DISCORDIA. Although it may have originated in the DEVIL'S ARSE, that terrible crack in the earth located beyond the nearby town of FEDIC, Roland thinks that their pursuer is more likely a monster that has broken through from TODASH space. The tunnel demon/tunnel monster is one of the ugliest creatures we've met in the Dark Tower series (SLOW MUTANTS aside, of course). It resembles a giant fanged centipede, but one whose round lump of a face is covered with pink albino eyes and whose gaping, trapdoor-sized mouth is filled with squirming tentacles. Luckily for our friends, this particular demon is photosensitive. VII:564, VII:566, VII:567–76, VII:579, VII:658 *(indirect)*

ZOMBIE FACES: SUSANNAH sees these dead faces staring at her from behind the strangely distorted windows and buildings of CASTLE-

TOWN, the ruined habitations located near LE CASSE ROI RUSSE. VII:592

DEMULLET (DEMULLET'S COLUMN)
DeMullet's Column was an army fighting on the side of the AFFILIATION. FARSON'S MEN defeated them at the fateful battle of JERICHO HILL.
V:170

DEPAPE, AMOS
See BIG COFFIN HUNTERS: DEPAPE, ROY

DEPAPE, ROY
See BIG COFFIN HUNTERS

DESCHAIN, ALARIC
Alaric Deschain was Roland's grandfather. He was known as "him of the red hair." Alaric went to GARLAN to slay a dragon, but that dragon had already been slain by another king, one who was later murdered. Since Alaric Deschain was known by the TOREN family of our world, it seems likely that he—like Roland—traveled between different levels of the DARK TOWER. If this is true, it seems even likelier that the dragon he wished to slay was none other than the dragon slain by King Roland of DELAIN, one of the main characters found in *The Eyes of the Dragon*. *(For further reflections on the similarities between Mid-World and the world of* The Eyes of the Dragon, *see* APPENDIX IV.)
VI:197

DESCHAIN, GABRIELLE
Gabrielle Deschain, daughter of CANDOR THE TALL, was Roland's mother. In *The Gunslinger* we found out that she had an affair with her husband's betraying enchanter MARTEN BROADCLOAK, and in *Wizard and Glass* that she attempted to kill STEVEN DESCHAIN for her lover. Although Roland prevented this disaster, he himself (tricked by a *glammer* thrown by RHEA OF THE CÖOS) committed matricide. (See *Stephen King's The Dark Tower: A Concordance, Volume I.*)

When Roland was a little boy sleeping in his nursery below the window of many colors (the spectrum of which represented the WIZARD'S RAINBOW), Gabrielle would sing the Baby-Bunting Rhyme to him. This little song becomes important at the end of the Dark Tower series, since the song's High Speech word *chassit* (NINETEEN) is the verbal code which opens the DOORWAY BETWEEN WORLDS linking the DIXIE PIG to the FEDIC DOGAN.

V:36 *(Roland's mother),* V:77 *(Roland's mother),* V:188, V:193 *(indirect),* V:410, V:415, V:605, V:659 *(mother),* VII:22–23, VII:179, VII:529, VII:801, VII:820, VII:821, VII:822, VII:823, VII:829
CANDOR THE TALL: Gabrielle Deschain's father. VII:529
ROLAND'S CRADLE AMAH: Roland's childhood nurse. V:188

DESCHAIN, MORDRED
See MORDRED

DESCHAIN, ROLAND (THE GUNSLINGER, THE REALLY BAD MAN, OLD WHITE DADDY, WILL-DEARBORN-THAT-WAS, GABBY)

Roland Deschain began life in our world as a version of Sergio Leone's Man with No Name, a wandering Clint Eastwood–type character traveling across a desert wasteland littered with the weapons, poisons, and machinery of an extinct civilization. However, as so often happens with characters, he soon morphed beneath the pen of his creator, STEPHEN KING, shook off the paper pulp, and stepped into the room, a full-fledged being in his own right.

The Roland we have come to know so well over the Dark Tower series is MID-WORLD's last hereditary gunslinger and the final human descendant of ARTHUR ELD, the ancient king of ALL-WORLD. Born in the IN-WORLD BARONY OF NEW CANAAN before the world moved on, Roland witnessed the toppling of his civilization and the drowning of his family and friends in the wave of anarchy that followed. Although he still carries the sandalwood-handled guns of his forefathers—guns whose barrels were forged from EXCALIBUR, the blade of Arthur Eld—Roland is a king without a kingdom. However, as a Warrior of the WHITE, he still has a quest—he will travel to the DARK TOWER, that linchpin of the time/space continuum, and climb to the room at the top, where he will question the God or Force that resides there.

Although he does not realize it, Roland, Warrior of the White, is a version of the eternal hero. Like his enemies who serve the Outer Dark, Roland *darkles* and *tincts*. He will relive his quest over and over, saving both Tower and BEAMS again and again, until he comes to understand that success must not be won at the cost of either the heart or the soul. Only when he remains true to his actual destiny (symbolized by the HORN OF ELD, which he must blow at the edge of CAN'-KA NO REY) will the Tower grant him the peace he so desires.

Since Roland is the main character of the Dark Tower series, his presence is implied in all other entries. For specific information about Roland's various adventures, look up the other characters or places involved. For example, if you want to read about Roland's interactions with DANDELO and PATRICK DANVILLE, look up both of those characters in the CHARACTERS section of the *Concordance*. If you wish to learn more about the battle of JERICHO HILL, look up JERICHO HILL in the MID-WORLD PLACES section.

RING-A-LEVIO (RINGO): Ringo was Roland's pet dog. He died when Roland was three. VII:824

DESCHAIN, STEVEN

Tall, thin Steven Deschain, father of Roland, was descended from one of ARTHUR ELD's forty jillies. During Roland's childhood, Steven took control of his tet—the Tet of the Gun—and was on the verge of becoming *dinh* of GILEAD, if not all of IN-WORLD. However, the last Lord of Light was betrayed by his sorcerer and counselor, MARTEN BROADCLOAK (also known as WALTER), and his own unfaithful wife, GABRIELLE DESCHAIN. Steven Deschain was murdered, the AFFILIATION fell, and the last of the gunslingers were slaughtered at JERICHO HILL. (See *Stephen King's The Dark Tower: A Concordance, Volume I.*)

Although Steven Deschain died while still relatively young, experience had transformed his face into one that was both hard and cruel. However, in the vision Roland has of him in one of the DARK TOWER's many rooms, his father's visage is still soft, and his eyes reflect his love for his only son.

V:85 *(Roland's father)*, V:105 *(knew of glass balls)*, V:193 *(indirect)*, V:215, V:242 *(father)*, V:392, V:400, V:410, V:415, V:481, V:482, V:541, V:579 *(father)*, V:590, V:597 *(father)*, VI:106, VI:162, VI:197, VI:295, VII:23 *(indirect)*, VII:50, VII:111, VII:134, VII:178, VII:442, VII:473, VII:499, VII:529, VII:769, VII:801, VII:822, VII:823–24, VII:827

DETTA
See DEAN, SUSANNAH

DEVAR-TOI CHARACTERS
See WARRIORS OF THE SCARLET EYE

DIANA'S DREAM
See MID-WORLD FOLKLORE

DICK, GRAY
See ORIZA, LADY

DILLON, MARSHALL
See DESCHAIN, ROLAND

DISCORDIA
See PRIM; *see also* DISCORDIA, *in* PORTALS

DISCORDIA, LORD OF
See CRIMSON KING

DIXIE PIG CHARACTERS
See WARRIORS OF THE SCARLET EYE: DIXIE PIG CHARACTERS/ FEDIC CHARACTERS

DOBBIE
See NORTH CENTRAL POSITRONICS

DOCTOR BUGS
See ELURIA CHARACTERS

DOG GUARDIAN
See GUARDIANS OF THE BEAM

DOOLIN, EAMON
See CALLA BRYN STURGIS CHARACTERS: WOLF POSSE

DOOLIN, MINNIE
See CALLA BRYN STURGIS CHARACTERS: ROONTS

DOOLIN, MOLLY
See ORIZA, SISTERS OF

DOOM, DR.
See WOLVES

DOROTHY
See WIZARD OF OZ

DRABNIK, CSABA
See DEAN, HENRY: HENRY DEAN'S KA-TET

DRETTO, 'CIMI
See BALAZAR, ENRICO: BALAZAR'S MEN

DUGAN, BISHOP
See CALLAHAN, FATHER DONALD FRANK: CALLAHAN'S OTHER PAST ASSOCIATES

E

EAGLE GUARDIAN
See GUARDIANS OF THE BEAM

EARNSHAW, DINKY
See BREAKERS

EAST DOWNE, WALKING WATERS OF
See MID-WORLD FOLKLORE

EAST STONEHAM CHARACTERS
See MAINE CHARACTERS

ECHEVERRIA
See CALLA BRYN STURGIS CHARACTERS: OTHER CHARACTERS

EDDIE
See DEAN, EDDIE

EISENHART, MARGARET
See ORIZA, SISTERS OF

EISENHART, TOM AND TESSA
See CALLA BRYN STURGIS CHARACTERS: RANCHERS: EISENHART, VAUGHN

EISENHART, VAUGHN
See CALLA BRYN STURGIS CHARACTERS: RANCHERS

EISENHART, VERNA
See CALLA BRYN STURGIS CHARACTERS: ROONTS

ELD, ARTHUR (THE ELD, LINE OF ELD, HORN OF ELD)
Arthur Eld—MID-WORLD's greatest mythical hero and the ancient king of ALL-WORLD—was a Warrior of the WHITE. Like the line of DESCHAIN, descended from one of his forty jillies, he was the Guardian of the DARK TOWER. (See *Stephen King's The Dark Tower: A Concordance, Volume I.*)

In story and tapestry, Arthur is often depicted as riding his white stallion, LLAMREI, and brandishing his great sword, EXCALIBUR. After his death and the dissolution of his kingdom, Arthur Eld's horse remained the sigul of IN-WORLD, and its image decorated the pennons of GILEAD. Although in *Wizard and Glass* we were told that Arthur Eld's unifying sword was entombed in a pyramid after the Eld's death, in the final book of the Dark Tower series we discover that it must have been the hilt that was entombed, since Roland's gun barrels were forged from the metal of that blade. As well as his guns, the young Roland carried another heirloom from the times of Eld—his ancestor's horn. Unluckily for him, Roland let his friend CUTHBERT ALLGOOD blow the Horn of Eld at the battle of JERICHO HILL, and Roland left it on the battlefield where it had tumbled from Cuthbert's dead hand, an oversight which he later comes to regret.

All descendants of Arthur Eld, as well as their gunslinger-knights, are sworn to uphold the Way of the Eld (also known as the Way of Eld) at all costs. The Way of Eld designates the proper conduct of gunslingers. It refers to their rigorous physical and mental training as well as to their sense of honor and duty. According to the Way of Eld, gunslingers must help those in distress if it is within their power to do so. According to FATHER CALLAHAN's books, they were forbidden to take reward.

Sometime during his long and eventful life, Arthur Eld must have had sexual relations with a demon of some sort, since the CRIMSON KING is also his descendant. This is not so surprising, since Mid-World is full of SPEAKING RINGS, LESSER DEMONS OF THE PRIM, and wily DEMON ELEMENTALS, all of whom are able to cast powerful *glammer*. In the final three books of the Dark Tower series, we see the two bloodlines of the Eld—of GAN and Gilead, and of the PRIM and the AM—reunited in the body of MORDRED DESCHAIN, son of two fathers and two mothers.

Although the human line of Eld serves the White, the demonic line of Eld serves the Outer Dark. Both bloodlines are obsessed with the Tower, which is their birthright, yet while the line of Deschain is sworn to preserve it, the Red King and his son—the *dan-tete*, or little king—have pledged to destroy it.

It seems likely that the Eld's two bloodlines—destined to battle each other—have each developed their own distinct mythologies about their ancestor. While in her dream-version of CASTLE DISCORDIA's BANQUETING HALL, SUSANNAH-MIO sees a screen, which depicts a heroic Arthur Eld charging through a swamp with three of his knight-gunslingers behind him, the corpse of the dangerous snake SAITA around his neck. Yet in the DIXIE PIG, a blasphemous tapestry depicts Arthur Eld and his court feasting on human flesh.

Not only do Arthur Eld's two bloodlines present two different views of the Eld, but the people of Mid-World also seem to have two versions of their greatest hero. The mythical Eld was the first king to arise after the Prim receded, hence he predated the time of the GREAT OLD ONES. The historical Arthur Eld lived approximately seven hundred years—or thirty generations—before Roland's birth. Perhaps Mid-World's King Arthur was, like the ARTHUR of our world, both the once and future king. Although born in an ancient world, he never died but only lay sleeping. After the Great Old Ones' terrible disasters, his people needed him and so he returned.

V:30–31, V:73, V:110 *(line of Eld)*, V:128 *(line of)*, V:153, V:156 *(way of Eld)*, V:162 *(Eld's way)*, V:170 *(horn)*, V:171, V:172 *(horn)*, V:181 *(way of Eld)*, V:203, V:215 *(line of)*, V:216, V:236, V:238, V:240 *(horn)*, V:284 *(horn only)*, V:321, V:324, V:333, V:373, V:388, V:410, V:497, V:542, V:567, V:605, V:609, V:624, V:686, V:709, VI:15, VI:39, VI:110, VI:111 *(Arthur Eld)*, VI:135 *(Lost Beasts of)*, VI:177, VI:183, VI:197, VI:252, VI:371–73 *(tapestry)*, VII:26, VII:50, VII:51, VII:111, VII:168, VII:176, VII:199, VII:253, VII:322, VII:473, VII:499, VII:501, VII:512, VII:549, VII:608, VII:766, VII:780, VII:791, VII:799, VII:800, VII:801, VII:819 *(horn)*, VII:820, VII:821, VII:822, VII:825 *(horn)*

ELD'S LAST FELLOWSHIP: A tapestry located in the DIXIE PIG depicts Eld's Last Fellowship. However, the feast it shows is a horrible parody of Eld and his knights' final meal. Instead of eating meat and drinking wine, Eld, his wife, and his followers are shown to be eating human flesh and drinking human blood. VII:6, VII:8, VII:10, VII:26 *(named)*, VII:28

EXCALIBUR: Like the blade carried by our world's mythical KING ARTHUR, Arthur Eld's sword was called Excalibur. The barrels of Roland's sandalwood-handled guns were cast from the metal of this blade. VII:608

HORN OF ELD: The horn which has been passed from father to son from the time of Arthur Eld to the time of Roland Deschain. Unfortunately, Roland left the Horn of Eld (also called the Horn of Deschain) next to CUTHBERT ALLGOOD's dead body on the battlefield of JERICHO HILL. *(For page references, see main entry.)*

LLAMREI: Arthur Eld's white horse. Llamrei's image was the sigul of all IN-WORLD and decorated the pennons of GILEAD. In the office of RICHARD P. SAYRE, located in the FEDIC DOGAN, Roland and SUSANNAH come across a painting of a young boy (probably MORDRED) standing triumphantly over the dead body of Llamrei, his foot on the horse's corpse. VII:549, VII:550, VII:780

LOST BEASTS OF ELD: The Lost Beasts of Eld were flying creatures. They may have resembled dragons. VI:135

ROWENA, QUEEN: Arthur Eld's lady-wife. In the blasphemous tapestry found in the DIXIE PIG, Queen Rowena is depicted drinking a goblet of blood. VI:371–73

SAITA: While MIA, daughter of none, searches for food in the deserted BANQUETING HALL located in her dream-version of CASTLE DIS-CORDIA, she sees a screen depicting Arthur Eld riding through a swamp with three of his knight-gunslingers behind him. Around his neck is Saita, the great snake, which he has just slain. V:373

SWORD OF ELD: *See* EXCALIBUR, *listed above*

ELURIA CHARACTERS

After the battle of JERICHO HILL, but before he found the trail of the MAN IN BLACK, Roland traveled through the deserted town of ELURIA. (See *Stephen King's The Dark Tower: A Concordance, Volume I.*) While searching for living inhabitants, Roland was captured by the MUTANT GREEN FOLK, who in turn handed him over to the LITTLE SISTERS OF ELURIA, a tribe of VAMPIRES who posed as a holy order of hospital nuns. Although most of the Little Sisters were hags who used potent *glammer* to appear young, one of their sisterhood was in actuality both youthful and beautiful. Dark-haired SISTER JENNA, an unwilling vampire, helped Roland to escape her kinswomen's clutches. When Jenna died, her body turned into CAM TAM, or DOCTOR BUGS. (For Green Folk and Sister Jenna, see *Stephen King's The Dark Tower: A Concordance, Volume I.*)

DOCTOR BUGS: The Doctor Bugs (called CAM TAM within "The Little Sisters of Eluria") were healing insects about the size of fat honeybees. Unlike the carrion-eating GRANDFATHER FLEAS, which follow TYPE ONE VAMPIRES, the Doctor Bugs were actually beneficial. VI:234

LITTLE SISTERS OF ELURIA: A tribe of female VAMPIRES that posed as a holy order of hospital nuns. Roland was their prisoner in the short story "The Little Sisters of Eluria." The Little Sisters dressed in billowing white habits and white wimples. Upon the breasts of their habits was embroidered a red ROSE. Beneath their *glammer*, the Little Sisters were about as attractive as RHEA OF THE CÖOS. However, unlike Rhea, the Little Sisters were not human but half-mortal and half-wraith. When they died, their bodies turned into the DOCTOR BUGS that served them. (For more information, see *Stephen King's The Dark Tower: A Concordance, Volume I.*) VI:234

EMERSON, SONNY
See TASSENBAUM, DAVID

ENGINEER BOB
See CHARLIE THE CHOO-CHOO: ENGINEER BOB

ESTRADA, DEELIE
See CALLA BRYN STURGIS CHARACTERS: FARMERS (SMALL-HOLD): ESTRADA, GEORGE

ESTRADA, GEORGE
See CALLA BRYN STURGIS CHARACTERS: FARMERS (SMALLHOLD)

ETHELYN, AUNTIE
See KING, STEPHEN: KING FAMILY

EURASIAN HOTEL CLERK
See PLAZA-PARK HYATT CHARACTERS: RECEPTIONISTS: EXOTIC HOTEL RECEPTIONIST

EVANS, BERYL
See CHARLIE THE CHOO-CHOO

EXCALIBUR
See ELD, ARTHUR

EX LIBRIS, MR.
See TOWER, CALVIN

F

FANNIN, RICHARD
See WALTER: WALTER'S ALIASES: R.F.

FARADAY, GEORGE
See CALLA BRYN STURGIS CHARACTERS: ROONTS

FARADAY, GEORGINA
See CALLA BRYN STURGIS CHARACTERS: FARMERS (SMALL-HOLD): FARADAY, NEIL

FARADAY, NEIL
See CALLA BRYN STURGIS CHARACTERS: FARMERS (SMALLHOLD)

FARDEN, WALTER
See WALTER

FARSON, JOHN (THE GOOD MAN)
When Roland was a boy, the harrier and stage-robber John Farson began to gain followers in the west. Originally from either GARLAN or DESOY, the Good Man opposed the inherited wealth and power of the aristocratic gunslingers as well as what he claimed were the unfair practices of the AFFILIA-TION, which supported them. Many were attracted to the Good Man's cause, including failed gunslingers, such as the BIG COFFIN HUNTER, ELDRED JONAS. In *The Gunslinger*, we saw GILEAD's head cook, HAX, hanged for his allegiance to Farson.

Despite his quasi-religious status, the Good Man was in actuality a madman who wanted nothing more than to bring death and destruction to MID-WORLD. (See *Stephen King's The Dark Tower: A Concordance, Volume I.*) Evidently, his favorite game was polo, but only when he could play it with his enemies' heads. Unlike the gunslingers, who knew that the OLD ONES' weapons were too dangerous to use, Farson and his men resurrected the Old People's weapons and tanks and planned to use them in their final battle against the Affiliation. Luckily, many of these pieces of machinery were destroyed by Roland, CUTHBERT ALLGOOD, and ALAIN JOHNS during their HAMBRY adventures. Ultimately, however, Farson and his men triumphed. At the battle of JERICHO HILL, they killed the last of Roland's gunslinger-companions, including our beloved Cuthbert Allgood.

One passage in *The Gunslinger* hints that Farson was actually STEVEN DESCHAIN's sorcerer, MARTEN BROADCLOAK, who in turn was none other than Roland's nemesis, WALTER O'DIM. However, by the end of the Dark Tower series it seems fairly certain that Farson—though mad as the CRIMSON KING himself—was not another incarnation of the demonic R.F., but one of his many pawns.

V:171, V:612 *(The Good Man)*, VII:135, VII:172, VII:174, VII:528, VII:550

FARSON'S MEN:

GRISSOM/GRISSOM'S MEN/BLUE-FACED BARBARIANS: Grissom was the leader of FARSON'S MEN during the battle of JERICHO HILL, where the AFFILIATION was defeated. Grissom's men are described as "blue-faced barbarians." V:169 *(Grissom's men)*, V:170, V:171 *(blue-faced)*, V:410 *(blue faces)*, VII:174 *(Walter fought with the "blue-faced barbarians")*

GRISSOM'S SON: V:169–70 *(eagle-eyed)*

LATIGO, GEORGE: V:576 *(men)*

FEDIC CHARACTERS

The unfortunate residents of FEDIC were annihilated by the Red Death more than two dozen centuries before the WOLVES began invading the BORDER-LAND CALLAS. SUSANNAH DEAN's demonic possessor, MIA (who haunted Fedic before she was incarnated in a human body by WALTER and his cohorts), describes the people of Fedic as stubborn. They must have been. Their town was caught between the haunted CASTLE DISCORDIA, the evil FEDIC DOGAN, and the DEVIL'S ARSE, a crack in the earth in which monsters bred. By the time Mia haunted Fedic, most of the women there were already giving birth to monsters, thanks to the poisons left by the GREAT OLD ONES. However, the one perfect baby born into that town—named MICHAEL—sowed the seeds of Mia's great child hunger and led to her Faustian pact with the WARRIORS OF THE SCARLET EYE.

ANDY LOOK-ALIKE ROBOT: *See* NORTH CENTRAL POSITRONICS

BABY MICHAEL: *See* MIA

FATHER: *See* MIA

MOTHER: *See* MIA

DEAD ROBOT: *See* NORTH CENTRAL POSITRONICS

HUCKSTER ROBOT: *See* NORTH CENTRAL POSITRONICS

RESIDENTS OF FEDIC: VI:243, VI:244

FEEMALO

See WARRIORS OF THE SCARLET EYE: CASSE ROI RUSSE: HUMANS: FEEMALO/FIMALO/FUMALO

FEENY, ANDREW

See DEAN, SUSANNAH: ODETTA HOLMES'S ASSOCIATES

FENNS

See MAINE CHARACTERS

FERMAN, ED
   See KING, STEPHEN

FILARO, RUDIN
   See WALTER: WALTER'S ALIASES: R.F.

FIMALO
   See WARRIORS OF THE SCARLET EYE: CASSE ROI RUSSE: HUMANS: FEEMALO/FIMALO/FUMALO

FINLI
   See TAHEEN: WEASEL-HEADED TAHEEN

FISH GUARDIAN
   See GUARDIANS OF THE BEAM

FLAGG, RANDALL
   See WALTER: WALTER'S ALIASES: R.F.

FLAHERTY, CONOR
   See WARRIORS OF THE SCARLET EYE: DIXIE PIG CHARACTERS/ FEDIC CHARACTERS: HUMANS

FLIP, MR.
   See CALLAHAN, FATHER DONALD FRANK: 'SALEM'S LOT CHARACTERS

FOOT SOLDIERS OF THE CRIMSON KING
   See WARRIORS OF THE SCARLET EYE

FORCE, THE
   See MANNI: OVER, THE

FORT LEE REGISTER AMERICAN
   See CALLAHAN, FATHER DONALD FRANK: CALLAHAN'S HIDDEN HIGHWAYS ASSOCIATES

FORTY
Like NINETEEN and NINETY-NINE, forty is a magic number. In hobo-speak, it refers to the bus that will take you as far away as possible. If you live in NEW YORK CITY and buy a ticket to FAIRBANKS, ALASKA, you are taking the forty bus.
   V:428

FOUNDING FATHERS
See TET CORPORATION

FOYLE, FRANKIE
See CALLAHAN, FATHER DONALD FRANK: 'SALEM'S LOT CHARACTERS

FRANK
See PUBES; *see also* CALLAHAN, FATHER DONALD FRANK

FREDERICKS, TOMMY
See DEAN, HENRY: HENRY DEAN'S KA-TET

FREEDOM RIDERS
See DEAN, SUSANNAH: ODETTA HOLMES AND THE CIVIL RIGHTS MOVEMENT

FREEMAN, NATHAN
See DEAN, SUSANNAH: ODETTA HOLMES'S ASSOCIATES

FULCHER, ANDY
See KING, STEPHEN

FUMALO
See WARRIORS OF THE SCARLET EYE: CASSE ROI RUSSE: HUMANS: FEEMALO/FIMALO/FUMALO

FURTH
See GUTTENBERG, FURTH, AND PATEL

G

GABBY
Gabby was the sarcastic nickname which the gunslinger apprentices' tutor, VANNAY, gave to Roland. The name came from Roland's childhood habit of being silent for prolonged periods.
VII: 20–21

GAI COCKNIF EN YOM, MR.
See TET CORPORATION: FOUNDING FATHERS: DEEPNEAU, AARON

GAN (VOICE OF THE BEAM, SPIRIT OF THE DARK TOWER)

According to MID-WORLD's oldest legends, Gan arose from the magical soup of creation known as the GREATER DISCORDIA, or the PRIM.[4] From his navel, he spun the universe, and once it had spun into the shape he desired, he set it rolling with his finger. This forward movement was time. After creating the world, Gan moved on. The universe would have plunged into the void had not the great TURTLE caught it and balanced it upon his back. And it is here the universe still sits, poised upon the Turtle's shell.[5]

The great god Gan is actually the animating spirit of the DARK TOWER. Although this smoky-black edifice and its spiral of electric-blue windows may appear to be made of stone and glass, it is, in actuality, a huge living body. Just as the ancient myths of Mid-World maintain that the world spun from Gan's navel, so both the BEAMS and the red ROSES of CAN'-KA NO REY spun out from the Tower. Together, Tower, Beams, and Roses form a living, singing force field which sits at the heart of END-WORLD, and it is toward this energy field that Roland, the last of the line of ELD, is inevitably drawn.

Gan is the Mid-World god most closely linked to the voice of the WHITE. As JAKE CHAMBERS says while in a trance state, "So speaks Gan, and in the voice of angels. Gan denies the CAN-TOI; with the merry heart of the guiltless he denies the CRIMSON KING and Discordia itself." In the prayer which Roland utters over Jake Chambers's grave, Gan is called upon to raise the dead from the darkness of the earth and to surround them with light.

Although Gan is a god, and though (as the spirit of the Tower) he rules the destiny of the multiverse, he seems to have a particular interest in Roland and the line of Eld. When Roland mounts Gan's steps in the final book of the Dark Tower series, what he sees in Gan's hundreds of rooms forces him to reflect upon his life, and how (if he gets the chance) he must choose to live differently.

In our world, the voice of Gan is often transmitted through artists and writers, who are called *kas-ka Gan*, which means one of the prophets, or singers, of Gan. For our tet, the most important of the KEYSTONE EARTH *kas-ka Gan* is the writer STEPHEN KING.

VI:294, VI:295 *("Gan bore the world and the world moved on")*, VI:298, VI:318 *("So speaks Gan along the Beam")*, VI:320, VI:321, VI:353 *(Gan the maker)*, VI:380, VI:394, VII:4, VII:33 *(birthed universe from his navel)*, VII:34 *(voice of Gan, voice of the Beam)*, VII:129, VII:168, VII:291, VII:295 *(Wolf-Elephant is Gan's Beam)*, VII:296 *(Beam)*, VII:300 *(Beam)*, VII:301 *(Beam)*, VII:303 *(Beam)*, VII:305, VII:306, VII:345, VII:348, VII:368, VII:371, VII:380, VII:388, VII:406, VII:447, VII:456, VII:457–58, VII:459, VII:474, VII:504, VII:505, VII:512, VII:513, VII:542, VII:543, VII:585,

---

4. In some variations of the legend, Gan was said to rise from either the void or the sea.

5. Interestingly, in the novel *It*, the Turtle claims that he created the universe on a day he had a bellyache. Hence, all of the evils we experience are the result of trapped wind.

VII:607, VII:609, VII:638, VII:757 *(Gan's Gateway)*, VII:798, VII:820, VII:821, VII:822, VII:823, VII:827

BLACK MAN IN JAIL CELL: While in 1999 NEW YORK, JAKE CHAMBERS has a vision of a black man in an OXFORD, MISSISSIPPI, jail cell. The man, who resembles a wizard in a fairy tale, has a toothbrush mustache, wears gold-rimmed glasses, and is listening to a radio, which is issuing a list of our world's dead. Jake thinks that this image was sent to him by the DARK TOWER, and that the man may be a human incarnation of Gan. However, the black man in question also resembles a younger version of MOSES CARVER, SUSANNAH DEAN's godfather, who is also a founding member of the TET CORPORATION. VI:320–21

GAN'S BEAM: Gan's BEAM is the ELEPHANT-WOLF Beam. *For page references, see* GUARDIANS OF THE BEAM

GAN'S GATEWAY: The yellow hearts of the CAN'-KA NO REY ROSES (roses which are identical to a certain flower in NEW YORK CITY's Vacant LOT) are called Gan's Gateways. *For page references, see* ROSE

GANGLI, DR.
See CAN-TOI

GAN'S BLACKBIRDS
See APPENDIX I

GARFIELD, BOBBY
See BREAKERS: BRAUTIGAN, TED

GARFIELD, LIZ
See BREAKERS: BRAUTIGAN, TED: GARFIELD, BOBBY

GARMA
See MUTANTS: CHILDREN OF RODERICK

GARTON, WILLIAM
See CALLAHAN, FATHER DONALD FRANK: CALLAHAN AND THE HITLER BROTHERS

GASHER
See GRAYS: GRAY HIGH COMMAND

GASKIE
See TAHEEN: OTHER TAHEEN

GEE (JEY)
See TAHEEN: BIRDMEN

GERBER, CAROL
See BREAKERS: BRAUTIGAN, TED

GILEAD WHORE
After his coming-of-age battle with CORT, Roland went to one of GILEAD's brothels and lost his virginity to this prostitute. (See *Stephen King's The Dark Tower: A Concordance, Volume I.*)
    VII:824

GIRL SCOUTS
See DEAN, SUSANNAH: SUSANNAH'S PRESENT ASSOCIATES

GIRL WITH BODACIOUS TA-TAS
See CHAMBERS, ELMER

GLICK, DANNY
See CALLAHAN, FATHER DONALD FRANK: 'SALEM'S LOT CHARACTERS

GODOSH
See PRIM

GODS OF CREATION
See GODS OF MID-WORLD

GODS OF MID-WORLD
MID-WORLD is home to many gods and goddesses, and it is from these older faiths that the MAN JESUS must win his followers. Although some, like LADY ORIZA, are described to us, most of these supernatural beings remain fascinating glimmers, half-seen, half-imagined. What follows is a list of the gods that are mentioned in the final three books of the Dark Tower series. For additional information about Mid-World's folklore, see the following subentries: For Mid-World heroes and antiheroes, see ELD, ARTHUR, and CRIMSON KING. For demons and devils, see DEMON ELEMENTALS and DEMONS/SPIRITS/DEVILS. For figures from Mid-World's folklore, see MID-WORLD FOLKLORE.
    V:10, V:313 *(Callahan calls Calla gods "second-rate")*, V:467 *(some listed)*
    APON: *See* OLD STAR, *listed below*
    BESSA: When things go according to plan, the people of Mid-World thank Bessa and GAN. We don't find out anything else about this god. VII:371
    BIG SKY DADDY: Some tribes of SLOW MUTANTS call the Father of the MAN JESUS "Big Sky Daddy." V:475
    BUFFALO STAR: Buffalo Star is one of the many gods of Mid-World. Roland once killed a preacher of Buffalo Star. V:467

PREACHER OF BUFFALO STAR: V:467

CAN-TAH: *See* CAN-TAH *and* GUARDIANS OF THE BEAM: TURTLE GUARDIAN

CHLOE: According to a Mid-World prayer said over the bodies of the dead (a prayer translated either from High Speech or from the MANNI tongue), the goddess Chloe gives strength to those who have passed over. VII:474

FORCE, THE: *See* MANNI: OVER, THE

GAN: *See* GAN, *listed separately*

GODS OF CREATION: VI:12

GRAY DICK: *See* ORIZA, LADY, *listed separately*

GRENFALL, LORD: *See* ORIZA, LADY, *listed separately*

GUARDIANS OF THE BEAM: *See* GUARDIANS OF THE BEAM, *listed separately*

LYDIA: *See* OLD MOTHER, *listed below*

LYDIA'S DIPPER: *See* OLD MOTHER, *listed below*

MAN JESUS: This is a Mid-World term for Jesus. Although Christianity exists in Roland's universe, it is not the dominant religion. CALLA BRYN STURGIS is predominantly Christian thanks to the efforts of FATHER CALLAHAN, but in other towns Christianity has been blended with pagan faiths. Father Callahan likes to call Mid-World's other deities "second-rate gods." V:2, V:6, V:7, V:14, V:27, V:39, V:143, V:146, V:224, V:311, V:318, V:325, V:376, V:398, V:475, V:477, V:484, V:601, V:647, VII:388, VII:617

MORPHIA: Morphia calls herself the Daughter of Sleep. Like SELENA, Daughter of the Moon, she is one of the female incarnations of Death. VII:460

NIS: Nis is both the dream-god of Mid-World and the name for the land of sleep and dreams. Nis is also the name of the CRIMSON KING's horse. V:500, V:549

OLD MOTHER (LYDIA, SOUTH STAR): Old Mother is Mid-World's South Star and is an important fixture of the night sky. (See *Stephen King's The Dark Tower: A Concordance, Volume I.*) According to an old legend, Old Mother was married to APON, also known as OLD STAR. The two of them had a crockery-throwing fight because of Apon's flirtations with younger goddesses. They still haven't forgiven each other. V:234, VI:250, VII:723, VII:764, VII:765 *(brightest)*, VII:766, VII:767, VII:770, VII:802, VII:826

   LYDIA'S DIPPER: Mid-World's term for the Big Dipper. VII:724

OLD STAR (NORTH STAR, APON): According to Mid-World's mythology, Old Star (also called North Star) was married to OLD MOTHER. His flirtations broke up their marriage. (See *Stephen King's The Dark Tower: A Concordance, Volume I.*) V:234, VI:250, VII:723, VII:802, VII:826

ORIZA, LADY: *See* ORIZA, LADY, *listed separately*

OVER, THE: *See* MANNI, *listed separately*

PRIM: *See* PRIM, *listed separately*

RAF: Raf is a magical being who has wings on his legs and/or feet. He seems to be similar to Mercury, the winged messenger of the Roman gods. V:173

SELENA: Selena calls herself the Daughter of the Moon. Like MORPHIA, the Daughter of Sleep, she is one of the female incarnations of Death. VII:460

SEMINON, LORD: *See* ORIZA, LADY, *listed separately*

S'MANA: According to a Mid-World death prayer (either translated from High Speech or from the MANNI tongue), the forgiving glance of S'mana heals the hearts of the dead. VII:474

SOUTH STAR: *See* OLD MOTHER, *listed above*

GOLDMAN, RICHARD
See GUTTENBERG, FURTH, AND PATEL: DAMASCUS, TRUDY: KIDZPLAY

GOLDOVER, SYLVIA
See DEAN, HENRY

GOOD MAN, THE
See FARSON, JOHN

GOODMAN, ANDREW
See DEAN, SUSANNAH: ODETTA HOLMES AND THE CIVIL RIGHTS MOVEMENT: VOTER REGISTRATION BOYS

GOOD-MIND FOLK, THE
See TET CORPORATION

GOODMOUTH KING
See WARRIORS OF THE SCARLET EYE: CASSE ROI RUSSE: HUMANS: FEEMALO/FIMALO/FUMALO

GRAHAM, TOMMY
See TOWER, CALVIN

GRANDFATHER FLEAS
See VAMPIRES: TYPE ONE (THE GRANDFATHERS)

GRANDFATHERS
See VAMPIRES: TYPE ONE (THE GRANDFATHERS)

GRAN-PERE JAFFORDS
See JAFFORDS FAMILY

GRANT, DONALD
See KING, STEPHEN

GRAPEFRUIT, THE
See MAERLYN'S RAINBOW

GRAY DICK
See ORIZA, LADY

GRAYS
We first met the sinister Grays in *The Waste Lands,* where they and their enemies, the PUBES, warred over the disintegrating city of LUD. GASHER, one of the Grays, kidnapped JAKE as our ka-tet crossed over the RIVER SEND on LUD BRIDGE. Jake was saved from these scoundrels by Roland, OY, and Lud's mad computer brain, BLAINE. (See *Stephen King's The Dark Tower: A Concordance, Volume I.*)
V:135, V:178, VI:152

GRAY HIGH COMMAND:

GASHER: When the disgusting buccaneer Gasher kidnapped JAKE on the far side of LUD BRIDGE, Roland could immediately tell that the man was dying of mandrus—one of Mid-World's venereal diseases. (See *Stephen King's The Dark Tower: A Concordance, Volume I.*) V:44, V:55, V:165, V:187, V:204, V:493, VI:184, VI:269, VI:337, VI:400, VII:502

HOOTS: Tall, skinny Hoots was GASHER's former lover. (See *Stephen King's The Dark Tower: A Concordance, Volume I.*) V:44, V:187, VI:269

QUICK, DAVID: David Quick, also known as the Outlaw Prince, was the original leader of the Grays. In *The Waste Lands,* our ka-tet found his mummified body in one of the GREAT OLD ONES' flying machines. (See *Stephen King's The Dark Tower: A Concordance, Volume I.*) V:265

TICK-TOCK (ANDREW QUICK): Tick-Tock, leader of the Grays, reminded JAKE CHAMBERS of the Morlocks from H. G. Wells's novel *The Time Machine.* This was probably due more to Tick-Tock's sense of cruelty than to his actual appearance. Although he looked like a cross between a Viking and a giant, he was one LUD's few healthy, vibrant inhabitants. Tick-Tock gained his name from the coffin-shaped clock he wore around his neck. The clock ran backward. (See *Stephen King's The Dark Tower: A Concordance, Volume I.*) V:36, V:44, V:55, V:187, V:204, V:535, V:573 *(as Morlock),* VI:269, VII:502

GREAT OLD ONES
See OLD ONES

GREAT ONES
See DEMONS/SPIRITS/DEVILS: TODASH DEMONS

GREATER DISCORDIA
See PRIM

GREEN KING
See WALTER

GREENCLOAKS
See WOLVES

GRENFALL, LORD
See ORIZA, LADY

GRISSOM
See FARSON, JOHN: FARSON'S MEN

GUARDIANS OF THE BEAM
In *The Waste Lands,* Roland drew a metaphysical map of MID-WORLD. The map was circular and looked like a clockface, but its circumference contained twelve X's rather than twelve numbers. Each X designated a Portal into, and out of, Mid-World. The twelve Portals were connected by six magnetic BEAMS. Each Beam, in turn, was guarded by two animal totems, or GUARDIANS. At the center of this map, in the place where all the Beams crossed, was the Thirteenth Gate or DARK TOWER, the linchpin of the macroverse. (See *Stephen King's The Dark Tower: A Concordance, Volume I.*)

When Roland was a little boy, HAX (the traitorous cook we met in *The Gunslinger*) told him a strange story about the framework of the universe. He believed that the Tower, Beams, and Guardians were man-made, not naturally or divinely created. They were the handiwork of the GREAT OLD ONES and were manufactured as a penance for the sins those ancient people had committed against the earth, and against each other. In the final book of the Dark Tower series, we find out that the Tower, Beams, and Guardians are simultaneously magical and mechanical.

Before the coming of the world of form, all that existed in the universe was the magical PRIM, or soup of creation. From this GREATER DISCORDIA arose GAN, the spirit of the Dark Tower. From his towering body he spun the Beams, the ROSES of CAN'-KA NO REY, and the physical substance of the multiple worlds, which the Beams bind together. Once the worlds were formed, the Prim receded, but the magic of Tower, Beams, and Guardians remained.

However, the Great Old Ones—those technological wizards who once ruled Roland's version of earth—mourned the passing of the Prim. Although enough magic remained in Tower and Beams to last for eternity, the Old People used their technology to remake the supporting structures of the macroverse, and to create doorways into, and out of, as many wheres and whens as possible. As we saw as early as *The Waste Lands,* the outcome of this misconceived folly was disastrous. Not only were the manufactured Beams destined to become unstable and the Old Ones' doorways fated to be used by the evil followers of the CRIMSON KING, but the cyborg Guardians themselves—much like BLAINE, that other psychotic NORTH CENTRAL POSITRONICS creation—were fated to descend into a vicious, malfunctioning madness.

By the time our tet reaches the DEVAR-TOI in the final book of the Dark Tower series, the Beams guarded by RAT and FISH, BAT and HARE, EAGLE and LION, and DOG and HORSE have all collapsed, and we can assume that their Positronics Guardians have already landed on the celestial junk pile. The only two guy-wires left holding the Tower in place are our tet's Beam—the BEAR-TURTLE—and Gan's Beam—the ELEPHANT-WOLF.

Luckily for all of us, the remaining magical Guardians, though weakened, are far from helpless. Just as GAN, the spirit of the Dark Tower, aids those who serve the WHITE, the Prim's Guardians aid those who serve the Beams. In both *Wolves of the Calla* and *Song of Susannah,* the Turtle Guardian (in the form of a little CAN-TAH) takes an active role in assuring our tet's success.

In *Song of Susannah,* we learn that the Tower, Beams, and Guardians have a shadow side as well. When the Prim receded, it left behind not only twelve Guardians to watch over the Beams, but also six mischievous, hermaphroditic DEMON ELEMENTALS. Just as the Guardians watch over the mortal world (including the world of men), these DEMON ASPECTS watch over the invisible world of spirits and demons. Although there are only six Demon Elementals, each of these demons has a male and a female aspect. Hence, there are twelve Demon Aspects, just as there are twelve Guardians. In the original version of *The Gunslinger,* we were told that a thirteenth Guardian, called the BEAST, guarded the Tower. If each of the Demon Elementals corresponds to one of the Guardians of the Beams, then the Crimson King, the polar opposite of GAN, must be (in his spider form at least) the Beast that guards the Tower. This would make perfect sense, since at least one of the Demon Elementals plays a large part in the Red King's plan to destroy both Tower and multiverse.

Throughout the Dark Tower series, our tet follows the Bear-Turtle Beam, specifically the Beam of the Bear, Way of the Turtle (sometimes called Path of the Bear, Way of the Turtle), which leads from SHARDIK's lair deep in the GREAT WEST WOODS to the Tower itself. Had our tet begun their journey on the same Beam, but from the Turtle's (or MATURIN's) end, they would have traveled along the Beam of the Turtle, Way of the Bear (Path of the Turtle, Way of the Bear).

V:405, VI:112, VI:296, VI:297

BAT: See *Stephen King's The Dark Tower: A Concordance, Volume I*

BEAR (SHARDIK/MIR): Our tet met this seventy-foot-tall cyborg Guardian at the beginning of *The Waste Lands.* By the time he attacked EDDIE DEAN in the GREAT WEST WOODS, this NORTH CENTRAL POSITRONICS version of the Bear Guardian had already been driven mad by the white worms tunneling through his body. SUSANNAH DEAN kills this raging monster by shooting the radar dish that spins on top of his head. (See *Stephen King's The Dark Tower: A Concordance, Volume I.*) Although Shardik dies early on in our tale, his Beam still holds, probably due in large part to the efforts of the magical TURTLE Guardian. According to STEPHEN KING, the *kas-ka Gan* of our tale, Shardik's name comes from a Richard Adams novel. V:37, V:45, V:166, V:378, V:512, V:573, V:649, V:665, V:681, VI:14, VI:83, VI:112, VI:296, VI:297, VI:359, VII:21, VII:34 *(by Shardik)*, VII:192, VII:232, VII:244, VII:272, VII:291, VII:295, VII:296, VII:301, VII:306, VII:307, VII:345, VII:409, VII:458, VII:466, VII:813

SERVOMECHANISMS (LITTLE GUARDIANS: TONKA TRACTOR, RAT, SNAKE, BLOCK, BAT): The servomechanisms were the small robots that served Shardik in his lair. When EDDIE lists these odd creatures in *Wolves of the Calla,* he names the snake, the Tonka tractor, the rat, and "some sort of mechanical bird" (it was a bat). The original list also contained a walking block. V:378 *(snake, Tonka tractor, stainless steel rat, flying thing)*, V:563 *(indirect)*, V:665, V:681, VII:195

BEAST, THE: In the original version of *The Gunslinger,* WALTER tells Roland that the DARK TOWER is guarded by a Beast, who stands watch over it. This Beast is the originator of all *glammer* and is an even more powerful force than MAERLYN. (For Maerlyn entry, see also *Stephen King's The Dark Tower: A Concordance, Volume I.*) According to Walter, Roland will have to confront this Beast before he reaches the Tower.

Although this Beast reference is cut from the 2003 version of *The Gunslinger,* the CRIMSON KING, in his spider shape, bears an uncanny resemblance to this terrible monster. For page references, see *Stephen King's The Dark Tower: A Concordance, Volume I.*

DOG: See *Stephen King's The Dark Tower: A Concordance, Volume I; see also* ROSE: UR-DOG ROVER

EAGLE: In *The Dark Tower* we find out that the BEAMQUAKE which our tet felt in CALLA BRYN STURGIS was caused by the snapping of the Eagle-LION Beam. VII:232

ELEPHANT: At the beginning of *The Dark Tower,* we find out that the only two BEAMS still intact are the BEAR-TURTLE Beam and the WOLF-Elephant Beam (also known as GAN's Beam). Together they form the only remaining guy-wires holding the TOWER in place. By the time Roland and his friends reach the DEVAR-TOI, the Devar's telemetry equipment has already picked up the first bends in the Bear-Turtle. Luckily for all of us in every world, our ka-tet defeats the CRIMSON KING's henchmen and the Beams are able to regenerate. VII:232, VII:295

FISH: VI:16

HARE: See *Stephen King's The Dark Tower: A Concordance, Volume I*

HORSE: See *Stephen King's The Dark Tower: A Concordance, Volume I*

LION: In *The Dark Tower* we find out that the BEAMQUAKE which our tet felt in CALLA BRYN STURGIS was caused by the snapping of the EAGLE-Lion Beam. VII:232

RAT: VI:16

TURTLE (MATURIN): According to MID-WORLD's legends, GAN bore the world and moved on. However, if the Turtle hadn't been there to catch it on his back as it fell, all of the known worlds would have ended in the abyss.

The Turtle Guardian's name is MATURIN. Unlike SHARDIK (Maturin's companion Guardian), the Turtle Guardian does not appear to be mad. In fact, he appears to be aiding our ka-tet in their search for the DARK TOWER.

In *Song of Susannah*, SUSANNAH-MIO finds a small SCRIMSHAW TURTLE in the lining of JAKE CHAMBERS's magical bowling bag (temporary home to BLACK THIRTEEN). This SKÖLDPADDA (as it is called by MATHIESSEN VAN WYCK) is actually one of the CAN-TAH, or little gods. Its good magic (probably derived from the Turtle Guardian, which it depicts) seems able to nullify some of the chaos wrought by Black Thirteen. Not only does it help Susannah/Mia to find shelter at the NEW YORK PLAZA-PARK HYATT, but it also later aids Jake and PERE CALLAHAN when they face the CAN-TOI, TYPE ONE VAMPIRES, and GRANDFATHERS at the DIXIE PIG.

The Turtle's beneficial influence is described in the following Mid-World poem *(for variations on the Turtle poem, see APPENDIX III)*:

> See the Turtle of enormous girth!
> On his shell he holds the earth.
> His thought is slow but always kind;
> He holds us all within his mind.
> On his back all vows are made:
> He sees the truth but mayn't aid.
> He loves the land and loves the sea,
> And even loves a child like me.

V:97 *(Turtle Bay)*, V:99, V:165 *(cloud)*, V:183, V:188 *(Turtle Bay)*, V:405, V:618–19 *(indirect; Eddie feels scrimshaw in bottom of bag; we don't find out what it is until later book)*, VI:15 *(Maturin)*, VI:57 *(fountain)*, VI:66, VI:68, VI:71, VI:81–98 *(scrimshaw in Susannah/Mia's possession)*, VI:112, VI:124 *(scrimshaw)*, VI:230 *(scrimshaw)*, VI:256 *(scrimshaw)*, VI:259 *(scrimshaw)*, VI:295 *(world born by Gan landed on Turtle's back)*, VI:296, VI:298, VI:299, VI:339–40 *(scrimshaw; indirect)*, VI:343 *(scrimshaw)*, VI:363 *(scrimshaw)*, VI:394, VI:398, VII:3 *(Maturin)*, VII:3–14 *(scrimshaw)*, VII:21, VII:25 *(can-tah)*, VII:26, VII:28, VII:51 *(can-tah)*, VII:143 *(scrimshaw)*, VII:144 *(scrimshaw)*, VII:147, VII:232, VII:244, VII:272, VII:291, VII:295, VII:409, VII:445, VII:446, VII:458, VII:488 *(New York sculpture)*, VII:489–90, VII:497, VII:513, VII:525–26 *(scrimshaw)*, VII:542, VII:813

SCRIMSHAW TURTLE (CAN-TAH): *For page references, see listing above; for more information about the can-tah, see CAN-TAH, listed separately*

WOLF: At the beginning of *The Dark Tower*, we find out that—thanks to the efforts of the BEAM BREAKERS—only two Beams are still intact. They are the BEAR-TURTLE Beam and the Wolf-ELEPHANT Beam (also known as GAN's Beam). Together they form the only remaining guy-wires holding the TOWER in place. By the time Roland and his friends reach the DEVAR-TOI, the Devar's telemetry equipment has already picked up the first bends in the Bear-Turtle. Luckily for all of us in every world, our ka-tet defeats the Crimson King's henchmen and the Beams are able to regenerate. VII:232, VII:295

GUTTENBERG, FURTH, AND PATEL
Guttenberg, Furth, and Patel is a NEW YORK CITY accountancy firm. TRUDY DAMASCUS works for them.
VI:47, VI:52–54
DAMASCUS, TRUDY: Until the first of June 1999, Trudy Damascus prided herself on being a hardheaded, no-nonsense accountant. Her professional goal was to become a partner in the firm of Guttenberg, Furth, and Patel. However, while returning from her lunch that fateful day, she witnesses SUSANNAH/MIA materialize on SECOND AVENUE. Mia—desperate to find a *telefung* so that she can contact RICHARD P. SAYRE and the other WARRIORS OF THE SCARLET EYE who have promised to let her bear her CHAP in safety—threatens Trudy and steals both her shoes and her *New York Times*. Trudy is never the same afterward. VI:47–58, VI:64 *(indirect)*, VI:65, VI:222

> **ANTASSI, OFFICER PAUL:** Officer Paul Antassi is the NEW YORK CITY police officer who arrives at Guttenberg, Furth, and Patel after Trudy Damascus reports being mugged on SECOND AVENUE. He is also the first person to hear Trudy's rather unlikely story about the abrupt appearance of SUSANNAH DEAN/MIA, daughter of none, into the New York of 1999. Like all the others who will listen later, Antassi refuses to believe Trudy's tale. VI:52–53, VI:54–55
>
> **KIDZPLAY:** This company owes Guttenberg, Furth, and Patel a large sum of money. RICHARD GOLDMAN is the company's CEO. VI:47, VI:48
>
>> **GOLDMAN, RICHARD:** Richard Goldman is the CEO for KidzPlay. Trudy Damascus is after his testicles. VI:48

GUTTENBERG, MITCH: Mitch Guttenberg is one of the partners of Guttenberg, Furth, and Patel. VI:54

H

HABER
See CAN-TOI

HAGGENGOOD TWINS
See CALLA BRYN STURGIS CHARACTERS: OTHER CHARACTERS

HAMBRY CHARACTERS
In *Wizard and Glass*, Roland tells his ka-tet about his fourteenth year, and the months he spent in the town of HAMBRY after he won his guns. (See *Stephen King's The Dark Tower: A Concordance, Volume I*.) In Hambry, Roland lost his heart to SUSAN DELGADO, and what remained of his innocence and trust to the duplicitous followers of the GOOD MAN. Under the false name of WILL DEARBORN, Roland and his two apprentice-gunslinger friends, CUTHBERT ALLGOOD (alias ARTHUR HEATH) and ALAIN JOHNS (alias RICHARD STOCKWORTH), discovered that the people of Hambry secretly supported John Farson. Roland and his friends destroyed the rebellion, whose forces were led by the BIG COFFIN HUNTERS and aided by the wicked witch RHEA OF THE CÖOS. They also stole John Farson's secret weapon, MAERLYN'S GRAPEFRUIT, for their fathers. Although Roland and his two friends survived, Roland (tricked by the *glammer* of Maerlyn's evil magic ball) deserted Susan and she was burned on a Charyou Tree fire.

SEAFRONT:
  TORRES, MIGUEL: A Seafront servant. V:166
TRAVELLERS' REST:
  PETTIE: An aging whore who wanted to be a bartender. VII:220, VII:333
  ROMP, THE: The two-headed MUTIE ELK whose double heads were mounted on the wall of the Travellers' Rest. VII:220
  RUIZ, STANLEY: Stanley Ruiz was the Travellers' Rest barkeep. He was also SHEEMIE RUIZ's father. When Roland and his tet meet Sheemie again in the DEVAR-TOI in the final book of the Dark Tower series, Sheemie is using his father's name. VII:218, VII:220, VII:333, VII:391
  SHEB: The Rest's piano player. In the 2003 version of *The Gunslinger*, we find out that he later became a piano player in TULL. VII:317, VII:333
  SHEEMIE: The mildly mentally retarded tavern boy who helped Roland, CUTHBERT, ALAIN, and SUSAN defeat the BIG COFFIN HUNTERS and the rest of FARSON'S MEN. In the final book of the Dark Tower series, we find out that Sheemie later became a BREAKER in THUNDERCLAP. *For more information, see* BREAKERS: RUIZ, STANLEY (SHEEMIE)
  THORIN, CORAL: Sister of Hart Thorin, Hambry's mayor. She and her brother owned the Rest, which was both an inn and a whorehouse. Coral became the lover of ELDRED JONAS, leader of the BIG COFFIN HUNTERS. (For information about Hart Thorin and additional information about Coral, see *Stephen King's The Dark Tower: A Concordance, Volume I*.) VII:333

OTHER CHARACTERS:
DELGADO, CORDELIA: *See* DELGADO, CORDELIA, *listed separately*
DELGADO, SUSAN: *See* DELGADO, SUSAN, *listed separately*
FARMER WITH LAMB SLAUGHTERER'S EYES: V:210, V:211
MEJIS COWPOKES: VII:455

HAMMARSKJÖLD PLAZA ASSOCIATION
See TET CORPORATION

HANDS FAMILY
See CALLA BRYN STURGIS CHARACTERS: OTHER CHARACTERS

HANSON, LUCAS
See PIPER SCHOOL CHARACTERS

HARE GUARDIAN
See GUARDIANS OF THE BEAM

HARLEM SCHOOL CHOIR (HARLEM ROSES)
At the end of the final book of the Dark Tower series, SUSANNAH DEAN travels through PATRICK DANVILLE's version of the UNFOUND DOOR and finds herself in an alternative version of NEW YORK CITY's CENTRAL PARK. There she hears the Harlem School Choir singing Christmas carols.
    VII:807, VII:809, VII:818 *(indirect)*

HARRIGAN, REVEREND EARL (CHURCH OF THE HOLY GOD-BOMB)
The Reverend Earl Harrigan is the preacher for the CHURCH OF THE HOLY GOD-BOMB. Although the rev is from Brooklyn, he tends to preach in front of the Vacant LOT on FORTY-SIXTH STREET and SECOND AVENUE. Harrigan, who is the twinner of HENCHICK, leader of the MANNI in CALLA REDPATH, is constantly harassed by OFFICER BENZYCK for parking his van illegally.
    Harrigan is instrumental in helping CALLAHAN, JAKE, and OY when they appear in 1999 NEW YORK. First, he silences a driver who threatens to report Jake for drawing a gun in public. Second, he gives Callahan a pair of shoes (one of the Pere's pair flew off during his flight through the UNFOUND DOOR). And third, he passes on the psychic message he received from SUSANNAH, stating that her tet-mates should go to the PLAZA-PARK HYATT before traveling on to the DIXIE PIG.
    VI:43 *(indirect)*, VI:258, VI:259–61, VI:307–20, VI:350, VII:90, VII:423, VII:503
    CROWD: VI:309–11 *(crowd grows when Jake freaks out)*, VI:315
        BLACK MAN IN GRAY FATIGUES: This man witnesses PERE CALLAHAN's sudden appearance into NEW YORK, 1999. VI:308

DRIVER NUMBER TWO (HORN HONKER): VI:310, VI:311, VI:312
DRIVER NUMBER THREE (LINCOLN): This bossy Lincoln driver stands six foot three inches and has a big belly. He threatens to report JAKE for carrying a gun but Harrigan silences him. VI:312–15
KID WITH HAT ON BACKWARD: VI:310
SCARED WOMAN: VI:310
SHOUTER: VI:309
TAXI DRIVER WHO ALMOST HIT OY: *See* TAXI DRIVERS: TAXI DRIVER NUMBER ONE
HARRIGAN'S FATHER: Harrigan's father was also a preacher. (Are you surprised?) VI:318

HATLEN, BURT
See KING, STEPHEN

HAUSER, FRED
See KING, STEPHEN

HAWK-HEADED MAN
See TAHEEN: BIRDMEN TAHEEN: JEY

HAX
Hax was Gilead's traitorous head cook. (See *Stephen King's The Dark Tower: A Concordance, Volume I.*) When they were only eleven, Roland and his friend CUTHBERT ALLGOOD found out that Hax planned to poison an entire town for the GOOD MAN. The two boys told their fathers and Hax was hanged. Roland and Cuthbert witnessed the hanging.
    V:590 *(indirect)*, VII:526, VII:585 *(cook)*, VII:748, VII:801

HAYCOX, LOUIS
See CALLA BRYN STURGIS CHARACTERS: FARMERS (SMALLHOLD)

HAYLIS OF CHAYVEN
See MUTANTS: CHILDREN OF RODERICK

HEATH, ARTHUR
See ALLGOOD, CUTHBERT

HEDDA JAFFORDS
See JAFFORDS FAMILY

HEDDON JAFFORDS
See JAFFORDS FAMILY

HEDRON
See MANNI

HENCHICK
See MANNI

HITLER BROTHERS
See CALLAHAN, FATHER DONALD FRANK: CALLAHAN AND THE HITLER BROTHERS

HO FAT II
Ho Fat II is the rickshaw which the robot STUTTERING BILL gives to SUSANNAH, Roland, PATRICK, and OY so that they can travel from THE FEDERAL (located on the edges of the WHITE LANDS OF EMPATHICA) to the DARK TOWER. Susannah christens it Ho Fat II after their previous vehicle.
VII:720–24, VII:725–50, VII:756–65, VII:767–82

HO FAT III
Ho Fat III is the small electric scooter which STUTTERING BILL makes for SUSANNAH DEAN so that she can ride the final miles toward the DARK TOWER. In many ways, it is the perfect replacement for Susannah's Cruisin Trike, which she left in the DEVAR-TOI. Susannah ends up taking Ho Fat III through PATRICK DANVILLE's version of the UNFOUND DOOR and over to an alternative version of NEW YORK CITY where everybody else is driving Takuro Spirits.
VII:720–50 *(742–43—Ho Fat III is named directly)*, VII:807–13

HO FAT'S LUXURY TAXI
Roland and SUSANNAH DEAN used this rickshaw while traveling through the BADLANDS beyond CASTLE DISCORDIA.
VII:579, VII:580–644 *(replaced by a travois in the snowlands)*, VII:697

HODJI, WALTER
See WALTER

HOLLINGS, ERNEST "FRITZ"
See CALLAHAN, FATHER DONALD FRANK: CALLAHAN'S HIDDEN HIGHWAYS ASSOCIATES

HOLMES, ALICE (SARAH WALKER HOLMES)
Alice Holmes (called Sarah Walker Holmes in *The Waste Lands*) was SUSANNAH DEAN's mother. She died before the accident which claimed her daughter's legs. Alice Holmes liked to use White Shoulders perfume.
V:101, V:121 *(mama)*, VI:80, VI:101, VI:237 *(white lie; this actually refers to Susannah/Odetta)*, VI:358 *(indirect)*, VI:361–63, VII:643 *(mother)*, VII:696 *(mother)*

HOLMES, DAN

Born into a poor Southern family, Dan Holmes rose to success despite the prejudices of a hostile and racist society. A trained dentist, an inventor, and later the founder of the phenomenally successful HOLMES DENTAL INDUSTRIES, Dan Holmes must have been an intelligent, resourceful, and resilient man. However, despite his many successes and the millions he made from his inventions and his business, his life was not without its tragedies. After the death of his wife and then the accident which claimed his daughter's legs, Dan Holmes suffered the first of a series of heart attacks for which his daughter, ODETTA HOLMES/SUSANNAH DEAN, felt personally responsible.

Until his health began to fail, Dan Holmes handled his business almost single-handedly. Then he turned financial responsibility over to his long-time friend MOSES CARVER. Carver continued to manage Holmes Dental after his friend's death.

In *The Dark Tower*, Moses Carver tells Roland that the western writer BEN SLIGHTMAN JR., author of CALVIN TOWER's valuable misprinted book, *The Dogan*, wrote science fiction under the name Dan Holmes.

V:100–101, V:103, V:122, V:181 *(father)*, V:597 *(father of Odetta)*, VI:268, VI:350, VI:361, VII:57, VII:497, VII:508, VII:534, VII:637, VII:657, VII:672, VII:732

HOLMES, ODETTA

See DEAN, SUSANNAH: SUSANNAH'S OTHER SELVES

HOLMES DENTAL INDUSTRIES

Holmes Dental Industries was founded by DAN HOLMES, father of SUSANNAH DEAN. Begun with the money Dan Holmes earned from his innovative dental-capping processes, Holmes Dental soon grew into a multimillion-dollar business. Until his first heart attack in 1959, Dan Holmes managed the financial aspects of his enterprise almost single-handedly. However, after this unfortunate event, he handed financial responsibility over to his close friend MOSES CARVER. Pop Mose continued to manage the business for ODETTA HOLMES (Susannah Dean's previous personality) after her father's death.

The success of Holmes Dental was a spectacular feat and speaks volumes for the cleverness and tenacity of its founder. Born into a poor Southern family, Dan Holmes became a dentist and built up both his practice and his business despite the oppression of a racist society.

Under the leadership of Moses Carver, JOHN CULLUM, and AARON DEEPNEAU, Holmes Dental merged with the TET CORPORATION—the brainchild of EDDIE DEAN—which was formed to protect the ROSE.

V:539, VI:188, VI:268 *(merger with Tet Corporation)*, VII:37, VII:40, VII:125

HOLSTEN, RAND

See KING, STEPHEN

HOONIK, ZALIA
See ORIZA, SISTERS OF: JAFFORDS, ZALIA

HOONIK, ZALMAN
See CALLA BRYN STURGIS CHARACTERS: ROONTS

HOOTS
See GRAYS: GRAY HIGH COMMAND

HORSE GUARDIAN
See GUARDIANS OF THE BEAM

HOSSA
See WARRIORS OF THE SCARLET EYE: DIXIE PIG CHARACTERS: HUMANS: JOCHABIM, SON OF HOSSA

HUCKMAN, WARD
See CALLAHAN, FATHER DONALD FRANK: CALLAHAN'S LIGHT-HOUSE SHELTER ASSOCIATES

HUCKSTER ROBOT
See NORTH CENTRAL POSITRONICS: FEDIC ROBOTS

HUMMA O' TEGO
See TAHEEN: OTHER TAHEEN

HYPERBOREAN WANDERER
See CHAMBERS, JAKE

I

IL ROCHE
See BALAZAR, ENRICO

IMMORTAL TIGER
See ROSE

INSIDE VIEW
Inside View is the kind of pseudo-news rag that prints stories about alligator-boys and Elvis sightings.
V:140

ISRAEL
See MAINE CHARACTERS

ITTAWAY, DAVE
See BREAKERS

J

JAFFORDS FAMILY (KA-JAFFORDS)
The Jaffords clan of CALLA BRYN STURGIS owns a smallhold farm near the banks of the RIVER WHYE. Unlike the other Calla *folken,* they have consistently resisted the WOLVES of THUNDERCLAP. Seventy years before our story began, JAMIE JAFFORDS and a *moit* of friends fought the Wolves on the EAST ROAD. Jamie was the only one of the WOLF POSSE to survive, but thanks to him, Roland and his tet find out that the Wolves are actually robots produced by the sinister company NORTH CENTRAL POSITRONICS. TIAN JAFFORDS, Jamie's grandson, is the first in his village to suggest that the town should stand against the Wolves, paving the way for Roland's battle against the child-stealing villains of Thunderclap. ZALIA, Tian's wife, is one of the SISTERS OF ORIZA. She and the other Sisters of the Plate fight with Roland and his tet during the East Road battle.
V:1, V:3, V:8, V:321, V:340, V:343, V:353, V:380, V:394, V:396, V:401, V:488, V:492, VI:178 *(Jaffords's Rentals in Maine),* VI:184 *(Jaffords's Rentals in Maine)*
HOONIK, ZALMAN: ZALIA JAFFORDS's roont brother, who lives with the Jaffords family. *See* CALLA BRYN STURGIS CHARACTERS: ROONTS
JAFFORDS, AARON: Aaron Jaffords is the two-year-old son of TIAN and ZALIA JAFFORDS. He is their youngest child, and a singleton. Unlike twins, singletons are safe from the WOLVES. V:9, V:10 *(children),* V:14 *(indirect),* V:15, V:25, V:143, V:146, V:162 *(indirect),* V:344–46, V:351–56, V:379 *(indirect),* V:380, V:397 *(indirect),* V:488–92 *(present),* V:494 *(baby)*
JAFFORDS, GRAN-PERE (JAMIE): Gran-pere Jaffords is the father of the deceased LUKE JAFFORDS and the grandfather of TIAN JAFFORDS. He is also the oldest person in the Calla. Although he is now toothless and spends most of his time dozing by the fire, in his youth he was full of thorn and bark. Seventy years before our story began, when Jamie was just NINETEEN years old, he and his friends MOLLY DOOLIN, EAMON DOOLIN, and POKEY SLIDELL formed a POSSE to defeat the WOLVES of THUNDERCLAP. Molly Doolin managed to kill one of the invaders with her ORIZA, but Jamie was the only human to survive the standoff.
Although Gran-pere lives with Tian and his family, he and his grandson have not spoken civilly for years. Their long feud began when Luke Jaffords

allowed seventeen-year-old Tian to site the family well with a drotta, or dowsing stick, against Jamie's wishes. Tian found water, but when his father tried to dig the well, the ground collapsed under him and he was buried alive in the clay-filled water.

Like many of the people of the Calla, Gran-pere Jaffords wears a Jesus-tree. However, he doesn't seem particularly pious. During dinner grace he picks his nose. Despite his advanced years, Jamie Jaffords still has an eye for pretty ladies. He especially likes his granddaughter-in-law, ZALIA. V:1, V:10, V:11, V:12, V:13, V:14, V:25, V:27, V:162, V:236–37, V:322, V:346–48, 352–69, V:377, V:396, V:401, V:405, V:419–20, V:485–86, V:484–92 (present), V:494, V:509, V:530, V:601–17 (present; mentioned directly on 601, 603, 608, 610, 611), V:621, V:664, V:679, VII:385

GRAN-PERE'S GRAN-PERE: V:12

GRAN-PERE'S TWIN: See CALLA BRYN STURGIS CHARACTERS: ROONTS

JAFFORDS, HEDDA: Hedda Jaffords is HEDDON JAFFORDS's twin. She and Heddon are the oldest of TIAN and ZALIA's five children. They are ten-year-old dark blonds. Hedda is the cleverer of the twins, but her brother is better tempered. Tian describes her as good but plain-faced. V:9, V:10, V:12, V:13, V:14 (children), V:15 (children), V:23, V:144–45, V:146, V:162 (indirect), V:344–46, V:351–56, V:357, V:379 (indirect), V:380 (indirect), V:397 (indirect), V:488–92 (present), V:494, V:601–17 (present; mentioned directly on 603, 605), V:662–67 (with children)

JAFFORDS, HEDDON: Heddon Jaffords is HEDDA JAFFORDS's twin. He is not as clever as his sister but is more agreeable. He and Hedda are ten-year-old dark blonds. V:9, V:10, V:12, V:13, V:14 (children), V:15 (children), V:23, V:144–45, V:146, V:162 (indirect), V:344–46, V:351–56, V:357, V:379 (indirect), V:380 (indirect), V:397 (indirect), V:488–92 (present), V:494, V:601–17 (present; mentioned directly on 603), V:662–67 (with children), V:696

JAFFORDS, JAMIE: See JAFFORDS, GRAN-PERE, listed above

JAFFORDS, LIA: Lia is LYMAN JAFFORDS's twin. She is five years old. V:9, V:10, V:12, V:14 (indirect), V:15 (indirect), V:23, V:146, V:162 (indirect), V:344–46, V:351–56, V:357, V:379, V:380 (indirect), V:397 (indirect), V:488–92 (present), V:494, V:662–67 (with children), V:693

JAFFORDS, LUKE: Luke Jaffords was the son of JAMIE JAFFORDS and the father of TIAN and TIA JAFFORDS. After Tia was taken to THUNDERCLAP and returned ROONT, Luke Jaffords doted on Tian. He even let his seventeen-year-old son site the family's new well, using a drotta, or dowsing stick, despite negative predictions by Jamie. Tian found the water they'd been searching for, but when his father dug the well, its clay sides collapsed and buried Luke alive. The grief and anger that resulted from this tragic and avoidable death set Tian and Jamie against each other forever after. V:8 (Tian's father), V:15, V:24, V:123, V:347, V:368, V:485

JAFFORDS, LYMAN: He is LIA JAFFORDS's twin. He is five years old. V:9, V:10, V:12, V:14 (indirect), V:15 (indirect), V:23, V:146, V:162 (indi-

rect), V:344–46, V:351–56, V:357, V:379, V:380 *(indirect),* V:397 *(indirect),* V:488–92 *(present),* V:494

JAFFORDS, TIA (ROONT): *See* CALLA BRYN STURGIS CHARACTERS: ROONTS

JAFFORDS, TIAN: Tian Jaffords is about thirty years old. He and his wife, ZALIA JAFFORDS, have five children—two sets of twins and one singleton. Tian is an anomaly in his village. Unlike most of the other smallhold farmers, he can read and write. He can also work with numbers. It is Tian Jaffords who calls the men of the Calla to meet at the TOWN GATHERING HALL so that they can try to save their children from the WOLVES. Tian and his GRAN-PERE have not spoken civilly in years. Each blames the other for LUKE JAFFORDS's death.

While Zalia Jaffords stands against the Wolves during the Calla's final battle, Tian acts as one of the CHILD-MINDERS. V:1–31, V:44 *(follows ka-tet),* V:45 *(follows ka-tet),* V:47 *(follows ka-tet),* V:88 *(new friends),* V:92 *(indirect),* V:106 *(indirect),* V:109 *(indirect),* V:111–13, V:116, V:122–37, V:142–60, V:162, V:201–10 *(present; mentioned directly on 208),* V:211–34 *(present; mentioned directly on 214, 216, 218, 222),* V:236 *(indirect),* V:237, V:319, V:343, V:344–57, V:359, V:360, V:368, V:376–77, V:379, V:380, V:397 *(indirect),* V:398–99, V:419, V:485, V:486–92 *(present),* V:494, V:572, V:587, V:589, V:601–17, V:629–35, V:641, V:644–50, V:652, V:654, V:662–67 *(present),* V:686, V:689 *(folken),* V:693–97 *(folken),* VI:204, VI:373

> **MOTHER:** Mentioned but unnamed. V:1
> **UNCLE:** While trying to break ground in SON OF A BITCH, TIAN's uncle was attacked by MUTANT WASPS. V:1

JAFFORDS, ZALIA: *See* ORIZA, SISTERS OF

JAFFORDS' RENTALS
> *See* MAINE (STATE OF): EAST STONEHAM, *in* OUR WORLD PLACES

JAKE
> *See* CHAMBERS, JAKE

JAKLI
> *See* TAHEEN: BIRDMEN TAHEEN

JAMIE
> *See* DECURRY, JAMIE

JAVIER, ANNABELLE
> *See* CALLA BRYN STURGIS CHARACTERS: FARMERS (SMALLHOLD): JAVIER, BUCKY

JAVIER, BUCKY
> *See* CALLA BRYN STURGIS CHARACTERS: FARMERS (SMALLHOLD)

JAVIER, BULLY
See CALLA BRYN STURGIS CHARACTERS: ROONTS

JAVIER, ROBERTA
See CALLA BRYN STURGIS CHARACTERS: FARMERS (SMALL-HOLD): JAVIER, BUCKY

JEFFY
See CALLAHAN, FATHER DONALD FRANK: CALLAHAN'S HOME SHELTER ASSOCIATES

JEMMIN
See MANNI

JENKINS
See WARRIORS OF THE SCARLET EYE: DEVAR-TOI CHARACTERS: UNKNOWN RACE

JESSERLING, PETRA
See PIPER SCHOOL CHARACTERS

JEY
See TAHEEN: BIRDMEN TAHEEN; *see also* WARRIORS OF THE SCARLET EYE: DIXIE PIG CHARACTERS: TAHEEN

JIM (UNCLE JIM)
See BREAKERS: BRAUTIGAN, TED

J.J. THE BLUE JAY
See BREAKERS: EARNSHAW, DINKY

JOCHABIM
See WARRIORS OF THE SCARLET EYE: DIXIE PIG CHARACTERS: HUMANS

JOHN LAWS
This bit of slang means "policeman."
   VI:65

JOHNS, ALAIN (RICHARD STOCKWORTH)
Alain Johns was Roland Deschain's childhood friend and fellow gunslinger. (See *Stephen King's The Dark Tower: A Concordance, Volume I.*) In *Wizard and Glass,* Roland recounts how stolid, blond-haired Alain and volatile CUTH-BERT ALLGOOD accompanied him to the town of HAMBRY in the BARONY OF MEJIS, where the three young boys had to battle the BIG COF-FIN HUNTERS and the other followers of JOHN FARSON.

Like all of the members of Roland's new ka-tet, Alain was strong in the touch. He also had an inbred sense of caution. After the fall of GILEAD, he, Roland, Cuthbert, and JAMIE DECURRY experienced one of MID-WORLD's BEAMQUAKES. Sadly, just before the battle of JERICHO HILL, Alain was shot by Roland and Cuthbert. The shooting was accidental, but nevertheless deadly.

V:41, V:59, V:78, V:79, V:85, V:98, V:164, V:170, V:182, V:184, V:389, V:400 *(indirect)*, VI:16 *(lived through Beamquake)*, VI:279, VII:219, VII:220, VII:271, VII:497, VII:503, VII:552, VII:762, VII:801

JOHNS, CHRISTOPHER (BURNING CHRIS): Alain Johns's father. V:85 *(father)*, V:195 *(father)*

JONAS, ELDRED
    See BIG COFFIN HUNTERS

K

KA-JAFFORDS
    See JAFFORDS FAMILY

KA-TET OF NINETEEN
    See NINETEEN

KA-TET OF NINETY-NINE
    See NINETY-NINE

KA-TET OF THE ROSE
    See TET CORPORATION

KELLY, TAMMY
    See WARRIORS OF THE SCARLET EYE: DEVAR-TOI CHARACTERS: HUMANS

KENOPENSKY, MARY LOU
    See DEAN, EDDIE: EDDIE'S PAST ASSOCIATES

KEYSTONE WORLD
    See entry in PORTALS

KEYSTONE YEAR
    See NINETEEN NINETY-NINE

KI'-DAM
   See WARRIORS OF THE SCARLET EYE: WARRIORS BY LOCATION: DEVAR-TOI CHARACTERS: HUMANS

KID SEVENTY-SEVEN
   See CHAMBERS, JAKE

KIDZPLAY
   See GUTTENBERG, FURTH, AND PATEL: DAMASCUS, TRUDY

KING, STEPHEN (THE WRITER, KAS-KA GAN)
Like TED BRAUTIGAN, Stephen King—our favorite *kas-ka Gan*—is actually a facilitator. However, whereas Ted's special talent increases the psychic abilities of those around him, sai King's special skill brings characters out of the PRIM and into the world of form. In over two hundred short stories and more than forty novels, King has created hundreds of doorways leading into, and out of, KEYSTONE EARTH. No wonder there is such a problem with WALK-INS in his part of the world.

When seven-year-old King was on punishment duty sawing wood in his uncle's barn, he was approached by the CRIMSON KING, Lord of Discordia. The Red King wanted to make little Stevie into a bard of the Outer Dark, but he was destined to be thwarted in this endeavor. Steve King was saved by CUTHBERT ALLGOOD and EDDIE DEAN, who convinced him to serve the cause of the WHITE instead. The Red King (never a good loser) has been gunning for King ever since.

Stephen King makes several guest appearances in the final books of the Dark Tower series. In *Song of Susannah,* King comes face-to-face with two of his "creations"—Roland of GILEAD and Eddie Dean of NEW YORK. King also plays a kind of *deus ex machina* by leaving JAKE CHAMBERS a key to SUSANNAH's room in the PLAZA-PARK HYATT so that Jake and PERE CALLAHAN can retrieve BLACK THIRTEEN. King plays this role again in *The Dark Tower,* when he warns Susannah Dean that the seemingly friendly JOE COLLINS is not what he seems. (He is actually the were-spider DANDELO.)

Although his characters form the TET CORPORATION to keep both King and the ROSE safe, the *todanna,* or death-bag, which Roland and Eddie saw around the writer in BRIDGTON, MAINE, is destined to have its day. In 1999—the KEYSTONE YEAR in the KEYSTONE WORLD—Stephen King is hit by a Dodge minivan driven by BRYAN SMITH. King's life is saved by Jake Chambers, who jumps between him and the oncoming vehicle. King survives the accident but Jake does not. As a badly hurt King lies on the side of SLAB CITY HILL, an angry Roland makes King promise to finish the Dark Tower series. True to his promise, King has done so.

   V:54, V:706, V:709, VI:167, VI:168–72, VI:207–8, VI:210 *(tale-spinner),* VI:211, VI:221, VI:270–303 *(294—possessed by Gan; his Beam is the*

Bear-Turtle Beam), VI:322–24, VI:336, VI:350, VI:389–411 *(journal extracts and article about accident)*, VII:17, VII:18, VII:33, VII:36, VII:39, VII:76, VII:120, VII:121, VII:125 *(writah)*, VII:143–44 *(telecaster)*, VII:145, VII:173–74, VII:266, VII:300, VII:301, VII:302, VII:303–7, VII:311, VII:312–14, VII:332, VII:336, VII:388, VII:405, VII:406, VII:409, VII:424, VII:434, VII:435, VII:436–39, VII:440, VII:441, VII:442, VII:444–62, VII:465, VII:467–68, VII:472, VII:475, VII:480, VII:485, VII:487, VII:505, VII:511–15, VII:524, VII:534, VII:542–45, VII:552, VII:601–13 *(uffis)*, VII:614, VII:627, VII:680–81, VII:689 *(enters tale again)*, VII:690–95 *(leaves poem)*, VII:706, VII:728, VII:802

BACHMAN, RICHARD: *See* BACHMAN, RICHARD, *listed separately*

CALDERWOOD, FLOYD: A friend or acquaintance of King's, Floyd Calderwood also makes a guest appearance in King's novel *It*. In that book, he appears in a flashback as a 1905 lumberjack who has a shady past. VI:276

CARLINER, MARK: VI:409

FAN MAIL/HATE MAIL: VI:401–3, VI:406

    SPIER, JOHN T.: VI:401

    VELE, MRS. CORETTA: VI:402–3, VI:406 *(Vermont gramma)*

FERMAN, ED: Editor in chief of *Fantasy and Science Fiction*. VI:390–91

FULCHER, ANDY: Babysitter. VI:391, VI:395

GRANT, DONALD: The publisher who first put King's novel *The Gunslinger* into print. VI:392, VI:395, VI:396, VI:403

HATLEN, BURT: Steve King's professor and friend who teaches at the UNIVERSITY OF MAINE. Burt Hatlen arranged for King to be a writer in residence at the University of Maine at ORONO. VI:391

HAUSER, FRED: VI:407

HOLSTEN, RAND: VI:409

JONES, BETTY: OWEN KING's babysitter. VI:289, VI:301

KING FAMILY (GENERAL): VI:272, VI:273 *(kids)*, VI:280 *(kids)*, VI:295 *(kids)*, VI:391 *(kids)*, VI:396 *(kids)*, VI:405 *(kids)*, VII:436, VI:438

    AUNTIE ETHELYN: King's aunt. VI:292, VI:389

    KING, DAVE: Stephen King's brother. VI:278, VI:292, VI:389, VI:399

    KING, JOE: King's eldest son. VI:280, VI:281, VI:283, VI:287 *(indirect)*, VI:296, VI:297, VI:301, VI:302, VI:389, VI:390, VI:406, VI:407, VI:408, VI:409

        WIFE: VI:406, VI:410

        ETHAN (SON): VI:409

    KING, NAOMI: King's daughter. VI:280, VI:390, VI:393, VI:405, VI:410

    KING, OWEN: King's youngest son. VI:280, VI:289, VI:389, VI:391, VI:392, VI:393, VI:404, VI:407, VI:408, VI:410

    KING, TABITHA (TABBY): King's wife. VI:273, VI:280, VI:285, VI:286, VI:289, VI:295, VI:389, VI:390, VI:391, VI:394, VI:398, VI:403–4, VI:406, VI:407, VI:408–9

FATHER: VI:280 *(poppa)*
MOTHER: VI:280 *(nanna)*, VI:389 *(nanna)*
KING'S MOTHER: VI:278, VI:286
UNCLE OREN: King's uncle. VI:292, VI:389
KOSTER, ELAINE: She worked for NAL. VI:393
MANSFIELD FAMILY (DAVIE, SANDY, MEGAN): VI:398
MARLOWE: King's dog, who resembles OY. VII:544–45
McCAULEY, KIRBY: King's agent. VI:390–91, VI:392, VI:393
McCAUSLAND, CHARLES (CHIP): *See* MAINE CHARACTERS, *listed separately*
McKEEN (GROUNDSKEEPER): Great-grandson of GARRETT McKEEN, who lived in the LOVELL area over one hundred years before our story takes place. The present Mr. McKeen is the groundskeeper for the Kings' family home, CARA LAUGHS. Roland thinks of him as King's bondsman. VII:437–38, VII:441–42, VII:443

McKEEN, GARRETT: Garrett McKeen lived in the LOVELL area of Maine at the turn of the twentieth century. His great-grandson is Stephen King's groundskeeper. VII:439, VII:443

McLEOD, GEORGE: One of King's old drinking buddies from his UNIVERSITY OF MAINE days. VI:409
MECUTCHEON, MAC: VI:276
ROUTHIER, RAY (REPORTER): This reporter writes King's obituary, which appears at the very end of *Song of Susannah*. Luckily, our tet prevents this disaster from taking place. However, altering ka always has its price. King survives being hit by BRYAN SMITH's van, but JAKE CHAMBERS dies in his place. VI:410
SMITH, BRYAN: Bryan Smith (who, we are told, is SHEEMIE's twinner) has two rottweilers, BULLET and PISTOL, and an extremely long list of motor vehicle offenses. In the KEYSTONE EARTH, Smith hits both JAKE CHAMBERS and STEPHEN KING with his 1985 Dodge minivan. King survives the accident but Jake does not. VII:433–34, VII:440–41, VII:443–44, VII:447, VII:448–62, VII:463, VII:467–68, VII:472, VII:528, VII:543

BULLET: VII:433–34, VII:441 *(indirect)*, VII:444, VII:448–49, VII:456, VII:461

HIPPIES WITH DRUGS: VII:433

PISTOL: VII:433–34, VII:441 *(indirect)*, VII:444, VII:448, VII:456, VII:461

SOYCHAK, MR.: King's algebra teacher. VI:289
THOMPSON, FLIP: King's old drinking buddy from his UNIVERSITY OF MAINE days. VI:409
VAUGHN, SAM: VI:393
VERDON, HENRY K.: The sociologist Henry K. Verdon authored the article on WALK-INS which Stephen King pasted in his journal. VI:397–98
VERRILL, CHUCK: Stephen King's New York editor. VII:448
ZOLTAN: *See* ZOLTAN, *listed separately*

KING DANDO
See DANDO (KING DANDO)

KOSTER, ELAINE
See KING, STEPHEN

L

LADY BLACKBIRD
See DEAN, SUSANNAH

LADY OF SHADOWS
See DEAN, SUSANNAH

LADY OF THE PLATE
See ORIZA, LADY

LADY OR THE TIGER, THE
See MID-WORLD FOLKLORE: DIANA'S DREAM

LADY ORIZA
See ORIZA, LADY

LADY RICE
See ORIZA, LADY

LAMERK INDUSTRIES
This sinister company is also known as LAMERK FOUNDRY and has ties to both NORTH CENTRAL POSITRONICS and SOMBRA REAL ESTATE. Like those other companies, LaMerk is probably part of the SOMBRA GROUP.

In one of the ALTERNATIVE AMERICAS that CALLAHAN travels through, a footbridge (just in the shadow of the GEORGE WASHINGTON BRIDGE) stretches across the HUDSON RIVER. This nineteenth-century bridge was repaired by LaMerk Industries during the bicentennial.

V:5, V:132, V:292–93, V:460, V:578, V:633, V:650

LAMLA
See TAHEEN: STOAT-HEADED TAHEEN

LLAMREI
See ELD, ARTHUR

LARS
See CALLAHAN, FATHER DONALD FRANK: CALLAHAN'S HIDDEN HIGHWAYS ASSOCIATES

LATIGO, GEORGE
See FARSON, JOHN: FARSON'S MEN

LAVENDER HILL MOB
According to SUSANNAH DEAN, in her when and where of early 1960s GREENWICH VILLAGE, the term *Lavender Hill Mob* was an oblique reference to homosexual men.
VII:549

LEABROOK REGISTER
See CALLAHAN, FATHER DONALD FRANK: CALLAHAN'S HIDDEN HIGHWAYS ASSOCIATES

LEEDS, TANYA
See BREAKERS

LESSER DEMONS OF THE PRIM
See DEMONS/SPIRITS/DEVILS

LEWIS
See MANNI

LIA JAFFORDS
See JAFFORDS FAMILY

LIGHTHOUSE SHELTER WORKERS AND CLIENTS
See CALLAHAN, FATHER DONALD FRANK: CALLAHAN'S LIGHTHOUSE SHELTER ASSOCIATES

LINCOLN, MR.
See HARRIGAN, REVEREND EARL

LION GUARDIAN
See GUARDIANS OF THE BEAM

LIPPY
See DANDELO

LISA
See CALLAHAN, FATHER DONALD FRANK: CALLAHAN'S HOME SHELTER ASSOCIATES

LITTLE SISTERS OF ELURIA
See ELURIA CHARACTERS

LOBSTROSITIES
These claw-snapping nasties live on the shores of the WESTERN SEA. (See
Stephen King's The Dark Tower: A Concordance, Volume I.) At the beginning
of *The Drawing of the Three,* one of them eats two of Roland's fingers and one
of his toes.
V:46, V:61, V:241, V:379, V:462 *(indirect),* V:525, V:540, V:686, VI:10,
VI:132, VI:295, VI:296, VI:395, VII:741, VII:797, VII:826

LONDON, JACK
See CAN-TOI

LORD GRENFALL
See ORIZA, LADY

LORD OF DISCORDIA
See CRIMSON KING

LORD OF THE SPIDERS
See CRIMSON KING

LORD PERTH
See MID-WORLD FOLKLORE

LORD SEMINON
See ORIZA, LADY

LOS
See CRIMSON KING

LOST BEASTS OF ELD
See ELD, ARTHUR

LOVELL, MAINE, CHARACTERS
See MAINE CHARACTERS

LOW MEN
See CAN-TOI

LUDDITES
On our level of the TOWER, the Luddites were a group of nineteenth-century
textile workers in the English manufacturing districts who rioted and destroyed
the machines which they believed were stealing their jobs. Contemporary

Luddites are people who are opposed to increased industry or new technology. In MID-WORLD, the Luddites are the inhabitants of the city of LUD. Like their namesakes in our world, their lives have been made unbearable by the totalitarianism of mad machines.

VI:287

LUNDGREN, DAHLIE
See DEAN, EDDIE: EDDIE'S PAST ASSOCIATES

LUSTER
See PUBES

LYDIA
See GODS OF MID-WORLD

LYDIA'S DIPPER
See GODS OF MID-WORLD: OLD MOTHER

LYMAN JAFFORDS
See JAFFORDS FAMILY

M

MAERLYN
Maerlyn is the magician responsible for the creation of the thirteen sinister magic balls that make up MAERLYN'S RAINBOW. (See *Stephen King's The Dark Tower: A Concordance, Volume I.*) In *Wolves of the Calla*, Roland wonders whether the Maerlyn of ancient legend is actually the sorcerer WALTER. Seductive as this idea is, it seems unlikely. According to MIA, once the magical PRIM receded and the sword of ELD gave way to the pistols of the gunslingers, the legendary Maerlyn retired to a magical cave. Like the Merlin of our world's folklore, he is probably still sleeping there.

V:36, V:412 *(as Walter/Marten/Flagg)*, VI:110

MAERLYN'S RAINBOW (BENDS O' THE RAINBOW, WIZARD'S RAINBOW, MAERLYN'S MAGIC BALLS)
There are thirteen glass balls in the Wizard's Rainbow, one for each GUARDIAN and one for the TOWER itself. (In the original version of *The Gunslinger*, we were told that the final ball—BLACK THIRTEEN—corresponded to the BEAST that guards the Dark Tower.) Some of these magic balls look into the future; others look into the past or into alternative realities. Still

others (chief among them being Black Thirteen) can act as doorways into other worlds. (See *Stephen King's The Dark Tower: A Concordance, Volume I.*)

The Wizard's Rainbow represents a corruption of the pure energy of the WHITE. Hence, it could be argued that the thirteen colored balls correspond not to the twelve Guardians and the Tower, but to the twelve aspects of the DEMON ELEMENTALS and the CRIMSON KING, the were-spider who wishes to bring the Tower crashing down.

When Roland was a boy, it was believed that only three or four of these magic balls were still in existence. In *The Dark Tower*, we realize there must have been more, since Roland has had temporary control of two of them (MAERLYN'S GRAPEFRUIT and Black Thirteen), and the Crimson King—until about halfway through *Wolves of the Calla*—owned six. (Never a good loser, the Red King smashed his once they foretold Roland's victories in both CALLA BRYN STURGIS and the DEVAR-TOI.)

V:79, V:80, V:89 *(glass balls)*, V:90, V:105, V:116, V:142, V:176, VI:8 *(bends o' the rainbow)*, VII:550, VII:606–7 *(Crimson King had six of them)*, VII:674, VII:770

BLACK THIRTEEN: According to Roland Deschain, Black Thirteen is the most terrible object left over from the days of ELD. In fact, Roland suspects that its wickedness even predates the time of his illustrious ancestor. If Roland is correct and the ancient magician MAERLYN is actually none other than our tet's nemesis, WALTER O'DIM, then this magic ball probably dates from the time of the GREAT OLD ONES, who tried, in their hubris, to unite magic and technology.

Black Thirteen enters our tale via an unlikely person—namely FATHER CALLAHAN, formerly of 'SALEM'S LOT, MAINE. Before coming to rest beneath the floorboards of Callahan's church in CALLA BRYN STURGIS, Thirteen was in Walter's possession. In fact, it seems likely that the ball was in Walter's hands throughout much of *The Gunslinger*, since when that nasty multifaced magician forces Thirteen upon an unwilling Callahan in the WAY STATION between worlds, we catch a glimpse of Roland and JAKE distantly struggling up an incline toward the CYCLOPEAN MOUNTAINS.

Before we see the malevolence of Thirteen at work, we are told that it looks like the slick eye of a monster that grew outside of God's shadow. As Callahan removes it from its hidey-hole beneath his church floor and unwraps it from its altar boy's surplice, Roland feels the ball's low hum vibrating in his bones, a sound and sensation he compares to a swarm of angry bees. Once Callahan removes the surplice, Roland sees Thirteen's ghostwood box, upon which is carved a ROSE, a stone, a door, and the word *unfound*. With the exception of the Rose, the engraved images come from Thomas Wolfe's novel *Look Homeward, Angel*. (In Wolfe's book, the "rose" is actually a leaf, but within the context of the Dark Tower series, a rose is a more appropriate image.) The word *unfound* refers to the UNFOUND DOOR, which Black Thirteen inevitably opens.

It seems likely that Thirteen's box (like the altar boy's surplice that

Callahan wraps it in) is meant to minimize the ball's evil vibrations. After Roland touches the magical ghostwood, his fingers smell of camphor, fire, and the flowers of the north country—the ones that bloom in the snow.

In both *Wolves of the Calla* and *Song of Susannah,* our tet carries Black Thirteen in a TODASH version of Jake's pink bowling bag. Although Jake's original bag bore the motto, "Nothing but Strikes at Mid-Town Lanes," the todash version reads, "Nothing but Strikes at Mid-World Lanes." Despite Thirteen's evil nature, our tet uses it to travel between Calla Bryn Sturgis and Calla NEW YORK. At the end of *Wolves of the Calla,* SUSANNAH DEAN (now under the control of her invading demon, MIA) uses Black Thirteen to escape through the Unfound Door to 1999, where Mia plans to give birth to her CHAP. With some help from STEPHEN KING, Jake and Callahan retrieve the magic ball from Susannah-Mio's room in the PLAZA-PARK HYATT before it can fall into the hands of the WARRIORS OF THE SCARLET EYE. The two of them store it in a locker located below the TWIN TOWERS. We can presume that the ball has since been destroyed.

Like the singing Rose, Thirteen's hum speaks of power, but it is the dangerous power of the void, a colossal malevolent emptiness which, if aroused, could send its unwary victims to all NINETEEN points of nowhere. Throughout the Dark Tower series, our tet believes that this nasty ball is the eye of the CRIMSON KING himself. Although the Red King may use Thirteen to spy upon our tet's movements, by the final book of the DARK TOWER series we realize that it is not his actual eye. Los's eyes are as red as the roses of CAN'-KA NO REY, and when we see him, shouting madly from the DARK TOWER's balcony, he has both his ruby orbs. In fact, once PATRICK DANVILLE erases the Red King from Mid-World, all that he leaves are the Lord of Discordia's floating eyes. V:31 *(indirect),* V:48–70 *(Eddie and Jake travel via todash; 53–56—reality of Black Thirteen),* V:114–16, V:117, V:142 *(worst of the bunch),* V:172–97 *(traveling in it/via todash; 176 origins, 180, 196),* V:235 *(indirect),* V:238 *(indirect),* V:252, V:271 *(thing in church),* V:311, V:313–18 *(described),* V:338, V:383 *(indirect),* V:393, V:400, V:409 *(box),* V:413 *(box),* V:414, V:415, V:461–65, V:468–70, V:502–5, V:506–49 *(Eddie's New York trip; 507–8—keep Black Thirteen in todash bag),* V:591–600 *(Callahan to our world),* V:618–27 *(Callahan to Stoneham, Maine),* V:688, V:697, V:704 *(indirect),* V:705, VI:4, VI:7, VI:8 *(and glammer, the sum of all the bends o' the rainbow),* VI:21 *(dark glass),* VI:28, VI:49 *(in bag),* VI:68 *(in box),* VI:74–97 *(in bag),* VI:178, VI:234, VI:300, VI:326–38, VI:342, VII:147, VII:302, VII:550, VII:689

MAERLYN'S GRAPEFRUIT (THE PINK ONE): Maerlyn's Grapefruit played a large part in Roland's MEJIS adventures, recounted in the novel *Wizard and Glass.* (See *Stephen King's The Dark Tower: A Concordance, Volume I.*) Like all of Maerlyn's magic glasses, the Grapefruit is hungry and feeds on the minds of those who use it. Roland was lucky to survive his travels within its pink glare. V:36, V:37, V:38, V:49, V:53 *(Wizard's Glass),* V:79, V:116, V:176

MAGRUDER, GEORGE
See CALLAHAN, FATHER DONALD FRANK: CALLAHAN'S HOME
SHELTER ASSOCIATES: MAGRUDER, ROWAN

MAGRUDER, ROWAN
See CALLAHAN, FATHER DONALD FRANK: CALLAHAN'S HOME
SHELTER ASSOCIATES

MAGRUDER, ROWENA
See CALLAHAN, FATHER DONALD FRANK: CALLAHAN'S HOME
SHELTER ASSOCIATES: MAGRUDER, ROWAN: RAWLINGS, ROWENA
MAGRUDER

MAINE CHARACTERS
   ANGSTROM, JUNIOR: Junior Angstrom is one of the many western
   Maine residents who sighted a WALK-IN. Angstrom's walk-in was a naked
   man, traveling up the center of ROUTE 5. *For more information on the
   supernatural walk-ins, those beings that "walk in" to our world from
   other worlds, see* WALK-INS. VI:151
   BARKER, GARY: Gary Barker has photographs of the bizarre weather pat-
   terns that affect KEZAR LAKE in LOVELL. VII:113
   BARKER, JUNIOR: Junior Barker runs JOHN CULLUM's caretaking
   business whenever Cullum is out of town. VII:44
   BECKHARDT, DICK/BECKHARDTS: Dick Beckhardt owns one of the
   many beautiful houses located along TURTLEBACK LANE in LOVELL.
   JOHN CULLUM is his caretaker. The Beckhardt cabin is the site of Cullum's
   final palaver with Roland Deschain and EDDIE DEAN. The Beckhardts are
   friends of the TASSENBAUMS. VII:117, VII:118, VII:120, VII:123, VII:126,
   VII:432, VII:518
   BEEMER, CHARLIE: He is the husband of RUTH BEEMER, one of the
   women killed in the EAST STONEHAM GENERAL STORE shoot-out in
   1977. VII:46
   BEEMER, RHODA: She is CHARLIE and RUTH BEEMER's daughter and
   is in the EAST STONEHAM GENERAL STORE when Roland and JAKE
   return in 1999. VII:424, VII:431
   BEEMER, RUTH: Ruth Beemer is one of the two elderly sisters killed by
   BALAZAR'S MEN in the EAST STONEHAM GENERAL STORE shoot-
   out in 1977. VI:130–31, VI:132, VI:193–94, VII:46, VII:425
      SISTER: VI:130–31, VI:132, VI:193–94, VII:46, VII:425 *(not named)*
   CENTRAL MAINE POWER GUY: VII:17–18
   CONVEIGH, REVEREND: A minister in the STONEHAM/LOVELL area
   of Maine. VII:426
   CROWELL, GARY: When JOHN CULLUM pretends to leave for VER-
   MONT so that he can escape from JACK ANDOLINI and BALAZAR's

other hardboys, he tells his clients to contact Gary Crowell if they need any work done on their properties. VII:44

CULLUM, JOHN: *See* TET CORPORATION: FOUNDING FATHERS

FENNS: The Fenns are one of the families who own a house along TURTLEBACK LANE in LOVELL. VII:115

FIREBUG LADY: VI:165

ISRAEL: Israel is the surname of one of the families living along TURTLE-BACK LANE in LOVELL, MAINE. VII:115

JOGGER: VII:49

McAVOY, CHIP: Owner of the EAST STONEHAM GENERAL STORE in EAST STONEHAM, MAINE. During the East Stoneham General Store battle, which takes place between Roland, EDDIE DEAN, and BALAZAR'S MEN in 1977, Chip is wounded and his store is almost destroyed. Luckily, he has good insurance. After Eddie Dean's death in the DEVAR-TOI, Roland and JAKE CHAMBERS make a second trip to Chip's store (this time they're searching for the writer STEPHEN KING). Chip isn't too pleased to see them. V:621, VI:123, VI:132–45 *(faints)*, VI:148, VI:177, VII:128, VII:423–30, VII:431, VII:435, VII:442, VII:445, VII:449, VII:469

    FATHER: VII:424, VII:425

    SON: Chip's son fought in Vietnam. VI:136

    UNNAMED SHOP PATRONS: VII:423–30 *(present)*, VII:431

McCAUSLAND, CHARLES (CHIP): Charles McCausland was a STONE-HAM man who was hit by a car while walking on ROUTE 7. VI:403–4

McCRAY FAMILY: The McCray family owned CARA LAUGHS, the house in LOVELL, MAINE, later purchased by STEPHEN KING. VII:116

McKEEN, GARRETT: *See* KING, STEPHEN, *listed separately*

PETERSON, REVEREND: Peterson is the reverend of the CHURCH OF THE WALK-INS, located in STONEHAM CORNERS. VII:435

PORTLAND SUNDAY TELEGRAM: On another level of the DARK TOWER, this paper carried STEPHEN KING's obituary. Praise GAN, the obituary wasn't needed. VI:410

POSTMISTRESS IN STONEHAM, MAINE: Although the postmistress of STONEHAM, MAINE, is never named, we know that she is in her late fifties or early sixties and has blue-white hair. V:622–24, V:627

ROYSTER, ELDON: Eldon Royster is the county sheriff for the area around EAST STONEHAM and LOVELL. VII:118

RUSSERT, DON: JOHN CULLUM's friend Don Russert is a retired history professor. Although his working life was spent at VANDERBILT COLLEGE, he presently lives in WATERFORD, MAINE. Like others living in the LOVELL/Waterford region, Russert has had firsthand experience of WALK-INS. In fact, Russert even managed to record one of them in his living room. Unfortunately, Russert couldn't decipher the language the man spoke, nor could his former colleagues in the Vanderbilt Languages Department. VI:151–53, VI:180–81, VI:200–201 *(indirect)*, VII:131

    PSYCHIC STUDIES PROFESSOR: This unnamed professor works at

DUKE UNIVERSITY. One of Russert's friends at Duke contacted her about MAINE's WALK-IN activity. VI:153

SARGUS, JANE: Jane Sargus owns a small store called COUNTRY COL-LECTIBLES, located near where the DIMITY ROAD branches off ROUTE 5 near EAST STONEHAM, MAINE. Jane sells furniture, glassware, quilts, and old books. Although he was supposed to be hiding from BALAZAR'S MEN, CALVIN TOWER went on a book-buying spree at her place, drawing unwanted attention to both himself and his companion, AARON DEEPNEAU. VI:165–66

SMITH, BRYAN: *See* KING, STEPHEN, *listed separately*

TASSENBAUM, DAVID: *See* TASSENBAUM, DAVID, *listed separately*

TASSENBAUM, IRENE: *See* TASSENBAUM, IRENE, *listed separately*

TOOTHAKER, ELVIRA: Elvira Toothaker attended VASSAR COLLEGE with her MAYBROOK, NEW YORK, friend JUSTINE ANDERSON. Elvira—now middle-aged—lives in LOVELL. She and Justine are out picking raspberries on ROUTE 7 when BRYAN SMITH careens by in his minivan. VII:439–41

> **ANDERSON, JUSTINE:** Justine Anderson is a friend of ELVIRA TOOTHAKER of LOVELL, MAINE. They attended VASSAR together and have remained friends ever since. Justine and Elvira are picking raspberries along ROUTE 7 when they see BRYAN SMITH career past in his minivan. Justine recognizes the make of Smith's 1985 Dodge Caravan because her son once owned a similar vehicle. VII:439–41
>
> > **SON:** VII:440

TRUCK DRIVER: VI:134–35

WIDOW: This woman sells used books in EAST FRYEBURG, MAINE. CALVIN TOWER buys books from her. VI:191

WILSON, TEDDY: Teddy Wilson lives on KEYWADIN POND in EAST STONEHAM, MAINE. He is the county constable and the game warden. VI:172

MAN IN BLACK
See WALTER

MAN JESUS
See GODS OF MID-WORLD

MANNI (SEEKING FOLK)
The Manni are one of MID-WORLD's strange religious sects. The first time we see the Manni of MANNI REDPATH, their village located north of CALLA BRYN STURGIS, they are crammed into a buckboard wagon drawn by a pair of MUTIE GELDINGS. Although in appearance they resemble both the Quakers and the Amish found in the America of our world, the Manni are not actually Christian. Their religion, which worships an entity called both THE FORCE and THE OVER, focuses on traveling between worlds via TODASH.

To induce the necessary state of mind to travel todash, the Manni use both magnets and plumb bobs, which they store in large boxes, called coffs. The coffs are covered in moons, stars, and odd geometric shapes. The largest and most powerful of the bobs is called the BRANNI BOB. This plumb bob is so powerful that it is used only by HENCHICK, the Manni *dinh*. As you might expect, Manni magic is extremely powerful. The Manni help Roland's ka-tet open the UNFOUND DOOR after MIA, SUSANNAH DEAN's demon-possessor, leaves Mid-World, taking BLACK THIRTEEN—and Susannah's body—with her.

Manni men are easily recognized. They wear dark blue cloaks and round-crowned hats, and they use the terms *thee* and *thou*. Manni men also have extremely long fingernails, since they are allowed to cut them only twice a year. Not only does their appearance set them apart from the other people of Mid-World, but the Seeking Folk's culture is also radically different from that of their neighbors. Manni men marry multiple wives and live in cabins called *kras*. Those who leave their clan to marry outsiders (such as MARGARET EISEN-HART) are called the forgetful. As far as their former brethren are concerned, these deserters are damned and will spend eternity in the depths of NA'AR, which is like Hell.

When the name of ARTHUR ELD is mentioned, the Manni whisper, "The Eld!" and lift their hands, raising their first and fourth fingers in the air. The movement is a sign of respect. When a Manni covers his eyes with his hands, it is a sigul of deep religious dread. When Manni folk shake their heads in negation, they do so slowly, sweeping their heads back and forth in wide arcs. The gesture is so common among them that Roland thinks it might well be genetic.

V:6, V:14–31 *(Town Gathering Hall; present)*, V:79, V:80, V:89, V:105, V:115, V:158, V:211–34 *(present; mentioned directly on 218, 219, 223)*, V:236, V:335, V:337, V:399 *(Seeking Folk)*, V:406, V:407 *(have ways of knowing)*, V:411 *(elder Manni seek other worlds for enlightenment)*, V:412, V:414 *(as travelers)*, V:422, V:465, V:483, V:566, V:573, V:601–17 *(present; mentioned directly on 602)*, V:654, V:677, VI:5, VI:7, VI:8, VI:9, VI:17, VI:21, VI:24–43 *(cloak folk)*, VII:149, VII:335, VII:413, VII:540, VII:756, VII:798, VII:817

ARRA: *See* CANTAB, *listed below*

BONY SHOULDERS, BALEFUL EYES: When the men of CALLA BRYN STURGIS meet in the TOWN GATHERING HALL to discuss what to do about the arrival of the WOLVES, this Manni states that they should have a festival for the children and then kill them. He thinks death is a more welcoming place for them than THUNDERCLAP. V:14–31 *(Town Gathering Hall; present but not mentioned until 16)*

BRANNI BOB: The Branni Bob is the largest and most potent of the magical plumb bobs that the Manni used to travel TODASH. It is kept in a four-foot-long ironwood coff, is about eighteen inches long, and looks a bit like a child's top, though it is made of a yellowish, greasy-looking wood. As EDDIE DEAN finds out, it is extremely powerful and becomes *dim* as it sways back and forth. The Branni Bob appears to have a will of its own. Perhaps this is why HENCHICK refers to it as a "he" rather than an "it." VI:28–43

CANTAB: When Roland asks FATHER CALLAHAN for the names of some adults that the children of the Calla trust implicitly, Callahan mentions Cantab of the Manni. Evidently, the children follow him as if he were the Pied Piper. Cantab and his wife, ARRA, are two of the CHILD-MINDERS during the final battle against the WOLVES. Cantab is also present when the Manni help Roland and the remains of his ka-tet open the UNFOUND DOOR. V:483, V:601–17 *(present; mentioned directly on 602, 603),* V:662–67 *(present; mentioned directly on 666),* V:677, V:689 *(folken),* V:693–97 *(folken),* VI:3–9, VI:24–43

> **ARRA:** Arra is CANTAB's wife. Like him, she is one of the CHILD-MINDERS during the final battle against the WOLVES. Like the SISTERS OF ORIZA, Arra throws the dish, but belonging to the Manni prohibits her fellowship with the other Sisters. V:662–67 *(present; mentioned directly on 666),* V:677, V:689 *(indirect),* V:693–97 *(folken),* VI:3 *(Henchick's granddaughter)*

ELDERS (GENERAL): VI:24–43

FORCE, THE: *See* OVER, THE, *listed below*

HEDRON: Hedron is a strong Sender. He is one of the Manni elders who helps HENCHICK open the UNFOUND DOOR for Roland and his ka-tet after their battle with the WOLVES. VI:41–43 *(present from 24, but not mentioned until 41)*

HENCHICK (SILKY WHITE BEARD): Henchick is the *dinh* of Manni Redpath. He is about eighty years old but is in marvelous physical shape, as Roland discovers when Henchick leads him up the steep incline to the DOORWAY CAVE. (Roland is fatigued by the exertion, but Henchick barely breaks a sweat.)

Like the other Manni, Henchick has multiple wives. (He has three.) MARGARET EISENHART (formerly Margaret of the Redpath clan) is either one of his daughters or one of his granddaughters. Bad blood still exists between them because Henchick opposed Margaret's marriage to a "heathen." Despite Margaret's having been with her husband, VAUGHN EISENHART, for more than twenty years, Henchick still believes she is destined for NA'AR.

In the end, Henchick proves to be one of Roland's greatest allies in CALLA BRYN STURGIS. He and his ka-tet help Roland, EDDIE, JAKE, and PERE CALLAHAN open the UNFOUND DOOR so that they can rescue SUSANNAH from the FEDIC DOGAN where MIA has escaped with her body.

Henchick has a twinner in our world. His name is REVEREND EARL

HARRIGAN. V:17–31 *(Town Gathering Hall; present)*, V:211–34 *(present; mentioned directly on 223, 224 not yet named)*, V:236, V:335, V:336, V:338 *(Margaret's da)*, V:389, V:393, V:399, V:400, V:401, V:406–16, V:421, V:466, V:508, V:510, V:601–17 *(present; mentioned directly on 602, 605, 608, 610)*, VI:3–9, VI:12, VI:17, VI:21, VI:23–43, VI:258, VI:288, VI:307, VI:311, VII:540

JEMMIN: Jemmin and HENCHICK were the Manni elders who discovered CALLAHAN lying by the UNFOUND DOOR in DOORWAY CAVE. Jemmin eventually died of a heart attack. V:411–14, V:466

LEWIS: Like THONNIE, Lewis is one of the younger Manni men. He is a strapping fellow with a short beard and hair that is pulled back in a long braid. VI:28–43

OVER, THE: This is the name for one of the GODS OF MID-WORLD, specifically the one worshipped by the MANNI. The other names for the Over are THE FORCE and the PRIM. V:406 *(The Force, The Over)*, V:412, V:414, VI:26, VI:108 *(as Discordia/Prim)*

REDPATH CLAN: They are the Manni clan that lives near CALLA BRYN STURGIS. MARGARET EISENHART was born into this family. V:335, V:399 *(Manni Redpath)*, VI:3, VI:5, VI:6, VI:7 *(sixty-eight men)*, VI:9, VI:38 *(Manni kra; Redpath-a-Sturgis)*

THONNIE: Like LEWIS, Thonnie is one of the younger Manni men. He is a strapping young man with a short beard and hair that is pulled back in a long braid. VI:28–43

YOUNG AND BEARDLESS: He is one of the younger members of the Manni delegation that comes to CALLA BRYN STURGIS's meeting at the beginning of *Wolves of the Calla*. He does not believe that the adults should let any children be taken by the WOLVES. V:18–31 *(Town Gathering Hall; present)*

MANPOWER
See CALLAHAN, FATHER DONALD FRANK: CALLAHAN'S HIDDEN HIGHWAYS ASSOCIATES

MANSFIELD FAMILY
See KING, STEPHEN

MANSION DEMON
See DEMONS/SPIRITS/DEVILS

MARGARET OF THE REDPATH CLAN
See ORIZA, SISTERS OF: EISENHART, MARGARET

MARIAN
See ORIZA, LADY

MARK CROSS BRIEFCASE BUSINESSMAN
See VAMPIRES: TYPE THREE

MARK CROSS PEN BUSINESSMEN
In *The Waste Lands*, JAKE CHAMBERS saw these two men playing tic-tac-toe on a NEW YORK CITY wall.
    V:51–52

MARLOWE
See KING, STEPHEN

MARTEN BROADCLOAK
See WALTER

MATURIN
See GUARDIANS OF THE BEAM: TURTLE

MAUDE AND JEEVES
See PUBES

McAVOY, CHIP
See MAINE CHARACTERS

McCANN, BIRDIE
See BREAKERS

McCAULEY, KIRBY
See KING, STEPHEN

McCAUSLAND, CHARLES (CHIP)
See MAINE CHARACTERS

McCOWAN, AL
See CALLAHAN, FATHER DONALD FRANK: CALLAHAN'S LIGHT-HOUSE SHELTER ASSOCIATES

McCRAY FAMILY
See MAINE CHARACTERS

McKEEN, GARRETT
See KING, STEPHEN: McKEEN (GROUNDSKEEPER)

McLEOD, GEORGE
See KING, STEPHEN

MEARS, BEN
See CALLAHAN, FATHER DONALD FRANK: 'SALEM'S LOT CHARACTERS

MECUTCHEON, MAC
See KING, STEPHEN

MEJIS CHARACTERS
See HAMBRY CHARACTERS

MENSO THE ESP WONDER
See CALLAHAN, FATHER DONALD FRANK: CALLAHAN'S HIDDEN HIGHWAYS ASSOCIATES

MERCY
See RIVER CROSSING CHARACTERS

MEXICAN IMMIGRANTS
See CALLAHAN, FATHER DONALD FRANK: CALLAHAN'S HIDDEN HIGHWAYS ASSOCIATES

MIA
In High Speech, Mia means "mother," and there could be no more appropriate name for this invading spirit that hijacks SUSANNAH DEAN's body in *Wolves of the Calla*. Unlike Susannah's previous split personalities of DETTA WALKER and ODETTA HOLMES, Mia does not come from a deep psychological schism within her host, but attaches herself to Susannah once she has conceived the CHAP in the demon-haunted SPEAKING RING of the RIVER BARONY plains. (See *Stephen King's The Dark Tower: A Concordance, Volume I.*)

Originally, Mia was one of the magical but disincarnate spirits left behind when the magical PRIM receded. In her wraith state, she was a sexual VAMPIRE who caused the deaths of many men, including AMOS DEPAPE, brother of the BIG COFFIN HUNTER ROY DEPAPE. For many years, Mia haunted the city of FEDIC. There, she saw and fell in love with a baby named MICHAEL. After the Red Death ravaged the city's populace and baby Michael was taken away by his parents, WALTER made the lovesick Mia a Faustian bargain. If she would give up her disincarnate immortality, Walter would give her a baby. Mia could not conceive (like all elemental beings, she was sterile), but if she could be given a body, then she could carry to term. After submitting herself to the horrid process of *becoming* (a technological and magical alchemy accomplished in the FEDIC DOGAN operating theater/torture chamber), Mia gained the necessary equipment for surrogate motherhood. All she needed was someone else's fertilized egg.

Mia's sole purpose is to nurture and bear the CHAP, the demonic offspring of herself, Susannah Dean, Roland Deschain, and the CRIMSON KING. As a servant of the Outer Dark, the *dan-tete*, or little king, is destined to destroy his White Daddy (Roland) and rule after his Red one. Although the fetal MORDRED is slowly being "faxed" into Mia's body located in END-WORLD, at first it is Susannah who experiences pregnancy's strange cravings. As an early service to the Red King, Mia occasionally hijacks Susannah's body to feed it the binnie bugs, frogs, and raw piglets that Susannah (in her waking state) would not have been able to stomach. However, like Detta Walker, the longer Mia is inside of Susannah, the more control-time she seems to require. By the beginning of *Song of Susannah*, Mia has seized the reins of the physical form she shares with her host.

Unfortunately for Mia (who goes mad upon the delivery of her chap), she never gets to raise the child for whom she has sacrificed so much. No sooner does MORDRED begin to suckle at his mother's breast than he turns into a were-spider and sucks all the moisture from her body. All that is left of Mother-Mia is a giant dust bunny.

V:71–81 *(hunts in Susannah's body)*, V:127, V:173, V:174, V:181, V:183, V:184, V:196, V:198, V:241, V:248, V:249, V:251, V:311 *(baby's keeper)*, V:318, V:329, V:341, V:370–76, V:376–80 *(Eddie knows she is in Susannah)*, V:382, V:383, V:385, V:390 *(indirect)*, V:391, V:392 *(indirect)*, V:394, V:396, V:472, V:478, V:479–83, V:488, V:583, V:617, V:628, V:629, V:648 *(Susannah-Mio)*, V:659, V:674, V:688, V:697, V:699–705, VI:8, VI:48–52, VI:53–125, VI:150, VI:190, VI:194, VI:210, VI:216, VI:219, VI:223, VI:224, VI:225–61, VI:241–45 *(Mia as elemental)*, VI:287, VI:316–17, VI:319 *(indirect)*, VI:320, VI:321, VI:322, VI:325, VI:326, VI:327, VI:339, VI:343, VI:347–85, VII:3, VII:4 *(Susannah-Mio)*, VII:21–22, VII:35, VII:47, VII:52, VII:55–75 *(by page 75 she is dried-out dust on a bed)*, VII:76, VII:81, VII:115, VII:141–42 *(a giant dust bunny)*, VII:145, VII:149, VII:160, VII:163, VII:168, VII:169, VII:170, VII:173, VII:175, VII:176, VII:302, VII:303, VII:315, VII:398, VII:399, VII:487, VII:488, VII:531, VII:538, VII:539, VII:554, VII:578, VII:595, VII:620 *(lunatic mother)*, VII:689, VII:741 *(body-mother)*, VII:766 *(dust-mummy)*

MIA'S ASSOCIATES:

BABY MICHAEL: Michael was one of the few healthy babies born in the town of FEDIC before the onset of the Red Death. In her incorporeal state, Mia saw this baby and fell in love with him, realizing that her true destiny was motherhood. Mia's longing for motherhood, a desire kindled by observing the untouchable Michael, was later used by WALTER, servant of the CRIMSON KING. He offered Mia motherhood in exchange for her incorporeal immortality. Mia, to her own undoing, accepted this most Faustian of bargains. VI:243–44, VI:249, VI:251, VI:254

MICHAEL'S FATHER: VI:243–44
MICHAEL'S MOTHER: VI:243–44
CHAP: *See* MORDRED, *listed separately*

RAT, MR.: During one of her food-raids in her dream-version of CAS-TLE DISCORDIA, Mia kills Mr. Rat and steals his dinner. They are competing over a roasted suckling pig, which appears, momentarily, to be a human baby. Mr. Rat is the size of a tomcat, so Mia is a fairly fierce fighter. As always happens in the Dark Tower series, Mia's foe has a twinner in Mid-World. Mr. Rat is also the rat which SUSANNAH DEAN kills in the JAFFORDS' barn. V:373–75, V:376, V:381–82, V:390, VI:373

MICHAEL (BABY MICHAEL)
See MIA

MID-WORLD FOLKLORE (HEROES, ANTIHEROES, MAGICAL FORCES, FAMOUS TALES)
For a list of Mid-World divinities, see GODS OF MID-WORLD
AM: See PRIM, listed separately
BEAMS: See BEAMS, PATH OF THE, in PORTALS
BEAMS, GUARDIANS OF THE: See GUARDIANS OF THE BEAM, listed separately
BLACK THIRTEEN: See MAERLYN'S RAINBOW, listed separately
CAN-TAH: See CAN-TAH and GUARDIANS OF THE BEAM, both listed separately
CHASSIT: See NINETEEN, listed separately
CHILDREN OF RODERICK: See MUTANTS: CHILDREN OF RODERICK
CRIMSON KING: See CRIMSON KING, listed separately
DEMON ELEMENTALS: See DEMON ELEMENTALS, listed separately
DIANA'S DREAM: This is an old Mid-World story which is very much like "The Lady or the Tiger?" V:39, V:442
ELD, ARTHUR: See ELD, ARTHUR, listed separately
GAN: See GAN, listed separately
GODOSH: See PRIM, listed separately
GRANDFATHERS: See VAMPIRES: TYPE ONE
GREATER DISCORDIA: See PRIM, listed separately
GREEN DAYS, QUEEN OF: The Queen o' Green Days is probably a figure from IN-WORLD folklore. When Roland tracks MIA through the BORDERLAND bogs, he mentions this figure. We don't learn anything else about her. V:81
GRENFALL, LORD: See ORIZA, LADY, listed separately
HORN OF ELD: See ELD, ARTHUR, listed separately
KAMMEN: See TODASH, in PORTALS
LLAMREI: See ELD, ARTHUR, listed separately
LOST BEASTS OF ELD: See ELD, ARTHUR, listed separately
MAERLYN (THE SORCERER): See MAERLYN, listed separately
MAERLYN'S GRAPEFRUIT: See MAERLYN'S RAINBOW, listed separately

OLD ONES (GREAT OLD ONES): *See* OLD ONES, *listed separately*

ORIZA, LADY: *See* ORIZA, LADY, *listed separately*

PERTH, LORD: The story of Lord Perth comes from one of MID-WORLD's old poems and is very much like our world's biblical tale of David and Goliath. According to tradition, Lord Perth was a giant who went forth to war with a thousand men, but he was still in his own country when a little boy threw a stone at him and hit him in the knee. He stumbled, the weight of his armor bore him down, and he broke his neck in the fall. (See *Stephen King's The Dark Tower: A Concordance, Volume I.*) V:10, V:39 *(like David and Goliath)*

ROWENA, QUEEN: *See* ELD, ARTHUR, *listed separately*

RUSTY SAM: Rusty Sam is the central character in one of MID-WORLD's folktales. In this story, Rusty Sam steals an old widow's best loaf of bread. VI:250

SAITA: *See* ELD, ARTHUR, *listed separately*

SEMINON, LORD: *See* ORIZA, LADY, *listed separately*

STUFFY-GUYS: Red-handed stuffy-guys, which can be found all over MID-WORLD, are a staple of Reaptide festivities. In the days of ARTHUR ELD, human beings were sacrificed during the autumn festival of REAP. However, by Roland's day, stuffy-guys, or human effigies, were burned instead. In Mid-World-that-was, stuffy-guys had heads made of straw, and their eyes were made from white cross-stitched thread. In the BORDER-LANDS, their heads are often made of SHARPROOT. In *Wolves of the Calla,* Roland has the SISTERS OF ORIZA prove their skills by aiming their sharpened plates at stuffy-guys. For more information, see *Stephen King's The Dark Tower: A Concordance, Volume I.* V:320, V:332–34, V:405

SWORD OF ELD: *See* ELD, ARTHUR, *listed separately*

TAHEEN: *See* TAHEEN, *listed separately*

TODASH: *See entry in* PORTALS

UFFIS: *Uffi* is an ancient term for a shape-changer. In LE CASSE ROI RUSSE, Roland and SUSANNAH come across three identical STEPHEN KINGs, who claim to be a single uffi. However, they are not FEEMALO/FIMALO/FUMALO as they pretend, but servants of the RED KING who have transformed themselves using *glammer.* Their leader is actually AUSTIN CORNWELL, a servant of the Red King who hailed from upstate NEW YORK in one of the MULTIPLE AMERICAS. *For page references, see* WARRIORS OF THE SCARLET EYE: LE CASSE ROI RUSSE: HUMANS

VAGRANT DEAD: *See* VAGRANT DEAD, *listed separately*

VAMPIRES: *See* VAMPIRES, *listed separately*

WALKING WATERS OF EAST DOWNE: Roland met the Walking Waters of East Downe during his travels through MID-WORLD. We never learn anything more about this intriguing entity. VI:234

WIZARD'S RAINBOW: *See* MAERLYN'S RAINBOW, *listed separately*

MID-WORLD GODS
See GODS OF MID-WORLD

MILLS CONSTRUCTION AND SOMBRA REAL ESTATE
Along with NORTH CENTRAL POSITRONICS and LAMERK INDUS-
TRIES, Mills Construction and Sombra Real Estate is part of the SOMBRA
GROUP, a corporate conglomerate which serves the CRIMSON KING. In our
world, Mills Construction and North Central Positronics were jointly respon-
sible for building the MIND-TRAP under the DIXIE PIG.

As JAKE CHAMBERS realized as far back as *The Waste Lands*, Sombra and
its subsidiaries want to destroy both the magical Vacant LOT and the ROSE
that grows there. *For more information, see* SOMBRA CORPORATION
V:96, V:188, VII:492

MINNIE
See CALLA BRYN STURGIS CHARACTERS: ROONTS: DOOLIN, MIN-
NIE

MIR
See GUARDIANS OF THE BEAM: BEAR GUARDIAN

MISLABURSKI, MRS.
See DEAN, EDDIE: EDDIE'S PAST ASSOCIATES

MOLLY (AUNT MOLLY)
See BREAKERS: BRAUTIGAN, TED

MOLLY (RED MOLLY)
See ORIZA, SISTERS OF

MONSTERS
See MUTANTS; *see also* DEMONS/SPIRITS/DEVILS

MOONS
See DEMON MOON, GOAT MOON, HUNTRESS MOON, PEDDLER,
all in APPENDIX I

MORDRED (THE CHAP, DAN-TETE, LITTLE RED KING, MORDRED DESCHAIN, MORDRED OF DISCORDIA, MORDRED RED-HEEL, MORDRED SON OF LOS, KING THAT WILL BE, SPIDER BOY)
As a father, Roland Deschain doesn't have much luck. His first child, conceived
with SUSAN DELGADO in HAMBRY, died in the womb when Susan was
burned upon a Charyou Tree fire. JAKE CHAMBERS, his adopted son, dies
three times—first beneath the wheels of a Cadillac on FIFTH AVENUE, NEW
YORK; second, beneath the CYCLOPEAN MOUNTAINS, where Roland let
him drop into an abyss; and finally in our world's LOVELL, MAINE, where he
steps in front of a van destined to kill the writer STEPHEN KING. Yet, however
terrible the fates of these two children may be, the destiny awaiting Roland's

third child is much more frightening to contemplate. He is the *dan-tete,* the "little savior" or "baby god" whose coming has been predicted for hundreds of years. Unlike the human line of ELD, from which he is (in part) descended, Mordred Deschain is a creature of the Outer Dark, and if his fate is fulfilled, he will destroy both the last of the gunslingers and all of the multiple worlds that spin like sequins upon the needle of the DARK TOWER.

For generations, the MANNI folk have prophesied the coming of Mordred Red-Heel, the were-spider who is the son of two fathers and two mothers. According to legend, this child—the last miracle spawned by the still-standing DARK TOWER—will be half-human, half-god, and will oversee the end of humanity and the return of the PRIM, or GREATER DISCORDIA.

Like the creature whose coming is apprehensively awaited by the Manni, Mordred Deschain unites both the mortal and nonmortal worlds. Two of his parents—Roland Deschain and his ka-tet mate SUSANNAH DEAN—are human. However, his two other parents—the CRIMSON KING and MIA, daughter of none—are not. The nature of Roland and Susannah's relationship (that of *dinh* and bondswoman, or leader and his symbolic daughter) also fulfills a MID-WORLD prophecy, which tells us even more about the destiny of this enfant terrible: "He who ends the line of Eld shall conceive a child of incest with his daughter, and the child will be marked, by his red heel shall you know him. It is he, the end beyond the end, who shall stop the breath of the last warrior." Like the fate of his namesake from the Arthurian legends of our world, Mordred is to destroy what is left of the WHITE and then kill the mortal hero who sired him.

As the series progresses, we come to realize that Mordred's conception was not an accident, but a carefully staged event that has been planned for eons. With his multiple destinies, Mordred is a valuable tool, which can be used by both WALTER, the Crimson King's prime minister, and the Crimson King himself. Not only can Mordred kill the seemingly unstoppable Roland, but the red, hourglass-shaped widow's brand, which sits upon his belly, will unlock the door to the Tower. (The only other key to GAN's body is Roland's pair of guns.) If the Crimson King wants to beat Roland to the Tower (and if Walter wants to climb to its top to become God of All), then both of them need the key, which rests upon the *dan-tete*'s body.

In retrospect, we realize that all of the seemingly random sexual encounters of the series—from Roland's copulation with the ORACLE OF THE MOUNTAINS to the rape of Susannah Dean in the SPEAKING RING—were actually planned by the servants of the Red King so that they could collect Roland's sperm, mix it with that of their master, and then use it to fertilize Susannah's egg. However, although Mordred is both the Crimson King's heir apparent and a potential A-bomb of a BREAKER, those who brought him into being misjudged the human aspects of Mordred's nature, a nature which both foils the Crimson King's plans and proves to be Mordred's undoing.

From the moment he is born in the FEDIC DOGAN to his body-mother, Mia, until the second he dies under Roland's guns on the TOWER ROAD,

Mordred is a creature of conflicting emotions. While his spider-self consists almost entirely of physical desires ("Mordred's a-hungry"), and although he seems to show no regret for either eating his birth mother just after emerging from her womb or cruelly devouring Walter O'Dim piece by piece, the small white node which connects Mordred's two selves is obviously capable of other modes of operating. No doubt, the black-haired, blue-eyed hume-Mordred is spiteful, cruel, and vicious, but his feelings for Roland combine hatred, jealousy, and rage with a sad and hungry love. Although he has several chances to arrange for Roland's demise (most notably he could have informed the guards of the DEVAR-TOI that their compound would soon be attacked), Mordred chooses instead to watch and wait. In this, he serves his own childlike curiosity, not the will of the Red King, who arranged for his arrival in the world. If Roland is to die, Mordred wants to be the one who kills him. However, Mordred does not choose to attack his White Daddy until he, himself, is dying of food poisoning. Perhaps he hopes to take Roland with him to the clearing at the end of the path? As unlikely as this may initially seem, we must remember the vision of Mordred which Roland sees within the Tower. This child is no monster, but a sad and lonely creature, one who never received any love at all.

V:71–87 *(fed by Mia)*, V:122, V:183 *(indirect)*, V:184, V:241 *(baby)*, V:370–76, V:377–78, V:382, V:383, V:391, V:393 *(baby)*, V:394, V:472 *(indirect)*, V:478, V:479–83 *(480—poison with a heartbeat)*, V:577, V:583–84 *(pregnancy)*, V:617, V:628–29 *(indirect)*, V:674, V:688, V:697, V:700–701, V:703, V:704, V:706, VI:5, VI:8, VI:10–11, VI:16, VI:50, VI:51–52 *(inside Susannah/Mia)*, VI:55, VI:56, VI:61–125, VI:194, VI:216, VI:222 *(as monster baby)*, VI:223 *(dream monster baby)*, VI:224 *(kid)*, VI:227 *(baby)*, VI:228, VI:229, VI:231, VI:233, VI:234, VI:235–56 *(Mia's pregnancy)*, VI:256–61 *(and trip to Dixie Pig)*, VI:297, VI:347–85, VI:408, VII:19 *(baby)*, VII:38 *(dan-tete)*, VII:47 *(baby)*, VII:52 *(baby)*, VII:55–71 *(birth; 71—leg shot off)*, VII:76 *(monster—Jekyll and Hyde, twin with two fathers)*, VII:141 *(chap)*, VII:149–50, VII:157, VII:160–64, VII:166–88 *(Roland's blue bombardier's eyes)*, VII:192, VII:226, VII:238, VII:261–63, VII:301, VII:314–18, VII:332 *(were-spider)*, VII:399, VII:406, VII:518, VII:537, VII:540, VII:549, VII:550, VII:589, VII:593–94, VII:595, VII:615–16, VII:618, VII:619–24, VII:625, VII:626, VII:627, VII:631–32, VII:639, VII:640, VII:648–50, VII:653, VII:667, VII:671, VII:710 *(stays in Dandelo's hut for two days; hears Tower sing in minor key)*, VII:721, VII:722, VII:725, VII:727, VII:730, VII:731, VII:741, VII:750, VII:751–56, VII:759, VII:762–63, VII:765–71 *(dual body's brain in white node; killed on 770)*, VII:774–75, VII:779, VII:822–23

MORKS
See BREAKERS

MORLOCKS
See GRAYS: GRAY HIGH COMMAND: TICK-TOCK

MORPHIA
See GODS OF MID-WORLD

MORT, JACK ("THE PUSHER")
In *The Drawing of the Three,* Roland entered the mind of this psychotic CPA through the BEACH DOOR labeled The Pusher. (See *Stephen King's The Dark Tower: A Concordance, Volume I.*) Jack Mort liked to "depth charge" people. In other words, he liked to kill them. It was Mort who dropped a brick on five-year-old ODETTA HOLMES's head, an accident which resulted in the birth of Odetta's second personality, DETTA WALKER. It was also Mort who pushed Detta/Odetta in front of the A train at CHRISTOPHER STREET STATION, severing their shared legs from the knee down. Mort was also responsible for JAKE CHAMBERS's first death in 1977 NEW YORK. (In the guise of a priest, he pushed Jake in front of an oncoming car.)
  V:72 *(indirect),* V:479, V:597, VI:221, VI:232, VII:567

MUCCI, TIMMY
See CHAMBERS, JAKE: JAKE'S ASSOCIATES

MUNOZ, ROSALITA
See ORIZA, SISTERS OF

MURRAY, PROFESSOR
See DEAN, SUSANNAH: ODETTA HOLMES'S ASSOCIATES

MUTANTS (MUTIES)
Although the GREAT OLD ONES and their destructive culture disappeared many generations before the rise of GILEAD, the poisons they left in soil, water, and air remained. We cannot be certain whether these destructive ancients engaged in all-out chemical and biological warfare, but it seems probable. By the end of their reign over MID-WORLD, most of their women were already giving birth to monsters, as the people of FEDIC could testify.
  By the time Roland was a young man, Mid-World was still full of genetically mutated beings which were commonly referred to as muties. As we learned in MEJIS, both domesticated and wild muties could carefully be bred to breed true. However, since this process was extremely slow, "threaded stock," or those that were born whole, were extremely valuable. (See *Stephen King's The Dark Tower: A Concordance, Volume I.*)
  VI:372, VII:670
  ALBINO BEES: VI:152
  ASSES (ALBINO): The MANNI own these beasts. VI:21, VI:23
  CHILDREN OF RODERICK (RODS): The Children of Roderick are a band of wandering slow mutants who originated in the distant SOUTH PLAINS, a land beyond those known to the people of GILEAD. Before the world moved on, they gave their grace to ARTHUR ELD and so owe allegiance to

the Eld's final human descendant, Roland Deschain. Despite their allegiance to the First Lord of Light, many of the Rods now serve as the CRIMSON KING's groundskeepers in the DEVAR-TOI. Their dirty little village is located about two miles from THUNDERCLAP STATION.

In appearance, the Rods resemble a cross between the radiation-sick SLOW MUTANTS and a band of lepers. Boogers are their favorite tasty treats. According to FINLI O'TEGO, it is not good to touch the skin of a Rod since many of the diseases they carry are easily transmittable.

In DINKY EARNSHAW's opinion, the Rods are untrustworthy, since their mouths tend to run at both ends. However, the Rods still remember their allegiance to the Eld, and at least one of their number—HAYLIS OF CHAYVEN—is instrumental in the destruction of the Devar. Many of the WALK-INS sighted in western MAINE are actually Rods. VII:50, VII:51, VII:114, VII:130, VII:180, VII:216–17, VII:223, VII:225, VII:234, VII:256–57, VII:300, VII:319, VII:321, VII:322, VII:323, VII:324, VII:329, VII:330, VII:338, VII:340, VII:341, VII:346, VII:347, VII:348, VII:351, VII:357

CHEVIN OF CHAYVEN: Green-skinned, lyre-carrying Chevin of Chayven is the first of the Children of Roderick that Roland and EDDIE encounter on their way to LOVELL, MAINE. His one double-yolked eye, fanglike booger, talon-toed feet, and urine stench are quite a shock to Eddie.

When Roland first sees this grim-looking creature scurrying into the roadside growth, he calls the Rod forth saying, "So come forth, ye child of Roderick, ye spoiled, ye lost, and make your bow before me, Roland, son of STEVEN, of the line of ELD." Chevin, who among his own people is a minstrel, comes forth. After questioning him about FEDIC and the DEVAR-TOI, Roland cuts short the Rod's slow and painful death by shooting him. VII:48–50, VII:52 *(indirect)*, VII:114, VII:120, VII:130, VII:142, VII:216, VII:217, VII:329

HAMIL: Father of Chevin of Chayven. VII:51

GARMA: Garma is HAYLIS OF CHAYVEN's female friend. She does the "pokey-poke" with him when he gives her snotty tissues. Talk about a cheap date. VII:349

HAYLIS OF CHAYVEN (CHUCKY): Haylis of Chayven is a red-haired Rod whose nose has been eaten away by a large, strawberry-shaped sore. EDDIE thinks he looks like Chucky—a nasty killer-toy from a horror movie—but when Haylis smiles he seems sweet and childlike. Like the rest of his kind, Haylis owes allegiance to Roland. Because of this allegiance, he plants sneetches in the DEVAR-TOI, initiating THUNDERCLAP's final battle. VII:319–24, VII:329–35, VII:337–42, VII:346–49, VII:351, VII:357, VII:406

ONE-EYED WOMAN WITH DEAD CHILD: EDDIE DEAN sees this walk-in by the magical doorway of CARA LAUGHS. VII:130

DEER (MUTANT DOE): VII:633

ELK: *See* HAMBRY CHARACTERS: TRAVELLERS' REST: ROMP, THE
MUTIE GELDINGS: The MANNI of CALLA BRYN STURGIS arrive at
the TOWN GATHERING HALL in a buckboard drawn by a pair of mutie
geldings. One of these muties has three eyes; the other has a pylon of raw
pink flesh poking out of its back. V:14
SLOW MUTANTS: Some tribes of Slow Mutants call the Father of the
MAN JESUS "BIG SKY DADDY." Many of MAINE's WALK-INS are
actually SLOW MUTANTS. Others are CHILDREN OF RODERICK.
V:475, VI:152 *(Maine walk-ins as slow mutants),* VI:243, VII:25, VII:51
WASPS: Some of the fields in CALLA BRYN STURGIS contain nests of
mutant wasps. The ones that attacked TIAN JAFFORDS's uncle had
stingers the size of nails. V:1–2
WILD DOGS: Packs of these dogs are known to wander the BORDER-
LANDS of MID-WORLD. They have no vocal cords so are silent predators.
V:397

MYSTERY NUMBER
See NINETEEN; *see also* NINETY-NINE

N

NIGEL THE BUTLER
See NORTH CENTRAL POSITRONICS

NINETEEN (CHASSIT, KA-TET OF NINETEEN)
As early as the 2003 revised edition of *The Gunslinger,* we began to suspect that
the number nineteen might have magical significance. In the town of TULL,
WALTER O'DIM resurrected the weed-eater NORT and implanted a secret
door in Nort's mind. Behind the door slept all of Nort's memories of being
dead. The password which opened this sinister door was the number nineteen.

At the beginning of *Wolves of the Calla,* our tet refers to the number nineteen
as the "mystery number." They find themselves gathering firewood in bundles
of nineteen branches and even see its double digits take shape in the sky's passing clouds. Many of the important figures they meet or otherwise have dealings
with—from DONALD FRANK CALLAHAN and CLAUDIA Y INEZ BACH-
MAN to RICHARD PATRICK SAYRE—have nineteen-letter names. When
EDDIE DEAN questions ANDY, CALLA BRYN STURGIS's Messenger Robot,
about how he predicts the WOLVES' cyclical invasions, Andy states that he cannot answer. The reason? Directive Nineteen.

And the coincidences continue. GRAN-PERE JAFFORDS was nineteen
years old when he and his WOLF POSSE faced down the Greencloaks on the
Calla's EAST ROAD. When Eddie saves CALVIN TOWER from BALAZAR's

thugs (Calla NEW YORK's version of the Wolves), he discovers that Tower's great-great-great-grandfather wrote about Roland Deschain in his will, a document drawn up on March 19, 1846. Both Father Callahan and his friend ROWAN MAGRUDER end up in room 577 of Riverside Hospital after being attacked by the HITLER BROTHERS (5+7+7 = 19). When SUSANNAH DEAN and her demon-possessor, MIA, travel to 1999 New York, they stay in room 1919 of the PLAZA-PARK HYATT hotel.

Although nineteen plays an important role throughout *Wolves of the Calla* and *Song of Susannah,* not until the final book of the Dark Tower series do we learn the full significance of this curious number. *Chassit* (High Speech for "nineteen") is the password for the OLD ONES' DOOR, which connects our world's New York with END-WORLD's FEDIC. When nineteen (the ka of our world) joins with ninety-nine (the ka of Roland's world), they form 1999, which happens to be the KEYSTONE YEAR in the KEYSTONE WORLD. Nineteen ninety-nine is the year that MORDRED DESCHAIN is born, and on June 19, 1999, our *kas-ka Gan,* STEPHEN KING, is hit by a minivan in LOVELL, MAINE. Hence, it is in 1999 that the fate of the DARK TOWER is decided.

V:37–38, V:41, V:52, V:55, V:68, V:94, V:95, V:98, V:99, V:108, V:111, V:117, V:119, V:130, V:141, V:142, V:164, V:165, V:166–67, V:169, V:175, V:179, V:201, V:215, V:232, V:257, V:284 *(Nineteenth Street),* V:302 *(Route 19),* V:315, V:350 *(Directive Nineteen),* V:357 *(Jamie Jaffords),* V:360, V:367, V:423, V:428 *(room),* V:443, V:447 *(Nineteenth Nervous Break-down),* V:449, V:451 *(and Callahan's death),* V:459, V:525, V:532, V:565, V:573, V:585, V:606, V:620, V:643, V:648, V:678, V:685, V:695, V:707, VI:48 *(time),* VI:53 *(time),* VI:84, VI:93, VI:95, VI:96, VI:118, VI:178, VI:184, VI:223, VI:225, VI:230, VI:270, VI:288, VI:325, VI:326, VI:328, VI:336 *(8+8+3 = 19),* VI:338, VII:7 *(plates),* VII:36, VII:130, VII:156 *(ka-tet of),* VII:302 *(ka of),* VII:303, VII:305, VII:399, VII:405, VII:418, VII:434, VII:436, VII:444, VII:453, VII:505, VII:551, VII:555, VII:556, VII:645, VII:665, VII:689, VII:761, VII:764, VII:821, VII:822, VII:825, VII:827

NINETEEN NINETY-NINE (KEYSTONE YEAR IN THE KEYSTONE WORLD)

The year 1999 is considered the Keystone Year in the KEYSTONE WORLD. In it, the number NINETEEN (the ka of our world) joins with NINETY-NINE (the ka of Roland's world). It is a year of transformation, either for good or dis. On our level of the TOWER, it is the year that sai KING is hit by a Dodge minivan. It is also the year that JAKE CHAMBERS passes into the clearing while trying to save him. It is to 1999 NEW YORK that MIA, the body-jacking mommy-bitch, takes SUSANNAH DEAN so that the two of them can give birth to MORDRED DESCHAIN, Roland's half-son and nemesis.

The fates of both the Dark Tower and the Dark Tower series depend upon what our tet can accomplish in this year. If they can save Stephen King and destroy Mordred, both Towers will survive. If they fail, then the multiverse will blink out of existence.

On the following pages, action takes place in the year 1999: V:648, V:695, VI:47–75, VI:66, VI:67, VI:72, VI:79–98, VI:86, VI:97, VI:119–25, VI:210, VI:219–34, VI:224, VI:256–61, VI:269, VI:307–85, VI:328, VI:333, VII:302, VII:303, VII:304, VII:305, VII:307, VII:405, VII:406, VII:418, VII:476, VII:485

NINETY-NINE (KA-TET OF NINETY-NINE)

Ninety-nine is another mystery number that continues to pop up throughout *Wolves of the Calla*. When he introduces himself to the *folken* of CALLA BRYN STURGIS, JAKE CHAMBERS claims to be of the ka-tet of ninety and nine. ANDY, the Calla's Messenger Robot (many other functions) will not disclose any information about his nasty programming until EDDIE DEAN recites his password, which is 1999. On the fence surrounding NEW YORK's VACANT LOT, our TODASH ka-tet sees a poem which reads, "Oh SUSANNAH-MIO, divided girl of mine, Done parked her RIG in the DIXIE PIG, in the year of '99."

Ninety-nine's true significance lies in that it is the ka of Roland's world, and of END-WORLD. It is also one-half of 1999, the KEYSTONE YEAR in the KEYSTONE WORLD, where the life of our ka-tet's facilitator—STEPHEN KING—is in grave danger. It is also the year that Roland's nemesis MORDRED DESCHAIN is born.

V:215, V:565, V:567, V:570, V:643, V:648, V:654, V:677, V:695, VI:73, VI:289, VII:302 *(ka of Mid-World)*, VII:303, VII:473, VII:485

NIS

See GODS OF MID-WORLD

NORT

See TULL CHARACTERS; *see also* CALLAHAN, FATHER DONALD FRANK: CALLAHAN AND THE HITLER BROTHERS

NORTH CENTRAL POSITRONICS

Like MILLS CONSTRUCTION AND SOMBRA REAL ESTATE and LAMERK INDUSTRIES, North Central Positronics is part of the SOMBRA GROUP—a cluster of companies which serve the CRIMSON KING. In the days of the GREAT OLD ONES, the brilliant (if mad) North Central Positronics technicians designed ANDY the Messenger Robot, BLAINE the Insane Mono, and SHARDIK, the rampaging BEAR GUARDIAN that SUSANNAH DEAN had to destroy in *The Waste Lands*. The brainy Positronics folks probably also designed the MIND-TRAP, which almost kills JAKE under the DIXIE PIG.

Although North Central Positronics was founded by the Old Ones on Roland's level of the TOWER, this company seems to exist in the MULTIPLE AMERICAS as well. The TASSENBAUMS have a North Central Positronics magnet on their refrigerator, and DINKY EARNSHAW, one of the DEVAR-TOI's BREAKERS, originally worked for a Positronics subsidiary that hired psychic assassins. North Central Positronics (in conjunction with Sombra) are also in the process of taking over the PLAZA-PARK HYATT, where SUSANNAH-MIO stays during her brief trip to 1999 NEW YORK.

No matter how beneficent the original NCP intended to be (after all, it seems likely that they were hired to redesign the Tower, BEAMS, and GUARDIANS), under the directorship of the CAN-TOI RICHARD P. SAYRE, it serves the purposes of the Outer Dark. Like the other subsidiaries of Sombra, they hope to destroy the ROSE and bring down the Dark Tower. Hence, it is little wonder that when EDDIE DEAN and Roland Deschain discuss the founding of the TET CORPORATION with JOHN CULLUM, they state that Tet must have three primary functions: save the Rose, protect STEPHEN KING, and sabotage both Sombra and North Central Positronics whenever possible. The future of all the worlds depends upon the destruction of this dangerous conglomerate.

V:5, V:72, V:132, V:564, V:702, VI:11, VI:72, VI:91–92, VI:109, VI:219, VI:235, VI:237, VI:238, VI:248, VI:269, VI:270, VI:336, VI:348, VI:377, VI:381, VII:37, VII:75, VII:87–88, VII:125, VII:126, VII:343 *(not directly mentioned, but they probably made the booby-trapped robots)*, VII:470 *(and Tassenbaums)*, VII:471, VII:498, VII:517, VII:664–65

ANDY: Andy is CALLA BRYN STURGIS's seven-foot-tall Messenger Robot. To EDDIE DEAN, he looks like C3PO from the film *Star Wars*. However, unlike C3PO, Andy's skinny legs and arms are made from a silvery material and his head is stainless steel. (Only his body is gold.) His eyes are described as electric-blue.

Like SHARDIK, the marauding man-made BEAR GUARDIAN, Andy bears the North Central Positronics stamp. Located on his chest, it reads as follows:

NORTH CENTRAL POSITRONICS, LTD.
IN ASSOCIATION WITH LaMERK INDUSTRIES
PRESENTS
ANDY
Design: MESSENGER (Many Other Functions)
Serial # DNF 34821 V 63

Although he is the last robot for wheels around, Andy never leaves the Calla. He wanders here and there, spreading gossip, singing songs, and telling horoscopes. (Despite his amazing strength, he rarely helps with any manual task more strenuous than cookery.) On the whole, the Calla *folken* consider Andy a nuisance; however, he does serve one important function. Each generation, he accurately predicts the coming of the WOLVES. No one has ever been able to find out how Andy knows this, since whenever they question him about it, he responds that he cannot answer unless they know the appropriate password. The reason? Directive NINETEEN.

In actuality, Andy works for the minions of the CRIMSON KING in THUNDERCLAP. Each generation, he finds a vulnerable adult who has parented only a single set of twins. Andy then infects one of the children with a deadly disease. (In the case of BENNY SLIGHTMAN's twin sister, the disease was hot-lung.) Once the parent has only one child left, Andy begins his emotional blackmail. If the parent acts as a spy for the Wolves, then his or her remaining child will be kept safe. Until the arrival of Roland and his ka-tet, Andy's ploy worked incredibly well. The people of the Callas felt powerless against the Greencloaks, since the child-snatchers seemed to predict their every act of resistance.

In the final book of the Dark Tower series, we learn that robots like Andy are called ASIMOV ROBOTS. Logic faults are quite common in such intelligent mechanical beings. However, whatever happened to make Andy such a traitorous monster seems to have less to do with logic faults and more to do with plain old meanness. V:1–2, V:3–8, V:10, V:15, V:18, V:25, V:29, V:31, V:129, V:131, V:132–33, V:134, V:137–42, V:144, V:150, V:151, V:154, V:155, V:161 *(indirect)*, V:168, V:207–8, V:211–34 *(present; mentioned directly on 218, 220)*, V:293, V:318, V:321–24 *(present with Jake and Benny)*, V:328, V:331, V:332, V:337, V:339, V:340, V:350–51, V:356, V:362, V:381, V:384–86, V:391, V:412, V:415, V:484, V:485, V:487, V:488, V:489–92, V:494–95, V:501, V:554, V:558, V:561, V:567–77, V:578, V:581, V:585, V:586–89, V:590, V:601–17 *(present; mentioned directly on 602, 603, 608, 610, 611)*, V:629, V:630–35, V:641, V:644–50, V:652, V:655 *(pard)*, V:656, V:658, V:659, V:660, V:678, V:702, V:704, VI:9, VI:67, VI:252, VII:65, VII:73, VII:146 *(indirect)*, VII:156 *(indirect)*, VII:157, VII:191, VII:708, VII:710, VII:722

ASIMOV ROBOTS: Intelligent robots created by North Central Positronics. They are prone to logic faults. In a working robot, such faults tend to be quarantined, like e-mail viruses that arrive on a computer protected by an antivirus program. However, as we see in the case of NIGEL, this quarantining process doesn't always seem to work, especially in instances where a robot's less stable emotional programming is involved. VII:156

BLAINE: Blaine the Insane Mono was the mad computer brain that controlled the city of LUD. As the ghost in the machines, he (with some help from the GRAYS) operated the god-drums which made the PUBES sacrifice each other. (For more information about the ghost in the machine, see *Stephen King's The Dark Tower: A Concordance, Volume I.*)

At the end of *The Waste Lands,* Blaine (animating his sleek, pink train body) agreed to take our tet to TOPEKA as long as they would take part in a riddling contest with him. If they won, they would reach their destination safely. If not, Blaine stated he would kill them, and himself, by crashing. Luckily, EDDIE DEAN fried Blaine's circuits with the Eddie Dean specialty—bad jokes. V:35, V:38, V:55, V:58, V:106, V:125, V:139, V:164 *(mono)*, V:220, V:258 *(indirect)*, V:291, V:478, V:508, V:565, V:567, V:572, V:573, V:639, VI:109, VI:117, VI:138, VI:244, VI:266, VI:269, VI:287, VI:358, VI:359, VI:404, VI:406, VII:19, VII:44, VII:160, VII:201, VII:407, VII:536, VII:645, VII:698, VII:808, VII:811

DELICIOUS RAIN: Delicious Rain and the other D-line trains run south from the DEVAR-TOI to the poisoned DISCORDIA. VII:411

DEVAR-TOI ROBOTS (UNNAMED):

   SIX-ARMED ROBOT: This robot has six pincerlike arms, which he waves about as he tours the DEVAR-TOI. VII:343, VII:351–52

DOBBIE: Dobbie is a type of domestic robot known as a house elf. She does much of TAMMY KELLY's work in the Devar-Toi Master's house. VII:354

FEDIC ROBOTS AND UNNAMED FEDIC DOGAN ROBOTS:

   CLASS A CONDUCTOR ROBOT (FEDIC STATION): VII:201

   DEAD ROBOT: VI:235

   HUCKSTER ROBOT: This robot travels up and down FEDIC's main street advertising humie and cybie girls, even though all of the potential johns are dead. Although we don't see the North Central Positronics stamp on this electronic pimp's body, we can be fairly certain that he was made by them. VI:235, VI:244, VII:536

   HUNTER-KILLER ROBOTS IN DOGAN: VII:159–60

   MAINTENANCE DRONE: DINKY EARNSHAW places this fried maintenance drone near the FEDIC/THUNDERCLAP STATION door to disguise our ka-tet's entrance into END-WORLD. VII:203, VII:222

   PLAYER PIANO: VI:235

   ROBOT THAT LOOKS LIKE ANDY: This robot is rusting in front of the FEDIC CAFÉ. VI:252

   STEEL BALL ON LEGS: SUSANNAH DEAN spots this mechanical foreman while the ASIMOV ROBOT NIGEL carries her through the FEDIC DOGAN. The foreman fried his boards eight hundred years earlier and all he can manage to say when they pass is, "Howp! Howp!" VII:75

FIRE-RESPONSE TEAM BRAVO: Although they are officially the DEVAR-TOI's mechanical firemen, Fire-Response Team Bravo are actually better at running people over with their fire engines than they are at putting out fires. VII:363, VII:369, VII:371–73, VII:389, VII:393

NIGEL THE BUTLER (CHUMLEY): When MORDRED DESCHAIN is due to be born in the FEDIC DOGAN, Nigel the Butler (DNK4932 DOMESTIC) arrives in the EXTRACTION ROOM bearing an incubator. However, as soon as he sees Mordred turn into a spider and devour his birth mother, Nigel realizes that such precautions probably aren't necessary. During the fray which follows Mordred's birth, SUSANNAH DEAN shoots out Nigel's eyes (an aggressive but understandable act, since Nigel closely resembles ANDY, CALLA BRYN STURGIS's treacherous Messenger Robot). Although both Nigel and Andy are ASIMOV ROBOTS, Nigel has a much more sensitive nature. Whereas Andy seems to take a vengeful pleasure in betraying the people of the Callas, Nigel seems positively pleased to help feed and house our tet once they are reunited in the Fedic Dogan. In fact, he finds feeding small animals to Spider-Mordred so distressing that his circuits blow. VII:65–80, VII:111, VII:145–46 *(sleeping until next entry),*

VII:148–49, VII:150–59 *(Asimov Robots)*, VII:160, VII:161, VII:162, VII:163–64, VII:166–67, VII:169 *(indirect)*, VII:171, VII:172 *(indirect)*, VII:176, VII:189, VII:250, VII:541, VII:707

PATRICIA: Sister to BLAINE the Insane Mono. Although back in *The Waste Lands* our tet saw the remains of her bright blue train body jutting out of the RIVER SEND near the city of LUD, in the distant past Patricia also embarked from the town of FEDIC in END-WORLD. VI:237, VI:244, VI:269, VII:89

PHIL: When TED BRAUTIGAN first arrived at the DEVAR-TOI, Phil was his robot driver. His favorite saying was, "My name's Phil, I'm over the hill, but the best news is I never spill." Not long after Ted met him, Phil ended up on the garbage dump. VII:289–90

SHARDIK: *See* GUARDIANS OF THE BEAM, *listed separately*

SPIRIT OF THE SNOW COUNTRY: Along with DELICIOUS RAIN, Spirit of the Snow Country is one of the D-line trains that runs from the DEVAR-TOI to the DISCORDIA. VII:411

SPIRIT OF TOPEKA: The Spirit of Topeka is the atomic engine (also called a hot-enge) which runs from the DEVAR-TOI to FEDIC. Like BLAINE, it doesn't require a human driver. VII:531, VII:536–37

STUTTERING BILL: Stuttering Bill (whose official name is William, D-746541-M, Maintenance Robot, Many Other Functions) is the kind-hearted robot that SUSANNAH and Roland meet after their terrible ordeal with DANDELO. Like the other ASIMOV ROBOTS we've met, Bill has rudimentary emotions. Hence, he is extremely happy to find out that our dwindling tet has freed PATRICK DANVILLE from his prison in Dandelo's basement. Stuttering Bill gives Roland, Susannah, and Patrick HO FAT II and HO FAT III to speed them along on their journey to the DARK TOWER. Roland fixes Bill's stutter using the power of suggestion. (It works, even though he doesn't have access to Bill's fix-it manual.) VII:661–62, VII:663, VII:664, VII:665, VII:670, VII:679, VII:705–10, VII:715–22, VII:753 *(indirect)*, VII:774 *(indirect)*, VII:801, VII:803

TURNIP-HEADED ROBOT: JAKE comes across this rundown robot in the passage between the DIXIE PIG and the FEDIC/NEW YORK doorway. Once he was a guard. Now all he can do is flash his eyes and croak. VII:89

NORTH STAR

See GODS OF MID-WORLD: OLD STAR

NORTON, SUSAN

See CALLAHAN, FATHER DONALD FRANK: 'SALEM'S LOT CHARACTERS

O

ODETTA
See DEAN, SUSANNAH: SUSANNAH'S OTHER SELVES

O'DIM, WALTER
See WALTER

OFFICER BOSCONI
See DEAN, EDDIE: EDDIE'S PAST ASSOCIATES

OLD FARTS OF THE APOCALPYSE
See TET CORPORATION: FOUNDING FATHERS

OLD FATTY
See TOWER, CALVIN

OLD FELLA
See CALLAHAN, FATHER DONALD FRANK

OLD MOTHER (SOUTH STAR, LYDIA)
See GODS OF MID-WORLD

OLD ONES (GREAT OLD ONES, THE MAKERS, OLD PEOPLE)
The Old Ones were the ancient rulers of Mid-World. (See *Stephen King's The Dark Tower: A Concordance, Volume I.*) The company they founded (namely NORTH CENTRAL POSITRONICS) was responsible for the creation of BLAINE the Insane Mono, ANDY the Messenger Robot, and SHARDIK, the cyborg BEAR GUARDIAN. The Great Old Ones desired to replace the magical DARK TOWER and the BEAMS with technological replicas, and it was their wars, weapons, and pollutants which created MID-WORLD's many MUTANTS.

The Old People may have been technological wizards, but in the long run, little good came from their experiments with the time/space continuum. They may have created DOORWAYS BETWEEN WORLDS, but they also built the DOGANS, the sinister equipment found in the DEVAR-TOI, and the diseases (such as the Red Death) which destroyed the people of FEDIC. Unfortunately, the Great Old Ones could well be our own descendants. As Roland so wryly notes when he visits NEW YORK, 1999, that city looks like a young and vibrant LUD. Occasionally, the term *Old Ones* is used for the ancient vampires known as the GRANDFATHERS.

V:100, V:108 *(Old People of the forest, not Great Old Ones)*, V:141, V:144, V:151, V:210, V:339, V:340, V:565, VI:252, VII:25, VII:77 *(indirect)*, VII:92, VII:100, VII:107, VII:108, VII:132, VII:152, VII:156, VII:238, VII:239, VII:537, VII:538, VII:566 *(mad)*, VII:721, VII:825

OLD PEOPLE
See OLD ONES

OLD STAR (NORTH STAR, APON)
See GODS OF MID-WORLD

OPOPANAX
See APPENDIX I

ORACLE OF THE MOUNTAINS
See DEMON ELEMENTALS

ORIZA, LADY (LADY OF THE PLATE, LADY RICE)
In some parts of MID-WORLD, Lady Oriza is considered a mythical heroine. However, in the BORDERLANDS, she is the pagan goddess of the rice. According to local folklore, Oriza gave birth to the first man, and from this man's breath came the first woman. To honor Oriza's part in the creation of the human race, the old folks of the Calla still say, *"Can-ah, can-tah, annah Oriza,"* which translates as, "All breath comes from the woman."

According to another old tale, Lady Oriza's father, LORD GRENFALL, was murdered by the infamous harrier GRAY DICK, and the beautiful Lady Oriza swore to take bloody vengeance. Cloaking her true motives in veils of seduction, she proposed that she and Dick share a conciliatory feast at WAYDON, her family castle. To prove her good intentions, she stated that they should each leave their weapons—and their clothes—at the door.

Not surprisingly, Dick accepted the offer. During the second toast, both Dicks stood at attention. "May your beauty ever increase," he said. To which Oriza replied, "May your first day in Hell last ten thousand years, and may it be the shortest." Then, flinging her specially sharpened dinner plate at him, she sliced off his head.

A female society called the SISTERS OF ORIZA was formed in honor of Lady Oriza's triumph. Although they may originally have been a sisterhood of warriors or priestesses, by the time our story begins, they are essentially a ladies' auxiliary that practices throwing their deadly, sharpened plates. Interestingly, their plates (known as Orizas) closely resemble DETTA WALKER's *forspecial* plate. However, the fine blue webbing which decorates the Orizas is in the form of the young oriza, or seedling rice plant. Two of the rice stalks cross at the edge of the plate, forming the great letter *ZN*, which means both "here" and "now." This segment of the rim is dull and slightly thicker so that the plate can be gripped without danger. The titanium Orizas are manufactured by the women of CALLA SEN CHRE and have a whistle underneath them so that they hum as they fly.

Like that of many gods and goddesses, Lady Oriza's vengeful nature surfaces frequently. Both she and her sister wished to marry LORD SEMINON, the god of the prewinter windstorms. However, Seminon preferred Oriza's sister and married her. Enraged that her love was rejected—and that a marriage between wind and rice would never take place—Oriza often blocks Seminon's passage over the RIVER WHYE. This pleases the people of the Calla since it protects them from Seminon's blasts.

V:313, V:321, V:325–27, V:329, V:330, V:331–37 *(throwing plate)*, V:338 *(plate)*, V:360 *(by 'Riza)*, V:361 *(reap charm)*, V:398, V:467, V:491 *('Riza)*, V:492, V:495, V:500, V:572 *('Riza)*, V:576, V:582 *(indirect)*, V:604, V:631, V:642–43, V:644 *(plate)*, V:662 *(plate)*, V:663, V:680, V:685, V:686, V:689, VI:68 *(plates)*, VI:92, VI:95, VI:97, VI:333 *(plates)*, VI:335 *(plates)*, VII:10 *(plates)*, VII:25 *(plates)*, VII:35 *(plates)*, VII:82 *(plates)*, VII:85 *(plates)*, VII:87 *(plates)*, VII:89 *(plates)*, VII:111 *(plates)*, VII:173 *(plates)*, VII:255 *(plates)*, VII:352 *(plates)*, VII:491 *(plates)*, VII:535 *(plates)*, VII:557 *(plates)*, VII:558 *(plates)*, VII:567 *(plates)*, VII:634 *(plates)*, VII:708–9 *(plates)*, VII:726 *(indirect)*

GRAY DICK: Gray Dick was an infamous harrier who killed LADY ORIZA's father, LORD GRENFALL. Oriza's revenge was both clever and seductive. Inviting her enemy to a meal at WAYDON, her family castle, she proposed that the two of them eat naked, to prove that they were each weaponless. Nevertheless, Oriza managed to decapitate Dick with one of her specially sharpened plates. V:325–27, V:332, V:398

GRENFALL, LORD: Lord Grenfall was Lady Oriza's father. Once he was known as the "wiliest lord in all the RIVER BARONIES," but when Oriza was still a young woman he was murdered by the infamous harrier GRAY DICK. Oriza decapitated her father's murderer. V:325, V:326, V:327 *(father)*

MARIAN: Marian was Lady Oriza's maid. After she left Oriza's service, she went on to have many of her own adventures. Unfortunately, we never hear about any of them. V:326

ORIZA'S SISTER: Lady Oriza and her sister both sought the love of LORD SEMINON, the BORDERLANDS' wind god, but Seminon preferred Oriza's sister and married her. Lady Oriza has never forgiven him. V:642–43

SEMINON, LORD: Lord Seminon is the personification of the prewinter winds that sweep across the RIVER WHYE and into CALLA BRYN STURGIS. According to one old story, Lord Seminon rejected Lady Oriza's love so that he could marry her sister. Out of spite, Oriza frequently refuses to let the harsh Seminon winds cross into the Callas. V:642–43

ORIZA, SISTERS OF (SISTERS OF THE PLATE)

The Sisters of Oriza, also known as the Sisters of the Plate, honor the goddess ORIZA's triumph over her enemy, the harrier GRAY DICK. Although in many ways the Sisters function as a ladies' auxiliary, they also practice throwing their deadly sharpened plates, known as Orizas. Seventy years before our story takes place, one of the Sisters—MOLLY DOOLIN—destroyed one of the Calla's child-stealing WOLVES. Unfortunately, she paid for the victory with her life.

The Sisters of Oriza are, by far, the fiercest fighters in the Calla. Three of them, MARGARET EISENHART, ZALIA JAFFORDS, and ROSALITA MUNOZ, stand with Roland's ka-tet against the final Wolf invasion. During that attack, Margaret Eisenhart is killed.

Like the mythical lady they are named for, the Sisters of Oriza are a multi-talented group of women. Not only are they the best fighters and cooks in the CRESCENT, but they also serve as the area's doctors and midwives.

V:331, V:338–39, V:358, V:489, V:493–94, V:496–500 *(competition)*, V:509 *(Ladies of)*, V:575, V:601–17 *(present; mentioned directly on 602, 607, 609, 611)*, V:630, V:641, V:642, V:662–68 *(present)*, V:674, V:679–97, VI:10

ADAMS, SAREY: Fat, jolly Sarey Adams is the wife of the rancher DIEGO ADAMS. Although surprisingly light on her feet, Sarey's aim is not as accurate as that of the other Sisters. Hence, Roland thinks it is too risky to place her on the front line of the EAST ROAD battle against the invading WOLVES. Instead, he asks this Sister of Oriza to lead the CHILD-MINDERS, who hide the Calla's children in the rice paddies near the DEVAR-TETE WHYE. V:338, V:341, V:399, V:419, V:421, V:483, V:493–94, V:496–500, V:575, V:658, V:662–67 *(present)*, V:677, V:689 *(folken)*, V:693–97 *(folken)*

DOOLIN, MOLLY (RED MOLLY): Molly Doolin was the wife of EAMON DOOLIN and was the only woman to stand with GRAN-PERE JAF-FORDS's WOLF POSSE against the GREENCLOAKS. Although Molly was seventy years dead by the time our ka-tet entered CALLA BRYN STURGIS, Gran-pere's memory of her flinging her plate at an oncoming Wolf—and destroying it—still burns bright. Molly died during her stand on the EAST ROAD, but what she managed to do with her Oriza inspired Roland to draft the Sisters of the Plate to join him in his own stand against those menacing, robotic horse-riders.

In life, Molly Doolin's fiery personality (not her blazing red hair) earned her the nickname Red Molly. She wore a silver reap charm around her neck which was shaped like Lady Oriza raising her fist in defiance. When Molly flung her Wolf-destroying plate, she shouted the name of her twin, MIN-NIE, whom the Wolves had taken to THUNDERCLAP during their previous raid and had returned ROONT. V:358–63, V:365, V:390, V:485, V:611, V:665, V:679

EISENHART, MARGARET (MARGARET OF THE REDPATH CLAN): Margaret Eisenhart was born Margaret of the REDPATH clan. Although her family was MANNI, she left the fold to marry VAUGHN EISENHART. According to her father (or grandfather) HENCHICK, she is destined for NA'AR because of it. Margaret is one of the three Sisters of Oriza that fight with Roland during the battle of the EAST ROAD. Sadly, she is decapitated by one of the WOLVES' light-sticks. We never find out whether she ends up in Na'ar. V:318 *(indirect)*, V:320 *(indirect)*, V:322–25, V:328–42 *(of Redpath clan)*, V:389, V:398, V:399, V:407–8, V:483, V:491, V:493–94, V:496–500, V:601–17 *(present; directly mentioned on 602, 607, 609)*, V:654, V:662–68, V:674 *(indirect)*, V:679–82 *(killed on 682)*, V:689, V:691–94, V:700, VI:3, VI:28, VI:73, VI:80, VI:205, VII:83

JAFFORDS, ZALIA (ZALLIE): Zalia Jaffords is the dark-skinned wife of TIAN JAFFORDS. The two of them have five children—two sets of twins and a singleton. Zalia's maiden name was HOONIK. Like the other people of the Calla, she lost a twin, ZALMAN, to the horrors of THUNDERCLAP. Though he was bright as polished agate when he was small, when Zalman returned from the dark lands of the east, he was ROONT.

Just as she stood by her husband in his decision to oppose the WOLVES, Zalia stands with Roland and his ka-tet during the Calla's final battle. Unlike her friend MARGARET EISENHART, Zallie survives. V:8–13, V:15, V:25, V:27, V:28, V:44 *(following ka-tet)*, V:45 *(following ka-tet)*, V:47 *(following ka-tet)*, V:88 *(new friends)*, V:92 *(indirect)*, V:106 *(indirect)*, V:109, V:111–13, V:116, V:122–37, V:142–60, V:162, V:201–10 *(present; mentioned directly on 207, 208)*, V:211–34 *(present; mentioned directly on 216, 218, 224)*, V:236–37, V:338, V:343–46, V:347 *(indirect)*, V:348 *(indirect)*, V:350, V:351–57, V:358, V:376–77, V:379, V:397–99, V:401, V:483, V:485, V:488–92 *(present)*, V:493–94, V:496–500, V:601–17, V:654, V:662–68, V:674 *(indirect)*, V:679–97, VI:205, VI:373

MUNOZ, ROSALITA (ROSITA, ROSA): Rosalita Munoz is PERE CALLA-HAN's housekeeper and (as EDDIE DEAN surmises) his executive secretary. Although Rosalita is a converted Catholic, this doesn't stop her from having an affair with Roland. Although she herself is childless, Rosalita's hatred of the WOLVES is ferocious, and she is one of the first people in the Calla to openly support Roland's ka-tet in their plan to resist these invaders from THUNDERCLAP. Not surprisingly, Rosalita is also one of the female warriors Roland chooses to be on the front line during the EAST ROAD battle.

Like many of the other Sisters, Rosalita is a healer as well as a fighter. Her cat-oil eases the pain of Roland's dry twist. She is also an accomplished midwife. V:236, V:242–44, V:245, V:250, V:251, V:252, V:281, V:293–94, V:310–12 *(present)*, V:320, V:331, V:338, V:341, V:399, V:417, V:418–19, V:420–21, V:438, V:442–51 *(present)*, V:467, V:475, V:476, V:477, V:480–83, V:484, V:493–94, V:496–500, V:584, V:589, V:601–17 *(present with Sisters of Oriza; mentioned on 602, 604, 609, 615)*, V:628, V:639, V:640–41, V:644, V:646–50, V:652, V:653, V:654, V:662–68, V:674 *(indirect)*, V:679–96, VI:4, VI:8, VI:9–10, VI:13–18, VI:24, VI:205, VI:281, VII:122, VII:152

OUTER DARK
See APPENDIX I

OUTWORLDERS
In *Wolves of the Calla*, outworlders are people who come from the lands west

of the BORDERLANDS. Roland, EDDIE, SUSANNAH, JAKE, and OY are all considered outworlders.
V:312, V:344, V:402, V:418

OVER, THE
See MANNI

OVERHOLSER, ALAN
See CALLA BRYN STURGIS CHARACTERS: FARMERS (LARGE FARMS): OVERHOLSER, WAYNE DALE

OVERHOLSER, WAYNE
See CALLA BRYN STURGIS CHARACTERS: FARMERS (LARGE FARMS)

OVERHOLSER, WELLAND
See CALLA BRYN STURGIS CHARACTERS: ROONTS

OVERMEYER, PROFESSOR
See DEAN, SUSANNAH: ODETTA HOLMES'S ASSOCIATES

OXFORD TOWN COPS
See DEAN, SUSANNAH: ODETTA HOLMES AND THE CIVIL RIGHTS MOVEMENT: ODETTA'S "MOVEMENT" ASSOCIATES

OY
Oy of Mid-World is JAKE CHAMBERS's pet billy-bumbler, but he is also a full-fledged member of Roland's ka-tet. (See *Stephen King's The Dark Tower: A Concordance, Volume I.*) Like all other bumblers, Oy looks like a cross between a raccoon, a woodchuck, and a dachshund. He has expressive, gold-ringed eyes and a little squiggle of a tail. Although he is not human, Oy is extremely intelligent. He can count, add, and even speak. Just as some kinds of terriers are bred to be ratters, in the days of old, billy-bumblers (also called THROCKENS) were kept to destroy GRANDFATHER FLEAS. Hence, by their very nature they serve the WHITE.

In the first four books of the Dark Tower series, we learned just how devoted Oy is to Jake. However, in the final book of the series, we discover that his allegiance is also to Roland and his quest. After Jake dies saving the writer STEPHEN KING, brave little Oy remains with Roland rather than lying down and expiring upon his master's grave. In fact, Oy makes it closer to the DARK TOWER than any other member of Roland's ka-tet.

Sadly, as was predicted back in *Wizard and Glass,* Oy dies impaled upon the branch of a tree. He is thrown there by MORDRED when he tries to foil the spider-boy's attempt to kill Roland.

V:8 *(strangers from Out-World)*, V:29–31 *(gunslingers)*, V:35, V:36, V:38–47,

V:48–70, V:77, V:78, V:80, V:81, V:87, V:88–119, V:125–37, V:138, V:139, V:142–60, V:176–86, V:189–91, V:193–98, V:201–34, V:238, V:318–24, V:381, V:383, V:384–87, V:400, V:402–5, V:417, V:418–19, V:444 *(sleeping)*, V:467, V:470, V:488, V:490–96, V:553–80, V:581–90 *(present)*, V:591 *(indirect)*, V:601–17, V:636–38, V:652, V:685, VI:3–8, VI:11–43, VI:68, VI:143, VI:216, VI:307–44, VI:402, VII:5–11, VII:14, VII:26–27, VII:28, VII:81–104 *(100 changes places with Jake!)*, VII:109–12, VII:141–59, VII:164–65, VII:168 *(circle)*, VII:169, VII:177, VII:186 *(ka-tet)*, VII:187, VII:188, VII:189–220, VII:247–61, VII:265–73, VII:276 *(indirect)*, VII:279–324 *(297–302 listening to Ted's story)*, VII:329–35, VII:337–42, VII:349 *(indirect)*, VII:352, VII:362–63, VII:369–70, VII:382–85, VII:387–418 *(sitting with Jake during Jake's long flashback)*, VII:421–33, VII:441–43, VII:444–45, VII:449–67, VII:472–90, VII:510, VII:513, VII:520–30, VII:532–42, VII:549–619, VII:620, VII:625–31, VII:632–44, VII:647–710, VII:716–24, VII:725, VII:737, VII:742–50, VII:752–53, VII:754 *(the mutt)*, VII:756–65, VII:768–75 *(killed)*, VII:780, VII:802, VII:818
TODDLER WHO SEES OY IN TODASH STATE: V:176

OZ THE GREEN KING
See WALTER: WALTER'S ALIASES

P

PADICK, WALTER
See WALTER

PANIC-MAN
When JAKE CHAMBERS enters an abandoned office closet in THUNDERCLAP STATION, he feels the fingers of the Panic-Man stroke his neck. In other words, Jake has claustrophobia.
VII:205

PATEL
See GUTTENBERG, FURTH, AND PATEL

PATRICIA
See NORTH CENTRAL POSITRONICS

PERTH, LORD
See MID-WORLD FOLKLORE

PETACKI, PETE
See CALLAHAN, FATHER DONALD FRANK: CALLAHAN'S HIDDEN HIGHWAYS ASSOCIATES

PETERSON, REVEREND
See MAINE CHARACTERS

PETRIE, MARK
See CALLAHAN, FATHER DONALD FRANK: 'SALEM'S LOT CHARACTERS

PETTIE
See HAMBRY CHARACTERS: TRAVELLERS' REST

PHIL
See NORTH CENTRAL POSITRONICS

PIED PIPER
See MANNI: CANTAB; see also GERMANY: HAMELIN, in OUR WORLD PLACES

PIMSY
See DEAN, SUSANNAH: ODETTA HOLMES'S ASSOCIATES

PINK
See MAERLYN'S RAINBOW: MAERLYN'S GRAPEFRUIT

PINKY PAUPER (PIGGY PECKER)
Pinky Pauper is the main character in a skip-rope rhyme sung by SUSANNAH DEAN while she's playing with the JAFFORDS FAMILY children. In the version that EDDIE DEAN sings, Pinky Pauper becomes Piggy Pecker.
   V:351–52

PIPER SCHOOL CHARACTERS
Piper was the name of JAKE CHAMBERS's private school back in NEW YORK CITY. He hated it. (For more information, see *Stephen King's The Dark Tower: A Concordance, Volume I.*)
   AVERY, BONNIE: Jake's English teacher. V:52, V:381, V:445, V:567, V:636, V:669, V:689
   GENERAL: VII:332 *(Piper kids)*, VII:395
   HANSON, LUCAS: Lucas Hanson was another Piper School student. He tried to trip JAKE whenever Jake walked past him. V:636
   JESSERLING, PETRA: She had a crush on Jake. V:636
   YANKO, MIKE: V:636

PISTOL
See KING, STEPHEN: SMITH, BRYAN

PLATE, LADY OF THE
See ORIZA, LADY

PLATE, SISTERS OF THE
See ORIZA, SISTERS OF

PLAZA-PARK HYATT CHARACTERS (NEW YORK)
The PLAZA-PARK HYATT is the FIRST AVENUE hotel where MIA takes a captive SUSANNAH once they land in 1999 NEW YORK. (Mia needs to find a *telefung* so that she can contact the evil RICHARD P. SAYRE, servant of the CRIMSON KING, who has promised to help her deliver her CHAP.) Since neither Susannah nor Mia has any money, Susannah uses her little CAN-TAH (in the shape of the TURTLE GUARDIAN) to mesmerize MATHIESSEN VAN WYCK into paying for their room.

Susannah stores BLACK THIRTEEN in the room safe, and JAKE and CALLA-HAN (with a little help from the deus ex machina STEPHEN KING) retrieve the ball from the safe so that they can stash it in New York's TWIN TOWERS.

> **DOORMEN:** VI:228, VI:257, VI:321
> **HOTEL MAID:** Like JAKE and CALLAHAN, this tiny, middle-aged Hispanic lady falls under the spell of BLACK THIRTEEN and remains hypnotized even after the evil ball falls back to sleep. A guilty Callahan robs her so that he and Jake have taxi fare. VI:330–32, VI:337
> **JAPANESE TOURISTS:** VI:226–29, VI:231–32
> > **MAN AND WIFE WITH CAMERA:** VI:226–27
> > **MAN WITH CAMERA:** VI:228
> > **SHOPPING WOMEN:** VI:227
> > **TWO WOMEN WITH CAMERA:** VI:228
> > **WOMEN IN RESTROOM:** VI:229, VI:231–32
>
> **PIANO PLAYER:** VI:91, VI:93 *(indirect)*, VI:95, VI:227 *(indirect)*, VI:229
> **PRETTY WOMEN IN LOBBY:** Despite his higher calling, PERE CALLA-HAN enjoys watching these attractive ladies. VI:324
> **RECEPTIONISTS:**
> > **EXOTIC HOTEL RECEPTIONIST:** This beautiful Eurasian woman checks SUSANNAH/MIA into room 1919 (*see* NINETEEN) of the PLAZA-PARK HYATT. Like MATHIESSEN VAN WYCK, she is hypnotized by Susannah's magical CAN-TAH, which looks like a scrimshaw version of the TURTLE GUARDIAN. VI:91–95, VI:109, VI:226, VI:257
> > **JAKE'S RECEPTIONIST (DAD-A-CHUM, DAD-A-CHEE, NOT TO WORRY, YOU'VE GOT THE KEY!):** When JAKE, OY, and CALLA-HAN arrive at the PLAZA-PARK HYATT, this hotel receptionist delivers a letter to them which is addressed to Jake. The letter is from STEPHEN

KING and contains a key to room 1919 (*see* NINETEEN), where Susannah stored MAERLYN's evil magic ball, BLACK THIRTEEN. VI:322–24
OTHER RECEPTIONISTS: VI:226
WOMEN IN SHORT SKIRTS: SUSANNAH DEAN is as shocked to see 1999 hemlines as she is to see women with bra straps and bellies on display. In her *when* of 1964, such dressing would have been considered risqué and may even have landed the exposed ladies in jail. VI:90–91

POLINO, JIMMY
    See HENRY DEAN: HENRY DEAN'S KA-TET

POP MOSE
    See TET CORPORATION: FOUNDING FATHERS: CARVER, MOSES

PORTLAND SUNDAY TELEGRAM
    See MAINE CHARACTERS

POSELLA, FARREN
    See CALLA BRYN STURGIS CHARACTERS: OTHER CHARACTERS

POSITRONICS
    See NORTH CENTRAL POSITRONICS

POST, THE
    See CALLAHAN, FATHER DONALD FRANK: CALLAHAN'S HIDDEN HIGHWAYS ASSOCIATES

POSTINO, TRICKS
    See BALAZAR, ENRICO: BALAZAR'S MEN

POSTMISTRESS, EAST STONEHAM
    See MAINE CHARACTERS

PRENTISS, PIMLI (DEVAR MASTER)
    See WARRIORS OF THE SCARLET EYE: DEVAR-TOI CHARACTERS: HUMANS

PRIM (AM, GADOSH, GREATER DISCORDIA)
In the final book of the Dark Tower series, we learn that MORDRED DESCHAIN, Roland's half-son and nemesis, was born of the joining of two worlds—the Prim and the AM, the GADOSH and GODOSH, GAN and GILEAD. *Prim, gadosh,* and *Gan* all refer to the primordial magical substance (or generating force) from which the multiverse arose. *Am, godosh,* and *Gilead* refer to the physical world, also known as the mortal world.

The people of MID-WORLD believe that, at the beginning of all things, there was only the Prim, or magical soup of creation. From the magical Prim arose Gan, the spirit of the DARK TOWER, whose body is the linchpin of existence. Gan spun the multiverse from his navel and then set it rolling with his finger. This forward movement was time. After the multiverse came into being, the Prim receded, leaving on the shores of existence not only the Tower and BEAMS but the DEMONS, DEMON ELEMENTALS, oracles, and succubi that haunt our world.

Like all magic, the Prim is neither good nor evil but contains the seeds of both. Hence, Gan, the magical creator, sired both the line of ELD (from which the DESCHAINs are descended) and the line of the CRIMSON KING.

According to the MANNI, Mordred Deschain's birth is intrinsically linked to the Prim. Their legends state that when this child, who is simultaneously half-human and half-god, descends into the world, humanity will be destroyed and the Prim will return. However, this particular apocalyptic view takes into consideration only the negative aspect of the Prim (that represented by the Crimson King in his Lord of Discordia guise). Ultimately, Mordred's birth—and early death—plays its part in the restoration of the Tower and the WHITE. Hence the good of the Prim, not its evil, ultimately triumphs.

VI:106, VI:108–14, VI:117, VI:242 *(and creatures of the Prim)*, VI:248, VI:249, VI:251, VII:25, VII:26, VII:35, VII:132, VII:168 *(am, gadosh, godosh)*, VII:176, VII:249, VII:291, VII:303, VII:334, VII:406, VII:447, VII:504, VII:515, VII:755, VII:756 *(return of the Prim)*

PUBES

Like their enemies, the GRAYS, the Pubes played a significant role in *The Waste Lands.* (See *Stephen King's The Dark Tower: A Concordance, Volume I.*) In the city of LUD, the Pubes ritually sacrificed each other whenever they heard the god-drums blasting over the city's many loudspeakers. The Pubes believed that such selective killing would save them from the ghosts in the machines, which, if not placated, would rise up and devour the living. In actuality, they were being manipulated by both the Grays and the city's psychotic computer brain, BLAINE.

V:135, VI:152
FRANK: V:226
LUSTER: V:226
MAUD AND JEEVES: V:226
TOPSY THE SAILOR: V:226, VI:118
WINSTON: V:226

Q

QUEEN O' GREEN DAYS
See MID-WORLD FOLKLORE

QUEEN ROWENA
See ELD, ARTHUR

QUICK, ANDREW
See GRAYS: GRAY HIGH COMMAND: TICK-TOCK

QUICK, DAVID
See GRAYS: GRAY HIGH COMMAND

R

RAF
See GODS OF MID-WORLD

RANDO THOUGHTFUL
See WARRIORS OF THE SCARLET EYE: CASSE ROI RUSSE: HUMANS:
FEEMALO/FIMALO/FUMALO: FIMALO

RANDOLPH, NORTON
See CALLAHAN, FATHER DONALD FRANK: CALLAHAN AND THE
HITLER BROTHERS

RASTOSOVICH, JOSEPH
See BREAKERS

RAT, MR.
See MIA

RAT GUARDIAN
See GUARDIANS OF THE BEAM

RAWLINGS, ROWENA MAGRUDER
See CALLAHAN, FATHER DONALD FRANK: CALLAHAN'S HOME
SHELTER ASSOCIATES: MAGRUDER, ROWAN

RED KING
   See CRIMSON KING

REDPATH CLAN
   See MANNI

REFEREE KING
   See WARRIORS OF THE SCARLET EYE: CASSE ROI RUSSE:
HUMANS: FEEMALO/FIMALO/FUMALO: FIMALO

REGULATORS
In *Wolves of the Calla*, we find out that the term *Regulator* refers to the LOW
MEN, or CAN-TOI, who serve the CRIMSON KING. In *Wizard and Glass*, we
learned that the BIG COFFIN HUNTERS were also sometimes called Regulators. In RICHARD BACHMAN's book entitled *The Regulators*, the Regulators
were a band of killers who were part cowboy and part *Motocops* cartoon characters. Their name came from a 1958 cowboy film about vigilantes on the ram-
page. Whereas STEPHEN KING's Regulators serve the Crimson King,
Bachman's Regulators ultimately serve a demon named Tak. Despite their
formal differences, all Regulators serve the Outer Dark.
   V:290–91

RENT-A-COP
JAKE and PERE CALLAHAN see this police officer when they store BLACK
THIRTEEN in the lockers below the TWIN TOWERS.
   VI:335

REYNOLDS, CLAY
   See BIG COFFIN HUNTERS: JONAS, ELDRED

RHEA OF THE CÖOS
The nasty old witch Rhea of the Cöos was one of Roland's most formidable
enemies during his time in the town of HAMBRY. (See *Stephen King's The Dark
Tower: A Concordance, Volume I.*) Vindictive Rhea was largely responsible for
SUSAN DELGADO's death upon a Charyou Tree bonfire. (She and Susan's
crazy, bewitched AUNT CORDELIA accused Susan of being a traitor to the
town, and to the AFFILIATION. Neither accusation was true.)
   V:40, V:55, V:71, V:411, V:703, VII:179, VII:219, VII:550

RICE, LADY
   See ORIZA, LADY

RING-A-LEVIO (RINGO)
   See DESCHAIN, ROLAND

RIVER CROSSING CHARACTERS

Roland and his ka-tet traveled through the town of RIVER CROSSING (located northwest of LUD) in *The Waste Lands,* the third novel of the Dark Tower series. (See *Stephen King's The Dark Tower: A Concordance, Volume I.*) Although all of River Crossing's inhabitants were extremely old, they were very hospitable. They gave our tet a feast and then warned them about Lud's ongoing civil war, and the dangers they might face there.

V:55, V:78, V:110, V:134, V:192, VI:111, VI:117, VI:182, VII:120

TALITHA, AUNT (TALITHA UNWIN): Aunt Talitha was the ancient matriarch of RIVER CROSSING. (See *Stephen King's The Dark Tower: A Concordance, Volume I.*) In *The Waste Lands,* Talitha (whom Roland calls Old Mother) gave Roland her cross so that he could lay it at the foot of the DARK TOWER. In the final book of the Dark Tower series, Roland does so. V:192, VI:118, VII:50, VII:123, VII:124, VII:518, VII:519, VII:802, VII:820

RODERICK, CHILDREN OF (RODS)

See MUTANTS: CHILDREN OF RODERICK

ROLAND

See DESCHAIN, ROLAND

ROLL CALL

See CALLAHAN, FATHER DONALD FRANK: CALLAHAN'S HIDDEN HIGHWAYS ASSOCIATES

ROMP, THE

See HAMBRY CHARACTERS: TRAVELLERS' REST

RONIN

See WARRIORS OF THE SCARLET EYE

RONK, DAVE VAN

See DEAN, SUSANNAH: ODETTA HOLMES'S ASSOCIATES

ROONT

See CALLA BRYN STURGIS CHARACTERS: ROONTS

ROSALITA

See ORIZA, SISTERS OF: MUNOZ, ROSALITA

ROSARIO, FREDDY

See CALLA BRYN STURGIS CHARACTERS: FARMERS (SMALLHOLD)

ROSE, THE

According to the three STEPHEN KINGs that Roland and SUSANNAH meet at LE CASSE ROI RUSSE, the wild, dusky-pink rose growing in the Vacant LOT in NEW YORK CITY is actually our world's incarnation of the DARK TOWER. In other worlds, the Tower can resemble an IMMORTAL TIGER or an UR-DOG named Rover. Although we don't know whether this uffi speaks truthfully (after all, the three Kings are not one creature at all but three separate servants of LOS, LORD OF DISCORDIA), we do know that the Rose, which JAKE, EDDIE, and Roland see in New York City's Vacant Lot, is almost identical to the beautiful red roses of CAN'-KA NO REY. Like them, it sings a song, which is simultaneously inexpressively lonely and inexpressively lovely, and its sun-yellow center contains faces and voices. However, unlike the healthy rose-song, which Roland hears as he approaches the Tower, threading into the song of our world's Rose is a note of discord.

In *The Dark Tower*, we find out that the roses, which grow in such profusion at the heart of END-WORLD, are a light pink shade on the outside but darken to a fierce red on the inside, a shade which Roland believes is the exact color of heart's desire. Their centers, which are called GAN'S GATEWAYS, burn such a fierce yellow that they are almost too bright to look upon. However, this yellow is the yellow of light and love, not destruction. What Roland comes to realize as he travels through their midst is that the roses feed the BEAMS with their songs and their perfume, and that the Beams, in turn, feed them. Roses and Beams are actually a living force field, a giving and taking, all of which spins out of the Tower. Interestingly enough, the roses (when mixed with Roland's blood) are the exact color of the Crimson King's eyes. Though in the case of the Red King, the red becomes the color of evil and greed, not pure, living energy.

In *Wolves of the Calla* and *Song of Susannah*, Eddie Dean discovers a way to save our world's Rose from the evil machinations of the Crimson King's many destructive companies, collectively known as the SOMBRA GROUP. Under the name of the TET CORPORATION, Eddie and his friends buy the magic lot from CALVIN TOWER, thus saving the Rose from being bulldozed by Sombra. When Roland visits New York 1999, in the final book of the Dark Tower series, he sees that Eddie's idea has worked. The Tet Corporation—founded by JOHN CULLUM, AARON DEEPNEAU, and SUSANNAH DEAN's godfather, MOSES CARVER—has erected a great black building around the Rose and has protected that most important of flowers in a small indoor garden called the GARDEN OF THE BEAM. Roland believes that the people who work in that building live long, happy, and productive lives.

V:51, V:58, V:59, V:97–106 *(how to save)*, V:174, V:177, V:179, V:181 *(begin to feel pull of it)*, V:182–85 *(183 effect described)*, V:187–89 *(effect described)*, V:190, V:191–94 *(Tower and rose)*, V:196, V:197, V:198, V:201 *(red as roses)*, V:249, V:291 *(Topeka roses)*, V:302 *(and lost worlds)*, V:314, V:315, V:317, V:335, V:377, V:389, V:393, V:513, V:528, V:531, V:539, V:555, V:594–95, V:598, V:706, VI:32 *(on knob)*, VI:35, VI:39, VI:40, VI:55–56, VI:73, VI:102, VI:171, VI:257, VI:265, VI:266, VI:267, VI:268, VI:270, VI:296, VI:308, VI:318 *(indirect)*, VI:319 *(still it sings)*, VI:324, VI:398–99 *(delivery to Stephen King)*, VII:121, VII:123, VII:125, VII:127,

VII:143, VII:301, VII:409–10, VII:475, VII:483, VII:488, VII:491–95 *(Garden of the Beam)*, VII:497, VII:499, VII:520, VII:524, VII:535, VII:550 *(roses)*, VII:609, VII:616 *(roses)*, VII:663 *(field)*, VII:666 *(field)*, VII:713 *(field)*, VII:721 *(field)*, VII:756–60 *(first they come across; twin of rose in Vacant Lot)*, VII:795–800 *(a rose from Can'-Ka No Rey used to paint the Red King's eyes)*. For additional rose references, see CAN'-KA NO REY, *in* PORTALS

HIPPIE WITH ACNE: PERE CALLAHAN meets this long-haired young man near the Vacant LOT on FORTY-SIXTH STREET and SECOND AVENUE in 1977 NEW YORK. This hippie-in-a-cowboy-hat believes that the Rose's emanations have cleared up his acne. In 1999, TRUDY DAMASCUS meets the same hippie outside 2 HAMMARSKJÖLD PLAZA. V:594–95, VI:55–56

   DERMATOLOGIST: V:594
   FATHER: V:594
IMMORTAL TIGER: VII:609
UR-DOG ROVER: VII:609

ROSITA
   See ORIZA, SISTERS OF: MUNOZ, ROSALITA

ROSSITER
   See CALLA BRYN STURGIS CHARACTERS: FARMERS (SMALLHOLD): STRONG, GARRETT

ROSTOV, DANEEKA (DANI)
   See BREAKERS

ROUTHIER, RAY
   See KING, STEPHEN

ROWENA, QUEEN
   See ELD, ARTHUR

ROYSTER, ELDON
   See MAINE CHARACTERS

RUBBERBAND AIRLINES
This is IRENE TASSENBAUM's airline of choice when she flies from NEW YORK CITY to MAINE.
   VII:521

RUDEBACHER, DICKY
   See CALLAHAN, FATHER DONALD FRANK: CALLAHAN'S HIDDEN HIGHWAYS ASSOCIATES

RUIZ, STANLEY (SHEEMIE)
  See BREAKERS

RUIZ, STANLEY (THE ELDER)
  See HAMBRY CHARACTERS: TRAVELLERS' REST

RUMBELOW, GRACE
  See BREAKERS

RUSSERT, DON
  See MAINE CHARACTERS

RUSTY SAM
  See MID-WORLD FOLKLORE

RUTA
  See CALLAHAN, FATHER DONALD FRANK: CALLAHAN'S HIDDEN HIGHWAYS ASSOCIATES

S

SACRAMENTO BEE
  See CALLAHAN, FATHER DONALD FRANK: CALLAHAN'S HIDDEN HIGHWAYS ASSOCIATES

SAITA
  See ELD, ARTHUR

'SALEM'S LOT CHARACTERS
  See CALLAHAN, FATHER DONALD FRANK: 'SALEM'S LOT CHARACTERS

SALLOW BRITISH MAN
  See BALAZAR, ENRICO: BALAZAR'S NASSAU CONNECTION

SAM THE MILLER
  See WALTER: WALTER'S ASSOCIATES

SARGUS, JANE
  See MAINE CHARACTERS

SAYRE, RICHARD P.
  See CAN-TOI

SCHWERNER, MICHAEL
See DEAN, SUSANNAH: ODETTA HOLMES AND THE CIVIL RIGHTS MOVEMENT: VOTER REGISTRATION BOYS

SCOWTHER
See WARRIORS OF THE SCARLET EYE: DIXIE PIG CHARACTERS: HUMANS

SCRIMSHAW TURTLE
See GUARDIANS OF THE BEAM: TURTLE

SEEKING FOLK
See MANNI

SEJ
See BREAKERS

SELENA
See GODS OF MID-WORLD

SEMINON, LORD
See ORIZA, LADY

SERGIO
See TOWER, CALVIN

SERVOMECHANISMS (LITTLE GUARDIANS)
See GUARDIANS OF THE BEAM: BEAR

SHARDIK
See GUARDIANS OF THE BEAM: BEAR

SHARPTON, MR.
See BREAKERS: EARNSHAW, DINKY

SHAW, GRETA
See CHAMBERS, JAKE: JAKE'S ASSOCIATES

SHEEMIE
See BREAKERS

SHOE SHINE BOY
See TOWER, CALVIN

SISTER BLUE
See DEAN, SUSANNAH: ODETTA HOLMES'S ASSOCIATES

SISTERS OF ORIZA
See ORIZA, SISTERS OF

SISTERS OF THE PLATE
See ORIZA, SISTERS OF

SKANK, BANGO
Although we never meet Bango Skank, Roland's tet sees his graffiti on the
MILLS CONSTRUCTION AND SOMBRA REAL ESTATE sign which they
find in JAKE's magic LOT in NEW YORK CITY. While having a seizure in a
TOPEKA JAIL CELL, Callahan also comes across Skank's signature, as does
Jake in the tunnels leading from the DIXIE PIG to the MIND-TRAP, which
guards the New York/FEDIC DOORWAY BETWEEN WORLDS. SUSANNAH
comes across Bango's writing when she and MIA visit one of the stalls in the
women's bathrooms located in the PLAZA-PARK HYATT hotel. This last bit
of graffiti reads, "Bango Skank awaits the King."
  V:189, V:447, V:619, VI:233 *(Bango Skank awaits the King)*, VI:256
  (Bango Skank awaits the King), VII:89

SKÖLDPADDA
See GUARDIANS OF THE BEAM: TURTLE

SLEEPY JOHN'S
See CALIFORNIA (STATE OF): SACRAMENTO: SLEEPY JOHN'S, *in*
OUR WORLD PLACES

SLIDELL, POKEY
See CALLA BRYN STURGIS CHARACTERS: WOLF POSSE

SLIGHTMAN, BEN
See CALLA BRYN STURGIS CHARACTERS: RANCHERS: EISENHART,
VAUGHN

SLIGHTMAN, BENNY
See CALLA BRYN STURGIS CHARACTERS: RANCHERS: EISENHART,
VAUGHN

SLIGHTMAN, EDNA
See CALLA BRYN STURGIS CHARACTERS: RANCHERS: EISENHART,
VAUGHN: SLIGHTMAN, BEN (EISENHART'S FOREMAN)

SLOW MUTANTS
See MUTANTS

S'MANA
See GODS OF MID-WORLD

SMITH, BRYAN
See KING, STEPHEN

SNEETCHES
See APPENDIX I

SNUGGLEBUT
See CALLAHAN, FATHER DONALD FRANK: CALLAHAN'S PRESENT
ASSOCIATES

SOBIESKI, MARY JEAN
See DEAN, EDDIE: EDDIE'S PAST ASSOCIATES

SOLDIERS OF THE CRIMSON KING
See WARRIORS OF THE SCARLET EYE

SOMBRA CORPORATION (SOMBRA GROUP)
NORTH CENTRAL POSITRONICS, LAMERK INDUSTRIES, and MILLS
CONSTRUCTION AND SOMBRA REAL ESTATE are all part of the Sombra
Group, a corporate conglomerate which serves the CRIMSON KING. Like its
subsidiary North Central Positronics, Sombra has been a leader in mind-to-mind
communication since the ten thousands. Mills Construction and North Central
Positronics were responsible for building the MIND-TRAP under the DIXIE PIG.
They are also refurbishing the PLAZA-PARK HYATT hotel where SUSANNAH-
MIO stays during her trip to 1999 NEW YORK.
    Incorporated in NASSAU, Sombra is a closed corporation that deals in tech-
nology, real estate, and construction. This dangerous conglomerate is after both
the Vacant LOT and the magical ROSE which grows there. As CALVIN
TOWER realizes when he hesitates selling the Vacant Lot to them, if Sombra
can't appeal to a person's greed, they will resort to terrorizing them. Just as the
servants of the Red King use the WOLVES of END-WORLD to steal the children of the BORDERLANDS, the Red King's men use BALAZAR and his thugs
to intimidate those who stand in their way in our world.
    Not only are Sombra's employees determined to destroy the DARK
TOWER, the lot, and the Rose, but they also bear grudges against those who
hunt down the VAMPIRES who serve the Outer Dark. When the vampire-killer
FATHER CALLAHAN is working at the LIGHTHOUSE SHELTER in
DETROIT, the Sombra Corporation lays a trap for him. Telling Callahan
and his associates that their shelter has been awarded a million dollars, they lure
the unsuspecting men to the TISHMAN BUILDING (982 Michigan Avenue),
so that they can pick up their check. However, rather than receiving the
money, Callahan finds himself in the hands of the evil RICHARD P. SAYRE, the
LOW MAN who is also Sombra's executive vice president. Rather than submitting to the bites of Sayre's AIDS-infected TYPE THREE VAMPIRES, Callahan jumps out the window. He awakes in Mid-World's WAY STATION.

V:68–69, V:95–106 *(and rose)*, V:188 *(Mills Construction and Sombra)*, V:451, V:453–57, V:503, V:522, V:527, V:528, V:539, V:550, VI:91–92, VI:109, VI:202, VI:219, VI:269, VI:336, VI:359, VI:381, VII:37, VII:48, VII:75, VII:125, VII:127, VII:492

SAYRE, RICHARD P.: *See* CAN-TOI, *listed separately*

SKANK, BANGO: *See* SKANK, BANGO, *listed separately*

SOMBRA ESCORT: V:451

SOMBRA SECRETARIES: V:454

SOMBRA SUBSIDIARIES:

> **MILLS CONSTRUCTION AND SOMBRA REAL ESTATE:** *Listed separately*
>
> **NORTH CENTRAL POSITRONICS:** *Listed separately*
>
> **LAMERK INDUSTRIES:** *Listed separately*

SONESH, TASSA OF

See WARRIORS OF THE SCARLET EYE: DEVAR-TOI CHARACTERS: HUMANS

SOO LINES

Once upon a time, the Soo Line trains ran to the DEVAR-TOI. By the time our tet reaches THUNDERCLAP, the line no longer runs. However, one of their boxcars is still stalled on the tracks just southwest of the Devar's fence. Roland, JAKE, and EDDIE hide behind this stalled car (as well as some of the others) while they are waiting to attack the Devar.

VII:340

SOUTH AMERICAN SEABEES

According to FRANK ARMITAGE, one of the humes who recruits BREAK-ERS to work in END-WORLD, back in 1946 a consortium of wealthy South American businessmen hired U.S. engineers, construction workers, and rough-necks to work for them. These workers were known as the South American Seabees. The consortium gave the North Americans four-year contracts. The workers were extremely well paid, but were not allowed to go home during their term of employment. Like the South American Seabees, Armitage explains, the workers that he hires also have to remain in their place of employment until their contracts expire. However, what this servant of the CRIMSON KING neglects to tell TED BRAUTIGAN and the other recruits is that their term of service in the DEVAR-TOI will not expire until the (literal) end of the world.

VII:284

SOUTH STAR

See GODS OF MID-WORLD: OLD MOTHER

SOYCHAK, MR.

See KING, STEPHEN

SPALTER
  See CALLA BRYN STURGIS CHARACTERS: OTHER CHARACTERS

SPEAKING-RING DEMON
  See DEMON ELEMENTALS

SPIDERS, LORD OF THE
  See CRIMSON KING

SPIER, JOHN T.
  See KING, STEPHEN: FAN MAIL/HATE MAIL

SPINELLI, FRANK
  See CALLAHAN, FATHER DONALD FRANK: CALLAHAN'S HOME
SHELTER ASSOCIATES

SPIRIT OF THE SNOW COUNTRY
  See NORTH CENTRAL POSITRONICS

SPIRIT OF TOPEKA
  See NORTH CENTRAL POSITRONICS

STOCKWORTH, RICHARD
  See JOHNS, ALAIN

STONEHAM, MAINE, CHARACTERS
  See MAINE CHARACTERS

STRAKER
  See VAMPIRES: TYPE ONE: BARLOW, KURT

STRAW
  See CAN-TOI

STREET ANGEL
  See CALLAHAN, FATHER DONALD FRANK: CALLAHAN'S HOME
SHELTER ASSOCIATES: MAGRUDER, ROWAN

STRONG, GARRETT
  See CALLA BRYN STURGIS CHARACTERS: FARMERS (SMALLHOLD)

STUFFY-GUYS
  See MID-WORLD FOLKLORE

STUTTERING BILL
  See NORTH CENTRAL POSITRONICS

SULLIVAN, JOHN (SULLY JOHN)
See BREAKERS: BRAUTIGAN, TED

SUSANNAH
See DEAN, SUSANNAH

SUSANNAH-MIO
See DEAN, SUSANNAH; *see also* MIA

SWEDISH AMBASSADOR TO THE UNITED NATIONS
See DEAN, SUSANNAH: SUSANNAH'S PRESENT ASSOCIATES: VAN WYCK, MATHIESSEN

SWORD OF ELD
See ELD, ARTHUR: EXCALIBUR

T

TAHEEN
The taheen servants of the CRIMSON KING have the heads of either beasts or birds but the bodies of men. Although JAKE, CALLAHAN, and SUSANNAH see several of these bizarre creatures while in NEW YORK CITY's DIXIE PIG, most of the taheen work in END-WORLD. (There, at least, they don't have to pass for human.) Unlike the rat-headed CAN-TOI (or low men), the taheen do not hide their beaks and snouts behind humanoid masks, nor do they believe that they are *becoming* human. Consistent with their appearance, the voices of mammal-headed taheen sound like yelps and growls. Although the taheen can speak and reason, their brains must be drastically different from ours, since their thoughts cannot be read by the psychic BREAKERS. (Any psychic trying to prog one of these creatures will only hear white noise.)

According to Roland, the taheen arose from neither the PRIM nor the natural world, but rather from somewhere in between the two. They are sometimes called the third people, though we are never told exactly what this means. Those taheen employed as guards at the DEVAR-TOI tend to man the watchtowers, since they have sharper eyes than either their hume or can-toi comrades.

If you thought the CHILDREN OF RODERICK's taste for snotty tissues was hard to stomach, you'll find taheen delicacies even worse. If you want to form an alliance with one of these creatures, offer him some pus. You'll make a friend for life, since the taheen think that pus is as sweet as candy. Unfortunately, they can't take advantage of the pimples and rashes that plague their human charges in THUNDERCLAP, since the dark land's emanations poison all human body fluids. Taheen don't get such blemishes themselves; however, those who work in the Devar do find that their skin tends to crack and ooze and their noses (or snouts) tend to bleed spontaneously.

V:26 *(indirect)*, V:150, V:660, VII:25, VII:126, VII:129–30, VII:200, VII:201, VII:204, VII:207, VII:209, VII:221, VII:223, VII:224, VII:225, VII:226, VII:229, VII:230, VII:231, VII:235, VII:239, VII:241, VII:244, VII:269, VII:281, VII:289, VII:292–93, VII:300, VII:326, VII:337, VII:352, VII:356–82 *(Devar-Toi battle)*, VII:392, VII:393, VII:394, VII:448, VII:554, VII:808

BEAR-HEADED TAHEEN: A taheen employed at the DEVAR-TOI. VII:381

BEAVER-HEADED TAHEEN: This taheen guards the DEVAR's east watchtower. He's shot by our ka-tet mate SUSANNAH DEAN. VII:350, VII:364

BIRDMEN TAHEEN:

CANARY/CANARYMAN/MEIMAN/TWEETY BIRD/WASEAU-TAHEEN: Meiman (who is called Canary by his friends, Canaryman by SUSANNAH DEAN, and Tweety Bird by JAKE CHAMBERS) has a feathered, dark yellow head, eyes like drops of liquid tar, and talon-hands. He is one of the first true taheen which Susannah Dean (and later Jake Chambers and PERE CALLAHAN) encounters in the DIXIE PIG.

Like the other true taheen, Canary does not wear a humanoid mask, even when he is in CALLA NEW YORK. However, he seems to like human clothing. When we encounter him in the Dixie Pig, Canary is wearing jeans and a plain white shirt, like any ordinary American.

Canary appears to be a fairly high-ranking WARRIOR OF THE SCARLET EYE. However, this does not prevent him from being mesmerized by the magical SCRIMSHAW TURTLE (or CAN-TAH) which Callahan uses to paralyze his enemies at the Pig. Unluckily for Jake and Callahan, Canary and his can-toi friends manage to break out of their paralysis. However, Callahan manages to shoot this nasty bird-man (as well as one of his can-toi accomplices) before turning his gun on himself. VI:366, VII:6–15, VII:26, VII:28, VII:104

JAKLI: This raven-headed taheen works at the DEVAR-TOI and is often in the company of FINLI O'TEGO and the Devar Master, PIMLI PRENTISS. Jakli has residual wings, which he flaps when he is excited or upset. We can assume that he has arms as well (otherwise he'd have a hard time wielding weapons). Like most of his comrades at the Devar, he is killed by our tet. VII:241, VII:352, VII:358–59, VII:362, VII:371–74, VII:379–82

JEY (GEE, HAWK-HEADED MAN): Hawk-headed Jey is one of the WARRIORS OF THE SCARLET EYE who accompanies SUSANNAH DEAN and MIA from the DIXIE PIG to the FEDIC DOGAN, where the two of them are destined to give birth to MORDRED of DISCORDIA. In the chaotic battle which transpires after Mordred's birth (and after the *dan-tete*'s first meal, which happens to be his mother, Mia), Susannah shoots Jey. VI:370–84, VII:22, VII:55–69, VII:71

ROOSTER-HEADED TAHEEN (FOGHORN LEGHORN): This taheen works at the DEVAR-TOI. Roland's tet doesn't kill him, but old Foghorn finds the thought of life outside of his THUNDERCLAP home extremely daunting. VII:392–93, VII:394

CAT ON LEGS (HOUSE-CAT TAHEEN, DISHWASHER NUMBER ONE): JAKE CHAMBERS decapitates this nasty, hissing dishwasher in the kitchens of the DIXIE PIG. VII:82

RAT-HEADED TAHEEN:

ALIA (NURSE): Although Alia has the head of a rat, she does not wear a humanoid mask. Hence, it seems likely that she considers herself taheen rather than CAN-TOI. As servants of the RED KING go, Alia doesn't seem so bad. While MIA groans with labor pains in the EXTRAC-TION ROOM of the FEDIC DOGAN, Alia offers what comfort she can. During the Fedic Dogan battle which takes place after Mordred's birth, Alia is wounded in the knee. She flees the fray and so survives. We never learn what happens to her. VI:378–84, VII:21, VII:22, VII:56–69, VII:75

ANDREW: *See* CAN-TOI

HABER: *See* CAN-TOI

SAYRE, RICHARD P.: *See* CAN-TOI

STRAW: *See* CAN-TOI

TIRANA: *See* CAN-TOI

STOAT-HEADED TAHEEN:

LAMLA OF GALEE: Lamla has the head of a stoat and narrow feet with thornlike nails. He, his hume companion FLAHERTY, and several LOW MEN pursue JAKE through the MIND-TRAP located below the DIXIE PIG. Although he survives Flaherty's murderous temper tantrum (which takes place just after Jake manages to elude their posse by slipping through the NEW YORK/FEDIC DOORWAY), Lamla is brought down by Roland's guns. VII:104–9, VII:111 *(posse),* VII:112, VII:129, VII:133–35, VII:528

WARTHOG TAHEEN:

DIXIE PIG CHEF: JAKE CHAMBERS encounters this imposing creature in the steamy kitchens of the DIXIE PIG. Warthog—dressed in a chef's whites—stands seven feet tall and speaks a dialect which is only margin-ally understandable. After Jake kills his HOUSE-CAT TAHEEN dish-washer, Warthog insists that Jake take up dish-scrubbing. Jake resumes his special art of dish-throwing instead and slices off Warthog's head. VII:81–83, VII:86

WEASEL-HEADED TAHEEN:

FINLI O'TEGO (FINLI OF THE TEGO CLAN, THE WEASEL, THE WEASE): Three-hundred-year-old Finli O'Tego is head of security at the DEVAR-TOI. He stands over seven feet tall, which is damn big, even by taheen standards. PIMLI PRENTISS, the Devar Master, thinks Finli would make a great basketball player. He is probably right, since a taheen like Finli could run up and down a basketball court for hours and not even get winded.

True to his nickname, "the Wease" has the head of a weasel complete with fur, large black eyes, and needle-sharp teeth. Like many of the other taheen at the Devar-Toi, Finli likes to wear lots of gold chains. At some point in the past he even docked his tail, a fashion statement he regrets since the act will probably ultimately land him in the HELL OF DARKNESS.

Although Finli is taheen and the Devar Master is hume, the two are close friends. In fact, when EDDIE DEAN puts a wounded Finli out of his misery by shooting him in the head, the dying Pimli Prentiss shoots Eddie. Our tet-mate dies from the resulting head wound. V:573–76, V:610, V:611, V:660, V:702, VII:200, VII:203, VII:204, VII:205, VII:207, VII:212, VII:215, VII:220–27, VII:230–45, VII:261, VII:272, VII:292, VII:297, VII:298–99, VII:300, VII:325, VII:341, VII:343–48, VII:358–59, VII:361–62, VII:371–74, VII:377, VII:380–82, VII:383–84, VII:385

OTHER TAHEEN (NOT DESCRIBED):
GASKIE O'TEGO: Gaskie is the DEVAR-TOI's deputy security chief—second only to FINLI O'TEGO. Since the two of them share the same clan name, it seems likely that they are related. During the Devar's final battle, Gaskie is shot by SUSANNAH DEAN. VII:300, VII:356–57, VII:362, VII:371–74
HUMMA O'TEGO: Humma was the Devar-Toi Master who sentenced the CAN-TOI rapist CAMERON to death. Humma lost his job (and possibly his life) after TED BRAUTIGAN escaped the BREAKER prison. VII:286, VII:297, VII:326, VII:343

TALITHA UNWIN
See RIVER CROSSING CHARACTERS

TASSA
See WARRIORS OF THE SCARLET EYE: DEVAR-TOI CHARACTERS: HUMANS

TASSENBAUM, DAVID SEYMOUR
David Tassenbaum is married to IRENE TASSENBAUM. According to his wife, David and his egghead friends created the Internet. Since Tassenbaum is associated with NORTH CENTRAL POSITRONICS (at least we see a Positronics magnet on his refrigerator), we can assume that the "information highway" is an incredibly sinister cultural force. (Hence, be wary of your keyboard.) Both David and Irene are staunch Republicans.
VII:423, VII:425 *(indirect)*, VII:429 *(indirect)*, VII:431, VII:435, VII:469, VII:470–71 *(North Central Positronics)*, VII:482, VII:486, VII:487, VII:490, VII:521, VI:522

EMERSON, SONNY: Sonny Emerson is David Tassenbaum's friend. They like to go fishing together. VII:470

TASSENBAUM, IRENE (IRENE CANTORA, DAUGHTER OF ABRAHAM)
Middle-aged Irene Tassenbaum, a staunch Republican, was born Irene Cantora in STATEN ISLAND, NEW YORK. Her computer-wiz husband, DAVID, helped to create the Internet. The two of them are extremely wealthy.

Although they live most of the year in MANHATTAN, Irene and David spend their summers in the old CULLUM cabin on KEYWADIN POND, located in EAST STONEHAM, MAINE. Hence, Irene is in the EAST STONE-HAM GENERAL STORE when Roland and JAKE appear there in 1999. Although she seems an unlikely heroine, Irene Tassenbaum plays her own small but important part in the Dark Tower saga.

Kidnapped by Roland, Jake, and OY, Irene drives our three tet-mates first to STEPHEN KING's house in LOVELL, Maine, then to SLAB CITY HILL, where King is about to be run down by a Dodge minivan. Thanks to her, our tet arrives just in time to save the writer, but since ka always demands that a blood-price be paid if a blood-price be owed, Jake dies in King's place. While driving bereaved Roland and Oy to New York City so that Roland can meet with the TET CORPORATION, Irene becomes Roland's lover. At the end of her adventure, Irene returns to her husband. However, she seems to be a changed person; the WHITE has touched her life.

VII:423–33, VII:434–38, VII:441–43, VII:444–45, VII:449–65, VII:469–71, VII:475–90, VII:504, VII:510, VII:520–25, VII:535, VII:573

TAVERY, FRANCINE
See CALLA BRYN STURGIS CHARACTERS: OTHER CHARACTERS

TAVERY, FRANK
See CALLA BRYN STURGIS CHARACTERS: OTHER CHARACTERS

TAXI DRIVERS
   TAXI DRIVER NUMBER ONE: When JAKE, CALLAHAN, and OY are propelled through the UNFOUND DOOR into 1999 NEW YORK, this dashiki- and fez-wearing driver almost hits Oy. Jake threatens to shoot him. VI:309–13, VI:322
   TAXI DRIVER NUMBER TWO: This Jamaican cabbie takes CALLA-HAN and JAKE to the TWIN TOWERS. They don't tip him very well. VI:333–34
   TAXI DRIVER NUMBER THREE: SUSANNAH/MIA's driver takes them to Sixtieth and Lexington, close to the DIXIE PIG. VI:347–49
   TAXI DRIVER NUMBER FOUR: This driver drops JAKE and CALLA-HAN off near the DIXIE PIG. VI:338

TELFORD, GEORGE
See CALLA BRYN STURGIS CHARACTERS: RANCHERS

TET CORPORATION (KA-TET OF THE ROSE)
In *Wolves of the Calla,* the Tet Corporation is nothing more than a white lie fabricated by EDDIE DEAN. Although the lie is for a good cause (Eddie wants CALVIN TOWER to sell the Vacant LOT to his spontaneously incorporated ka-tet so that they can save the magical ROSE from the destructive SOMBRA CORPORATION), it is nonetheless an untruth. No Tet Corporation exists, and although SUSANNAH DEAN is an heiress in her own where and when, the newly formed Tet has no way to access her HOLMES DENTAL INDUSTRIES fortune to pay for the expensive SECOND AVENUE plot which they wish to buy.

However, sometimes ka's will works through such odd twists of chance (and through the seemingly silly utterances that escape the mouth of a ka-mai). Although in 1977 (when Eddie spins his tale in the back room of the MANHATTAN RESTAURANT OF THE MIND) Tet is no more than a pipe dream, by 1999 (the KEYSTONE YEAR in the KEYSTONE WORLD), the Tet Corporation is a powerful reality.

Through the efforts of JOHN CULLUM (the *dan-tete* that Roland and Eddie meet in EAST STONEHAM, MAINE, in 1977), the lawyerly skills of Calvin Tower's friend AARON DEEPNEAU, and the financial clout of MOSES CARVER, Susannah Dean's godfather, Tet takes form in our world. When Roland visits the corporation in 1999, it is housed in 2 HAMMARSKJÖLD PLAZA, a towering black building located on the former Vacant Lot. Just inside the building's lobby is a small, protected garden called the GARDEN OF THE BEAM. In it grows the sacred Rose. Just as Eddie and Roland had envisioned and hoped back in 1977, when they held their final long palaver with John Cullum in LOVELL, Maine, Tet has accomplished its three major tasks. It has protected the Rose; it has watched out for the writer STEPHEN KING; and it has screwed Sombra Corporation whenever possible.

When Roland holds palaver with Moses Carver, MARIAN CARVER, and NANCY DEEPNEAU in Tet's headquarters in 1999, they give our gunslinger a Patek Philippe pocket watch engraved with three symbols—a key, a Rose, and a Tower. According to the psychic GOOD-MIND FOLK whom Tet employs, the watch will either stop or run backward once Roland gets close to the DARK TOWER. These three leaders of the Tet Corporation also give our gunslinger a copy of the book *Insomnia* and return AUNT TALITHA's gold crucifix to him (the one Roland gave to John Cullum and which spoke to Moses Carver in the voice of Susannah Dean). The book is the only one of the three gifts which Roland does not take on his journey. (He leaves it with IRENE TASSENBAUM.) True to the Good-Mind Folk's prediction, the Patek Philippe runs backward once Roland reaches the end of his journey.

V:527, V:538 VI:189, VI:201, VI:202, VI:267–70 *(merger with Holmes Dental),* VI:319, VII:37, VII:48, VII:123, VII:125, VII:146, VII:479, VII:490, VII:496–520, VII:586, VII:812

CALVINS, THE: The Calvins (who took their name in honor of the grumpy bibliophile CALVIN TOWER) are a group of researchers hired by the Tet Corporation to read all of STEPHEN KING's books. These scholars spend their working time cross-referencing King's novels by character, setting, and theme. They also trace any of King's characters who live or may once have lived on KEYSTONE EARTH.

According to the Calvins, the novel *Insomnia* is of central importance to Roland's quest since it contains a direct reference to the CRIMSON KING, and since it predicts that the artist PATRICK DANVILLE may play an important part in Roland's future. VII:509, VII:511–14

CARVER, MARIAN ODETTA: Marian Odetta Carver was born when her father, MOSES CARVER, was seventy. She is a tall, stately black woman with the beautiful but hard face of a warrior. (She stands six foot six.) Marian has been president of the Tet Corporation since her father retired in 1997, at the age of ninety-eight. VII:498–520

CARVER, MOSES: *See* FOUNDING FATHERS, *listed below*

CULLUM, JOHN: *See* FOUNDING FATHERS, *listed below*

DEEPNEAU, AARON: *See* FOUNDING FATHERS, *listed below*

DEEPNEAU, ED: *See* DEEPNEAU, ED, *listed separately*

DEEPNEAU, NANCY REBECCA: Nancy Rebecca Deepneau is the granddaughter of AARON DEEPNEAU's older brother. She is also a high-ranking member of the Tet Corporation. According to Roland, she is a green-eyed beauty. VII:492–520

FOUNDING FATHERS (KA-TET OF THE ROSE, OLD FARTS OF THE APOCALYPSE, THREE TOOTHLESS MUSKETEERS): VII:496–98, VII:499

> **CARVER, MOSES ISAAC (DADDY MOSE, POP MOSE):** Moses Carver (called POP MOSE by his goddaughter, SUSANNAH DEAN) was DAN HOLMES's accountant and friend. After Dan Holmes's first heart attack, Moses handled the financial side of HOLMES DENTAL INDUSTRIES.
>
> Moses Carver is one of the three men that Roland and EDDIE choose to found the Tet Corporation. By the time Roland arrives in 1999 NEW YORK, one-hundred-year-old Moses is the only living member of the original founding fathers. He has officially retired, but his daughter, MARIAN ODETTA CARVER, runs the corporation. V:43, V:101, V:102, V:103, VI:268, VI:270, VII:36, VII:37, VII:38, VII:48, VII:119, VII:123, VII:124, VII:125–27, VII:141, VII:496–520, VII:579, VII:654, VII:656
>
> **CULLUM, JOHN (SAI YANKEE FLANNEL SHIRT, JOHN OF EAST STONEHAM):** John Cullum, called John of East Stoneham by Roland, is the elderly bachelor who becomes Roland and EDDIE's ally when they fight BALAZAR'S MEN at the EAST STONEHAM GENERAL STORE in EAST STONEHAM, MAINE, in 1977. At first, Eddie refers to him as Mr. Flannel Shirt, but by the end of their acquaintance Cullum has won the respect of both gunslingers. Though he is far from young, Cullum is tough and resilient. A caretaker by trade, he eventually becomes (at least on our level of the DARK TOWER) one of the most important

guardians of the Rose. Although Cullum helps Roland and Eddie defeat Balazar's men, his role in the larger war between Light and Dark is sizable. It is Cullum who shows Eddie and Roland CARA LAUGHS, the magic door spun from the substance of the PRIM. It is also Cullum whom Eddie and Roland name as executive vice president of the Tet Corporation, the company formed to protect the Rose. Cullum dies of a gunshot wound in 1989. VI:130–82, VI:186, VI:200, VI:209, VI:210, VI:215, VI:270, VI:271, VI:274, VI:285, VI:301, VII:18, VII:19, VII:20, VII:24, VII:31, VII:34, VII:38–48 *(38—Waterford dan-tete?)*, VII:52, VII:114, VII:115–31, VII:141, VII:305, VII:414, VII:423, VII:428, VII:429, VII:432, VII:434, VII:438, VII:469, VII:487, VII:496–98 *(498—died in 1989 of a gunshot wound)*, VII:499, VII:519

> **AIDAN (YOUNG NEPHEW):** John Cullum's grandnephew. In 1977, he is three years old and full of questions. VI:180
>
> **FATHER:** VI:158 *(folks)*
>
> **GRANDPARENTS:** VI:158
>
> **MOTHER:** VI:158 *(folks)*, VI:160 *(ma)*
>
> **NEPHEW (UNNAMED SMOKING NEPHEW):** In John Cullum's opinion, his nephew is too young to smoke, so he gives the boy's stale cigarettes to Roland. Since Roland isn't used to filters, he thinks that people on our level of the DARK TOWER like to inhale murky air. VI:160
>
> **NIECE:** VII:41
>
> **RUSSERT, DONNIE (FRIEND):** *See* MAINE CHARACTERS, *listed separately*
>
> **VERMONT FRIEND:** Cullum used to work with this man at the Maine State Prison. VI:181, VI:182

DEEPNEAU, AARON (CHEMOTHERAPY KID, AIRY, MR. GAI COCKNIF EN YOM, VOICE NUMBER TWO): Aaron Deepneau, a close friend of CALVIN TOWER's, appeared briefly in the earlier Dark Tower volume *The Waste Lands*. Although he is about seventy years old and ill with cancer, Aaron has no shortage of healthy courage. When BALAZAR'S MEN threaten Tower's life because he will not sell the magical Vacant LOT to the SOMBRA CORPORATION, Aaron escapes with his friend to MAINE. Later, and despite Tower's protests, Aaron writes up the "selling papers," which bestow ownership of the lot upon Roland, EDDIE, and the newly created Tet Corporation, a company which he then helps to develop. (On a humorous note, Deepneau draws up the contract on a piece of paper that has a cartoon of a beaver on it and the caption "Dam Important Things to Do.")

In *Wolves of the Calla,* we learn that Deepneau and Tower are destined to save FATHER CALLAHAN's life when he is attacked by the HITLER BROTHERS in the TURTLE BAY WASHATERIA in 1981. During this adventure, Deepneau and Tower keep their identities secret. Callahan calls Deepneau both "Voice Number Two" and "Mr. Gai Cocknif En Yom."

(The latter name comes from the Yiddish insult which Deepneau screams at the Hitler Brothers. It means, "Go shit in the ocean.")

When Roland visits Tet's headquarters in 1999, he meets Aaron's grandniece, NANCY REBECCA DEEPNEAU. Unfortunately, Aaron succumbed to his cancer in 1992. V:56, V:58, V:62–64, V:100, V:168–69, V:437–42 *(as cavalry, as Voice Number Two, and as Mr. Gai cocknif en yom)*, V:447–48 *(cavalry)*, V:471, V:518, V:528, V:530, V:537, V:538, V:542, V:544, V:545, V:550, V:584–85, V:600 *(friend)*, V:623–24, V:626–28, V:703–4, V:705, V:706, V:709, VI:35, VI:36, VI:81, VI:142, VI:163–68, VI:177, VI:183–212, VI:214–16, VI:269, VI:270, VII:18, VII:19, VII:34, VII:37–38, VII:39, VII:48, VII:122, VII:123, VII:125, VII:126, VII:128, VII:141, VII:495, VII:496–98 *(lived until 1992)*, VII:499, VII:513

    MOTHER (UNNAMED): VI:202

    SISTER AND TWO BROTHERS: V:538

GOOD-MIND FOLK: Like the CALVINS, the Good-Mind Folk are a group of researchers hired by the Tet Corporation. Whereas the Calvins are scholars, the Good-Mind Folk are psychics. Their headquarters are located on a ranch in TAOS, NEW MEXICO. Although they squabble a lot, the Good-Mind Folk and the Calvins work together. VII:507–8, VII:510, VII:517, VII:586 *(watch)*

    FRED TOWNE: Fred is the most talented of the Good-Mind Folk. His predictions are many and they are rarely wrong. Fred is the Tet employee who states that Roland's Patek Philippe watch will either stop or run backward once he nears the DARK TOWER. VII:517, VII:518

GUARD AT DIXIE PIG: VII:523

HAMMARSKJÖLD PLAZA ASSOCIATION: VII:505

LIMOUSINE DRIVER: VII:520–21

OLD FARTS OF THE APOCALYPSE: See FOUNDING FATHERS, *listed above*

SECRETARY: VII:504

SECURITY GUARDS AT HEADQUARTERS: VII:495 *(rose)*, VII:496 *(Tet headquarters)*, VII:505 *(Tet headquarters)*

THREE TOOTHLESS MUSKETEERS: See FOUNDING FATHERS, *listed above*

THINNY
See entry in PORTALS

THOMPSON, FLIP
See KING, STEPHEN

THONNIE
See MANNI

THORIN, CORAL
   See HAMBRY CHARACTERS: SEAFRONT

THREE TOOTHLESS MUSKETEERS
   See TET CORPORATION: FOUNDING FATHERS

THROCKEN
   See OY; *see also* APPENDIX I
   BABY THROCKEN: Under extreme duress, NIGEL, the robotic butler we
   meet in the FEDIC DOGAN, gives this baby billy-bumbler to MORDRED
   so that the spider-boy can suck it dry. Softhearted Nigel suffers a complete
   mechanical meltdown because of it. VII:163–64, VII:166, VII:180, VII:182

TIA JAFFORDS
   See CALLA BRYN STURGIS CHARACTERS: ROONTS

TIAN JAFFORDS
   See JAFFORDS FAMILY

TICK-TOCK
   See GRAYS: GRAY HIGH COMMAND

TIGER, IMMORTAL
   See ROSE

TIRANA
   See CAN-TOI

TODASH DEMONS
   See DEMONS/SPIRITS/DEVILS

TOOK, EBEN
   See CALLA BRYN STURGIS CHARACTERS: OTHER CHARACTERS

TOOK, OLD
   See CALLA BRYN STURGIS CHARACTERS: OTHER CHARACTERS

TOOK FAMILY
   See CALLA BRYN STURGIS CHARACTERS: OTHER CHARACTERS

TOOTHAKER, ELVIRA
   See MAINE CHARACTERS

TOPSY THE SAILOR
   See PUBES

TOREN, CALVIN
See TOWER, CALVIN

TOREN, EDDIE
See DEAN, EDDIE

TOREN, JAKE
See CHAMBERS, JAKE

TOREN, STEPHAN
Stephan Toren was CALVIN TOWER's great-great-great-grandfather. His will (written on March 19, 1846), included a piece of paper addressed to *ROLAND DESCHAIN, OF GILEAD/THE LINE OF ELD/GUNSLINGER.* Although the will itself no longer remains, the piece of paper addressed to Roland survives, as does the dead letter's envelope. The envelope bears the symbols for "unfound," symbols which also appear on BLACK THIRTEEN's box and upon the UNFOUND DOOR.
    V:541–42, V:546, VI:187, VI:195

TORRES, MIGUEL
See HAMBRY CHARACTERS: SEAFRONT

TOWER, CALVIN (CALVIN TOREN, MR. EX LIBRIS, OLD FATTY, VOICE NUMBER ONE)
Calvin Tower (born Calvin Toren) is the owner of the MANHATTAN RESTAURANT OF THE MIND, located on SECOND AVENUE. In *The Waste Lands,* he sold *Charlie the Choo-Choo* and *Riddle-De-Dum* to JAKE CHAMBERS. (See *Stephen King's The Dark Tower: A Concordance, Volume I.*)
    The Toren family (a Dutch name which means "tower") were the original custodians for the Vacant LOT, located on FORTY-SIXTH STREET and Second Avenue, and for the wild, dusky-pink ROSE which grows there. Not surprisingly, the Toren family (who are custodians for the Rose) are linked to the DESCHAIN family (who are custodians for the DARK TOWER). In fact, there is a good chance that one of Calvin's ancestors met one of Roland's forefathers, or perhaps even met Roland himself. When EDDIE DEAN visits the Manhattan Restaurant of the Mind in 1977 to convince Tower to sell the lot to the TET CORPORATION instead of to the CRIMSON KING's evil SOMBRA CORPORATION, Calvin shows him the envelope in which his great-great-great-grandfather kept his will. Although the dead letter has long disappeared, a single brittle sheet of paper remains, and that sheet is addressed to Roland Deschain, of GILEAD, the line of ELD.
    Just as Eddie Dean saves Calvin Tower from BALAZAR's thugs when they try to force him to sell the lot to Sombra, Tower and his friend AARON DEEPNEAU are destined to rescue FATHER CALLAHAN as he is being

attacked by the HITLER BROTHERS in the TURTLE BAY WASHATERIA in 1981. Since Deepneau and Tower try to keep their identities secret during this escapade, Callahan can only identify Tower as "Voice Number One" and "Mr. Ex Libris," the latter name derived from the words engraved on the signet ring he wears.

In *Song of Susannah*, a reluctant Tower agrees to sell both Vacant Lot and Rose to Roland and Eddie. Although Tower has little to do with the Tet Corporation once it is formed, he does make one extremely valuable contribution. Borrowing an idea he found in a science-fiction novel written by BEN SLIGHTMAN JR. (who wrote sci-fi under the name DANIEL HOLMES), he tells Aaron Deepneau and the other FOUNDING FATHERS to hire precogs and telepaths to help them battle their archenemies (the Sombra Corporation) and to protect their two charges (the Rose and STEPHEN KING). These psychic GOOD-MIND FOLK prove to be extremely useful. However, another group of more ordinary researchers—hired to catalog and index the works of Stephen King—are the ones who acknowledge Tet's debt to Tower the most openly. They christen themselves the Calvins in honor of this grumpy old bibliophile. Calvin Tower dies of a heart attack in 1990.

V:54, V:55–58, V:62–70, V:92, V:93, V:94–106 *(rose and Sombra)*, V:118, V:168–69, V:196, V:338, V:437–42 *(as cavalry, as Voice Number One, and as Mr. Ex Libris)*, V:447–48 *(cavalry)*, V:471, V:503–5, V:517, V:518–50, V:584–85, V:591, V:593, V:595, V:597, V:599, V:600, V:618, V:622–24, V:626–28, V:703–4, V:705, V:706, V:709, VI:7, VI:35, VI:36, VI:81, VI:84, VI:136–37, VI:139, VI:140, VI:141, VI:142, VI:154 *(indirect)*, VI:163, VI:171, VI:177–80, VI:183–212, VI:214–16, VI:269, VI:334, VII:19, VII:37–38, VII:39, VII:122 *(indirect)*, VII:123, VII:128, VII:495, VII:507–8, VII:509, VII:821

BRICE, MR.: One of Calvin Tower's clients. V:543
FATHER (UNNAMED): VI:195
FIRST WIFE: V:530–31
GRAHAM, TOMMY: He owned TOM AND GERRY'S ARTISTIC DELI, which once sat on the Vacant LOT located on SECOND AVENUE and FORTY-SIXTH STREET. When the deli went bust, Tower paid for it to be torn down. V:531
GRANDFATHER (UNNAMED): VI:195
HARRIED-LOOKING WOMAN: V:593–94
MIDDLE-AGED COUPLE: V:596
SERGIO: Shop cat. He lives at the MANHATTAN RESTAURANT OF THE MIND. V:67, V:525, V:543, V:548, V:549
SHOE SHINE BOY: V:593
TOREN, STEPHAN: *See* TOREN, STEPHAN, *listed separately*

TOWNE, FRED
See TET CORPORATION: GOOD-MIND FOLK

TRAMPAS
See CAN-TOI

TRELAWNEY
See CAN-TOI

TRISTUM, DR. GANGLI
See CAN-TOI

TUBTHER, MR.
See DEAN, EDDIE: EDDIE'S PAST ASSOCIATES

TULL CHARACTERS
At the beginning of *The Gunslinger,* Roland traveled through the dying town of Tull, located on the edges of the MOHAINE DESERT. Here he battled the followers of SYLVIA PITTSTON, who was herself an acolyte of the MAN IN BLACK. Before pushing into the desert, Roland killed everyone in Tull, including his lover, ALICE. (For further information about Tull, Sylvia Pittston, and Alice, see *Stephen King's The Dark Tower: A Concordance, Volume I.*) According to STEPHEN KING, the town of Tull was named after the rock band Jethro Tull.
   ALICE (ALLIE): Roland's lover. She owned a honky-tonk called Sheb's. During his battle against the mad followers of the preacher SYLVIA PITTSTON, Roland accidentally shot her. (See *Stephen King's The Dark Tower: A Concordance, Volume I.*) VI:288
   NORT: Nort was a weed-eater brought back to life by the MAN IN BLACK (otherwise known as WALTER.) V:253, VI:284, VII:826 *(weed-eater mentioned. Reference actually refers to Brown, the border dweller; see* BROWN, *listed separately).*
   PITTSTON, SYLVIA: See *Stephen King's The Dark Tower: A Concordance, Volume I.*

TUNNEL DEMON
See DEMONS/SPIRITS/DEVILS: TODASH DEMONS

TURTLE GUARDIAN
See GUARDIANS OF THE BEAM

U

UFFIS
See WARRIORS OF THE SCARLET EYE: CASSE ROI RUSSE: HUMANS; *see also* APPENDIX I

UNCLE JIM
See BREAKERS: BRAUTIGAN, TED

UNWIN, TALITHA
See RIVER CROSSING CHARACTERS

UPS GUY
See CHAMBERS, JAKE: JAKE'S ASSOCIATES

UR-DOG ROVER
See ROSE

V

VAGRANT DEAD (VAGS)
When our ka-tet travels to NEW YORK CITY via TODASH at the beginning of *Wolves of the Calla,* they see a number of these forlorn creatures wandering around the city. A vag (or one of the vagrant dead) is a person who died so suddenly that he or she does not yet comprehend that he/she is dead. Sooner or later the vag will pass on, but seeing one walking around with his or her death wounds still oozing is disconcerting (to say the least). A vag who died in a frontal collision walks the streets bleeding, his head split like a melon. One who died on an operating table may still have his or her incisions hanging open. When Roland was a boy, BURNING CHRIS (father of ALAIN JOHNS) warned him that traveling todash meant such meetings were possible.
V:195, V:284, V:285, V:286, V:288, V:289, V:290, V:297 *(walking dead),* V:302 *(bewildered dead people),* V:304 *(dead folks),* V:506, V:516, VI:147
BURNED WOMAN MISSING ARM AND LEG: Seen by FATHER CALLAHAN on Park Avenue. V:284
DEAD WOMAN: Seen by SUSANNAH DEAN in TODASH NEW YORK. She has a white face, empty, black eye sockets, and a black, moss-splotched dress. V:186, V:190, V:194

LITTLE GIRL: Seen by SUSANNAH DEAN and then by her ka-tet in TODASH NEW YORK. She died in a car accident. V:194–95, V:196

MAN WITHOUT EYES: Seen by FATHER CALLAHAN while on Park Avenue. V:284

NAKED MAN: Seen by SUSANNAH DEAN and then by her ka-tet in TODASH NEW YORK. V:191, V:194, V:196, V:197

VAMPIRES

In *Wolves of the Calla,* the people of CALLA BRYN STURGIS state that THUNDERCLAP is a land of vampires. They call these bloodsuckers "broken-helm undead ronin" or the "WARRIORS OF THE SCARLET EYE." Although we later learn that END-WORLD is actually populated by CAN-TOI and TAHEEN—animal-headed creatures who serve the CRIMSON KING— MID-WORLD and End-World contain plenty of vampires, though not all of them subsist on blood alone. In the short story "The Little Sisters of Eluria" (discussed in *Stephen King's The Dark Tower: A Concordance, Volume I*), we met the vampiric LITTLE SISTERS, a tribe of blood- and semen-drinking wraiths that wandered the land posing as a religious sect of healers. In *The Gunslinger* and *The Waste Lands,* we learned about the Speaking-Ring spirits that required a sexual payment from any human who dared to pause within the circumference of their enchanted circles. (While in her wraith form, MIA, Susannah's demon-possessor, was a similar type of sexual vampire.) And finally, in *The Dark Tower,* we encounter DANDELO, a giant were-insect who feeds upon human emotion.

However, even if we narrow our present category so that it includes only the bloodsucking variety of vamps, we can still add three more types of vampires to our list. They are called (quite appropriately) TYPE ONE vampires, TYPE TWO vampires, and TYPE THREE vampires (*see below*).

V:26, V:150, V:256–57, V:266, V:269–71, V:273, V:285, V:289, V:297, V:299, V:302, V:306, V:423, V:430, V:452, V:610, VI:22, VI:64, VI:122, VI:172, VI:231, VI:253, VI:293, VI:303, VI:320, VI:326, VI:337, VI:364–84 *(Dixie Pig),* VII:5, VII:55–70 *(in birth room),* VII:104–9 *(following Jake),* VII:111 *(posse),* VII:133–35, VII:146, VII:147, VII:259, VII:332, VII:473, VII:526

TYPE ONE (THE GRANDFATHERS): According to FATHER CALLA-HAN, there are only about a dozen Type One vampires in the world. They live extremely long lives and can survive periods of up to two hundred years in deep hibernation. These creatures, also known as Grandfathers, were some of the nastiest demons to survive once the magical PRIM receded. When JAKE and Callahan travel to the DIXIE PIG in NEW YORK CITY, they discover approximately a dozen of these monsters feeding behind a blasphemous tapestry depicting ARTHUR ELD and his court taking part in a cannibals' feast.

The Grandfathers do not just drink blood. They eat human flesh as well, and their appearance is as revolting as their appetites. Their evil, shriveled, apple-doll faces are twisted by age, and their mouths are filled with huge numbers of teeth, which are so pronounced and so numerous that they cannot close their lips. Their eyes are black and oozing, and their skin is yellow, scaled with teeth, and covered with patches of diseased-looking fur. Their auras are of a poisonous violet so dark that they appear almost black. When Type One vampires feed on humans, they create TYPE TWO vampires. V:261, V:269–70, V:292, V:396, V:708, VI:365, VI:372–73, VI:376, VII:8 *(not seen)*, VII:11–16, VII:26, VII:28, VII:32, VII:86, VII:145, VII:166, VII:168

> **BARLOW, KURT:** Kurt Barlow, the bloodsucker who spread his infection throughout the town of 'SALEM'S LOT, MAINE, is an example of a Type One vampire. (See STEPHEN KING's novel *'Salem's Lot.*) Although Barlow was not quite as ugly as the Type Ones that JAKE and CALLAHAN meet in the DIXIE PIG, he was every bit as dangerous. When a much younger Father Callahan challenged Barlow in the PETRIE family kitchen back in Maine, he found that his faith in the WHITE was not strong enough to defeat this servant of the Outer Dark. Barlow broke the arms of Callahan's cross and forced him to drink his contaminated blood. Despite this victory, Barlow was eventually destroyed by Callahan's companion BEN MEARS. V:257, V:258–61, V:266, V:268, V:269, V:270 *(vampire-demon)*, V:271, V:275 *(vampire-demon)*, V:280, V:283 *(indirect; blood taste)*, V:291, V:292 *(indirect)*, V:306, V:423, V:437, V:451, V:456, V:463, V:465, V:591 *(filthy bloodsucker)*, V:706 *(vampire)*, V:708, VI:329, VI:330, VII:12, VII:16, VII:28 *(indirect)*

> **STRAKER:** Straker was BARLOW's half-human accomplice. V:258

> **CROSS OF MALTA VAMPIRE:** This vile creature looks like a deformed skeleton in a moss-encrusted dinner suit. Around its neck it wears an ancient award, which CALLAHAN believes is the Cross of Malta.

> The Cross of Malta Vampire is the first of the Grandfathers to attack Callahan during the DIXIE PIG battle. As the vamp attacks, Callahan stabs the end of his crucifix into the creature's forehead and burns through the flesh. The vampire's vile aura whiffs out like a candle, leaving nothing but liquefying flesh spilling out of his dinner jacket and pants. VII:12

> **GRANDFATHER FLEAS:** These horrible insects, which are roughly the size of mice, accompany the Grandfathers and feed upon their leftovers. They are the parasites of parasites and are both blood-drinkers and camp followers. BILLY-BUMBLERS hunt them the way some terriers hunt rats. Whenever you see Grandfather Fleas, you can be sure that the Grandfathers are close. (Watch your neck.) VI:366, VI:381, VII:8–16, VII:26

TYPE TWO: Type Two vampires are created by TYPE ONE vampires. They are more intelligent than zombies, but not much. Though they can't go out in daylight, they make up for it at night by feeding voraciously. Thanks to their unquenchable hunger and diminished intellect, Type Twos rarely survive for long. V:269–70, V:396

TYPE THREE: Type Three vampires are like mosquitoes. They are made by TYPE TWO vampires but don't seem to be able to create more of their kind.

However, they feed voraciously and are dangerous. Type Threes are more intelligent than Type Twos (perhaps because they retain a bit more of their humanity). Hence, they can pass for human. Like ordinary mortals, they withstand daylight and can eat food. However, psychic individuals (such as FATHER CALLAHAN) can identify them by their burned-onion smell and by the blue haze which surrounds them.

While they feed, Type Threes secrete an enzyme, which simultaneously numbs the skin and keeps the blood flowing freely. It also seems to create a temporary amnesia that prevents their victims from remembering the attack. Type Three vampires can spread HIV. Also, once a person has been bitten by a Type Three, they become a magnet for more bloodsuckers. V:266, V:269–70, V:273, V:274–79, V:280–81, V:284, V:286, V:289, V:290, V:291, V:301, V:303, V:304 (bloodsucking folks), V:444, V:451, V:455–57, VII:5, VII:14–16, VII:55–70 (in birth room), VII:104–9 (following Jake), VII:111 (posse), VII:133–35

INDIVIDUAL TYPE THREE VAMPIRES AND THEIR VICTIMS:

BATTERY PARK VAMPIRE: PERE CALLAHAN stabbed this vampire four times—once in the kidneys, once between the ribs, once in the back, and once in the neck. V:287

   DOMINICAN TEENAGER (VICTIM): V:287–88

DIXIE PIG VAMPIRE GUARDS (GUARDING SUSANNAH/MIA): VI:364–66, VI:368, VI:377–84, VII:8–16

DIXIE PIG VAMPIRES: VI:365–71

EAST VILLAGE VAMPIRE: V:274–75

   VICTIM: V:275

MARK CROSS BRIEFCASE BUSINESSMAN: He attacks LUPE DELGADO outside the HOME shelter. V:276–79, V:281

   DELGADO, LUPE: See CALLAHAN, FATHER DONALD FRANK: CALLAHAN'S HOME SHELTER ASSOCIATES

MOTORCYCLE MESSENGER: PERE CALLAHAN killed this vampire and then took his boots. V:288

OLD WOMAN FEEDING SQUIRRELS: CALLAHAN encountered this Type Three in a NEW YORK CITY park. V:285–86, V:287

PETE PETACKI'S VAMPIRE GIRL: CALLAHAN saw this seventeen-year-old girl while he was working as a gravedigger in rural KENTUCKY. His fellow worker PETE PETACKI thought she was hot. He was wrong. She was probably cold. Callahan killed her before she could cause any damage. Pete Petacki never found out. V:302

SOMBRA CORPORATION VAMPIRES: These Type Threes work for RICHARD P. SAYRE. Some of them are HIV-positive. V:455–57

TIMES SQUARE MOVIE THEATER VAMPIRE (YOUNG MAN): The Times Square movie theater vampire was the first Type Three that CALLAHAN encountered. Although the vamp and his victim first appeared to be lovers, Callahan saw the telltale blue light hovering around both of them. V:268–69, V:270–71 (homosexual), V:276 (indirect)

VICTIM (OLDER MAN): V:268–69, V:270–71 *(homosexual)*, V:276 *(indirect)*
WOMAN IN MARINE MIDLAND BANK: This Type Three flirted with CALLAHAN. V:275, V:288, V:289

VAN RONK, DAVE
See DEAN, SUSANNAH: ODETTA HOLMES'S ASSOCIATES

VAN WYCK, MATHIESSEN
See DEAN, SUSANNAH: SUSANNAH'S PRESENT ASSOCIATES

VANNAY (VANNAY THE WISE)
Vannay was Roland's gentle tutor and was often called Vannay the Wise. While CORT taught apprentice gunslingers how to fight, Vannay believed that violence often caused more problems than it solved. Vannay gave Roland the sarcastic nickname GABBY because—as a young boy—Roland was given to prolonged silences. Vannay had a son named WALLACE, who died of the falling sickness.
    V:78–80 *(described)*, V:81, V:86, V:89, V:90, V:204, V:388, V:392, VII:20–21, VII:33, VII:589, VII:742, VII:801 *(Vannay the Wise)*, VII:829
WALLACE: Wallace, son of Vannay, was one of Roland's childhood friends. He died of the falling sickness, also known as King's Evil. Like the TAVERY twins, Wallace was a child prodigy. V:78–79

VAUGHN, SAM
See KING, STEPHEN

VELE, MRS. CORETTA
See KING, STEPHEN: FAN MAIL/HATE MAIL

VERDON, HENRY
See KING, STEPHEN

VERRILL, CHUCK
See KING, STEPHEN

VOICE NUMBER ONE
See TOWER, CALVIN

VOICE NUMBER TWO
See TET CORPORATION: FOUNDING FATHERS: DEEPNEAU, AARON

VOICE OF THE BEAM
See GAN

VOTER REGISTRATION BOYS
See DEAN, SUSANNAH: ODETTA HOLMES AND THE CIVIL RIGHTS
MOVEMENT: VOTER REGISTRATION BOYS

W

WALKER, DETTA
See DEAN, SUSANNAH: SUSANNAH'S OTHER SELVES

WALKIN' DUDE
See WALTER: WALTER'S ALIASES

WALKING WATERS OF EAST DOWNE
See MID-WORLD FOLKLORE

WALK-INS
Walk-ins are people (and sometimes animals) that seem to *walk in* to our world
from other wheres or whens. Often they are dressed in old-fashioned clothes
and speak indecipherable languages. Some of these walk-ins are disfigured
(JOHN CULLUM calls them ROONT, or ruined) and are probably either
SLOW MUTANTS or CHILDREN OF RODERICK. Others have a bleeding
hole in the center of their forehead and appear to be CAN-TOI servants of the
CRIMSON KING.
    In *Song of Susannah,* we find out that the towns near LOVELL, MAINE,
are plagued by walk-ins. In the final book of the Dark Tower series, we discover that these walk-ins are entering our world through the doorway of
CARA LAUGHS, the home which the writer STEPHEN KING is destined to
buy. Obviously, our *kas-ka Gan* uses his imagination to create DOORWAYS
BETWEEN WORLDS, doorways which the walk-ins can use.
    VI:151–54, VI:161, VI:170–71, VI:172, VI:180–81 *(center),* VI:182,
    VI:285, VI:301, VI:397–98, VI:407, VI:409, VII:46, VII:49, VII:50, VII:116,
    VII:129–30 *(taheen),* VII:131, VII:173, VII:305, VII:433, VII:434, VII:438
    BIRDS: VI:153
    CHEVIN OF CHAYVEN: *See* MUTANTS: CHILDREN OF RODERICK
    ONE-EYED WOMAN WITH DEAD CHILD: *See* MUTANTS: CHIL-
    DREN OF RODERICK
    WOMAN WITH BALD HEAD AND BLEEDING EYE IN FOREHEAD:
    VI:153, VI:171

WALK-INS, CHURCH OF THE
See MAINE (STATE OF): OXFORD COUNTY: STONEHAM: STONE-

HAM CORNERS: LOVELL-STONEHAM CHURCH OF THE WALK-INS, *in* OUR WORLD PLACES

WALLACE
See VANNAY

WALTER (THE DARK MAN, THE MAN IN BLACK, WALTER OF ALL-WORLD, WALTER OF END-WORLD, WALTER O'DIM, THE CRIMSON KING'S PRIME MINISTER, WALTER PADICK, WALTER HODJI, WALTER FARDEN, WALTER THE BLIND)
As far back as *The Gunslinger,* Walter O'Dim (also known as the Man in Black) has been Roland's nemesis. (See *Stephen King's The Dark Tower: A Concordance, Volume I.*) Under the name MARTEN BROADCLOAK, he served as STEVEN DESCHAIN's betraying sorcerer, the man who seduced Roland's mother and shamed Roland into taking his test of manhood years too early. While in the service of JOHN FARSON, he helped to bring down GILEAD, the last bastion of civilization, in a tide of blood and murder.[6] Under the name RUDIN FILARO, he fought with the BLUE-FACED BARBARIANS at JERICHO HILL and shot CUTHBERT ALLGOOD through the eye with an arrow.

An accomplished sorcerer and a devoted servant of the Outer Dark, Walter has many infernal skills. In the first book of the Dark Tower series, we saw him restore the weed-eater NORT to life; we watched him prophesy with his stacked tarot deck; and we witnessed the incredible vision of the macroverse which he imposed upon Roland's unprepared mind. Although Walter pretended to die in the GOLGOTHA, located near the shores of the WESTERN SEA, he did not actually travel to the clearing at the end of the path. Oh, no. He is too much of a trickster and a survivor to meet such a simple end.

Changing both his name and his face, Walter can travel through time and between worlds, spreading destruction and disaster like plague or poison. As MOTHER ABAGAIL states in the related novel *The Stand,* whereas ordinary mortals wish to live and create, dark creatures such as Walter (aka RANDALL FLAGG) only want to uncreate or destroy. Wherever goodness or hope exists, or wherever tragedy has taken place and the forces of the WHITE are needed to rebuild human society, Walter will turn up, dragging his shadow of chaos behind him.

In the provinces south of GARLAN, Walter was known as Walter Hodji, the latter word meaning both "dim" and "hood." When Roland and his tet met him in the GREEN PALACE back in *Wizard and Glass,* he claimed to be both OZ

---

6. In *The Gunslinger,* Stephen King hints that the Good Man may be just another of Walter's aliases. However, by the time we reach *The Dark Tower,* it is fairly apparent that this bit of information was a red herring. John Farson and Walter are separate beings. Farson was one of Walter's many pawns.

THE GREEN KING and Randall Flagg, the demonic sorcerer whose nefarious deeds are recorded in STEPHEN KING's novels *The Eyes of the Dragon* and *The Stand*.

Although CONSTANT READERS have long been familiar with Walter and his multiple masks (many of which begin with the initials R.F.), not until the final book of the Dark Tower series do we find out the true identity of this multifaced sorcerer. Born Walter Padick, the son of a simple miller in DELAIN, a town located in the EASTAR'D BARONY of a world much like Roland's, Walter chose at a young age to avoid the path most humans travel. At the age of thirteen he ran away from home and refused to return even after being raped by a fellow wanderer. Instead, he pursued his dark destiny, using and abusing his magical powers so that he gained a kind of quasi-immortality. Despite having belonged to numerous cliques and cults through the ages, often espousing conflicting causes, Walter, like Roland, has only ever had one ultimate goal. He longs to climb to the top of the DARK TOWER and enter the room at its summit. However, whereas Roland wants to hold palaver with whatever god controls that linchpin of existence, Walter secretly hopes to take up residence there and become God of All.

By the time our series begins, Walter has taken up another cause in pursuit of his own secret ambition and has become the prime minister of the mad CRIMSON KING. In the name of the Lord of Discordia, Walter convinces MIA to give up her immortality so that she can give birth to MORDRED, who (according to legend) is destined to murder Walter's longtime enemy and ultimate rival, Roland. However, in creating Mordred (whose amputated foot he hopes to use to unlock the Tower) Walter finally overplays his hand. Once Mordred realizes Walter's true intentions, he eats him.

V:314, V:410, V:412 *(as Maerlyn/Marten/Flagg)*, V:460–65 *("I am what ka and the King and the Tower have made me")*, V:470, V:702, VI:239–40, VI:245–55 *(prime minister of the Crimson King)*, VI:282, VI:283, VI:284, VI:288, VI:337, VI:405, VII:13 *(O'Dim)*, VII:106, VII:107, VII:141 *(Crimson King's chancellor)*, VII:148, VII:171–87, VII:188, VII:192, VII:250, VII:442, VII:515, VII:518, VII:531, VII:535, VII:762, VII:829, VII:830

WALTER'S ALIASES:

BROADCLOAK, MARTEN: Under the name of Marten Broadcloak, Walter served as STEVEN DESCHAIN's betraying sorcerer. (See *Stephen King's The Dark Tower: A Concordance, Volume I.*) Marten became GABRIELLE DESCHAIN's lover and tricked young Roland into taking his test of manhood years too early. V:36, V:412 *(as Walter/Maerlyn, Flagg)*, VII:178, VII:184, VII:822, VII:824

GREEN KING, THE: Oz, otherwise known as Oz the Great and Terrible, was the sorcerer of the Emerald City in the children's book *The Wizard of Oz*. Walter occasionally uses this disguise as well. VII:173

PADICK, WALTER: Walter's birth name was Walter Padick. He was the son of SAM THE MILLER and grew up on a farm in DELAIN, located in EASTAR'D BARONY. At thirteen, Walter was raped by another wanderer, but refused to return home. Instead, he pursued his dark destiny. VII:184

R.F.: As we discovered in the first four novels of the Dark Tower series, many of Walter's aliases use the initials R.F. We are never told why. (I try not to be paranoid about it.) VII:194

FANNIN, RICHARD: VII:184

FILARO, RUDIN: Walter fought at JERICHO HILL under this name. VII:174, VII:184

FLAGG, RANDALL: Under the name of Randall Flagg, Walter played a major role in both *The Eyes of the Dragon* and *The Stand*. In the first of these two books, he framed Peter (King Roland's eldest son) for his father's murder and placed the king's weaker-willed younger son, Thomas, on the throne. (Walter hoped to bring the kingdom to ruin by manipulating Thomas.) In *The Stand*, Flagg becomes a truly demonic force. After more than 99 percent of America's population dies of the superflu, Flagg gathers the dregs of the survivors to him in Las Vegas. There, he accumulates both technological and biological weapons so that he can annihilate those people who live in the Free Zone and who still honor the WHITE. Although in this incarnation Walter/Flagg seems almost as powerful as the CRIMSON KING himself, his ambitions are ultimately thwarted. V:36, V:37, V:187, V:412 *(also Walter, Maerlyn)*, VI:246, VI:249, VI:251, VI:337, VI:405, VII:43, VII:125, VII:148, VII:172, VII:173, VII:176, VII:178, VII:184, VII:185, VII:250

WALKIN' DUDE: This epithet was used by RANDALL FLAGG in STEPHEN KING's novel *The Stand*. V:291

WALTER'S ASSOCIATES

CRIMSON KING, THE: *See* CRIMSON KING, *listed separately*

FARSON, JOHN: *See* FARSON, JOHN, *listed separately*

SAM THE MILLER: Walter's father. He was from EASTAR'D BARONY. VII:184

WARRIORS OF THE SCARLET EYE (MEN OF THE EYE)
The Warriors of the Scarlet Eye are the FOOT SOLDIERS OF THE CRIMSON KING. Like their master, they oppose the WHITE and serve the Outer Dark. *See also* BIG COFFIN HUNTERS, CAN-TOI, NORTH CENTRAL POSITRONICS, REGULATORS, SOMBRA CORPORATION, TAHEEN, VAMPIRES, WOLVES.

V:26 *(Broken-helm undead ronin)*, VI:64 *(indirect)*, VI:73 *(indirect)*, VI:74 *(indirect)*, VI:75 *(indirect)*, VI:114–15, VI:117, VI:233, VI:244–45, VI:246–47 *(indirect)*, VI:248, VI:326, VI:364–84 *(Dixie Pig)*

WARRIORS BY LOCATION:

CASSE ROI RUSSE: Le Casse Roi Russe is the palace of the CRIMSON KING. Roland and SUSANNAH pass it on their way to the DARK TOWER.

HUMANS (HUMES):

BRASS: *See* FEEMALO/FIMALO/FUMALO: FEEMALO, *listed below*

COMPSON: *See* FEEMALO/FIMALO/FUMALO: FUMALO, *listed below*

CORNWELL, AUSTIN: *See* FEEMALO/FIMALO/FUMALO: FIMALO (RANDO THOUGHTFUL), *listed below*

FEEMALO/FIMALO/FUMALO (UFFIS): Roland and SUSANNAH meet these three STEPHEN KING look-alikes on the stone moat-bridge of LE CASSE ROI RUSSE. At first the three Stephen Kings claim to be one being—an uffi, or shape-changer—who was once employed as the CRIMSON KING's court jester. However, in reality they are three separate men, all servants of the Red King. Their names are BRASS (Feemalo), COMPSON (Fumalo), and RANDO THOUGHTFUL (Fimalo). The most important of these three is FIMALO/RANDO THOUGHTFUL.

According to this false, three-faced uffi, once the Crimson King discovered that Roland and his tet would defeat both the WOLVES of CALLA BRYN STURGIS and the DEVAR-TOI guards in THUNDERCLAP, he realized that the BEAMS would regenerate and that all of his dreams of murder and mayhem were destined to fail. Being an extremely bad loser, the Red King threw a temper tantrum. First he forced his castle servants to swallow rat poison, then he smashed the six Bends o' the WIZARD'S RAINBOW which were in his possession, and finally he killed himself by swallowing a sharpened spoon. Once he was undead, he galloped toward the DARK TOWER so that he could (he hoped) prevent Roland from achieving his life's goal.

Pretending to be conciliatory (since they alone had survived the Red King's pique), the triple uffi offers Roland, Susannah, and OY two wicker baskets, which appear to contain warm clothes and food. Not surprisingly, the real contents (disguised by *glammer*) are much more disgusting. What the uffis offer are poisonous snakes and human body parts.

Susannah and Roland shoot Feemalo and Fumalo but leave Fimalo (who—once the *glammer* is broken—looks like an extremely ill old man) to confront the were-spider MORDRED, who is following them. The bodies of both Feemalo and Fumalo rot unnaturally fast.

FEEMALO (BRASS/GOODMOUTH KING/EGO): As well as being called Goodmouth King, Feemalo is also referred to as STEPHEN KING Number Two and Right-Hand Stephen King. Unlike Fumalo, he is polite. He claims to be the uffi's ego. VII:600–613, VII:614, VII:615, VII:619

FIMALO (RANDO THOUGHTFUL, AUSTIN CORN-

WELL/REFEREE KING/SUPEREGO): During his years as the CRIMSON KING's minister of state, Fimalo (who originally claims to be the uffi's superego) was called Rando Thoughtful. Rando (who is actually an ordinary hume) was born AUSTIN CORNWELL in one of the MULTIPLE AMERICAS' upstate NEW YORKs. Once upon a time, he ran the NIAGARA MALL. He also had a successful career in advertising. (He proudly tells our tet that he worked for both the Nozz-A-La and the Takuro Spirit accounts.)

Once his *glammer* disperses, Austin Cornwell looks like a very ill old man. His skull is covered in peeling eczema and his face is lumped with pimples and open, bleeding sores. Roland and Susannah choose not to kill him. Instead, they leave him to greet MORDRED, who arrives soon after they leave. Mordred feeds Austin's eyes to the castle rooks and then eats the rest of him. VII:600–617, VII:619–24, VII:627, VII:632

CORNWELL, ANDREW JOHN: Austin Cornwell's father from TIOGA SPRINGS, NEW YORK. VII:616

FUMALO (COMPSON/BADMOUTH KING/ID): Fumalo, also called STEPHEN KING Number One, Left-Hand Stephen King, and Badmouth King, is supposed to be the uffi's id. VII:600–613, VII:614, VII:615, VII:619

DEVAR-TOI CHARACTERS: The Devar-Toi is the BREAKER prison located in THUNDERCLAP.

BREAKERS: *See* BREAKERS, *listed separately*
BRAUTIGAN, TED
EARNSHAW, DINKY
RUIZ, STANLEY (SHEEMIE)

CAN-TOI (LOW MEN): *See* CAN-TOI, *listed separately*
ALEXANDER, BEN
CAGNEY, JAMES
CAMERON
CONROY
LONDON, JACK
TRAMPAS
TRELAWNEY
TRISTUM, DR. GANGLI

HUMANS (HUMES):
ARMITAGE, FRANK: Frank Armitage is a hume who recruits BREAKERS from the parallel earths. Real humans have to do this work since the CAN-TOI (despite their aspirations) don't make very convincing men and women. VII:281, VII:283–90, VII:297

BURKE, DAVID: A stupid human guard who was lobotomized for throwing peanut shells at BREAKERS working in the STUDY. VII:241

KELLY, TAMMY: Tammy Kelly is PIMLI PRENTISS's housekeeper. She has a large bottom. VII:347, VII:348, VII:352–55, VII:358, VII:361, VII:371, VII:381

PRENTISS, PIMLI (DEVAR MASTER): Pimli Prentiss (formerly Paul Prentiss of RAHWAY, NEW JERSEY) is the Master of the DEVAR-TOI. Among the more discontented BREAKERS, he is known as the Devar-Toi's ki'-dam or "shit-for-brains." Sai Prentiss stands six foot two inches, has an enormous sloping belly, long legs, and slab thighs. He is balding and has the turnip nose of a veteran drinker. When he arrived at the Devar-Toi, he was a former prison warden and approximately fifty years old. He still looks the same age, though he has been in END-WORLD for decades. Although he is working to bring about the end of all the worlds, Pimli spends every Mother's Day in tears. (He misses his ma.) Prentiss (who took a TAHEEN name) is good friends with the taheen security chief, FINLI O'TEGO.

During the final battle at the Devar-Toi, Roland shoots Prentiss and leaves him for dead. However, the prostrate and bleeding Devar Master still has enough life left to shoot EDDIE DEAN in the head. Roland quickly dispatches Prentiss, but Eddie dies. VII:197, VII:207, VII:212, VII:215, VII:221–46, VII:261, VII:262, VII:270, VII:271, VII:275, VII:292, VII:295, VII:298–99, VII:325, VII:340, VII:341, VII:343–48, VII:352–53, VII:354 (*indirect*), VII:358–59, VII:361–62, VII:371–75, VII:377, VII:380–81 (*shot*), VII:383–90, VII:396, VII:398 (*indirect*)

    GRANDFATHER: VII:232

    MOTHER: VII:228, VII:229, VII:235, VII:246

PROCTOR OF CORBETT HALL: We never meet the proctor of CORBETT HALL, but EDDIE DEAN, who has been shot in the head, dies in his rooms. JAKE believes that SUSANNAH used the proctor's nail-care gadget to clean Eddie's fingernails before she buried him. VII:409

SONESH, TASSA OF: Tassa of Sonesh is PIMLI PRENTISS's houseboy. He is slim and willowy and likes lipstick. He and TAMMY KELLY (Prentiss's housekeeper) do not get along at all. (Tammy dislikes homosexual men.) Tassa is one of the few servants of the CRIMSON KING to survive the DEVAR-TOI battle. VII:299, VII:352–55, VII:358, VII:366, VII:371, VII:375, VII:400, VII:407

ROBOTS: *See* NORTH CENTRAL POSITRONICS, *listed separately*

    DOBBIE

    FIRE-RESPONSE TEAM BRAVO

    PHIL

    SIX-ARMED ROBOT

TAHEEN: *See* TAHEEN, *listed separately*

    FINLI O' TEGO CLAN (HEAD OF SECURITY)

GASKIE O' TEGO
HUMMA O' TEGO
JAKLI
UNKNOWN RACE:
JENKINS: Jenkins is the DEVAR-TOI's chief technician. We don't know whether he is TAHEEN, CAN-TOI, or hume. VII:343–44, VII:345

DIXIE PIG CHARACTERS/FEDIC CHARACTERS: After the EAST ROAD battle in CALLA BRYN STURGIS, MIA, daughter of none, steals SUSANNAH DEAN's body so that she can keep her appointment with RICHARD P. SAYRE at the Dixie Pig restaurant in NEW YORK CITY. Sayre has promised to help Mia deliver her CHAP. When Susannah/Mia enter the Pig, they are met by approximately fifty men and seventy-five women. Most of these guards are LOW MEN, though some are also TYPE THREE VAMPIRES. In a separate dining room (located behind a tapestry depicting ARTHUR ELD partaking in a cannibal's feast) are a group of ancient TYPE ONE vampires.

Below the Dixie Pig is a DOORWAY, which leads from our world to the FEDIC DOGAN. Here, in the Dogan's EXTRACTION ROOM, Mia gives birth to MORDRED. VI:365–84

CAN-TOI (LOW MEN): *See* CAN-TOI, *listed separately*
ANDREW
DOORMEN
HABER
STRAW
TIRANA
HUMANS (HUMES):
FLAHERTY, CONOR (HUME FROM BOSTON): Along with a TAHEEN named LAMLA and a number of LOW MEN, Conor Flaherty pursues JAKE CHAMBERS through the MIND-TRAP which lies beneath the Dixie Pig. VII:93 *(indirect)*, VII:104–9, VII:111 *(posse)*, VII:112, VII:129, VII:133–35, VII:528
     FATHER: VII:106
JOCHABIM, SON OF HOSSA (DISHWASHER NUMBER TWO): This young boy originally came from LUDWEG, a town north of the city of LUD. He now works in the kitchens of the Dixie Pig. Jochabim is none too bright; however, he does manage to warn JAKE about the MIND-TRAP he will encounter on his way to the NEW YORK/FEDIC DOOR. VII:82–86, VII:99, VII:526
     HOSSA: VII:84
LIMO DRIVERS: VI:341–42
SCOWTHER (DOCTOR): Scowther is the impudent hume doctor who delivers baby MORDRED. He is described as a stoutish man with brown eyes, flushed cheeks, and hair combed back against his skull. He wears a scarlet cravat decorated with the red eye of the

CRIMSON KING. VI:378–84, VII:22, VII:55–68 *(shot by Susannah)*, VII:71 *(automatic)*, VII:149, VII:152
ROBOTS: *See* NORTH CENTRAL POSITRONICS, *listed separately*
NIGEL THE BUTLER (DNK4932 DOMESTIC)
TAHEEN: *See* TAHEEN, *listed separately*
ALIA (NURSE)
CANARYMAN (MEIMAN)
DIXIE PIG CHEF (WARTHOG)
JEY
LAMLA
VAMPIRES: *See* VAMPIRES, *listed separately*
TYPE ONE (GRANDFATHERS)
GRANDFATHER FLEAS
TYPE THREE
WOLVES: *See* WOLVES, *listed separately*

WAVERLY
See BREAKERS

WEASEL, THE
See TAHEEN: WEASEL-HEADED TAHEEN

WEED-EATER
See TULL CHARACTERS: NORT

WERE-SPIDER
See MORDRED

WHITE, THE
The White is the force of good. It is akin to faith in God, but it is both larger and more elemental than a belief in any particular religion or creed. To the beleaguered inhabitants of MID-WORLD, the aristocratic gunslingers are knights of the White. Although the ancient hero ARTHUR ELD is often associated with the White, the term is not limited to a particular political faction, allegiance, or social class. Its true meaning relates back to the philosophy of wholeness and unity embedded in the language of High Speech. Like white light and white magic, the White contains all colors within its balance and is the opposite of the evil Outer Dark.
V:101, V:104, V:605, V:709, VII:4, VII:6, VII:10, VII:12, VII:13, VII:27, VII:127, VII:607, VII:748

WILSON, TEDDY
See MAINE CHARACTERS

WINKLER
See CALLA BRYN STURGIS CHARACTERS: OTHER CHARACTERS

WINSTON
  See PUBES

WIZARD OF OZ
The Wizard of Oz, which tells the tale of DOROTHY, TOTO, the Cowardly Lion, and the Tin Woodsman, is mentioned quite often in the Dark Tower series. (See *Stephen King's The Dark Tower: A Concordance, Volume I.*) Like JAKE, SUSANNAH, and EDDIE, Dorothy Gale was blown from a world much like ours to one where witches and magic are real. However, had *The Wizard of Oz* taken place in MID-WORLD, the Tin Woodsman would have been manufactured by NORTH CENTRAL POSITRONICS, and the Cowardly Lion would have been a MUTIE of some sort.
  V:166
  DOROTHY: V:567
  TOTO: V:296

WIZARD'S GLASS
  See MAERLYN'S RAINBOW

WIZARD'S RAINBOW
  See MAERLYN'S RAINBOW

WOLF POSSE
  See CALLA BRYN STURGIS CHARACTERS: WOLF POSSE

WOLVES (GREENCLOAKS)
Once every generation, the CALLAS of MID-WORLD's BORDERLANDS are invaded by giant, green-cloaked horse-riders from THUNDERCLAP. These servants of the CRIMSON KING steal one of each pair of prepubescent twins and deliver them en masse to their masters in the dark land. Although the people of the Callas don't know exactly what happens to their young children once they are kidnapped, they do know that those who survive the journey home upon the train-pulled flatcars come back ROONT, or mentally ruined.

Although the Wolves' coming is always foretold by ANDY, CALLA BRYN STURGIS's one remaining Messenger Robot, before the arrival of our gunslinger tet the *folken* have never successfully rebuffed an attack. As they so morosely state during their meeting at the TOWN GATHERING HALL, they are a village of farmers, not fighters, and the Greencloaks who come galloping across the RIVER WHYE, bearing their terrible light-sticks and sneetches, are more than a match for a bunch of clod-turners.

By anyone's standards, the Wolves (named for the gray wolf masks they wear) are truly terrifying. As they gallop through the town on their huge gray steeds, wearing their green, swirling cloaks and black, cruel-looking boot spurs, they seem unassailable. No weapon penetrates the armor they wear beneath their clothes, and the ones they wield are the deadly technological creations of the GREAT OLD ONES. Their light-sticks burn the skin black and stop the heart, and their flying metal buzz-balls strip a man of skin in five seconds.

In truth, the Wolves are neither men nor beasts but robots manufactured by NORTH CENTRAL POSITRONICS. However, by the time our tet rides into Calla Bryn Sturgis on their borrowed horses, only one of the Calla's *folken* knows the true nature of the town's terrible adversaries. This person—GRAN-PERE JAFFORDS—has guarded his secret for years, afraid that he will be disbelieved by his fellows or (worse yet) killed by Andy and whatever other traitors lurk in the town. Because, as becomes clear in *Wolves of the Calla,* the Calla always contains traitors—adults willing to sell information to Thunderclap as long as their own children are guaranteed safety.

At the EAST ROAD battle, which takes place at the end of *Wolves of the Calla,* our tet defeats these terrible invaders and ends a cycle of violence which has been playing out for six generations. They kill these monsters not by shooting them through the heart, but by destroying the small radar dishes, or thinking caps, which revolve above their heads, but which are hidden by the hoods of their cloaks. (In this one vulnerability, they resemble SHARDIK, the cyborg BEAR GUARDIAN, which SUSANNAH killed at the beginning of *The Waste Lands.*) When EDDIE and JAKE remove the mask from one of their metallic enemies, they discover that he looks much like DR. DOOM from the *Spider-Man* comic books. He has lenses for eyes, a round mesh grille for a nose, and two sprouted microphones for ears.

V:5–31 *(coming to Calla),* V:113, V:117, V:132, V:135, V:139, V:142–60 *(149—described),* V:161, V:163, V:164, V:207, V:214, V:217, V:220, V:221–22, V:224, V:236, V:237, V:247, V:257–91, V:295, V:318, V:319, V:321, V:322, V:328, V:339, V:340, V:341, V:342, V:347–49, V:350, V:356, V:357–69, V:382, V:383, V:390 *(killed),* V:393, V:394, V:396, V:397, V:413, V:416, V:420, V:434 *(Hitler Brothers and Wolves),* V:479, V:481, V:483, V:484, V:490, V:491, V:492, V:494, V:501, V:509, V:536 *(Balazar's men as),* V:537 *(Wolves of our world),* V:554, V:555, V:561, V:567, V:572, V:574, V:575, V:580, V:581, V:582, V:584, V:586, V:590, V:602, V:603, V:604, V:606, V:607–17, V:629, V:632–35, V:636–38, V:642, V:645, V:650, V:656, V:658, V:659, V:661, V:663–97, V:700, VI:4, VI:6, VI:10, VI:23–26, VI:27, VI:61, VI:64, VI:81, VI:237, VI:238 *(horses),* VI:243, VI:245, VI:246, VI:247, VI:248, VI:337, VI:365, VII:21, VII:43, VII:81, VII:149, VII:151–53, VII:173, VII:179, VII:191, VII:192, VII:193–94, VII:206, VII:214, VII:232, VII:233, VII:234, VII:239, VII:252, VII:272, VII:407, VII:538, VII:540

WORTHINGTON, FRED
See BREAKERS

Y

YANKO, MIKE
See PIPER SCHOOL CHARACTERS

YOUNG AND BEARDLESS
See MANNI

Z

ZALIA JAFFORDS
See ORIZA, SISTERS OF

ZALMAN HOONIK
See CALLA BRYN STURGIS CHARACTERS: ROONTS

ZOLTAN
Zoltan was the pet raven of BROWN, a border dweller who lived in the desert beyond the town of TULL. (See *Stephen King's The Dark Tower: A Concordance, Volume I.*) Zoltan was also the name of a folksinger and guitarist that STEPHEN KING knew at the University of Maine.
VI:283, VII:826

ZOMBIS
In *Wolves of the Calla,* Roland must hide his knowledge of the WOLVES' true nature from whatever traitors lurk in CALLA BRYN STURGIS. He does this by telling the *folken* that the Greencloaks are zombis (spelled without the usual *e*), not robots.
V:610, V:616

MID-WORLD PLACES
AND BORDERLAND PLACES

*Eddie slept. There were no dreams. And beneath them as the night
latened and the moon set, this borderland world turned like a dying
clock.*

V:239

A

ALL-WORLD
In the time of Roland's semimythical ancestor ARTHUR ELD, MID-WORLD,
IN-WORLD, and END-WORLD were united. This unified land was ruled by
the Eld himself. In *Wizard and Glass,* we learned that Arthur Eld's original
kingdom (known as the ancient land of Eld) was located in the northwestern
section of the lands united under the AFFILIATION. Ironically (or perhaps
quite pointedly) these western baronies were the first to fall to the GOOD MAN
during Roland's youth. See also *Stephen King's The Dark Tower: A Concordance, Volume I.*
   V:486, VI:251

APPLE, THE BIG
   See NEW YORK CITY, *in* OUR WORLD PLACES

ARC
   See BORDERLANDS: GRAND CRESCENT

ARROYO COUNTRY
   See BORDERLANDS: CALLA BRYN STURGIS

B

BADLANDS
See CALLA BADLANDS *and* DISCORDIA, *both in* PORTALS

BANQUETING HALL
See CASTLE DISCORDIA, *in* PORTALS

BEACH (LOBSTROSITY BEACH)
See WESTERN SEA

BEACH DOORS
See DOORWAYS BETWEEN WORLDS: MAGICAL DOORWAYS, *in* PORTALS

BIG RIVER
See BORDERLANDS: RIVER WHYE

BOG
See MID-FOREST (MID-FOREST BOG)

BOOM-FLURRY HILL
See CALLA BADLANDS, *in* PORTALS

BORDERLANDS (THE RIM, ARC O' THE BORDERLANDS, THE CRESCENT)
The Arc o' the Borderlands is the crescent of land that separates MID-WORLD-that-was from END-WORLD, location of both THUNDERCLAP and the DARK TOWER. In CALLA BRYN STURGIS (setting for the novel *Wolves of the Calla*), the RIVER WHYE divides the green lands of the Callas from the desolate wastes of Thunderclap.

Although the world has most definitely moved on, and the borderlands have moved on with it, the Callas of the Crescent have remained more civilized than the other areas of Mid-World which our tet has visited so far. Unlike the mad, warring citizens of LUD (whom we learned about in *The Waste Lands*), the Calla *folken* have roads, law enforcement, and a system of government reminiscent of the democratic process found in New England town meetings. Perhaps the borderlands have managed to hold on to an older way of life because—even before IN-WORLD fell to JOHN FARSON—life in the Rim was always strange.

Despite having remained civilized, the people of the Callas have had to face a menace which those towns farther from the dark land of Thunderclap have never had to contemplate. Every generation, for the past six generations, masked riders have galloped over the River Whye and entered the Callas to steal one of every pair of prepubescent twins. (In the Callas, most children are born as twins, not as singletons.) These GREENCLOAKS, or WOLVES, deliver the children to the servants of the CRIMSON KING, who cull their brains for the chemical which causes twin-telepathy. When the children are returned to their homes (and most are sent back), they are ROONT, or ruined.

V:11, V:113, V:135, V:386, VI:7, VI:122, VII:21, VII:214, VII:716 *(Arc o' the Borderlands)*

ARC, THE: *See* GRAND CRESCENT, *listed below*

ARC QUADRANT: According to the rusted steel plate of the CALLA DOGAN, the area of the borderlands which our tet visits was once known as the Northeast Corridor Arc Quadrant. *See also* DOGAN, *in* PORTALS. V:564, V:565

BIG RIVER: *See* RIVER WHYE, *listed below*

BOG: *See* MID-FOREST (MID-FOREST BOG), *listed separately*

BOOM-FLURRY HILL: *See* CALLA BADLANDS, *in* PORTALS

CALLA (CALLAS): According to SUSANNAH DEAN, the word *Calla* means street or square. In the borderlands, Callas are towns. There are approximately seventy Callas in the borderlands. They form a mild arc, known locally as the GRAND CRESCENT. This crescent is approximately six thousand miles from tip to tip. As you travel north, toward the lands where snow falls, the towns are smaller. The people who live in them wear wooden shoes and make good cheese. They tend to farm and raise sheep. CALLA BRYN STURGIS (situated approximately one-third of the way down the Crescent) is a farming and ranching Calla. Farther south, the Callas consist of vast tracks of ranchland. There are mining Callas, manufacturing Callas, and pleasure Callas. All of the Callas near Calla Bryn Sturgis are attacked by the WOLVES of THUNDERCLAP once each generation. V:135–36 *(Callas in a mild arc, north and south of Calla Bryn Sturgis)*, V:332, VI:88, VI:377, VII:21, VII:52, VII:142, VII:152, VII:232, VII:233 *(Calla-bound)*, VII:300, VII:412, VII:558, VII:594

CALLA AMITY: Located north of CALLA BRYN STURGIS, Calla Amity is a farming and ranching Calla. V:135, V:397

CALLA BOOT HILL: We never learn where Calla Boot Hill is located. However, if EDDIE DEAN ever got the chance, he would slap leather and blow EBEN TOOK all the way to Calla Boot Hill. V:402

CALLA BRYN BOUSE: This Calla consists mainly of ranches. V:135

CALLA BRYN STURGIS: Calla Bryn Sturgis is located approximately one-third of the way down the GRAND CRESCENT. A town has existed on this site for over one thousand years, though its citizens have only been losing their children to THUNDERCLAP's green-cloaked WOLVES for about six generations. In the novel *Wolves of the Calla*, Roland and his tet defeat these robotic child-stealers. In the final EAST ROAD battle, where the horse-riders from Thunderclap are defeated, three members of the SIS-TERS OF ORIZA fight beside Roland and his friends.

The people of Calla Bryn Sturgis ride donkeys and burros. The men dress in white pants, long, colorful shirts, and dusty sombreros. Both women and men wear the clodhoppers known as shor'boots. There are approximately 140 men in the Calla, if one does not count either ROONTS or the very old. Since some of these men are unmarried farmhands; the female population is probably somewhat smaller. At the time our story takes place, approximately NINETY-NINE prepubescent children are in the town.

At times, Calla Bryn Sturgis is reminiscent of HAMBRY, the setting for *Wizard and Glass,* but at other times it bears a strong resemblance to STONEHAM, MAINE, and even 'SALEM'S LOT, MAINE. Perhaps they are all variations of the same town, just ones that exist on different levels of the DARK TOWER. The accent found in Calla Bryn Sturgis is similarly mixed. Some Calla words sound almost Scottish; others are reminiscent of Maine's Yankee dialect.

CALLA BRYN STURGIS DIRECTLY NAMED ON THE FOLLOWING PAGES: V:2, V:4, V:5, V:11, V:20, V:24, V:27, V:28, V:29, V:31, V:106, V:109 *(Calla),* V:111, V:113, V:114, V:115, V:119, V:123–24, V:128, V:129, V:142, V:143, V:147, V:148, V:151, V:153, V:154, V:156, V:158, V:159, V:160, V:161 *(Calla-folk),* V:166, V:174, V:180, V:188, V:201, V:204, V:206–7 *(ka-tet's first view),* V:208, V:210–34 *(pavilion),* V:237, V:296, V:321, V:339, V:340, V:359 *(indirect),* V:362, V:382, V:385, V:393, V:398, V:406, V:442, V:467, V:469, V:479, V:481, V:489, V:490, V:493, V:497, V:498, V:499, V:502, V:516, V:547, V:551, V:552, V:555, V:557, V:561, V:562, V:572, V:577, V:580, V:581, V:584, V:592, V:601, V:602, V:606, V:607, V:618, V:623, V:625, V:627, V:637, V:641, V:642, V:648, V:650, V:654, V:655, V:658, V:679, V:686, V:700, V:703, V:707, V:708, VI:3–43 *(setting),* VI:63, VI:67, VI:81, VI:84, VI:88 *(Calla),* VI:92, VI:103, VI:115, VI:122, VI:131, VI:178, VI:179, VI:184, VI:185, VI:187, VI:203, VI:222, VI:237, VI:247, VI:248, VI:252, VI:268, VI:272, VI:273, VI:281, VI:329, VI:339, VI:350, VII:4, VII:14, VII:26, VII:44, VII:73, VII:75, VII:81, VII:120, VII:126, VII:143, VII:146, VII:150, VII:152, VII:153, VII:156, VII:173, VII:207, VII:339, VII:398, VII:404, VII:423, VII:428, VII:473, VII:493, VII:518, VII:540, VII:602, VII:606, VII:627, VII:703, VII:708, VII:710, VII:722, VII:726, VII:743, VII:744, VII:748

ARRA'S SMALLHOLD PATCH: V:361

ARROYO COUNTRY (COMMALA DRAWS, MAGNETIC HILLS, BATTLE SITE): The arroyo country is the hilly land located northeast of Calla Bryn Sturgis. Here, in a worn-out garnet mine located at the end of a long dead-end canyon, Roland proposes that the Calla *folken* hide their children while he and his tet ambush the green-cloaked, child-stealing WOLVES. (Roland doesn't really plan to hide the children in such a dangerous place, but the Calla has too many informants for him to reveal his true strategy.)

The hills above the Calla are magnetic. Not only are they full of old garnet mines, but they are also riddled with many DOORWAYS BETWEEN WORLDS. The DOORWAY CAVE, where the MANNI found an unconscious PERE CALLAHAN, is located deep in the arroyo country. The EAST ROAD battle, where Roland, his tet, and the SISTERS OF ORIZA make a final stand against the Wolves, is located on a stretch of road that also winds north into this hilly land. V:340–42, V:406–9, V:508–9, V:548–52, V:575–76, V:662–97, V:700, VI:23–27, VI:30. *See also* MAGNETIC HILLS *and* DOORWAY CAVE, *both in* PORTALS

GLORIA MINE and REDBIRD TWO MINE: These two mines are located at the far end of a dead-end canyon. Roland tells the Calla *folken* that they should hide their children here when the WOLVES attack the town. (In actuality, Roland plans to hide the children in the rice paddies located near the RIVER WHYE.) V:508, V:575–76, V:608, V:615–16, V:663–97

UNFOUND DOOR: *See* DOORWAY CAVE, *in* PORTALS

UNFOUND DOOR (PATH TO THE): As HENCHICK warns Roland, this long, twisty path which leads through the arroyo country to the UNFOUND DOOR is rather "upsy." Despite this, the going is clear (and contains some spectacular views). However, the mouth of the DOORWAY CAVE is blocked by a large boulder. Anyone who wishes to enter this cave must first ease himself or herself around this rock. Unfortunately, the bit of free ledge is so small that a visitor's boot heels will have to hang free over a two-thousand-foot drop as he or she inches toward the cave mouth. (Ten feet farther down, where EDDIE DEAN almost falls, the drop from path to ground reduces to a mere seven hundred feet!) V:406–9, V:508–9, V:548–52, V:699–703, VI:6, VI:8, VI:23–27, VI:33, VI:41, VI:63–64

BADLANDS: *See* CALLA BADLANDS, *in* PORTALS

BLUFF: The bluff is located near a bend in the RIVER WHYE. JAKE and BENNY SLIGHTMAN go camping here. Not far from this spot, Jake overhears SLIGHTMAN THE ELDER having a suspicious conversation with ANDY, the Calla's traitorous Messenger Robot. V:323, V:380–87 *(camping)*, V:558 *(tenting place)*

BOOM-FLURRY HILL: *See* CALLA BADLANDS, *in* PORTALS

BUCKHEAD RANCH: This is GEORGE TELFORD's ranch. V:553

CAUSEWAY: *See* CALLA BADLANDS, *in* PORTALS

CAVE OF VOICES: *See* DOORWAY CAVE, *in* PORTALS

CAVERRA HOUSE: Home of the Caverra family. V:15

COMMALA DRAWS: *See* ARROYO COUNTRY, *listed above*

DOGAN: *See* DOGAN, *in* PORTALS

DOORWAY CAVE: *See* DOORWAY CAVE, *in* PORTALS

EAST ROAD: East Road is Calla Bryn Sturgis's major artery. Although for most of its length it runs from the west to the east, once it approaches the western shore of the RIVER WHYE, it turns and heads roughly north/northeast. (During his trip to the CALLA DOGAN, JAKE CHAMBERS discovers that the East Road originally continued east into THUNDERCLAP. For quite obvious reasons, the Calla *folken* no longer use this section and it has fallen into disrepair.)

Many years before our story takes place, JAMIE JAFFORDS and his WOLF POSSE killed a Wolf on the East Road. (Unfortunately, all of the human fighters, save for Jamie, died as well.) In *Wolves of the Calla*, the East Road is the site of our tet's final stand against Thunderclap's child-stealers. V:237 *(says west, should say east)*, V:348, V:360–65 *(Wolf posse)*, V:390–96, V:399–402, V:487, V:492 *(main road)*, V:508, V:561–62 *(continues into Thunderclap)*, V:629–35 *(junction with River Road)*, V:638–44 *(directly mentioned on 641)*, V:654–97, V:703, VI:5, VI:6, VI:10, VI:21–27, VI:31, VI:67, VII:126, VII:142, VII:558

GARNET MINES: *See* ARROYO COUNTRY, *listed above*

GATHERING HALL: *See* TOWN GATHERING HALL, *listed below*

GLORIA MINE: *See* ARROYO COUNTRY, *listed above*

HIGH STREET: During his brief but terrifying visit to the CALLA DOGAN, JAKE CHAMBERS discovers that either BEN SLIGHTMAN SR. or ANDY the Messenger Robot planted two spy cameras along the Calla's High Street. (However, it is also possible that an earlier spy planted these cameras.) V:9, V:10, V:13, V:210–12, V:213, V:234, V:238, V:618 *(two cameras)*, VII:423

JAFFORDS' LAND (JAFFORDS' BARN, JAFFORDS' HOME, RIVER FIELD, ROADSIDE FIELD, SON OF A BITCH): The JAFFORDS' family home place is located on RIVER ROAD. As well as their house and barn, the Jaffordses own three fields. River Field grows rice; Roadside Field grows sharproot, pumpkin, and corn; and Son of a Bitch produces nothing but rocks, blisters, and busted hopes. This final bit of information is hardly surprising since Son of a Bitch sits on loose ground. (Bogarts probably live below it.) V:1–13, V:343–69, V:376–80 *(barn)*, V:396–99, V:401, V:488–92, V:649

LIVERY: V:159, V:210

MAGNETIC HILLS: *See* ARROYO COUNTRY, *listed above; see also* DOORWAY CAVE *and* DOORWAYS BETWEEN WORLDS, *both in* PORTALS

MANNI CALLA (MANNI REDPATH, REDPATH KRA-TEN, REDPATH-A-STURGIS): Manni Calla, home of the local Manni sect, is located approximately two hours north of Calla Bryn Sturgis. In the CALLA DOGAN, JAKE discovers that someone planted two spy cameras in Manni Calla. V:6 *(indirect)*, V:213, V:399, V:566 *(two cameras)*, VI:3, VI:5, VI:6, VI:7, VI:9, VI:35 *(indirect)*, VI:38

> **HENCHICK'S KRA (CABIN):** Henchick's home. He lives here with his three wives. V:466

> **TEMPA (MANNI MEETING HALL):** The MANNI's Tempa is equivalent to the Calla's TOWN GATHERING HALL. VI:6

OUR LADY OF SERENITY (CHURCH, CHURCH RECTORY and ROSALITA'S COTTAGE): Our Lady of Serenity is FATHER CALLAHAN's church. Locally, it is also known as the MAN JESUS Church. As well as a house of worship, the church grounds contain Callahan's rectory, his small garden, and ROSALITA's cottage. Like many other places in the Calla, Pere Callahan's living room contains a spy camera. (This camera must have been placed by either BEN SLIGHTMAN SR. or ANDY, since Our Lady of Serenity was built relatively recently.)

Although the spies for THUNDERCLAP probably don't know it, Callahan's modest wooden church contains a secret. Under its floorboards sleeps BLACK THIRTEEN, the most evil of all MAERLYN's magic spheres. V:8, V:27 *(indirect)*, V:128 *(indirect)*, V:158 *(indirect)*, V:221 *(indirect)*, V:234 *(indirect)*, V:235–53 *(setting)*, V:254–309 *(Callahan tells his story here)*, V:309–17, V:337 *(indirect, bedroom)*, V:338, V:381, V:383, V:402, V:415, V:417–72 *(428–65 Callahan's story)*, V:475–86, V:487, V:488, V:494, V:496–505, V:506–8, V:566 *(one camera in church and one in rectory)*, V:584, V:589, V:598, V:617, V:628–29 *(privy)*, V:639–41, V:644–50, V:653 *(indirect)*, V:685, VI:3–18 *(setting)*, VI:67, VI:336

PAVILION and TOWN COMMON: All of the Calla's outdoor festivities are held on the town's common. When our tet first arrives in the village, the *folken* hold a welcoming party for them here, and Roland dances the Commala on the pavilion's bandstand. On Wolf's Eve (the night before the WOLVES are due to raid the town), Roland requests that all of the Calla's children come here to camp. One of the DOGAN's spy cameras records all that goes on in this place. Luckily, Roland and his tet know it and so only spread misleading information here. V:13, V:204, V:205, V:208, V:209, V:211–34, V:238, V:322, V:331, V:403, V:566 *(camera)*, V:567, V:581–90 *(palaver)*, V:601–17 *(green and musica)*, V:638, V:641, V:650–53, V:662 *(common)*, VI:12 *(common)*, VI:21 *(common)*, VI:67, VI:339

PEABERRY ROAD: V:360

RANCH ROAD: V:487

REDBIRD MINE TWO: *See* ARROYO COUNTRY, *listed above*

RIVER ROAD: River Road branches off the EAST ROAD. Many of the smallhold farms (including the JAFFORDS' FAMILY home) are located here. V:343, V:345, V:360, V:603, V:629–35 *(junction with East Road)*

RIVER STREET: River Street is located in the central part of Calla Bryn Sturgis. V:585

ROCKING B RANCH: The Rocking B Ranch, situated south of Calla Bryn Sturgis, is owned by VAUGHN EISENHART. The traitorous BEN SLIGHTMAN SR. is Eisenhart's foreman. JAKE's friend BENNY lives at the Rocking B. V:13, V:153, V:203, V:205, V:223, V:234, V:294, V:318–42, V:385, V:388, V:407, V:487, V:491, V:495, V:500, V:552, V:553–58, V:569, V:578, V:579–80, V:636–39, VI:17

SEVEN MILE: This is OVERHOLSER's farm. It is the largest in the Calla. V:157, V:213

TOOK'S GENERAL STORE (TOOKY'S): EBEN TOOK, owner of Took's General Store, is one of the most important men in Calla Bryn Sturgis. He is also one of the richest. Many years before the events of *Wolves of the Calla* take place, Tooky's was burned flat because some of the townsfolk tried to hide children there. Now the Tooks are too afraid of the WOLVES (and of lost profits) to stand up to the monsters of THUNDERCLAP.

According to both PERE CALLAHAN and Roland, Tooky's closely resembles the EAST STONEHAM GENERAL STORE located in EAST STONEHAM, MAINE. (Perhaps the biggest difference is that, at Tooky's, you can pay for your purchases with garnets as well as coins.) Like so many of the other gathering places of the Calla, Tooky's contains a hidden camera, probably planted by either BEN SLIGHTMAN SR. or ANDY the Messenger Robot.

In the STEPHEN KING story "Return to 'Salem's Lot," Tooky's is the name of a bar. V:13, V:14, V:19, V:147, V:150, V:211, V:359–60, V:400, V:401, V:402–6 *(mercantile and grocery)*, V:417, V:418, V:487, V:497, V:502 *(mercantile)*, V:534, V:545, V:566 *(camera)*, V:585, V:621, VI:67, VI:130, VI:162, VII:423

TOWN COMMON: *See* PAVILION, *listed above*

TOWN GATHERING HALL: All of Calla Bryn Sturgis's town meetings are held in the Town Gathering Hall, which stands at the end of HIGH STREET, beyond TOOK'S GENERAL STORE. Only men attend these gatherings. When one of the townsmen wants to call a meeting, he sends round the opopanax feather. If enough men touch the feather, the meeting is called. V:12, V:13–31, V:135, V:150, V:210, V:214, V:225, V:311, V:331, V:354, V:582, V:604, V:620

TRAVELERS' REST: This boardinghouse and restaurant is owned by the TOOK family. Unlike the TRAVELLERS' REST found in HAMBRY, the Calla's Travelers' Rest is spelled with only one L. *See also* MEJIS, BARONY OF: HAMBRY, TOWN OF: TRAVELLERS' REST. V:158 *(indirect)*, V:210

CALLA DIVINE: This Calla is located south of CALLA BRYN STURGIS. We know that the SISTERS OF ORIZA have members here too, since they buy ORIZAS from the women of CALLA SEN CHRE. V:332 *(as far south as the Orizas travel)*

CALLA LOCKWOOD: This Calla is located just south of CALLA BRYN STURGIS. It consists of farms and ranches. V:27, V:135, V:207, V:397

CALLA SEN CHRE: The people of this Calla farm and raise sheep. The women also make the titanium plates thrown by the SISTERS OF ORIZA. V:135, V:331–32 *(plates made here)*

CALLA SEN PINDER: The people of this Calla are farmers and sheep breeders. V:135

CALLA STAFFEL: This Calla consists mainly of ranchland. V:135

EASTERN PLAIN: *See* CALLA BADLANDS, *in* PORTALS

GRAND CRESCENT (ARC, ARC QUADRANT, MIDDLE CRESCENT, RIM): The Grand Crescent, also known as the Arc, contains all of the borderland Callas. It stretches for six thousand miles. CALLA BRYN STURGIS is located one-third of the way down the Crescent. V:135 *(indirect),* V:143, V:149, V:158, V:211, V:322, V:328, V:360, VII:300 *See also* OUTER ARC, *listed separately*

GREAT ROAD: *See* MEJIS, BARONY OF

MIDDLE CRESCENT: *See* GRAND CRESCENT, *listed above*

MID-FOREST: *See* MID-FOREST (MID-FOREST BOG), *listed separately*

RIVER WHYE (BIG RIVER, DEVAR-WHYE, DEVAR-TETE WHYE): Northwest of CALLA BRYN STURGIS, the River Whye divides into two branches. The western branch, located close to where the borderlands meet MID-WORLD-that-was, is known as the Devar-Whye. During the town meeting which takes place at the beginning of *Wolves of the Calla,* BUCKY JAVIER suggests that the Calla *folken* try to escape the WOLVES by heading in this direction. The eastern branch of the River Whye is known as the Devar-Tete Whye, or the Little Whye. The Devar-Tete Whye divides Calla Bryn Sturgis from the dead lands of THUNDERCLAP. The River Whye (which runs roughly north-south) is an important trade route for the people of the borderlands. Lake-boat marts often travel along it. Both branches of the River Whye empty into the SOUTH SEAS.
V:18, V:136, V:153 *(river),* V:206, V:211, V:238, V:242 *(river),* V:311, V:322 *(indirect),* V:331, V:338 *(indirect),* V:377, V:381, V:495, V:496, V:553, V:557, V:558–61, V:562, V:566, V:611, V:632, V:641, V:642, V:643, V:655, V:659, V:665–67, V:672, V:702, VI:10 *(riverbank),* VI:23, VI:24, VI:64 *(should say east side of Whye),* VI:67, VI:72, VII:151, VII:191, VII:203, VII:412

C

CAIN

We don't know where Cain is located. However, we do know that it figures prominently in a song sung by the servants of the CRIMSON KING as they chase JAKE CHAMBERS and OY through the passage located beneath the DIXIE PIG:

> We don't care how far you run!
> We'll bring you back before we're done!
> You can run to Cain or Lud!
> We'll eat your balls and drink your blood!
> VII:109

CALLA
  For all Callas and Calla entries, see BORDERLANDS

CALLA BRYN STURGIS
  See BORDERLANDS

CAUSEWAY (DEVIL'S CAUSEWAY)
  See CALLA BADLANDS, *in* PORTALS

CAVE OF VOICES
  See DOORWAY CAVE, *in* PORTALS

CLEAN SEA
In *Wizard and Glass,* we learned that the Clean Sea is located east of HAM-
BRY. In *Wolves of the Calla,* Roland tells us that JERICHO HILL lies at least
five hundred miles farther north along the Clean Sea's shores.
  V:170

COMMALA DRAWS
  See BORDERLANDS: CALLA BRYN STURGIS: ARROYO COUNTRY

CÖOS
  See MEJIS, BARONY OF

CRADLE OF LUD
  See RIVER BARONY: LUD

CRESCENT
  See BORDERLANDS: GRAND CRESCENT

CYCLOPEAN MOUNTAIN RANGE
While traveling across these mountains at the end of *The Gunslinger,* Roland
and JAKE encountered the sex-hungry ORACLE OF THE MOUNTAINS. In
the abandoned subway tunnels below the range, they battled the disfigured
SLOW MUTANTS. Jake met his second death in the tunnels below the Cyclo-
pean Mountains. (For more information, see *Stephen King's The Dark Tower:
A Concordance, Volume I.*)
  V:462 *(indirect)*

D

DARK TOWER
See entry in PORTALS

DELAIN
See EASTAR'D BARONY

DOGAN
See entry in PORTALS

DOORWAY CAVE
See entry in PORTALS

E

EAST DOWNE
East Downe was one of the many lands Roland traveled through during his years as a MID-WORLD wanderer. In East Downe, there are walking waters. Unfortunately, they are never described.
VI:234

EAST ROAD
See BORDERLANDS: CALLA BRYN STURGIS

EASTAR'D BARONY
VII:184
DELAIN: According to *The Dark Tower,* WALTER was born in Delain. This kingdom is also the setting for STEPHEN KING's novel *The Eyes of the Dragon.* In the short story "The Little Sisters of Eluria," we were told that Delain was also known as Dragon's Lair and Liar's Heaven. VII:184

EASTERN PLAIN (CALLA BADLANDS)
See CALLA BADLANDS, *in* PORTALS

ELURIA
The town of Eluria was the setting for the Dark Tower–related short story "The Little Sisters of Eluria." When Roland traveled through it, all the human

inhabitants were dead. The only remaining creatures were the mutant GREEN FOLK and the vampiric LITTLE SISTERS. (For more information about the town of Eluria as well as the GREEN FOLK and the LITTLE SISTERS, see *Stephen King's The Dark Tower: A Concordance, Volume I.*)
VI:234

EYEBOLT CANYON
See MEJIS, BARONY OF

G

GARLAN, BARONY OF
The distant kingdom of Garlan plays an indirect, but interesting, part in the Dark Tower series. In the first four books of the series, we learn that Garlan is the home of the Grand Featherex, that its citizens have brown skin, and that many poisons are produced there. (See *Stephen King's The Dark Tower: A Concordance, Volume I.*) Not surprisingly, the accomplished poisoner RANDALL FLAGG (in his *Eyes of the Dragon* incarnation) once lived in Garlan, though (according to *The Dark Tower*) he was using the name WALTER HODJI at the time. In *Song of Susannah,* we learn that Roland's grandfather ALARIC went to Garlan to slay a dragon.
VI:197, VII:39, VII:183

GARNET MINES
See BORDERLANDS: CALLA BRYN STURGIS: ARROYO COUNTRY

GATHERING HALL
See BORDERLANDS: CALLA BRYN STURGIS: TOWN GATHERING HALL

GILEAD
See NEW CANAAN, BARONY OF

GILEAD, BARONY OF
See NEW CANAAN, BARONY OF

GLASS PALACE
See GREEN PALACE, *in* PORTALS

GLORIA MINE
See BORDERLANDS: CALLA BRYN STURGIS: ARROYO COUNTRY

GOLGATHA, THE
See entry in PORTALS

GRAND CRESCENT
See BORDERLANDS

GREAT HALL
See NEW CANAAN, BARONY OF: GILEAD

GREAT ROAD
See MEJIS, BARONY OF

GREAT WEST WOODS (SHARDIK'S WOODS)
At the beginning of *The Waste Lands,* Roland, EDDIE, and SUSANNAH
traveled through the Great West Woods. Here, Susannah shot the cyborg
BEAR GUARDIAN, SHARDIK. At Shardik's lair, our tet discovered the start-
ing point of the BEAR-TURTLE BEAM. (For more information, see *Stephen
King's The Dark Tower: A Concordance, Volume I.*)
    V:37, V:110, V:512 *(clearing),* V:563 *(clearing),* V:573 *(Shardik's woods),*
VII:466 *(indirect)*

GREEN PALACE
See entry in PORTALS

H

HILL OF STONE FACES
See JERICHO HILL

I

IN-WORLD (INNER BARONIES/IN-WORLD BARONIES)
When the author STEPHEN KING refers to the whole of Roland's version of
earth, he uses the term *Mid-World.* However, when he refers to specific regions
of Mid-World, he uses the terms IN-WORLD, OUT-WORLD, MID-WORLD,
END-WORLD, and the BORDERLANDS. During Roland's youth, the term *In-
World* was used to refer to those baronies which sat at the center of human culture, where the old civilized ways still held and where some of the old electrical
machinery still worked. Roland and the gunslinger elite ruled In-World from the

walled city of GILEAD, barony seat of NEW CANAAN. The sigul of In-World was ARTHUR ELD's horse, LLAMREI. An image of Llamrei decorated Gilead's pennons. (For more information, see *Stephen King's The Dark Tower: A Concordance, Volume I.*)

V:11, V:13, V:94, V:243, V:604 *(In-World-that-was)*, VI:97, VI:247, VII:210, VII:549 *(Llamrei, Arthur Eld's horse, is the sigul for all In-World)*, VII:550, VII:594, VII:607, VII:664

J

JAFFORDS' LAND
See BORDERLANDS: CALLA BRYN STURGIS

JERICHO HILL (near the HILL OF STONE FACES)
The last great battle between the tattered remnants of the AFFILIATION and the remains of FARSON's army took place on Jericho Hill. CUTHBERT ALL-GOOD died here, shot through the eye by an arrow aimed at him by Roland's old enemy WALTER O'DIM. JAMIE DECURRY was also brought down here, though he was killed by a sniper (probably GRISSOM's eagle-eyed son). Roland (the only gunslinger to survive) saved his skin by hiding in a cart filled with the dead. He crept out of the slaughter pile at sundown, just before the whole works were set alight.

The east side of Jericho Hill was a shale-crumbly drop to the CLEAN SEA. Its western edge, known as the Hill of Stone Faces, was a long, sloping field filled with great, gray-black, sculptured visages. Roland's horn, the HORN OF ELD, was dropped on Jericho Hill by a dying Cuthbert. Roland never retrieved it, which he regrets greatly by the time he reaches the DARK TOWER.

V:153, V:169–72, V:173, V:240, V:284, V:347, V:410, VI:134, VI:219, VII:144, VII:174–75, VII:465, VII:552, VII:748, VII:762, VII:819, VII:825, VII:829

L

LOBSTROSITY BEACH
See WESTERN SEA

LUD
See RIVER BARONY

LUDWEG
See RIVER BARONY

M

MANNI CALLA (MANNI REDPATH)
See BORDERLANDS: CALLA BRYN STURGIS

MEJIS, BARONY OF
The Barony of Mejis was the setting for most of *Wizard and Glass*. (See *Stephen King's The Dark Tower: A Concordance, Volume I*.) Roland and his two childhood friends CUTHBERT ALLGOOD and ALAIN JOHNS were sent to Mejis by their fathers to keep them safe from JOHN FARSON and his traitorous cohort, the enchanter MARTEN BROADCLOAK. (As CONSTANT READERS will remember, Marten shamed Roland into taking his test of manhood years too early.) While in Mejis, Roland and his two friends confronted the BIG COFFIN HUNTERS, who (along with most of Mejis's population) secretly served Farson. While in HAMBRY, Roland fell in love with SUSAN DELGADO, made an enemy of the evil witch RHEA OF THE CÖOS, and retrieved MAERLYN'S GRAPEFRUIT for the gunslingers. Susan Delgado was eventually killed on a Charyou Tree fire, falsely accused of treason.
V:35, V:85, V:92, V:116, V:117, V:166, V:170, V:181, V:195, V:202, V:210, V:211, V:341, V:400, V:405, VI:184, VI:242, VI:279, VI:404 *(and Mexico)*, VII:84, VII:175, VII:219, VII:270, VII:271, VII:317, VII:321, VII:331, VII:333, VII:455, VII:468, VII:524, VII:552, VII:651, VII:695, VII:802
CÖOS: A ragged hill located five miles from HAMBRY, ten miles from EYEBOLT CANYON. RHEA lived here. V:40, V:55, V:71, V:703, VII:179, VII:219
DROP: A long, grassy slope which stretched for thirty wheels toward the sea. It was used as a horse meadow. V:202, VI:184, VII:762
EYEBOLT CANYON: A short, steep-walled box canyon shaped like a chimney lying on its side. A THINNY had eaten its way into the far end of it. Roland destroyed FARSON's followers by laying a trap for them in Eyebolt Canyon. V:341, V:508, V:576, VII:524
GREAT ROAD: V:210
HAMBRY, TOWN OF: Hambry (Barony Seat of Mejis and setting for the novel *Wizard and Glass*) was a beautiful town located on the edge of the CLEAN SEA. Its citizens were fishermen and horsebreeders. It was here that Roland, CUTHBERT ALLGOOD, and ALAIN JOHNS battled the BIG COFFIN HUNTERS and the other followers of JOHN FARSON. *(For page references, see MEJIS, listed above.)*
  SEAFRONT: Mayor HART THORIN's house. (For HART THORIN

entry, see *Stephen King's The Dark Tower: A Concordance, Volume I.*)
V:166

TRAVELLERS' REST: The Travellers' Rest was Hambry's bar and
whorehouse. It was owned by CORAL THORIN and her brother HART
THORIN. SHEEMIE RUIZ worked here doing odd jobs. When Sheemie
(now a BREAKER in THUNDERCLAP) meets the BEAM BOY in the
final book of the Dark Tower series, he does so in a dream-version of the
Travellers' Rest. *See also* BORDERLANDS: CALLA BRYN STURGIS:
TRAVELERS' REST. For more information about Hambry's version of
the Travellers' Rest, and entries for Coral and Hart Thorin, see *Stephen
King's The Dark Tower: A Concordance, Volume I.* VII:219, VII:220,
VII:271 *(indirect)*, VII:333, VII:336

RIM: *See also* BORDERLANDS: GRAND CRESCENT. VI:184

SILK RANCH ROAD: V:210

MIA'S CASTLE
See CASTLE DISCORDIA, *in* PORTALS

MID-FOREST (MID-FOREST BOG)
The wooded region which our tet travels through at the beginning of *Wolves
of the Calla* is known as Mid-Forest. It marks the beginning of the BORDER-
LANDS. While following the PATH OF THE BEAM through this fairy-tale
wood, Roland and his ka-tet are tracked by FATHER CALLAHAN and the
other representatives from CALLA BRYN STURGIS. Our tet makes their first
trip to NEW YORK, via TODASH, from their Mid-Forest campsite.

V:38–47 *(traveling through; mentioned on 41, 45)*, V:66–68 *(Roland follows Susannah)*, V:80–169 *(setting)*, V:197–206 *(setting)*, V:246 *(woods)*,
V:406, V:604 *(named)*, V:681, VI:30, VII:594

BOG: While Roland's ka-tet travels through Mid-Forest, MIA, daughter of
none, takes over SUSANNAH DEAN's body so that she can feed her CHAP
in the Mid-Forest bogs. Although she is actually eating frogs and binnie bugs,
Susannah-Mio dreams that she is dining in CASTLE DISCORDIA's BAN-
QUETING HALL. V:82–86, V:88

MID-WORLD
When the author STEPHEN KING refers to the whole of Roland's version of
earth, he uses the term *Mid-World*. However, when he refers to specific regions
of Mid-World, he uses the terms IN-WORLD, OUT-WORLD, MID-WORLD,
END-WORLD, and the BORDERLANDS. In the Mid-World version of earth
which our tet travels through in the Dark Tower series, both time and directions
are in drift. Hence, ANDY (CALLA BRYN STURGIS's Messenger Robot) often
refers to it as Mid-World-that-was.

In *The Waste Lands,* Roland drew a metaphysical map of Mid-World,
which was meant to encompass all the known lands of his reality. According to
this map, Mid-World was shaped like a sequin impaled upon a central needle.

The center of the needle—or the hub of the earth-wheel—was the DARK TOWER, or the nexus of the time/space continuum. Radiating out from the Tower were the BEAMS, those invisible high-tension wires which simultaneously held all of the universes together and maintained the divisions between them. According to this map, End-World (home of the Tower) sat at the center of everything, like a bull's-eye, and In-World (the hub of human civilization when Roland was a boy) didn't even appear on the map. Although the terms *End-World* and *In-World* are confusing when viewed in this manner, readers must remember that Roland's map was meant to be figurative, not literal. It was a teaching tool used to explain universal forces, not actual geography. (For an explanation of why In-World was called In-World, see the IN-WORLD entry, listed separately.)

Although the term *Mid-World* is usually used in its most general form, the word originally applied to a specific kingdom—one which tried to preserve culture and knowledge in a time of darkness. Mid-World's ancient boundaries stretched from a marker near the edge of the GREAT WEST WOODS to MID-FOREST, the wooded area which abuts the borderlands. The city of LUD (which our tet traveled through in *The Waste Lands*) was Mid-World's largest urban center. Since King often implies that Lud is a future version of our world's NEW YORK, and since the BEAR-TURTLE BEAM runs through both New York and Lud, it seems likely that the ancient kingdom of Mid-World was (geographically at least) more closely linked to the northeastern part of the United States than to the Southwest, which it resembles.

V:4, V:13, V:18, V:25 *(the Mids)*, V:31, V:35, V:39, V:44 *(term for Roland's world)*, V:48, V:49 *(term for Roland's world)*, V:51 *(term for Roland's world)*, V:56, V:58, V:61, V:71, V:89, V:100, V:108, V:111 *(term for Roland's world)*, V:137, V:138 *(Mid-World-that-was)*, V:165, V:202, V:214, V:478, V:501, V:631, VI:7, VI:30, VI:40, VI:67, VI:84, VI:122, VI:148, VI:247, VI:403, VI:404, VI:405, VI:407, VII:12, VII:37, VII:51, VII:84, VII:103, VII:141, VII:234, VII:260, VII:262, VII:300, VII:336, VII:382, VII:395, VII:398, VII:555, VII:580, VII:594, VII:598, VII:601, VII:607, VII:668, VII:669, VII:670, VII:715, VII:802, VII:810, VII:817

MOHAINE DESERT

In *The Gunslinger*, Roland pursued his nemesis the MAN IN BLACK (also known as WALTER) across this deadly expanse of desert. Although the border dwellers lived on the edges of this wasteland, nothing could survive within its desiccated heart. The WAY STATION (which is actually a way station between worlds) is located in the Mohaine. (For more information, see *Stephen King's The Dark Tower: A Concordance, Volume I.*)

VI:180 *(indirect)*, VI:283 *(not directly named)*, VI:288, VII:175, VII:515, VII:594, VII:827–30

N

NA'AR
See entry in PORTALS

NEW CANAAN, BARONY OF
The Barony of New Canaan, ruled by the gunslinger descendants of ARTHUR ELD, shares its name with the biblical land of milk and honey. Before the fall of the AFFILIATION, New Canaan (and its barony seat of GILEAD) was the hub of IN-WORLD. Like the ancient kingdom of MID-WORLD (the kingdom for which Roland's version of earth is named), New Canaan tried to keep alive the ideals of hope, knowledge, and light. *For page references, see* GILEAD, *listed below.* (For more information, see *Stephen King's The Dark Tower: A Concordance, Volume I.*)

GILEAD: Roland remembers his home city of Gilead as a jewel set amid New Canaan's green-gold fields and serene, blue rivers. Before IN-WORLD fell to JOHN FARSON, the ancient walled city of Gilead was MID-WORLD's last great urban center. The color of Gilead's royal court was dark blue. LLAMREI, who was both ARTHUR ELD's horse and the sigul of all In-World, decorated the city's pennons. V:30, V:49, V:50, V:85, V:94 *(most inner of inner baronies)*, V:109, V:124, V:128, V:143, V:153, V:162, V:171, V:175, V:182, V:195, V:214, V:215, V:218, V:221, V:230, V:243, V:318, V:321, V:322, V:392, V:406, V:416, V:500, V:527, V:528, V:542, V:604, V:605 *(low-town)*, V:612, V:641, V:654, V:679, VI:16, VI:17, VI:63, VI:106, VI:129, VI:149, VI:183, VI:197, VI:234, VI:271, VI:275, VI:277, VI:279, VI:299, VI:319, VI:328, VI:370, VI:395, VI:396, VII:24, VII:35, VII:43, VII:50, VII:111, VII:122, VII:134, VII:135, VII:159, VII:166, VII:168, VII:172, VII:174, VII:176, VII:178, VII:179, VII:199, VII:219, VII:266, VII:270, VII:317, VII:322, VII:323, VII:333, VII:349, VII:381, VII:382, VII:384, VII:393, VII:411, VII:415, VII:439, VII:443, VII:487, VII:492, VII:494 *(Great Letters)*, VII:496, VII:499, VII:516 *(dark blue is the royal color)*, VII:549 *(Llamrei on pennons)*, VII:552, VII:601, VII:607, VII:651, VII:657, VII:711, VII:727, VII:749, VII:759, VII:801, VII:802, VII:821, VII:824, VII:828

BABY FOREST: The Baby Forest was located west of Gilead's castle. In it took place one of the apprentice gunslingers' tests of manhood, overseen by none other than the infamous CORT. Cort maintained that neither clocks nor sundials could be depended upon all of the time, so his students had to learn to keep a timepiece ticking inside of their minds. Summer evening after summer evening, the apprentices were sent out to spend an uncomfortable night in the forest until they could return to the yard behind the GREAT HALL at exactly the moment that Cort specified. As Roland testified to SUSANNAH, it took a great while to get that internal clock ticking, but once it did, it ran true. Roland lost this ability when the BEAMS began collapsing, but after the battle at the DEVAR-TOI, the skill returned. VII:587

BLOSSWOOD FORESTS (BLOSSIE FARMS): While he and his ka-tet are trying to explain to the people of CALLA BRYN STURGIS why it is important to fight the WOLVES, even at the risk of losing everything, Roland tells the story of the Blosswood Forests, which he knew and loved as a boy. The thousand-acre Blosswood Forests were located in the eastern part of the Barony of New Canaan. The blossies were farmed and so stood in neat rows, which were overseen by the barony forester. Blosswood was strong, yet so light that a thin piece could practically float on the air. Hence, it was the best possible wood for making boats. The rule of the foresters was always the same—for every two trees harvested, three must be planted. That way, the barony was assured a good crop for all time.

However, when Roland was a boy, a terrible plague fell upon the Blosswood Forests. Spiders spun webs in their crowns, killing the upper branches and rotting them. Most of the trees fell before the plague could reach their roots. Seeing what was happening, the foresters ordered that all the trees be cut down, to save what wood was still usable. Within a year, the Blossie Forests no longer existed. In Roland's opinion, the Wolves are like the foresters. Since end-times are so close, the Wolves will take *all* the children when they next arrive, not just one of every pair of twins. V:612–13

GREAT HALL: Gilead's Great Hall was a grand place. It had great balconies and a central dancing area illuminated by electric flambeaux. The Spring Ball (also known as the Sowing Night Cotillion) was held here. (For more information about the Great Hall, and to see further page references, see *Stephen King's The Dark Tower: A Concordance, Volume I.*) V:50, VII:587

> **YARD BEHIND THE GREAT HALL:** Here, CORT awaited those apprentice gunslingers who had spent the night in the BABY FOREST. VII:587

NORTH FIELD: Apprentice gunslingers practiced bow-shooting in North Field. V:248

ROLAND'S NURSERY (CONTAINS THE ROOM OF MANY COLORS): The windows of Roland's childhood nursery were made of stained glass colored to represent the BENDS O' THE RAINBOW. When he hears the High Speech word *chassit,* Roland has a vivid memory of this room, and of his mother singing the Baby-Bunting Rhyme to him. (*For the words of the Baby-Bunting Rhyme, see* APPENDIX III.) VII:22, VII:23, VII:329

NORTH CENTRAL POSITRONICS (FACTORY)
See NORTH CENTRAL POSITRONICS, *in* CHARACTERS

O

OUR LADY OF SERENITY
See BORDERLANDS: CALLA BRYN STURGIS

OUTER ARC
In *Wizard and Glass,* we learned that geographical terms such as *Outer Arc* were metaphorical rather than literal. During Roland's youth, backwater baronies such as MEJIS, which existed far from the civilized hub of the IN-WORLD baronies, were known as OUT-WORLD baronies or Outer Arc baronies. These relative terms of *in, out,* and *outer* make sense when you consider them in terms of the metaphysical map of MID-WORLD which Roland drew in *The Waste Lands.* On that map, the DARK TOWER sat at the center of the world-circle, and the PORTALS (watched over by the GUARDIANS) sat at its periphery. If this metaphor of the world-circle is applied to the human world, then In-World, and the In-World baronies such as NEW CANAAN, sit at the center of the map, since they form the hub of civilization. Cultural backwaters, which are both physically and psychically distant from the hub, are considered part of the Outer Arc. In *Wolves of the Calla,* we learn that most of Mid-World's coffee was grown in the southern reaches of the Outer Arc.
V:89

OUT-WORLD
In *Wizard and Glass,* we learned that, during Roland's youth, geographical terms such as *Out-World* were more metaphorical than literal. To the IN-WORLD citizens of GILEAD (barony seat of NEW CANAAN), those baronies located far from the hub of civilization were part of Out-World. They existed "out there," on the OUTER ARC of human culture. In *Wolves of the Calla,* the same metaphorical use of terms applies, but the center, or hub, of the world changes. To the people of CALLA BRYN STURGIS, the Callas of the BORDERLANDS form the hub of the known world. Hence, any people who travel to the borderlands from other parts of MID-WORLD are considered *outworlders.*
V:8, V:312 *(outworlders),* V:344 *(outworlders),* V:402 *(outworlders),* V:418 *(outworlders),* VII:176

P

PEABERRY ROAD
   See BORDERLANDS: CALLA BRYN STURGIS

PORTALS
   See DOORWAYS BETWEEN WORLDS *and* BEAMS, PATH OF THE,
both in PORTALS

R

REDBIRD TWO MINE
   See BORDERLANDS: CALLA BRYN STURGIS: ARROYO COUNTRY

REDPATH KRA-TEN
   See BORDERLANDS: CALLA BRYN STURGIS: MANNI CALLA

REDPATH-A-STURGIS
   See BORDERLANDS: CALLA BRYN STURGIS: MANNI CALLA

RIM, THE
   See BORDERLANDS: GRAND CRESCENT

RIMROCKS
A few days before the final gunslinger battle of JERICHO HILL, Roland's rein-
forcements (DEMULLET'S COLUMN) were ambushed and slaughtered here.
ALAIN JOHNS heard the news, but when he galloped back to camp after midnight to inform his friends about the disaster, he was accidentally shot. Alain
died under Roland and CUTHBERT's guns.
   V:170

RIVER BARONIES (and WAYDON CASTLE)
According to the stories Roland heard as a child, LADY ORIZA, the rice god-
dess, was born in Waydon Castle near the RIVER SEND. However, in the
BORDERLANDS Oriza is associated with the RIVER WHYE. Although Lady
Oriza is always associated with a river (rice only grows in flooded paddies), the
particular River Barony she rules may vary from region to region and from folk-
tale to folktale.
   V:325–26 *(Waydon Castle)*

RIVER BARONY
River Barony, which our ka-tet traveled through in *The Waste Lands,* took its
name from the RIVER SEND, which flowed through it. According to some
Mid-World folktales, LADY ORIZA came from River Barony. *(For page references, see RIVER BARONIES, listed separately.)*

> **LUD:** Our ka-tet traveled through the war-torn city of Lud in *The Waste
> Lands.* Although it was once the greatest city in the kingdom of MID-
> WORLD, by the time our tet arrived, this once thriving metropolis was a
> battlefield fought over by the warring PUBES and GRAYS, rival gangs
> manipulated by BLAINE, Lud's psychotic computer brain. On another
> level of the DARK TOWER, Lud is a version of our world's NEW YORK
> CITY. V:35, V:135, V:141, V:165 *(and Mid-World),* V:166, V:178–79 *(and
> New York),* V:225, V:246, V:319 *(The Great City),* V:377, V:379, V:512,
> V:565, V:610, VI:14, VI:67, VI:91, VI:118, VI:152, VI:184, VI:206, VI:244,
> VI:287, VII:84, VII:109, VII:120, VII:160, VII:502, VII:521, VII:558,
> VII:590, VII:594, VII:725

> > **CRADLE OF LUD (BLAINE'S CRADLE):** When BLAINE, Lud's mad
> > computer brain, animated the city's pink Monorail, he was known as
> > Blaine the Mono. Blaine the Mono slept in the Cradle of Lud, which was
> > the GREAT OLD ONES' version of our world's Grand Central Station.
> > (For more information about the Cradle of Lud, and about Blaine, see
> > *Stephen King's The Dark Tower: A Concordance, Volume I.)* V:38,
> > VII:77, VII:492

> > **LUD BRIDGE:** *See* SEND RIVER: SEND RIVER BRIDGE

> **LUDWEG:** The town of Ludweg is located north of Lud. JOCHABIM, the
> hume dishwasher whom JAKE CHAMBERS meets in the kitchens of the
> DIXIE PIG, originally came from Ludweg. VII:84

> **RIVER CROSSING:** In *The Waste Lands,* our tet had a grand meal with the
> ancient residents of River Crossing, then held palaver with them. Although
> the River Crossing *folken* had to hide their gardens and homes behind
> ruined building facades (otherwise LUD's harriers would have come to
> burn and raze), these elderly people maintained a level of civilization
> unknown in the nearby metropolis. The residents of River Crossing were led
> by AUNT TALITHA, who gave Roland a gold cross to place at the foot of
> the DARK TOWER. V:55, V:78, V:110, V:134, V:192, VI:111, VI:117,
> VI:118, VI:182, VII:50, VII:120, VII:126 *(a forgotten town),* VII:473,
> VII:802

> **RIVER SEND:** *See* SEND RIVER, *listed separately*

RIVER CROSSING
See RIVER BARONY

RIVER FIELD
See BORDERLANDS: CALLA BRYN STURGIS: JAFFORDS' LAND

RIVER ROAD
  See BORDERLANDS: CALLA BRYN STURGIS

RIVER SEND
  See SEND RIVER

RIVER STREET
  See BORDERLANDS: CALLA BRYN STURGIS

ROADSIDE FIELD
  See BORDERLANDS: CALLA BRYN STURGIS: JAFFORDS' LAND

ROCKING B RANCH
  See BORDERLANDS: CALLA BRYN STURGIS

ROSALITA'S COTTAGE
  See BORDERLANDS: CALLA BRYN STURGIS: OUR LADY OF SERENITY

S

SEND RIVER
The Send River flows through RIVER BARONY. Our tet had to cross the Send
to reach the city of LUD.
  V:325
  SEND RIVER BRIDGE (CROSSING TO LUD): In *The Waste Lands,* our
  tet had to cross this dilapidated bridge to enter the city of LUD. Unfortu-
  nately, the child-snatcher GASHER was waiting for them on the far side.
  VII:502

SEVEN MILE
  See BORDERLANDS: CALLA BRYN STURGIS

SHARDIK'S WOODS
  See GREAT WEST WOODS; *see also* BEAMS, PATH OF THE, *in* POR-
TALS

SILK RANCH ROAD
  See MEJIS, BARONY OF

SON OF A BITCH
  See BORDERLANDS: CALLA BRYN STURGIS: JAFFORDS' LAND

SOUTH PLAINS

The MUTANT minstrel CHEVIN OF CHAYVEN—one of the CHILDREN OF RODERICK—once called the South Plains his home. Although his tribe originated in lands far from those Roland ever knew, Chevin's people gave their grace to Roland's ancestor ARTHUR ELD in the days before the world moved on. EDDIE DEAN assumes that the South Plains are in MID-WORLD, so I have placed them here as well.

VII:51

SOUTH SEAS

The RIVER WHYE, which runs through the BORDERLANDS, eventually flows into the South Seas.

V:136

SWAMP

See MID-FOREST (MID-FOREST BOG)

T

TEMPA

See BORDERLANDS: CALLA BRYN STURGIS: MANNI CALLA

THINNIES

See THINNY, *in* PORTALS

THUNDERCLAP

See entry in PORTALS

TOOK'S GENERAL STORE

See BORDERLANDS: CALLA BRYN STURGIS

TOWN COMMON

See BORDERLANDS: CALLA BRYN STURGIS

TOWN GATHERING HALL

See BORDERLANDS: CALLA BRYN STURGIS

TRAVELERS' REST/TRAVELLERS' REST

See BORDERLANDS: CALLA BRYN STURGIS; *see also* MEJIS, BARONY OF: HAMBRY, TOWN OF

TULL
While following the trail of the MAN IN BLACK in *The Gunslinger,* Roland traveled through the depressingly dilapidated town of Tull. While in Tull, Roland had to battle the followers of the evil preacher SYLVIA PITTSTON. Unfortunately, Roland ended up shooting all of Tull's residents, including his lover, ALICE. (For more information, see *Stephen King's The Dark Tower: A Concordance, Volume I.)*
   V:253, VI:283, VI:284, VI:288

U

UNFOUND DOOR
   See DOORWAY CAVE, *in* PORTALS

UNFOUND DOOR (PATH TO THE)
   See BORDERLANDS: CALLA BRYN STURGIS: ARROYO COUNTRY

W

WASTELANDS
   See CALLA BADLANDS *and* DISCORDIA, *both in* PORTALS

WAY STATION
   See entry in PORTALS

WAYDON
   See RIVER BARONIES

WESTERN PLAINS
   See BORDERLANDS

WESTERN SEA and LOBSTROSITY BEACH
The opening section of *The Drawing of the Three* (the second novel of the Dark Tower series) takes place on the barren, gray shores of the Western Sea. Here, Roland loses two of his right fingers and part of his great toe to the monstrous LOBSTROSITIES. On these deserted shores Roland also discovers the magical BEACH DOORS, which lead him to the Prisoner (EDDIE DEAN), the Lady of Shadows (ODETTA HOLMES/DETTA WALKER), and the Pusher (JACK

MORT). For more information about the Western Sea, see *Stephen King's The Dark Tower: A Concordance, Volume I.*

V:77, V:105, V:409, V:445, V:701, VI:132, VI:284, VI:295, VI:395, VII:177 *(shore),* VII:339, VII:594, VII:723, VII:741, VII:749

WHYE
  See BORDERLANDS: RIVER WHYE

WILLOW JUNGLE
The Willow Jungle, located high in the CYCLOPEAN MOUNTAINS, was the home of the ORACLE OF THE MOUNTAINS. In *The Gunslinger*, Roland gained prophecy from this spirit, but her price was sexual intercourse. Although Roland didn't know it at the time, this creature was no mere wraith but the female aspect of a DEMON ELEMENTAL. Once she collected Roland's sperm, she gave it to the servants of the CRIMSON KING, who used it to create MORDRED. (For more information about the Willow Jungle, see *Stephen King's The Dark Tower: A Concordance, Volume I.*)
  V:46 *(indirect)*

X

XAY RIVER
ALAIN JOHNS, CUTHBERT ALLGOOD, and Roland Deschain crossed the Xay River while returning to GILEAD from HAMBRY. To cross the Xay, Roland and his friends had to clamber across a rope bridge. To make sure that no enemies followed, Alain severed the rope after they used it, and the remains of the bridge fell into the water a thousand feet below. Despite there being no bridge to cross, SHEEMIE managed to follow Roland's tet all the way back to GILEAD. In *The Dark Tower*, we find out that Sheemie (a powerful BREAKER) teleported himself.
  VII:271

OUR WORLD PLACES
AND THE MULTIPLE AMERICAS[1]

Look, there are a billion universes comprising a billion realities. . . .
Those realities are like a hall of mirrors, only no two reflections are
exactly the same. I may come back to that image eventually, but not
yet. What I want you to understand for now—or simply accept—is
that reality is *organic*, reality is *alive*.

VII:270

Maybe instead of forty-two continental United States on the other
side of the Hudson, there are forty-two hundred, or forty-two *thousand*, all of them stacked in vertical geographies of chance.
    And he understands instinctively that this is almost certainly true.
He has stumbled upon a great, possibly endless, confluence of worlds.
They are all America, but they are all different. There are highways
which lead through them, *and he can see them*.

V:298–99

A

AKRON
  See OHIO (STATE OF)

ALABAMA (STATE OF)
In SUSANNAH DEAN's *when* of 1964, Alabama cops were more than willing
to sic dogs on black marchers protesting for voting rights. The world might be
moving on, but some things have improved.
  V:75, VI:109
  BIRMINGHAM/BOMBINGHAM: V:75

1. For definitions of the terms *Multiple Americas* and *Alternative Americas*, see
APPENDIX I, MID-WORLD DIALECTS. Also see the entry MULTIPLE AMERICAS in
this section of the *Concordance*.

ALASKA (STATE OF)
V:428, VII:41, VII:229
FAIRBANKS: The FORTY BUS is hobo-speak for the bus that will take you as far away as possible. If you're living in NEW YORK CITY, the forty bus will probably drop you off somewhere near Fairbanks, Alaska. V:428, VII:41

ALBUQUERQUE
See NEW MEXICO (STATE OF)

ALDERSHOT
See ENGLAND

ALTERNATIVE AMERICAS
See MULTIPLE AMERICAS, *below in this section; see also* ALTERNATIVE AMERICAS, *in* APPENDIX I

ARCTIC
JAKE CHAMBERS doesn't envy people who live in arctic countries, since they have to deal with long periods of darkness each year. He thinks such a life would be even worse than one spent under the artificial sun of THUNDER-CLAP.
VII:256

ARIZONA (STATE OF)
V:57, V:118, V:305
BLACK FORK: In the kind of western novels which CALVIN TOWER likes to read, heroes always blow into towns like Black Fork, Arizona, clean up the town, then blow on like tumbleweeds. V:57, V:118
GRAND CANYON: VI:241
PHOENIX: V:305

ATLANTIC CITY
See NEW JERSEY (STATE OF)

ATTICA STATE PRISON
See NEW YORK (STATE OF)

AUSCHWITZ
See POLAND

AUSTRIA
VIENNA: Sigmund Freud, author of *Ego and Id* (1923), studied medicine in Vienna and joined the staff of the Vienna General Hospital in 1882. In *Ego and Id,* Freud discussed his theories concerning the division

of the unconscious mind into the id, the ego, and the superego. AUSTIN CORNWELL and his fellow fake UFFIS must have read this book. VI:231 *(Viennese)*

B

BABYLON
VI:319

BACK BAY
See MASSACHUSETTS (STATE OF)

BAHAMAS
In *The Drawing of the Three*, EDDIE DEAN traveled to NASSAU as a drug runner for ENRICO BALAZAR. (See *Stephen King's The Dark Tower: A Concordance, Volume I.*) Luckily for Eddie, Roland entered his mind during his plane ride home and convinced him to dump his stash on the bleak shores of the WESTERN SEA. Otherwise, Eddie would have ended up in prison. However, Balazar was none too pleased about Eddie's little side trip.
V:453, VI:212, VII:19
NASSAU: V:453, V:524, VII:19

BALAZAR'S OFFICE
See NEW YORK CITY: MANHATTAN: LEANING TOWER

BANGOR
See MAINE (STATE OF)

BARCELONA LUGGAGE STORE
See NEW YORK CITY: MANHATTAN: SECOND AVENUE

BECKHARDT COTTAGE
See MAINE (STATE OF): LOVELL: TURTLEBACK LANE

BERGEN-BELSEN
See GERMANY

BERMUDA
LAMLA, a TAHEEN servant of the CRIMSON KING, likes to wear Bermuda shorts (close-fitting shorts which reach the knees). I don't know what connection Bermuda shorts have to Bermuda, but I figure it's worth mentioning.
VII:104

BERNIE'S BARBER SHOP
See NEW YORK CITY: BROOKLYN

BLACK FORK
See ARIZONA (STATE OF)

BLACK HOLE OF CALCUTTA
See INDIA

BLACK TOWER (2 HAMMARSKJÖLD PLAZA)
See LOT, THE: 2 HAMMARSKJÖLD PLAZA, *in* PORTALS

BLACKSTRAP MOLASSES CAFÉ
See NEW YORK CITY: MANHATTAN

BLEECKER STREET
See NEW YORK CITY: MANHATTAN

BOLIVIA
Back in *The Drawing of the Three,* EDDIE DEAN tried to smuggle cocaine into NEW YORK CITY for ENRICO BALAZAR. This high-grade white powder originated in Bolivia. Eddie refers to it as Bolivian marching powder.
   V:525

BOSTON
See MASSACHUSETTS (STATE OF)

BRAZIL
According to FRANK ARMITAGE, secret servant of the CRIMSON KING, most of the South American businessmen who hired the SOUTH AMERICAN SEABEES were Brazilian.
   VII:284
   RIO: VII:285

BRIDGTON
See MAINE (STATE OF)

BROOKLYN
See NEW YORK CITY: BROOKLYN

BROOKLYN BRIDGE
See NEW YORK CITY: BROOKLYN

BRYCE
See COLORADO (STATE OF)

BUCHENWALD
See GERMANY

C

CAIRO
See EGYPT

CALIFORNIA (STATE OF)
During his years following the HIGHWAYS IN HIDING, PERE CALLAHAN spent quite a bit of time in California. His longest drunken period (four full days) took place in this state. While in SACRAMENTO, Callahan discovered that his old friend ROWAN MAGRUDER had been attacked by the HITLER BROTHERS.

Callahan's twinner, TED BRAUTIGAN, applied for his *job of a lifetime* while in California. He got the position, but it ended up being a life sentence as a BREAKER in THUNDERCLAP.

V:179, V:305, V:306–309, V:424, VI:13, VI:211, VII:707
DEATH VALLEY: V:461
DISNEYLAND: V:152, VII:369
FORT ORD: V:101
HOLLYWOOD: V:451, V:640, VII:207
LOS ANGELES: V:451
SACRAMENTO: CALLAHAN spent the spring of 1981 in Sacramento. He read about ROWAN MAGRUDER's terrible injuries in the *Sacramento Bee*. V:296 *(Bee),* V:306–309, V:422, VII:281, VII:283
    CRAZY MARY'S: FATHER CALLAHAN and his Mexican workmates like the enchiladas made at this take-out restaurant. V:307
    SLEEPY JOHN'S: FATHER CALLAHAN worked here while living in Sacramento. V:307
SAN BERDOO: V:102
SAN FRANCISCO: In the back of an out-of-business dance studio, surrounded by filmy pink tutus, FRANK ARMITAGE, a hume servant of the CRIMSON KING, offered TED BRAUTIGAN the *job of a lifetime*. The job turns out to be a life sentence in the DEVAR-TOI of THUNDERCLAP. V:255, V:451, VI:188, VII:7, VII:211, VII:281, VII:283, VII:285, VII:286, VII:289, VII:657
    MARK HOPKINS HOTEL: VII:286
    SANTA MIRA: A door here leads from our world to THUNDERCLAP. VII:287–89, VII:297
    SEAMAN'S SAN FRANCISCO BANK: VII:285, VII:287, VII:289
SANTA MONICA: VII:471
    SANTA MONICA ASPCA: IRENE and DAVID TASSENBAUM began

their romance here amid the howls and yaps of homeless pets. Irene arrived looking for a kitten; David came to drop off a stray dog. Irene may not have found her kitten, but she did find a beau. VII:471
YOSEMITE: VI:242

CALTECH
DAVID TASSENBAUM attended CalTech. According to his wife, IRENE, David and his CalTech friends invented the Internet.
VII:429

CANADA
VII:94
MONTREAL: VII:94

CANNIBAL ISLANDS
See entry in PORTALS

CARA LAUGHS
See DOORWAYS BETWEEN WORLDS, *in* PORTALS

CHEW CHEW MAMA'S
See NEW YORK CITY: MANHATTAN: SECOND AVENUE

CHICAGO
See ILLINOIS (STATE OF)

CHINA
V:561

CHRISTOPHER STREET STATION
See NEW YORK CITY: MANHATTAN

CHURCH OF THE HOLY GOD-BOMB
See NEW YORK CITY: BROOKLYN

CHURCH OF THE WALK-INS
See MAINE (STATE OF): STONEHAM

CITY HALL
See NEW YORK CITY: MANHATTAN

CLEMSON UNIVERSITY
Clemson University is located in Clemson, SOUTH CAROLINA. DAMLI HOUSE of the DEVAR-TOI would look at home on the Clemson campus.
VII:230

CLEVELAND
  See OHIO (STATE OF)

COLORADO (STATE OF)
  V:192, VII:283, VII:811
  BRYCE: The BREAKER TANYA LEEDS was born and raised in Bryce.
  VII:283
  DENVER: V:192

COLUMBIA UNIVERSITY
ODETTA HOLMES attended this university. During a late-night college hen
party, she heard the story of a girl on a road trip who was too shy to tell her
friends that she had to stop and pee. As a result, her bladder burst in the car.
(Messy!)
  During her college years, Odetta (later Susannah) took Psych I with PRO-
FESSOR OVERMEYER. In this class she learned the fantastic visualization
technique which helps her see, and enter, her internal DOGAN. While at
Columbia, she also took a medieval history course with PROFESSOR MUR-
RAY. Professor Murray taught his students the story of KING ARTHUR and his
betraying son/nephew MORDRED.
  VI:62, VI:116, VI:221

CONEY ISLAND
  See NEW YORK CITY: BROOKLYN

CONNECTICUT (STATE OF)
When TED BRAUTIGAN escaped from the DEVAR-TOI through a door
made for him by his fellow BREAKER, SHEEMIE, he landed in Connecticut.
The story of Ted's Connecticut adventure—and of his friendship with BOBBY
GARFIELD—is the subject of the short story "Low Men in Yellow Coats,"
which can be found in the STEPHEN KING book *Hearts in Atlantis.*
  In the recorded tale which our ka-tet listens to in their camp on STEEK-
TETE in THUNDERCLAP, Ted confides that he was born in MILFORD,
Connecticut, in 1898. However, in *Hearts in Atlantis,* he tells Bobby Garfield
that he was born in Teaneck, NEW JERSEY. (In the latter case, Ted must have
been talking about a parallel version of himself.)
  VI:389, VII:212, VII:233, VII:234, VII:270, VII:273, VII:297, VII:298,
  VII:304, VII:326, VII:339, VII:357, VII:376, VII:415
  BRIDGEPORT: This is where the LOW MEN caught TED BRAUTIGAN
  at the end of his Connecticut adventure. They dragged him back to the
  DEVAR-TOI. For more information about Ted's little vacation in Con-
  necticut, see *Hearts in Atlantis.* VII:376
  HARTFORD: V:263, VII:274–76, VII:282, VII:297
    EAST HARTFORD HIGH: During World War One, TED BRAUTI-
    GAN visited a recruitment office here. He was rejected because of health

problems but *also* because he was a telepath. His uncanny abilities frightened the doctors. VII:275

HARWICH: VII:483

   MOTEL 6: VII:483

MILFORD: In the final book of the Dark Tower series, TED BRAUTIGAN tells our tet that he was born in Milford in 1898. VII:212, VII:273, VII:415

NORWICH: PATRICK DANVILLE's pencils (complete with erasers) were bought in a Norwich Woolworth's in 1958. Hence, Norwich played its own small but significant part in Roland's ultimate triumph over the CRIMSON KING. VII:800

WESTPORT: V:544, VI:185

CO-OP CITY
   See NEW YORK CITY: BROOKLYN

COPIAH
   See MISSISSIPPI (STATE OF)

COSTA DEL SOL
   See SPAIN

CROSS BRONX EXPRESSWAY
   See NEW YORK CITY: BRONX

CUBA
   VII:599

CULLUM'S CABIN
   See MAINE (STATE OF): EAST STONEHAM

CUYAHOGA RIVER
   See OHIO

D

DALE'S FANCY BUTCHER SHOP
   See OHIO (STATE OF): AKRON

DEAN FAMILY APARTMENT
   See NEW YORK CITY: BROOKLYN

DELAWARE (STATE OF)
During his years traveling along the HIGHWAYS IN HIDING, PERE
CALLAHAN worked for a while as an apple-picker in Delaware.
V:302
ROUTE 71: V:302

DENMARK
VII:603
See also MAINE (STATE OF)

DENMARK, MAINE
See MAINE (STATE OF)

DENNIS'S WAFFLES AND PANCAKES
See NEW YORK CITY: MANHATTAN: CHEW CHEW MAMA'S

DES MOINES
See IOWA (STATE OF)

DETROIT
See MICHIGAN (STATE OF)

DIMITY ROAD
See MAINE (STATE OF): EAST STONEHAM

DIXIE PIG
See entry in PORTALS

DODGE
See KANSAS

DUBLIN
See IRELAND

DUKE UNIVERSITY
Duke University has a department of Psychical Research. According to JOHN
CULLUM, one of the subjects they study is WALK-IN activity.
VI:152

DUTCH HILL
See NEW YORK CITY: BROOKLYN

E

EAST CONWAY VILLAGE
See NEW HAMPSHIRE (STATE OF)

EAST FRYEBURG
See MAINE (STATE OF)

EAST STONEHAM
See MAINE (STATE OF)

EGYPT
VII:115
CAIRO: V:140
PYRAMIDS: VII:115

ENGLAND
GRACE RUMBELOW, an incredibly annoying BREAKER, came from ALDERSHOT, ENGLAND.
VI:390, VII:394
HAMPSHIRE: VII:394
   ALDERSHOT: VII:394
LONDON: V:91, V:506, VII:242
STONEHENGE: VII:777

ETHIOPIA
VII:732

EVEREST
See MOUNT EVEREST

F

FLORIDA (STATE OF)
V:305, VI:408, VII:570, VII:674

FORMOSA (TAIWAN)
Originally known by its aboriginal name, Pakan, this island was renamed For-

mosa when an early Dutch navigator (sailing on a Portuguese ship) saw it and exclaimed, "Ilha formosa" or "beautiful island." The contemporary name *Taiwan* is an adaptation of the word *tayouan*, which means "terrace bay."
VII:115

FORT ORD
See CALIFORNIA (STATE OF)

FRANCE
VII:275, VII:276
NOTRE DAME CATHEDRAL: V:595
PARIS: VI:242
   LOUVRE: VII:242

FRENCH LANDING
See WISCONSIN (STATE OF)

FRYEBURG
See MAINE (STATE OF)

G

GAGE PARK
See KANSAS (STATE OF): TOPEKA

GAIETY
See NEW YORK CITY: MANHATTAN: TIMES SQUARE

GARDEN OF THE BEAM
See LOT, THE, *in* PORTALS

GERMANY
VII:276
BERGEN-BELSEN: A Nazi concentration camp located in northwest Germany, near the village of Belsen. VII:698
BUCHENWALD: A Nazi concentration camp located in eastern Germany, near the village of Buchenwald. VII:698
HAMELIN: In *Wolves of the Calla*, EDDIE DEAN compares ANDY, CALLA BRYN STURGIS's duplicitous Messenger Robot, to the Pied Piper of Hamelin. Eddie draws this comparison because the children of the Calla love Andy and follow him everywhere, but another, more sinister meaning is behind Eddie's statement. According to the old folktale, the town of

Hamelin was afflicted by a plague of rats, and the people of the town could not get rid of the terrible, flea-bitten rodents. However, just as they were about to go out of their minds, along came a piper in a parti-colored suit who agreed to solve their problem as long as they paid him what he wanted. The Pied Piper and the townsfolk agreed on an amount, but once the rats were gone, the stingy *folken* refused to honor their pledge. The Piper left, only to return the following Saint John's Day. This time when he played his pipe, he charmed the children away. None of them were ever seen again. Only two little children remained in the village—one who was blind and could not see the Piper to follow him, and one who was lame and could not keep up with his little fellows. Like the Pied Piper, Andy steals children. He doesn't do it himself—the WOLVES OF THUNDERCLAP do it for him—however, he is every bit as guilty as they are. V:586–87

GRAND ARMY PLAZA
See NEW YORK CITY: BROOKLYN

GRAND CANYON
See ARIZONA (STATE OF)

GRAND COULEE DAM
See WASHINGTON (STATE OF)

GRAND RIVER MEN'S WEAR
See MICHIGAN (STATE OF): DETROIT

GRANT PARK
See NEW YORK CITY: BROOKLYN

GREEN BAY
See WISCONSIN (STATE OF)

GREENWICH VILLAGE
See NEW YORK CITY: MANHATTAN

GUTTENBERG, FURTH, AND PATEL
See NEW YORK CITY: MANHATTAN

GUYANA
The Reverend Jim Jones established the People's Temple in Jonestown, Guyana. Almost one thousand people committed suicide there by drinking poisoned Kool-Aid. While they downed their final drinks, the reverend stood on his porch and, holding a bullhorn to his lips, recounted stories about his mother.
    VII:211

H

HAMELIN
See GERMANY

HAMMARSKJÖLD PLAZA (2 HAMMARSKJÖLD PLAZA)
See NEW YORK CITY: MANHATTAN: SECOND AVENUE

HAMPSHIRE
See ENGLAND

HARRIGAN'S STREET CORNER
See NEW YORK CITY: MANHATTAN: SECOND AVENUE

HARVARD
TED BRAUTIGAN attended Harvard.
   VII:212, VII:273, VII:276
   HARVARD BUSINESS SCHOOL: VII:126

HAWAII (STATE OF)
   V:48, V:89

HIDDEN HIGHWAYS/HIGHWAYS IN HIDING
See HIDDEN HIGHWAYS, *in* PORTALS

HOBOKEN
See NEW JERSEY (STATE OF)

HOME
Home was a wet shelter for homeless people located on FIRST AVENUE and FORTY-SEVENTH STREET in MANHATTAN, NEW YORK. The owner and chief supervisor was PERE CALLAHAN's friend ROWAN MAGRUDER. Unlike many of New York City's shelters, Home accepted both men and women and allowed in people who were drunk as well as sober. At Home, the drunks weren't locked up, the booze was. If somebody came in suffering from the d.t.'s, he or she would be given a shot, and probably a sedative chaser to keep him or her quiet. Despite—or more probably because of—its unusual policies, Home became one of the city's most successful, and highly regarded, shelters. In 1977, Mother Teresa visited it, and in 1980, Magruder was named Man of the Year by New York City's Mayor Ed Koch. (Magruder even made the cover of *Newsweek*.)

After his terrible encounter with the VAMPIRE BARLOW, Pere Callahan traveled to New York and ended up at this shelter. Although he began as a resident, he ended up as an employee. Pere worked for Home from October of 1975 until June of 1976. However, in June of 1976, just after his friend and fellow Home employee LUPE DELGADO died from AIDS (contracted through the bite of a TYPE THREE VAMPIRE), a distraught Callahan went back on the booze. Pere left Home and—bottle in hand—began his inebriated journeys along America's HIGHWAYS IN HIDING.

V:106, V:266–68, V:271–82, V:287, V:292, V:308–309 *(Magruder and Hitler Brothers)*, V:422, V:424 *(flophouse)*, V:425, V:426, V:427, V:428–29, V:443, V:445, V:452, V:466, VI:332

HUDSON RIVER
See NEW YORK (STATE OF)

HUNGRY I
See NEW YORK CITY: MANHATTAN

I

ILLINOIS (STATE OF)
CHICAGO: V:423
GREENTOWN: To Ray Bradbury fans, Greentown is a well-known and well-loved place. Based upon Bradbury's hometown of Waukegan, Illinois, it represents all that is best in small-town America. However, in the Dark Tower series, Greentown becomes a sinister place.

According to SUSANNAH DEAN, the DEVAR-TOI (or BREAKER prison) is reminiscent of Bradbury's idealized Midwestern town. Its cozy Main Street and nearby college campus look like snapshots out of an album of Americana—places where there is no crime, where girls wearing dresses with hemlines safely below the knee kiss their boyfriends a chaste goodnight and then return to their college dorms early so that their dormitory moms (as well as their actual mothers) will think well of them. Its low buildings and friendly streets make the viewer daydream about a time before the world *moved on*—an era predating world wars and cold wars, when the sun always shone and old folks sat happily on their porches, drinking lemonade.

However, as our tet knows all too well, the apparent friendliness of THUNDERCLAP's Greentown is an illusion. The sun is an artificial spotlight, run by a technological egg timer. The town is surrounded by barbed wire and all of the citizens are prisoners, who have become so accustomed to their lot that they no longer question the terrible job that they have been brought here to do. In truth, the psychic residents of the Devar-Toi are eroding the BEAMS so that the DARK TOWER—the linchpin of existence—will collapse. The instability of the multiverse is being generated from this outpost owned by the CRIMSON KING. VII:209

INDIA
CALCUTTA:
BLACK HOLE OF CALCUTTA: In the annals of imperialist history, the Black Hole of Calcutta is infamous. Following the capture of Calcutta by Siraj-ud-Dawalah, nawab of Bengal, in 1756, one hundred and forty-six British defenders were placed in this narrow, airless dungeon, twenty feet by twenty feet. According to the story, only twenty-three survived the night. The actual details of the event remain controversial, and many historians believe that the true number of Englishmen jailed was probably smaller. However, as SUSANNAH DEAN discovers when she is imprisoned by MIA, the Black Hole of Calcutta remains a fairly accurate description of the horror and desperation a person feels when she is imprisoned without hope of escape or rescue. VI:124
NEW DELHI: VII:127

IOWA (STATE OF)
V:192
DES MOINES: VII:279

IRELAND
V:465
DUBLIN: The crucifix which FATHER CALLAHAN used to stave off the VAMPIRE BARLOW in 'SALEM'S LOT, MAINE, originally came from Dublin. Callahan's mother bought it in a souvenir shop, probably at a scalper's price. During his confrontation with Barlow, Callahan learned that the trappings of religion have no intrinsic worth if the one wielding them does not have faith. V:459

ISRAEL
JERUSALEM: *See also* MAINE (STATE OF): JERUSALEM'S LOT. V:192

ISSAQUENA COUNTY
See MISSISSIPPI (STATE OF)

ITALY
LEANING TOWER OF PISA: In *The Waste Lands,* JAKE CHAMBERS glued a photograph of this tower to the final page of his English-class essay entitled "My Understanding of Truth." Though he didn't realize it at the time, the Leaning Tower (which he had covered in black crayon scribbles) was his unconscious mind's version of the DARK TOWER. See *Stephen*

King's The Dark Tower: A Concordance, Volume I. See also NEW YORK CITY: MANHATTAN: LEANING TOWER (BALAZAR'S OFFICE) V:56

J

JAFFORDS RENTALS
  See MAINE (STATE OF): EAST STONEHAM

JAPAN
  SAPPORO: VI:226

JERUSALEM
  See ISRAEL; *see also* MAINE (STATE OF): JERUSALEM'S LOT

JERUSALEM'S LOT
  See MAINE (STATE OF): JERUSALEM'S LOT

JFK AIRPORT
  See NEW YORK CITY: QUEENS

JOHN CULLUM'S CABIN
  See MAINE (STATE OF): EAST STONEHAM

JONESTOWN
  See GUYANA

K

KANSAS (STATE OF)
The state of Kansas (initial setting for *The Wizard of Oz*) plays an important part in the Dark Tower series. At the beginning of *Wizard and Glass*, BLAINE the Insane Mono crashed into an alternative version of our world's TOPEKA, one devastated by the superflu virus. (The story of the superflu, which killed off more than 99 percent of America's population, is told in STEPHEN KING's novel *The Stand*.)

Like HAMBRY—the MID-WORLD town where Roland, CUTHBERT ALLGOOD, and ALAIN JOHNS battled the BIG COFFIN HUNTERS and the other traitors to the AFFILIATION—this alternative Topeka contained a

THINNY. The sight and sound of this warbling DOORWAY BETWEEN WORLDS enticed Roland to tell his new friends about the trials he faced in Hambry, and about his ill-fated love affair with the beautiful, young SUSAN DELGADO. Also in this alternative version of Kansas, our tet entered the GREEN PALACE and confronted OZ the Great and Terrible—a wizard who turned out to be none other than Roland's longtime nemesis, WALTER (aka RANDALL FLAGG). (See *Stephen King's The Dark Tower: A Concordance, Volume I.*)

Kansas continues to play a significant role in the final books of the Dark Tower series. In late winter of 1982, PERE CALLAHAN reeled drunkenly through the city of Topeka and landed in a JAIL CELL there. While incarcerated, he had an alcohol-related seizure. Although Callahan joined Alcoholics Anonymous and managed to sober up, he was not destined to settle in this state. In the fall of that year, Callahan saw the first of the LOW MEN's "lost pet" posters advertising for information about his whereabouts. Callahan left Topeka for DETROIT.

V:35, V:106, V:296, V:447, V:456, VI:298, VI:401
    DODGE: VII:811
    LAWRENCE: VI:401
    TOPEKA: V:36, V:106, V:440, V:445–49, VI:25, VI:103, VII:531
        GAGE PARK: V:291, V:449, VII:335
            REINISH ROSE GARDEN: In Reinish Rose Garden (home of the infamous toy version of CHARLIE THE CHOO-CHOO) PERE CALLAHAN saw some of the LOW MEN's "lost pet" posters, offering a reward to anyone who could disclose his whereabouts. Callahan left Kansas in a hurry. V:449
    JAIL CELL: FATHER CALLAHAN was held here for assaulting an officer. While incarcerated, he had an alcohol-related seizure. V:445–49
    KANSAS CITY: V:36
    KANSAS TURNPIKE (I-70): V:35, V:36, V:291, V:516

KANSAS CITY BLUES
See NEW YORK CITY: MANHATTAN

KANSAS ROAD
See MAINE (STATE OF)

KENTUCKY
While traveling along the HIGHWAYS IN HIDING, CALLAHAN worked as a gravedigger in Kentucky. His shovel-buddy was a digger named PETE PETAKI. Pete had a taste for seventeen-year-old jailbait. However, the girl who caught his eye turned out to be a TYPE THREE VAMPIRE. Callahan destroyed her before she could sink her teeth into Petaki's all-too-willing throat.
    V:302
    ROUTE 317: V:302

KEYSTONE EARTH/KEYSTONE WORLD
See KEY WORLD/KEYSTONE WORLD, *in* PORTALS

KEYWADIN POND
See MAINE (STATE OF): EAST STONEHAM

KEZAR LAKE
See MAINE (STATE OF): LOVELL

KIDZPLAY
See GUTTENBERG, FURTH, AND PATEL, *in* CHARACTERS

KING'S CHILDHOOD BARN
See entry in PORTALS

KING'S HOUSE IN LOVELL
See DOORWAYS BETWEEN WORLDS: CARA LAUGHS, *in* PORTALS

KLATT ROAD
See MAINE (STATE OF)

KOREA
VII:280

L

LA GUARDIA AIRPORT
See NEW YORK CITY: QUEENS

LAS VEGAS
See NEVADA (STATE OF)

LAWRENCE
See KANSAS (STATE OF)

LEANING TOWER (BALAZAR'S OFFICE)
See NEW YORK CITY: MANHATTAN

LEANING TOWER OF PISA
See ITALY

LEWISTON
See MAINE (STATE OF)

LIGHTHOUSE SHELTER

CALLAHAN worked at this wet shelter (located in DETROIT) from the late autumn of 1982 until December of 1983. According to Pere, it was an almost exact replica of the HOME shelter he'd worked at in NEW YORK CITY, although one without ROWAN MAGRUDER to manage it. Callahan's workmates at Lighthouse were WARD HUCKMAN and AL MCCOWAN. In early December of 1982, Ward received a letter from the SOMBRA CORPORATION, saying that Lighthouse had been awarded a million-dollar grant. However, when the three men arrived at SOMBRA's corporate headquarters to discuss the details of their windfall, they discovered that the whole thing was a setup. Huckman and McCowan were knocked unconscious by electrical stunners, and Callahan was left to face the evil RICHARD P. SAYRE and the other servants of the CRIMSON KING alone. Rather than submit to the bites of Sayre's HIV-infected TYPE THREE VAMPIRES, Callahan jumped out the window of the TISHMAN BUILDING. He died in our world only to awake in MID-WORLD's WAY STATION.

V:270, V:449, V:450–57 *(up to Sayre's trickery)*, V:466

LONDON
See ENGLAND

LOS ZAPATOS
See MEXICO

LOT, THE
See LOT, THE, *in* PORTALS

LOUISIANA (STATE OF)
NEW ORLEANS: V:305, V:621

LOVELL
See MAINE (STATE OF)

LOWELL
See MASSACHUSETTS (STATE OF)

M

MACY'S
See NEW YORK CITY: MANHATTAN

MADISON SQUARE GARDEN
See NEW YORK CITY: MANHATTAN

MAINE (STATE OF)

Maine is the home state of our *kas-ka Gan*, STEPHEN KING. It is also the setting for several scenes in *Wolves of the Calla* and significant stretches of *Song of Susannah*. When CALVIN TOWER flees NEW YORK CITY to escape from BALAZAR'S MEN, he and his sidekick, AARON DEEPNEAU, take up temporary residence in EAST STONEHAM, Maine. When Roland and EDDIE DEAN travel through CALLA BRYN STURGIS's UNFOUND DOOR to find the anally retentive bibliophile, they land in front of the EAST STONEHAM GENERAL STORE, where Balazar's men already lie in wait for them.

In Maine, Roland and Eddie meet JOHN CULLUM, their *dan-tete*. Cullum leads them to Calvin Tower (from whom they finally buy the Vacant LOT), and also directs them to the home of Stephen King, where these two members of our tet finally meet their maker. In addition, Cullum brings Roland and Eddie to CARA LAUGHS, the magical DOORWAY BETWEEN WORLDS, which is the center of western Maine's WALK-IN activity.

When Roland and JAKE CHAMBERS return to Maine in 1999 to save Stephen King from the Dodge minivan which is destined to hit him, Jake dies. He is buried on a Maine roadside. Over his grave, IRENE TASSENBAUM promises to plant a ROSE. *For further information about walk-in activity, see also* NEW HAMPSHIRE (STATE OF).

V:106, V:256, V:537, V:598, V:627, VI:4, VI:35, VI:123, VI:130–54, VI:158–216, VI:265–303, VI:397, VI:408, VII:17–53, VII:113–32, VII:266, VII:421–79, VII:521, VII:522, VII:559

ALTERNATIVE AMERICAS AND THE STATE OF MAINE: The following towns don't exist on KEYSTONE EARTH, hence we cannot assign them to specific counties. However, they do exist on other levels of the TOWER, and in a number of other STEPHEN KING novels.

JERUSALEM'S LOT ('SALEM'S LOT): In one of the ALTERNATIVE AMERICAS, Jerusalem's Lot is located in CUMBERLAND COUNTY. Jerusalem's Lot (usually referred to as 'Salem's Lot) was the VAMPIRE-infested setting for STEPHEN KING's novel *'Salem's Lot*. Our good friend PERE CALLAHAN, whom we meet in *Wolves of the Calla,* was the Lot's boozing Catholic priest.

Although initially skeptical, Callahan eventually joined forces with BEN MEARS, MATTHEW BURKE, JAMES CODY, and MARK PETRIE to destroy the TYPE ONE VAMPIRE, BARLOW, who initiated all of the Lot's problems. Although Callahan managed to save Mark Petrie (if not the boy's parents) from this servant of the Outer Dark, the priest's faith ultimately proved too weak to stand up against his enemy. Callahan was forced to drink Barlow's blood, and though it did not turn him into a vampire, it disgraced him in the eyes of God. Outcast from the WHITE, Callahan fled 'Salem's Lot for NEW YORK CITY. V:31, V:106, V:109, V:119, V:234, V:256–62, V:269, V:270, V:291, V:298, V:299, V:454, V:468, V:470, V:706, VI:171, VI:177, VI:211, VI:271, VI:280, VI:307, VI:329, VII:3, VII:15, VII:28, VII:593, VII:802

MARSTEN HOUSE: The evil Marsten House was built by Hubie Marsten, the president of a 1920s trucking company that specialized in running Canadian whiskey into Massachusetts. Hubie and his wife, Birdie, settled in the Lot in 1928, but they lost most of their money in the stock market crash of 1929. In the ten years between the disaster of 1929 and the rise of Adolf Hitler, Hubie and his wife became hermits, and Hubie went mad. In 1939, one of the Lot's residents smelled something foul issuing from the building and so entered the house through the back door. He found booby traps (set for unwanted visitors) all over the place. He also found the body of Birdie sprawled on the kitchen floor (her husband had shot her in the head), and the remains of Hubie himself dangling from a rafter. When the VAMPIRE BARLOW and his servant STRAKER decided to take up residence in 'Salem's Lot, they chose this scene of a murder-suicide as their abode. V:257, V:291–92 *(indirect)*

PETRIE HOUSE AND KITCHEN: MARK PETRIE's home. The fateful confrontation between PERE CALLAHAN and the VAMPIRE BARLOW took place here. V:258–61, V:280, VII:11

SAINT ANDREW'S CHURCH: CALLAHAN's church. After drinking BARLOW's blood, Callahan was too polluted to enter this sacred space. V:261

> **RECTORY:** VI:307

SPENCER'S DRUGS: Spencer's Drugs doubled as the town's bus station. V:261, V:262

DERRY: STEPHEN KING's version of BANGOR, MAINE. Like JERUSALEM'S LOT, it exists on one of the other levels of the DARK TOWER. Many of King's novels (including *Insomnia* and *It*) take place in Derry. VII:412

EAST OVERSHOE: East Overshoe is EDDIE DEAN's humorous nickname for the town of EAST STONEHAM. V:627

'SALEM'S LOT: *See* JERUSALEM'S LOT, *above*

ANDROSCOGGIN COUNTY:

AUBURN: VII:118

LEWISTON: VI:403, VII:480, VII:485

> **CENTRAL MAINE GENERAL HOSPITAL:** STEPHEN KING was taken to this hospital after being hit by BRYAN SMITH's Dodge minivan. VII:480, VII:485 *(indirect)*

LISBON:

> **LISBON HIGH:** VI:289

CUMBERLAND COUNTY:

BRIDGTON: In 1977, STEPHEN KING and his family lived in this town, which is located twenty-five miles from EAST STONEHAM. In *Song of Susannah,* EDDIE and Roland meet King here. Like many other western Maine towns, Bridgton is plagued by WALK-INS. VI:151, VI:170, VI:172, VI:207, VI:209, VI:211, VI:265–303, VI:389, VI:391,

VI:411, VII:17, VII:20, VII:24, VII:33–48 *(Eddie and Roland on road)*,
VII:119, VII:123, VII:159, VII:435, VII:457, VII:476, VII:573
  BRIDGTON HIGH STREET: VII:40
  BRIDGTON SHOPPING CENTER: VI:265, VI:267, VII:41
    BRIDGTON PIZZA AND SANDWICHES: VII:41
    DEPARTMENT STORE (RENY'S): VII:41
    DRUGSTORE: VI:265, VII:41
    LAUNDRY: VI:265
    MAGIC LANTERN (MOVIE THEATER): VII:41
  HIGHLAND LAKE: VII:40
  KANSAS ROAD: VI:266–67, VII:19, VII:24, VII:32–40
  KING HOUSE: Roland and EDDIE visit STEPHEN KING here, in his family home. King is so shocked to see them that he tries to run into the nearby lake. Afterwards, he faints. VI:273–300, VI:301–2, VI:350 *(bedroom)*, VII:17, VII:36
  LONG LAKE: VI:276, VII:24
  NORTH CUMBERLAND MEMORIAL HOSPITAL: VII:411
  SLAB CITY HILL: *See* ROUTE 7
HARRISON: VI:280, VII:40, VII:433
NORTH WINDHAM: VI:392
  DISCOUNT BEVERAGE: VI:392
PORTLAND: V:598, VI:409, VI:410, VII:521
  BOOKLAND: VI:169, VI:208
RAYMOND: VI:172
  SEBAGO LAKE (BIG SEBAGO): VI:172
  WINDHAM: VI:172
KENNEBEC COUNTY:
  WATERVILLE: VI:389
    THE SILENT WOMAN RESTAURANT: VI:389
KING'S CHILDHOOD BARN: *See entry in* PORTALS
KING'S HOME: *See* BRIDGTON, *under* CUMBERLAND COUNTY; LOVELL, *under* OXFORD COUNTY; *and* ORRINGTON, *under* PENOB-SCOT COUNTY
KNOX COUNTY:
  MAINE STATE PRISON: Until it closed its doors in 2002, the Maine State Prison was located in Thomaston, Knox County. Hence, within the state it was known simply as Thomaston. VI:181
OXFORD COUNTY: VII:18
  DENMARK: Like many of the towns in its immediate vicinity, Denmark was plagued by WALK-INS during the 1970s. This strange phenomenon may still be going on. VI:151
  EAST FRYEBURG: VI:181, VI:191
  EAST STONEHAM: East Stoneham is a small town located forty miles north of PORTLAND. This is where CALVIN TOWER and AARON DEEPNEAU go to hide from BALAZAR'S MEN. It is also where Roland

and EDDIE are ambushed by these WOLVES of NEW YORK. In 1999, Roland and JAKE return to East Stoneham in search of STEPHEN KING, whose life they wish to save. With the help of IRENE TASSENBAUM, they find King walking down ROUTE 7 in LOVELL. Our dwindling tet manages to save King from being killed by BRYAN SMITH's Dodge minivan, but at the cost of Jake's life. V:598, V:620–24, V:627, VI:123, VI:130–54, VI:158–216, VI:265, VII:17–18, VII:24, VII:39, VII:123, VII:124, VII:465

COUNTRY COLLECTIBLES: JANE SARGUS owns this shop. VI:165

DIMITY ROAD: Dimity Road branches off of ROUTE 5. CALVIN TOWER and AARON DEEPNEAU stay near here on the ROCKET ROAD. VI:165, VI:167, VI:171, VI:178

> **ROCKET ROAD:** TOWER and DEEPNEAU's cabin (number NINETEEN of JAFFORDS RENTAL CABINS) is on this small dirt road which branches off Dimity Road. VI:178, VI:184, VI:194, VI:216

>> **JAFFORDS RENTAL CABINS:** During their brief but eventful stay in East Stoneham, CALVIN TOWER and AARON DEEPNEAU stay in number NINETEEN of these lakeside cabins. Here Deepneau draws up the bill of sale which transfers ownership of New York's magic LOT from Tower to the TET CORPORATION. VI:166, VI:167, VI:178–216, VII:128

EAST STONEHAM GENERAL STORE: The East Stoneham General Store, owned by CHIP McAVOY, is the site of Roland and EDDIE's battle with BALAZAR'S MEN in 1977. In 1999, it is the site of JAKE and Roland's entrance into our world. They meet IRENE TASSENBAUM here. V:621, V:624–25, V:707, VI:130–47, VI:162, VII:46, VII:87, VII:124, VII:128, VII:417, VII:421–29, VII:431, VII:437, VII:438, VII:442 *(indirect)*, VII:468 *(indirect)*, VII:479

EAST STONEHAM POST OFFICE: V:621, V:622–24 *(one mile from General Store)*, VI:133, VI:166, VI:177

EAST STONEHAM TOWN GARAGE: VI:132

EAST STONEHAM TOWN OFFICE: VI:132

EAST STONEHAM VOLUNTEER FIRE DEPARTMENT: VI:158

KEYWADIN POND: JOHN CULLUM's cabin is located on Keywadin Pond. VI:148–54, VI:161, VI:163, VI:169, VI:179, VII:44, VII:423, VII:469, VII:470

> **CULLUM'S CABIN (SUNSET COTTAGE):** John Cullum's cabin is a tidy little bachelor pad located on the shores of Keywadin Pond. It reminds EDDIE DEAN of a hobbit hole. Years later, after Cullum leaves Maine to become one of the FOUNDING FATHERS of the TET CORPORATION, the cabin is bought by IRENE AND DAVID TASSENBAUM. They rename it Sunset Cottage. VI:149, VI:158–73, VII:39, VII:44, VII:469–71

FRYEBURG: Home of the annual Fryeburg Fair. VI:166, VI:181, VI:407, VI:410, VII:40, VII:446

    YOUR TRASH, MY TREASURE: During his stay in Maine, CALVIN TOWER goes book hunting here. VI:166

KLATT ROAD: VII:422

LOVELL: Lovell is one of the many Maine towns plagued by WALK-IN activity. CARA LAUGHS (a home located on TURTLEBACK LANE in Lovell) is the DOORWAY BETWEEN WORLDS through which the walk-ins enter our world. Not surprisingly, this house is destined to be the home of STEPHEN KING. VI:151, VI:165, VI:180, VI:181, VI:210, VI:285, VI:394, VI:397, VI:398, VI:404, VI:405, VII:17, VII:18, VII:34, VII:35, VII:40, VII:45, VII:46, VII:47, VII:48–53, VII:115, VII:127, VII:142, VII:329, VII:339, VII:414, VII:422, VII:424, VII:428, VII:429, VII:432, VII:434, VII:439, VII:441–43, VII:520

    BERRY HILL: VII:446

    CENTER LOVELL STORE: BRYAN SMITH loves the Mars bars that are sold here. VII:433

    KEZAR LAKE: The KING family home is located on beautiful Kezar Lake. According to locals, Kezar is famous for its bizarre weather patterns. A section of its shoreline is also the center of western Maine's WALK-IN activity. VI:181, VII:113, VII:117, VII:120, VII:128, VII:132, VII:438, VII:443

        SCHINDLER PLACE: VII:438

        TURTLEBACK LANE: Turtleback Lane is the center of western Maine's WALK-IN activity. The lane is a loop which runs off ROUTE 7 and follows the shores of KEZAR LAKE. STEPHEN KING's house, CARA LAUGHS, is located on this lane. VI:180, VI:210, VI:285, VI:301, VI:394, VI:397, VI:403, VI:404, VI:405, VI:407, VI:408, VI:409, VII:17, VII:34, VII:35, VII:46, VII:47, VII:49, VII:53, VII:113–32, VII:173, VII:304, VII:428, VII:429, VII:432, VII:434, VII:436–39, VII:441–43, VII:444, VII:445, VII:446, VII:542

            BECKHARDT COTTAGE: JOHN CULLUM is the caretaker for the Beckhardt Cottage. He, Roland, and EDDIE hold their final palaver here. VII:115, VII:117–27, VII:518

            CARA LAUGHS (KING HOUSE): *See* DOORWAYS BETWEEN WORLDS, *in* PORTALS

            FENN COTTAGE: VII:115

            ISRAEL COTTAGE: VII:115

LOVELL-STONEHAM CHURCH OF THE WALK-INS: *See* STONEHAM, *below, in the* MAINE *subsection*

MILLION DOLLAR BRIDGE: This rickety wooden bridge spans the water near the MILLION DOLLAR CAMPGROUND. Hippies often go there to sell drugs. VII:433

MILLION DOLLAR CAMPGROUND: This campground is located just over the Lovell/STONEHAM town line. BRYAN SMITH stays here with his two rottweilers, BULLET and PISTOL. VII:432, VII:433, VII:434, VII:443

SLAB CITY HILL: *See* ROUTE 7

WARRINGTON ROAD: This road leads to ROUTE 7. VII:441, VII:443, VII:446, VII:447, VII:449

NORWAY: VI:166, VI:185

HOSPITAL: Despite CALLAHAN's written warning that CALVIN TOWER and AARON DEEPNEAU should keep a lower profile, Tower refuses to sleep in his rental cabin's boathouse. He says that the damp there will land his wheezy friend Deepneau in Norway's shitpot little hospital. VI:185

NOTIONS: Although he should be in hiding, CALVIN TOWER insists on going book hunting here. VI:166

OXFORD: VI:407, VII:425

VIKING MOTORS: "The Boys with the Toys." They sell Jet Skis here. CHIP McAVOY has ordered some. VII:425

ROUTE 5: JUNIOR ANGSTROM saw a naked WALK-IN on this road. VI:151, VI:165, VI:178

ROUTE 7 (OLD FRYEBURG ROAD): Route 7 is a dangerous place to walk. In July of 1994, a Stoneham man named CHARLES McCAUS-LAND was struck by a car and killed here, an event which foreshadows STEPHEN KING's accident. King's accident (and JAKE CHAMBERS's death) takes place on the section of tarmac known as SLAB CITY HILL. In 1977, Roland and EDDIE meet CHEVIN OF CHAYVEN, a CHILD OF RODERICK, while they are driving along this road. VI:181, VI:403, VI:406, VI:410, VII:46, VII:48–53 *(Roland and Eddie see Child of Roderick),* VII:113, VII:422, VII:424, VII:430–33 *(driving),* VII:439–41, VII:443, VII:444, VII:446, VII:447, VII:449–68, VII:472–75

MELDER'S GERMAN RESTAURANT AND BRATHOUSE: VII:440

SLAB CITY HILL: This section of Route 7 is extremely dangerous because of its short sight-lines. Worse yet, there is nowhere to jump if a car goes off the road and ends up on the shoulder. Slab City Hill is the place where STEPHEN KING is hit by BRYAN SMITH's Dodge minivan. VI:403, VI:406, VI:411, VII:446, VII:451–68, VII:472–75

WOODS OFF ROUTE 7: JAKE CHAMBERS manages to save the life of STEPHEN KING by grabbing King around the waist and using his own body to shield the writer from BRYAN SMITH's oncoming Dodge minivan. Although King survives, Jake is killed. Roland buries his adopted son in the woods off Route 7. VII:465–68, VII:472–75

ROUTE 93 (BOG ROAD): VII:17

SOUTH PARIS: VI:302

SOUTH STONEHAM: VII:45

SOUTH STONEHAM SHOE: VII:45

STONEHAM: Like DENMARK, EAST CONWAY, EAST STONE-

HAM, LOVELL, SOUTH STONEHAM, and SWEDEN, the town of Stoneham in western Maine is plagued by WALK-IN activity. *(See also EAST STONEHAM, above, in the MAINE subsection.)* VI:151, VI:165, VI:180, VI:280, VI:403, VI:404, VII:422, VII:432

> **FIRST CONGREGATIONAL CHURCH:** This church is located on the corner of ROUTE 7 and KLATT ROAD. VII:422, VII:423
> **STONEHAM CORNERS:** VII:435
>> **LOVELL-STONEHAM CHURCH OF THE WALK-INS:** Given the number of WALK-INS in this part of Maine, it's not surprising that a church has grown up around the phenomenon. The Church of the Walk-Ins is located in STONEHAM CORNERS. Its pastor is REVEREND PETERSON. The church's sign reads, "We Seek the Doorway to Heaven—Will You Seek With Us?" VII:422
> **STONEHAM FIRE AND RESCUE:** VI:132

SWEDEN: Sweden is another Maine town plagued by WALK-INS. VI:151, VI:181, VII:40, VII:433

WATERFORD: Waterford is one of the many Maine towns plagued by WALK-INS. VI:151 *(walk-ins)*, VI:165, VI:181, VII:40, VII:433

> **DON RUSSERT'S HOUSE:** Don Russert, a friend of JOHN CULLUM's, is a retired history professor who once worked at VANDERBILT COLLEGE. Don actually interviewed a WALK-IN in his living room. VI:151–52

PENOBSCOT COUNTY:

BANGOR: TABITHA KING's family lives in Bangor. VI:280, VI:389 *(Nanatown)*, VI:398, VI:404, VII:512, VII:513, VII:545

ORONO:

> **PAT'S PIZZA:** A pizza joint located close to the UNIVERSITY OF MAINE. They make great pizza. (The beer is good too.) I especially recommend the jalapeño-and-garlic pizza—it's guaranteed to keep vampires away (unfortunately, it will probably drive away most of your friends as well). VI:409
> **UNIVERSITY OF MAINE:** *See* MAINE, UNIVERSITY OF, *listed separately*

ORRINGTON: STEPHEN KING lived in this town while teaching at the UNIVERSITY OF MAINE. VI:391

SAGADAHOC COUNTY:

TOPSHAM: VI:290, VI:399

UNIVERSITY OF MAINE: *See* MAINE, UNIVERSITY OF, *listed separately*

WHITE MOUNTAINS: *See* WHITE MOUNTAINS, *listed separately*

MAINE, UNIVERSITY OF

STEPHEN KING attended the University of Maine located in ORONO. Thanks to BURT HATLEN, he also taught creative writing there for a year. VI:283, VI:391

MAJESTIC THEATER
See NEW YORK CITY: BROOKLYN

MAMARONECK
See NEW YORK (STATE OF): WESTCHESTER

MANHATTAN RESTAURANT OF THE MIND
See NEW YORK CITY: MANHATTAN: SECOND AVENUE

MANSION, THE
See DOORWAYS BETWEEN WORLDS, *in* PORTALS

MARINE MIDLAND BANK
See NEW YORK CITY: MANHATTAN

MARSTEN HOUSE
See MAINE (STATE OF): JERUSALEM'S LOT

MASS GENERAL
See MASSACHUSETTS: BOSTON, *below*

MASSACHUSETTS (STATE OF)
V:254, VII:479
BOSTON: V:254, V:255, VI:166, VI:200, VI:408, VII:104, VII:115, VII:134
   BACK BAY: CONOR FLAHERTY, a servant of the CRIMSON KING,
   has a Back Bay accent. VII:108
   FILENE'S: VII:612
   HARVARD: *See* HARVARD, *listed separately*
   HYATT HARBORSIDE: VI:408
   MASS GENERAL (MASSACHUSETTS GENERAL HOSPITAL):
   VI:402
LOWELL: V:254, V:255, V:593, VI:200
SEA BREEZE INN: During their trek from MAINE to NEW YORK CITY,
Roland, OY, and IRENE TASSENBAUM stay at this roadside motel.
Although we don't know exactly where the Sea Breeze is located, we do
know that it sits somewhere off Route I-95. As far as Roland can tell, there
are no sea breezes at the Sea Breeze. VII:479–83

MELDER'S GERMAN RESTAURANT AND BRATHOUSE
See MAINE (STATE OF): OXFORD COUNTY: ROUTE 7

MERCURY LOUNGE
See NEW YORK CITY: MANHATTAN

MERRITT PARKWAY
VII:297, VII:298

MEXICO
V:236, V:469 *Also see* TODASH: MEXICO, *in* PORTALS
LOS ZAPATOS: While in the TODASH state, PERE CALLAHAN attended the funeral of BEN MEARS here. V:236, V:469

MICHIGAN (STATE OF)
V:53, V:106
DETROIT: PERE CALLAHAN's five years traveling along America's HIGHWAYS IN HIDING finally led him to the LIGHTHOUSE SHELTER in Detroit. Callahan worked at Lighthouse from the late fall of 1982 until December of 1983. On December 19 of that year, Callahan and his two Lighthouse workmates—WARD HUCKMAN and AL MCCOWAN—were tricked by RICHARD SAYRE of the SOMBRA CORPORATION into entering the company's local headquarters on MICHIGAN AVENUE. Huckman and McCowan were rendered unconscious, but Callahan was forced to face the wrath of Sayre's HIV-infected TYPE THREE VAMPIRES. Rather than submit to their bites, Callahan threw himself out a window. V:106, V:270, V:449, V:450–57, V:464, VI:122
>   GRAND RIVER MENSWEAR: In anticipation of his meeting with SOMBRA, CALLAHAN actually bought a suit here. All things considered, it turned out to be a waste of money. V:456, V:458
>   HOLY NAME HIGH SCHOOL: The LIGHTHOUSE SHELTER held its annual Thanksgiving Day festivities in this Catholic high school located on West Congress Street. V:450–51
>   JEFFERSON AVENUE: V:452
>   LIGHTHOUSE SHELTER: *See* LIGHTHOUSE SHELTER, *listed separately*
>   MICHIGAN AVENUE: V:453–57 *(setting)*, V:466
>>   TISHMAN BUILDING: The Tishman Building was the Detroit headquarters of the CRIMSON KING's SOMBRA CORPORATION. When CALLAHAN was attacked here by the Red King's TYPE THREE VAMPIRES, he jumped out the window. V:453–57
>   WEST FORT STREET: V:452

MID-TOWN LANES
See NEW YORK CITY: MANHATTAN

MIDTOWN TUNNEL
See NEW YORK CITY: MANHATTAN

MID-WORLD LANES
See entry in PORTALS

MILLION DOLLAR BRIDGE
See MAINE (STATE OF): OXFORD COUNTY: LOVELL

MILLION DOLLAR CAMPGROUND
See MAINE (STATE OF): OXFORD COUNTY: LOVELL

MILLS CONSTRUCTION AND SOMBRA REAL ESTATE
See entry in CHARACTERS

MISSISSIPPI (STATE OF)
Back in 1964, ODETTA HOLMES (one of SUSANNAH DEAN's previous personalities), spent three days in an OXFORD, Mississippi, jail. She was incarcerated for her participation in the Civil Rights Movement. In *Song of Susannah,* we learn that Susannah was part of the voter registration campaign which took place in this state during the summer of '64, nicknamed Freedom Summer. On June 21, 1964, three VOTER REGISTRATION BOYS—JAMES CHANEY, ANDREW GOODMAN, and MICHAEL SCHWERNER—were attacked and killed by the Ku Klux Klan.

During his travels along the HIGHWAYS IN HIDING, PERE CALLAHAN spent some time in Mississippi. His experiences in the state were much better than Susannah's.

V:305, V:403, V:445, VI:256, VI:321, VI:350, VI:351–55, VI:361, VII:62, VII:76, VII:145, VII:587, VII:716

ADAMS COUNTY:
  NATCHEZ: V:304
COPIAH COUNTY: V:304
  SHADY GROVE: V:305
ISSAQUENA COUNTY: V:303, V:445
  ROUTE 3: V:303–305
LAFAYETTE COUNTY:
  OXFORD: ODETTA HOLMES spent three days in an Oxford jail cell. She was imprisoned because of her participation in the Civil Rights Movement. V:445, VI:11, VI:219–22 *(jail cell)*, VI:223, VI:256, VI:321, VI:350, VI:351, VI:352–55, VI:356, VI:361, VII:62, VII:76, VII:145, VII:259

  BLUE MOON MOTOR HOTEL: ODETTA HOLMES and her VOTER REGISTRATION friends stayed in the Blue Moon Motor Hotel during their time in Mississippi. VI:352, VI:353, VI:355, VI:357

  JOHN BAMBRY'S CHURCH (FIRST AFRO-AMERICAN METHODIST CHURCH): VI:352

  OLE MISS: See MISSISSIPPI, UNIVERSITY OF, *listed separately*
NESHOBA COUNTY: VI:356
  LONGDALE: VI:351, VI:354, VI:355
  PHILADELPHIA: VI:351, VI:352, VI:355
UNIVERSITY OF MISSISSIPPI (OLE MISS): See MISSISSIPPI, UNIVERSITY OF (OLE MISS), *listed separately*
YAZOO COUNTY:
  YAZOO CITY: V:303, V:304

MISSISSIPPI, UNIVERSITY OF (OLE MISS)
Ole Miss was the site of the 1962 riots which Bob Dylan immortalized in his song "Oxford Town." The riots were the result of the university's forced acceptance of its first black student, James Meredith. We are told that DAMLI HOUSE, located in the DEVAR-TOI in END-WORLD, would look at home on the campus of Ole Miss.
VI:354, VII:230

MISSOURI (STATE OF)
V:308

MONTANA (STATE OF)
V:532, V:534

MONTREAL
See CANADA

MOREHOUSE
Founded in 1867, Morehouse College is a highly respected private liberal arts college for African-American men. Morehouse is located three miles from downtown Atlanta and has strong ties with Spelman College (also located in Atlanta), a prestigious private liberal arts college for African-American women.
V:76, V:85, V:375, VI:106, VI:116, VI:150, VI:221, VI:230, VI:363

MORNINGSIDE HEIGHTS
See NEW YORK CITY: MANHATTAN

MOROCCO
TANGIERS: VII:115

MOUNT EVEREST
VII:244

MOZAMBIQUE
V:179

MULTIPLE AMERICAS (ALTERNATIVE AMERICAS)
Although the DARK TOWER contains only one KEYSTONE EARTH, and that Keystone Earth contains only one United States, other levels of the Tower contain alternative versions of the North American superpower. These multiple Americas are subtly different from the United States that we know. In some, people drive Takuro Spirits and drink Nozz-A-La cola. In at least one of them, more than 99 percent of the American population was wiped out by the superflu virus. As PERE CALLAHAN discovers during his five years along the

HIGHWAYS IN HIDING, which connect these various United States, politics also vary from one version of America to another. While in one *where*, Jimmy Carter may have been elected president, in two other *wheres* (but the same *when*) Ronald Reagan and George Bush were elected instead of him.

Landscapes and town names also change from one Alternative America to another. In one version, FORT LEE sits across the HUDSON RIVER from NEW YORK CITY, yet in a different America, a town named LEABROOK sits in its place. In *Song of Susannah,* a somewhat disturbed EDDIE DEAN discovers that he is not from the Keystone World at all, but from one of these Alternative Americas. (In his version of the Big Apple, CO-OP CITY is located in BROOKLYN, not the BRONX.)

At the end of *The Dark Tower,* SUSANNAH DEAN decides to abandon her quest for the Tower and goes to live in one of these alternative versions of America. The reason? Even though her beloved husband, Eddie, died in the DEVAR-TOI, in this other *where* and *when* he is alive and well, though his name isn't Eddie Dean anymore but Eddie TOREN. Unlike the former junkie Eddie Dean, Eddie Toren doesn't have a bullying big brother named HENRY, but a wonderful kid brother named JAKE.

V:298–310, V:423 *(indirect)*, V:456, V:463 *(prisms of America)*, V:543, VI:199–200 *(Eddie discovers Co-Op City is in the Bronx)*, VI:204 *(Co-Op City)*, VI:271 *(Co-Op City)*, VII:807–13 *(Susannah in an alternative New York)*

N

NASSAU
See BAHAMAS

NATCHEZ
See MISSISSIPPI (STATE OF)

NATHAN'S
See NEW YORK CITY: MANHATTAN

NATIONAL GRAMOPHONE INSTITUTE
See NEW YORK CITY: MANHATTAN: SECOND AVENUE

NEBRASKA (STATE OF)
(Also see ROCKY MOUNTAINS)
V:149
OMAHA: VII:657

NEEDLE PARK
   See NEW YORK CITY: MANHATTAN: GREENWICH VILLAGE

NEVADA (STATE OF)
   V:305
   ELKO: V:305
   LAS VEGAS: EDDIE DEAN thinks that "Roland the Hypnotist" could make a fortune in Vegas plying his trade. V:59, VII:94
   RAINBARREL SPRINGS: V:305

NEW DELHI
   See INDIA

NEW ENGLAND
   V:135, V:256, V:537, V:538, V:544, V:584, VI:207, VI:208, VI:265, VII:487

NEW GUINEA
   PAPUA: VI:52

NEW HAMPSHIRE (STATE OF)
Some New Hampshire towns located just over the border from western MAINE are also prone to WALK-IN activity.
   V:537, VI:181, VI:397
   EAST CONWAY VILLAGE: Like many of the towns located in OXFORD COUNTY, MAINE, East Conway is plagued by the sinister WALK-INS. VI:153
   NORTH CONWAY: VI:397, VI:406
   PORTSMOUTH: VII:435

NEW JERSEY (STATE OF)
During his travels through the MULTIPLE AMERICAS, PERE CALLAHAN spends much time flipping between two versions of New Jersey. In the KEY-STONE version of this state, he lives in FORT LEE and works at the FORT LEE HOMESTYLE DINER. In an alternative version of New Jersey, he lives in LEABROOK and works at the LEABROOK HOMESTYLE DINER. In both cases, his boss is named DICKY RUDEBACHER. PIMLI PRENTISS, the Master of the DEVAR-TOI, was originally from one of the New Jerseys. We don't know if he hailed from the Keystone World or not.
   V:264, V:292, V:296–301 *(Callahan is there)*, VI:165, VII:212, VII:225, VII:239, VII:297, VII:324, VII:362
   ATLANTIC CITY: V:181–82, V:537
   FORT LEE: During his travels through the MULTIPLE AMERICAS, PERE CALLAHAN spends time in Fort Lee. However, sometimes he wakes up in the morning to find himself in LEABROOK instead. V:296, V:298, V:299, V:427

FORT LEE HOMESTYLE DINER: DICKY RUDEBACHER owns this diner. (He owns its LEABROOK twinner as well.) V:302

SUNRISE HOTEL: One of the ways that PERE CALLAHAN can figure out whether he has awoken in Fort Lee (in the Sunrise Hotel) or in LEABROOK (in the SUNSET MOTEL) is to examine the color of his bedspread. In Fort Lee, it's orange. V:300

HACKENSACK: V:297

HOBOKEN: V:524, VI:141

LEABROOK: On another level of the TOWER, FORT LEE is called Leabrook. V:296–301

LEABROOK HOMESTYLE DINER: An alternative version of DICKY RUDEBACHER owns this diner. (The KEYSTONE WORLD Dicky lives in Fort Lee.) V:299–301

LEABROOK TWIN CINEMA: V:301

MAIN STREET: V:299

SUNSET MOTEL: In the Sunset Motel, PERE CALLAHAN has a pink bedspread. (His alternative bed, located in FORT LEE, has an orange spread.) V:300

LEEMAN/LEIGHMAN/LEE-BLUFF/LEE PALISADES/LEGHORN VILLAGE: These are all versions of FORT LEE. V:298

NEWARK AIRPORT: VI:226

PERTH OIL AND GAS: When he was in high school, EDDIE DEAN went on a field trip to this oil refinery. The smell was so terrible that two of the visiting girls, and three of the visiting boys, puked. Evidently, the defunct factories located south of the DEVAR-TOI smell a bit like Perth Oil and Gas. VII:324–25

RAHWAY: PAUL PRENTISS (who later becomes PIMLI PRENTISS, the Devar Master) originally came from Rahway. VII:225, VII:226, VII:227, VII:229

TEANECK: In one of the MULTIPLE AMERICAS, the War of Kites takes place in Teaneck. V:297

NEW MEXICO (STATE OF)
V:305, VII:497, VII:510, VII:514, VII:517

ALBUQUERQUE: VII:287

TAOS: The FOUNDING FATHERS of the TET CORPORATION sometimes held executive retreats in Taos. (The company owns a ranch there.) Tet's GOOD-MIND FOLK—a group of psychics who rival the CRIMSON KING's BREAKERS—have their headquarters at this ranch. VII:497, VII:507, VII:509

NEW ORLEANS
See LOUSIANA (STATE OF)

NEW YORK (STATE OF)
  V:68, VII:614 *(upstate)*, VII:615 *(upstate)*
  ATTICA STATE PRISON: VII:229
  HUDSON RIVER: V:292, V:296–99, V:427, V:522
  NEW YORK CITY: *See* NEW YORK CITY, *below*
  NIAGARA FALLS: VII:237
  NIAGARA MALL: We don't know exactly where the Niagara Mall is located, just that it is situated in upstate New York in one of the ALTER-NATIVE AMERICAS. (In other words, you won't find it in the KEY-STONE WORLD, where we live.) VII:614
  STATEN ISLAND: IRENE TASSENBAUM was born on Staten Island. VII:430
  TIOGA SPRINGS: RANDO THOUGHTFUL, the CRIMSON KING's minister of state, was born Austin Cornwell, son of ANDREW JOHN CORNWELL. Andrew Cornwell came from Tioga Springs. VII:616
  VASSAR COLLEGE: *See* VASSAR COLLEGE, *listed separately*
  WHITE PLAINS: When SUSANNAH DEAN abandons her quest for the DARK TOWER and departs MID-WORLD via the magical DOOR drawn for her by PATRICK DANVILLE, she enters one of the ALTERNATIVE AMERICAS. Although her tet-mates EDDIE DEAN and JAKE CHAMBERS are both dead (one passed on in the DEVAR-TOI and the other entered the clearing on ROUTE 7 in MAINE), in her new America both are alive and well. These alternative versions of Eddie and Jake are the TOREN brothers, and they hail from White Plains. Although Susannah knows that this *where* is not the KEYSTONE WORLD (people drive Takuro Spirits and drink Nozz-A-La cola), nevertheless she is overjoyed to be there with her resur-rected loved ones. VII:812
  WOODSTOCK: V:527

NEW YORK CITY (CALLA NEW YORK, THE BIG APPLE)
The city of New York plays a central role in the Dark Tower series. All three of Roland's human companions—EDDIE DEAN, SUSANNAH DEAN, and JAKE CHAMBERS—come from this late-twentieth-century metropolis. Although they all hail from New York, each of our friends was drawn from a slightly dif-ferent version of the city. Roland brought Susannah from the New York of 1964; he took Jake from that of 1977, and Eddie from 1987. Although our tet-mates were drawn from their home places through magical DOORWAYS BETWEEN WORLDS (doors which were, in one way or another, derived from the magical substance of the PRIM), in the final book of the Dark Tower series, we learn that the city is absolutely lousy with mechanical doorways as well. These mechanized portals, which Roland often refers to as the OLD ONES' doors, lead to multiple time periods and multiple worlds, and at least a score of them open onto paral-lel versions of New York itself. Unfortunately, most of these mechanical portals are controlled by the servants of the CRIMSON KING.

New York City is important for other reasons as well. It is the home of the magical ROSE, which is the KEYSTONE WORLD's manifestation of the Dark Tower. It is also the home of the TOREN family (custodians for the Rose), and the future corporate headquarters of the TET CORPORATION, the company whose job it is to guard that most sacred of flowers.

Although the New York City we know is alive and well, the Dark Tower series hints that it may have a less than happy future. Over and over, the Big Apple is compared to the city of LUD, which was (once upon a time) the thriving central metropolis of RIVER BARONY. Even though our New York City is thriving, its futuristic twinner, LUD, has been torn apart by warfare and gang rivalry. If Lud provides a glimpse of what New York will look like in about two thousand years, then the technological and biochemical disasters which almost destroyed Roland's world may yet happen to ours.

ACTION TAKES PLACE IN NEW YORK CITY ON THE FOLLOWING PAGES: V:48–70 *(todash)*, V:172–97 *(todash)*, V:264–93 *(Callahan's story)*, V:423–43 *(Callahan's story)*, V:515–47 *(through door)*, V:592–98 *(through door)*, VI:47–58, VI:73–98, VI:119–25, VI:225–34, VI:256–61, VI:307–63 *(characters move to the* DIXIE PIG—*entries in* PORTALS*)*, VII:3–5 *(characters move to the* DIXIE PIG—*entries in* PORTALS*)*, VII:485–525, VII:724–25 *(Susannah's dream)*, VII:807–13

DIRECT REFERENCES: V:40, V:47, V:48–70 *(todash)*, V:97, V:98, V:101, V:103, V:105 *(New York in all its multiples)*, V:106, V:108, V:110 *(Big A)*, V:131 *(Calla New York)*, V:135, V:138 *(Calla York)*, V:141, V:167, V:172–97 *(todash, 179 as Lud)*, V:201, V:221, V:223, V:231, V:247, V:260, V:263, V:264–93 *(Callahan's story)*, V:296, V:298, V:308, V:309, V:314, V:321, V:338, V:352, V:360, V:377, V:382, V:383, V:393, V:394, V:395, V:400, V:427, V:494, V:502, V:503, V:508, V:509, V:511, V:512, V:513, V:514–48, V:549, V:550, V:558, V:561, V:573, V:593, V:622, V:631, V:633, V:646, V:648, V:649, V:687, VI:11, VI:12, VI:13, VI:14, VI:28, VI:31, VI:35, VI:42, VI:43, VI:47–61, VI:64, VI:65–98 *(67–72 Susannah's dogan)*, VI:102, VI:104, VI:107, VI:108, VI:117, VI:118–25, VI:147, VI:149, VI:163, VI:165, VI:180, VI:185, VI:188, VI:210, VI:223, VI:225–34, VI:238, VI:239, VI:243, VI:248, VI:256–61, VI:275, VI:288, VI:296, VI:300, VI:307–63, VI:405, VI:407, VII:3–5, VII:21 *(todash)*, VII:36, VII:47, VII:56, VII:84, VII:87, VII:90, VII:93 *(under it)*, VII:104, VII:105, VII:110, VII:111, VII:119, VII:121, VII:122, VII:133, VII:135, VII:146, VII:201, VII:208, VII:266, VII:297, VII:309, VII:325, VII:381, VII:396, VII:398, VII:399, VII:405, VII:424 *(Jew York)*, VII:443, VII:477, VII:478, VII:485–525 *(502—City of Lud in its prime; 526, 527, 521—young and vital Lud)*, VII:550, VII:555, VII:559, VII:586, VII:591, VII:601, VII:604, VII:652, VII:657, VII:676, VII:687, VII:689, VII:724–25 *(Susannah's dream)*, VII:728, VII:743, VII:747, VII:762, VII:802, VII:807–13, VII:818

BRONX: In the KEYSTONE WORLD, CO-OP CITY is located in the Bronx. However, in EDDIE DEAN's New York, it is located in BROOKLYN. VI:43, VI:199, VI:200, VI:204, VI:271, VII:812

CO-OP CITY: *See* BROOKLYN, *listed below*

CROSS BRONX EXPRESSWAY: V:264

BROOKLYN: EDDIE DEAN originally hailed from Brooklyn. The Sicilian mobster ENRICO BALAZAR was also a Brooklyn boy. V:50, V:62, V:65, V:162, V:203, V:207, V:443, V:512, V:525, V:527, V:537, V:544, V:548, V:637, VI:150, VI:153, VI:154, VI:199, VI:200, VI:204, VI:206, VI:214, VI:271, VI:277, VI:312, VII:17, VII:305, VII:381, VII:668, VII:807, VII:812

    BERNIE'S BARBERSHOP: BALAZAR plays poker here. V:537

    BROOKLYN AVENUE: *See* BROOKLYN AVENUE BEAT *and* MAJESTIC THEATER, *both below*

    BROOKLYN AVENUE BEAT: BOSCO BOB, a slightly mad officer of the law, patrolled this beat when EDDIE DEAN was a boy. V:140

    BROOKLYN BRIDGE: VI:96

    CASTLE AVENUE MARKET: VII:102

    CHURCH OF THE HOLY GOD-BOMB: Although the Reverend EARL HARRIGAN lives in Brooklyn, he often preaches on SECOND AVENUE in MANHATTAN. VI:312

    CONEY ISLAND: V:37, V:443, V:701, VI:90, VI:157

    CO-OP CITY: EDDIE DEAN (who was obviously born in one of the ALTERNATIVE AMERICAS) was born in Co-Op City. Although in the KEYSTONE WORLD Co-Op City is located in the BRONX, in Eddie's New York it exists in Brooklyn. V:203, VI:199, VI:200, VI:204, VI:214, VI:271, VI:277, VII:17, VII:102, VII:305, VII:807

    DAHLIE'S: Dahlie's, a shop located in EDDIE DEAN's old neighborhood, was owned by Dahlie Lundgren. Dahlie's sold great fried dough, and its comic books were fairly easy to steal. The Dean brothers and their friends used to smoke cigarettes behind Dahlie's back door. V:187, V:257

    DEAN FAMILY APARTMENT: VI:157

    DUTCH HILL: Dutch Hill was the site of the infamously evil DUTCH HILL MANSION. When EDDIE DEAN was a boy, he was afraid of this place, and for good reason. Its reputation rivaled that of the MARSTEN HOUSE, found in 'SALEM'S LOT, MAINE. In *The Waste Lands,* JAKE CHAMBERS had to travel to this demon-infested house to reenter MID-WORLD. V:50, V:93, V:104, V:204, V:258, V:476, VII:143, VII:144–45, VII:249, VII:592

        MANSION IN DUTCH HILL (DUTCH HILL MANSION): *See* DOORWAYS BETWEEN WORLDS, *in* PORTALS

    GRAND ARMY PLAZA: New York has two Grand Army Plazas—one in MANHATTAN and one in Brooklyn. Midtown Manhattan's Plaza is located on Fifth Avenue, between Fifty-eighth and Sixtieth Streets. Brooklyn's Grand Army Plaza is located at the main entrance to Prospect Park, near the main branch of the Brooklyn Public Library. Brooklyn's Grand Army Plaza is best known for the Soldiers and Sailors Memorial Arch, which is Brooklyn's rival to Paris's Arc de Triomphe.

    In *Wolves of the Calla,* EDDIE DEAN saves CALVIN TOWER's

bacon by telling JACK ANDOLINI that if he and his nasty boss, BAL-AZAR, don't leave Tower alone, Eddie will fill Grand Army Plaza with dead gangsters from Brooklyn. Whichever Grand Army Plaza Eddie is talking about, that's a lot of carnage. V:528, V:536, VI:193

MAJESTIC THEATER: This theater is located in Brooklyn, on Brooklyn and Markey Avenues. V:152, V:209, V:257, VI:285

MARKEY AVENUE: *See* MAJESTIC THEATER, *above*

MARKEY AVENUE PLAYGROUND: VII:336

ROOSEVELT ELEMENTARY SCHOOL: This was EDDIE DEAN's elementary school. V:352

WOO KIM'S MARKET: V:140

MANHATTAN: V:48–70 *(todash, mentioned directly on 62, 68)*, V:93, V:96, V:97, V:99, V:172–97 *(todash)*, V:264–93 *(Callahan's story)*, V:297, V:299, V:308, V:422, V:423–43 *(Callahan's story)*, V:451, V:512, V:515–47 *(door)*, V:592–98 *(door)*, VI:57, VI:225–34 *(setting)*, VI:256–61 *(setting)*, VI:307–63 *(setting—directly mentioned on 338)*, VII:3–5 *(setting)*, VII:33, VII:240 *(Manhattan Project)*, VII:430, VII:486–525

ALPHABET CITY: VI:11

AVENUE B: VI:43

AMERICANO BAR: This is where PERE CALLAHAN fell off the wagon, even though he'd managed to stay sober during his months of employment at the HOME shelter, located on FIRST AVENUE. Despite the strain LUPE DELGADO's death placed on him, Callahan did not return to the bottle until he saw some VAGS (or VAGRANT DEAD) walking along PARK AVENUE. V:285, V:444

BARCELONA LUGGAGE STORE: *See* SECOND AVENUE, *below*

BATTERY PARK: V:287

BLACK TOWER (2 HAMMARSKJÖLD PLAZA): *See* LOT, THE: 2 HAMMARSKJÖLD PLAZA, *in* PORTALS

BLACKSTRAP MOLASSES CAFÉ: The Blackstrap Molasses Café is located on Sixtieth Street and Lexington, not far from the DIXIE PIG. The young BUSKER who plays "Man of Constant Sorrow" for SUSANNAH DEAN and MIA, daughter of none, sits in front of this café. VI:350

BLARNEY STONE: V:283, V:444

BLEECKER STREET: As well as being known for its music, Bleecker Street houses one of New York's many DOORWAYS BETWEEN WORLDS. This particular door connects the MULTIPLE AMERICAS to one another. In some versions of New York, the door is located in an abandoned warehouse. In other New Yorks, it is located in an eternally half-completed building. V:169, VII:105

BLIMPIE'S: V:175, V:515

BLOOMINGDALE'S: V:53

BORDERS: During her lunch hour, TRUDY DAMASCUS carries her good shoes in a canvas Borders bag. Unfortunately for her, shoeless MIA (who is in control of SUSANNAH DEAN's body) mugs her on

SECOND AVENUE. She steals Trudy's bag, shoes, and *New York Times*. VI:50, VI:65, VI:87, VI:97

BROADWAY: V:283, VII:405

CENTRAL PARK: As she and Roland near the DARK TOWER, SUSANNAH DEAN begins to have repeating dreams about her two dead ka-tet mates, EDDIE and JAKE. The scenario she sees is always the same. Eddie and Jake stand in Central Park wearing two woolly hats, one of which says "Merry" and one of which says "Christmas." Although they can't give her many clues about how she can manage the transition, they want her to leave MID-WORLD and join them (otherwise, she will probably die like all of Roland's previous companions).

Traveling through the magical UNFOUND DOOR which PATRICK DANVILLE draws for her, Susannah abandons the quest. Riding HO FAT III, she idles into Central Park, where the HARLEM ROSES sing Christmas carols in the snow. As in her dreams, Eddie is there to greet her, a cup of hot chocolate in hand. V:290 *(Central Park, west side of the Ramble)*, VII:208, VII:554, VII:555, VII:559, VII:581, VII:645–46, VII:724–25, VII:728, VII:743, VII:749, VII:807–13 *(Susannah arrives in 1987)*, VII:818

CHEW CHEW MAMA'S (DENNIS'S WAFFLES AND PANCAKES): *See* SECOND AVENUE, *below*

CHRISTOPHER STREET STATION: VI:221, VI:232 *(indirect)*

CITY HALL: V:517, V:520, VI:256

CITY LIGHTS BAR: After LUPE DELGADO's death, but before he began to be actively hunted by the LOW MEN, PERE CALLAHAN spent a lot of time in this bar. It was located on Lexington Avenue. V:290

COLUMBIA UNIVERSITY: *See* COLUMBIA UNIVERSITY, *listed separately*

DENNIS'S WAFFLES AND PANCAKES: *See* SECOND AVENUE: CHEW CHEW MAMA'S, *below, under* MANHATTAN

DIXIE PIG: *See entry in* PORTALS

EMPIRE STATE BUILDING: V:286, V:321, VII:18, VII:47

FIFTH AVENUE: V:271, VI:41, VII:724, VII:811

   BRENDIOS: VII:811

   BRENTANO'S BOOKSTORE: VII:811

   PLAZA HOTEL: During the day, LUPE DELGADO worked as part of the maintenance crew at the Plaza Hotel. However, his real calling was working with homeless people at the HOME shelter. V:271, V:280

FIRST AVENUE: V:266, V:429, V:433, V:531, VI:57, VI:74, VI:86

   NEW YORK PLAZA-PARK HYATT (U.N. PLAZA, U.N. PLAZA HOTEL, REGAL U.N. PLAZA): The Plaza-Park Hyatt is the First Avenue hotel where MIA takes a captive SUSANNAH once they land in 1999 New York. (Mia needs to find a *telefung* so that she can contact the evil RICHARD P. SAYRE, servant of the CRIMSON KING,

who has promised to help her deliver her CHAP.) Although neither
Mia nor Susannah has any money to pay for their room, Susannah
uses her little CAN-TAH to mesmerize MATHIESSEN VAN WYCK
into paying for their stay. She also uses it to hypnotize the EXOTIC
HOTEL RECEPTIONIST into giving her the room key even though
she has no identification. Later on in *Song of Susannah,* JAKE
CHAMBERS and PERE CALLAHAN travel to the Plaza-Park Hyatt
to retrieve BLACK THIRTEEN from the hotel room safe where
Susannah has hidden it. According to the sign located in the Plaza-
Park's lobby, as of July 1st, 1999, SOMBRA REAL ESTATE and
NORTH CENTRAL POSITRONICS are going to rename the hotel
the Regal U.N. Plaza. V:595, VI:57, VI:74, VI:86, VI:89, VI:90–98,
VI:107, VI:109, VI:118–25, VI:219, VI:223–34, VI:251, VI:256–57,
VI:297 *(U.N. Plaza Hotel),* VI:317, VI:320–33, VII:67, VII:143 *(indi-
rect),* VII:145, VII:303, VII:689

FORTY-EIGHTH STREET: *See* SECOND AVENUE: EIGHT MAGIC
BLOCKS, *below*

FORTY-FIFTH STREET: *See* SECOND AVENUE: EIGHT MAGIC
BLOCKS, *below*

FORTY-SEVENTH STREET: *See* SECOND AVENUE: EIGHT MAGIC
BLOCKS, *below*

FORTY-SIXTH STREET: *See* SECOND AVENUE, *below, and* LOT,
THE, *in* PORTALS

GAIETY: *See* TIMES SQUARE, *below*

GEORGE WASHINGTON BRIDGE: The George Washington Bridge is
our world's version of LUD BRIDGE. V:292, V:297, V:298, V:444,
VII:503 *(Lud Bridge)*

> **FOOT BRIDGE (LAMERK INDUSTRIES):** According to PERE
> CALLAHAN, in one of the ALTERNATIVE AMERICAS a foot-
> bridge (not far from the George Washington Bridge) crosses the HUD-
> SON RIVER. The footbridge was manufactured by LAMERK
> INDUSTRIES. V:292–93, V:296–99, V:444

GRAND ARMY PLAZA: There are two Grand Army Plazas, one in
Brooklyn and one in Manhattan. *See entry in* BROOKLYN *subsection*

GRAND CENTRAL STATION: VII:77, VII:201, VII:537

GREENWICH VILLAGE: V:89, V:168, V:169, V:275 *(East Village),*
V:276, V:290, V:544, VII:653

> **NEEDLE PARK (WASHINGTON SQUARE PARK):** Washington
> Square Park was one of PERE CALLAHAN's hangouts during his
> drunken vagrant days. When he first arrived in the Big Apple (just after
> his terrible confrontation with the VAMPIRE BARLOW), he slept on
> one of its benches. He became a Needle Park vagrant once more
> after the death of his friend LUPE DELGADO and after the shock of
> seeing the VAGRANT DEAD wandering around the city.
>
> In Needle Park, Callahan discovered the first of the LOW MEN's

"lost pet" posters advertising for information about him. The writing, spray-painted across the back of one of the benches, said, "He comes here. He has a burned hand." As a result, Callahan has to leave the city in a hurry.

It's not surprising that Washington Square Park became a haunt for the low men, given its less than savory history. Before the park was built in 1826, it was a burial ground and then an execution site (public gallows were situated there). During the 1980s, when Callahan would have frequented it, it was a well-known drug-dealing center (hence its nickname). It has cleaned up its act since then, but (as Roland and his ka-mates know all too well) the dead of such places don't rest easy. V:89, V:265, V:289, V:290

GUTTENBERG, FURTH, AND PATEL: The accountant TRUDY DAMASCUS works for this firm. VI:47, VI:52–54 *(setting)*

HAMMARSKJÖLD PLAZA: *See* LOT, THE: 2 HAMMARSKJÖLD PLAZA, *in* PORTALS

HARLEM: VII:807, VII:809

HOME (WET SHELTER): *See* HOME, *listed separately*

HUDSON RIVER: *See* NEW YORK (STATE OF)

HUNGRY I: A café that ODETTA HOLMES frequented. A lot of folk musicians preformed there during the early 1960s. VI:351, VII:533

JAKE CHAMBERS'S APARTMENT: V:565–66 *(Elmer's study)*

KANSAS CITY BLUES: A midtown saloon located on Fifty-fourth Street, just around the corner from SECOND AVENUE. When Jake travels TODASH to New York City at the beginning of *Wolves of the Calla,* he finds himself standing in front of this bar. V:49

KIDZPLAY: *See* GUTTENBERG, FURTH, AND PATEL: DAMASCUS, TRUDY, *in* CHARACTERS

LEANING TOWER (BALAZAR'S OFFICE): Although ENRICO BALAZAR is one of BROOKLYN's resident thugs, his head offices are in a midtown saloon known as the Leaning Tower. The first time Roland saw the sign for this den of iniquity (back in *The Drawing of the Three*), he assumed that the sign depicted the DARK TOWER itself. EDDIE DEAN informed him that it was merely a picture of the LEANING TOWER OF PISA. V:61, V:92, V:104, V:164, VI:134, VI:139, VI:334

LEXINGTON AVENUE (AND THE DIXIE PIG): *See* DIXIE PIG, *in* PORTALS

LEXINGTON AVENUE AND SIXTIETH STREET: In *Song of Susannah,* SUSANNAH and MIA stop to listen to a BUSKER performing on this street corner. VI:338–39, VI:347–57

LOT, THE (FORTY-SIXTH STREET AND SECOND AVENUE): *See entry in* PORTALS

MACY'S: V:174, V:703

MADISON SQUARE GARDEN: VI:311

MANHATTAN RESTAURANT OF THE MIND: *See* SECOND AVENUE, *below*

MARINE MIDLAND BANK: V:275, V:288, V:289 *(indirect)*

MERCURY LOUNGE: V:183

MIDTOWN: VI:73

MID-TOWN LANES: The bowling alley that JAKE CHAMBERS frequented while he lived in New York. While traveling to New York via TODASH, Jake and his tet-mates discover a version of his Mid-Town Lanes bowling bag in the Vacant LOT on SECOND AVENUE. (It is the perfect size for carrying BLACK THIRTEEN.) However, whereas Jake's original bag said, "Nothing but Strikes at Mid-Town Lanes," the bag he finds while in the todash state says, "Nothing but Strikes at Mid-World Lanes." V:198, V:694, VI:49, VI:73, VI:97, VII:143

MILLS CONSTRUCTION AND SOMBRA REAL ESTATE: *See entry in* CHARACTERS

NATHAN'S HOT DOGS: V:46

NATIONAL GRAMOPHONE INSTITUTE: *See* SECOND AVENUE, *below*

NEEDLE PARK (WASHINGTON SQUARE PARK): *See* GREENWICH VILLAGE, *listed above*

NETWORK, THE: JAKE CHAMBERS's father, ELMER CHAMBERS, works at the Network. VII:95, VII:299, VII:398

NEW YORK GENERAL HOSPITAL: *See also* RIVERSIDE HOSPITAL. V:282

NEW YORK PUBLIC LIBRARY: V:596, V:598 *(indirect)*, V:619–23, V:621

NEW YORK UNIVERSITY: V:424

NINETEENTH STREET: V:284

PARK AVENUE: V:283, V:284 *(vags)*

PENN STATION: VII:194

PIPER SCHOOL: *See* PIPER SCHOOL, *listed separately*

PLAZA HOTEL: *See* FIFTH AVENUE, *listed above*

PLAZA-PARK HYATT: *See* FIRST AVENUE, *listed above*

POCKET PARK: *See* SECOND AVENUE, *below*

PORT AUTHORITY: V:264, V:428

RADIO CITY MUSIC HALL: V:183, VI:53, VII:47

RIVERSIDE HOSPITAL, ROOM 577 (NEW YORK GENERAL HOSPITAL): Both ROWAN MAGRUDER and PERE CALLAHAN end up in this hospital room after being attacked by the HITLER BROTHERS. (Quite appropriately, if you add up the room's digits, they equal NINETEEN.) V:422, V:423–27, V:442, V:443

SECOND AVENUE: According to EDDIE DEAN and JAKE CHAMBERS, the eight Second Avenue blocks which stretch from Forty-sixth Street to Fifty-fourth Street function as a kind of magic portal. This area contains both the MANHATTAN RESTAURANT OF THE MIND and the magic LOT, home of the ROSE. V:47, V:49–70 *(todash)*, V:174–97, V:284 *(and Nineteenth Street)*, V:429–33 *(setting)*, V:502, V:511, V:514, V:515–48 *(setting)*, V:590, V:592–96 *(setting)*, VI:43, VI:47–52, VI:53, VI:54–58, VI:68, VI:65–69 *(pocket park)*, VI:189 *(buying Vacant Lot)*, VI:195 *(Vacant Lot)*, VI:308–20, VII:423 *(Harrigan)*

EIGHT MAGIC BLOCKS (FIFTY-FOURTH STREET TO FORTY-SIXTH STREET): V:49–50 *(we learn that these are the "magic blocks" later)*, V:57, V:58, V:95, V:173, V:175, V:178, V:181, V:182, V:502–503 *(magic blocks and key world)*, V:592, V:594–96

BARCELONA LUGGAGE STORE: V:49 *(todash)*

BLACK TOWER: *See* LOT, THE: 2 HAMMARSKJÖLD PLAZA, *in* PORTALS

CHEW CHEW MAMA'S (DENNIS'S WAFFLES AND PAN-CAKES): Chew Chew's is located at Second Avenue and Fifty-second Street. In *The Waste Lands,* both EDDIE DEAN and JAKE CHAMBERS passed by this restaurant—Eddie in a dream, and Jake on his way to see the ROSE. In *Wolves of the Calla,* our entire ka-tet strolls past this restaurant while traveling to New York City via TODASH.

Not surprisingly, PERE CALLAHAN also has a connection to Chew Chew's. During his days at the HOME shelter, he and some of his friends would occasionally eat there. After visiting ROWAN MAGRUDER in RIVERSIDE HOSPITAL, Callahan decided to return to Chew Chew's for one final bite before leaving New York. When he is attacked by the HITLER BROTHERS, it is a Swiss-burger from Chew Chew's that Callahan vomits onto his clothing.

In 1994, Chew Chew's changed its name to Dennis's Waffles and Pancakes, but still managed to retain its central significance to our ka-tet's story. After eating at Dennis's, TRUDY DAMASCUS witnesses SUSANNAH/MIA suddenly appear on the corner of Second Avenue and Forty-sixth Street, and Mia promptly confiscates her shoes.

As we all know from the earlier books of the series, Chew Chew's isn't an entirely benevolent place. *Chew Chew* sounds a lot like *Choo-Choo,* as in *Charlie the Choo-Choo,* a sinister storybook starring CHARLIE, the nasty train. V:60, V:178, V:429, V:432, V:503, V:514, VI:47, VI:52, VI:313

DENNIS'S WAFFLES AND PANCAKES: *See* CHEW CHEW MAMA'S, *listed above*

FORTY-SIXTH STREET: The corner of Forty-sixth Street and Second Avenue is an important place. On one side of the road is the magical Vacant LOT. On the other (at least in 1999) there is a POCKET PARK, which contains a fountain and a statue of the TURTLE GUARDIAN *(see* POCKET PARK, *below; and* LOT,

THE, *in* PORTALS). VI:47–51, VI:53, VI:54–58, VI:65–89, VI:90, VI:104, VI:189, VI:195

> **HAMMARSKJÖLD PLAZA (2 HAMMARSKJÖLD PLAZA, THE BLACK TOWER):** *See* LOT, THE, *in* PORTALS
>
> > **GARDEN OF THE BEAM:** *See* LOT, THE: 2 HAMMARSKJÖLD PLAZA, *in* PORTALS
>
> **POCKET PARK:** This little pocket park is located across the street from 2 HAMMARSKJÖLD PLAZA, the 1999 home of the ROSE. Inside the park is a fountain containing a metal sculpture of the TURTLE GUARDIAN. In this park SUSANNAH DEAN enters her internal DOGAN so that she can delay the birth of baby MORDRED. Here also she charms MATHIESSEN VAN WYCK with her little CAN-TAH. In the final book of the Dark Tower series, IRENE TASSENBAUM waits for Roland in this peaceful place while he visits the TET CORPORATION across the street. Those visiting the pocket park sometimes hear singing, reminiscent of the Rose's song. For all who go there, it is a refreshing place. VI:57–58, VI:65–89 *(in dogan—67–77),* VII:488–91, VII:497

HARRIGAN'S STREET CORNER (SECOND AND FORTY-SIXTH STREET): The Reverend EARL HARRIGAN likes to preach on this corner. VI:257–61, VI:308–20, VII:423

LOT, THE: *See entry in* PORTALS

MANHATTAN RESTAURANT OF THE MIND: This is CALVIN TOWER's bookshop. Back in *The Waste Lands,* Jake bought *Riddle-De-Dum!* and *Charlie the Choo-Choo* here. In *Wolves of the Calla,* Eddie visits the Manhattan Restaurant of the Mind and arrives just in time to save Tower from BALAZAR'S MEN. After Eddie beats up Balazar's thugs, telling them that Tower will not sell the Vacant LOT to them, the WOLVES of New York burn this shop down. Luckily, Tower isn't there when they do it. We don't know whether the shop cat, SERGIO, survives the blaze. V:51, V:54–70 *(todash),* V:91, V:92–100 *(discussed),* V:177, V:178, V:503, V:516, V:518–48, V:592–93, V:709, VI:35 *(indirect),* VI:84 *(indirect),* VI:139, VI:140, VI:183 *(indirect),* VI:192 *(indirect),* VI:196 *(indirect),* VI:399, VII:495

NATIONAL GRAMOPHONE INSTITUTE: This place doesn't really exist. EDDIE DEAN makes it up to show that any old institution can exist on the Vacant LOT as long as the ROSE is protected from harm. VI:270

POCKET PARK: *See* FORTY-SIXTH STREET, *listed above*

STATION SHOES AND BOOTS: Located on Second Avenue and Fifty-fourth Street. V:517, V:593

TOM AND JERRY'S ARTISTIC DELI: *See* LOT, THE, *in* PORTALS

QUEENS MIDTOWN TUNNEL: V:525
WESTCHESTER:
    MAMARONECK: VII:103

NEWARK
See NEW JERSEY (STATE OF)

NIAGARA FALLS
See NEW YORK (STATE OF)

NIAGARA MALL
See NEW YORK (STATE OF)

NORTH CONWAY
See NEW HAMPSHIRE (STATE OF)

NORTH WINDHAM
See MAINE (STATE OF)

NORWAY
See MAINE (STATE OF)

NORWICH
See CONNECTICUT

NOTIONS
See MAINE (STATE OF): NORWAY

NOTRE DAME
See FRANCE

O

OHIO (STATE OF)
V:255, VI:336, VII:673
AKRON: In Akron, Ohio, in 1935, TED BRAUTIGAN became a murderer.
As Ted stood on the corner of STOSSY AVENUE, a brown bag containing
a pork chop in his hand, a mugger ran past, drove Ted face-first into a telephone pole, and stole his wallet from his pocket. Enraged, Ted threw a mind-
spear at the man. He dropped dead. VII:277, VII:376, VII:657
    STOSSY AVENUE: VII:277–78
        DEFUNCT CANDY STORE: VII:277, VII:283

MR. DALE'S FANCY BUTCHER SHOP: Ted bought his pork chop here. He never ate it. VII:277

CLEVELAND: VI:336, VII:669, VII:673, VII:674, VII:676

JANGO'S NIGHT CLUB: JOE COLLINS (who is actually the were-insect DANDELO) tells Roland and SUSANNAH that he performed his comedy act in this club. VII:669, VII:673, VII:674

CUYAHOGA RIVER: VII:674

DAYTON: V:255

SPOFFORD: V:255

OKLAHOMA (STATE OF)
V:309
ENID: V:309

OLD FRYEBURG ROAD
See MAINE (STATE OF): OXFORD COUNTY: ROUTE 7

OLE MISS
See MISSISSIPPI, UNIVERSITY OF

OMAHA
See NEBRASKA (STATE OF)

OREGON (STATE OF)
V:305
FOSSIL: During his years traveling the HIGHWAYS IN HIDING, PERE CALLAHAN passed through Fossil. V:305

ORONO
See MAINE (STATE OF)

ORRINGTON
See MAINE (STATE OF)

OXFORD, MAINE
See MAINE (STATE OF)

OXFORD TOWN
See MISSISSIPPI (STATE OF)

P

PACIFIC
    VII:286

PAPUA
    See NEW GUINEA

PARIS
    See FRANCE

PARK ON SECOND AVE
    See NEW YORK CITY: MANHATTAN: SECOND AVENUE

PARKLAND MEMORIAL HOSPITAL
    See TEXAS: DALLAS

PECOS RIVER
    VII:325

PENN STATION
    See NEW YORK CITY: MANHATTAN

PENNSYLVANIA (STATE OF)
    PITTSBURGH: VII:668
    WILKES-BARRE: VII:285

PENTAGON
    See WASHINGTON, D.C.

PERTH OIL AND GAS
    See NEW JERSEY (STATE OF)

PERU
    V:561

PIPER SCHOOL
During his years in NEW YORK CITY, JAKE CHAMBERS attended this
exclusive private MANHATTAN middle school. He hated it.
    V:51, V:52, V:502, V:669, V:689, VI:40, VII:85, VII:332, VII:395

PITTSBURGH
See PENNSYLVANIA

PLAZA HOTEL
See NEW YORK CITY: MANHATTAN: FIFTH AVENUE

PLAZA-PARK HYATT
See NEW YORK CITY: MANHATTAN: FIRST AVENUE

POCKET PARK
See NEW YORK CITY: MANHATTAN: SECOND AVENUE

POLAND
AUSCHWITZ: A Nazi concentration camp located near the town of Auschwitz. VII:698

PORTALS
See entry in PORTALS

PORTLAND
See MAINE (STATE OF)

Q

QUEENS
See NEW YORK CITY

R

RAHWAY
See NEW JERSEY (STATE OF)

RAYMOND
See MAINE (STATE OF)

REINISH ROSE GARDEN
See KANSAS (STATE OF)

RHODESIA
V:179

RIVERSIDE HOSPITAL
See NEW YORK CITY: MANHATTAN

ROCKET ROAD
See MAINE (STATE OF): EAST STONEHAM

ROCKY MOUNTAINS (ROCKIES)
The Rocky Mountains stretch from the U.S. border with Mexico to the Yukon Territory in northern Canada. Their peaks form the backbone of the Continental Divide, separating the Great Plains from the Pacific Coast. This range also separates the rivers which flow eastward into the Atlantic from those which flow westward into the Pacific. JAKE thinks that the mountains beyond THUN-DERCLAP must look like the Rocky Mountains. In actuality, the peaks of the DISCORDIA resemble the WHITE MOUNTAINS of MAINE and NEW HAMPSHIRE.
V:149

ROUTE 5
See MAINE (STATE OF)

ROUTE 7
See MAINE (STATE OF)

RUSSIA
VI:274, VII:290, VII:598

S

SACRAMENTO
See CALIFORNIA (STATE OF)

SAINT ANDREW'S CHURCH
See MAINE (STATE OF): JERUSALEM'S LOT

'SALEM'S LOT
See MAINE (STATE OF): JERUSALEM'S LOT

SAN BERDOO
See CALIFORNIA (STATE OF)

SAN FRANCISCO
See CALIFORNIA (STATE OF)

SAPPORO
See JAPAN

SCANDINAVIA
VI:84–85

SEATTLE
See WASHINGTON (STATE OF)

SEBAGO LAKE
See MAINE (STATE OF)

SECOND AVENUE PARK
See NEW YORK CITY: MANHATTAN: SECOND AVENUE: EIGHT MAGIC BLOCKS: FORTY-SIXTH STREET: POCKET PARK

SHADY GROVE
See MISSISSIPPI (STATE OF)

SILENT WOMAN, THE
See MAINE (STATE OF): WATERVILLE

SLAB CITY HILL
See MAINE (STATE OF)

SLEEPY JOHN'S
See CALIFORNIA (STATE OF): SACRAMENTO

SMILER'S MARKET
See NEW YORK CITY: MANHATTAN

SOMBRA REAL ESTATE
See SOMBRA CORPORATION, *in* CHARACTERS

SOUTH AMERICA
The SOUTH AMERICAN SEABEES were a group of North American engineers, construction workers, and roughnecks hired to work in South America for a group of South American businessmen.
VII:284

SOUTH CAROLINA (STATE OF)
V:232

SOUTH DAKOTA (STATE OF)
V:262
HOT BURGOO: After the bloody Eucharist served to him by BARLOW
the VAMPIRE in 'SALEM'S LOT, MAINE, FATHER CALLAHAN was so
desperate to leave town that he claims he would even have fled to Hot Burgoo, if he could have hopped on a bus heading in that direction. I don't
know whether this place exists, but I can define *burgoo* for you. A burgoo
is a hot soup made from chicken, beef, and vegetables. It is cooked for several hours so that the flavors blend and the consistency becomes stewlike.
According to the burgoo Web site (yes, there is one), burgoo was probably
originally just a thin gruel served by sailors in the seventeenth century.
Early burgoos probably also included such tantalizing ingredients as squir-
rel. V:262

SOUTH PARIS
See MAINE (STATE OF)

SPAIN
COSTA DEL SOL: The Costa del Sol is a resort region located on southern
Spain's Mediterranean coast. At the beginning of *Wolves of the Calla*,
JAKE CHAMBERS believes that MOSES CARVER (SUSANNAH DEAN's
godfather) probably funneled all of Susannah's HOLMES DENTAL INDUS-
TRIES fortune into his own accounts and moved to the Costa del Sol.
(After all, that's the kind of thing that happens in mystery novels.) However,
as we learn in the final book of the Dark Tower series, Pop Mose did no such
thing. V:102

STATION SHOES AND BOOTS
See NEW YORK CITY: MANHATTAN: SECOND AVENUE

STONEHAM
See MAINE (STATE OF)

STONEHAM FIRE AND RESCUE
See MAINE (STATE OF): EAST STONEHAM

STONEHENGE
See ENGLAND

STOSSY AVENUE
See OHIO (STATE OF): AKRON

STOWE
  See VERMONT (STATE OF)

SUNSET COTTAGE
  See MAINE (STATE OF): EAST STONEHAM: CULLUM'S CABIN

SWEDEN (TOWN OF)
  See MAINE (STATE OF)

SWEDEN
  VI:85, VI:88

SWITZERLAND
  VI:213

T

TANGIERS
  See MOROCCO

TENNESSEE (STATE OF)
  MEMPHIS: VII:78

TEXAS (STATE OF)
  V:31, V:305, VII:697
  DALLAS: V:468
    PARKLAND MEMORIAL HOSPITAL: While being driven through Dallas, Texas, in an open car in November of 1963, President John F. Kennedy was shot by an assassin. He was rushed to Parkland Memorial Hospital, but could not be saved. Two days later, the alleged assassin, Lee Harvey Oswald, was shot at point-blank range by Jack Ruby. In the vivid dream which SUSANNAH DEAN experiences while locked inside the body she shares with MIA, Susannah hears Walter Cronkite announce the president's death. VI:219
  LUFKIN: V:305

THERMOPYLAE
The pass of Thermopylae is located in Greece; it leads between mountains and the sea. Although much wider now, in ancient times it was (at its narrowest) only twenty-five feet across. In 480 BC, the pass of Thermopylae was the site of a famous confrontation between the Greeks and the Persians. Although they were vastly outnumbered, the Greek defenders held the pass against a huge

army of invaders. Eventually, all the Greeks were betrayed and killed, but their stand was heroic. Jake's DIXIE PIG battle strategy is based on the Greek plan used at Thermopylae. Luckily, Jake doesn't die.
VII:85, VII:86, VII:110

TISHMAN BUILDING
See MICHIGAN (STATE OF): DETROIT

TOM AND JERRY'S ARTISTIC DELI
See LOT, THE, *in* PORTALS

TOPEKA
See KANSAS (STATE OF)

TOWER OF POWER RECORDS
See NEW YORK CITY: MANHATTAN: SECOND AVENUE

TURTLE BAY CONDOMINIUMS
See NEW YORK CITY: MANHATTAN

TURTLE BAY WASHATERIA
See NEW YORK CITY: MANHATTAN

TURTLEBACK LANE
See MAINE (STATE OF): LOVELL

TWIN TOWERS
See NEW YORK CITY: MANHATTAN

U

UNITED NATIONS
See NEW YORK CITY: MANHATTAN

UNITED NATIONS PLAZA-PARK HYATT
See NEW YORK CITY: MANHATTAN: FIRST AVENUE

UNIVERSITY OF MAINE AT ORONO
See MAINE, UNIVERSITY OF

UTAH (STATE OF)
V:305

V

VACANT LOT
See LOT, THE, *in* PORTALS

VANDERBILT COLLEGE
JOHN CULLUM's friend DON RUSSERT was a history professor at Vanderbilt College before he retired and moved to WATERFORD, MAINE.
VI:151, VI:152, VI:180

VASSAR COLLEGE
JUSTINE ANDERSON and ELVIRA TOOTHAKER, the two women who see BRYAN SMITH careening along ROUTE 7 in LOVELL, MAINE, met at Vassar College.
VII:439–40

VERMONT (STATE OF)
JOHN CULLUM once worked at the MAINE STATE PRISON with a man who later moved to Vermont. When Roland states that it is no longer safe for Cullum to stay in EAST STONEHAM, MAINE (after all, he helped our tet battle BALAZAR'S MEN, and those folks aren't exactly forgiving), John says that he will go visit his friend and former coworker. Not surprisingly, Cullum never makes it across the state border. Instead, he helps EDDIE and Roland find CARA LAUGHS, a magical DOORWAY BETWEEN WORLDS. Roland calls the state of Vermont "Vermong."
V:308, VI:181, VI:182, VI:211, VII:38 *(Vermong)*, VII:39, VII:41, VII:45, VII:47, VII:128
MONTPELIER: VII:46
STOWE: VI:402

VIENNA
See AUSTRIA

VIETNAM
EDDIE DEAN's bossy older brother, HENRY DEAN, fought in Vietnam. He returned home with a bad knee and a worse drug habit.
V:254, V:264, V:468, VI:136, VI:285, VI:407, VI:409, VII:173

W

WASHINGTON (STATE OF)
   GRAND COULEE DAM: The Grand Coulee Dam is located on the
   Columbia River in central Washington. It is the largest concrete structure in
   the United States. VI:241, VI:242
   SEATTLE: VI:241

WASHINGTON, D.C.
   VII:116
   PENTAGON: VI:41

WATERFORD
   See MAINE (STATE OF)

WATERVILLE
   See MAINE (STATE OF)

WEST VIRGINIA (STATE OF)
   V:302
   ROUTE 19: V:302

WESTPORT
   See CONNECTICUT (STATE OF)

WHITE MOUNTAINS
New England's White Mountains, located in northern NEW HAMPSHIRE and
southwestern MAINE, are part of the Appalachian system. The White Moun-
tains of our world parallel the dry, poisoned mountains of the DISCORDIA in
END-WORLD.
   VI:397, VII:117

WILKES-BARRE
   See PENNSYLVANIA (STATE OF)

WINDHAM
   See MAINE (STATE OF)

WISCONSIN (STATE OF)
   BELOIT: V:425, V:426, VII:183
   FRENCH LANDING: French Landing, Wisconsin, is the setting for the

King/Straub novel *Black House*. Evidently, the nasty WALTER traveled there to get his "thinking cap." Unfortunately for him, the thinking cap (so effective in the DEVAR-TOI) cannot keep baby MORDRED from spying on his thoughts. VII:183
GREEN BAY: V:102

WORLD TRADE CENTER
See NEW YORK CITY: MANHATTAN

Y

YAZOO
See MISSISSIPPI (STATE OF)

YOSEMITE
See CALIFORNIA (STATE OF)

Z

ZABAR'S
See NEW YORK CITY: MANHATTAN

ZION
VI:319

PORTALS, MAGICAL PLACES,
AND END-WORLD PLACES

This is a place between . . . a place where shadows are canceled and time holds its breath.

VI:240

A

ABYSS
According to the *Oxford English Reference Dictionary*,[1] the word *abyss* has several related meanings. They are: 1. A deep or seemingly bottomless chasm. 2a. An immeasurable depth (as in *an abyss of despair*). 2b. A catastrophic situation as contemplated or feared *(his loss brought him a step nearer the abyss)*. And finally, when preceded by the word *the* (as in *the abyss*): 3. Primal chaos, or Hell.

In the Dark Tower series, all of these definitions apply. When Roland first touches the ghostwood box containing BLACK THIRTEEN, the voice of MAERLYN's evil magic ball warns him that if he is not careful, his mind, body, and soul could all be swallowed by its dark magic. "Do you see how little it all matters?" it says. "How quickly and easily I can take it all away, should I choose to do so? Beware gunslinger! Beware shaman! The abyss is all around you. You float or fall into it at my whim."

CASTLE DISCORDIA, which abuts the town of FEDIC, is also known as the Castle on the Abyss. The abyss for which it is named is actually a great crack in the earth, located just beyond its adjoining town. This abyss is filled with terrible monsters that cozen, diddle, and plot to escape. Although we cannot be completely certain, it seems likely that these creatures originated in the TODASH darkness located between worlds.

According to Mid-World folklore, GAN bore the world and then moved on. If the great TURTLE had not caught the plummeting universe on his back, all of the worlds would have landed in yet another version of the abyss.

1. *Oxford English Reference Dictionary*, 2nd ed., rev. (Oxford: Oxford University Press, 2002).

Finally, in *The Gunslinger*, JAKE CHAMBERS died for the second time when his adopted father, Roland, let him fall into an abyss located below the CYCLOPEAN MOUNTAINS. While he fell, Jake uttered the famous phrase "There are other worlds than these." In Jake's case, perhaps the abyss turned out to be yet another DOORWAY BETWEEN WORLDS.

V:317, VI:105 *(Castle on the Abyss)*, VI:295 *(and Turtle)*, VI:299 *(and Jake)*

AFTERLIFE, PLANET

See PLANET AFTERLIFE

ALGUL SIENTO

See DEVAR-TOI

ALL-A-GLOW

The All-A-Glow is the magical kingdom which children inhabit. As adults, we spend years trying to return to this place.

VII:23

ALLURE

See CASTLE DISCORDIA

ALTERNATIVE AMERICAS

See MULTIPLE AMERICAS, *in* OUR WORLD PLACES; *see also* ALTERNATIVE AMERICAS *and* MULTIPLE AMERICAS, *in* APPENDIX I

ARC 16 EXPERIMENTAL STATION (FEDIC DOGAN)

See DOGAN: FEDIC DOGAN

ARC 16 STAGING AREA

See DOGAN: FEDIC DOGAN

AVEN KAL

See APPENDIX I; *see also* BEAMS, PATH OF THE, *below*

AYJIP

According to the Book of the MANNI, when the Angel of Death passed over Ayjip, he killed the firstborn in every house where the blood of a sacrificial lamb hadn't been daubed on the doorposts. The Book of the Manni sounds very much like the Bible, and this story, which the Manni recount in CALLA BRYN STURGIS's TOWN GATHERING HALL, is similar to one found in the Book of Exodus. According to Exodus, God imposed ten plagues upon the Egyptians because Pharaoh would not release the Israelites from captivity. The smiting of the firstborn was the tenth of these plagues.

V:16

B

BADLANDS (CALLA BADLANDS)
See CALLA BADLANDS

BADLANDS (THE BADS)
See DISCORDIA

BADLANDS AVENUE
See DISCORDIA: BADLANDS AVENUE

BANQUETING HALL, THE
See CASTLE DISCORDIA

BEACH DOORS
See DOORWAYS BETWEEN WORLDS

BEAM, GARDEN OF THE
See LOT, THE: GARDEN OF THE BEAM

BEAMQUAKE
See BEAMS, PATH OF THE

BEAMS, PATH OF THE (BEAM PORTALS, BEAMQUAKE)
In *The Waste Lands,* Roland drew a metaphysical map of his world. According
to this map, MID-WORLD is shaped like a wheel. At the hub of this earth-
wheel sits the DARK TOWER, the linchpin of the time/space continuum. The
spokes radiating out from this hub are BEAMS. Each end of a Beam terminates
in a PORTAL, which is a doorway leading into, and out of, Mid-World. The
twelve Portals are watched over by twelve animal GUARDIANS.

The six Beams, which connect opposite Portals and which pass through the
nexus of the Dark Tower, are like invisible high-tension wires. Their energy can
be felt by those who pass close to them, and their streamlike paths can be
detected in the movement of nearby clouds. As well as affecting gravity and the
proper alignment of time, space, size, and dimension, the Beams hold the
Dark Tower in place.

In *Wolves of the Calla,* Roland and his tet discover just how far the crazed
CRIMSON KING has progressed in his desire to destroy both the Beams and
the Tower. For approximately 140 years, the servants of the Red King have been
sending robotic WOLF-masked horse-riders into Mid-World's BORDER-
LANDS to steal one of every pair of prepubescent twins born there. From the

brains of these innocent victims, the workers in the FEDIC DOGAN withdraw the chemical which causes twin-telepathy. This chemical is then fed to the psychic BREAKERS, whose wild talents are being used to erode the Beams.

Although Roland has only experienced two Beamquakes in his life (Beamquakes are similar to earthquakes, but are caused by the snapping of a Beam), many more must have taken place over the centuries. By the time our tet reaches the Devar-Toi, the Beams guarded by RAT and FISH, BAT and HARE, EAGLE and LION, and DOG and HORSE have all collapsed. The only two Beams left to hold the Tower in place are our tet's Beam (the Bear-Turtle) and GAN's Beam (the ELEPHANT-WOLF). These two remaining Beams are in place, but they are not healthy, as the wounded and disfigured BEAM BOY can attest. Luckily, Roland and his tet manage to destroy the Devar-Toi and stop the terrible erosion of the macroverse's framework before the whole thing comes crashing down. We readers are also assured that the future of the Tower is secure. Either the collapsed Beams will regenerate, or the two existing Beams will generate more Beams to support the macroverse's linchpin.

In the final book of the Dark Tower series, we learn that Tower, Beams, and the red ROSES of CAN'-KA NO REY (the Red Fields of None in which the Tower sits) are all part of one living force-field. The song and perfume of the Roses feed the Beams, and the Beams, in turn, feed the Roses. Both Roses and Beams spin out from Gan, the living body of the Dark Tower. As Roland approaches his life's goal, he sees two jutting steel posts atop the Tower. The Beams emanate from these posts. (For more information about the Beams, see *Stephen King's The Dark Tower: A Concordance, Volume I*. For information about the AVEN KAL, or tidal wave along the Beam, see the HIGH SPEECH section of APPENDIX I.)

V:8, V:29, V:31, V:36, V:37–47 *(following; 38 near it but not on it, 39)*, V:72, V:93, V:97, V:99, V:101–169 *(on or near Path; directly mentioned on: 101, 110, 121–22, 126, 129, 160)*, V:183, V:192 *(indirect)*, V:193, V:539, V:562, V:563, V:604, V:638, V:660, V:661, VI:3, VI:12–18 *(Beamquake; 14—Beam portals; 16—fish and rat)*, VI:21, VI:33, VI:40, VI:83, VI:108, VI:109–144 *(discussed)*, VI:117, VI:118, VI:148, VI:211, VI:265–303 *(heart of the Beam; 265, barrel of the Beam and King's house)*, VI:318, VI:319, VI:336, VI:353, VI:359, VI:394, VII:17, VII:20–28 *(aven kal—Beamquake; 21—Bear/Turtle Beam; 22—voice of the Beam)*, VII:32 *(Beamquake)*, VII:33, VII:34, VII:40, VII:77, VII:92, VII:117, VII:121, VII:148, VII:150 *(Beamquake)*, VII:188 *(Beamquake)*, VII:195 *(Shardik's portal)*, VII:208, VII:212, VII:214, VII:232 *(Bear/Turtle, Eagle/Lion, Wolf/Elephant)*, VII:234, VII:237, VII:244 *(Shardik/Maturin)*, VII:251, VII:272 *(Bear/Turtle)*, VII:291 *(Bear/Turtle)*, VII:292 *(Wolf/Elephant)*, VII:295 *(Bear/Turtle is Shardik's Beam; Elephant/Wolf is Gan's Beam)*, VII:296, VII:297, VII:300, VII:301 *(Shardik's/Gan's)*, VII:304, VII:305, VII:306 *(Gan, Shardik)*, VII:317, VII:330, VII:333–36 *(Beam Boy)*, VII:360, VII:378, VII:381, VII:387–88 *(Gan's)*, VII:389, VII:391, VII:392, VII:401, VII:406, VII:409

(Bear/Turtle), VII:428 *(Beamquake)*, VII:438, VII:442, VII:455, VII:458, VII:476, VII:477, VII:505, VII:506, VII:518 *(Beamquake)*, VII:551 *(following it toward place of Turtle)*, VII:574, VII:577–803 *(Roland and his companions follow the Beam through the badlands, the White Lands of Empathica, and all the way to the Tower. Page numbers that follow are for direct references)*, VII:582, VII:587, VII:592, VII:593, VII:594, VII:606, VII:609, VII:610, VII:617, VII:620, VII:624, VII:647, VII:658, VII:661, VII:663, VII:670, VII:691, VII:705, VII:706, VII:757, VII:780, VII:782, VII:786, VII:813, VII:819, VII:825

BLACK THIRTEEN
See MAERLYN'S RAINBOW, *in* CHARACTERS

BLUE HEAVEN
See DEVAR-TOI

BLUETOWN
See DEVAR-TOI

BOG
See MID-FOREST (MID-FOREST BOG), *in* MID-WORLD PLACES

BOOM-FLURRY HILL
See EASTERN PLAIN (CALLA BADLANDS)

BREAKER U
See DEVAR-TOI

BRIDGE OVER THE ABYSS
See CASTLE DISCORDIA *and* FEDIC

C

CALLA BADLANDS (EASTERN PLAIN)
Located east of the RIVER WHYE, the dry wastes of the Eastern Plain form a border zone between CALLA BRYN STURGIS and THUNDERCLAP. The CALLA DOGAN is situated here. Although the Calla *folken* maintain that they could once see mountains beyond the Eastern Plain, by the time our tet reaches the BORDERLANDS, all that is visible beyond the plain is a vast darkness. The train which returns ROONT children must cross this desert land before it reaches the banks of the Whye.

V:149, V:153 *(plains)*, V:207, V:386, V:445, V:574 *(region leading to Thunderclap)*, VI:72

BOOM-FLURRY HILL: The giant, carnivorous, cactuslike BOOM-FLURRY guard this wrecked section of the EAST ROAD, which leads from the RIVER WHYE to the CALLA DOGAN. V:561–62, V:567–68, V:571, V:577

CALLA DOGAN (NORTH CENTRAL POSITRONICS NORTHEAST CORRIDOR ARC QUADRANT OUTPOST 16): *See* DOGAN, THE, *listed separately*

DEVIL'S CAUSEWAY: The Devil's Causeway is the train bridge which crosses the RIVER WHYE. The CALLA's ROONT children cross it in flatcars once they are released from THUNDERCLAP. V:562

CALLA DOGAN
>   *See* DOGAN: CALLA DOGAN (NORTH CENTRAL POSITRONICS NORTHEAST CORRIDOR ARC QUADRANT OUTPOST 16)

CAN CALYX
>   *See* DARK TOWER

CAN STEEK-TETE
>   *See* DEVAR-TOI: STEEK-TETE

CANDY HOUSE
>   *See* GINGERBREAD HOUSE

CAN'-KA NO REY
>   *See* DARK TOWER

CANNIBAL ISLES
According to EDDIE DEAN, the people of the BORDERLANDS are so civilized that they make the city of LUD, with its warring GRAYS and PUBES, look like the Cannibal Isles in a boy's sea story.
>   V:135

CARA LAUGHS
>   *See* DOORWAYS BETWEEN WORLDS

CASSE ROI RUSSE (LE CASSE ROI RUSSE, LE CASSE ROI ROUGE, COURT OF THE CRIMSON KING, FORGE OF THE KING, RED KING'S CASTLE, CASTLE OF THE KING)
According to the old legends, the CRIMSON KING's castle is called Le Casse Roi Russe. When SUSANNAH DEAN first sees its pulsing crimson glow from the ALLURE of CASTLE DISCORDIA, MIA tells her not to stare at the Forge of the King, since the Lord of Discordia can fascinate, even at a distance.

By the time Susannah, OY, and Roland reach its cobbled forecourt, the forge has been extinguished and the Red King has galloped toward the DARK TOWER, but the castle is not completely deserted. Left to greet the remaining members of our tet is an uffi, or shape-shifter, who has split himself into three and taken on the form of our *kas-ka Gan,* STEPHEN KING (albeit in triplicate). In the end, this false uffi proves not to be a shape-shifter at all, but three servants of the Red King (AUSTIN CORNWELL, BRASS, and COMPTON) disguised by *glammer.*

The Crimson King's wide cobbled forecourt is painted with the King's sigul, a staring crimson eye, and is guarded by two deserted watchtowers. Before this outer courtyard is an unpleasant-smelling river (which serves as a moat), and beyond the moat, an inner courtyard. Beyond the courtyard, the castle rises in a jumble of towers, turrets, and walkways, which remind Susannah of turnpike entrances and exits. However, the center of the castle, from which this mind-boggling architecture sprouts, is quite plain, its only decoration being the staring eye carved into the keystone of the main entrance's arch.

As its name suggests, Le Casse Roi Russe is built of deep red stone, which, over the years, has darkened to a near black. The sills of its oddly narrow windows are haunted by castle rooks (birds known to feed from bodies of hanged men). Crossing the castle's yellow-foamed moat-river is a humped stone bridge. Here, the false uffis await our friends, and it is here that two of them die under Roland and Susannah's guns.

V:236, V:470, VI:13 *(Court of the Crimson King),* VI:102 *(Forge of the King),* VI:105 *(King's Eye),* VII:47, VII:150, VII:173, VII:300, VII:559, VII:580, VII:581, VII:585 *(Roi Rouge),* VII:589, VII:590, VII:592, VII:595 *(described),* VII:599–617 *(600, described),* VII:618, VII:619–24, VII:625, VII:703, VII:823 *(indirect)*

CASSE ROI RUSSE RIVER: This foul-smelling river flows around a number of fangy black rocks. Its foam is yellow instead of white. VII:597, VII:600

CASTLE TOWN: This evil town surrounds Le Casse Roi Russe. The cottages are narrow and steep-roofed; the doorways are thin and abnormally high. Many of the buildings are haunted by *housies.* VII:590 *(ruined city near castle),* VII:591, VII:592–600, VII:619, VII:624 *(named),* VII:630, VII:631, VII:703

CASTLE DISCORDIA (CASTLE ON THE ABYSS, THE LAST CASTLE, MIA'S CASTLE, ROOMS OF RUIN)

The first time SUSANNAH DEAN hears the name of this castle is when it is spoken by her demon-possessor, MIA. However, even before she and Mia wander along the castle's ALLURE, Susannah (possessed by Mia) had journeyed to the Castle's phantom BANQUETING HALL so that she could feed the CHAP growing inside her. (At the time, we knew of this imposing architectural nightmare only as Mia's castle.) Although throughout much of *Wolves of the Calla* we assume that this castle is a dream place which Susannah-Mio visits to fool herself into thinking that the bog frogs and binnie bugs she eats are actually succulent roasts and caviar, in *Song of Susannah* and *The Dark Tower,* we discover that Castle Discordia is a real place, located deep in END-WORLD.

The version of Castle Discordia which Susannah visits to feed her chap is illuminated by electric flambeaux and has long stone corridors floored with black and red marble. It contains the Rooms of Ruin, which we already know about from EDDIE DEAN's poem fragment, recited first at SHARDIK's portal and then later on his deathbed in the PROCTOR'S SUITE of the DEVAR-TOI. Beneath the castle lie crypts, as well as some slo-trans engines created by NORTH CENTRAL POSITRONICS. From the Allure, or wall-walk around the inner keep, one can see southeast to the FORGE OF THE CRIMSON KING.

In its heyday, Castle Discordia would have been well-defended. Behind its inner keep is a terrible drop leading to the huge, needlelike rocks of the DISCORDIA. On the other side of the ruined keep are two towers (one of them broken), and beyond the towers is the deserted village of FEDIC. Beyond the village is an outer wall, and beyond the outer wall is the DEVIL'S ARSE, a great crack in the earth filled with monsters that cozen, diddle, increase, and plot to escape. The bridge that once crossed this abyss exists no longer.

Like Fedic, Castle Discordia is located on the far side of THUNDERCLAP, on the PATH OF THE BEAM, on V SHARDIK, V MATURIN. It is the last castle (besides that of the RED KING himself) before reaching the soot-colored TOWER, which rises in its field of shouting red ROSES. According to NIGEL THE BUTLER, Castle Discordia and the FEDIC DOGAN are connected by underground passages. Together, they contain 595 operational DOORWAYS BETWEEN WORLDS. At least one of these doors leads to TODASH SPACE. Another leads to THUNDERCLAP STATION.

V:71–77 *(Mia is there)*, V:370–76, V:385, V:390, V:391, V:478, VI:79, VI:101–118 *(on the Allure)*, VI:124, VI:229, VI:230, VI:232 *(Allure)*, VI:236, VI:240 *(Allure)*, VI:243, VI:247 *(passages)*, VI:248 *(Rooms of Ruin)*, VI:249, VI:254, VI:255 *(Allure)*, VI:364, VI:371, VI:373, VI:374–76 *(walkway)*, VII:52, VII:67, VII:151, VII:158, VII:531 *(Allure)*, VII:539, VII:540, VII:549, VII:554, VII:560–76 *(tunnels beneath)*, VII:577, VII:580, VII:590, VII:595 *(Allure)*, VII:619, VII:658, VII:808

BANQUETING HALL: For MIA and SUSANNAH, the Banqueting Hall is the most important room in Castle Discordia. Here, the dreaming pair comes to feed the CHAP growing inside their shared womb. The Banqueting Hall is forty yards wide, seventy yards long, and is illuminated by brilliant electric torches in crystal sheaths. It also contains a vast ironwood table laden with delicacies both hot and cold. Before each of the several hundred chairs is a white plate with delicate blue webbing. These plates resemble both the deadly weapons flung by the SISTERS OF ORIZA and the *forspecial* plate given by Odetta Holmes's mother to SISTER BLUE. Standing before the Banqueting Hall where Mia/Susannah feasts is a statue of ARTHUR ELD. It is made of chrome and rose-colored marble. Somewhere in this castle

stands an old throne drenched in ancient blood. V:71–77, V:83, V:85, V:174, V:198, V:370–76, V:478, V:659, V:674, VI:79
DOOR TO TODASH DARKNESS: *See* DOORWAYS BETWEEN WORLDS: MAGICAL DOORWAYS
PASSAGES BENEATH DOGAN AND CASTLE: VII:151, VII:553–54, VII:558–76 *(tunnels beneath)*
ROOMS OF RUIN: V:72, V:371, VI:248, VII:397
ROTUNDA: *See* DOGAN: FEDIC DOGAN
WOLF STAGING AREA: *See* DOGAN: FEDIC DOGAN

CASTLE OF OZ
See OZ

CASTLE OF THE KING
See CASSE ROI RUSSE

CATACOMBS
See DEVAR-TOI

CAVE OF VOICES
See DOORWAY CAVE

CHAYVEN
See RODERICK, CHILDREN OF, *in* CHARACTERS

CLEARING AT THE END OF THE PATH
See entry in APPENDIX I

COFFAH
Coffah is another term for "Hell" and is a particularly potent Hell for men like Roland. Unlucky adventurers fall into this pit by following the white-robed bitch-goddess who beckons them forward, always assuring them that the goal they seek will be attained. She lures them on and on, and then, once the goal is in sight, she tricks them into the black pit where they must spend eternity— forever seeing, but not reaching, their desire. According to Roland, this goddess will be laughing when the world finally comes to an end.
   VII:265

COURT OF THE CRIMSON KING
See CASSE ROI RUSSE

D

DANDELO'S HOUSE
  See EMPATHICA, WHITE LANDS OF

DARK TOWER (CAN CALYX, HALL OF RESUMPTION)
As every CONSTANT READER knows, the Dark Tower, located deep in
END-WORLD, is the focus of Roland Deschain's lifelong quest. (It could
also be argued that it is the focus of STEPHEN KING's creative quest as well,
since he has been writing about it, in one guise or another, for more than thirty
years.)

Sitting in the red field of ROSES known as CAN'-KA NO REY, this loom-
ing gray-black edifice rears six hundred feet into the sky. (When one enters it,
however, it grows exponentially taller.) Narrow, slit windows emitting an
eldritch blue glow decorate its barrel in an ascending spiral. The oriel window
at its top blazes with many colors, though its black glass center peers at those
who approach like the very eye of TODASH. Two steel posts jut from the
Tower's top; the two working BEAMS flow away from their tips, making a great
X-shape in the sky. The Tower's door is a steel-banded slab of black ghostwood,
upon which is the ancient symbol for UNFOUND. TOWER ROAD, which follows the course of the BEAR-TURTLE Beam through the WHITE LANDS OF
EMPATHICA, leads directly to this most important of edifices. In fact, Tower
Road leads directly onto the circular road which encircles the Tower—a road
which appears white against the red of the surrounding rose field. Like both
Beams and Roses, the Tower sings in a thousand voices. Its song is a musical
tapestry weaving together the names of all the worlds.

When Roland approaches the Tower at the end of the final book of the
Dark Tower series, the CRIMSON KING (in his human form) has taken possession of one of its many balconies. There he waits with his piled boxes of
sneetches, hoping to keep Roland from achieving his life's dream. However, ka
has other plans. With the help of PATRICK DANVILLE, the young artist
whom he and SUSANNAH DEAN rescued from the were-spider DANDELO,
Roland *uncreates* the Red King, leaving nothing but his red eyes floating above
the balcony's waist-high railings. Once Roland lays AUNT TALITHA's cross,
along with his ancient six-shooter, at the Tower's base, the word *Unfound*,
written upon its door, becomes Found. Roland enters.

Although the Dark Tower appears to be made of gray-black stone, it is actually the body of GAN the creator, initiator of ka, and the first being to rise out
of the PRIM. Not only is Gan's body the axis of all worlds, but it is the linchpin of the time/space continuum as well. All realities, and all possible realities,
exist on its many levels. However, when Roland enters the Tower and climbs

its spiral staircase, what he sees in room after room is not the incarnations of the macroverse's many worlds, but the story of his own life. It seems that the Tower—which welcomed him in its windlike voice as the son of both GILEAD and ELD—has a lesson to teach him, a lesson which Roland has been slow in learning.

Like the Crimson King, Roland *darkles* and *tincts*. He is eternal and can live in all worlds and all times. However, although he was born to serve the WHITE, at many times Roland has not fulfilled his obligation to the code of Eld. Due to his lack of foresight as well as his ambitious heart and preternaturally fast hands, he has often, unintentionally, served the death-drive of Discordia rather than the cause of life.

The revelation which awaits Roland in the room located at the apex of the Tower is that he has reached the Tower not just once but at the end of many, many long journeys. He is caught in a loop. Each time his hand touches the knob of the Tower's final door—the one marked Roland—he does so without memory, without recall. Yet invariably, this door does not lead him to that silent place where the God of All resides, but to the beginning of his own unquestioning pursuit of the MAN IN BLACK across the wastes of the MOHAINE DESERT.

Like so many of us, Roland is caught in a trap. To escape that trap, Roland must first understand that it is of his own creation. According to Gan, Roland's journey must endlessly repeat because he does not have the Horn of Eld with him. (He left it on the battlefield of JERICHO HILL next to the body of his dead childhood friend CUTHBERT ALLGOOD.) This lack of foresight, and Roland's inability, at times, to see the long-term consequences of his actions, is one personal fault which Roland must correct before he can reach the true end of his quest.

The second lesson that Roland has to learn before he finds peace is that life itself, not just the blind pursuit of the quest, is valuable. We often think that the ends justify the means, but what Roland finds when he reaches his life's goal is that the means can taint the end. Each Tower room represents an event from Roland's life, but each one contains a loss and a betrayal. What Roland begins to realize as he ascends toward the Tower's top is that every floor is a place of death, but they are only like this because his fast hands and single-mindedness have made them so.

What Roland must learn, if the Tower's topmost door is to lead him to a place of final redemption, is forethought and respect for life. And these are the very two lessons which, over the Dark Tower series, he has struggled to learn. Gone is the man who let JAKE CHAMBERS fall into the abyss below the CYCLOPEAN MOUNTAINS, and who killed all the people of TULL, even his lover ALICE, without guilt. And although Gan will not let Roland's journey end quite yet (ka is never so merciful) he acknowledges our gunslinger's progress by allowing him to resume his journey with the horn of his fathers at his hip. To an extent at least, Roland has learned forethought, has learned mercy, has learned (once more) to love. Hence, he has regained the right to wear yet another powerful symbol of the White. Perhaps, then, the story we read in the Dark Tower series is Roland's penultimate journey to the Tower. Maybe, if he is careful, Roland's next journey to End-World will be his last.

V:36, V:53, V:56, V:72, V:93, V:105, V:110, V:163, V:170, V:171, V:192–94 *(described)*, V:410, V:413, V:463, V:464, V:465, V:481, V:525 *("along this track of possibility"—on this level of the Tower)*, V:533, V:539, V:555, V:626, V:634, V:660, V:686, V:689, V:706, V:708, VI:13, VI:15, VI:16, VI:17, VI:18, VI:35, VI:38, VI:43, VI:50 *(black tower)*, VI:83, VI:89, VI:91, VI:95, VI:103, VI:106, VI:109–114 *(discussed)*, VI:118, VI:132, VI:147, VI:148, VI:199, VI:200, VI:210, VI:266, VI:269–70, VI:271, VI:275, VI:278, VI:279, VI:280, VI:281, VI:282, VI:283, VI:289, VI:293 *(tower-pent)*, VI:298, VI:302 *(title)*, VI:303 *(title)*, VI:321, VI:339, VI:378, VI:389 *(title)*, VI:390 *(title)*, VI:391 *(title)*, VI:392 *(title)*, VI:393 *(title)*, VI:394 *(title)*, VI:396 *(title)*, VI:398 *(title)*, VI:399 *(title)*, VI:404 *(title)*, VI:407, VI:408 *(title)*, VI:409, VII:16, VII:25, VII:32, VII:37, VII:40, VII:51, VII:76, VII:77, VII:111, VII:112, VII:116, VII:127, VII:138, VII:147, VII:148, VII:150, VII:159, VII:161, VII:169, VII:173, VII:174, VII:175, VII:176, VII:177, VII:179, VII:210, VII:224, VII:228, VII:229, VII:232, VII:238, VII:244, VII:250, VII:253, VII:259, VII:262, VII:266, VII:270, VII:271, VII:279, VII:292, VII:294, VII:296, VII:305, VII:332, VII:338, VII:387, VII:406, VII:410, VII:442, VII:446, VII:447, VII:452, VII:456, VII:483, VII:486, VII:488, VII:506, VII:511, VII:512, VII:513, VII:514, VII:517, VII:519, VII:535, VII:545, VII:550, VII:551, VII:552, VII:555, VII:559, VII:586, VII:588, VII:589, VII:595, VII:606, VII:607, VII:608, VII:609, VII:610, VII:615, VII:616, VII:617, VII:618, VII:626, VII:630, VII:650, VII:655, VII:662–66 *(painting of it)*, VII:670, VII:672, VII:695, VII:706, VII:710, VII:711, VII:717, VII:718 *(100 miles/120 wheels from the Federal)*, VII:719, VII:720, VII:721, VII:725, VII:727, VII:728, VII:729, VII:740, VII:741, VII:745, VII:747, VII:750, VII:752, VII:753, VII:754, VII:755, VII:756, VII:759, VII:760, VII:762, VII:767, VII:771, VI:772, VII:775, VII:777, VII:779–803 *(begin to see it)*, VII:813, VII:817, VII:818–28, VII:830

CAN'-KA NO REY (THE RED FIELDS OF NONE): Can'-Ka No Rey is the great sea of ROSES which grows at the heart of END-WORLD, around the base of the Dark Tower. The single Rose which grows in the Vacant LOT of our world's NEW YORK CITY is an exact replica of one of these roses. However, whereas the song sung by our world's Rose contains a note of discord (or at least it did before our tet saved both BEAMS and Tower by destroying the DEVAR-TOI), the song sung by the roses of Can'-Ka No Rey is sweet and pure.

Like the lot's Rose, the roses which grow in such profusion at the heart of End-World are a light pink shade on the outside but darken to a fierce red on the inside, a shade which Roland believes is the exact color of heart's desire. Their centers, which are called GAN'S GATEWAYS, burn such a fierce yellow that they are almost too bright to look upon. However, this yellow is the yellow of light and love, not destruction. What Roland comes to realize as he travels through their midst is that the roses feed the Beams with their song and perfume, and that the Beams, in turn, feed them. Roses and Beams are actually a living force-field, a giving and taking, all of which spins out of the Tower. Interestingly enough, the roses (when mixed with Roland's blood) are the exact color of the Crimson King's eyes. Though in the case of the Red King, the red becomes the color of evil and greed, not pure, living energy. *See* ROSE, *in* CHARACTERS. *For the representation of this field in* KEYSTONE WORLD, *see* GARDEN OF THE BEAM. VII:127, VII:447, VII:483, VII:486, VII:488 *(indirect)*, VII:513, VII:550, VII:551, VII:663, VII:666, VII:721, VII:756–57 *(first rose described)*, VII:759, VII:760–81 *(roses begin to grow densely)*, VII:782–803 *(786, they speak)*, VII:818–20, VII:824

LEVEL NINETEEN OF THE DARK TOWER: According to EDDIE DEAN, the KEYSTONE WORLD is level NINETEEN of the Dark Tower. V:525

TOWER KEYSTONE: *See* KEYSTONE WORLDS, *listed separately*

DERRY

See MAINE (STATE OF), *in* OUR WORLD PLACES

DERVA

What little we know about the Derva comes from NIGEL THE BUTLER, a friendly robot who unfortunately looks much like ANDY, CALLA BRYN STURGIS's Messenger Robot. According to Nigel, the FEDIC DOGAN is deserted because most of its workers have moved on to the Derva. He can't explain what the Derva is or what purpose it serves, since such information is classified.

VII:76

DEVAR-TETE

See DOGAN: FEDIC DOGAN

DEVAR-TOI (ALGUL SIENTO, BLUE HEAVEN, PLEASANTVILLE, BREAKER U, ELMVILLE, THUNDERCLAP STATION)

The Devar-Toi (which means Big Prison or BREAKER prison) is located in the desert wastes of THUNDERCLAP, the first, sunless region of END-WORLD. It lies on the SHARDIK/MATURIN BEAM and is six miles from THUN-DERCLAP STATION.

To the CAN-TOI guards who live and work there, the Devar-Toi is known as Algul Siento, or Blue Heaven. In fact, to anyone looking down upon its cheerful blue roofs from the nearby butte, STEEK-TETE, the Devar looks like a delightful slice of Americana set amid the dry, dead lands of End-World. Half of the Devar is modeled upon a quiet American college campus, and the other half resembles the Main Street of an old-fashioned Midwestern town, complete with a local movie theater and a drugstore/soda fountain.

However, despite its idyllic appearance, the Devar-Toi is a horrible place. Its ground and air are poisonous, a lingering toxicity left over from the deadly gas set off by the mad CRIMSON KING generations before. All who live there—hume, TAHEEN, or can-toi—suffer from skin irritations, frequent infections, and general bad health. Since Thunderclap itself has no real sunlight (a permanent darkness left over from the mad king's gas), the daylight which illuminates the compound is artificially generated by an electric (or perhaps atomic) sun. Like everything else in MID-WORLD and End-World, the machinery that runs this false sun is wearing down, hence days usually last more than twenty-four hours and are often disrupted by moments of complete darkness, like a foretaste of the Void.

True to its real name, the Devar-Toi is a prison, not a holiday camp. It employs 180 full-time personnel, all of whom serve the Crimson King and his ultimate goal of destroying the macroverse. Surrounding the campus and town are three runs of electric fence (guarded by humes) and six watchtowers (guarded by armed taheen). Both campus and Main Street are watched over by wandering can-toi guards, known as floaters.

The purpose of the Devar-Toi is to house (and cage) the psychic BREAKERS, whose powers are enhanced by the twin-telepathy chemicals culled from the brains of the BORDERLANDS' prepubescent children. Whether they want to or not, the Breakers are forced to use their powerful minds to weaken the BEAMS, which hold the DARK TOWER in place. Unfortunately, few of the Breakers have the moral integrity needed to stand up against their captors' desires. Most are in complete denial, but even those who suspect what they are doing are unwilling to rock the proverbial boat. The food is good, the sim-sex is excellent, and most of them were outcasts in the hume world anyway, so why should they care if the universe ends in fire or in ice? However, luckily for our tet, a few of the Breakers (including TED BRAUTIGAN, DINKY EARNSHAW, and SHEEMIE RUIZ) find the job they do morally reprehensible. They help Roland and his friends destroy the Devar, saving the Tower, and the macroverse, from almost certain annihilation.
V:573, VII:151, VII:152, VII:153, VII:178, VII:181, VII:207–216, VII:221–46, VII:250, VII:254–59 (map), VII:261, VII:266, VII:272, VII:292–302, VII:309, VII:312, VII:323, VII:325 (indirect), VII:326, VII:329, VII:331, VII:340–42, VII:343–416, VII:421, VII:455, VII:535 (Blue Heaven), VII:559, VII:560, VII:606 (Algul), VII:627 (Algul), VII:629 (dorms)
BREAKER U: The section of the Devar that resembles a college campus. The Breakers' luxurious accommodations are located here, as are the INFIRMARY and the all-important STUDY. VII:209, VII:257
   CORBETT HALL (DORMS, PROCTOR'S SUITE): Corbett Hall is one of the Breaker dorms. (SHEEMIE lives here.) After he is fatally wounded, EDDIE DEAN is brought to Corbett's PROCTOR'S SUITE. He dies here. VII:267, VII:366, VII:378, VII:387, VII:394, VII:395, VII:396, VII:399, VII:400–404, VII:408–16, VII:411–14

PROCTOR'S SUITE: EDDIE DEAN dies here. VII:394, VII:395–97, VII:400, VII:401–404, VII:408–10

DAMLI HOUSE (HEARTBREAK HOUSE): This large Queen Anne–style house is home to both the CAN-TOI and TAHEEN guards. It also contains the STUDY, the INFIRMARY, and the CAFETERIA. All of the Devar's deep telemetry equipment (which measures psychic activity, among other things) is located here. On Roland's instructions, HAYLIS OF CHAYVEN (a CHILD OF RODERICK) plants two sneetches in Damli. VII:201, VII:209, VII:230, VII:231, VII:232, VII:233, VII:234, VII:235–45, VII:256–57, VII:258, VII:293, VII:300, VII:345, VII:347, VII:349, VII:356–57, VII:358, VII:359, VII:361, VII:362, VII:363 *(indirect)*, VII:366, VII:367–68, VII:370, VII:371, VII:372, VII:373, VII:374, VII:375, VII:389, VII:395, VII:414, VII:577

> **INFIRMARY:** The infirmary is located on the third floor of Damli and is overseen by the much feared DR. GANGLI. V:367–68

> **THE STUDY:** This plush room, which looks much like a richly endowed Victorian gentlemen's club, is located in the center of Damli House. It is a long, high, oak-paneled room decorated with Turkish rugs, Tiffany lamps, and expensive art. Through its glass ceiling, the Breakers can see THUNDERCLAP's false sun.

> Any guard in a bad mood will jump at the chance to take a stroll onto the Study's third-floor balcony. Watching the Breakers work in their sumptuous room is pleasurable. However, this pleasure doesn't arise from the beauty of the room itself but from the "good mind" vibe which the Breakers exude while they're working. VII:236, VII:239, VII:241–45, VII:272, VII:290, VII:291, VII:295, VII:337, VII:343, VII:353, VII:357, VII:359–61, VII:364

FEVERAL HALL: This Breaker dorm is located directly behind DAMLI HOUSE. Roland instructs HAYLIS OF CHAYVEN, a CHILD OF RODERICK, to plant a sneetch here. VII:349, VII:356, VII:357–58, VII:359, VII:362, VII:371, VII:389

MALL: The Mall is the large green lawn located at the center of the campus section of the Devar-Toi. DAMLI HOUSE and SHAPLEIGH HOUSE both overlook the Mall. VII:224, VII:230–34, VII:236, VII:241, VII:245, VII:343, VII:352, VII:358, VII:371, VII:372, VII:393, VII:400, VII:404–408, VII:411, VII:414, VII:416–17

SHAPLEIGH HOUSE (DEVAR MASTER'S HOUSE, WARDEN'S HOUSE, SHIT HOUSE): This tidy Cape Cod belongs to PIMLI PRENTISS and sits on the opposite side of the MALL from DAMLI. The Breakers call it SHIT HOUSE. HAYLIS OF CHAYVEN plants the last of his sneetches in Shapleigh. VII:221–30, VII:245–46, VII:256, VII:258, VII:299, VII:343–49, VII:352–55, VII:358, VII:361, VII:371, VII:377, VII:389, VII:400

PLEASANTVILLE (ELMVILLE): Pleasantville (which our tet originally calls

Elmville) is the town section of the Devar-Toi. It looks like an old-fashioned Main Street taken from small-town-anywhere, USA. VII:209, VII:255, VII:257, VII:293, VII:299, VII:310–11, VII:327, VII:351, VII:362, VII:363, VII:381, VII:387, VII:399, VII:491

> **CLOVER TAVERN:** Located at the end of Main Street in Pleasantville. After the Devar's final battle (and after EDDIE DEAN is mortally wounded), JAKE CHAMBERS waits here until it is time for him to go to Eddie's deathbed. VII:387–99 *(Jake waits here for Roland's call; his flashback happens here)*
>
> **GAY PAREE FASHIONS:** VII:370, VII:380
>
> **GEM THEATER:** VII:210, VII:272, VII:293, VII:370, VII:382
>
> **HAIR TODAY:** VII:370, VII:381
>
> **HENRY GRAHAM'S DRUG STORE AND SODA FOUNTAIN:** VII:272, VII:369
>
> **MAIN STREET:** VII:208, VII:293, VII:299, VII:327, VII:352, VII:369, VII:374, VII:378, VII:379, VII:380, VII:382, VII:387, VII:391
>
> **PLEASANTVILLE BAKESHOP:** VII:378, VII:380
>
> **PLEASANTVILLE BOOKSTORE:** VII:369
>
> **PLEASANTVILLE HARDWARE:** This shop also contains Pleasantville's robotic firemen. VII:363, VII:369
>
> **PLEASANTVILLE SHOES:** VII:370, VII:380
>
> **STORAGE SHEDS:** These empty sheds are located north of the Devar, just beyond the electric fence. SUSANNAH hides behind them at the beginning of our ka-tet's attack upon the Breaker prison. V:341, V:349

ROD VILLAGE: The CHILDREN OF RODERICK live in this small, dirty village located about two miles beyond THUNDERCLAP STATION. The Rods do grounds work at the Devar. VII:216

STEEK-TETE (CAN STEKE-TETE): In English, *Can Steek-Tete* means "The Little Needle." Steek-Tete is a butte located about six or eight miles from THUNDERCLAP STATION. While planning their attack on the Devar-Toi, Roland's ka-tet stays in one of the butte's many caves. This hideout was prepared for them by TED BRAUTIGAN and his comrades. VII:203–220 *(setting)*, VII:247–342 *(setting; our ka-tet listens to Ted's tapes here)*

THUNDERCLAP STATION: Thunderclap's deserted train station, located approximately six miles from the Devar-Toi, is a green-roofed structure adjacent to a huge, glass-roofed switching yard. Although we do not actually see Thunderclap Station until the final book of the Dark Tower series, it is an ominous, unseen presence as early as *Wolves of the Calla.*

To reach the CALLAS of the BORDERLANDS, the robotic, child-stealing WOLVES travel through a MECHANICAL DOORWAY (located beneath the FEDIC DOGAN) and come out in Thunderclap Station. It is from here that they gallop toward the Callas on their child-stealing mission. After they are made ROONT in the Fedic Dogan's EXTRACTION ROOM, the Callas' ruined children pass through this same door so that they can be loaded onto one of Thunderclap Station's remaining flatcars. This train returns the children to the Borderlands so that they can live out the remainders of their brief (and painful) shadow-lives. VII:151, VII:152, VII:153, VII:200–205, VII:206, VII:207, VII:208, VII:213, VII:214, VII:215, VII:221–22, VII:225–26, VII:261, VII:288, VII:297, VII:300, VII:411, VII:531

DEVIL'S ARSE
See FEDIC

DISCORDIA, THE (BADLANDS, THE BADS, NOWHERE LANDS)
The Discordia badlands, located deep in END-WORLD, lie between the southeastern side of CASTLE DISCORDIA and the northwestern edge of the WHITE LANDS OF EMPATHICA. When SUSANNAH DEAN first sees the broken rocks and gaping crevices of the Discordia from Castle Discordia's ALLURE, she thinks it is the most forbidding landscape she has ever seen. Unfortunately for her, she and her *dinh*, Roland, are destined to travel through these poisoned lands on their way to LE CASSE ROI RUSSE, castle of the CRIMSON KING. According to Roland, the badlands were poisoned by the Crimson King himself.

The dead, needlelike mountains of the Discordia are the twinners of our world's beautiful WHITE MOUNTAINS. Interestingly, the term *Greater Discordia* is sometimes used for the PRIM, the magical, chaotic soup from which all life arose.

VI:93, VI:95, VI:98, VI:101–118 *(near castle)*, VI:219, VI:221, VI:222, VI:229, VI:232, VI:234, VI:244, VI:254, VI:290, VI:291, VI:294 *(and Dis)*, VI:295 *(and Dis)*, VI:318, VI:352, VI:353, VI:354, VI:357, VI:374, VI:384, VI:408, VI:409, VII:51, VII:52, VII:76, VII:96, VII:97, VII:127, VII:144, VII:150, VII:223 *(lands beyond Fedic)*, VII:246, VII:259, VII:300, VII:303, VII:378, VII:406, VII:411, VII:533, VII:539, VII:554, VII:577, VII:580–627 *(Badlands Avenue; 588, Nowhere Lands)*, VII:644, VII:658, VII:670, VII:677, VII:709, VII:710, VII:746

BADLANDS AVENUE (KING'S WAY): Badlands Avenue is SUSANNAH DEAN's name for the path which winds through the Discordia. Badlands Avenue follows the PATH OF THE BEAM. As it nears LE CASSE ROI RUSSE, it is also known as KING'S WAY. VII:580–99 *(591—named King's Way)*, VII:617–19, VII:624–27

DISCORDIA (CASTLE OF)
See CASTLE DISCORDIA

DISCORDIA CHECK-POINT DOGAN
See DOGAN: DISCORDIA CHECK-POINT DOGAN

DIXIE PIG
The first time we hear a reference to the Dixie Pig is when Roland's entire ka-tet travels to NEW YORK CITY via TODASH. Written on the fence surrounding the Vacant LOT, located on Forty-sixth Street and SECOND

AVENUE, is the following rhyme: "Oh, SUSANNAH-MIO, divided girl of mine, Done parked her RIG in the Dixie Pig, in the year of '99." Our second hint that the Pig will play an important part in our tale comes while Mia hunts for food in CASTLE DISCORDIA's deserted BANQUETING HALL (a dining room which is, in reality, just the JAFFORDS' FAMILY barn). While Mia struggles with sai RAT over a suckling pig, we see that she is wearing a Dixie Pig T-shirt.

In *Song of Susannah,* we learn that the Dixie Pig is a restaurant located on Lexington Avenue and Sixty-first Street in New York City. According to a todash version of *Gourmet* magazine, they have the best ribs in town. Unfortunately, the ribs are human, and the high-class clientele are actually the GRANDFATHERS, those hideous TYPE ONE VAMPIRES left over by the receding PRIM. Besides its two dining rooms (the second of which is secreted away behind a blasphemous tapestry depicting ARTHUR ELD'S court partaking in a cannibal feast), the Dixie Pig contains a kitchen, a pantry, and an underground tunnel containing a MIND-TRAP. Beyond the mind-trap is a MECHANICAL DOORWAY leading to the FEDIC DOGAN.

V:183, V:376 *(Lexington and Sixty-first),* V:648, VI:120 *(Sixty-first and Lexington),* VI:125, VI:143, VI:227, VI:229, VI:254, VI:255, VI:256, VI:317, VI:320, VI:327, VI:333, VI:334, VI:337, VI:339, VI:340–44 *(Jake and Callahan outside),* VI:360–78 *(through door!),* VI:382, VII:3, VII:4–16, VII:23 *(via aven kal),* VII:25–28 *(via aven kal),* VII:32, VII:34, VII:81–112 *(86—mind-trap; 87–112—tunnel beneath Dixie Pig),* VII:133–38 *(tunnel beneath Dixie Pig),* VII:145, VII:146, VII:147, VII:152, VII:297, VII:303, VII:309, VII:522–29, VII:531, VII:538

MIND-TRAP: To guard the NEW YORK/FEDIC DOOR, the GREAT OLD ONES fitted the Dixie Pig's subterranean tunnel with a mind-trap, which, when activated, will (quite literally) stop unwanted visitors dead in their tracks. This mind-trap accesses a person's deepest and oldest fears, then makes those fears manifest. Of course, the vision is an illusion, but the body reacts to the visual stimuli as if they were real and the victim dies of heart failure. When JAKE and OY travel through the mind-trap, Jake sees the dinosaur-infested landscape of a film entitled *The Lost Continent.* Oy saves Jake's life by switching places with him. Taking over Jake's body, Oy carries his friend (who is hiding in his own furry skin) to safety. VII:81–112

DOGAN, THE

The first time we encounter the term *Dogan,* it is merely a misprinted title on the cover of one of CALVIN TOWER's rare books. (*The Dogan,* which is supposed to read *The Hogan,* was a western novel written by our world's version of BEN SLIGHTMAN JR.) Although, in our world, the word *Dogan* is no more than a typing error, in END-WORLD it has a particular and sinister meaning.

End-World's Dogans are a series of military-like control centers and are shaped like Quonset huts. (As any CONSTANT READER knows, STEPHEN

KING's Quonset huts are invariably nasty places.[2]) In these Dogans, technology still works. Some of these Dogans (such as the CALLA DOGAN) are used as spy centers for the CRIMSON KING's followers in THUNDERCLAP. In others, such as the FEDIC DOGAN, magic and technology can be merged. The series of Dogans which run along the BEAR-TURTLE BEAM were built by the OLD ONES' sinister company NORTH CENTRAL POSITRONICS. V:532 *(Tower's rare book)*, V:533 *(rare book)*, V:552 *(rare book)*, V:553 *(chapter title)*, VI:32

CALLA DOGAN (NORTH CENTRAL POSITRONICS NORTHEAST CORRIDOR ARC QUADRANT OUTPOST 16): The Northeast Corridor Arc Quadrant Dogan is the END-WORLD control center located on the THUNDERCLAP side of the DEVAR-TETE WHYE. JAKE CHAMBERS and his pet BILLY-BUMBLER, OY, discover it when they follow BEN SLIGHTMAN SR.'s back trail through the CALLA BADLANDS. (Jake and Oy had seen Ben senior and ANDY, the CALLA's devious Messenger Robot, holding a suspicious conversation near the Whye.)

What Jake discovers is that Calla Bryn Sturgis is full of secret cameras, and that all of these images are projected onto monitor screens in the Dogan. From this Northeast Corridor Arc Quadrant Outpost, Ben Slightman and Andy report useful information about hidden children to FINLI O'TEGO, chief of security at the DEVAR-TOI. Obviously, Finli then feeds this information to the invading WOLVES. V:561–78, V:582 *(indirect)*, V:656, V:678, V:702–703, VI:64 *(should say on east side of River Whye)*, VI:67, VI:171, VI:247 *(Jake's Dogan)*, VII:151, VII:191

DISCORDIA CHECK-POINT DOGAN: SUSANNAH DEAN and Roland Deschain discover this Quonset hut in the wastelands of the DISCORDIA. (It sits next to the crumbling hillside arch where CASTLE DISCORDIA's subterranean tunnels exit into the open air.) This Quonset hut looks similar to the ARC 16 Experimental Station found across the WHYE from CALLA BRYN STURGIS, only it is smaller and in even worse shape. The roof of the Discordia Check-Point Dogan is covered with rust, and piles of bones are scattered in a ring around its front. Both Roland and Susannah think that it was the site of a terrible battle. VII:577–80, VII:620

FEDERAL OUTPOST 19: TOWER WATCH (THE FEDERAL): Federal Outpost 19 (which the robot STUTTERING BILL refers to as the Federal) sits on the edge of the WHITE LANDS OF EMPATHICA. Like all the other Dogans, it is a lonely-looking Quonset hut. The Federal is located 120 wheels from the DARK TOWER. Until the CRIMSON KING took up residence on one of the Tower's balconies and blew the observation cameras, one of the Federal's TV surveillance screens projected images of that linchpin of the worlds. VII:709, VII:715, VII:717–22, VII:801, VII:803

---

2. In the novel *Desperation*, Diablo Mining has its headquarters in a Quonset hut in the Nevada desert. The military experiment stations, where the superflu virus was developed in *The Stand*, were Quonset huts.

FEDIC DOGAN (NORTH CENTRAL POSITRONICS LTD, FEDIC HEADQUARTERS, ARC 16 EXPERIMENTAL STATION; THE DOGAN OF ALL DOGANS): According to MIA, the Fedic Dogan is the Dogan of all Dogans. Located deep in the heart of END-WORLD, it was once the Fedic headquarters of NORTH CENTRAL POSITRONICS. Just as we readers have long suspected, the GREAT OLD ONES' company learned how to fuse the magic of the PRIM with their own rancid technology, and the Fedic Dogan was a center for such dangerous research. Once there may have been many such magical/technological Dogans in IN-WORLD, MID-WORLD, and END-WORLD, but by the time our story begins, the Fedic Experimental Station is the only outpost of its kind left. To Mia, it is a place both wonderful and terrible.

As the followers of the CRIMSON KING know all too well, at the Fedic Dogan, magic and technology can still be merged. This Dogan's technological magic made possible MIA's transformation from spirit to flesh. This Dogan's technological magic also made the conception and birth of MORDRED (child of four parents) possible.

Although we do not know the original purpose of the Fedic Dogan, like most of the other wreckage left by the Old Ones, it is now being used for evil ends. Several centuries after the Red Death decimated Fedic's human population, the Crimson King's servants began to use this experimental station to extract the twin-telepathy enzyme from the children of the BORDERLAND CALLAS. They did this in the EXTRACTION ROOM, which is also the room in which Mia gives birth to Mordred. Roland calls this place *devar-tete* or "little torture chamber."

The Fedic Dogan is connected to CASTLE DISCORDIA by a series of subterranean tunnels. According to NIGEL THE BUTLER, the Fedic Dogan and the adjacent castle contain 595 operational DOORWAYS BETWEEN WORLDS. At one time, 30 one-way doors connected Fedic to NEW YORK CITY, but after Door #7 (leading to the Extraction Room) burns out, all that is left is Default Door #9, located in the ROTUNDA. VI:237–38, VI:244–45, VI:247, VI:249, VI:251, VI:378–84, VII:21–23 *(Extraction Room via aven kal)*, VII:27, VII:55–80 *(77–80—Rotunda)*, VII:141–96 *(141–58—Extraction Room setting)*, VII:206, VII:222, VII:232, VII:532, VII:537–40, VII:549–52 *(kitchen, pantry, office)*, VII:553, VII:557, VII:558–70 *(tunnels under Discordia; 559—Rotunda; 563—Main Street)*, VII:591, VII:708

> **CONTROL CENTER ("THE HEAD"):** The Arc 16 Experimental Station's nerve center is located four levels down from the EXTRACTION ROOM. During his short stay in the Fedic Dogan, baby MORDRED installs himself here so that he can view the Dogan's many monitors. (He uses them to spy on Roland's ka-tet.) Mordred kills and eats WALTER here. VII:159–64, VII:166–86
>
> **EXTRACTION ROOM:** According to Roland, the Extraction Room's true name is the *devar-tete,* or "little torture chamber." The NEW

YORK/FEDIC door (#7), which SUSANNAH is dragged through at the end of *Song of Susannah*, leads directly to this room. The Extraction Room gained its terrible name from the awful procedures done on its many beds. The BORDERLANDS children were brought to this room so that the twin-telepathy chemical could be extracted from their brains. MORDRED was also born here. VI:378–84, VII:21–23, VII:27 *(indirect)*, VII:55–75, VII:141–58

NIGEL'S QUARTERS: Nigel's three-room apartment is located near the Fedic Dogan's kitchen. It contains no bedroom, but it does have a living room and a butler's pantry full of monitoring equipment. It also contains a book-lined study. Nigel is a big fan of STEPHEN KING's novels. VII:158–59, VII:164–66, VII:189–90, VII:538

ROTUNDA: Deep below the Fedic Dogan and CASTLE DISCORDIA is a Rotunda, whose shape reminds SUSANNAH DEAN both of GRAND CENTRAL STATION in NEW YORK CITY and of BLAINE'S CRADLE in LUD. Around the circumference of this rotunda are a series of doors that lead to other *wheres* and *whens*. Among them are portals labeled SHANGHAI/FEDIC, BOMBAY/FEDIC, DALLAS (NOVEMBER 1963)/ FEDIC, and NEW YORK/FEDIC. All these doors are one-way. *(For more information, see DOORWAYS BETWEEN WORLDS, listed separately.)* VII:77–80, VII:559

STAGING AREA: Deep in the entrails of the Fedic Dogan, our tet finds a hangar-sized door marked *To Horses*. Beyond this is a door marked *Staging Area*. When our tet enters this staging area, they find that it is thick with hanging WOLVES awaiting repair, as well as the utility bays used to fire them up. To the left of the utility bays is the DOORWAY leading to THUNDERCLAP STATION. VII:192–96, VII:207, VII:232

JAKE'S MIND-DOGAN: While trying to escape the CRIMSON KING's gunbunnies in the tunnels below the DIXIE PIG, Jake feels an unseen hand fiddling with his mind's control center. He slams all doors shut, but the damage has been done. By the time Jake realizes what has happened, the OLD ONES' MIND-TRAP has already located a memory which it can use to scare Jake to death. (The memory is of a dinosaur film called *The Lost Continent*.) The only way Jake survives the mind-trap is by switching bodies with OY. Oy's mind-Dogan isn't affected by the Old Ones' machinery. In fact, he finds the controls of Jake's mind-Dogan to be much more mesmerizing. Luckily, he ignores them. VII:88 *(mind-trap)*, VII:101 *(Oy)*

SUSANNAH'S MIND-DOGAN: This Dogan, which actually exists within SUSANNAH DEAN's mind, is a version of the CALLA DOGAN, which JAKE CHAMBERS entered in *Wolves of the Calla*. (Susannah uses a visualization technique to create it.) Susannah's Dogan acts as a kind of inner control room. From this place she can see the CHAP growing inside her body, and can control (or at least regulate) the birth contractions racking her body. She can also use this control room to send urgent psychic messages to EDDIE DEAN. Much to Susannah's dismay, some of the Dogan's machinery is stamped with the NORTH CENTRAL POSITRONICS insignia. VI:62, VI:64, VI:67–72, VI:82, VI:89, VI:107, VI:124, VI:150, VI:171, VI:210, VI:222–29 *(Susannah in it)*, VI:247, VI:259–60, VI:321, VI:348, VI:351 *(gulag)*, VI:357–61, VII:142, VII:182, VII:239

WALTER'S MIND-DOGAN: According to baby MORDRED, the controls in WALTER's mind-Dogan are similar to the ones in SUSANNAH's MIND-DOGAN. However, instead of switches labeled *Emotional Temp* and the *Chap,* Walter's switches control functions such as ambulation. Mordred turns this latter switch off. VII:182

YOUNG THROCKEN'S MIND-DOGAN: According to baby MORDRED, the machinery inside a young billy-bumbler's mind-Dogan is no more complicated than a series of granny knots. OY might disagree. VII:164, VII:182

DOORWAY CAVE (CAVE OF VOICES, KRA KAMMEN)

CALLA BRYN STURGIS's Doorway Cave, high in the garnet-veined hills of the BORDERLANDS' ARROYO COUNTRY, plays a major part in *Wolves of the Calla* and *Song of Susannah*. Located about three hours north of Calla Bryn Sturgis and an hour north of MANNI CALLA, this cave contains two significant magical features. The first, situated about twenty feet from the cave's mouth, is the freestanding UNFOUND DOOR *(for more information about the Unfound Door, see* DOORWAYS BETWEEN WORLDS, *listed below)*. The second, placed much deeper in the cave, is the noxious-smelling Pit of Voices. Before the sudden appearance of the magical Unfound Door (which came to the Calla at the same time as FATHER CALLAHAN), this nasty cavern was known to the people of Calla Bryn Sturgis as the Cave of Voices. To the Manni folk, it was Kra Kammen, or the House of Ghosts.

As HENCHICK, the Manni *dinh,* warns Roland, the twisting arroyo PATH which leads to Doorway Cave is "rather upsy." The cave itself is not much more welcoming. Its ragged mouth, measuring nine feet by five feet, is partially blocked by a fallen boulder, so to enter it a seeker must ease his way around this huge stone, letting his heels hang over a two-thousand-foot drop. Once inside, the seeker is assailed by the Pit's noxious fumes, as well as the terrible voices which rise from it, accusing him of any misdeed (real or imaginary) which he has ever committed.

The chasm known as the Pit of Voices functions as a kind of distorted psychic mirror. It is almost as if the cave (or some entity or mechanical device haunting the cave) can hear the voices that play through an individual's mind. When a person stands in the cave, all of his ghosts scream up from the depths of the pit, accusing him of all his most painful failings and awful wrongdoings.

Despite the horror of the Pit of Voices and the dangers of using BLACK THIRTEEN (MAERLYN's evil magic ball, which opens the otherwise locked Unfound Door), in *Wolves of the Calla* and *Song of Susannah,* every member of our tet travels to this cavern. EDDIE uses the Unfound Door to travel to NEW YORK CITY, circa 1977. Pere Callahan travels through it to visit both

New York City and EAST STONEHAM, MAINE. At the end of *Wolves of the Calla*, SUSANNAH DEAN (controlled by her demon, MIA) wheels her way up to the cave so that Mia can escape through the door to 1999 New York, where she is destined to bear her CHAP. (In this final instance, Mia takes Black Thirteen with her.)

At the beginning of *Song of Susannah*, Roland, Eddie, JAKE, OY, and Callahan travel to the Doorway Cave once more. Although the door initially seems to have lost its magic, and though the voices in the Pit of Voices seem to have tipped over into complete insanity, our tet (with quite a bit of help from the Manni) manage to use the Unfound Door two more times. Jake, Oy, and Callahan are propelled to 1999 New York, to pursue Susannah-Mio. Roland and Eddie are sent to East Stoneham, Maine (circa 1977), to track down CALVIN TOWER.

> V:335, V:399–400, V:407 *(indirect)*, V:408–416 *(two thousand feet up; 408–410—described; 411—previously Cave of Voices)*, V:421, V:458–65 *(Unfound Door only)*, V:466, V:468, V:505, V:508, V:509–548 *(Roland waiting there)*, V:549, V:550–51, V:573, V:584, V:590–600 *(door)*, V:618–27, V:642, V:687, V:699, V:702, V:703–709, VI:3–8 *(under discussion)*, VI:12, VI:21, VI:26 *(cave)*, VI:28–43 *(34—kra kammen means "house of ghosts")*, VI:49 *(indirect)*, VI:64, VI:80–82, VI:122 *(Unfound Door)*, VI:124, VI:129, VI:142, VI:164, VI:167, VI:307, VI:308, VII:36 *(Cave of Voices)*, VII:88 *(Cave of Voices)*, VII:123 *(Unfound Door)*, VII:143, VII:196, VII:239, VII:416, VII:447 *(inside sai King's head)*, VII:540, VII:743

DOORWAYS BETWEEN WORLDS

Both MID-WORLD and KEYSTONE EARTH contain numerous doorways between worlds. These doorways can be divided into two types—MAGICAL and MECHANICAL. Magical doorways can be formed either from the same substance as the PRIM (the magical soup of creation), or from the magical tension between two people. STEPHEN KING's home, CARA LAUGHS, is an example of the first type of magical door. The BEACH DOORS through which Roland drew EDDIE and SUSANNAH DEAN are examples of the latter. Most magical doors are two-way. Others (such as the UNFOUND DOOR found in the BORDERLANDS) are doors to anywhere. What world or time period they open onto depends completely upon the mind-set, and desire, of the user.

Unlike Magical Doorways, Mechanical Doorways are *dedicated*. In other words, they always open onto the same location, if not the same time period. The majority we see in the Dark Tower series were created by the GREAT OLD ONES' sinister company NORTH CENTRAL POSITRONICS. Few are in good working order. Unlike Magical Doorways, most Mechanical Doorways are one-way only. Both NEW YORK CITY and the subterranean tunnels joining the FEDIC DOGAN with CASTLE DISCORDIA are lousy with Mechanical Doorways.

> **GENERAL REFERENCES:** V:72 *(indirect)*, V:89, V:97, V:102, V:104, V:105–106 *(doors you can aim in time)*, VI:40–41 *(Jake must imagine*

them), VI:147 *(need to find one),* VI:247–48, VI:251 *(Mia's doorway to mortality),* VII:73–74 *(595 doorways in Castle Discordia and Fedic Dogan)*
MAGICAL DOORWAYS:
    ARTIST'S DOOR (UNFOUND DOOR, EBERHARD-FABER DOOR): *See* UNFOUND DOOR, *below*
    BEACH DOORS (WESTERN SEA): In *The Drawing of the Three,* Roland Deschain encountered the three magical Beach Doors. These doors, located on the LOBSTROSITY-infested beach of the WESTERN SEA, were the result of the magical tension that existed between Roland and his nemesis WALTER. The first door, labeled *The Prisoner,* led him to EDDIE DEAN. The second, labeled *The Lady of Shadows,* opened into the mind of ODETTA HOLMES/DETTA WALKER. The final door, named *The Pusher,* led to the exceedingly seedy personality of the sociopath JACK MORT. All three of these doors were made of ironwood and stood six and a half feet tall. None had any visible support. (For more information, see *Stephen King's The Dark Tower: A Concordance, Volume I.*) V:105, V:409, V:410 *(indirect),* V:411, V:478, V:479, V:597, VII:177, VII:560, VII:724, VII:741
    BEAM PORTALS: *See* BEAMS, PATH OF THE, *listed separately*
    BLACK THIRTEEN: *See* MAERLYN'S RAINBOW, *in* CHARACTERS
    CARA LAUGHS: Cara Laughs is the name of the house located at 19 TURTLEBACK LANE in LOVELL, MAINE. In 1979, two years after JOHN CULLUM takes EDDIE and Roland there so that they can use it to transport themselves to the subterranean tunnels below the 1999 DIXIE PIG, STEPHEN KING purchases it. Obviously, either King has a nose for magic, or magic has a nose for him.
    Like the BEACH DOORS, Cara Laughs is a magical doorway. However, unlike them, it is created not by the magical tension between two people but from the pure, undifferentiated magic of the PRIM. The Cara Laughs Doorway is the source of the many WALK-INS found throughout western Maine and northern NEW HAMPSHIRE. The name *Cara Laughs* is very similar to SARA LAUGHS, the summer home of Mike Noonan, the main character of *Bag of Bones.* VI:394–95, VI:397, VI:403, VI:405, VI:408, VI:410, VII:116–17, VII:129–32, VII:304, VII:435–39, VII:441–43, VII:444, VII:446, VII:453, VII:463 *(indirect),* VII:542–45
    CHEWING DOOR: This doorway (and its hidden chewing monster) is located in the tunnels beneath the FEDIC DOGAN and CASTLE DISCORDIA. VII:560–61
    DOOR TO EVERYWHERE: *See general entry for* DOORWAYS BETWEEN WORLDS, *listed above*
    DOOR TO TODASH DARKNESS: This door is located beneath CASTLE DISCORDIA. The CRIMSON KING sends his worst enemies through it to be devoured by TODASH's many hideous monsters. VI:248–49
    DOORWAY CAVE: *See* DOORWAY CAVE, *listed separately*

JAKE'S DOOR (DOOR #4: THE BOY): *See* MANSION DOOR, *below, and* STONE CIRCLES (SPEAKING RINGS): SPEAKING RING ALONG THE PATH OF THE BEAM, *listed separately*

MANSION DOOR (JAKE'S DOOR): Like many magical portals, the door that JAKE CHAMBERS used to reenter MID-WORLD in *The Waste Lands* took a different form in our world than it did in Roland's world. In our world, the door appeared in a haunted house called THE MANSION, located in DUTCH HILL, BROOKLYN. In Mid-World, it existed within a SPEAKING RING located on the BEAR-TURTLE BEAM. V:50 *(indirect)*, V:93, V:104, V:246 *("pulling Jake through" and demon of the stone circle)*, V:258 *(stone-circle demon/doorkeeper in Dutch Hill)*, V:478 *(stone-circle demon/doorkeeper in Dutch Hill)*, VII:143, VII:144–45, VII:249

SHEEMIE'S MAGIC DOORS: Although teleportation is a talent forbidden in THUNDERCLAP's DEVAR-TOI, Roland's old friend SHEEMIE RUIZ can make Doorways with his mind. When Roland was young, Sheemie used this skill to follow our gunslinger and his original ka-tet to GILEAD. Sheemie used this ability again to help TED BRAUTIGAN escape the Devar-Toi and return to his home state of CONNECTICUT. Unfortunately, when Sheemie uses this skill (as he does several times to help our tet), he has tiny strokes. *See* BREAKERS: RUIZ, STANLEY (SHEEMIE), *in* CHARACTERS

THINNY: *See* THINNY, *listed separately*

TODASH: *See* TODASH, *listed separately*

UNFOUND DOOR: In the Dark Tower series, the Unfound Door has three manifestations. The first time we see it, it is a freestanding ironwood door located in DOORWAY CAVE, high in the ARROYO COUNTRY of the BORDERLANDS. In this incarnation, it bears a strong resemblance to the BEACH DOORS, through which Roland drew EDDIE and SUSANNAH DEAN into MID-WORLD. Like the portals Roland found on the shores of the WESTERN SEA, the Unfound Door stands six and a half feet high and has no visible support, its hinges apparently fastened to nothing. However, whereas the Beach Doors were marked with the High Speech words for *The Prisoner*, *The Lady of Shadows*, and *The Pusher* (the final of these being the door which led Roland to the evil JACK MORT), the Unfound Door is marked with hieroglyphs. These hieroglyphs mean *Unfound* and also appear on the ghostwood box containing BLACK THIRTEEN. Etched upon the Unfound Door's crystal knob is a ROSE.

By the time our tet arrives in CALLA BRYN STURGIS, the Unfound Door has been in Doorway Cave as long as PERE CALLAHAN has been in the Calla (probably between five and ten years). In fact, the two of them appeared together in that cavern, which, before their arrival, had been known as the Cave of Voices. Callahan, the Unfound Door, and Black Thirteen were transported to the arroyo cave from the MOHAINE DESERT's WAY STATION. The magician who did the transporting was Roland's old nemesis WALTER. Since the Unfound Door had not previously existed in the Way Station (otherwise Roland and JAKE would have seen it during their sojourn there), we can assume that Walter conjured it from another where and when. This would be completely consistent with the Unfound Door's later appearances in the series.

While in the Cave of Voices/Doorway Cave, the Unfound Door is locked. Although it has no keyhole, it does have a key. That key is MAERLYN's most dangerous magic ball, Black Thirteen. Despite the many risks involved in waking Thirteen, our tet uses it to open the door so that they can travel to other wheres and whens. With Roland's help, Eddie uses ball and door to travel to NEW YORK CITY, 1977. With Roland and Eddie's aid, Pere Callahan uses them to travel to New York and to STONEHAM, MAINE. At the end of *Wolves of the Calla*, MIA, Susannah's demon-possessor, opens the door for what she hopes will be a final time. Taking Black Thirteen with her, she escapes to New York City, 1999, where the servants of the CRIMSON KING await her arrival.

However, the Unfound Door's job in the Callas is not over yet. With the help of the MANNI, our remaining tet-mates reopen the door so that they can complete their quest. Callahan, Jake, and OY travel to New York City, 1999, to pursue Susannah-Mio. Roland and Eddie travel to Stoneham, Maine, circa 1977, to track down CALVIN TOWER (owner of the Vacant LOT) and to meet our *kas-ka Gan*, STEPHEN KING.

We next encounter the Unfound Door in the final book of the Dark Tower series. Only three members of our tet—Roland, Susannah, and Oy—still struggle onward toward their goal. Although Eddie and Jake are dead, Susannah begins to dream about them. In her dream, Eddie and Jake are in a snowy CENTRAL PARK. Behind them is the Unfound Door. This ironwood dream-door looks exactly like the Unfound Door in Doorway Cave, only below the hieroglyphs for *Unfound* are the words *The Artist*. The knob is no longer crystal but solid gold, and filigreed with the shape of two crossed pencils—#2's whose erasers have been cut off. When they are but a few days' journey from the Tower, PATRICK DANVILLE, the artist whom Susannah and Roland rescued from DANDELO in the WHITE LANDS OF EMPATHICA, draws this second version of the Unfound Door so that Susannah can escape Mid-World. Although the door he draws does not have *The Artist* written upon it, and though the knob is of a plain shiny metal, not filigreed gold, it bears the necessary hieroglyphs and so works perfectly well. Susannah leaves Mid-World through this ironwood portal and joins her beloved ka-tet mates (who in this particular ALTERNATIVE AMERICA are named Eddie and Jake TOREN) in a wintertime Central Park.

The final time we encounter the Unfound Door is at the base of the DARK TOWER itself. Roland's long journey ends at a ghostwood door banded with black steel. Upon it, engraved three-quarters of the way up, is the hieroglyphic sigul meaning *Unfound*. As Roland lays AUNT

TALITHA's cross and his final remaining six-gun at the Tower's base, the hieroglyphs change. The door which Roland has been seeking all of his life transforms from UNFOUND to FOUND. Through this, the Found Door, Roland enters the Tower.

UNFOUND DOOR AND DOORWAY CAVE/CAVE OF VOICES: V:335, V:399–400, V:407 *(indirect)*, V:408–416 *(two thousand feet up; 408–410—described; 411—previously Cave of Voices)*, V:421, V:458–65 *(Unfound Door only)*, V:466, V:468, V:505, V:508, V:509–548 *(Roland waiting there)*, V:549, V:550–51, V:573, V:584, V:590–600 *(door)*, V:618–27, V:642, V:687, V:699, V:702, V:703–709, VI:3–8 *(under discussion)*, VI:12, VI:21, VI:26 *(cave)*, VI:28–43 *(34—kra kammen means "house of ghosts")*, VI:49 *(indirect)*, VI:64, VI:80–82, VI:122 *(Unfound Door)*, VI:124, VI:129, VI:142, VI:164, VI:167, VI:307, VI:308, VII:36 *(Cave of Voices)*, VII:88 *(Cave of Voices)*, VII:123 *(Unfound Door)*, VII:143, VII:196, VII:239, VII:416, VII:447 *(inside sai King's head)*, VII:540, VII:743

UNFOUND DOOR DRAWN BY PATRICK DANVILLE (ARTIST'S DOOR, EBERHARD-FABER DOOR): VII:724–25, VII:729, VII:738–50, VII:751–52

UNFOUND DOOR TO THE DARK TOWER: VII:820–21

MECHANICAL DOORWAYS (OLD ONES' DOORWAYS): Both our world and MID-WORLD are riddled with mechanical doorways left over by the GREAT OLD ONES. At one time, 595 working mechanical doors existed below CASTLE DISCORDIA and the FEDIC DOGAN alone. Over 30 of them were one-way ports leading from NEW YORK CITY to FEDIC. Unlike magical doors, mechanical doorways are *dedicated*. In other words, they always open onto the same place.

The Great Old Ones (who, as we all know, learned to merge technology and magic) built doorways to other *wheres* and *whens* for mere entertainment. For example, anyone wishing to witness the assassination of President John F. Kennedy had merely to enter the ROTUNDA portal (located below Castle Discordia and the Fedic Dogan) marked DALLAS (NOVEMBER 1963)/FEDIC. Anyone wishing to see the Lincoln assassination had only to go though the door marked FORD'S THEATER. Like the cyborg GUARDIANS, ANDY the Messenger Robot, and BLAINE the Insane Mono, the mechanical doorways between worlds were manufactured by NORTH CENTRAL POSITRONICS. VII:73–74, VII:200

BOMBAY/FEDIC DOOR: VII:78

DALLAS (NOVEMBER 1963)/FEDIC DOOR: VII:78, VII:538

DOOR TO TODASH DARKNESS: According to MIA, below CASTLE DISCORDIA is a door that goes TODASH, or to the no-place between worlds. Although this door was probably created by mistake, the CRIMSON KING uses it to punish his worst enemies. Anyone unfortunate enough to be pushed through this door will wander, blind and insane, until eaten by one of todash's many monsters. VI:248–49, VII:562

FEDIC/THUNDERCLAP STATION DOOR: This doorway leads from the ARC 16 WOLF STAGING AREA to THUNDERCLAP STATION, six miles from the DEVAR-TOI. Although the robotic WOLVES have been using it for decades, this portal is in terrible shape. Any human unlucky enough to pass through it feels as though he or she is being turned inside out. Once on the other side, he/she is overcome with a terrible, gut-spewing nausea. Unlike the other magical and mechanical doorways we have encountered so far, this one is made of steel, not ironwood. It is painted green and bears a sigul which resembles a cloud with a lightning bolt. VII:151–52, VII:179, VII:187–88 *(marked with a cloud and lightning sigul)*, VII:190, VII:194–200, VII:203

FORD'S THEATER DOOR: This door leads to Ford's Theater, in WASHINGTON, D.C. We can also assume that it always opens onto April 14, 1865—the day on which President Lincoln was assassinated. (He was killed while attending the play *Our American Cousin.*) VII:538, VII:561, VII:562

FORTY-SEVENTH STREET DOOR (BLEECKER STREET, NEW YORK CITY): Like the NINETY-FOURTH STREET door, NEW YORK CITY's Forty-seventh Street door links both the MULTIPLE AMERICAS and the multiple New Yorks. In all of its manifestations, this door is located on BLEECKER STREET, between FIRST and SECOND AVENUES. However, in some versions of New York, the door stands in an empty warehouse. In other versions of the city, it stands in an eternally half-completed building. VII:105

NEW YORK #7/FEDIC DOOR: This door leads from the tunnels below the DIXIE PIG to the EXTRACTION ROOM in the ARC 16 EXPERI-MENTAL STATION in FEDIC. It is made of ghostwood. After SUSAN-NAH DEAN is dragged through this door by SAYRE and his *closies,* it burns out. Hence, when our other tet-mates travel from the Dixie Pig to Fedic, they are rerouted to a default door (NEW YORK #9/FEDIC), located in the ROTUNDA below CASTLE DISCORDIA and the FEDIC DOGAN. Susannah has the robot NIGEL carry her from the Extraction Room to the Rotunda so that she can meet her friends. VI:373 *(indirect)*, VI:377–79, VII:74

NEW YORK#9/FEDIC/FINAL DEFAULT DOOR: At one time, over 30 one-way portals led from NEW YORK CITY to FEDIC. However, after the FEDIC DOGAN's EXTRACTION ROOM door (NEW YORK #7/FEDIC) burns out, only #9 Final Default remains. All operational doors leading from New York to Fedic now transport to this doorway. VII:74, VII:78–80, VII:110 *(New York side)*, VII:133–38, VII:146, VII:529, VII:538

NINETY-FOURTH STREET DOOR (NEW YORK CITY): This door-way connects alternative versions of NEW YORK CITY. Unfortunately, it is usually on the blink. VII:105

SANTA MIRA/THUNDERCLAP DOOR: TED BRAUTIGAN and his

fellow BREAKERS—TANYA LEEDS, JACE McGOVERN, DAVE ITTAWAY, and DICK of the forgotten last name—were all brought to END-WORLD through this door. VII:287–89, VII:297
SHANGHAI/FEDIC DOOR: VII:78
SPEAKING RINGS: *See* STONE CIRCLES (SPEAKING RINGS), *listed separately*
WIZARD'S RAINBOW (MAERLYN'S MAGIC BALLS): *See* MAERLYN'S RAINBOW, *in* CHARACTERS

DRAWERS
The Drawers are a kind of wasteland. According to SUSANNAH DEAN, they are places that are spoiled, useless, or both. However, they are also places of tremendous psychic power. (For more information about the Drawers, see *Stephen King's The Dark Tower: A Concordance, Volume I.*)
VII:733

E

EASTERN PLAIN (CALLA BADLANDS)
See CALLA BADLANDS

ELMVILLE
See DEVAR-TOI

EMPATHICA, WHITE LANDS OF (WESTRING, SNOWLANDS)
The White Lands of Empathica are the snow-laden lands located southeast of the DISCORDIA BADLANDS. Unlike the Badlands, which were poisoned by the CRIMSON KING, the White Lands still contain living creatures. After their terrible encounter with the false uffi at LE CASSE ROI RUSSE, Roland, SUSANNAH, and OY travel into the hilly White Lands where they hunt deer, make themselves some winter clothes, and build a travois. (Susannah even makes snowshoes for Roland.)

However, from the beginning, the careful reader realizes that something is fishy about any land called Empathica. When you empathize with someone, you identify completely with that person's mind-set and emotions. In a place called Empathica, someone or something is using this power. On ODD'S LANE, our threesome meets the empath living in Empathica. However, he is anything but empathetic.

DANDELO, the were-insect who uses *glammer* to disguise himself as a cheery old man named JOE COLLINS, eats other people's emotions. For years he has been milking fear and laughter out of PATRICK DANVILLE, a young artist whom Dandelo keeps in his basement. Dandelo tries to feed from Roland, but SUSANNAH (warned by the deus ex machina STEPHEN KING) kills him first.

VII:545, VII:607, VII:609 *(pass into them)*, VII:611, VII:612, VII:618, VII:625, VII:647–711 *(action takes place here)*, VII:715, VII:746

CAMPSITE WHERE HIDES ARE PREPARED: Roland and SUSANNAH prepare deer hides here. They use the "brain-tanning" method. Gross but effective. VII:636–45

FEDERAL, THE (FEDERAL OUTPOST 19): *See* DOGAN: FEDERAL OUTPOST 19

ODD LANE (ODD'S LANE): Three weeks after entering the White Lands of Empathica, SUSANNAH, Roland, and OY emerge from a snowy tract of upland forest and see, below them, an inverted *T* carved in the snow. Much to their delight, they realize that this letter is actually the crossing point of two roads. The long body of the *T*, which continues over the hump of the horizon, is TOWER ROAD, but the relatively short cross-arm is Odd's Lane, home of JOE COLLINS and his horse, LIPPY.

The self-proclaimed "Odd Joe of Odd's Lane" seems as friendly and welcoming as his house is cozy. However, in the White Lands of Empathica, not everything is as it seems. In reality, Odd Joe is none other than the dangerous were-spider DANDELO. Dandelo disguises his appearance (as well as the rundown facade of his cottage) using *glammer*. In actuality, Dandelo is a vampire, but one who drinks human emotion. Fearful that our tet will discover that *Odd Lane* is an anagram of *Dandelo*, this tricky were-spider painted an *S* onto the end of his lane's name. (It doesn't work.) VII:651–60 *(corner)*, VII:661, VII:666, VII:671, VII:680, VII:682, VII:683, VII:690, VII:696, VII:707, VII:710 *(intersection)*, VII:751

   DANDELO'S HOUSE: VII:652–711, VII:731, VII:755

   DESERTED VILLAGE: VII:652

STONE'S WARP: According to the improvised life's tale which the false JOE COLLINS spins for our tet, Joe awoke in an END-WORLD town called Stone's Warp after being beaten up by three NBA-size men in our world's CLEVELAND. VII:670

TOWER ROAD: Tower Road runs from DANDELO's house, in the White Lands of Empathica, all the way to the DARK TOWER itself. VII:651–60 *(corner)*, VII:664, VII:671, VII:682, VII:705, VII:707, VII:709, VII:710 *(intersection)*, VII:711, VII:715–17, VII:718 *(discuss traveling along it)*, VII:726–27 *(on it)*, VII:729–803 *(on it; 777, 779, 781—description of road near Tower)*

END-WORLD

The RIVER WHYE marks the end of the BORDERLANDS and the beginning of End-World, home of the DARK TOWER. Moving southeast along the PATH OF THE BEAM, Roland and his dwindling tet travel through the following End-World regions: THUNDERCLAP (containing the CALLA DOGAN, the DEVAR-TOI, and THUNDERCLAP STATION), the DISCOR-

DIA (containing FEDIC, CASTLE DISCORDIA, the DISCORDIA BAD-LANDS, and LE CASSE ROI RUSSE), the WHITE LANDS OF EMPATHICA (containing DANDELO's house and the FEDERAL), and finally CAN'-KA NO REY, the red ROSE fields containing the DARK TOWER.

ACTION TAKES PLACE IN END-WORLD ON THE FOLLOWING PAGES: VI:379–84, VII:55–80, VII:137–418, VII:531–803, VII:827–28

END-WORLD DIRECTLY NAMED ON THE FOLLOWING PAGES: V:558, VI:13, VI:103, VI:247, VI:251, VI:406, VI:407, VII:176, VII:407, VII:555, VII:594, VII:696, VII:715, VII:798, VII:800, VII:818

END-WORLD PLACES, MOVING SOUTHEAST ALONG THE PATH OF THE BEAM, FROM THE BORDERLANDS TO THE DARK TOWER:

CALLA BADLANDS (EASTERN PLAIN): See CALLA BADLANDS, *listed separately*

   BOOM-FLURRY HILL: See CALLA BADLANDS, *listed separately*
   DEVIL'S CAUSEWAY: See CALLA BADLANDS, *listed separately*
   CALLA DOGAN (NORTH CENTRAL POSITRONICS NORTH-EAST CORRIDOR ARC QUADRANT OUTPOST 16): See DOGAN, THE, *listed separately*

THUNDERCLAP: See THUNDERCLAP, *listed separately*
   CAN-STEKE-TETE (STEKE-TETE): See DEVAR-TOI, *listed separately*
   DEVAR-TOI (ALGUL SIENTO, BLUE HEAVEN): See DEVAR-TOI, *listed separately*
   THUNDERCLAP STATION: See DEVAR-TOI, *listed separately*
   THUNDERCLAP BADLANDS: See THUNDERCLAP, *listed separately*
   BRIDGE OVER THE ABYSS: See FEDIC: DEVIL'S ARSE AND FALLEN BRIDGE
   DEVIL'S ARSE: See FEDIC: DEVIL'S ARSE AND FALLEN BRIDGE
   FEDIC: See FEDIC, *listed separately*
      FEDIC DOGAN: See DOGAN, *listed separately*
   CASTLE DISCORDIA: See CASTLE DISCORDIA, *listed separately*
      BANQUETING HALL: See CASTLE DISCORDIA, *listed separately*

DISCORDIA (BADLANDS): See DISCORDIA, *listed separately*
   KING'S WAY (BADLANDS AVENUE): This is the coach road between CASTLE DISCORDIA and LE CASSE ROI RUSSE.
CASSE ROI RUSSE, LE: See CASSE ROI RUSSE, *listed separately*
REGION OF THE UNDERSNOW: See EMPATHICA, WHITE LANDS OF, *listed separately*
WHITE LANDS OF EMPATHICA: See EMPATHICA, WHITE LANDS OF, *listed separately*
   ODD LANE (ODD'S LANE): See EMPATHICA, WHITE LANDS OF, *listed separately*

DANDELO'S HOUSE AND BARN: *See* EMPATHICA, WHITE LANDS OF, *listed separately*
FEDERAL, THE: *See* EMPATHICA, WHITE LANDS OF, *listed separately*
CAN'-KA NO REY: *See* DARK TOWER, *listed separately*
DARK TOWER, THE: *See* DARK TOWER, *listed separately*

EXTRACTION ROOM
See DOGAN: FEDIC DOGAN, *above*

F

FEDERAL, THE (FEDERAL OUTPOST 19)
See DOGAN: FEDERAL OUTPOST 19

FEDIC (FEDIC O' THE DISCORDIA)
The deserted village of Fedic (also known as FEDIC O' THE RED DEATH and FEDIC O' THE DISCORDIA) lies on the far side of THUNDERCLAP, on the PATH OF THE SHARDIK-MATURIN BEAM. Fedic sits within the outer wall of the CASTLE ON THE ABYSS (also known as CASTLE DISCORDIA). It consists of a single street, which terminates against the castle's inner wall. The town contains several deserted shops as well as a number of bars and brothels. (Before the Red Death obliterated its population, boozing and prostitution were popular distractions on this far-flung edge of the world.) In the days of the GREAT OLD ONES, PATRICIA, BLAINE's twin Mono, terminated at FEDIC STATION. Beyond both village and outer castle wall is a great fissure in the earth called THE DEVIL'S ARSE. Demons breed here. Long ago, a bridge crossed this crack, but by the time Roland and SUSANNAH visit the town, the bridge is long gone.

Fedic also contains one extremely sinister building, which is still in use. This place is the FEDIC DOGAN, which MIA calls the Dogan of all Dogans. Within the walls of the Fedic Dogan is the ARC 16 EXPERIMENTAL STATION, which is run by the minions of the RED KING. The Fedic Dogan is unique, since it is one of the few places where magic and technology have been integrated successfully.

VI:105, VI:229, VI:234–55, VI:382, VII:13, VII:51, VII:52, VII:89, VII:106, VII:110, VII:111, VII:146, VII:149, VII:150, VII:152, VII:153, VII:158, VII:167, VII:206, VII:207 *(staging area)*, VII:223, VII:246, VII:297, VII:300, VII:306, VII:407, VII:409, VII:477 *(Faydag)*, VII:485, VII:520, VII:531–42, VII:553, VII:554, VII:556–58, VII:559, VII:590, VII:594
DEVAR-TETE: *See* DOGAN: FEDIC DOGAN
DEVIL'S ARSE AND FALLEN BRIDGE: The Devil's Arse is a great crack in

the earth located just northeast of the town of Fedic. It contains horrific monsters that cozen, diddle, and plot to escape. According to TED BRAUTIGAN and the other BREAKERS who travel to Fedic with SUSANNAH, the monsters from the Devil's Arse have been tunneling through to the catacombs beneath CASTLE DISCORDIA and the FEDIC DOGAN for years, and they are close to breaking through. VI:105 *(not yet named)*, VI:243 *(not yet named)*, VI:244, VII:536, VII:539, VII:557, VII:567

EXTRACTION ROOM: *See* DOGAN:FEDIC DOGAN

FEDIC CAFÉ: VI:252

FEDIC DOGAN: *See* DOGAN, *listed separately*

FEDIC GOOD-TIME SALOON AND DANCE EMPORIUM: VI:235, VI:245 *(where Mia met Walter)*, VII:557 *(saloon next door to hotel)*

FEDIC HOTEL: VI:235, VII:534, VII:553, VII:556–58

FEDIC STATION: Although it appears somewhat derelict, Fedic Station plays its own small but important role in the plans of the CRIMSON KING. After the WOLVES arrive in THUNDERCLAP with the CALLAS' kidnapped children, they and their prisoners board a train at THUNDERCLAP STATION. This train terminates at Fedic's Station. From here, the children are brought to the FEDIC DOGAN's EXTRACTION ROOM, where a twin-telepathy chemical is extracted from their brains, leaving them ROONT. Once upon a time (before she threw herself into the RIVER SEND), BLAINE's twin, the blue Mono called PATRICIA, ran from LUD to Fedic Station. VI:237, VII:531, VII:537

GAIETY BAR AND GRILLE: VII:536

GIN PUPPY SALOON: VI:239–55 *(sitting outside)*, VII:149, VII:532

LIVERY: VI:235

MILLINERY AND LADIES WEAR (FEDIC MILLINERY AND LADIES WEAR): VI:239, VII:534

SERVICE'S MALAMUTE SALOON: VI:235–36

FEDIC DOGAN
　　See DOGAN: FEDIC DOGAN (ARC 16 EXPERIMENTAL STATION)

FIELD O' END-WORLD
　　See DARK TOWER: CAN'-KA NO REY

FIELD OF RED ROSES
　　See DARK TOWER: CAN'-KA NO REY

FORGE OF THE KING
　　See CASTLE DISCORDIA *and* CASSE ROI RUSSE

FOUND DOOR
　　See DOORWAYS BETWEEN WORLDS: MAGICAL DOORS: UNFOUND DOOR

G

GAGE PARK
See KANSAS (STATE OF), *in* OUR WORLD PLACES

GALEE
See TAHEEN: STOAT-HEADED TAHEEN, *in* CHARACTERS

GARDEN OF THE BEAM
See LOT, THE, *below*

GEM THEATER
See DEVAR-TOI

GINGERBREAD HOUSE
The Gingerbread House, where TED BRAUTIGAN, DINKY EARNSHAW, and SHEEMIE RUIZ go to escape the constant surveillance of the DEVAR-TOI guards, was actually created by Roland's old friend Sheemie. Unlike any of the other Breakers, Sheemie can create fistulas in time, which are like balconies on the DARK TOWER. Since the Gingerbread House exists outside the time/space continuum, our rebel Breakers can spend many hours recuperating there and yet return to the Devar at the same instant in which they left. Hence, no one ever detects their absence.

Like the edible witch's cottage in *Hansel and Gretel*, Sheemie's Gingerbread House is made entirely of sweets. The walls are of green, yellow, and red candy. The stairs are chocolate; the banister is a candy cane. VII:266–302 *(Ted Brautigan tells his story here)*

    TWIZZLER AVENUE: Although it is impossible to step outside the Gingerbread House and onto this licorice-like street, you can see it from the Gingerbread House window. The cars that drive along Twizzler Avenue look suspiciously like bonbons. VII:267

GLASS·PALACE
See GREEN PALACE

GOLGOTHA, THE
At the end of *The Gunslinger*, Roland and WALTER held palaver in this ancient killing ground located on the western slopes of the CYCLOPEAN MOUNTAINS. During an interminable night, Walter told Roland's fortune here. (For more information, see *Stephen King's The Dark Tower: A Concordance, Volume I.*)
    V:314, VI:284, VII:176–77 *(indirect)*

GREEN PALACE (GLASS PALACE)

In the ALTERNATIVE version of KANSAS which our tet travels through in *Wizard and Glass,* the Green Palace is located on the I-70, near TOPEKA's warbling THINNY. When our tet enters this palace of green glass, they confront RANDALL FLAGG (yet another version of WALTER), who is posing as the Wizard of OZ. While here, our tet travels through MAERLYN'S GRAPEFRUIT back to GILEAD, where they witness Roland's matricide. At the beginning of *Wolves of the Calla,* we find out that just before our tet arrived in the BORDERLANDS, a green palace appeared and then disappeared near the western branch of the RIVER WHYE.

V:18, V:36, V:121, V:166, VI:290, VII:173 *(Castle of Oz)*

GREY HAVENS

According to STEPHEN KING, the Grey Havens is the place that tired characters go to rest.

VII:817

H

HALL OF RESUMPTION
See DARK TOWER

HEAD, THE
See DOGAN: FEDIC DOGAN (ARC 16 EXPERIMENTAL STATION)

HEARTBREAK HOUSE
See DEVAR-TOI

HELL OF DARKNESS

This is where bad TAHEEN go after death, especially ones who have had their tails docked.

VII:224

HENRY GRAHAM'S DRUG STORE AND SODA FOUNTAIN
See DEVAR-TOI: PLEASANTVILLE

HIDDEN HIGHWAYS (HIGHWAYS IN HIDING, TODASH TURNPIKES, SECRET HIGHWAYS, DARKSIDE ROADS)

Although the DARK TOWER contains only one KEYSTONE EARTH and that Keystone Earth contains only one North America and one United States, other levels of the Tower also contain ALTERNATIVE AMERICAS, or alternative versions of North America and of the United States. These Alternative Americas are linked by hidden highways.

The hidden highways are not just bridges between worlds. They are darkside roads where people can lose themselves, their memories, and their identities. To ordinary people, these roads are *dim,* or almost invisible, but to those in need of their slightly poisonous freedom, they are an escape route. After the death of his dear friend LUPE DELGADO in NEW YORK CITY, PERE CALLAHAN traveled these highways for five years. In *The Stand,* we find out that RANDALL FLAGG follows America's hidden highways as well.

V:260, V:263–64, V:289, V:292–93, V:299 *(and multiple Americas),* V:300–310 *(302—and Rose),* V:444, V:461, V:543

HIGHWAYS IN HIDING
See HIDDEN HIGHWAYS

HOGAN HOUSE
See DEVAR-TOI

J

JAKE'S DOOR
See DOORWAYS BETWEEN WORLDS

JAKE'S MIND-DOGAN
See DOGAN

JERUSALEM'S LOT
See MAINE (STATE OF), *in* OUR WORLD PLACES

K

KANSAS
See KANSAS (STATE OF), *in* OUR WORLD PLACES

KEYSTONE EARTH
See KEYSTONE WORLDS

KEYSTONE WORLDS
KEY WORLD, KEYSTONE EARTH, REAL WORLD: The Keystone World is the version of Earth that STEPHEN KING inhabits and is the one

in which he writes his books. (I assume it is also the world in which you and I read them.) Keystone Earth has many twinners—EDDIE DEAN and TED BRAUTIGAN both come from such parallel realities—but Keystone World is the only true version of Earth. On Keystone, time flows in one direction only, and what is done there can't be undone. In other words (to quote Dorrance Marstellar, one of my favorite characters from the novel *Insomnia*), on Keystone, what's "done-bun can't be undone."

Keystone Earth is the true twin of Roland's world, which is also known as TOWER KEYSTONE. The ka of Keystone Earth is NINETEEN. VI:200, VI:270 *(no do-overs)*, VI:271 *(only world that matters)*, VII:121 *(twin of Roland's world)*, VII:174 *(indirect)*, VII:242 *(Keystone Earth)*, VII:280 *(Keystone Earth)*, VII:300 *(Real World)*, VII:302–303, VII:304, VII:305, VII:307, VII:339, VII:400 *(Real World)*, VII:405, VII:416, VII:488, VII:493, VII:511, VII:528, VII:627 *(Stephen King's world)*, VII:728, VII:773, VII:807

TOWER KEYSTONE: Tower Keystone is Roland's world (MID-WORLD). It is the true twin of KEYSTONE EARTH. Tower Keystone takes its name from the DARK TOWER, which exists here in its true form, not disguised as a ROSE, as it is on Keystone Earth. The ka of Tower Keystone is NINETY-NINE. VII:121 *(called key world)*, VII:609, VII:773

KING'S CHILDHOOD BARN
The first time STEPHEN KING saw the CRIMSON KING, he was seven years old and sawing wood in his uncle and aunt's barn. (He and his brother were on punishment duty because they had tried to run away.) This barn was also the site of our author's first meeting with CUTHBERT ALLGOOD and EDDIE DEAN.
    VI:292–93, VI:389

KING'S HOUSE IN LOVELL
    See DOORWAYS BETWEEN WORLDS: CARA LAUGHS

KING'S WAY
    See DISCORDIA

KRA KAMMEN
    See DOORWAY CAVE

L

LAND OF DARKNESS
    See THUNDERCLAP

LAND OF NINETEEN
The Land of NINETEEN is the land of bizarre coincidences. Sometimes it seems to be the land of failed plans as well. *See* NINETEEN, *in* CHARACTERS
V:169, VII:36

LAND OF UNDERTABLE
A strange kingdom of wet mud and scampering feet. It exists below the feast-laden table of MIA's BANQUETING HALL. (Although Mia dreams she is in CASTLE DISCORDIA, in actuality, Mia's Banqueting Hall is nothing but a BOG.)
V:74

LE CASSE ROI RUSSE
See CASSE ROI RUSSE

LICORICE AVENUE
See GINGERBREAD HOUSE

LOS ZAPATOS
See MEXICO, *in* OUR WORLD PLACES

LOT, THE (VACANT LOT)
"The lot" refers to the magical Vacant Lot, located on the corner of FORTY-SIXTH STREET and SECOND AVENUE in NEW YORK CITY. The lot contains the magical singing ROSE, which is our world's version of the DARK TOWER. It was also once the home of TOM AND JERRY'S ARTISTIC DELI. The lot (also known as LOT #298, BLOCK 19, in MANHATTAN) is owned by CALVIN TOWER (also known as Calvin TOREN).
   In 1977, SOMBRA REAL ESTATE (secret servants of the CRIMSON KING) approached Calvin Tower about buying the lot. In fact, they paid him $100,000 for first right of sale. Luckily, their plans to buy the lot and bulldoze the Rose are foiled by EDDIE DEAN, our ka-mai, whose brilliant flash of intuition leads him to spontaneously create the TET CORPORATION while palavering with Calvin Tower in the back room of his bookshop.
   By 1999, the lot is no longer vacant, but the site of 2 HAMMARSKJÖLD PLAZA, headquarters of Eddie's spontaneously incorporated corporation. Tet, whose major purpose is to protect the Rose, has done its job well. This most important flower still grows, and sings, in its original locale. The only difference is that the Rose now grows in an indoor garden called the GARDEN OF THE BEAM.
   V:51, V:58 (*Second Avenue and Forty-sixth*), V:66–67, V:68 (*Lot #289, Block #19*), V:69 (*indirect*), V:95, V:96, V:98, V:174, V:177, V:181, V:182–97, V:312, V:316, V:431, V:432 (*hears Rose*), V:502, V:503, V:504, V:507, V:517, V:522, V:527, V:528, V:530, V:531, V:538–42 (*Eddie and Tower discuss selling*), V:544–45, V:584, V:594, V:706, VI:35, VI:47, VI:56,

VI:147, VI:171, VI:187, VI:189, VI:195–216 *(and bill of sale)*, VI:267, VI:270, VI:297, VII:26, VII:33, VII:36, VII:37, VII:122, VII:143, VII:487, VII:492, VII:495, VII:526, VII:756, VII:757

HAMMARSKJÖLD PLAZA (2 HAMMARSKJÖLD PLAZA, THE BLACK TOWER, HOUSE OF THE ROSE): This tall black building was erected by the TET CORPORATION on what was once the Vacant Lot. It serves as Tet's headquarters and is the home of the ROSE. VI:47, VI:50, VI:51, VI:53, VI:54–56, VI:89, VI:91–92, VI:257, VI:308, VI:315, VI:318, VII:487, VII:488, VII:489, VII:490–520

> **GARDEN OF THE BEAM:** When he visits 1999 NEW YORK, near the end of *The Dark Tower,* Roland sees this small garden shrine on the ground-floor lobby of 2 HAMMARSKJÖLD PLAZA. The Garden of the Beam is surrounded by ropes of wine-dark velvet. At its center, separate from the dwarf palm trees and Spathiphyllum plants which surround it, is the ROSE. In front of this garden is a small brass sign bearing the following dedication: "Given by the Tet Corporation, in honor of Edward Cantor Dean and John 'Jake' Chambers. Cam-a-cam-mal, Pria-toi, Gan delah" ("White over Red, thus Gan wills ever" or "God over evil, this is the will of God"). Before Eddie and Jake died, the plaque read, "Given by the Tet Corporation, in honor of the Beam family, and in memory of Gilead." Like the Rose, this sign is magical. No matter what language a person speaks, the plaque translates itself so that its message can be understood. VII:491–95, VII:503–505, VII:520

TOM AND JERRY'S ARTISTIC DELI: Before the Vacant Lot became vacant, it was the home of this deli. Tom and Jerry's was run by TOMMY GRAHAM, though the ground landlord was CALVIN TOWER. V:51, V:61 *(deli)*, V:99, V:266, VI:47, VI:297, VI:318 *(indirect)*

M

MAERLYN'S GRAPEFRUIT
> *See* MAERLYN'S RAINBOW, *in* CHARACTERS

MAERLYN'S RAINBOW
> *See* MAERLYN'S RAINBOW, *in* CHARACTERS

MAGICAL DOORS
> *See* DOORWAYS BETWEEN WORLDS

MAGNETIC HILLS
> *See* BORDERLANDS, *in* MID-WORLD PLACES

MALL
See DEVAR-TOI; *see also* NEW YORK (STATE OF): NIAGARA MALL, *in* OUR WORLD PLACES

MANSION, THE
See DOORWAYS BETWEEN WORLDS

MECHANICAL DOORS
See DOORWAYS BETWEEN WORLDS

MEXICO
See MEXICO, *in* OUR WORLD PLACES; *see also* TODASH, *below*

MIA'S CASTLE
See CASTLE DISCORDIA

MID-WORLD LANES
When JAKE CHAMBERS lived in NEW YORK CITY, he liked to go bowling at MID-TOWN LANES. When he and his tet travel TODASH to the magical Vacant LOT at the beginning of *Wolves of the Calla*, Jake finds a twinner of his old bowling bag amid the trash and weeds growing near the singing ROSE. This todash bag looks almost exactly like his New York bowling bag, except his New York bag said, "Nothing but Strikes at Mid-Town Lanes," while his todash bag reads "Nothing but Strikes at Mid-World Lanes." Our tet uses this bag to carry BLACK THIRTEEN. *See also* NEW YORK: MANHATTAN: MID-TOWN LANES, *in* OUR WORLD PLACES
   V:198, V:316, V:506, V:704, VI:329, VI:335, VII:143

MIND-TRAP
See DIXIE PIG, *above*

MULTIPLE AMERICAS (ALTERNATIVE AMERICAS)
See entry in OUR WORLD PLACES

N

NA'AR
This is the MANNI name for Hell. Roland wonders whether the voices issuing up from the Pit of Voices (located in the DOORWAY CAVE) are actually the voices of the damned rising out of Na'ar. According to the Manni, all of the For-

getful Folk (those who leave their tribe to marry heathens) are doomed to spend eternity in Na'ar.
V:408, V:511, VII:384

NEW YORK, TODASH
See NEW YORK CITY, *in* OUR WORLD PLACES; *see also* TODASH, *below*

NIS
Nis is the name of Mid-World's dream god. It is also the name of his realm of sleep and dreams. The CRIMSON KING's horse is also named Nis.
V:500 *(god)*, V:549, VII:601 *(Land of sleep and dreams, also Red King's horse)*

NORTH CENTRAL POSITRONICS NORTHEAST CORRIDOR ARC QUADRANT OUTPOST 16
See DOGAN: CALLA DOGAN

NOWHERE LANDS
See DISCORDIA

O

ODD LANE (ODD'S LANE)
See EMPATHICA, WHITE LANDS OF

ORACLE OF THE MOUNTAINS
See STONE CIRCLES (SPEAKING RINGS)

OZ
Oz is the magical land which the cyclone-blown Dorothy visited in the famous book-turned-film *The Wizard of Oz*. At the end of *Wizard and Glass*, our tet visited a version of Oz's GREEN PALACE.
V:70, V:166 *(Wizard of)*, V:567, VI:223, VI:308, VII:173

OUTER DARK
See entry in APPENDIX I

P

PALACE OF GREEN GLASS
 See GREEN PALACE, THE

PINK ONE, THE
 See MAERLYN'S RAINBOW, *in* CHARACTERS

PLANET AFTERLIFE
This is PERE CALLAHAN's term for death. After he falls from the window of SOMBRA CORPORATION's headquarters in DETROIT, Callahan wonders whether he's landed on Planet Afterlife. He hasn't. He's landed in the MOHAINE DESERT's WAY STATION.
 V:458

PLEASANTVILLE
 See DEVAR-TOI

POCKET PARK
 See NEW YORK (CITY): SECOND AVENUE, *in* OUR WORLD PLACES

PORTALS
 See DOORWAYS BETWEEN WORLDS *and* BEAMS, PATH OF THE

PORTALS OF THE BEAM
 See BEAMS, PATH OF THE

PRIM
 See entry in CHARACTERS

Q

QUONSET HUT
 See DOGAN

R

RED KING'S CASTLE
   See CASSE ROI RUSSE

RED ROSES, FIELD OF
   See DARK TOWER: CAN'-KA NO REY

REINISCH ROSE GARDEN
   See KANSAS (STATE OF): TOPEKA: GAGE PARK, *in* OUR WORLD PLACES

ROOMS OF RUIN
   See CASTLE DISCORDIA

ROTUNDA
   See DIXIE PIG; see *also* CASTLE DISCORDIA *and* DOGAN: FEDIC DOGAN

S

'SALEM'S LOT
   See MAINE (STATE OF), *in* OUR WORLD PLACES

SHARDIK'S LAIR
   See BEAMS, PATH OF THE; see *also* GREAT WEST WOODS, *in* MID-WORLD PLACES, *and* GUARDIANS OF THE BEAM, *in* CHARACTERS

SNOWLANDS
   See EMPATHICA, WHITE LANDS OF

SOUTH PLAINS
   See entry in MID-WORLD PLACES

SPEAKING RINGS
   See STONE CIRCLES (SPEAKING RINGS)

STAGING AREA (WOLF STAGING AREA)
See DOGAN: FEDIC DOGAN

STEEK-TETE
See DEVAR-TOI

STONE CIRCLES (SPEAKING RINGS)
MID-WORLD contains many ancient stone circles. These circles (also known as Speaking Rings) are the haunts of spirits and oracles. In these demonic places, the boundaries between the visible and invisible worlds are thin. Although we don't know who built these stone circles, or whether they predate the GREAT OLD ONES, we can be fairly certain that they are hundreds—and perhaps thousands—of years older than the IN-WORLD BARONIES. (For more information, see *Stephen King's The Dark Tower: A Concordance, Volume I.*)

ORACLE OF THE MOUNTAINS: In *The Gunslinger,* Roland had sexual intercourse with this oracle in exchange for prophecy. In *Song of Susannah,* we learn that this oracle, who seemed to be trapped in her Speaking Ring high in the Willow Jungles of the CYCLOPEAN MOUNTAINS, was no run-of-the-mill demon sexpot. In fact, she was the female aspect of a DEMON ELEMENTAL and had been sent to her Speaking Ring specifically to collect Roland's sperm for the servants of the CRIMSON KING. (Our gunslinger's seed was then used to create MORDRED DESCHAIN.) VI:112–13 *(Place of the Oracle)*

SPEAKING RING ALONG THE PATH OF THE BEAM (JAKE'S DOOR): In *The Waste Lands,* Roland, EDDIE, and SUSANNAH drew JAKE CHAMBERS into MID-WORLD through a door which Eddie sketched on the ground of this Speaking Ring. (The ring itself was located on the GREAT ROAD leading to LUD.) While Eddie and Roland helped Jake battle the DUTCH HILL MANSION DEMON, who tried to block Jake's passage from our side, Susannah kept the Speaking Ring's male demon trapped in a sexual vise. Unfortunately, this demon impregnated her.

In *Song of Susannah,* we discover that Susannah's pregnancy was no accident, but had long been planned by the servants of the CRIMSON KING. The demon who shot seed into Susannah's core was none other than the male aspect of the DEMON ELEMENTAL who had collected Roland's sperm many years before as the ORACLE OF THE MOUNTAINS. V:46, V:246 *("pulling Jake through" and demon of the stone circle),* V:258 *(stone-circle demon/doorkeeper in Dutch Hill),* V:478 *(stone-circle demon/doorkeeper in Dutch Hill),* VI:113, VI:116 *(demon of the ring),* VI:253

STONE'S WARP
See EMPATHICA, WHITE LANDS OF

STUDY, THE
See DEVAR-TOI

SUSANNAH'S MIND-DOGAN
See DOGAN

T

THINNY
A thinny is a place where the fabric of existence has worn almost entirely away. Thinnies look like silvery, shimmering water and make a nauseating, atonal squalling. In many ways, they seem like watery, animate demons, since they have both a kind of body and a definite, malign presence. Thinnies can elongate their essence and create arms, which can snatch birds out of the air. They can also whisper like sirens, luring humans into their dead embrace. Roland first encountered a thinny in the town of HAMBRY, when he was fourteen years old. Our tet stumbles across another one in the ALTERNATIVE TOPEKA which they travel through in *Wizard and Glass*. The monster-filled fog which David and Billy Drayton have to face in STEPHEN KING's short story "The Mist" is a cross between a thinny and TODASH space.
    V:36, V:48, V:130–31, V:341, V:508, V:516, V:597

THUNDERCLAP (THE LAND OF DARKNESS, THE DARK LAND)
The dark land of Thunderclap sits on the lip of END-WORLD, just east of THE BORDERLANDS but west of CASTLE DISCORDIA. (Castle Discordia marks the beginning of the arid DISCORDIA BADLANDS.) In Thunderclap, the world has already ended. It is described as "a great darkness, like a rain cloud on the horizon." Despite the rain-cloud analogy used by the CALLA *folken,* Thunderclap is a dry, rainless desert.
    Thunderclap is the home of the DEVAR-TOI, or Big Prison, where the CRIMSON KING keeps the psychic BREAKERS. The Breakers (who are human) are forced to use their wild talents to erode the BEAMS so that the foundering DARK TOWER will collapse, causing the macroverse to blink out of existence. Long before our story began, the insane Red King released poison gas over the whole of this area. Hence, the Breakers, as well as their CAN-TOI and TAHEEN guards, are plagued by skin diseases and other illnesses. (It seems likely that they suffer some of the effects of radiation sickness as well.) Even the most minor skin abrasions can turn septic and deadly.
    Since there is no sun in Thunderclap, the Devar-Toi's residents are dependent upon a mechanical (or atomic) sun, which runs on what might as well be the world's largest egg timer. Unfortunately for them, it is wearing down and

occasionally goes on the blink, creating pseudo-eclipses and general depression and panic.

V:5, V:6, V:7, V:12, V:16, V:22, V:26, V:113, V:117, V:136–37, V:144, V:149, V:150 *(vampires, bogarts, taheen),* V:152, V:182, V:207, V:225, V:226, V:249, V:291, V:312, V:368, V:390, V:401, V:413, V:422, V:452 *(dark land is root of association between vampires and low men),* V:481, V:484, V:509, V:557, V:562, V:574, V:586, V:601, V:610, V:615, V:655, V:659, V:703, VI:13, VI:246, VI:247, VI:248, VII:51, VII:52, VII:58, VII:148, VII:152, VII:178, VII:190, VII:195, VII:200–416 *(setting; individual references are as follows: 200, 203, 210, 215, 223, 230, 247, 258, 261, 266, 282, 288, 289, 290, 306, 333, 337, 356, 357, 404, 416),* VII:485, VII:494, VII:507, VII:510, VII:514, VII:531, VII:536, VII:559, VII:563, VII:581, VII:594, VII:736

CAUSEWAY, THE: *See* CALLA BADLANDS, *listed separately*
DEVAR-TOI: *See* DEVAR-TOI, *listed separately*
DOGAN, THE: *See* DOGAN, *listed separately*
THUNDERCLAP STATION: *See* DEVAR-TOI, *listed separately*

THUNDERCLAP STATION
See DEVAR-TOI

TODASH
In *Wolves of the Calla,* we are told that traveling *todash* is similar to the state of lucid dreaming. However, unlike lucid dreaming, both body and mind travel todash. As we see when EDDIE and JAKE travel to NEW YORK CITY via todash at the beginning of *Wolves,* the body of a person in the todash state fades out of existence in a series of jerky pulses and is replaced by a dull gray glow. Those not traveling, but sleeping or sitting near a todash traveler, may hear a kind of low crackling or electrical buzzing. Entry into the todash state is signaled by the chiming of the *kammen,* or the todash CHIMES.

The blue-cloaked MANNI are well acquainted with traveling todash. Many (such as the Manni *dinh,* HENCHICK) have even seen the *todash tahken,* or the holes in reality. Some of MAERLYN'S BALLS also facilitate the todash state. Most notorious of these is BLACK THIRTEEN. A person can also travel todash from our world. During the five years following the death of his beloved friend LUPE DELGADO, FATHER CALLAHAN traveled along the todash turnpikes of America, also known as the HIGHWAYS IN HIDING.

Although traveling todash is practiced by the magnet- and plumb-bob-wielding Manni, it is not without risks. Todash space is the void place between worlds, or the equivalent of the monster-filled hollows between the walls and floors of the DARK TOWER. Below CASTLE DISCORDIA is a doorway that leads directly to todash space. Although the Old Ones considered this door a mistake, the CRIMSON KING makes good use of it. He has his bitterest enemies thrown into the null lands, so that they will wander in that nothingness, blind and mad, until they are devoured by todash's many monsters.

According to MORDRED DESCHAIN, the nastiest of the todash monsters are known as the GREAT ONES. CONSTANT READERS familiar with STEPHEN KING's short story "The Mist" will probably recognize these todash monsters. In that tale, the military personnel responsible for the Arrowhead Project ripped a hole in reality. What leaked through was a cross between todash space and the horror of a monster-infested THINNY.

V:48–70 *(New York)*, V:78–81 *(described)*, V:84, V:88–97 *(89—Manni; 90—Wizard's Rainbow; 91–97—Eddie and Jake describe)*, V:105 *(holiest of rites, most exalted of states)*, V:110, V:114–16, V:139, V:165 *(like being stoned)*, V:166, V:172–97 *(New York)*, V:201, V:236, V:257, V:271, V:275, V:284, V:314, V:469, V:470, V:502, V:505, V:507, V:511, V:515, V:516, V:539, V:546, V:549, V:558, V:599, V:709, VI:12, VI:18, VI:37, VI:81, VI:82, VI:119, VI:131, VI:248–49 *(doors to todash darkness or todash space)*, VI:251, VI:265 *(Beams as antitodash)*, VI:281, VI:301, VI:307, VI:326 *(can get lost forever there)*, VI:328–31 *(Black Thirteen brings todash darkness; it disappears when Thirteen sleeps)*, VI:375, VI:378, VII:20, VII:21, VII:23 *(chimes)*, VII:32, VII:38, VII:196, VII:407, VII:531, VII:539, VII:542 *(writing as a benign todash)*, VII:557, VII:559, VII:567, VII:582, VII:711, VII:747 *(todash space)*, VII:749, VII:754, VII:779

CHIMES, THE (KAMMEN): In the MANNI tongue, *kammen* means "ghosts." Hence, the DOORWAY CAVE is known as *kra kammen*, or "house of ghosts," because of the voices that echo within it. Those traveling todash are assailed by the beautiful but bone-vibrating sound of the *kammen*, or todash bells. Their painful music is reminiscent of the warble of the THINNY. Evidently, when the box containing BLACK THIRTEEN is opened, the *kammen* begin to chime. The sound is both overwhelming and maddening. V:48, V:53, V:65, V:67, V:68, V:69, V:90, V:139, V:167–68 *(bells)*, V:171, V:174, V:184, V:196, V:197, V:268–69, V:275, V:283, V:299, V:317, V:413, V:414, V:432, V:457, V:458, V:459, V:462, V:515, V:516, V:540, V:546, V:591, V:592, V:597, VI:81, VI:98, VI:307, VI:326, VI:327, VI:328, VI:378, VII:20, VII:21, VII:23, VII:28, VII:36, VII:288, VII:539, VII:540, VII:562, VII:564

DOOR TO TODASH DARKNESS: *See* CASTLE DISCORDIA

END-WORLD (VIA BLACK THIRTEEN): *See* END-WORLD, *listed separately*

    CASTLE OF THE KING (VIA BLACK THIRTEEN): *See* CASSE ROI RUSSE, *listed separately*

MAINE (VIA BLACK THIRTEEN): *For page references, see* MAINE (STATE OF), *in* OUR WORLD PLACES

    EAST STONEHAM: East Stoneham is a small town forty miles north of PORTLAND. This is where CALVIN TOWER and AARON DEEPNEAU go to hide from BALAZAR'S MEN. PERE CALLAHAN visits East Stoneham courtesy of Black Thirteen and the UNFOUND DOOR. This town is also the site of Roland and EDDIE's battle with Balazar's thugs. *For page references, see* MAINE (STATE OF): STONEHAM, *in* OUR WORLD PLACES

EAST STONEHAM GENERAL STORE: *For page references, see* MAINE (STATE OF): STONEHAM, *in* OUR WORLD PLACES
METHODIST MEETING HALL: *For page references, see* MAINE (STATE OF): STONEHAM, *in* OUR WORLD PLACES
POST OFFICE: *For page references, see* MAINE (STATE OF): STONEHAM, *in* OUR WORLD PLACES

MEXICO (VIA BLACK THIRTEEN):

LOS ZAPATOS (VIA BLACK THIRTEEN): In the years before our tet reached CALLA BRYN STURGIS, FATHER DONALD CALLAHAN traveled here, propelled by BLACK THIRTEEN. Los Zapatos is also the village where we find BEN MEARS and his eleven-year-old companion, MARK PETRIE, at the beginning of *'Salem's Lot.* (The body of the novel is told in retrospect.) *Los zapatos* means "the shoes." *For page references, see* MEXICO: LOS ZAPATOS, *in* OUR WORLD PLACES

NEW YORK (VIA BLACK THIRTEEN): *For page references, see* NEW YORK CITY, *in* OUR WORLD PLACES

DIXIE PIG: *See* DIXIE PIG, *listed separately*
GEORGE WASHINGTON BRIDGE: *For page references, see* NEW YORK CITY, *in* OUR WORLD PLACES
FOOTBRIDGE (LAMERK INDUSTRIES): *For page references, see* NEW YORK CITY, *in* OUR WORLD PLACES
LOT, THE (FORTY-SIXTH STREET AND SECOND AVENUE): *See* LOT, THE, *above; see also* ROSE, THE, *in* CHARACTERS
SECOND AVE—FORTY-SIXTH STREET TO FIFTY-FOURTH: According to EDDIE DEAN and JAKE CHAMBERS, these eight blocks function as one large DOORWAY BETWEEN WORLDS. *For page references, see* NEW YORK CITY, *in* OUR WORLD PLACES

TODASH HOSPITAL (ROOM NINETEEN): V:423
TODASH TAHKEN: The holes in reality. V:413
TODASH TURNPIKES (USA): *See* HIDDEN HIGHWAYS, *listed separately*

TOWER
See DARK TOWER

TOWER KEYSTONE
See DARK TOWER *and* KEY WORLDS/KEYSTONE WORLDS

TOWER ROAD
See EMPATHICA, WHITE LANDS OF

U

UNDERSNOW
See EMPATHICA, WHITE LANDS OF

UNFOUND DOOR
See DOORWAYS BETWEEN WORLDS: MAGICAL DOORS: UNFOUND DOOR; *see also* DOORWAY CAVE

UNFOUND DOOR TO LAND OF MEMORY
Inside each of us there is an UNFOUND DOOR, and memory is the key which opens it. When we find that door, we find forgotten parts of ourselves. VI:352–53, VI:362

UPLANDS
See EMPATHICA, WHITE LANDS OF

V

VACANT LOT
See LOT, THE

W

WALTER'S MIND-DOGAN
See DOGAN

WASTELANDS EAST OF THE RIVER WHYE
See CALLA BADLANDS

WAY STATION
Both JAKE CHAMBERS and FATHER CALLAHAN end up in the MOHAINE DESERT's Way Station after they "die" in our world. According to Roland's longtime nemesis WALTER, this Way Station is "a little rest stop between the hoot of [our] world and the holler of the next." When Callahan arrives in the

Way Station, Walter is waiting for him. Walter gives Callahan BLACK THIR-TEEN, then forces him to enter the UNFOUND DOOR. When Callahan regains consciousness, he finds himself with the MANNI of CALLA BRYN STURGIS.

V:458–65 *(460—hoot and holler)*, V:470, VI:290, VI:327, VI:389, VI:391, VI:399, VII:826

WAYDON CASTLE
See RIVER BARONIES, *in* MID-WORLD PLACES

WESTRING
See EMPATHICA, WHITE LANDS OF

WHITE LANDS OF EMPATHICA
See EMPATHICA, WHITE LANDS OF

WIZARD'S GLASS
See MAERLYN'S RAINBOW, *in* CHARACTERS

WOLF GARAGE
See DOGAN: FEDIC DOGAN *and* CASTLE DISCORDIA

WOLF STAGING AREA
See DOGAN: FEDIC DOGAN *and* CASTLE DISCORDIA

APPENDIX I:
MID-WORLD DIALECTS

CONTENTS

A BRIEF NOTE ON THE USE OF APPENDIX I

For each word or phrase listed in this appendix, I have provided at least one page reference so that you can view the relevant word, object, or phrase in the context of the Dark Tower series. My hope, in so doing, is to enrich your enjoyment of Mid-World's diverse dialects. In instances where the word or phrase under discussion receives a lengthier description elsewhere in the *Concordance,* I give a brief definition or translation, then direct you to the entry and section where an in-depth discussion of the subject is available. A word in all capitals within an entry indicates that word has an entire entry devoted to it within the appendix.

Since in Mid-World, as in our world, dialects often share words and expressions, some terms could be placed with equal validity in more than one subsection. In such cases, I have tried to place the questionable term in the most general category. (For example, if a word is used in the Calla but is also used elsewhere in Mid-World, it can be found in the "Mid-World Argot" subsection. Similarly, if a word is used by the Manni but is also related to a High Speech term, then the word will be found in the "High Speech" subsection.)

If you are unsure where to find a particular word or phrase, the following guidelines may help. For words and phrases that sound similar to ones from our world, begin in "Mid-World Argot." If you don't find what you're searching for there, move to "Calla Bryn Sturgis Dialect." Finally, try "End-World Terms." For words and phrases that are definitely in High Speech or a similar language, begin searching in "High Speech," then proceed to "Manni Terms." Last of all, try "End-World Terms."

I apologize to those Constant Readers who would have preferred a single, straightforward alphabetical listing of all the unusual words and phrases found in the final three books of the Dark Tower series. That was one organizational option, but in the end, I decided that it would be more enjoyable—both for me and for you—if I tried to capture at least a bit of Mid-World's magic, a *glammer* cast as much by the variety of cultures we encounter there as by the story line itself.

HIGH SPEECH TERMS AND SYMBOLS

Note: Throughout the Dark Tower series, High Speech is also called the Tongue.

    ᐃ᭙ᑕ ᑫ᭗: This scrollwork means UNFOUND. VII:739, VII:820

    ᭙ᑕ ᑫ᭗: This scrollwork means FOUND. VII:820

    CR : This scrollwork means WHITE. It was Arthur Eld's DINH mark and is found near the muzzle of Roland's guns. VII:501

AM: *See* PRIM, *in* CHARACTERS

ANRO CON FA; SEY-SEY DESENE FANNO BILLET COBAIR CAN: These words are spoken by Chevin of Chayven, a CHILD OF RODERICK, to Roland of Gilead. The words are never translated. Here is Chevin's complete statement: "Anro con fa; sey-sey desene fanno billet cobair can. I Chevin devar dan do. Because I felt sad for dem. Can-toi, can-tah, can Discordia, aven la cam mah can. May-mi. Iffin lah vainen eth—" His words are cut short by Roland's guns. Roland considers this a mercy killing. VII:50–51

AN-TET: *An-tet* implies intimacy of all kinds. To speak an-tet to someone is to be completely honest and open, to share all. It also means to sit in council. Roland and his trailmates are both ka-tet and an-tet. V:115, V:216, V:394, V:472, VII:22

ANTI-KA: That force which works against one's ka, or destiny. It is a counterforce which tries to stop a person from fulfilling his or her life-mission. The anti-ka which works against Roland's ka-tet was set in motion by the Crimson King. VII:266

AVEN KAL: An aven kal is a kind of tidal wave that runs along the path of the Beam. Literally translated, *aven kal* means "lifted on the wind" or "carried on the wave." The use of *kal* rather than the more usual form *kas* implies a natural force of disastrous proportions. In other words, not a hurricane but a tsunami. VII:20

AVEN-CAR: A hunting term which refers to carrying the kill and preparing to make it into something else. VII:635

BONDSMAN: *See entry in* MID-WORLD ARGOT

CAM-A-CAM-MAL, PRIA-TOI, GAN DELAH: "White over Red, This God Wills Ever." This is written on the plaque in front of the Garden of the Beam. It also translates as "Good over evil, this is the will of God." VII:504

CAN CALAH: The can calah are angels. VI:318

CAN-AH, CAN-TAH, ANNAH, ORIZA: "All breath comes from the woman." This is a saying repeated in Calla Bryn Sturgis. Although mortal woman was made from the breath of mortal man, the first man came from Lady Oriza. V:631

CANDA: That distance (never the same in any two situations) which assures a pair of outnumbered gunslingers will not be killed by a single shot. VII:25

CAN STEEK-TETE: The Little Needle. Can Steek-Tete (also called Steek-Tete) is a butte located near the DEVAR-TOI. VII:205

CAN-TAH: According to Roland, the tiny scrimshaw turtle which Susannah Dean finds hidden in a pocket of Jake Chambers's bowling bag is one of the can-tah, or little gods. Constant Readers have met the can-tah before, namely in Stephen King's novel *Desperation*. In *Desperation*, the little can-tah were tiny demonic sculptures depicting the can-toi, or coyotes, snakes, etc., which served Tak the Outsider. (*Tak* is short for *can-tak*, which means "big god.") *See also* CAN-TAH, *in* CHARACTERS

CAN-TOI: *Can-toi* is another term for the low men. The can-toi are rat-headed beings who wear humanoid masks. (The masks are grown and so are made of a living substance.) Unlike the TAHEEN, the can-toi worship the human form and believe that they are slowly transforming into humans themselves. They call this process "becoming." In the novel *Desperation*, the can-toi were the coyotes, spiders, snakes, and other dangerous creatures that obeyed the will of Tak the Outsider. (*Tak* is short for *can-tak*, which means "big god.") *See also* CAN-TOI, *in* CHARACTERS

CAN-TOI-TETE: Roland uses the term *can-toi-tete* to refer to the desert dogs of Thunderclap. *Can-toi-tete* translates roughly as "little can-toi" or "tiny can-toi." In Stephen King's novel *Desperation*, the can-toi were the coyotes, spiders, snakes, and other dangerous creatures that obeyed the will of Tak the Outsider. (*Tak* is short for *can-tak*, which means "big god.") *See also* CAN-TAH, *above.* VII:255, VII:261

CHAR: Most words in High Speech have multiple meanings. However, *char* is an exception to this general rule. *Char* has one meaning only, and that is death (III:382). *Char* is the root of many Mid-World terms, including Big Charlie Wind and CHARYOU TREE. The definition of *char* is not given in the final three books of the Dark Tower series, but because of its importance, I have included a page reference listed in *Stephen King's The Dark Tower: A Concordance, Volume I.* III:382

CHARY (YOU CHARY MAN): As we all know, the High Speech term *char* means "death." Hence, a chary man is one who courts death, brings death, or deals death. Think of him as the Grim Reaper's deputy. V:335, V:612

CHARY-KA: This insult is thrown at Roland by one of the Crimson King's TAHEEN just before Roland kills him. It most likely means somebody who is one of death's ka-mates, or one whose ka is aligned with death. It may also imply that although the chary-ka is destined to deal death, he is also destined to suffer from death's nasty sense of humor. VII:135

CHARYOU TREE: Charyou Tree was the ritual bonfire made on the Festival of REAP. In the days of Arthur Eld, people were burned on this fire. By Roland's day, STUFFY-GUYS were burned instead. V:124, V:210 *(Reap fair of the Old People)*, VI:219

CHASSIT (CHUSSIT, CHISSIT, CHASSIT): *Chussit, Chissit, Chassit* are the numbers seventeen, eighteen, and nineteen. They are used in the BABY-BUNTING RHYME, one of Mid-World's childhood rhymes. *See also entry in* MID-WORLD ARGOT *and* APPENDIX III. VII:22, VII:23, VII:57

CHILDREN OF RODERICK: *See entry in* MID-WORLD ARGOT

COFFA: This is another term for Hell. *See also entry in* PORTALS

COMMALA DAN-TETE: The coming of the little god. VII:61

DAN SUR, DAN TUR, DAN ROLAND, DAN GILEAD: We are never given a translation of this phrase. However, since Roland tells Ted Brautigan to say it to one of the mutant CHILDREN OF RODERICK, we know it must refer to the vow of allegiance which that race once swore to the line of Eld. VII:216

DAN-DINH: "May I open my heart to your command" is the literal interpretation of this ancient term. Roland's tutor Vannay maintained that the phrase predated Arthur Eld by centuries. To ask your leader a question dan-dinh means to seek your leader's advice on an emotional problem. However, when you turn to your DINH in this way, you agree to do exactly as the *dinh* advises, immediately and without question. Men and women usually address their leader dan-dinh about love-affair problems, but in *Wolves of the Calla,* Jake speaks to Roland dan-dinh about the problem of Susannah/Mia and her chap. V:388

DAN-TETE: (The second part of this word is pronounced *tee-tee.*) *Dan-tete* means "little savior" or "baby god." Mordred is End-World's dan-tete. Roland calls John Cullum his KA-TET's dan-tete. VI:182, VII:38

DARKLES and TINCTS: In *The Gunslinger,* we were told that Maerlyn (also known as the Ageless Stranger) *darkles* and *tincts.* In other words, he lives backward in time and can live simultaneously in all times. In *The Dark Tower,* we learn that the Crimson King also *darkles* and *tincts.* This makes it difficult for the artist Patrick Danville to draw him. At the very end of this final book of the Dark Tower series, we learn that Roland also *darkles* and *tincts.* Roland will not die but will go on forever, repeating his journey to the Tower over and over, until he learns the lessons ka wishes him to learn. VII:789

DASH-DINH: A dash-dinh is a religious leader. Henchick of the Manni is a dash-dinh. V:389

DEATH PRAYER: Roland translates this prayer for us and recites it over Jake's grave:

> Time flies, knells call, life passes, so hear my prayer.
> Birth is nothing but death begun, so hear my prayer.
> Death is speechless, so hear my speech.
> This is Jake, who served his ka and his tet. Say true.
> May the forgiving glance of S'mana heal his heart. Say please.
> May the arms of Gan raise him from the darkness of the earth. Say please.
> Surround him, Gan, with light.
> Fill him, Chloe, with strength.
> If he is thirsty, give him water in the clearing.
> If he is hungry, give him food in the clearing.
> May his life on this earth and the pain of his passing become
> as a dream to his waking soul, and let his eyes fall upon
> every lovely sight; let him find the friends that were lost to him,
> and let every one whose name he calls call his in return.
> This is Jake, who lived well, loved his own, and died as ka would have it.
> Each man owes a death. This is Jake. Give him peace.
> VII:474

DEH: Pronunciation of the letter *D* in High Speech. V:130

DELAH: Many. V:148, V:598, V:642, VI:268, VI:294, VII:50

DEVAR: Prison. VII:142

DEVAR-TETE: Little prison or torture chamber. VII:142

DEVAR-TOI: *See entry in* END-WORLD TERMS

DINH: Leader or father (as in "father of his people"). V:31, V:203, V:368, VI:252

FAN-GON: The exiled one. This term is used to describe Eddie Dean when he returns to New York via the Unfound Door. VII:515

GODOSH: *See* PRIM, *in* CHARACTERS

GUNNA (GUNNA-GAR): All of one's worldly possessions. In the case of a traveler, it is what he or she carries. V:404, VI:33, VI:73, VII:134

HAD HEET ROL-UH, FA HEET GUN, FA HEET HAK, FA-HAD GUN? This is a phonetic translation of something which Calvin Tower says to Roland. We know that these words are probably in the Tongue, but we never find out what they mean. VI:197

HODJI: *Hodji* means both "dim" and "hood." In the southern provinces of Mid-World, Walter O'Dim was known as Walter Hodji. He was given this nickname for two reasons—first for the hooded cloak he often wore and second for his ability to make himself DIM so that he could move unnoticed. VII:183

HOUKEN: *Houken* is a descriptive term. If someone comments on your *sad houken's eyes* they are talking about your waif eyes, or your melodramatically sad eyes. When Mordred calls Oy a "little furry houken," he's calling him a sad little furry waif. VI:753

IRINA: The healing madness that comes after terrible loss. VII:466

JIN-JIN: Quickly. As in "Get me a piece of chalk and do it jin-jin." VII:149

KA: Like many words in High Speech, *ka* has multiple meanings and so is difficult to define precisely. It signifies life force, consciousness, duty, and destiny. In the vulgate, or low speech, it also means a place to which an individual must go. The closest terms in our language are probably *fate* and *destiny,* although ka also implies karma, or the accumulated destiny (and accumulated debt) of many existences. We are the servants of ka, but we are also its prisoners. Ka's one purpose is to turn, and we turn with it, albeit sometimes under different names and in different bodies. In the final volume of the Dark Tower series, ka is compared to a train hurtling forward, one which may not be sane. The ka of our world is NINETEEN. The ka of Roland's world is ninety-nine. V:31, V:91, VI:293, VI:341, VII:169, VII:302, VII:307

KA-DINH: Oy believes that Jake is his ka-dinh. VII:92

KA-GAN: Gan himself. Writers and artists are *kas-ka Gan.* VII:458

KA-HUMES: *See entry in* END-WORLD TERMS

KA-MAI (KA-MAIS): Ka's fool, or destiny's fool. Roland uses this term to describe both Eddie Dean and Cuthbert Allgood. The servants of the Crimson King call Jake and Callahan *Gilead's ka-mais.* Those who are designated ka-mais are often safe from harm, or at least until ka tires of their antics and swats them out of the world. V:527 *(opposite of ka-me),* VI:358, VII:6, VII:427

KA-MATES: Your ka-mates are those people whose fates (or destinies) are entwined with your own. It is another term for the members of your KA-TET. V:405

KA-ME: Wisely. It is the opposite of KA-MAI, which means foolishly. V:527

KAMMEN: The TODASH chimes, or the bells you hear when you travel todash. This word has special significance for the Manni, since they travel between worlds so frequently. *See* TODASH: KAMMEN, *in* PORTALS

KA-SHUME: This rue-laden term does not have an exact translation. It describes the dark emotion one feels when a break in one's KA-TET looms. Ka-tets can only be broken by death or betrayal. Some argue, however, that these things are also aspects of KA. If this is the case, then *ka-shume* implies a sense of approaching disaster involving the members of a ka-tet. Ka-shume is the price paid for attempting to change or divert ka. VII:247, VII:250, VII:259, VII:307

KAS-KA GAN: Prophets of Gan or singers of Gan. All artists—whether they are writers, painters, sculptors, poets, or composers—are *kas-ka Gan.* VII:458

KA-TET: *Ka-tet* means "one made from many." *Ka* refers to destiny; *tet* refers to a group of people with the same interests or goals. Ka-tet is the place where men's lives are joined by fate. Ka-tet cannot be changed or bent to any individual's will, but it can be seen, known, and understood. The philosophers of Gilead stated that the bonds of ka-tet could be broken only by death or treachery. However, Roland's teacher Cort maintained that neither death nor treachery are strong enough to break the bonds of ka-tet, since these events are also tied to ka, or fate. Each member of a ka-tet is a piece of a puzzle. Each individual piece is a mystery, but when put together, the collective pieces form a greater picture. It takes many interwoven ka-tets to weave a historical tapestry. Ka-tets overlap, often sharing members.

A ka-tet is not always bound by love, affection, or friendship. Enemies are also ka-tet. Although usually referred to as positive or at least inevitable, the forces of ka and ka-tet can cast a sinister shadow over our lives. As Roland says to his friends when the shadow of KA-SHUME falls over their lives, "We are ka-tet . . . we are one from many. We have shared our water as we have shared our lives and our quest. If one should fall, that one will not be lost, for we are one and will not forget, even in death" (VII:260). V:108, V:149, VI:341

KES: Pronouced like *kiss*. A person's kes is linked to his or her vitality. Even the Beams have kes. VII:334

KHEF: Literally speaking, *khef* means "the sharing of water." It also implies birth, life force, and all that is essential to existence. Khef can only be shared by those whom destiny has welded together for good or ill—in other words, by those who are KA-TET.

Khef is both individual and collective. It implies the knowledge a person gains from dream-life as well as his or her life force. Khef is the web that binds a ka-tet. Those who share khef share thoughts. Their destinies are linked, as are their life forces. Behind the multiple meanings of this word lies a philosophy of inter-connectedness, a sense that all individuals, all events, are part of a greater pattern or plan. Our fates, for good or dis, are the result of both our own and our shared khef. V:15, V:92, V:98, V:149, V:296, VI:7, VI:341, VII:259

KI'BOX: *See entry in* CALLA BRYN STURGIS DIALECT

KI'COME: *See entry in* CALLA BRYN STURGIS DIALECT

KI'-DAM: *See entry in* END-WORLD TERMS

MA'SUN: A war chest. Roland uses this word to describe the cave in STEEK-TETE where Ted Brautigan, Sheemie Ruiz, and Dinky Earnshaw have stored weapons for his KA-TET. VII:253

MIA: Mother. V:248

MIM: Mother Earth. VII:798

PRIM: The Prim is the original magical Discordia, or soup of creation, from which the MULTIVERSE arose. *See also entry in* CHARACTERS

PROPHECY: In High Speech, prophecy is the information a person gains by having intercourse with a supernatural being. The term does not necessarily imply sexual intercourse, although, as we saw in *The Gunslinger,* many demons will not give prophecy unless a sexual price is paid. Prophecy is, as its name implies, prophetic. It describes events—in the distant future, a distant past, or in a distant place—which the seeker could learn about in no other manner. To seek prophecy is dangerous and should not be embarked upon lightly. VI:112

PROPHECY FOR THE LINE OF ELD: Mordred Deschain's birth fulfills an ancient prophecy which foretold the destruction of the last gunslinger:

> He who ends the line of Eld shall conceive a child of incest with his sister or his daughter, and the child will be marked, by his red heel shall you know him. It is he who shall stop the breath of the last warrior.

As we know from the Dark Tower series, Roland was tricked into conceiving a child with his KA-TET mate Susannah Dean. Roland's sperm was taken by a Demon Elemental (posing as the Oracle of the Mountains), which then turned itself into a male and impregnated Susannah in the Speaking Ring where she, Roland, and Eddie drew Jake Chambers into Mid-World. Although Roland is not actually Susannah's father, he is her DINH, or leader, and so is the father of their ka-tet. VI:252

RODERICKS (CHILDREN OF RODERICK, RODS): *See entry in* MID-WORLD ARGOT

SEE-LAH: We aren't given a translation of this term, which is used by the Reverend Harrigan of our world. VI:318, VI:319

SEPPE-SAI: Seppe-sai was the name Roland's mother gave to the pie seller in the low-town of Gilead. It meant death-seller. During the heat of summer, his pies often became poisonous. V:605

SH'VEEN: A jilly, or mistress. V:120

SO SPEAKS GAN, AND IN THE VOICE OF THE CAN CALAH, WHICH SOME CALL ANGELS: In its entirety, this quote reads as follows: "So speaks Gan, and in the voice of the can calah, which some call angels. Gan denies the can-toi; with the merry heart of the guiltless he denies the Crimson King and Discordia itself." Jake utters these words in a trance state. It seems likely that they are translated from the Tongue. VI:318

STEEK-TETE: *See* CAN-STEEK-TETE, *above*

TAHEEN: The taheen are creatures that belong neither to the natural (physical) world nor to the magical PRIM. According to Roland, they are misbegotten creatures from somewhere between the two. The taheen have the bodies of men but the heads of beasts. They are also known as the third people or the CAN-TOI. The can-toi (or low men) are rat-headed taheen that believe they are becoming human. *See entry in* CHARACTERS

TELAMEI: This term means to gossip about someone you shouldn't gossip about. V:389

TELEMETRY: *See entry in* END-WORLD TERMS

TET-KA GAN: The navel. When babies were born in the In-World baronies, the umbilical cord was cut and a cedar clip was placed just above the newborn's tet-ka Gan, or navel. The clip would be wrapped in blue silk if the baby was a boy, or pink if the baby was a girl. VII:821

THROCKEN: This is an old term for a billy-bumbler. Bumblers were bred to hunt down Grandfather Fleas. *See* BILLY-BUMBLER, *in* MID-WORLD ARGOT

TODANA: The term *todana* is a variation of the word *todash*. *Todana* means "death-bag." Eddie and Roland see one around Stephen King when they visit him in Bridgton in 1977. We also encounter death-bags in Stephen King's novel *Insomnia*. VI:290, VI:301

TODASH: Todash is a state similar to that of lucid dreaming. However, unlike lucid dreaming, both the body and the mind travel todash. The sounding of the chimes, or KAMMEN, signal entry into the todash state. The blue-cloaked Manni often travel to other worlds via todash. Some of Maerlyn's magic balls can also send the unwilling into this place between worlds. Traveling via todash is not without risks. Many monsters live in the crevices between realities. *See entry in* PORTALS

TODASH TAHKEN: The holes in reality. V:413

TRIG DELAH: *See entry in* MID-WORLD ARGOT

TRUM: *See entry in* MID-WORLD ARGOT

TWIM: This means "two." It can also refer to a twin. VI:35, VI:39, VI:319, VII:141

URS-KA GAN: The Song of the Bear. *Urs-A-Ka Gan* means the scream of the Bear. VII:458

VES'-KA GAN: The Song of the Turtle. VII:446, VII:458

Zn: The Great Letter *Zn* stands for both "eternity" and "now," but it also means "come," as in *come-commala*. The green rice tendrils which decorate the ornate plates thrown in honor of Lady ORIZA take the shape of this letter. V:372

MID-WORLD ARGOT, ROLAND'S VERSIONS OF OUR WORDS, AND TERMS USED IN THIS CONCORDANCE

A LADY'S ROSES: A light menstrual period. V:121

A MAN CAN'T PULL HIMSELF UP BY HIS OWN BOOTSTRAPS NO MATTER HOW HARD HE TRIES: This is one of Cort's sayings. Roland doesn't agree with it. VII:33

A ONE-EYED MAN SEES FLAT: This was one of Cort's sayings. It means that a person must use both eyes to gain a true perspective. In other words, it is best to try to see a situation from several angles before judging it. V:204

A RUSTIE JUST WALKED OVER MY GRAVE (A RUSTIE HAD JUST WALKED OVER HIS GRAVE): *See* RUSTIE WALKED OVER MY GRAVE, *below*

A SOFTENING OF TIME: In Mid-World, time is no longer constant. It runs erratically. A day is no longer twenty-four hours, the sun doesn't always rise in the east, etc. V:105

A WORD TO TUCK BENEATH YOUR HATS: Here's something to think about, or to remember. V:336

ABOUT THE GREAT MATTERS, YOU HAVE NO SAY: In other words, sometimes it is fate, and not the individual, who decides which events are to take place. All we mere mortals can do is hope and pray. This phrase is often used along with THERE WILL BE WATER IF GOD WILLS IT. V:87

ACHES AND MOLLIES: Aches and pains. VII:314

ADELINA SAYS SHE'S RANDY-O: This is part of a Mid-World drinking song. VII:520

AFTER A WHILE TALK SICKENS: There's only so much to say before you need to stop discussing a matter. V:142

AGE OF MAGIC/AGE OF MACHINES: According to the ancient history of Mid-World, the universe spun from Gan's navel, but Gan himself arose from the magical soup of creation called the PRIM. Eventually, the magical tide of the Prim receded, but it left on the shores of the mundane worlds the demons and spirits which human beings occasionally encounter, as well as the Tower and the Beams, which hold the multiverse together. Although the Prim left enough magic to uphold both Tower and Beams for eternity (and enough demons and spirits to give mankind trouble for ages to come), human beings suffered a great loss of faith and sought to replace the magical Beams with manufactured machinery. Unfortunately, machines—like the men who make them—are mortal. Hence, the Age of Magic began the universe, but it seems likely that the Age of Machines will end it. VI:108–112

AIM TIME LIKE A GUN (TO AIM TIME LIKE A GUN): To time-travel, but to do so with a specific date in mind. V:116

AIM WITH THE EYE, SHOOT WITH THE MIND, KILL WITH THE HEART: This is the essence of the gunslinger litany, or what a gunslinger must learn to do to become an accomplished killer. V:110

ALL THINGS SERVE KA AND FOLLOW THE BEAM: A phrase similar to ALL THINGS SERVE THE BEAM. In other words, all things work in harmony with the greater tides of fate. V:706

ALL THINGS SERVE THE BEAM: All things work in harmony with the greater tides of fate. All events serve a greater purpose, even if we can't understand what that purpose might be. V:93, VI:266, VII:304

ALL-A-GLOW: This is a Mid-World term for the imaginative and magical kingdom which children inhabit. VII:23

ALLEYO (PLANNING ALLEYO): Someone who is planning alleyo is planning to run away. V:395

ALLURE: The name given to a castle wall-walk. VI:103

ALTERNATIVE AMERICAS: Many levels of the Dark Tower contain versions of the United States, but each version is unique. Hence, when I refer to the many incarnations of America (the versions that are similar to the one found on KEYSTONE EARTH but which are not exactly the same), I use this term. *See* MULTIPLE AMERICAS, *below*

ALWAYS CON YOUR VANTAGE: This was Cort's rule. In other words, always stop and examine your whereabouts. VII:778

AMERICA-SIDE: When our tet-mates use the term "America-side," they are usually referring to New York City, the metropolis where Eddie, Jake, and

Susannah lived before entering Mid-World. However, this term could just as easily refer to any of the MULTIPLE AMERICAS. VII:758

AND MAY YOU HAVE TWICE THE NUMBER: *See* MAY YOUR DAYS BE LONG UPON THE EARTH, *below*

ANTI-TODASH: According to Roland and Eddie, the heightened reality of our world is like an anti-TODASH force. Our world exists at the heart of the Beam, probably because Stephen King, the creator of Mid-World and the Beams, lives here. VI:265

ANY RO': Anyhow. V:407, VI:33, VII:239

ASSUME MAKES AN ASS OUT OF U AND ME: This particular phrase comes from Eddie Dean of New York. Basically, it means that if you assume something, there's a good chance that you'll be proven wrong, and in an embarrassing fashion. V:583

ASTIN: Roland's pronunciation of the word *aspirin.* V:104, VI:209, VII:41

AUTO-CARRIAGE: A car. V:518

AVEN-CAR: *See entry in* HIGH SPEECH

AYE: Yes. V:161

BABY-BUNTING RHYME:

> Baby-bunting, baby-dear,
> Baby, bring your berries here.
> Chussit, chissit, chassit!
> Bring enough to fill your basket.

When Roland was a little boy, his mother sang this song to him. *Chussit, chissit, chassit,* are the High Speech words for the numbers seventeen, eighteen, and NINETEEN. VII:23

BAG-FOLKEN: Bag-people. Unfortunately, many bag-people sleep rough in the cities of our world. VI:80

BAH AND BOLT: The bah is a crossbow. (It shoots bolts instead of arrows.) Like the people of Calla Bryn Sturgis, Roland's old friend Jamie DeCurry favored bah and bolt. V:20, V:204, V:324

BAH-BO: A bah-bo is a baby. It is a term of endearment. VII:149, VII:487

BANNOCK: Bannocks are herd beasts. They look like buffalo. VII:734, VII:745

BARN RUSTIES: *See* RUSTIES, *below*

BARREL OF THE BEAM (HEART OF THE BEAM): The energy that flows through the center of the Beam. If you are caught in the barrel of the Beam, you are in the heart of that ceaseless, powerful current. Your hair will probably be standing on end! VI:265, VI:269

BARREL-SHOOTERS: A type of gun. Vaughn Eisenhart owns two of them. Roland and his childhood friends called these firearms barrel-shooters because of their oversize cylinders. Unlike the cylinders of many other handguns, the cylinder of a barrel-shooter must be revolved by hand after each shot. V:319

BASTED IN A HOT OAST: A Mid-World saying which basically means "our goose is cooked." Roland likes to use it. VII:195

BATTLES THAT LAST FIVE MINUTES SPAWN LEGENDS THAT LIVE A THOUSAND YEARS: This is one of Roland's sayings. VII:5

BEAM BREAKERS: The Beam Breakers are powerful psychics who were kidnapped by the Crimson King and brought to End-World. The Red King stationed them in the Devar Toi—a kind of luxurious prison—and set them to the task of destroying the Beams and bringing down the Dark Tower. Although a few of the Breakers rebel against their fate, most of them are pretty comfortable doing their job. Sad but true. *See* BREAKERS (BEAM BREAKERS), *in* CHARACTERS

BEAMQUAKE: A Beamquake feels like an earthquake, but it is a tremor felt in all of the worlds. A Beamquake takes place when one of the Tower's support Beams snaps. *See also* AVEN KAL, *in* HIGH SPEECH. VI:14

BEFORE VICTORY COMES TEMPTATION. AND THE GREATER THE VICTORY TO WIN, THE GREATER THE TEMPTATION TO WITHSTAND: This was one of Vannay's sayings. He called it "the one rule with no exceptions." VII:589, VII:601

BIG SKY DADDY: Some tribes of slow mutants call God "Big Sky Daddy." V:475

BILLY-BUMBLER (BUMBLER, THROCKEN): Billy-bumblers (also called throcken) look like a cross between a raccoon, a woodchuck, and a dachshund. Their eyes are gold-black and they wag their little corkscrew tails like dogs. Bumblers are intelligent. In the days they lived with men, they could parrot the words they heard, and some could even count and add. Few wild ones seem to remember how to speak, although Jake's pet, Oy, does. Originally, Bumblers were bred to keep down vermin, including the nasty Grandfather Fleas. If Oy is anything to go by, they are devoted to those they love and fiercely protective of them. *See also* OY, *in* CHARACTERS

BINNIE BUGS: These bugs hover over the swamps of Mid-Forest. While she is possessed by Mia, Susannah snatches them out of the air and gobbles them to feed her chap. (Yum.) V:82

BIT O' TAIL: "Bit of ass." A man's bit o' tail is his woman on the side, or his mistress. V:411

BLACK THIRTEEN: Black Thirteen is the last and worst of Maerlyn's magic balls. According to Roland, it is the most terrible object left over from the days of Arthur Eld, although it probably even predates Roland's illustrious and semimythical ancestor. *See also* MAERLYN'S RAINBOW, *in* CHARACTERS

BLACKMOUTH: Cancer. Or as Roland pronounces it, *can't sir.* VII:141

BLOSSIES: When Roland was young, Blossie trees were grown on farms east of Gilead. Their light, strong wood was used for boatbuilding. However, when Roland was still a boy, a terrible plague wiped them out. V:612

BLOW-WEED: Tobacco. VII:310

BLUE CAR SYNDROME: According to Susannah Dean, a person develops Blue Car Syndrome when he or she buys a blue car and then suddenly begins to see blue cars everywhere. Our ka-tet has not Blue Car Syndrome but "Nineteen Syndrome." V:98

BLUEBACKS: Roland's term for police officers. VII:463, VII:472

BOLA: A Mid-World weapon. According to Mid-World mythology, the harrier Gray Dick thought that his enemy, Lady ORIZA, would try to murder him with a bola. She killed him with a sharpened dinner plate instead. V:326

BONDSERVANT: A servant. VII:437

BONDSMAN: One who is bound to serve the DINH of his or her KA-TET. VII:258

BOUGIE: A reanimated corpse. VII:764

BUCKA (BUCKA WAGGON, BUCKBOARD): A buckboard wagon is a horse-drawn vehicle whose body is formed by a plank of wood fixed to the axles. The ones driven by the Manni have rounded canvas tops. V:14, V:21, V:477, V:654, VI:62

BUMBLER: *See* BILLY-BUMBLER, *above*

BUMBLER GOT YOUR TONGUE? Mia uses this term during her PALAVER with Susannah. It translates as "Cat got your tongue?" In other words, why are you so quiet? VI:246

BUMHUG: *Bumhug* is an amusing word that Jake and Eddie made up. Although we don't hear it as often in the final books of the Dark Tower series, we still occasionally come across it. A bumhug is a jerk, a poop-head, etc. VII:144, VII:173

BY SHARDIK: This is the equivalent of saying "By God!" VII:34

CANDA: *See entry in* HIGH SPEECH

CAN'EE SEE HOWGIT ROSEN-GAFF A TWEAK IT BETTER: Roland utters this phrase while talking to Patrick Danville about one of the roses of Can'-Ka No Rey. Basically, it means "Can you see that-there goddamn rose a little better?" VII:759

CARTOMOBILE: This is Roland's word for a car. VI:166, VII:426

CASTLE ROOKS: *See* GAN'S BLACKBIRDS, *below*

CASTLES: A game similar to chess. V:530

CHASSIT: *See entry in* HIGH SPEECH

CHEFLET: Roland's pronunciation of the antibiotic Keflex. VII:635

CHERT: A stone much like quartz, which can be used to scrape hides. Hunters say it breaks lucky. VII:636, VII:638

CHILDREN OF RODERICK (RODS): The Children of Roderick (also known as Rods) are a band of mutants who swore allegiance to Arthur Eld in the long-ago. They are from lands beyond those known to Roland. *See* MUTANTS: CHILDREN OF RODERICK, *in* CHARACTERS

CLEARING AT THE END OF THE PATH (THE CLEARING AT THE END OF THE PATH): This is the place we all go to in the end, though each of us arrives there by a different route. The clearing at the end of the path is death—the snip at the end of the life-cord. V:374, VI:34, VI:243, VI:259

CLOAK FOLK: This is Eddie Dean's term for the Manni. VI:24

CLOUTS: A clout is a cloth that can be used for cleaning, as in a dish-clout, or for diapering a BAH-BO. VII:22, VII:91

COME FORWARD, GOOD STRANGER, AND TELL US OF YOUR NEED: Come forward and speak. V:107

COME TO ME: This is actually an arm gesture. Roland uses it frequently. V:116

COME-COME-COMMALA: *See* COMMALA, *in* CALLA BRYN STURGIS DIALECT

COMMALA: *See entry in* CALLA BRYN STURGIS DIALECT

COZEN (COZENING, COZENING BASTARDS): To cozen is to deceive. A cozening bastard is a deceitful bastard. V:647, VI:74

CRADLE-AMAH: A nanny or childhood nurse. V:188

CRADLE-STORY: Nursery tale. V:341

CRY YOUR PARDON (CRY PARDON): I ask (or beg) your forgiveness. V:157, V:226, V:471, VI:22

CUJO: Although King fans may associate this word with mad dogs, in Mejis, *cujo* means "sweet one." VII:468

CULLIES (CULLY): In Mid-World, the word *cully* can be used positively. So much so that it seems roughly equivalent to the British term *lad*. However, you can also use the term *cully* or *cullies* to refer to a callow youth, or to foolish young men. In our world, a cully is someone who is easily duped or deceived. V:44, V:362, VII:84

DAB HAND: If you have a dab hand at an activity, you are good at it. Susannah Dean proves to have a dab hand at throwing ORIZAS. V:491

DANDY-O BALL: Although we are not given an exact definition, we know that a dandy-o ball is similar to the white silk of a milkweed. After Mordred sucks all of the moisture out of his second mother, Mia, we are told that her head looks like a dandy-o ball. It seems likely that a dandy-o ball is the fluffy seed-head of a dandelion. VII:141

DEAD LETTER: A will. V:319

DEAD-LINE: A dead-line is a line that you cannot cross. The Crimson King set a dead-line around his castle walls so that none of his servants could leave. VII:605

DELAH: *See entry in* HIGH SPEECH

DEMON MOON: The Demon Moon is the demonic, red-faced moon that rises during the season of REAP. *See also* REAP MOON, *below.* VII:659

DEVIL GRASS: A grass which grows on waste ground; it can be smoked or chewed for a narcotic effect. Devil grass is extremely addictive but eventually poisons those who use it. *See* DEMONS/SPIRITS/DEVILS: DEVIL GRASS, *in* CHARACTERS

DIANA'S DREAM: Diana's Dream is a folktale similar to our story "The Lady or the Tiger?" *For page references, see* MID-WORLD FOLKLORE, *in* CHARACTERS

DIM: *Dim* has several meanings. Sorcerers and witches can make themselves dim, or difficult to see. When Henchick of the Manni was close to BLACK THIRTEEN, Maerlyn's evil magic ball, he began to feel dim. In this latter case, dim implies going TODASH, or slipping between worlds. In *Wizard and Glass* (book four of the Dark Tower series), we learned that feeling dim can also mean having a sense of déjà vu. V:414, VI:31

DINH: *See entry in* HIGH SPEECH

DIPOLAR: As we learned in *The Waste Lands,* Lud's computers ran on either dipolar or unipolar circuits. In fact, it seems as though Mid-World's technology was based on slo-trans engines as well as dipolar and unipolar circuitry. V:72, V:563

DO YOU CALL ME DINH? WILL YOU SHARE KHEF WITH ME AND DRINK THIS WATER? Once they feel the impending weight of KA-SHUME upon them, Roland's KA-TET performs this ritual to reaffirm the bonds between them. Roland asks each of his ka-tet mates, in turn, these two questions. They answer in the affirmative and then share KHEF with him, symbolized by a sip of water. VII:258

DO YOU COME FOR AID AND SUCCOR? *See* WILL YOU OPEN TO US IF WE OPEN TO YOU?, *below*

DO YOU SEE US FOR WHAT WE ARE, AND ACCEPT WHAT WE DO? *See* WILL YOU OPEN TO US IF WE OPEN TO YOU?, *below*

DO YOU SET YOUR WATCH AND WARRANT ON IT? Do you guarantee it? VI:283

DOCKER'S CLUTCH: Roland's term for a gunholder. He uses this term for both hidden gunholders and shoulder holsters. V:490, V:559

DOES THEE ASK IF I PLAY THE TOADY? This phrase has several possible meanings. It could translate as "Are you calling me a liar?" but it seems more likely that it means "Do you really think I'm sucking up to you?" V:416

DON'T SHILLY-SHALLY: Don't mess about; don't waste time. V:116

DRAWERS: The Drawers are places that are spoiled or useless or both. However, they are also places of extreme power, like psychic trash middens. VII:733

DROMEDARY: A camel. VI:160

DRY TWIST (OLD BONE-TWIST MAN): Arthritis. V:241, V:243, VI:10, VI:273

DUST-DEVILS: Dust that rises up in little tornado-like shapes. Dust-devils appear to be animated by evil spirits. V:642

ELD (THE WAY OF ELD, THE WAY OF THE ELD, ELD'S WAY): "It's no trick," Roland said. "Never think it. It's the Way of the Eld. We are of that an-tet, khef and kin, watch and warrant." The Way of the Eld signifies the way in which true gunslingers must conduct themselves. Gunslingers must protect the weak if it is at all within their power to do so. *For additional discussion and page references, see* ELD, ARTHUR, *in* CHARACTERS

ELD'S LAST FELLOWSHIP: The tapestry in the Dixie Pig depicts Arthur Eld's last fellowship. However, in that tapestry, Eld's rite is blasphemed, as it shows Arthur, his lady, and his knights taking part in a cannibal's feast. VII:26

ELE-VAYDORS: Roland's word for elevators. VII:494

FAIR AND TRUE: If you say Roland and his KA-TET are gunslingers "fair and true," you mean that they are—without a doubt—true gunslingers. V:230

FAIR-DAY GOOSE: In Roland's world, a person won the Fair-Day goose if he or she won a Fair-Day riddling contest. In *Song of Susannah*, we find out that this phrase has a special significance for Stephen King. When he and his brother finished all their chores and did them well, his mother would tell them both that they'd won the Fair-Day goose. VI:277–78

FAIR-DAY SHOOTING CONTEST: A shooting gallery found at fairs both in our world and Mid-World. The usual targets are clay birds. The usual prize (in our world at least) is a stuffed toy. In Mid-World, you might win a FAIR-DAY GOOSE. VI:146

FALLING SICKNESS (KING'S EVIL): This is the disease that killed Roland's childhood friend Wallace. Wallace was the son of Vannay, Roland's tutor. V:78

FAN-GON: *See entry in* HIGH SPEECH

FAR ON THE OTHER SIDE OF TIME'S HORIZON: Long, long ago. VI:162

FASHED: Riled up. *See also* BOOM-FLURRY, *in* CALLA BRYN STURGIS DIALECT

FEAR ME NOT, BUT HEAR ME WELL: Don't be afraid, but listen well to what I have to say. V:250

FIRST THE SMILES, THEN THE LIES. LAST COMES GUNFIRE: Both Roland's father and Cuthbert Allgood's father followed this rule when maneuvering in potentially hostile territory. It shows that the gunslingers had to use guile as well as diplomacy. V:590

FIST TO FOREHEAD: This is actually a gesture much like bowing. To be polite to a new Mid-World acquaintance, you should raise your fist to your forehead and (if you want to be extra polite) bow over your bended leg. VII:130, VII:175, VII:236, VII:442

FIVE MINUTES' WORTH OF BLOOD AND STUPIDITY: Roland's description of battle. V:679

FLOWER (TO FLOWER): When disease grows, it flowers. Irene Tassenbaum had a lump removed from her breast before cancer could flower. VII:482

FOLKEN: Folks, or ordinary people. VII:242, VII:350

FOOD AND PALAVER DON'T MIX: Food and heavy discussion don't mix. V:134

FOO-LIGHTS: *See* HOBS, *below*

FOR THESE ARE MINE, SURE AS I AM THEIRS. WE ARE ROUND AND ROLL AS WE DO: Essentially, this means "We are family." V:110

FOR YOUR FATHER'S SAKE: Roland often uses this phrase. It means "Do it for your honor's sake." In Mid-World, or at least in the In-World baronies, culture was patriarchal. A gunslinger did not just bring honor (or disgrace) upon himself, but upon his father and all of his father's fathers. V:91, V:245

FORSPECIAL (FORSPECIAL PLATE): The plate which Odetta Holmes/Susannah Dean's mother gave to Susannah's aunt (Sister Blue) as a wedding present. Soon after the wedding, little Odetta was hit on the head by a brick dropped by the psychopath Jack Mort, giving birth to Odetta's second personality, Detta Walker. For some reason, Detta Walker blamed Sister Blue for her accident and so broke the *forspecial* plate. The *forspecial* bore a marked resemblance to a Mid-World ORIZA. V:74, V:329, V:370

FOTTERGRAFS (FOTTERGRAFFS): Roland's term for photographs. V:104, VII:41, VII:496

FRESH EYES SEE CLEAR: This is actually Susannah Dean's saying. It means that a person seeing a situation for the first time has a clearer understanding because he or she isn't bogged down in small details. VII:121

FULL EARTH: Full Earth is the season which comes after MID-SUMMER but before REAP. It is the time of ripening. According to Andy, the Calla Bryn Sturgis's duplicitous Messenger Robot, it is a propitious time for finishing up old business and meeting new people. The red HUNTRESS MOON is a Full Earth moon. V:2, V:6

FULL OF HOT SPIT AND FIRE: Full of life and energy, but in this case, the energy is like lightning. VII:509

GAMRY BOTTLED GAS: The Old People used this to fire up their talking grills. Our KA-TET is forced to use some while hunkering down in a campsite on Can-Steek-Tete, near the DEVAR-TOI. Eddie Dean finds the talking grill exceptionally annoying. VII:318

GAN BORE THE WORLD AND THE WORLD MOVED ON: A saying often used in Mid-World. Gan gave birth to the world from his navel, then tipped it with his finger and set it rolling. This forward movement is what we perceive to be time. *For more information about Gan, see GAN, in CHARACTERS.* VI:295

GAN'S BLACKBIRDS (CASTLE ROOKS): Gan's blackbirds are scavenger birds which feed upon the bodies of the dead. Often called Castle Rooks (though never Royal Rooks), they haunt execution yards. Le Casse Roi Russe is home to many, many of these sinister birds. Their cry sounds like "Croo, croo!" VII:585

GHOSTS ALWAYS HAUNT THE SAME HOUSE: This explains why ghosts don't take vacations. A person who dies in a place under unhappy circumstances remains there, quite possibly because he or she does not understand that he or she is dead. Roland uses this term to explain why the VAGS (or vagrant dead) always remain close to the places where they died. V:288

GHOSTWOOD: Ghostwood is another name for black ironwood, which is heavier than the usual ironwood. Black Thirteen's box is made of ghostwood. V:316, VI:83

GILLY: *See* JILLY, *below*

GIVE YOU PEACE: A short blessing, or prayer, to be said over the bodies of the dead. It should be accompanied by a simple gesture—pronging the fingers and drawing them down over the face of the corpse. Roland performs this ritual over the remains of Chevin of Chayven, CHILD OF RODERICK. VII:51

GLAMMER: Magic or enchantment. Susannah Dean thinks that *glammer* has its own rules. Unfortunately, we mere mortals rarely comprehend them. *See also entry in* MANNI TERMS. V:469, VII:690

GOAT MOON: Also known as "Goat with beard." In our world, it would be the February moon. It is the moon under which Eddie Dean was born. V:138, V:530

GOD-DRUMS: As we learned in *The Waste Lands,* the Grays of Lud broadcasted the god-drums throughout the city so that their enemies, the Pubes, would kill each other. The Pubes believed that the god-drums were the voices of the ghosts in the machines, which demanded human sacrifice. If they didn't ritually sacrifice one of their band each time the drums began, the dead would rise up and devour the living. In actuality, the Grays only thought they played the god-drums. The whole sadistic scenario was the creation of Blaine, Lud's mad computer brain. (Lud's Blaine was the same as Blaine the Mono.) Sadly, the god-drums were nothing more than the backbeat of ZZ Top's song "Velcro Fly." As Eddie Dean wryly observed, the Pubes killed each other for a song that never even made it as a single. VI:205

GODS-A-GLORY: "Oh my God" or "Oh my gosh!" V:332

GONE DAYS: Those days are gone, and you can't do anything to change them. V:101

GONE WORLD, THE: This phrase refers to the world from which our own world has "moved on." It is equivalent to "the olden days." For the people of Mid-World and the borderlands, the gone world was a better world. Gilead is part of the gone world, hence Roland himself is also part of the gone world. V:214

GONICKS: This is Mia's word. We are not given a translation. VII:64

GOOSE JUST WALKED OVER YOUR GRAVE (A GOOSE JUST WALKED OVER YOUR GRAVE): This phrase is equivalent to "A cat just stepped on my grave." In other words, you had a sudden eerie, inexplicable chill. VII:315

GRAF: Apple beer. V:127

GRANDFATHER FLEAS (LITTLE DOCTORS): Grandfather Fleas are the parasitic bugs which feast on the GRANDFATHERS' leftovers. If you see Grandfather Fleas, you know that the Grandfathers can't be far away. *For more information, see* VAMPIRES: TYPE ONE: GRANDFATHER FLEAS, *in* CHARACTERS

GRANDFATHERS: The Grandfathers are TYPE ONE VAMPIRES. They are the nastiest of the demons that the receding PRIM left stranded upon the shores of Mid-World. The Grandfathers are monstrous-looking creatures. They have shriveled faces and black, oozing eyes. They have so many teeth that they can't close their lips, and even their skin is scaled with teeth. These Type Ones don't just drink human blood—they eat human flesh as well. *For more information, see* VAMPIRES: TYPE ONE, *in* CHARACTERS

GRASS-EATERS, GRASS-EATING LOOK: Roland thinks that most civilians look more like grass-eaters, or sheep, than people. VI:131, VII:39

GREAT LETTERS: The letters of High Speech. V:93, VII:494

GREATER DISCORDIA: *See* PRIM, *below*

GREEN CORN A-DAYO: *See entry in* CALLA BRYN STURGIS DIALECT

GREENSTICKING: To put pressure on someone, or "to twist an arm." V:92

GROW BAG: A grow bag is a magical purse that grows money. Roland's grow bag was given to him by his father, Steven Deschain. Roland's purse can be emptied three times, as we see in Calla Bryn Sturgis when Roland gives money to his three KA-TET mates. The first time the purse spills silver, the second time it spills gold, and the third time it spills garnets. We don't know whether the grow bag always grows the same riches or whether it responds to the needs of the receiver. V:401

GUARD, THE: This is a gun-holding position used by gunslingers. In the guard position, the gun barrel rests on the hollow of the left shoulder. VII:192

GUARD O' THE WATCH: An officer of the law. VI:258, VII:463

GUNNA: *See entry in* HIGH SPEECH

GUNSLINGER BURRITOS: The vegetarian wraps which Roland makes for his KA-TET while they are traveling. Eddie Dean prefers meat. V:134

GUNSLINGER LITANY: Every gunslinger must learn to recite the following litany: "I do not aim with my hand; he who aims with his hand has forgotten the face of his father. I aim with my eye. I do not shoot with my hand; he who shoots with his hand has forgotten the face of his father. I shoot with my mind. I do not kill with my gun; he who kills with his gun has forgotten the face of his father. I kill with my heart." V:155–56

HARD RAIN MAKES FOR QUEER BEDFELLOWS AT THE INN (A HARD RAIN MAKES FOR QUEER BEDFELLOWS AT THE INN): We have a version of this saying in our world too: "Necessity makes for strange bedfellows." VII:791

HARRIERS: Bandits or outlaws. V:92, VI:131

HE KEPT HIS FACE WELL: His face didn't betray his emotions. V:205

HEAD CLEAR. MOUTH SHUT. SEE MUCH. SAY LITTLE: Roland's advice to Jake when the boy is about to go and stay at Eisenhart's ranch. V:205

HEAR HIM VERY WELL: Listen to what he's saying. VI:193

HEART OF THE BEAM: *See* BARREL OF THE BEAM, *above*

HERE WE ARE, AND KA STANDS TO ONE SIDE AND LAUGHS. WE MUST DO AS IT WILLS OR PAY THE PRICE: Sometimes it is fate, and not free will, which decides our destinies. If we try to buck fate, we will be punished for it. V:395

HILE: A formal greeting. V:107

HILE AND MERRY-GREET-THE-DAY: A form of "Good morning." The response is "Merry see, merry be." VII:310

HOBS (FOO-LIGHTS): A hob is like a will-o'-the-wisp. Susannah sees these orange lights swirling while she and Roland travel through the White Lands of Empathica. A hob is also a kind of demon. Roland calls the Crimson King a hob. VII:630, VII:730, VII:799

HODJI: *See entry in* HIGH SPEECH

HOLLERED LIKE AN OWL: This is Roland's phrase. It expresses disapproval of those who aren't stoic enough to withstand pain. VII:191

HOLLOW CHAMBER, THE: Roland's gentle tutor, Vannay, taught his pupils that violence worsened problems more often than it solved them. He called violence the hollow chamber where all true sounds become distorted by echoes and can no longer be clearly understood. V:78–79

HOO-HOO BIRD: A nocturnal bird, probably an owl. VII:164

HOT-ENJ: This is the Old People's term for an atomic locomotive. VII:531, VII:678

HOT-LUNG: *See entry in* CALLA BRYN STURGIS DIALECT

HOUKEN: *See entry in* HIGH SPEECH

HOUSIES: Ghosts or whispering voices that murmur in the shadows. Housies are quite nasty, and although they can't usually hurt humans, they can harm small animals like BILLY-BUMBLERS. VII:590

HUMES: *See entry in* END-WORLD TERMS

HUMPIES: Roland uses this term for the cowboys that work Eisenhart's ranch. V:489

HUNCH-THINK: To go on a hunch. VII:217

HUNKER (TO HUNKER): To crouch down or squat. V:509

HUNTRESS MOON: The red Huntress Moon is the first moon of FULL EARTH. It marks the end of summer. V:4, V:138

I CRY YOUR PARDON: I beg your forgiveness. V:154

I HAVE JUST BEEN CASTLED: "I've just been stumped" or "I've just been outdone." It's similar to saying "touché" or "checkmate." V:482

I ONLY DO AS KA WILLS: I do only what fate demands of me, and what honor demands of me. V:336

I SEE YOU VERY WELL: "I see you," but it also implies a deeper and more profound focus upon the person being viewed. This phrase seems to imply that the speaker sees the whole person—their past and present, their needs and desires. VII:115

I SET MY WATCH AND WARRANT ON IT: I bet my life on it. V:30, V:538, VI:7

I SWEAR ON THE FACE OF MY FATHER: I swear upon all I hold sacred. VI:188

I TELL YOU TRUTH: This is actually a hand gesture made by laying the forefinger of the left hand across a circle made by the thumb and pinkie of the right. VII:311

I WON'T WORRY THAT OLD KNOT: I won't go back and dig up that old business. V:477

I WOULD SPEAK TO YOU AN-TET: I would speak to you in private, of important matters, etc. When you speak AN-TET, you speak honestly and intimately. V:117

IF KA WILL SAY SO, LET IT BE SO: This was one of Steven Deschain's phrases. VII:442, VII:516

IF—THE ONLY WORD A THOUSAND LETTERS LONG: The word *if* encompasses a thousand possibilities. V:109

I'LL HAVE YOUR WORD, SWORN UPON THE FACE OF YOUR FATHER: If you ask someone to swear in this way, it's like asking them to swear an oath upon a sacred book. V:481

ILL-SICK VAPORS: According to Roland, tobacco keeps away ill-sick vapors. In other words, it chases away all those nasty viruses and diseases. Eddie Dean doesn't think that the Surgeon General would believe such a statement. VI:299

IRINA: *See entry in* HIGH SPEECH

IRONWOOD (BLACK IRONWOOD): Ironwood trees grow in many of Mid-World's forests. Their wood is hard and durable. In fact, it's too hard to burn. Many of the doors between worlds are made of ironwood, but Black Thirteen's box is made of black ironwood, which is also known as GHOST-WOOD. V:74, V:81, V:316

IT'S THE WAY OF THE ELD. WE ARE OF THAT AN-TET, KHEF AND KA, WATCH AND WARRANT: Roland uses this phrase. In other words, he and his KA-TET are descended from the Eld and follow the Way of Eld in this life and every life. V:156

I-WANT LINES: The lines that carve their course from the sides of the nose down to the chin. V:122

JILLY: The term *jilly* is another spelling of the word *gilly,* which was used frequently in *Wizard and Glass.* Whichever way you spell it, *jilly* means "mistress." This particular use of *jilly* should not to be confused with the jilly of Punch and Jilly (a Mid-World version of Punch and Judy). V:7, V:632

JIN-JIN: *See entry in* HIGH SPEECH

KA HAS NO HEART OR MIND: Ka does what it must do without considering the emotions of mere mortals. VI:16

KA LIKE A WIND: Ka comes with a force of its own. V:31

KA SPEAKS AND THE WIND BLOWS: Ka is the force behind all events. VII:305

KA WAS OFTEN THE LAST THING YOU HAD TO RISE ABOVE: Ka doesn't always bring what we want it to bring. It can bring death and failure too. V:661

KA WORKS AND THE WORLD MOVES ON: Roland utters this phrase in anger after Ben Slightman apologizes for supplying information to the WOLVES of Thunderclap and their masters. Roland's exact response is "Balls to your sorry. Ka works and the world moves on." V:658

KA WOULD TELL. IT ALWAYS DID: In the end, ka has the final say over our fates. V:160

KA-DADDY: A slang term for one's boss. VI:144

KA-DINH: *See entry in* HIGH SPEECH

KAFFIN TWINS: Identical twins who are joined at the body. In our world, we often use the term "Siamese twins." V:675

KAMMEN: *See entry in* HIGH SPEECH

KA-SHUME: *See entry in* HIGH SPEECH

KENNIT: *See entry in* CALLA BRYN STURGIS DIALECT

KEY WORLD: Our world is the key world because Stephen King, the key maker, lives in it. *See also* KEYSTONE EARTH *in* END-WORLD TERMS. VI:200

KI'BOX: *See entry in* CALLA BRYN STURGIS DIALECT

KI'COME: *See entry in* CALLA BRYN STURGIS DIALECT

KI'-DAM: *See entry in* END-WORLD TERMS

KING'S EVIL: *See* FALLING SICKNESS, *above*

LADY OF THE PLATE: *See entry in* CALLA BRYN STURGIS DIALECT

LET BE WHAT WILL BE, AND HUSH, AND LET KA WORK: Roland learned this saying from his mother, Gabrielle Deschain. VII:729

LET EVIL WAIT FOR THE DAY ON WHICH IT MUST FALL: This saying comes from Gilead. It means that you shouldn't borrow trouble from the future since it will arrive soon enough. V:162

LIFE FOR YOU AND FOR YOUR CROP: A Mid-World greeting. V:72

LIFE IS A WHEEL AND WE ALL SAY THANKYA: Life, like ka, is a wheel. We seem to move forward, but in the end we find ourselves back just where we began. VII:4

LINEOUT: This is Roland's word for an outline. VI:285

LOAD (THE LOAD): *See entry in* CALLA BRYN STURGIS DIALECT

LOG OF EASE: The log which campers sit on to dump the proverbial dinner. I suppose some people find it easier than squatting to poop. VII:635

LONG AGO (THE LONG AGO): The time before the world moved on. VII:9, VII:161, VII:178

LONG DAYS AND PLEASANT NIGHTS: A Mid-World greeting. The proper response is, "May you have twice the number." In Calla Bryn Sturgis, this greeting is accompanied by three taps to the throat. V:3, VI:149

LOOKS: *See* THREE LOOKS TO THE HORIZON, *below*

LORD PERTH: Mid-World's story of Lord Perth bears a strong resemblance to our biblical tale of David and Goliath. *See also* MID-WORLD FOLK-LORE, *in* CHARACTERS. V:39

LOS ÁNGELES: This Mejis term describes fat, white, fair-weather clouds. VII:455, VII:477

LOUTKIN: A lout; an ill-mannered person. VI:180

LOVE STUMBLES: This is Roland's mother's phrase. It is roughly equivalent to our saying "love is blind." V:77

MACROVERSE: A term often used in Stephen King's fiction for all the known worlds that spin about the Tower. I use it frequently in this *Concordance,* even though Stephen King doesn't use it in the Dark Tower series. *See also* MULTI-VERSE

MADAME DEATH: Lady Death. In decks of cards, she is often represented by the Queen of Spades. VI:18

MAGDA-SEENS: Roland's misprounciation of the word *magazines.* V:677, VII:494

MAKE WATER (TO MAKE WATER): To urinate. V:86

MANY AND MANY-A: A long time ago. V:131, V:328

MAY IT SERVE THEM VERY WELL: May it make them healthy, or may it make them prosper. V:74

MAY THE SUN NEVER FALL IN YOUR EYES: Good luck to you. V:402

MAY WE BE WELL-MET ON THE PATH: *See* WELL-MET, *below*

MAY WE MEET IN THE CLEARING AT THE END OF THE PATH WHEN ALL WORLDS END: May we meet after death. May we meet again in the next world. VII:801

MAY YOU DO WELL: May you prosper. VI:182

MAY YOU HAVE TWICE THE NUMBER: *See* LONG DAYS AND PLEAS-ANT NIGHTS, *above*

MAY YOUR BEAUTY EVER INCREASE/AND MAY YOUR FIRST DAY IN HELL LAST TEN THOUSAND YEARS, AND MAY IT BE THE SHORTEST: This testy interchange is part of the story of Lady ORIZA and her suitor/enemy Gray Dick. *See* ORIZA, LADY, *in* CHARACTERS

MAY YOUR DAYS BE LONG UPON THE EARTH: A Mid-World greeting. The proper reply to this is "And may you have twice the number." V:123

MAY YOUR FIRST DAY IN HELL LAST TEN THOUSAND YEARS: *See* MAY YOUR BEAUTY EVER INCREASE, *above*

MAYHAP: Perhaps. V:328

MAYHAP SOME OF THE OLD WAYS STILL HOLD: Perhaps some of the old ways have survived. V:126

MERRY SEE, MERRY BE: *See* HILE AND MERRY-GREET-THE-DAY, *above*

METALED/METAL: A metaled road is a paved road. V:291

MID-SUMMER: The season of Mid-Summer marks the hottest part of the year. V:2

MIM: *See entry in* HIGH SPEECH

MIND-SPEAR: A mind-spear is a focused thought which can kill the person at whom it is aimed. The BREAKER Ted Brautigan is especially good at throwing mind-spears. VII:278, VII:376

MOIT: A group of five or six. It is also part of an expression: "Surely you've got a moit more guts than that." V:237, V:358, VII:808 *(expression)*

MORE THAN ONCE-UPON-A: More than once. V:367

MORTATA: *See entry in* CALLA BRYN STURGIS DIALECT

MUFFIN-BALLS: Although they look like mushrooms, muffin-balls are actually a kind of edible ground berry. V:42

MULTIPLE AMERICAS: Although the Tower contains only one keystone earth and that keystone earth contains only one North America and one United States, other levels of the Tower also contain alternative Americas, or alternative versions of North America and of the United States. These alternative Americas are subtly different from ours. (For example, in those alternative Americas people drive Takuro Spirits and drink Nozz-A-La cola.) When I refer to the many Americas, including the one found on keystone earth, I use the term *Multiple Americas*. *See also entry in* OUR WORLD PLACES

MULTIVERSE: A term I often use in this *Concordance* when I am referring to the many worlds which spin around the Dark Tower.

MUMBLETY-PEG: A game in which players throw or flip a jackknife in various ways so that the knife sticks in the ground. We play this game in our world too. V:227

MUSICA: In Calla Bryn Sturgis, a musica is a bandstand on a town green. In other parts of Mid-World, a wandering musica is a wandering musician. V:210, VII:51

MUTIE: A mutant. Mutants are common in Mid-World. *See* MUTANTS, *in* CHARACTERS

MY TONGUE TANGLES WORSE THAN A DRUNK'S ON REAP-NIGHT: Roland's way of saying that he isn't good with words. V:216

NAUGHT BE ZERO, NAUGHT BE FREE, I OWE NOT YOU, NOR YOU OWE ME: Nothing has been decided yet, and no one owes anyone else anything, at least as yet. V:110

NE'MINE: Never mind. VI:50

NEVER IN LIFE: Not on your life. V:403

NEVER MIND SPLITTING NAILS TO MAKE TACKS: Don't split hairs. The gist of whatever is being said is correct. V:167

NEVER SPEAK THE WORST ALOUD: This was one of Cort's sayings. Don't speak your worst fears. VII:589

NEW EARTH: New Earth is the spring plowing season. Mother Nature is just waking from her long sleep. V:3

NINETEEN: Nineteen is the number which haunts our KA-TET throughout the last three books of the Dark Tower series. *See* NINETEEN, NINETY-NINE, *and* NINETEEN NINETY-NINE, *all in* CHARACTERS

NO QUARTER: *See* WE WILL ACCEPT NO QUARTER, *below*

NOON (TO NOON): To noon in the saddle is to spend noontime (or the afternoon) riding. You can also "noon with" someone, which means to spend the afternoon with them. V:205

NOT BY MY WARRANT: Not if it's up to me. V:47

NOT JUST ONE POINT OF WHEN: Not just one point in time, but more than one. V:103

NOW WHILE WE BIDE: Now while we stay here. V:230

NOZZ-A-LA: The Great Old Ones must have preferred Nozz-A-La cola to either Coke or Pepsi, since some of the cans are still kicking around End-

World. Nozz-A-La may also be found in many of the ALTERNATIVE AMER-ICAS. V:36, V:560, VII:724

OAST: *See* BASTED IN A HOT OAST, *above*

OGGAN: *See entry in* CALLA BRYN STURGIS DIALECT

OLD BONE-TWIST MAN: *See* DRY-TWIST, *above*

OLD ONES: The Old Ones (also called the Old People or the Great Old Ones) were the technologically advanced inhabitants of Mid-World. By Roland's time, they were long gone, and all that remained of them were their weapons and dangerous, half-fried technology. *See* OLD ONES, *in* CHARACTERS

OLD ONES' DOOR: This is Roland's term for a mechanical door made by the Old Ones. Unlike the magical doors left over from the PRIM, or the enchanted doors created by ka or art, the Old Ones' doors are dedicated and always come out at the same place. Few are in good condition, so passing through them can make a person physically sick. *See also* DOORWAYS BETWEEN WORLDS, *in* PORTALS. VII:35

OLD RED FURY (THE OLD RED FURY): Battle fury. V:171

ORIZA: *See entry in* CALLA BRYN STURGIS DIALECT

OTHER WHERE-AND-WHEN: On some other level of the Dark Tower. In some other where-and-when, Lud is a version of New York City. V:179

OUTER DARK: Chaos. Evil. The Crimson King serves the Outer Dark. Roland and his fellow gunslingers serve the WHITE. V:115

PAIN RISES, FROM THE HEART TO THE HEAD: This is one of Roland's sayings. Eddie has a strange feeling that he's heard similar sentiments in cowboy flicks. When Roland removes a bullet from Eddie's leg, he tells Eddie to bite down on a belt so that he can catch the pain as it rises. The trick seems to work. VI:203

PALAVER: To hold palaver is to hold counsel. *Palaver* tends to imply the exchange of important ideas. V:108, V:158, VI:66, VI:183

PARTI: A brand of cigarettes once smoked by the inhabitants of End-World. V:560

PASEAR: To take a little pasear around town is to take a short tour of the town, or a short wander around the town. V:584

PATH OF THE BEAR, WAY OF THE TURTLE: The section of the Bear/Turtle Beam which leads from Shardik's portal to the Dark Tower. Once the Dark Tower is reached and you begin to travel toward Maturin's portal, you're on the Path of the Turtle, Way of the Bear. In the final book of the Dark Tower series, the Path of the Bear, Way of the Turtle is called Beam of the Bear, Way of the Turtle. VI:15, VII:295

PEAK SEAT: The seat at the front of a BUCKA WAGGON, where the driver sits. V:655

PEDDLER: The late-summer moon. When the moon is full, you can see the squint-and-grin of the Peddler upon its face. This moon is also called Old Cheap Rover Man's moon. V:37, VII:165

PEELED OFF: Turned off, or left the path. V:42

PENNY FOR EM, DIMMY-DA: Penny for your thoughts. VII:316

PENNY, POSY, JACK'S A NOSY! DO YA SAY SO? YES, I DO-SO! HE'S MY SNEAKY, PEEKING DARLING BAH-BO! This bit of "cradle nonsense" was sung to children in Mid-World. Roland would have known it well. VII:171

PERT: Impertinent or impertinently. VI:104

POINTS: A Mid-World game much like baseball. It is also called Wickets. V:236

POKEBERRIES: Waxy-skinned berries that taste like sweet cranberries. V:245, VI:102, VII:716

POPKIN: A sandwich. V:175, VII:42, VII:503

POSSE: A strong force, a company of men. VI:51

PRAYER AFTER A SUCCESSFUL HUNT: Roland recites this prayer after he and Susannah successfully hunt down deer. The prayer is addressed to the head of a dead deer.

> We thank you for what we are about to receive.
> (Father, we thank thee.)
> Guide our hands and guide our hearts as we take life from death.
> VII:636–37

PRIM: The magical soup of creation from which all life arose. It is sometimes called the Greater Discordia or the OVER. *See also entry in* CHARACTERS

PRINK-A-DEE: A trinket. V:661

PUBES: A Pube is a young person. In Lud, which our KA-TET had to pass through during their *Waste Lands* journeys, the Pubes were the descendants of the city's original inhabitants. Originally, the term *Pube* had been short for "pubescent"; however, by the time Roland and his ka-tet arrived in the city, the original Pubes had grown older than GAN and had marched to the CLEARING AT THE END OF THE PATH. Like their enemies the Grays, the descendants of the Pubes were riddled with diseases and were half-mad. They also played a game of chance in which the winner was lynched to please the demonic GOD-DRUMS. *For more information about the Pubes, see entry in* CHARACTERS. VII:84

PURSE: Roland's scuffed swag-bag. V:45

QUICKENED: A child quickens in the womb when it begins to move. V:480

RANCHER'S DINNER: A big dinner, which is meant to fill you up for your chores. V:134

REAP: Reap is both the season and the festival of harvest. In the days of Arthur Eld it was celebrated with human sacrifice, but by the time Roland was born, STUFFY-GUYS were thrown onto Reap bonfires instead of people. Although it is followed by the Year's End festival, Reap is the true closing of the year. V:13

REAP CRACKERS: Reaptide firecrackers. V:226

REAP MOON: The Reap Moon is the DEMON MOON. VII:229

REAPTIDE: The time of Reap. V:202

RED DEATH: The Red Death can be found in Edgar Allan Poe's famous tale "Masque of the Red Death." In Poe's story we learn the symptoms of this awful plague. First, the sufferer complains of sharp pains, then of a sudden dizziness, and finally he or she begins to bleed profusely from all pores. The entire seizure—from first symptom until death—takes one-half hour. The people of Fedic were decimated by this terrible disease. VI:105, VI:243, VI:244

RED PLAGUE: The Red Plague is probably the same as the RED DEATH. VII:429

RHEUMATIZ: Rheumatoid arthritis. *See also* DRY TWIST, *above.* V:240

RICE SONG: *See* RICE SONG *and* COMMALA, *both in* CALLA BRYN STURGIS DIALECT

RIDING DROGUE: Riding behind. V:128

ROCK-CATS: *See entry in* CALLA BRYN STURGIS DIALECT

RODERICK, CHILDREN OF: *See* CHILDREN OF RODERICK, *above*

ROOST ON (TO JUST ROOST ON): To remain in place. It implies pointless waiting and a sense of futility. V:172

RUSTIES (BARN RUSTIES): A large Mid-World blackbird. The bird's name derives from its harsh squalling cry, a call slightly shriller than that of a crow. V:7, V:154, V:162, VI:23, VII:193 *(barn rusties),* VII:793

RUSTIE WALKED OVER MY GRAVE (A RUSTIE HAD JUST WALKED OVER HIS GRAVE): "A cat stepped on my grave." These kinds of phrases describe the deep chill or shiver we feel when someone's statement (or something we experience) resonates with a deep, internal foreboding. V:103

SANDITCH: Roland's pronunciation of *sandwich.* VII:42

SAWBONES' BAG: A doctor's bag. VII:468

SCRIP: A lawyer. VI:186

SEE ME! SEE ME VERY WELL: Look at me. *See also* I SEE YOU VERY WELL, *above.* V:172, VII:115

SEE THE TURTLE OF ENORMOUS GIRTH: This is the first line of a well-known and well-loved Mid-World poem which invokes the spirit of the Turtle Guardian. Although there are many variations, Rosalita Munoz's version goes like this:

> See the Turtle of enormous girth!
> On his shell he holds the earth,
> His thought is slow but always kind;
> He holds us all within his mind.
> On his back the truth is carried,
> And there are love and duty married.
> He loves the earth and loves the sea,
> And even loves a child like me. (VI:15)

For more information and for page references, see GUARDIANS OF THE BEAM, *in* CHARACTERS

SEEN THE BOAT SHE CAME IN: *See entry in* CALLA BRYN STURGIS DIALECT

'SENERS: Keroseners, or kerosene lights. V:438, V:506, V:561, VI:14

SEND YOU WEST WITH THE BROKEN ONES WHO HAVE FORGOT-TEN THE FACES OF THEIR FATHERS (TO SEND YOU WEST): In In-World-that-was, failed gunslingers were sent west in disgrace. Hence, this saying arose. V:568

SEPPE-SAI: *See entry in* HIGH SPEECH

SET MY WATCH AND WARRANT ON IT: You bet. I know it's true. V:214

SEVEN DIALS OF MAGIC: Vannay, Roland's tutor, taught him about the Seven Dials of Magic. We have not, as yet, found out what they are. V:79

SHARPROOT: This is one of Mid-World's crops. V:1, V:151

SHEEVIN (SH'VEEN): Side-wife or mistress. V:120

SHINNARO: In the alternative America where Eddie Dean is actually Eddie Toren, Shinnaro cameras are popular. VII:728

SHOOTING-IRON: A gun. V:20, V:319, VII:47

SHORT BEER: *See entry in* CALLA BRYN STURGIS DIALECT

SHORTS: Half-sized smokes. VII:310

SHUCKIES: Corn shucks used to roll smokes. VI:299

SIGUL: A sigul is a sign, symbol, or insignia which is secret but full of meaning. It often has religious, political, or magical significance. VI:14, VI:65, VI:327, VII:26

SILVER METAL: What you paint on warts to make them go away. V:479

SINGLETS: A singlet is an undershirt or vest worn under other clothes. V:403

SKÖLDPADDA: A turtle. *See* GUARDIANS OF THE BEAM: TURTLE GUARDIAN, *in* CHARACTERS

SLEWFEET: Roland's term for noisy trackers. V:44

SLINKUM: An old man's strap-style undershirt. VII:518

SLO-TRANS ENGINES: Mid-World's technology was one of unipolar circuits, dipolar circuits, and slo-trans technology. V:72, V:371

SLOW MUTANTS: Slow Mutants are creatures damaged by radiation poisoning. They were the result of the Old Ones' disastrous wars. *See* MUTANTS: SLOW MUTANTS, *in* CHARACTERS

SLUT OF THE WINDS: Roland's term for the female spirits who have sex (consensual or not) with traveling men. Often, these demonic sluts are deadly. VI:370

SMALLHOLDS: *See entry in* CALLA BRYN STURGIS DIALECT

SNIVELMENT: To snivel is to show weak or tearful resentment. It can also imply hypocrisy. A young snivelment is a sniveler. *Snivelment* can also be used as a noun, as in "stop your snivelment." VI:29, VI:295

SOH: *See entry in* CALLA BRYN STURGIS DIALECT

SONG OF THE TURTLE, CRY OF THE BEAR: Roland tells a hypnotized Stephen King that whenever he hears the Song of the Turtle or the Cry of the Bear he must turn his attention back to the Dark Tower series and continue writing it. VI:296

SONGS: The following songs are known both in Mid-World and our world: "Careless Love" and "Hey Jude." The major difference is that, in Mid-World, "Hey Jude" begins "Hey Jude, I see you, lad." V:37

SPARK-A-DARK, WHO'S MY SIRE? Roland repeats this old catechism whenever he sets a campfire alight. It goes, "Spark-a-dark, who's my sire? Will I lay me? Will I stay me? Bless this camp with fire." VII:761

SPARKLIGHTS: Electric lights. V:90, V:561

SPATHIPHILIUM: A plant that grew in Gilead. It also grows in the Garden of the Beam. VII:492

SPEAK QUIET, BUT SPEAK PLAIN: Speak quietly, but state what you mean. V:43

SPEED-SHOOTER: A machine gun. VI:130, VI:228

SPIRIT-MAN: The spirit that lingers near the body after death. VII:474

SQUIREEN: Owner of a small landed property. Also a knight's attendant. V:383

STAND TRUE: Remain true to your mission, your beliefs, etc. V:163

STEM: A stem is a man of affairs. VI:268

STRAWBERRY COSY: A tasty dessert. V:134

STUFFY-GUYS: Red-handed stuffy-guys can be found all over Mid-World and are a staple of REAPTIDE festivities. In the days of Arthur Eld, human beings were sacrificed during the festival of REAP. However, by Roland's day, stuffy-guys, or human effigies, were burned instead. In Mid-World-that-was, stuffy-guys had heads made of straw, and their eyes were made from white cross-stitched thread. In the BORDERLANDS, their heads are often made of SHARPROOT. *See also entry in* CHARACTERS

SUCH WOULD PLEASE ME EVER: Yes, that would make me happy. VII:137

SUMMA LOGICALES: Roland studied this subject with Vannay. We don't know what it is, but its theories encompassed both the anatomy of the Beams and the Bends o' the Rainbow. VII:33

SUPERFLU: The genetically engineered disease that killed off more than 99 percent of the human population in Stephen King's novel *The Stand*. This disease also wiped out the citizens of the alternative Topeka, which Roland, Eddie, Susannah, Jake, and Oy traveled through in *Wizard and Glass*. The superflu is also called Captain Trips. VI:110

SURELY YOU'VE GOT A MOIT MORE GUTS THAN THAT: Surely you've got more guts than that. VII:808

SWAG-BAG: Another name for Roland's scuffed old purse. V:512

TACK-SEES: Roland's word for taxis. V:104, V:172, VII:426

TAHEEN: End-World creatures that have the bodies of men but the heads of birds or beasts. *See entry in* HIGH SPEECH; *see also entry in* CHARACTERS

TAKE THE KING'S SALT (TO TAKE THE KING'S SALT): To make a deal with someone and to be in their pay. When you take the Crimson King's salt, you make a bargain with the devil. V:550

TAKURO (TAKURO SPIRIT): A Takuro Spirit is a type of car found in some of the alternative versions of America. Takuro (along with North Central Positronics and Honda) manufactured the Cruisin Trike that Susannah Dean uses during the attack on the Devar-Toi. VII:250, VII:724

TALE-SPINNER: A storyteller. VI:210, VI:275

TEARS OF MY MOTHER: Roland utters this phrase when he and Susannah discover tongueless Patrick Danville in a prison cell below Dandelo's house. The only other time Roland uttered this phrase (within Susannah's presence at least) was when the two of them stumbled upon a deer that had fallen in the woods and broken its legs. The flies had eaten its still-living eyes. VII:697–98

TELEFUNG: This is Mia's mispronunciation of the word *telephone*. VI:73

THANKEE-SAI: Thank you. V:28

THAT'S AS CLEAR AS EARTH NEEDS: This phrase was used by Cort and by Roland's father, Steven Deschain. It means "that's as clear as we need" or "that's obvious." VII:473

THAT'S AS KA WILLS: Whether it happens depends on fate's decree. V:167

THE WAY OF KA IS ALWAYS THE WAY OF DUTY: Basically, duty comes first. V:181

THE WISE MAN DOESN'T POKE A SLEEPING BEAR WITH A STICK: The wise man doesn't make a bad situation worse. Also, you shouldn't awaken dangerous forces—they may turn against you. V:316

THE WORLD HAS MOVED ON: *See* WORLD HAS MOVED ON, *below*

THERE ARE OTHER WORLDS THAN THESE: Jake Chambers's famous saying. In the final three books of the Dark Tower series, we learn just how true this statement is. V:105

THERE WILL BE WATER IF GOD WILLS IT (THERE WOULD BE WATER IF GOD WILLED IT): What is meant to happen will happen. V:81, V:87, V:113, V:569

THIN: When something feels thin, it feels dangerous, or full of tricks. A thin place is one where the fabric of reality has almost worn through and other worlds are close. The word *thin* is related to the word *thinny*, that nasty demonic entity which Roland encountered in Eyebolt Canyon in Mejis, and then again in the alternative Topeka. VII:114, VII:524

THINKING CAPS: *See* END-WORLD TERMS

THOSE WHO DO NOT LEARN FROM THE PAST ARE CONDEMNED TO REPEAT IT: Vannay often repeated this maxim. VII:829

THREADED: Threaded stock is normal stock, or animals born without mutations. MUTIES abound in Mid-World, so threaded stock is extremely valuable. Threaded stock can be bred with other threaded stock to keep the bloodlines pure, but threaded stock can also be born from late-generation muties. In Mid-World-that-was, they called this latter process "clarifying." V:2, V:613

THREE IS A NUMBER OF POWER: This particular belief is held in our world as well. V:110

THREE LOOKS TO THE HORIZON: This is a saying used to describe distance, as in "You should travel at least three looks to the horizon." Three looks is roughly equivalent to one hundred WHEELS. VI:151

THROAT TAPS: Throat tapping is an important custom in Mid-World. A person taps his throat as a sign of respect, as Roland does when he meets Aunt Talitha in *The Waste Lands*. Roland also taps his throat three times before crossing water. V:205, V:356, VI:148

THROCKEN: *See* BILLY-BUMBLER, *above*

TIME HAS SOFTENED (TIME HAD BEGUN TO SOFTEN, TIME HAD GROWN SOFT): In Mid-World, time does not flow evenly but moves forward erratically. Like the points of the compass, time itself is in drift. V:23, V:35, V:318

TIME IS A FACE ON THE WATER: Mejis proverb. Time is an illusion. V:35

TIME O' THE GOAT: Time of the Goat Moon, which is equivalent to the month of February in our world. Eddie Dean was born during Goat Moon. V:140

TODASH: *See entry in* HIGH SPEECH

TODASH TAHKEN: *See entry in* HIGH SPEECH

TOUCH (THE TOUCH): The ability to read minds, also to see into the past and the future. It is similar to ESP and is half-empathy, half-telepathy. Jake is strong in the touch. V:296, V:381, V:389, VI:71, VII:190

TRAIL-FRAYED: This was Cuthbert Allgood's description of someone who has been on the road so long that he or she looks thin and worn. You treat this disorder with sassafras and salts. VII:758

TRIG: Clever. *Trig* also implies craftiness. V:114, V:575

TRIG COVE: A clever bastard. Believe it or not, this term can be used as a compliment. VII:121

TRIG DELAH: Extremely clever. VII:176

TRUCKOMOBILE: A truck. VII:426

TRUE AS EVER WAS: True as ever. This statement is also uttered when an ORIZA flies true to its mark. V:334

TRUE THREAD, THE: This is Cort's phrase. It refers to a person's most basic and fundamental skills. A gunslinger's true thread is his ability to use weapons. VII:250

TRUM: In the Callas, a person is trum when he or she can convince other people to do dangerous things. However, a "big and painful trum" is a terrible disease, like cancer. V:348, VII:413

TWINNER: The term *twinner* actually comes from the novels *The Talisman* and *Black House,* which Stephen King cowrote with Peter Straub. Although King doesn't use this term in the Dark Tower series, I frequently use it in this *Concordance* to describe the "twin" phenomenon, which occurs so frequently in the Dark Tower books. A person's twinner is the version of that person that exists in another world, or on another level of the Dark Tower. For example, Eddie Dean dies in Mid-World, but Susannah Dean meets one of his twinners— Eddie Toren—in an alternative version of New York. Places can have twinners too. For example, Mid-World's Lud is the twinner of our world's New York, albeit in a distant future where terrible disasters have taken place.

TWIRLING HAND: A somewhat impatient gesture. Roland frequently uses it. It means "carry on" or "hurry up." V:701

UFFIS: This ancient term means shape-changer. VII:602

UNDERMIND: The unconscious mind. VII:513

UNIVERSAL TRUTHS, THE: Cort gave his apprentices lectures on what he called "the universal truths." We are not told what they are. V:78

VAGS: Vagrant dead. *See* VAGS, *in* CHARACTERS

WALK-INS: Certain parts of western Maine are plagued by walk-ins, or beings that enter our world from other worlds. *See* WALK-INS, *in* CHARACTERS

WATCH AND WARRANT: *See* DO YOU SET YOUR WATCH AND WARRANT ON IT?, *above*

WATCH ME: A Mid-World card game. V:559, VI:17

WATCH ME CHIP (A WATCH ME CHIP): A Watch Me chip is like a poker chip. V:627

WATCH ME FACE: A Watch Me face is like a poker face. It is a face devoid of expression—one that can't be read because it doesn't expose emotion. The person behind the Watch Me face guards his or her secrets well. VI:38

WE ARE AT PEACE, YOU AND I: We are at peace. There is no argument between us. V:111

WE ARE KA-TET, WE ARE ONE FROM MANY: We are joined by fate, and our destinies are woven together. *See* KA-TET, *in* HIGH SPEECH. V:581

WE DEAL IN LEAD: A statement made by Steve McQueen in *The Magnificent Seven*, but Roland also uses it. Gunslingers are fighters first and foremost, but they are not mere hired guns. They are lawmakers and lawmen, and the bullet is the tool of their trade. V:115

WE MAY BE CAST ON . . . BUT NO MAN MAY CAST US BACK: Once we begin, we cannot be stopped. V:111

WE SPREAD THE TIME AS WE CAN, BUT IN THE END THE WORLD TAKES IT ALL BACK: We do what we can during a life, but in the end the world takes our lives along with everything we've accomplished. V:244

WE WILL ACCEPT NO QUARTER (NO QUARTER): We will neither accept nor give mercy. V:171, V:679

WE'LL KEEP HIM VERY WELL: We'll take care of him. VI:37

WELL-MET (WE WERE WELL-MET, MAY WE BE WELL-MET ON THE PATH): We met, and that is important. Good has come from our meeting (implying an element of fate). "May we be well-met" means "let good come of this meeting." V:107, V:215, V:229, VI:9, VI:181

WELL-MET OR ILL, IT MAY BE YOU WILL FIND WHAT YOU SEEK: Whether good or evil comes of our meeting, you may find what you originally set out to find. V:107

WHAT I KEN: What I understand. V:205

WHATEVER THE GODS MAY BE, THEY HAVE FAVORED THIS PLACE: Similar to saying "God has favored this place," but it makes allowances for Mid-World's many deities. V:208

WHEELS: An archaic form of measurement still used throughout Mid-World and the BORDERLANDS. In *The Waste Lands,* Blaine tells us that a distance of eight thousand wheels is roughly equivalent to seven thousand miles. In that case, there are about 1.143 wheels to a mile. However, in *Wizard and Glass,* tricky Blaine tells us that 900 mph is the same as 530 wheels per hour. In this instance, one wheel is equal to 1.7 miles. (See *Stephen King's The Dark Tower: A Concordance, Volume I.*) In *The Dark Tower* (the final volume of the Dark Tower series), we are told that 120 wheels is roughly equivalent to 100 miles, hence a wheel equals about .83 of a mile, but slightly later we are told that twelve wheels is equal to nine or ten miles, hence a wheel is approximately .75 of a mile. Obviously, wheels, like the points of the compass, are in drift. V:4, VII:718–19

WHEN YOU ARE UNSURE, YOU MUST LET KA ALONE TO WORK ITSELF OUT: If you are unsure about what to do, leave the decision in the hand of God, the gods, or Lady Fate. V:392

WHERE AND WHEN (THIS WHERE AND WHEN): Your *where* and *when* refers to the specific level of the Dark Tower you are on (or which world you are in), and what time you are inhabiting. Each *where* has many *whens,* and each *when* has many *wheres.* VII:36

WHITE: In our world, the White is an elemental force akin to faith and can mean faith in God or in a just universe. Before he lost his calling, Father Callahan knew the White well, and that energy was returned to him at the end of his life. To the beleaguered inhabitants of Mid-World and the BORDERLANDS, the descendants of Arthur Eld and their fellow gunslingers are the knights of the White. In an unstable and violent present, they represent a stable and peaceful past. However, *the White* implies more than a particular political faction, allegiance, or social class. The White represents wholeness, unity, and health and is the opposite of the OUTER DARK—that force of chaos and destruction championed by the Crimson King. V:101, V:104, V:115, VI:270, VII:4

WHY DON'T YOU STOP BEATING YOUR BREAST AND GET STARTED: Stop pulling your hair out and begin. V:559

WICKETS: *See* POINTS, *above*

WIDE EARTH: One of Gilead's Fair-Days. It takes place in late winter/early spring. Wide Earth was famous for its riddling contests. V:687, VII:64

WIDOWER'S HUMP: An older man's curved spine. VII:427

WIDOWMAKER: A gun. VII:49

WILL YOU NOT SEND ME ON WITH A WORD: Won't you speak to me? VII:760

WILL YOU OPEN TO US IF WE OPEN TO YOU? If you ask a gunslinger to defend you in the name of the WHITE, he will ask you three questions. This is the first of them. The next questions is "Do you see us for what we are and accept what we do?" The final question is "Do you seek aid and succor?" V:109, V:230, V:397, VI:275

WINTER'S SNOW IS FULL OF WOE, WINTER'S CHILD IS STRONG AND WILD: A Mid-World saying. V:138

WIT GREEN WIT: A canned drink, which Eddie tastes in the Fedic Dogan. He finds it utterly foul. VII:155

WITCHLIGHT: In the tunnels beneath Castle Discordia, the puddles glow with what might be either radiation or witchlight. VII:562

WOODS TEA: Tea Roland brews from forest plants. V:107

WORDSLINGER: A writer. Roland calls Stephen King a wordslinger. VI:300

WORK-STOOP: A Gilead term for a porch located behind the main house and which faces both barn and fields. V:318

WORLD HAS MOVED ON (THE WORLD HAS MOVED ON): This phrase is used throughout the Dark Tower series. It means that things have changed, and that the world is now profoundly different from what it once was. The change has not been for the better. V:126

WORLD NEXT DOOR (THE WORLD NEXT DOOR): Those worlds which are similar to ours but which are not exactly the same. Eddie must come from one of the worlds next door, since in his version of New York, Co-Op City is in Brooklyn, not the Bronx. V:106

WOULD'EE HAVE THE PEACE OF THE CLEARING? Would you like to pass on to the next world? VII:50

WRIT OF TRADE: A legal document conveying ownership. VII:37

YAR: Yes. VI:179, VII:83

YE CHARY GUNSTRUCK MAN: *See* CHARY, *in* HIGH SPEECH

YEAR END GATHERING: Year End Gathering is one of Mid-World's Fair-Days. Although REAP is the year's true end and marks the beginning of winter, Year End marks the end of the calendar year. V:21

YESTEREVE: Yesterday evening. V:410

YOU HAVE FORGOTTEN THE FACE OF YOUR FATHER: Gunslinger culture was patriarchal, and a man was expected to uphold the honor of his father, and his father's fathers, at all costs. V:661, VI:144

YOU MUST NEVER DRAW UNTIL YOU KNOW HOW MANY ARE AGAINST YOU, OR YOU'VE SATISFIED YOURSELF THAT YOU CAN NEVER KNOW, OR YOU'VE DECIDED THAT IT'S YOUR DAY TO DIE: This rather bleak statement comes from Roland. VII:55

YOU NEEDN'T DIE HAPPY WHEN YOUR DAY COMES, BUT YOU MUST DIE SATISFIED, FOR YOU HAVE LIVED YOUR LIFE FROM BEGINNING TO END AND KA IS ALWAYS SERVED: This is another of Roland's sayings. VII:5

YOU SAY TRUE, I SAY THANKYA: *See entry in* CALLA BRYN STURGIS DIALECT

YOU WIN THE FAIR-DAY GOOSE: *See* FAIR-DAY GOOSE, *above*

YOUR HEART SURELY SAID TRUE: Your heart guided you well. V:316

Zn: *See entry in* HIGH SPEECH

MANNI TERMS

ANYROA' (ANY RO'): *See entry in* MID-WORLD ARGOT

BAYDERRIES: Batteries. V:415

BEFORE THE SUN GOES ROOFTOP: Before the sun is high. VI:7

BOOK OF THE MANNI: The Manni's sacred book. It seems to be a version of the Bible. V:16

BRANNI BOB AND BRANNI COFF: The Branni Bob is the most powerful of the magical plumb bobs used by the Manni of Calla Redpath. As the Branni Bob swings, it gains weight and the space it passes through becomes

DIM. The Branni Bob is carried in the Branni Coff. *See* MANNI: BRANNI BOB, *in* CHARACTERS

COFFS: Coffs are the boxes in which Manni carry their plumb bobs and magnets. They are large wooden boxes covered in stars, moons, and odd geometric shapes. The undersides of the coffs are fitted with long metal sleeves, which house long wooden rods. The rods can then be placed on the shoulders so that the coffs and their contents can be carried like coffins. VI:26

DIM: *See entry in* MID-WORLD ARGOT

FORCE, THE: *See* OVER, THE, *below*

FORGETFUL, THE (THE FORGETFUL FOLK): Those who have left the Manni tribe to marry heathens. They will spend the rest of eternity in NA'AR, or the Manni Hell. V:407, VI:6, VI:28

GLAMMER: Although *glammer* is a term found throughout Mid-World, it has particular importance for the Manni, whose religion makes use of magic to travel between worlds. As the Manni say, "Magic and *glammer*, both are one, and they do unroll from the back. From the past, do'ee ken." VI:5

IN TIME OF LOSS, MAKE GOD YOUR BOSS: A Manni song. V:6

KAMMEN: *See entry in* HIGH SPEECH

KAVEN: The persistence of magic. The greater the magic, the longer it persists. Magic unrolls from the back, which means from the past. Hence, even when an object or a place seems to have lost its magic, a seed of that magic remains and can be awakened by those (like the Manni) who know how. VI:4, VI:26

KRA: A Manni cabin. Manni men live in a kra with all of their wives and offspring. When a Manni speaks of the "men of his kra," he means the men of his village, who are probably all kinsfolk. V:466, VI:34

KRA KAMMEN: This is the Manni term for the Doorway Cave. Jake thinks it means "house of bells," but it actually means "house of ghosts." To the Manni, the KAMMEN (TODASH chimes) are ghost bells. VI:34

MAGS AND BOBS: The magical tools which the Manni use to travel between worlds. *For more information, see* BRANNI BOB, *above, and* MANNI, *in* CHARACTERS. VI:7

MANNI KRA REDPATH-A-STURGIS: The Manni clan that lives in a village near Calla Bryn Sturgis. It is also the name of that village. VI:38

MANNI MANNERISMS: The Manni have many mannerisms which are as unique to their sect as are their blue cloaks, thick beards, and long fingernails. When a Manni covers his face with his hands, it is a gesture of deep religious dread (V:413). When Manni men have lost face, they tug their beards (VI:21). When Manni folk say, "The Eld," they raise their fists in the air with the first and fourth fingers pointed (V:31). Finally, when Manni folk shake their heads, they do so in long, sweeping arcs (V:414).

MANNI REDPATH: Another name for Manni Calla, the Manni village located two hours north of Calla Bryn Sturgis. V:399

NA'AR: The Manni term for Hell. V:408

NAY: No. V:411

OVER, THE: Manni term for the divine force. According to Mia, the Over is identical to the PRIM, or the primordial soup of creation. *For page references, see* MANNI: OVER, THE, *in* CHARACTERS

OVER-SAM KAMMEN! CAN-TAH KAMMEN! CAN-KAVAR KAMMEN! OVER-CAN-TAH! This is the praise-prayer Henchick gives when the Unfound Door opens. We are not given a translation. VI:42

OVER-SAM, OVER-KRA, OVER-CAN-TAH: A Manni prayer. We are not given a translation. VI:26

PASS OVER (TO PASS OVER): To time-travel or to travel between worlds. V:115

REDPATH KRA-TEN: Another term for Manni Calla, or the Manni village. VI:6, VI:7

SEEKING FOLK: Another descriptive term for the Manni. They are called seeking folk, far-seers, and far travelers because they travel between worlds. V:399

SENDERS: The senders are the most powerful of the Manni psychics and travelers. When Henchick and his followers reactivate the magic of the Unfound Door, they use the psychic strength of their strongest senders. VI:7, VI:39

SNIVELMENT (YOUNG SNIVELMENT): This is a Manni insult. Henchick calls Eddie Dean a young snivelment when he questions the power of the BRANNI BOB. *See entry in* MID-WORLD ARGOT. VI:29

TEMPA: The Tempa is the Manni Meeting Hall. VI:6

'TIS A GOOD NAME, AND A FAIR: Henchick says this to Roland. It is a way of saying that his name is good and honorable. V:416

TODASH: *See entry in* HIGH SPEECH

TODASH TAHKEN: *See entry in* HIGH SPEECH

WE ARE FAR-SEERS AND FAR TRAVELERS. WE ARE SAILORS ON KA'S WIND: This is how Henchick, the DINH of the Manni, describes his people. VI:38

CALLA BRYN STURGIS DIALECT

A HARD PULL THAT'D BE (THAT'D BE QUITE A PULL): That will be a tough one to pull off. V:224

A MAN WHO CAN'T STAY A BIT SHOULDN'T APPROACH IN THE FIRST PLACE: A man who can't spend the time to finish a conversation (or a visit) should have the sense not to begin one. V:477

A STONE MIGHT DRINK, IF IT HAD A MOUTH: This statement comes from Rosa Munoz, and is equivalent to "if pigs had wings, they would fly." VI:8

ADDLED (HE AIN'T HALF-ADDLED): Confused. *Addled* can also imply senility. V:346

ALL GODS IS ONE WHEN IT COMES TO THANKS: In other words, it doesn't matter which of Mid-World's gods you thank, as long as you thank one of them. V:206

AND MAY YOU HAVE TWICE THE NUMBER: *See* PLEASANT DAYS, AND MAY THEY BE LONG UPON THE EARTH, *below. See also* MAY YOUR DAYS BE LONG UPON THE EARTH, *in* MID-WORLD ARGOT

AND WITH THE BLESSING, WHAT AIN'T FINE WILL BE: With God's blessing, what isn't right will be put right. V:346

ANT-NOMIC: The people of the Calla use this word instead of *atomic*. V:151, V:340

ANY RO': *See entry in* MID-WORLD ARGOT

ARC: *See* GRAND CRESCENT, *below*

ARMYDILLO: Armadillo. V:578

ASK PARDON: I beg your pardon. V:123

BABBIES: Children. V:611

BABY BANGERS (LITTLE BANGERS): Small fireworks or Reap-crackers set off during festivals or holidays. Children love them. V:227

BAH AND BOLT: *See entry in* MID-WORLD ARGOT

BARREL-SHOOTERS: *See entry in* MID-WORLD ARGOT

BEG-MY-EAR? This phrase is equivalent to "Excuse me?" or "Pardon me?" V:124

BIDE (TO BIDE): To bide is to stay. V:322

BIG-BIG: Very much. It is usually heard in the context of "thankya big-big." It can also mean "a lot" or "a lot of." V:312, V:368

BLOODMUCK: Blood poisoning. V:651

BOAT, THE: *The boat* is a Calla term for the rear part of a cowboy's saddle, or the place where bedrolls are tied. V:557

BOLA: *See entry in* MID-WORLD ARGOT

BOOM-FLURRY: *Boom-flurry* is the Calla term for the nasty cacti which live in the desert dividing Calla Bryn Sturgis from Thunderclap. Boom-flurry eat humans. When they get all riled up (usually because a potential meal is passing by), they are said to be FASHED. V:571

BORDERLANDS: Calla Bryn Sturgis and the other Callas of the GRAND CRESCENT are located in the area known as the borderlands. The borderlands sit between Mid-World-that-was and End-World. *For page references, see entry in* MID-WORLD PLACES

BRIGHT OR DIM, THAT'S A LOT OF MEAT IN MOTION: Tian's da, Luke Jaffords, coined this phrase. He used it to describe his daughter Tia (Tian's twin), who was taken to Thunderclap by the Wolves and returned ROONT. Like the other roonts, Tia is a giantess, but her mental capabilities are extremely limited. V:8

BROWNIE: Eben Took uses this nasty phrase to describe Susannah Dean. (Gran-pere Jaffords uses it too, but Susannah doesn't take offense in Gran-pere's case, probably because he is so old and ADDLED that she figures he doesn't know any better.) Although many people in the CALLAS are dark-skinned, the term *brownie* refers specifically to a person who (in terms of our world's geography) is of African, or Afro-Caribbean, descent. V:359, V:405

BUCKA WAGGONS: *See entry in* MID-WORLD ARGOT

BUCKBOARD: *See entry in* MID-WORLD ARGOT

BUMPER: A bumper is a brimful glass of wine or beer. V:219

BUZZ-BALLS: *See* SNEETCHES, *below*

CALLA: According to Susannah Dean, the word *calla* means street or square. All of the villages in the BORDERLANDS are called callas. *For more information, see* BORDERLANDS, *in* MID-WORLD PLACES

CALLUM-KA: A callum-ka is a simple pullover worn by both the men and the women of the BORDERLANDS when the weather turns chilly. It looks like a boatneck. VI:229

CAN-AH, CAN-TAH, ANNAH, ORIZA: *See entry in* HIGH SPEECH

CAT-OIL: Rosa Munoz makes this arthritis rub. It contains mint and spriggum from the swamp, but its secret ingredient is ROCK CAT bile. It's potent stuff. V:242–43

CAVE OF VOICES: The Cave of Voices is located high in the arroyo country north of Calla Bryn Sturgis. Its name comes from the deep, noxious-smelling pit it contains—a pit that echoes with horrid, accusatory voices. What voices are heard depends upon who is there to hear them. Essentially, the demon of the cave (or its animating mechanism) taps into a listener's most guilty memories and then plays back the sobbing or angry voices of all those whom the listener believes he or she has wronged. Once Pere Callahan entered the Calla, the Cave of Voices was renamed Doorway Cave. This renaming came about because the freestanding magical door which Callahan used to enter the Calla (or was forced to use to enter the Calla) became a permanent fixture of the Cave. The door itself is known as the Unfound Door. *For more information, see* DOORWAY CAVE, *in* PORTALS

CHARY (YOU CHARY MAN): *See entry in* HIGH SPEECH

CHRIST AND THE MAN JESUS: The people of the Calla are a little confused about whether the Man Jesus is the same as Christ. V:6

COMMALA: The Commala is another name for the RICE SONG, which was known and sung throughout Mid-World, In-World, and the BORDERLANDS. On our KA-TET's first night in Calla Bryn Sturgis, Roland dances the Commala and wins the hearts (if not the trust) of the Calla FOLKEN.

In the borderlands, the term *commala* has more meanings than anywhere else in Roland's world. Here is a fairly complete collection of those definitions: 1. A variety of rice grown at the farthermost eastern edge of All-World. 2. Sexual intercourse. 3. Sexual orgasm (Q: Did'ee come commala? A: Aye, say thank ya, commala big-big.) 4. The commencement of a big, joyful feast. 5. A fork. 6. Schmoozing. 7. TO STAND COMMALA: literally speaking, this means to stand belly-to-belly. It is a slang term which translates as "to share secrets." 8. COME STURGIS COMMALA or COME BRYN COMMALA: literally speaking, to stand belly-to-belly with the entire community. 9. TO WET THE COMMALA: to irrigate the rice in a dry time. It can also mean to masturbate. 10. COMING COMMALA: a man who is losing his hair. 11. DAMP COMMALA: putting animals out to stud. 12. DRY COMMALA: gelded animals. 13. GREEN COMMALA: a virgin. 14. RED COMMALA: a menstruating woman. 15. SOF' COMMALA: a man who can no longer get an erection. 16. THE COMMALA DRAWS: the rocky arroyos north of Calla Bryn Sturgis. 17. COME-COME-COMMALA: the Rice Dance. 18. LOW COMMALA: *see* KI'BOX. 18. FUCK-COMMALA: a curse. 19. COMMALA-MOON: to stare aimlessly, or to be inattentive; to moon about. 20. STRONG COMMALA: a hard boy, or potentially dangerous man. V:208, V:230–33, V:325, V:484, V:486–87, V:489, V:587–89 *(words for the Commala)*, V:699, VI:229 *(Commala-moon)*

COOL EYES SEE CLEAR: A person who has an emotional distance from a situation will be able to see it in a more balanced way. V:323

COSY (A GOOD COSY, I HAVE A COSY FOR HIM): In our world, a cosy is a canopied corner seat for two. When Rosa Munoz says she has a "cosy" where Roland can sleep, she means she has a cot or a bed for him in a corner of her cabin. However, the sexual connotations of this phrase are fairly obvious. V:359, V:467

COWARDLY CUSTARDS: Cowards. V:360, V:362

COZENING BASTARDS: *See entry in* MID-WORLD ARGOT

CROSS-WAY: A person who holds to the Cross-way is a Christian. In other words, he or she follows the teachings of the crucified God. V:477

CRUSIE-FIX: *See* JESUS-TREE, *below*

CRY PARDON (CRY YOUR PARDON): *See entry in* MID-WORLD ARGOT

CULLIES: *See entry in* MID-WORLD ARGOT

DAIRTY: Dirty. V:402

DEEP HAIRCUT (A DEEP HAIRCUT): Margaret Eisenhart's term for the damage that can be done by an ORIZA. VII:83

DEVIL GRASS: *See entry in* MID-WORLD ARGOT; *see also* DEMONS/SPIR-ITS/ DEVILS: DEVIL GRASS, *in* CHARACTERS

DINH: *See entry in* HIGH SPEECH

DIVE DOWN: Like *yer bugger, dive down* is an exclamation often heard in the Calla. V:223

DO YA (IF IT DOES YA; DO YA, I BEG; MAY IT DO YA): This is one of the Callas' all-purpose terms. It is often used rhetorically. Depending on the circumstances, it can mean "if you want," "if you know what I mean," or "Beg pardon?" V:22, V:129, V:209, V:353, V:477

DO YA EITHER WAY: This term translates loosely as "It's up to you" or "Do whichever you feel like doing." V:310

DO YA FINE: *See* MAY IT DO YA FINE, *below*

DO YA KEN: *See* KEN, *below*

DO YA TAKE NO OFFENSE, I BEG: "No offense intended." It can also mean "please." V:123, V:139

DO YE, I BEG: This is a polite way to demand what you want. For example, if you are in the Town Gathering Hall and the speaker is saying something with which you strongly disagree, you might demand the OPOPANAX feather by saying, "I'd have the feather, do ye, I beg!" V:22

DO'EE: "Do you." V:154

DO'EE FOLLER? Do you follow what I'm saying? V:360

DON'T HURT A BOY TO SEE A WOMAN DO WELL: It's good for a boy to see a woman succeed. V:332

DOORWAY CAVE: *See* CAVE OF VOICES, *above*

DROTTA STICK: Dowsing stick. V:368

DRY-TWIST: *See entry in* MID-WORLD ARGOT

DUSTER: A duster is a kind of coat or rain-poncho. V:557

EARTHSHAKE: An earthquake. V:22

'EE (TO TELL 'EE): You (to tell you). V:417

EVEN HAND/ODD HAND: This is a way to take turns. For example, when Jake and Benny share Benny's room, Jake gets the bed on "odd hand" nights and Benny gets it on "even hand" nights. V:554

FAR-SEER: A telescope. V:573

FASHED: *See entry in* MID-WORLD ARGOT

FER GOOD OR NIS (FOR GOOD OR DIS): For good or ill. V:603

FOLKEN: *See entry in* MID-WORLD ARGOT

FOR GOOD OR DIS: *See* FER GOOD OR NIS, *above*

FOR THAT WE ALL SAY THANKYA: For that we are all grateful. V:350

FUCK-COMMALA: *See* COMMALA, *above*

FULL EARTH: *See entry in* MID-WORLD ARGOT

GALOOT: We have this word in our world too. It means a clumsy person. V:703

GARN (GARN, THEN): Go on. V:319, V:325, V:344

GET: When a man speaks of his get, he is referring to his begotten children. V:21

GITS: This word is used in our world too, especially in Britain. It translates loosely as "jerk." Neil Faraday calls Roland, his tet, and the townies who support them "numb gits" for thinking that they can defeat the WOLVES. V:612

GIVE YOU EVERY JOY OF THEM: May you enjoy them. V:173

GONE WORLD, THE: *See entry in* MID-WORLD ARGOT

GOODISH WANDER: Andy the Robot's term for a long walk. V:3

GRAF: *See entry in* MID-WORLD ARGOT

GRAND CRESCENT: The Grand Crescent (also known as the Arc, the Middle Crescent, and the Rim) is a mild arc of land located in the BORDERLANDS. It stretches for approximately six thousand miles and contains seventy CALLAS, or towns. Many of the Callas of the Crescent suffer from the predations of the WOLVES. Calla Bryn Sturgis, setting for *Wolves of the Calla,* is located about one-third of the way down from the Arc's northern tip. *See* BORDERLANDS: GRAND CRESCENT, *in* MID-WORLD PLACES

GRAN-PERE: Grandfather. V:251

GREEN CORN A-DAYO, THE: A popular song often sung in the Calla. It has twenty or thirty verses. V:5

GUT-TOSSERS: Doctors. V:630

HE NEVER HAD NO SHORTAGE OF THORN AND BARK: He never had a shortage of guts. V:348

HEAR ME, I BEG (HEAR, I BEG; HEAR ME WELL, DO YA, I BEG): If you're staying in the Calla and want people to listen to what you're about to say, or to contemplate what you've just said, then use this phrase. It can loosely be translated as "Hey" or "Listen up." The stock response (whether your listeners agree with you or not) is "We say thankee-sai." V:15, V:111, V:113, V:131, V:213, V:229

HOT-LUNG: This disease killed Benny Slightman's twin sister. Jake thinks hotlung is similar to pneumonia. V:385

HOW FROM HEAD TO FEET, DO YA, I BEG? This is the Calla way of saying "How are you doing?" The stock response is "I do fine, no rust, tell the gods thankee-sai." V:113

HOWGAN: Hogan or home. V:612

HUNTRESS MOON: *See entry in* MID-WORLD ARGOT

I BEG: *I beg* is a term which, in the Calla, is often tacked on to the end of sentences. *See* DO YA (DO YA, I BEG), *above*

I DO FINE, NO RUST, TELL THE GODS THANKEE-SAI: *See* HOW FROM HEAD TO FEET, DO YA, I BEG?, *above*

I SET MY WATCH AND WARRANT ON IT: *See entry in* MID-WORLD ARGOT

I WISH YOU JOY OF HIM: "I hope you enjoy dealing with him." Although this statement sounds pleasant enough, it is usually used sarcastically. In other words, "I hope you like dealing with the old bastard more than I do." V:347

I'D DO THAT MUCH, GODS HELP ME, AND SAY THANKEE: I'd do that much. V:128

IF IT DO YA FINE: This is another rhetorical statement. It can be used to mean "if that's all right by you," "if you want to," etc. V:127

IN THE END THE GROUND CURES ALL: In the end, death puts an end to all suffering. V:630

IT SPLIT THROG: It split three ways. V:359

IT'S TRIG AS A COMPASS: It sure is clever. V:130

JESUS-TREE: A Jesus-tree is a crucifix. Pere Callahan makes crucifixes (or "crusie-fixes") for the Christian converts of the Calla. V:2

JILLY: *See entry in* MID-WORLD ARGOT

KA-BABY (KA-BABBY, KA-BABBIES): This term can be used for little brothers and sisters or for young KA-TET mates. It can also be used to insult a person who appears to be too young for the title he or she holds. For example, George Telford refuses to acknowledge Jake as a gunslinger. Instead, he refers to him as Eddie's ka-babby. V:9, V:223

KAFFIN TWINS: *See entry in* MID-WORLD ARGOT

KEN (AS YE KEN, DO YE KEN, DO YA KENNIT, I KEN, I DON'T KEN-NIT, YE KEN): To ken is to know. "Do ye ken?" is the equivalent of both "Do you know?" and "You know what I mean?" V:23, V:131, V:158, V:347, V:659

KI'BOX: Tian Jaffords explains human motivation to Eddie Dean in terms of a man's (or a woman's) body parts. Tian states that a human being consists of three boxes—a HEADBOX (also called a thoughtbox), a TITBOX (also called a heartbox), and a SHITBOX (also known as a ki'box). A person strives highest when he or she is motivated by the head or the heart. Nastiness, selfishness, lust, etc., all come from the ki'box. Actions motivated by the ki'box are LOW COMMALA, or base actions born of base desires. V:630–31

KI'COME: Jake Chambers learned this term from his Calla friend Benny Slightman. *Ki'come* means "utter nonsense." It is probably related to KI'BOX. VII:396

KILLIN (YE FOOLISH KILLIN): Gran-pere Jaffords calls his grandson Tian a "foolish killin" for proposing that the men of the Calla stand up and fight the WOLVES. (According to Gran-pere, drunken men will stand up and fight, but sober men are cowards.) Although we are not given a literal translation of *killin,* we know that Granpere thinks Tian's idea is admirable but unfeasible. Stephen King tells us that *killin* is a harsh word, but it can obviously be used in sadness as well. V:13

LADY OF THE PLATE: The Lady of the Plate is no other than Lady ORIZA, the rice goddess. Although the story of Lady Oriza was known throughout Mid-World-that-was, the tale of her confrontation with the harrier Gray Dick has special significance in the BORDERLANDS. In honor of Lady Oriza's clever revenge against her father's murderer, many of the Calla's women practice throwing sharpened plates. Their deadly aim helps Roland's ka-tet win their battle against the WOLVES. *See both* ORIZA, LADY *and* ORIZA, SISTERS OF, *both in* CHARACTERS

LADY ORIZA: *See* LADY OF THE PLATE, *above, and* ORIZA, *below*

LAKE-BOAT MART: The lake-boat marts are wide flatboats that are paddle-wheel-driven and gaily painted. They are covered with shops and float down the River Whye, selling wares. According to Gran-pere Jaffords, some of the women who work on these boats are as dark-skinned as Susannah Dean. V:211

LAST TIME PAYS FER ALL: Gran-pere Jaffords uses this term to express his desire for vengeance against the WOLVES. When the Wolves descend this last time, he says, the people of the Calla will pay them back for all their previous attacks. V:369

LEG-BREAKERS (LEG-SMASHERS): These are the holes found in LOOSE GROUND. Leg-breakers are often nestled in innocent-looking weeds and high grass, so they can easily trap unwary or hurried people. Animals fall foul of them as well. There are many leg-breakers in Son of a Bitch, Tian Jaffords's worthless field. V:2, V:347

LEGBROKE: If you are lying on the ground legbroke, you have broken your leg. V:1

LEG-SMASHER: *See* LEG-BREAKERS, *above*

LIGHT-STICKS: These are the fire-hurling weapons used by the WOLVES. They look like the light sabers used in the *Star Wars* films. V:26, V:151

LOAD (THE LOAD): This term describes the stance taken by a woman (or boy) about to throw two ORIZAS at once. The stance was invented by Susannah Dean, but it was named by Margaret Eisenhart. VII:83

LONG DAYS AND PLEASANT NIGHTS: *See entry in* MID-WORLD ARGOT

LOOK HERE AT US, DO YA, AND SAY THANKEE: "Look at this" or "Look at what we've done." V:156

LOOSE GROUND: This term is used by the old folks of Calla Bryn Sturgis to describe ground riddled with holes and underground caves. The holes are called LEG-BREAKERS. Some of the Calla FOLKEN believe that bogarts live in the caves under loose ground. V:2

LOW COACHES: Like BUCKA WAGGONS, a low coach is a type of horse-drawn vehicle used in the CALLAS. (*For* BUCKA WAGGON, *see entry in* MID-WORLD ARGOT) V:21

LOW COMMALA: *See* KI'BOX *and* COMMALA, *both above*

MADRIGAL: Tian Jaffords wants to grow this valuable crop in his field known as Son of a Bitch. But like PORIN, which his mother dreamed would grow in this rock-strewn waste-ground, it will probably die. The only thing that Tian is likely to grow in Son of a Bitch is a good crop of blisters. V:1

MAN JESUS: This is the Callas' term for Jesus. It can also be used as a curse. V:6

MANY AND MANY-A: *See entry in* MID-WORLD ARGOT

MAY I SPELL YE A BIT? Shall I take a turn? V:129

MAY IT DO YA FINE: This can be used in place of "you're welcome." V:133, V:219, V:320, V:373

MAY THE SUN NEVER FALL IN YOUR EYES: *See entry in* MID-WORLD ARGOT

MAYHAP: *See entry in* MID-WORLD ARGOT

MIDS, THE: Another term for Mid-World, which lies to the west of the BORDERLANDS. V:25

MID-SUMMER: *See entry in* MID-WORLD ARGOT

MILK-SICK: This disease affects milk cows. It can kill them. V:8

MOIT: *See entry in* MID-WORLD ARGOT

MORTATA: Literally speaking, the mortata is the death dance. It is the opposite of the RICE DANCE (or COME-COME-COMMALA), which celebrates the fecundity of the rice. Some of the Calla FOLKEN suspect that Roland dances the mortata even better than he dances the commala. They have a point. V:607

MUMBLETY-PEG: *See entry in* MID-WORLD ARGOT

MUSICA: *See entry in* MID-WORLD ARGOT

NAR: No. V:332

NAY (NAYYUP): No. V:225, V:402

NEW EARTH: *See entry in* MID-WORLD ARGOT

NOBBUT (HE WON'T HAVE NOBBUT TO DO WITH ME): Nothing (he won't have anything to do with me). V:346

NUMMORE: No more, or no longer. V:322

NUP: No. V:209

OGGAN: This is the smooth-packed dirt used to make roads. V:654, VI:25, VI:272

OPOPANAX: Whenever a male resident of Calla Bryn Sturgis has something important to share with the *folken,* he sends around the opopanax feather. If enough men touch the feather, then a meeting is held at the Town Gathering Hall. The feather is a rust-red, ancient plume. In our world, the opopanax is not a kind of bird but a gum resin used in perfumery. In the novel *Black House,* the word *opopanax* becomes a sinister mantra for the main character, Jack Sawyer. As he states near the beginning of the book, "I'm falling apart. Right here and now. Forget I said that. The savage opopanax has gripped me in its claws, shaken me with the fearful opopanax of its opopanax arms, and intends to throw me into the turbulent Opopanax River, where I shall meet my opopanax." V:20–21

ORIZA: An Oriza is a plate made from a light metal alloy, probably titanium. Unlike most plates, Orizas aren't made for dining but for flinging. In fact, the deadly Orizas—which are manufactured by the ladies of Calla Sen Chre and thrown by the SISTERS OF ORIZA—are the deadliest weapons found in any of the Callas.

The Sisters of Oriza practice plate-throwing in memory of Lady Oriza, Goddess of the Rice, who invited her father's murderer over to dinner and then sliced off his head by flinging her specially made plate at him. Orizas are decorated with a delicate blue webbing which depicts the seedling rice plant. Two of the rice stalks on the edge of the plate cross, forming the Great Letter *Zn*, which means both "here" and "now." Luckily, the letter *Zn* also marks the one edge which is safe to hold. (Otherwise, an unwary person might absentmindedly pick up a plate and slice off a finger.) Beneath the plate is a small whistle, so the plate sings as it flies through the air. Interestingly enough, the Orizas bear a strong resemblance to a plate once owned by Susannah Dean's maternal aunt, Sister Blue. Detta Walker broke this *forspecial* plate in a fit of temper. *For page references, see* ORIZA, SISTERS OF, *in* CHARACTERS

OTTEN ELSE (I NEVER CONSIDERED OTTEN ELSE): Anything else (I never considered anything else). V:615

OUT-WORLD: To the people of Calla Bryn Sturgis, Out-World refers to the area west of the BORDERLANDS, close to Mid-World-that-was. V:8

PARD: Pardner, partner, or comrade. V:655

PEAK SEAT: *See entry in* MID-WORLD ARGOT

PLEASANT DAYS AND MAY THEY BE LONG UPON THE EARTH: This greeting is a variant of MAY YOUR DAYS BE LONG UPON THE EARTH, a phrase heard all over Mid-World. If someone greets you in this manner, your response should be "And may you have twice the number." V:3

PLOW-BREAKER (PLOW-BUSTER): A large fieldstone. V:2, V:349

POISON FLURRY: Poison flurry is a lot like poison ivy—the bane of Boy Scouts. If you find yourself needing to squat in Mid-Forest, make sure you don't wipe with this particular plant. Otherwise, you will develop a rash in a very uncomfortable place. V:137, V:644

PORIN: This is a spice of great worth. Tian Jaffords's mother thought it would grow in the family field known as Son of a Bitch. Unfortunately, the only things able to grow in that field are rocks, blisters, and busted hopes. V:1

PULLS: Corn-shuck wraps used for rolling tobacco. V:320

REAP: *See entry in* MID-WORLD ARGOT

REMUDA: A remuda is a corral. V:321, V:336

RICE SONG/RICE DANCE: The Rice Song and the Rice Dance (jointly known as the COMMALA) are sung, danced, and loved throughout Mid-World. They celebrate the planting of rice and are (in essence) a fertility rite. *For page references, see* COMMALA *in* CALLA BRYN STURGIS DIALECT

RIM: *See* GRAND CRESCENT *in* CALLA BRYN STURGIS DIALECT

'RIZA (BY 'RIZA): Lady Oriza is the rice goddess, who is worshipped all over Mid-World. *By 'Riza* is equivalent to *by God.* It can also be used in a stronger fashion. If you cry out because your "by 'Riza" eyes have been hurt, you mean your "goddamned eyes" have been hurt. Also, when the Sisters of Oriza throw their sharpened plates (known as ORIZAS), they often cry "'Riza!" as they fling. V:360, V:572

ROCK CAT: *Rock cat* is the Calla term for the wild cats that live in the desert east of the River Whye. Roland thinks they are probably pumas or cougars. Rock cat bile is the secret ingredient in Rosa Munoz's arthritis rub. V:340

ROONT: In Calla Bryn Sturgis, as in the other CALLAS of the CRESCENT, twins are the norm and singletons are rarities. Once a generation, the green-cloaked WOLVES sweep out of Thunderclap to kidnap one of every pair of pre-pubescent twins. Most of the children are returned, but they are returned roont, or ruined.

A roont child is a mentally handicapped child. Few of them can speak. Some cannot be toilet-trained. No matter how bright children were before being taken to Thunderclap, they return mentally challenged and with a central part of themselves missing. The roonts grow to prodigious size, but they die young. For roonts, both growing and dying is excruciatingly painful. *For page references, see* CALLA BRYN STURGIS CHARACTERS: ROONTS, *in* CHARACTERS

RUSTIES: *See entry in* MID-WORLD ARGOT

SALIDE: Although we're not told exactly what a salide is, it seems likely that it's either a blanket or cloak. V:234

SAUCY SUSAN: Saucy Susan is a flower with a lemony, faintly astringent smell. Rosa Munoz keeps a few sprigs of Saucy Susan in her privy. V:475

SAY SORRY: Sorry. VI:209

SAY THANKYA (SAY THANKEE, SAY THANKYA BIG-BIG): "Thank you," "thanks," or "thanks a lot!" V:124, V:130, V:143, V:265

SAY TRUE? Do you mean it? Really? V:583, VII:129

SEEN THE BOAT SHE CAME IN: Although Roland thinks about this phrase in New York, it originates in Calla Bryn Sturgis. It comments on striking family resemblances. VII:493

SEMINON: This is the name given to the Calla's late-autumn windstorms, the ones that come just before true winter. In the Calla they say, "Seminon comin', warm days go runnin'." Lord Seminon is also the name of a God whom Lady ORIZA wanted to marry. However, Lord Seminon preferred Oriza's sister, and Oriza never forgave him. *See* SEMINON, LORD, *and* ORIZA, LADY, *both under* ORIZA, LADY, *in* CHARACTERS

'SENERS: *See entry in* MID-WORLD ARGOT

SET US ON WITH A WORD: Say grace for us. *See also* WILL YOU NOT SET ME ON WITH A WORD, *in* MID-WORLD ARGOT. V:354

SHARPROOT: *See entry in* MID-WORLD ARGOT

SHOOTING-IRON: *See entry in* MID-WORLD ARGOT

SHOR'BOOTS: The heavy clodhoppers, or short boots, worn in the Calla. V:14, V:18, V:21, V:136

SHORT BEER: In Calla Bryn Sturgis, a short beer is a beer served in a small water glass. V:656

SINCE TIME WAS TOOTHLESS: A great phrase that basically means "since before anyone can remember" or "forever." V:360

SINGLETON: A child born without a twin. In Calla Bryn Sturgis, singletons, and not twins, are the rarities. V:21, V:113, V:344

SINGLETS: *See entry in* MID-WORLD ARGOT

SISTERS OF ORIZA: The Sisters of Oriza are a female society, or network, found throughout the CALLAS of the BORDERLANDS. Although they function like a ladies' auxiliary—catering for town events, gossiping, etc.—their true purpose is to practice throwing sharpened, platelike ORIZAS in honor of Lady Oriza, goddess of the rice. The deadly skills of the Sisters help Roland and his KA-TET defeat the WOLVES in the final showdown on East Road. *For page references, see* ORIZA, SISTERS OF, *in* CHARACTERS

SLAGGIT! A curse. It must be a bad one, since Gran-pere Jaffords's use of it at the dinner table makes the children giggle. V:355

SMALLHOLDS: The small family-run farms of the Calla. Most of them are located on the fertile banks of the River Whye. V:208

SMALL-SMALL (SAY ANY SMALL-SMALL, AN' SNAY DOWN SMALL-SMALL): Very small. V:347, V:353, V:361

SMOKEWEED: Tobacco. V:403

SNEETCHES (BUZZ-BALLS, STEALTHIES): These flying metal balls are some of the most fearsome weapons used by the invading WOLVES against the people of the Callas. The sneetches seek their targets, and once they lock on, they put forth whirling blades that are as sharp as razors and can strip a man of flesh in five seconds. As Jake Chambers and Eddie Dean find out when they take a close look at one of these weapons, they are based upon the snitches found in the *Harry Potter* novels. Although neither Eddie nor Jake know who Harry Potter is (they left our world too early), both would have been interested to find out that the original snitches are little gold balls used in the game of Quidditch and aren't dangerous at all. (That is, unless you fall out of the sky while chasing one.) V:26, V:151, VI:25

SNUG: A snug is a small cottage. VI:13

SO I DO: This is yet another of the rhetorical phrases used in the Calla. People tack it on the end of sentences. For example, someone might look at a dying fire and maintain, "I see a few sparks yet, so I do." V:127

SO IT IS: This is another phrase which the Calla FOLKEN tack on the end of sentences. It emphasizes what a person has just uttered. This phrase can also mean "you're right." V:226

SOF' CALIBERS: Sof'calibers are guns which are too old or too rusty to shoot. Given that *sof' commala* refers to a man who can no longer make iron at the proverbial feminine forge, you'd better be pretty damn sure that a man's calibers *are* sof' before you tell him they are. Otherwise, he might be so insulted that he shoots you. V:20

SOH (YOUNG SOH): The people of the Calla seem to use the term *soh* rather than *sai* when they are addressing a young person. Hence they often call Jake *Jake-soh*. V:150, V:417, V:489

SPEAK A WORD O' BEGGARY: If you speak a word o' beggary to someone, you're crossing them, defying them, or arguing with them. V:359

SPEAK YOU WELL: This can either mean "you speak well" or be a request that you "speak well." V:216

SPEAKIES: A breed of demon found in the caves beneath LOOSE GROUND. V:2

SPELL YE (MAY I SPELL YE ON THAT CHAIR A BIT?): *See* MAY I SPELL YE, *above*

SPRIGGUM: Rosalita Munoz puts spriggum from the swamp into her CAT-OIL (her arthritis rub). We're not told what spriggum is, but we know it must be potent. V:243

SQUABBOT: This is part of a phrase uttered by an angry Neil Faraday during one of the Town Gathering Hall meetings held in Calla Bryn Sturgis. When Roland and his tet try to convince the townsfolk to stand up to the WOLVES, a cynical Faraday responds, "'Ay'll take 'een babbies anyroa' and burn 'een squabbot town flat." Roland and his friends find Faraday's accent almost incomprehensible, but it's obvious that he thinks that the Wolves, and not our tet, will triumph. Luckily, he's wrong. V:611

STEALTHIES: *See* SNEETCHES, *above*

STUBBORN AS A STICK: Incredibly stubborn. V:329

STUFF YOUR PRATTLE: Shut up. V:572

STUFFY-GUYS: *See entry in* MID-WORLD ARGOT

SURELY YOU'VE GOT A MOIT MORE GUTS THAN THAT: *See entry in* MID-WORLD ARGOT

SWARD (GREENSWARD): A sward is an expanse of short grass. Hence, a greensward is an expanse of short green grass. V:614

TA'EN: Taken. V:149

TELL GODS THANKEE (TELL THE GODS THANKEE): "Thank God" or "praise be to God" or "thankfully." V:149, V:206

TELL IT ANY OLD WAY IT DOES YA FINE: This is a soothing and reassuring phrase which is meant to set a person at ease so that he or she can tell the tale that needs telling. V:265

TELL ME, I BEG: Tell me. V:225

THANKEE-SAI: *See entry in* MID-WORLD ARGOT

THANKYA BIG-BIG: "Thank you very much!" V:312

THAT BEATS THE DRUM! DON'T IT JUST: This saying is equivalent to a rather strange phrase found in our world—"that just takes the cake." V:353

THE JIMMY JUICE I DRANK LAST NIGHT: A song sung in the Calla. Andy the Messenger Robot likes to sing it. V:141

THOSE WHO HOLD CONVERSATION WITH THEMSELVES KEEP SORRY COMPANY: In other words, you shouldn't talk to yourself. V:207

THROAT-TAPPING: *See entry in* MID-WORLD ARGOT

THROG: *See* IT SPLIT THROG, *above*

TIME HAS SOFTENED: *See entry in* MID-WORLD ARGOT

TO LEAD US ALL TO BLUNDER WI' NO WAY BACK: To lead us into imminent danger with no way out. V:133

TODASH: *See entry in* HIGH SPEECH

TONGUE-WHIPPING: A tongue-lashing. V:572

TRIG: Clever. *Trig* implies an ability to read and understand other people's thoughts and motivations. It can also imply slyness. V:656

TRUE AS EVER WAS: Absolutely true. V:367

TRUM: *See entry in* MID-WORLD ARGOT

'TWERE: "It was." For example, "'Twere his eyes that frightened me." V:131

TWIN-TELEPATHY: *Twin-telepathy* describes the telepathy—or thought-sharing—which twins often experience. In the later books of the Dark Tower series, we find out that the WOLVES steal twins so that the servants of the Crimson King can harvest the brain chemical which causes twin-telepathy. They then feed this chemical (in pill form) to the BREAKERS working in the DEVAR-TOI. V:580

UNFOUND DOOR: An Unfound Door has the symbol for "unfound" written upon it. The magical portal in the CAVE OF VOICES bears this mark. *For page references, see* DOORWAY CAVE *and* DOORWAYS BETWEEN WORLDS: THE ARTIST'S DOOR, *both in* PORTALS

WEIRDLING WEATHER: Strange or ominous weather. V:601

WELL-MET: *See entry in* MID-WORLD ARGOT

WHAT IS IT FASHES AND DIDDLES THEE S'SLOW, OAFING: What is it that upsets you and makes you so slow? V:603

WILL IT DRAW WATER?: Will it work? V:491

WITTLES AND RATIONS: Food. V:358

WOLF'S EVE: The night before the WOLVES attack. V:608

WOLVES: The green-cloaked predators who come sweeping out of Thunderclap every generation to steal one of each pair of prepubescent twins born into the CALLAS of the GRAND CRESCENT. The Wolves ride gray horses and wear masks which look like the faces of snarling wolves, yet their bodies resemble those of giant men. At the end of *Wolves of the Calla,* we find out that the Wolves are actually robots, and beneath their clothing they look a lot like Andy, Calla Bryn Sturgis's treacherous Messenger Robot. *For page references, see* WOLVES, *in* CHARACTERS

YAR: Yes. V:131

YE: You. V:411

YE DARE NOT: You wouldn't dare. V:411

YEAR END GATHERING: *See entry in* MID-WORLD ARGOT

YER BUGGER: The equivalent of "You bet your ass." V:149, V:151, V:222–23

YON: "Over yonder." V:207

YOU SAY TRUE AND I SAY THANKYA (YOU SPEAK TRUE AND I SAY THANKEE): "You speak truth and I say thank you." Also, "I agree with you." V:310

Zn: *See entry in* HIGH SPEECH

END-WORLD TERMS

ALGUL SIENTO: *See* DEVAR-TOI, *below*

ASIMOV ROBOTS: Intelligent robots, such as Nigel and Andy, built by North Central Positronics. Logic faults are quite common in these models. VII:156

BASCOMB: A type of wicker basket that has a lid and handles. It is a TAHEEN word. VII:347

BECOMING: For Mia, "becoming" was the process of becoming human, or for transforming from a creature of the PRIM into a being of flesh and blood. The bizarre surgery which made this transformation possible took place in the Fedic Dogan. *Becoming* is also the term that the CAN-TOI use for their own process of becoming human. However, despite all their efforts, the only thing that the can-toi are becoming is uglier. It is probably almost impossible for the can-toi to become human since they can't comprehend true human emotion. Hence, their humanoid faces—made from a kind of living latex—will never be more than masks to cover their lice-infested rat snouts. VI:251, VII:235, VII:293

BHST: Blue Heaven Standard Time. This is the way they measure time in the DEVAR-TOI. VII:271

BLUE HEAVEN: *See* DEVAR-TOI, *below*

BREAKERS (BEAM BREAKERS): The Beam Breakers are a group of psychics who were tricked by servants of the Crimson King into taking the perfect "job of a lifetime." It certainly turns out to be a lifetime job, since none of them can leave the DEVAR-TOI, or Breaker prison, until the universe collapses. Each day, the Breakers go to the Devar-Toi STUDY, where they focus their special skills on eroding the weakened Beams. *For page references, see* BREAKERS, *in* CHARACTERS

CHILDREN OF RODERICK: *See entry in* MID-WORLD ARGOT

CLAN-FAM: *Clan-fam* denotes a CAN-TOI clan family. The clan-fam gives a low man or low woman a human name as part of their process of BECOM-ING. The clan-fam name is a maturity-marker. VII:293, VII:617

CLOSIES: A term used by a washerboy in the Dixie Pig who warns Jake Chambers about Sayre and his "closies" or henchmen. VII:84

CRAZY, THE: This form of madness afflicts many in Thunderclap, especially the RODS. VII:300

CUT-EM-UP-MAN: A coroner. VII:106

DARKS: A dark is a unit of expelled psychic energy and is used to describe units of Breaker Force. In other words, it is a way to measure the amount of psychic energy which the Breakers emit at any one time—a force which is trained to erode the Beams. Ted Brautigan's talent as a facilitator means that he raises the Breaker Force exponentially every time he enters the STUDY where the Breakers do their work. With Ted around, the Breaker Force radiating from this room can jump from fifty breaks an hour to five hundred breaks an hour. VII:236, VII:295

DEEP TELEMETRY: *See* TELEMETRY, *below*

DESERT DOGS: This is the End-World term for coyotes. VII:289

DEVAR-TETE: *See entry in* HIGH SPEECH

DEVAR-TOI: The BREAKER prison located in End-World. *For page references, see entry in* PORTALS.

DON'T WORRY ABOUT THE EGGS UNTIL YOU'RE ALMOST HOME: This phrase was originally used by the grandfather of Pimli Prentiss, the Devar Master. VII:232

EAR-STYKE: Like boils, eczema, headaches, and nosebleeds, this is one of the many ailments that can affect people in Thunderclap. VII:494

EATING SICKNESS: A nasty cancer that moves quickly and painfully through the body. The RODS often suffer from it. VII:300

END-TIMES: According to those who work in the DEVAR-TOI, End-Times are almost upon us. This is because the Tower and the Beams are almost ready to collapse. VII:226

ENJOY THE CRUISE, TURN ON THE FAN, THERE'S NOTHING TO LOSE, SO WORK ON YOUR TAN: This saying is popular among the BREAKERS. Rather disturbing when you consider that they are working to destroy all the known universes. VII:289

FACILITATOR: A facilitator is a psychic whose gift includes the ability to increase the power of other psychics. Ted Brautigan is a facilitator. VII:243

FLOATERS: CAN-TOI guards that roam about the DEVAR-TOI. VII:293

GMS: GMS stands for the General Mentation Systems, found in North Central Positronics robots. There are two such systems—rational and irrational. VII:155–56

GOOD MIND: Good Mind is what rises from the BREAKERS when they work. It is a kind of psychic happy-gas. Not only does it dispel depression and pique, but it also increases the telepathic abilities of ordinary HUMES. VII:242

HINKY (HINKY-DI-DI): This is a term used by Finli O'Tego. (He picked it up from the HUME crime novels which he likes to read.) When something feels hinky-di-di, it means that it doesn't feel quite right. Trouble is on the wind. VII:226, VII:239

HUME: This term refers to humans. The CAN-TOI, who believe they are BECOMING human, find it demeaning. VII:9, VII:235

I TELL YOU TRUTH: This TAHEEN gesture is similar to the one used by Roland. The taheen (assuming he has hands) lays his right forefinger over a circle made by his left thumb and index finger. VII:238

KA-HUME: A term used by the GRANDFATHERS for human beings. VII:9

KEYSTONE EARTH: Keystone Earth, also called Keystone World, is our world—the one where Stephen King writes his books and where we read them. Keystone Earth is the only world in which time flows in a singular direction, or where (in the words of Dorrance Marstellar, a character from Stephen King's novel *Insomnia*) things that are "Done-bun-can't-be-undone." Keystone Earth is real in the same way that Mid-World was real before the Beams began to weaken. The ka of our world is NINETEEN. The ka of Mid-World/End-World is ninety-nine. When the two come together, as in the year 1999, cataclysmic events can take place. *For page references, see* KEYSTONE WORLDS, *in* PORTALS

KI'CAN: Shit-people or shit-*folken*. This is Ted Brautigan's term for the guards at the DEVAR-TOI. VII:286

KI'-DAM: Shit-for-brains. This is Dinky Earnshaw's term for sai Prentiss, the Devar Master. VII:197, VII:207, VII:262

LIGHT-STICKS: *See entry in* CALLA BRYN STURGIS DIALECT

MAKERS: The term that the ASIMOV ROBOTS use for the Old Ones. VII:156

MOMPS: A HUME disease. VII:356

MORKS: This is another term for a BREAKER. It comes from the 1970s American sitcom *Mork & Mindy*. Like the alien Mork of the series, Breakers don't have the same emotional makeup as other human beings. They tend to be disconnected from their fellow humans and so cannot form the emotional bonds that others feel. As a result, many of them are sociopaths. According to Ted Brautigan, most morks are selfish introverts masquerading as rugged individualists. Ted Brautigan, Dinky Earnshaw, and Sheemie Ruiz are three exceptions to this rule. VII:268–69

OTHER-SIDE WORLDS: To the Warriors of the Scarlet Eye living in End-World, our world is one of many other-side worlds. VII:300

PRECOG/POSTCOG: Precogs are psychics who see events before they happen. Postcogs are psychics who pick up on events that have already taken place. VII:238, VII:271

PROG: Dinky Earnshaw's word for reading thoughts. VII:292

REAL WORLD: Keystone Earth. VII:300

RED DEATH: *See entry in* MID-WORLD ARGOT

SHEEP GOD ('HEEP GOD): The GRANDFATHERS' term for the Christian God. VII:12

SHUFFLEFOOT BAH-BO: This is Pimli Prentiss's term for the CHILD OF RODERICK named Haylis. VII:346

SIM SEX: The kind of sex which most of the BREAKERS end up having. You can have sim sex with anyone you like. The only problem is that it's an illusion. The other person will seem real enough, but if you blow on them, the part your breath touches disappears. (Not a very nice thought.) In essence, sim sex is a fancy form of masturbation. VII:210–11

SNEETCHES: *See entry in* CALLA BRYN STURGIS DIALECT

STUDY, THE: The room in the DEVAR-TOI where the BREAKERS work on breaking the Beams. It looks like a library in a nineteenth-century men's club. *See* DEVAR-TOI, *in* PORTALS

SWING-GUARDS: The guards of the DEVAR-TOI. The term probably refers to either a particular rotation on the compound or to the changing of the guards. VII:237

TELEMETRY: Telemetry (or Deep Telemetry) is the machinery used in the DEVAR-TOI to detect psychic bursts. No one is sure exactly what this machinery was originally made to measure, but one suspects it was to detect telepathy, teleportation, or even deep tremors in the fabric of reality. VII:344

TELEPATH: Someone who can read other people's thoughts. VII:275

TELEPORTS: Teleports are psychics who can teleport, or move from one place to another using mind energy. Teleportation is the one wild talent that the DEVAR staff fear. VI:238–39

THINKING CAPS: The thinking caps are, in actuality, antithinking caps. The HUME and CAN-TOI guards at the DEVAR-TOI wear them so that the BREAKERS can't read their thoughts. The small radar dishes located on top of the heads of the robotic WOLVES are also called thinking caps. VII:171, VII:288

VAI, VAI, LOS MONSTROS PUBES, TRE CANNITSEN FOUNS: These words (which are never translated) are spoken by a huge warthog-headed chef at the Dixie Pig just before Jake Chambers cuts off its head with an ORIZA. The quote continues, "San Fai, can dit los! . . . Can foh pube ain-tet can fah! She-so pan! Vai! And eef you won'd scrub, don'd even stard!" VII:82

WE MUST ALL WORK TOGETHER TO CREATE A FIRE-FREE ENVI-RONMENT: These signs are posted all over the DEVAR-TOI. VII:236

WILD TALENT: A pulp-fiction term for psychic ability. Wild talents can manifest as precognition, postcognition, telepathy, or even teleportation. VII:238–39, VII:277

APPENDIX II:
A BRIEF HISTORY OF MID-WORLD[1]
(ALL-WORLD-THAT-WAS)
AND OF ROLAND DESCHAIN,
WARRIOR OF THE WHITE

In the beginning there was only the Prim, the magical soup of creation. From the Prim arose Gan, spirit of the Dark Tower, who spun the physical universe from his navel. Gan tipped the world with his finger and set it rolling. This forward movement was Time.

The magical tide of the Prim receded from the earth but left behind it the Tower and the Beams, the fundamental structures which hold the macroverse together. Enough magic was left in Tower and Beams to last for eternity, but the Great Old Ones, in their hubris, decided to remake Beams and Tower using their technology. Magic is eternal, but machinery (like the men who build it) is mortal. Hence, the great technological advances of the Old People made possible not just the destruction of one level of the Tower but the obliteration of all of them.

The Great Old Ones had the knowledge of gods, and so, like reckless demiurges, they assumed that they had the right to manipulate reality with impunity. For their own decadent entertainment, they created doorways that led from their world to other *wheres* and *whens* on every level of the Tower. They built great cities where centralized computers and Asimov robots catered to their every need.

But still, it wasn't enough. The Old People designed Dogans, where magic and technology could be joined. Here, their scientists/alchemists created new diseases, such as the Red Death, and terrible weapons which they launched against their enemies, poisoning earth, air, and water. Soon every living creature on the surface of the earth became contaminated. Animals and humans gave birth to mutants, and Mid-World was reduced to a great poisoned wasteland.

The time of the Great Old Ones was almost over. But before they disappeared from their level of the Tower, the Old People made a final act of atonement. To

1. As readers of the Dark Tower series know, Mid-World was originally the name of an ancient kingdom, one that tried to preserve culture and knowledge during a great age of darkness. However, throughout the series Stephen King also uses *Mid-World* as a general term for Roland Deschain's level of the Tower. I have followed this practice.

make amends for their atrocities and to pay penance for the sins they had committed against the earth and against each other, they built twelve giant mechanical Guardians to watch over the twelve entrances into, and out of, Mid-World. These Guardians—Bear and Turtle, Elephant and Wolf, Rat and Fish, Bat and Hare, Eagle and Lion, Dog and Horse—were cyborg versions of the twelve immortal animal totems left by the Prim to guard the Beams.

Yet even this final act of atonement proved misguided. The fabric of reality, rewoven by the Great Old Ones, was destined to fray. Less than three thousand years after being built in the farthest reaches of Out-World, the giant cyborg Bear Guardian, Shardik, ran mad. The mechanical Beams (already eroded) began—one by one—to topple. The computers and robots built by the ancient company North Central Positronics (a leader in mind-to-mind communications since the ten thousands) became dangerously psychotic and either murdered their masters' descendants or joined forces with the Crimson King, that ancient Lord of Chaos. And as the Old Ones' technological web collapsed, whole worlds were destroyed by plagues like the superflu.

But life is striving to be life, and against all odds it will defy the Outer Dark. The Tower had more than a little of its old magic left, and from its ancient gray-black foundations deep in the red rose-fields of End-World, it sent out a call. From In-World-that-was, it drew forth the world's last gunslinger—final descendant of Arthur Eld, King of All-World-that-was, Warrior of the White, and Guardian of the Tower. Although this gunslinger believed that his only ambition was to climb to the top of the Tower to meet whatever being resided there, ka had greater plans for him.

Like his enemy the Red King, Lord of Discordia, Roland Deschain of the White both *darkles* and *tincts*. Leaping from one level of the Tower to another, he pursues his vision and his quest. With the help of a ka-tet drawn from other levels of the Tower (ones where the great city of Lud is called New York, and where North Central Positronics and the Sombra Corporation have not yet poisoned the ambitions of their culture), he opposes Discordia and fulfills the will of the White.

What began, in *The Gunslinger,* as the journey of a goal-obsessed loner, becomes, in *The Dark Tower,* a great journey of redemption and sacrifice. End-World lies ahead, and the Tower waits.

TIME LINE FOR THE DARK TOWER SERIES

Books I–VII and "The Little Sisters of Eluria"

B.R.B.—Before Roland's Birth
A.R.B.—After Roland's Birth

2,700–1,700 B.R.B.
The Great Old Ones, rulers of All-World-that-was, create the cyborg
Guardians to atone for their sins against the earth and against each other.[2]

2,200 B.R.B.
Due to radiation poisoning and other types of fallout, most humans are
already sterile. Women who can conceive give birth to mutants.[3]
Although rumor states that Castle Discordia, in End-World,
is haunted again, a few stoic individuals continue to occupy End-World's
towns and villages. They will soon regret it.
A jar of the Great Old Ones' demonstuff cracks open, loosening plague.
The Red Death wipes out the people of Fedic.[4]

1,800 B.R.B.
The Great Old Ones finally destroy themselves.
They disappear from the earth.[5]

---

2. III:33—Shardik is two thousand to three thousand years old when our ka-tet finds him in the Great West Woods. III:38—Creating the cyborg Guardians was the Great Old Ones' final act of atonement for the harm they had done to the earth, and to each other. To pinpoint a time-line date, I counted backward from our ka-tet's adventures in the Great West Woods. At that point, Roland is approximately 336 years old. (I explain Roland's age in footnote 27.) Since Shardik's age is approximate, I thought this date should be approximate also. 3,000 − 336 A.R.B. = 2,664 B.R.B. 2,000 − 336 A.R.B. = 1,664 B.R.B., or approximately 2,700 B.R.B. to 1,700 B.R.B.

3. VI:243—The Red Death affected Fedic two dozen centuries, or twenty-four hundred years, before the coming of the Wolves. Most people were already birthing monsters. Mid-World's many mutants came into being thanks to the Great Old Ones' disastrous wars. For more information, see MUTANTS, in CHARACTERS.

4. VI:243—The Red Death may have come out of the deep crevice beyond Fedic, called the Devil's Arse, but given the name of the disease (taken from a fictional plague created by Edgar Allan Poe), and the terrible practices of the Great Old Ones, it seems most likely that it was created by biological engineers and accidentally released.

5. III:38—See footnote 2. For date on the time line, I counted backwards. The Great Old Ones disappeared two thousand years before the Wolves began raiding the Callas (V:339). In *Wolves of the Calla*, we find out that the Wolves have been preying on the children of the borderlands for six generations (V:339). In the Calla, one generation is twenty-three years (V:15). Six generations equals 138 years. If Roland is approximately 336 at the time that *Wolves of the Calla* takes place, he was 198 when the Wolves started raiding (198 A.R.B.). I counted back from this date.

Human society fragments, and the old knowledge is forgotten.
Mutants roam the wastelands.
Mid-World's Dark Age begins.

690 B.R.B.

Arthur Eld rises to power and rules the Kingdom of All-World.[6]
The people practice human sacrifice as part
of the Charyou Tree Festival of Reap.

464 B.R.B.

The Great Old Ones' technological web—supporting Beams
and Tower—continues to decay.
Blaine's computerized monitoring equipment in End-World collapses.[7]

464–64 B.R.B.

The Kingdom of All-World fragments and is replaced
by a loose Affiliation of Baronies.
The In-World Barony of New Canaan is the Affiliation's hub.
New Canaan, and its barony seat of Gilead, is ruled by the gunslingers,
the descendants of Arthur Eld.

64 B.R.B.–36 A.R.B.

Civil War erupts in the distant baronies of Garlan and Porla.
Wars continue for a hundred years.[8]
The Affiliation begins to destabilize.

ROLAND IS BORN

John Farson, a harrier from Garlan and Desoy, gains power
in the lands west of New Canaan. His followers call him the Good Man.
Farson resurrects the Great Old Ones' killing machines so that
he can overthrow the Affiliation and the aristocratic gunslingers.

---

6. There appear to be two Arthur Elds—the mythical Arthur Eld, who was the first king to arise after the Prim receded and who was the ancestor of both the line of Deschain and the Crimson King (VII:176), and the historical Arthur Eld, forefather of Steven Deschain. Steven Deschain was twenty-ninth, on a side-line of descent, from the historical Arthur Eld. Roland, then, is thirtieth. If a generation is approximately twenty-three years (see V:15), and if Steven Deschain was approximately twenty-three when Roland was born, then 30 x 23 = 690.

7. III:412—At the time *The Waste Lands* takes place, eight hundred years have passed since Blaine's monitoring equipment went down in End-World. If Roland is 336 years old when he and his tet riddle with Blaine, 800 – 336 = 464 B.R.B.

8. III:242—Civil war erupts in Garlan/Porla three hundred to four hundred years before our ka-tet reaches River Crossing.

Failed gunslingers from Gilead and the In-World baronies,
sent west in disgrace, begin to join Farson's cause.

11 A.R.B.

Roland's father, Steven Deschain, is on the verge of becoming *dinh*
of Gilead, and possibly *dinh* of all In-World.[9]
Roland and his friend Cuthbert Allgood discover that Gilead's head cook,
Hax, is poisoning people for John Farson. They tell their fathers.
Hax is hanged for treason. Roland and Cuthbert
witness his hanging.[10]

14 A.R.B.

West of Gilead, near the edge of the civilized world,
fighting breaks out between Farson's rebels and the Affiliation.[11]
Roland finds out that his mother is having an affair
with his father's sorcerer (Marten Broadcloak/Walter O'Dim),
who also happens to be a secret supporter
of the Good Man. Needing guns to exact revenge,
Roland goes for his test of manhood five years too early.
Roland succeeds.

14–14.5 A.R.B.

Roland and his two friends Cuthbert Allgood and Alain Johns
are sent east to Hambry, in the Barony of Mejis, to keep them safe
from Farson's treachery.[12]
They discover a plot against the Affiliation and defeat some
of the Good Man's forces.
They find Maerlyn's Grapefruit, the Pink One of the Wizard's Rainbow,
and steal it for their fathers.
Roland is captivated by the Pink One's *glammer* and gazes
into its depths. He sees his pregnant lover, Susan Delgado,
burned to death on a Charyou Tree fire.[13]

---

9. I(2003):160.

10. I(1988):159, I(2003):170—Roland is fourteen when he finds out that Marten Broadcloak is having an affair with his mother. Roland challenges his teacher, Cort, and wins his guns. Hax hanged by the neck three years before Roland's test of manhood.

11. I(2003):169.

12. See footnote 10. I(1988):163—Roland goes for his test five years too early. Steven Deschain sent Roland east because he thought that the Good Man and his followers were in the west. IV:112.

13. Events of *Wizard and Glass*.

14.5 A.R.B.

Roland and his friends return to Gilead.
Roland is given his father's guns.
Gabrielle Deschain, lately back from a retreat in Debaria,
is still in Marten Broadcloak's power. She secretly plans
to kill her husband, but Roland prevents it.[14]
Roland accidentally shoots his mother.[15]

16 A.R.B.

Much of In-World falls to the Good Man.
Roland's father is murdered.[16]

19 A.R.B.

Roland's ka-tel (or graduating class) of gunslingers
load their guns for the first time.
Only thirteen remain out of a class of fifty-six.
Cort is too ill to attend the Presentation Ceremony.
Nine weeks later, Cort dies of poisoning.[17]

21 A.R.B.

Two years after Cort's death, the red slaughter reaches Gilead,
the last bastion of civilization.
The final civil war begins.[18]

24 A.R.B.

The battle of Jericho Hill is fought.[19]
Cuthbert Allgood dies, shot through the eye
by Rudin Filaro (aka Walter O'Dim).[20]
Roland is the only gunslinger to survive.[21]
Roland leaves the Horn of Deschain (the Horn of Eld)
on Jericho Hill.

---

14. IV:655–56.

15. Ibid.

16. I(2003):118—The land falls to Farson five years after Hax's hanging. Roland's father is dead by this time. I(2003):161—Steven Deschain was killed by a knife.

17. I(1988):163—Roland won his guns five years too early. He was fourteen at the time. Hence, the average age for gunslingers to win their guns is nineteen. II:177—We are told that Cort dies of poison nine weeks after the gunslinger apprentices' Presentation Ceremony.

18. II:177.

19. V:347—Cuthbert was twenty-four when he died at Jericho Hill. If he and Roland were approximately the same age, then Roland must have also been about twenty-four when this battle was fought.

20. VII:174.

21. VII:174–75.

24–36 A.R.B.

Roland casts about for Walter's trail.[22]
He visits the ruins of Gilead, now overrun with timothy and wild vines.
The old castle's kitchens are infested with Slow Mutants.[23]
Roland travels to Eluria, is captured by the Green Folk,
and ends up in the clutches of the vampiric Little Sisters of Eluria.
He escapes.[24]

36 A.R.B.[25]

Roland is hot on the trail of the Man in Black.
He enters Tull and is besieged by the followers of the mad preacher
Sylvia Pittston, servant of the Crimson King and lover of the Man in Black
(aka Walter O'Dim).
Roland kills everyone in Tull, including his lover, Alice.
Roland crosses the Mohaine Desert and at the Way Station
meets Jake Chambers.
In the Cyclopean Mountains, Roland sees the Man in Black
for the first time in twelve years.
Roland allows Jake to fall into an abyss below the mountains,
then enters the golgotha with Walter.
Roland and Walter enter a fistula of time and Roland has a vision
of the Tower's many levels.[26]
When he awakes, Roland has aged ten years,
but three hundred years have passed in Mid-World-that-was.[27]
While Roland dreams, the remains of Mid-World collapse.

140 A.R.B.

River Barony Castle (near the town of River Crossing) falls to harriers.[28]

---

22. I(2003):152—Roland catches sight of Walter, presumably after the battle of Jericho Hill, and then does not see him again for twelve years, or until he and Jake enter the passages beneath the Cyclopean Mountains. Twenty-four years plus twelve years equals thirty-six years.

23. I(2003):146.

24. Events of "The Little Sisters of Eluria."

25. Events from *The Gunslinger.* For explanation of Roland's age, see footnote 22.

26. VII:176–77.

27. I(2003):230–31—Roland appears to be ten years older when he wakes. II:47—at least one hundred years pass while Roland is in the golgotha. III:375—According to Blaine, by the time our ka-tet reaches Lud, it has been three hundred years since any gunslinger walked either In-World or End-World. Since Roland is the last gunslinger, Roland must have disappeared for about three centuries. Roland was approximately twenty-four at the battle of Jericho Hill. (See footnote 19.) He was approximately thirty-six when the events of *The Gunslinger* took place. (See footnote 22.)

28. According to Si of River Crossing, the last tribute was sent to River Barony Castle in the time of his great-grand-da, but they found the castle in ruins. Si is at least seventy by the time he tells his story.

198 A.R.B.

The Wolves begin invading the Callas of the Borderlands.[29]
The Crimson King's followers are feeding a "twin-telepathy" chemical
(extracted from the brains of prepubescent twins) to the Breakers
of End-World so that these telepaths can speed the destruction
of the Beams and the collapse of the Tower.

246 A.R.B.

David Quick, the outlaw prince, leads an attack on the city of Lud.
This city (Mid-World's version of New York) is caught in
a constant cycle of warfare.
Quick dies trying to use one of the Old Ones' flying machines.[30]

266 A.R.B.

Patricia (Blaine's twin mono) stops running.[31]

336 A.R.B.

Roland awakens in the golgotha and travels to the Western Sea,
where two of his right fingers and one of his toes are eaten by lobstrosities.
He draws forth Eddie Dean and then Odetta Holmes
(along with Odetta's second personality, the nasty Detta Walker).
Roland forces Odetta and Detta to unite,
and they become Eddie Dean's great love, Susannah Dean.
In the Great West Woods, our tet finds the Bear-Turtle Beam
and follows it to the ancient kingdom of Mid-World.
Jake is drawn, once more, onto Roland's level of the Tower.
While drawing Jake, Susannah becomes pregnant by the demon
of the Speaking Ring (actually a Demon Elemental)
and conceives "the chap."
Oy joins the ka-tet.
Our tet travels to River Crossing, then to Lud, and finally boards Blaine
the Insane Mono on his mad hurtle toward Topeka.
Blaine says he will kill them all, and himself,
unless they can beat him in a riddling contest.
Eddie defeats Blaine with the illogic of his bad jokes.

29. V:339—By the time *Wolves of the Calla* takes place, the Wolves have been invading the Calla for six generations, or 138 years. On V:15, we learn that a generation is approximately twenty-three years.

30. III:244—Ninety years before our ka-tet reached River Crossing, Quick rode into Lud with his harriers. III:273–75—Our ka-tet finds the remains of both Quick and the flying machine.

31. III:246—The mono under discussion stopped running seventy years before our ka-tet reached the town of River Crossing. On this page, our tet seems to think that the stalled mono is Blaine. Later in the story they realize that Patricia stopped running, not Blaine.

Blaine crashes, destroying himself, but our ka-tet survives.
They enter an alternative version of our Kansas and encounter a thinny.
There, by the warble of the thinny, Roland recounts the story
of his time in Mejis and of his love affair with Susan Delgado.
Our tet enters the Green Palace and faces down the infamous R.F.
(aka Walter O'Dim).
They awake in a clearing of white winter grass,
once more on the Path of the Beam.

336–337 A.R.B.[32]

Our tet journeys along the Path of the Beam and enters the borderlands.
Susannah, pregnant with the chap, develops another personality,
that of Mia (High Speech for "mother").
Roland and his companions enter Calla Bryn Sturgis
and battle the Wolves, saving the Calla's twins
from being made "roont" in End-World.
The Crimson King foresees our ka-tet's victory,
so kills himself and all but three of his followers.
Undead, the Crimson King rides to End-World and positions himself
on a balcony of the Dark Tower.

After the battle with the Wolves, Mia takes control of Susannah's body
and escapes through the magical portal of the Doorway Cave.
She travels to the Dixie Pig in New York, 1999, so that she can rendezvous
with the servants of the Crimson King and bear her demonic chap.
In the Extraction Room of the Fedic Dogan, Mordred Red-Heel is born.
Mordred immediately eats his body-mother, Mia.
Susannah Dean kills her captors and shoots off one of Mordred's
eight spider legs.

Jake, Oy, and their new tet-mate, Father Donald Callahan, track Susannah
to the Dixie Pig in the *where* of New York City and the *when* of 1999.
Pere Callahan is killed.
Pursued by the henchmen of the Crimson King,
Jake and Oy reach the New York/Fedic Door.

Roland and Eddie pass through the Unfound Door to Maine, 1977.
After battling Balazar's thugs, they track down
Calvin Tower and Aaron Deepneau.
Calvin Tower sells Roland and Eddie the magic Vacant Lot,
home of the Rose.

---

32. Throughout *Wolves of the Calla*, we are told that Jake is twelve years old. In the previous books he was eleven. Hence, a year (or a good part of a year) must pass between the events of *The Waste Lands/Wizard and Glass* and *Wolves*.

Roland and Eddie meet their maker, Stephen King,
in the *when* of 1977 and the *where* of Bridgton, Maine.
With the help of John Cullum, Roland and Eddie
form the Tet Corporation to protect the Rose in our world.

Our tet is reunited in the Fedic Dogan
and passes through the Wolves' Door to Thunderclap Station.
Mordred eats Walter O'Dim and follows them.
Our ka-tet defeats the servants of the Crimson King in the Devar-Toi.
Eddie is shot by the Devar Master and dies.

Roland, Jake, and Oy travel through a magic door made
by the Breakers to Maine, 1999.
They save the life of their maker, Stephen King.
Jake dies.
Roland meets the executives of the Tet Corporation and sees the Rose.

Roland, Oy, and Susannah are reunited in Fedic.
They travel through the Discordia to Le Casse Roi Russe.
Mordred follows.
Roland, Oy, and Susannah destroy the were-insect Dandelo
and free the mute artist Patrick Danville.

On the road to the Tower, Patrick draws the Unfound Door for Susannah.
Susannah abandons the quest and enters an alternative version of New York.
Mordred—dying of food poisoning—attacks Roland.
Oy dies defending Roland.
Mordred dies under the gun of his White Daddy.

Roland and Patrick reach the Tower, but the Red King is waiting for them.
Patrick uses his magical drawing skills to draw,
and then erase, the Crimson King.
Roland climbs the Tower and finds . . .
himself.

Commala come-come,
The journey's never done.

Or is it?

The man in black fled across the desert, and the gunslinger followed.

But this time, Roland has his horn, and he will sound it when he reaches
the distant fields of Can'-Ka No Rey, and the Tower which calls him.

APPENDIX III:
MID-WORLD RHYMES,
SONGS, PRAYERS,
AND PROPHECIES

I: RHYMES

1. BABY-BUNTING RHYME

When Roland was a little boy, his mother sang this song to him. *Chussit, chissit, chassit* are the High Speech words for the numbers seventeen, eighteen, and nineteen. (VII:23, VII:767)

Baby-bunting, darling one,
Now another day is done.
May your dreams be sweet and merry,
May you dream of fields and berries.

Baby-bunting, baby-dear,
Baby, bring your berries here.
Chussit, chissit, chassit!
Bring enough to fill your basket.

2. BREAKER RHYME

This little rhyme is popular among the Breakers of End-World. I suppose it helps them justify their part in the destruction of the macroverse. (VII:289)

Enjoy the cruise,
turn on the fan,
there's nothing to lose,
so work on your tan.

3. ORIZA RHYME

We learn this High Speech rhyme in Calla Bryn Sturgis. In the Calla they believe that mortal woman was made from the breath of mortal man, but that the first man came from Lady Oriza. The translation is "All breath comes from the woman." (V:631)

417

Can-ah,
can-tah,
annah,
Oriza

4. PENNY POSY

This bit of "cradle nonsense" was sung to children in Mid-World. Roland
would have known it well. (VII:171)

Penny, posy,
Jack's a-nosy!
Do ya say so?
Yes I do-so!
He's my sneaky, peeky, darling bah-bo!

5. SEE THE TURTLE OF ENORMOUS GIRTH

This well-known and well-loved Mid-World poem invokes the spirit of the Turtle Guardian. Each region repeats a slightly different version, but despite this,
the poem remains essentially the same. *For more information and for page references, see* GUARDIANS OF THE BEAM, *in* CHARACTERS

BORDERLANDS VERSION (VI:15)

See the Turtle of enormous girth!
On his shell he holds the earth,
His thought is slow but always kind;
He holds us all within his mind.
On his back the truth is carried,
And there are love and duty married.
He loves the earth and loves the sea,
And even loves a child like me.

IN-WORLD VERSION (VII:490)

See the Turtle of enormous girth!
On his shell he holds the earth,
His thought is slow but always kind;
He holds us all within his mind.
On his back all vows are made;
He sees the truth but mayn't aid.
He loves the earth and loves the sea,
And even loves a child like me.

6. SEMINON RHYME

Seminon is the name given to the Calla's late-autumn windstorms, the ones that
come just before true winter. Lord Seminon is also the name of a god whom

Lady Oriza wanted to marry. However, Lord Seminon preferred Oriza's sister, and Oriza never forgave him. *See* SEMINON, LORD, *and* ORIZA, LADY, *under* ORIZA, LADY, *in* CHARACTERS

> Seminon comin',
> warm days go runnin'.

7. SPARK-A-DARK, WHO'S MY SIRE
Roland repeats this old catechism whenever he sets a campfire alight. (VII:761)

> Spark-a-dark, who's my sire?
> Will I lay me?
> Will I stay me?
> Bless this camp with fire.

II: SONGS
Throughout the Dark Tower series, we learn about many of Mid-World's popular songs. Some of them are versions of songs found in our world (reinforcing the belief that Mid-World is one of our earth's many possible futures). However, quite a few have never been heard in our world.

A list of those songs which appear in *The Gunslinger, The Drawing of the Three, The Waste Lands,* and *Wizard and Glass* can be found in Appendix II of *Stephen King's The Dark Tower: A Concordance, Volume I.* Below are listed those songs which appear in the final three books of the series.

1. ADELINA SAYS SHE'S RANDY-O
We never learn the words to this Mid-World drinking song. (VII:520)

2. BUY ME ANOTHER ROUND YOU BOOGER YOU
Pere Callahan sings this song on the night of the Calla's welcoming fiesta, put on in honor of Roland and his ka-tet. We never learn the words. (V:228)

3. CARELESS LOVE
"Careless Love" has special significance, since we associate the song with Roland's first and only true love, Susan Delgado. Although "Careless Love" is mentioned in the final three books of the Dark Tower series, the extract we have comes from *Wizard and Glass.* (IV:121)

> Love, O love, O careless love,
> Can't you see what careless love has done?

4. THE COMMALA SONG
The Commala Song is probably one of the most important songs found in Mid-World. It is sung in the Calla, but it was also sung in In-World during Roland's youth. The version which the Calla *folken* sing during their welcoming fiesta

(and to which Roland dances at the beginning of *Wolves of the Calla*) can be found at the front of this volume. Below are listed some of the Commala's variants, found throughout the rest of the series.

CALLA CHILDREN'S VERSION

Roland's tet overhears the Calla's prepubescent twins singing this version while they march behind Andy the Messenger Robot. (V:587–88)

Commala-come-one!
Mamma had a son!
Dass-a time 'at Daddy
Had d'mos' fun!

Commala-come-come!
Daddy had one!
Dass-a time 'at Mommy
Had d'mos' fun!

Commala-come-two!
You know what to do!
Plant the rice commala,
Don't ye be . . . no . . . foo'!

Commala-come-two!
Daddy no foo'!
Mommy plant commala
cause she know jus' what to do!

Commala-come-t'ree!
You know what t'be
Plant d'rice commala
and d'rice'll make ya free!

Commala-come-t'ree!
Rice'll make ya free!
When ya plant the rice commala
You know jus' what to be!

EAST ROAD BATTLE VERSION

The people of the Calla add this verse to the Commala Song after the battle of the East Road. It honors Lady Oriza for hiding the Calla's children in her rice. (V:689)

Come-come-commala
Rice come a-falla
I-sissa 'ay a-bralla
Dey come a-folla
We went to a-rivva
'Riza did us kivva

SONG OF SUSANNAH VERSION

One stave and response from this version of the Commala Song can be found at the end of each Stanza section in *Song of Susannah*. (VI:18, VI:43–44, VI:58, VI:75, VI:98, VI:154, VI:173, VI:216, VI:261, VI:303, VI:344, VI:384–85, VI:411)

STAVE

Commala-come-come
There's a young man with a gun.
Young man lost his honey
When she took it on the run.

RESPONSE

Commala-come-come!
She took it on the run!
Left her baby lonely but
Her baby ain't done.

STAVE

Commala-come-coo
The wind'll blow ya through.
Ya gotta go where ka's wind blows ya
Cause there's nothing else to do.

RESPONSE

Commala-come-two!
Nothin' else to do!
Gotta go where ka's wind blows ya
Cause there's nothing else to do.

STAVE

Commala-come-key
Can ya tell me what ya see?

Is it ghosts or just the mirror
That makes ya want to flee?

RESPONSE

Commala-come-three!
I beg ya, tell me!
Is it ghosts or just your darker self
That makes ya want to flee?

STAVE

Commala-come-ko
Whatcha doin at my do'?
If you doan tell me now, my friend,
I'll lay ya on de flo'.

RESPONSE

Commala-come-fo'!
I can lay ya low!
The things I done to such as you
You never want to know.

STAVE

Commala-gin-jive
Ain't it grand to be alive?
To look out on Discordia
When the Demon Moon arrives.

RESPONSE

Commala-come-five!
Even when the shadows rise!
To see the world and walk the world
Makes ya glad to be alive.

STAVE

Commala-mox-nix!
You're in a nasty fix!
To take the hand in a traitor's glove
Is to grasp a sheaf of sticks!

RESPONSE

Commala-come-six!
Nothing there but thorns and sticks!
When you find your hand in a traitor's glove
You're in a nasty fix.

STAVE

Commala-loaf-leaven!
They go to Hell or up to Heaven!
When the guns are shot and the fire's hot,
You got to poke em in the oven.

RESPONSE

Commala-come-seven!
Salt and yow' for leaven!
Heat em up and knock em down
And poke em in the oven.

STAVE

Commala-ka-kate.
You're in the hands of fate.
No matter if you're real or not,
The hour groweth late.

RESPONSE

Commala-come-eight!
The hour groweth late!
No matter what the shade ya cast
You're in the hands of fate.

STAVE

Commala-me-mine
You have to walk the line.
When you finally get the thing you need
It makes you feel so fine.

RESPONSE

Commala-come-nine!
It makes ya feel fine!

But if you'd have the thing you need
You have to walk the line.

STAVE

Commala-come-ken
It's the other one again.
You may know her name and face
But that don't make her your friend.

RESPONSE

Commala-come-ten!
She is not your friend!
If you let her get too close
She'll cut you up again.

STAVE

Commala-come-call
We hail the One who made us all,
Who made the men and made the maids,
Who made the great and small.

RESPONSE

Commala-come-call!
He made the great and small!
And yet how great the hand of fate
That rules us one and all.

STAVE

Commala-come-ki,
There's a time to live and one to die.
With your back against the final wall
Ya gotta let the bullets fly.

RESPONSE

Commala-come-ki!
Let the bullets fly!
Don't 'ee mourn for me, my lads
When it comes my day to die.

Sing your song, O sing it well,
The child has come to pass.

Commala-come-kass,
The worst has come to pass.
The Tower trembles on its ground;
The child has come at last.

Commala-come-come,
The battle's now begun!
And all the foes of men and rose
Rise with the setting sun.

SUSANNAH'S DREAM VERSION

Susannah Dean hears this version of the Commala Song
in her dream version of Central Park. (VII:724)

Rice be a green-o,
Seen what we seen-o,
Seen-o the green-o,
Come-come-commala!

5. THE GREEN CORN A-DAYO

We never hear this song, though we do learn that Andy likes to sing all twenty
or thirty verses of it. It may be yet another version of the Commala Song. (V:5)

6. HEY JUDE

"Hey Jude" exists in our world too. The major difference between the Mid-
World version and the Beatles' version is that Mid-World's begins "Hey Jude,
I see you, lad." (V:39)

7. IN TIME OF LOSS, MAKE GOD YOUR BOSS

Andy the Messenger Robot (Many Other Terrible Functions) learned this
song from the Manni. We never get to hear him sing it. (V:6)

8. THE JIMMY JUICE I DRANK LAST NIGHT

This is an amusing song sung in the Calla. (We never hear it.) Since Andy the
Messenger Robot offers to sing it to Eddie not long after Eddie almost wipes

his bottom with poison flurry, I can't help but wonder whether Jimmy juice is a bit like prune juice. (V:141)

9. MAID OF CONSTANT SORROW
Susannah Dean sings this song from our world at the Calla fiesta. It goes down well. (V:228)

10. STREETS OF COMPARA
A pair of nine-year-old twins sings this song at the Calla fiesta. Since the Calla *folken* believe that the better part of one of the girl's brains is destined to be made into Breaker-food, it's not surprising that the song makes them cry. We never learn the words. (V:227)

III: PRAYERS

1. DEATH PRAYER
Roland translates this prayer for us and recites it over Jake's grave. (VII:474)

Time flies, knells call, life passes, so hear my prayer.
Birth is nothing but death begun, so hear my prayer.
Death is speechless, so hear my speech.
This is Jake, who served his ka and his tet. Say true.
May the forgiving glance of S'mana heal his heart. Say please.
May the arms of Gan raise him from the darkness of the earth. Say please.
Surround him, Gan, with light.
Fill him, Chloe, with strength.
If he is thirsty, give him water in the clearing.
If he is hungry, give him food in the clearing.
May his life on this earth and the pain of his passing become
as a dream to his waking soul, and let his eyes fall upon
every lovely sight; let him find the friends that were lost to him,
and let every one whose name he calls call his in return.
This is Jake, who lived well, loved his own, and died as ka would have it.
Each man owes a death. This is Jake. Give him peace.

2. GUNSLINGER LITANY
Every gunslinger must learn to recite the following litany. (V:155–56)

I do not aim with my hand; he who aims with his hand has forgotten the face of his father. I aim with my eye. I do not shoot with my hand; he who shoots with his hand has forgotten the face of his father. I shoot with my mind. I do not kill with my gun; he who kills with his gun has forgotten the face of his father. I kill with my heart.

3. MANNI PRAYER (I)
This is the praise-prayer Henchick gives when the Unfound Door opens. We are not given a translation. (VI:42)

> Over-sam kammen!
> Can-tah, can-kavar kammen!
> Over-can-tah!

4. MANNI PRAYER (II)
The Manni repeat this short prayer after Henchick prays to the Over in front of the Unfound Door. Henchick's prayer to the Over was for safe passage and success of endeavor with no loss of life or sanity. He also begged the Over to enliven their mags and bobs, and for *kaven,* or the persistence of magic. We are not given Henchick's words, and we are not given a translation of the short prayer which follows, as below. (VI:26)

> Over-sam,
> Over-kra,
> Over-can-tah.

5. PRAYER AFTER A SUCCESSFUL HUNT
Roland recites this prayer after he and Susannah successfully hunt down deer. The prayer is addressed to the head of a dead deer. (VII:636–37)

> We thank you for what we are about to receive.
> (Father, we thank thee.)
> Guide our hands and guide our hearts as we take life from death.

IV: PROPHECIES

1. PROPHECY ABOUT THE CRIMSON KING
When Roland was a boy, he heard a bit of doggerel which predicted the death of the Crimson King. According to this prophecy, the Red King would kill himself with a spoon. The second part of the prophecy stated that Los the Red could be killed by Roland's guns, since their barrels were made from Arthur Eld's great sword, Excalibur. However, by swallowing the sharpened spoon, the Crimson King made himself Undead, and so safe from even Roland's guns. It's a shame we never get to hear the actual prophecy. (VII:607–608)

2. PROPHECY FOR THE LINE OF ELD
Mordred Deschain's birth fulfills an ancient prophecy which foretells the destruction of the last gunslinger—Roland Deschain. As we know from the Dark Tower series, Roland was tricked into conceiving a child with his ka-tet

mate Susannah Dean. Roland's sperm was taken by a Demon Elemental (posing as the Oracle of the Mountains), which then turned itself into a male and impregnated Susannah in the Speaking Ring where she, Roland, and Eddie drew Jake Chambers into Mid-World. Although Roland is not actually Susannah's father, he is her *dinh,* or leader, and so is the father of their ka-tet. (VI:252)

> He who ends the line of Eld shall conceive a child of incest with his sister or his daughter, and the child will be marked, by his red heel shall you know him. It is he who shall stop the breath of the last warrior.

APPENDIX IV:
THE TOWER, THE QUEST,
AND *THE EYES OF THE DRAGON*

A question recently arose on the King Web site message board concerning the relationship between the Dark Tower books and *The Eyes of the Dragon*. The Constant Reader who posted the query wanted others to share their thoughts about where *The Eyes of the Dragon* should be placed on the Dark Tower time line. Does *Eyes* take place before or after the rule of Roland's illustrious ancestor Arthur Eld? Is our Roland a descendant of King Roland? And, by extension, is the house of Delain related to the house of Deschain? Having just completed a Dark Tower time line (it should be posted on-site soon), this question really interested me, so I thought I'd throw in my own two cents' worth of commentary.

My first job was to reread *Eyes*. I too had always assumed that *The Eyes of the Dragon* took place in Roland's world, albeit in the distant past. However, once I took a good long look at my time line, at Volume I of my *Concordance*, and at the many, many notes and maps spread about my workroom, I realized that I had a very big problem. Namely, *The Eyes of the Dragon* doesn't fit into the history of Roland's world. Before you reach for your six-gun to shoot me, hear me out. Then decide what you think. As you read, keep in mind that familiar phrase, the essence of which I will return to at the end of my entry: *There are other worlds than these.* As Jake Chambers so eloquently stated before his free fall into the abyss below the Cyclopean Mountains, no world stands alone. A universe consists of many worlds, and the Dark Tower contains all of them. Some levels of the Dark Tower may be unique, some may be dangerous or downright deadly, but the majority of them seem like slightly distorted echoes of each other.

As we've seen over and over in the Dark Tower series, the multiverse is almost like a rabbit warren, with many secret entrances and byways leading from one "earth" or "Mid-World" to another. As the Manni know so well, unwary travelers must beware. If you dare to click the heels of your ruby slippers together (or in the case of the Manni, set your plumb bob swinging), there is no guarantee that you will be able to return to the world that you left. There may be only one Keystone Earth, but there are many variants of that earth. Eddie Dean may think that he comes from the same New York City as Calvin

Tower, but in Eddie's world, Co-Op City is in Brooklyn. In Calvin's, it's in the Bronx.

As Callahan discovered during his five years traveling along the highways in hiding, and as our ka-tet found out in the alternative Kansas, the worlds-next-door may look the same as ours, but upon close scrutiny they prove to be subtly, but significantly, different. Though their landscapes are almost identical, and though they seem to share our history and culture, at some point in time those worlds, and ours, diverged. In *Wolves of the Calla,* Pere Callahan recounts his travels through the multiple Americas, which he calls the vertical geographies of chance (V:298). In Callahan's version of earth, as in ours, Fort Lee sits on the far side of the George Washington Bridge, yet during his travels through the alternative Americas, he leaves New York City via the G.W. only to find himself in a town called Leabrook, where the face of someone named Chadborne decorates the ten-dollar bill and a politician named Earnest "Fritz" Hollings is elected president (V:300, V:305). Similarly, Susannah, Eddie, and Jake disembark from Blaine the Insane Mono into what they think is our world's Kansas, only to find that the Takuro Spirit–driving and Nozz-A-La-cola-drinking inhabitants have all been killed off by a disease called superflu.

Certainly, what holds true for our world also holds true for Roland's. We live on Keystone Earth, the template for all of the alternative earths, but Roland comes from Tower Keystone, the template for all of the multiple Mid-Worlds. If there are many worlds similar to ours spinning about the central needle of the Dark Tower, then surely there are alternative versions of Roland's world to be found there as well. However, even by stating this obvious fact, I leave out a very important point. Related worlds can have differences that are as arresting as their similarities. After all, as Eddie Dean states in *The Dark Tower,* Roland's world and our world are also twins. Despite their divergent histories and apparent differences, they are protected by the same divine forces and are attacked by the same enemies.

As we all know, there *are* many striking similarities between the world depicted in *The Eyes of the Dragon* and the one we travel in during the Dark Tower series. In both tales, *Roland* is a royal name. The halls of the rich and powerful are adorned with Kashamin rugs, and the weapons of kings are made of sandalwood. In Delain, as in Gilead, Old Star shines in the night sky. People wonder about the semimythical Grand Featherex, and magicians (both good and evil) have the power to make themselves *dim.* Those born to aristocratic families are said to be of High Blood, and records are written, and read, using the Great Letters. Gunpowder is rare, and extremely valuable.

In both Delain and Gilead, the distant (and somewhat sinister) land of Garlan is well-known for its poisons. Both the Dragon Sand used to kill King Roland of Delain, and the poisoned knife meant to murder Steven Deschain of Gilead, originated in Garlan. John Norman, whom we met in the Dark Tower novella "The Little Sisters of Eluria," was born in Delain (a land also known as Dragon's Lair and Liar's Heaven), which also seems to imply that *The Eyes of the Dragon* and the Dark Tower series both take place on the same level of the Tower.

But even the similarities between *The Eyes of the Dragon* and the Dark Tower series raise their own problems. For example, both Delain and Gilead are referred to as In-World baronies, yet how can this be so if Roland Deschain seems unaware of the places so frequently mentioned in *The Eyes of the Dragon*—the Sea of Tomorrow, the Far Forests, the Northern, Eastern, Western and Southern Baronies? Wouldn't they have appeared on the map Roland saw as a boy, the one which depicted the Greater Kingdoms of the Western Earth? And why is the Delain that we learn about in "The Little Sisters of Eluria" closer to Eluria—an Out-World town—than to Gilead? And if the worlds of *The Eyes of the Dragon* and the Dark Tower series are the same, why are their gods so dissimilar? The people of King Roland's Delain worship at the Church of the Great Gods; the Man Jesus, and his Father, seem unknown. Yet the medallion worn by James Norman (of Mid-World's Delain) specifically mentions the One God, and it is this sigul which saves our gunslinger, Roland, from the bloodthirst of the Little Sisters.

And the questions continue. If the great city of Delain is part of In-World, why is it unaffected by the Great Old Ones' mutations and horrible munitions? And why are the Beams, the Guardians, and the Dark Tower never mentioned? The only hint given to us, suggesting that the people of *The Eyes of the Dragon* know of the Tower, is the existence of the Needle, a three-hundred-foot-tall stone prison located in the center of Delain's Plaza. And if all this can be explained away by temporal distance, by "long, long ago," how then did Dennis and Thomas, two of the main characters from *The Eyes of the Dragon,* make their way to Gilead during Roland Deschain's youth, and just after that great city's fall? How, except through some kind of magic door—the kind of magic door favored by their quarry, the magician Randall Flagg?

To any Constant Reader, Randall Flagg is a familiar, if slippery, figure. His name changes, as does his face, but his purpose always remains the same. Whether he calls himself Walter, Marten, or one of the many variations of "R.F.," his Chaotic Calling remains unchanged. He must search out lands where the White flourishes and bring them to ruin. His attempt to reduce Delain to anarchy failed, but in Roland's world, he triumphed. Somehow, he leapt from the In-World of *The Eyes of the Dragon* to the In-World of Roland's youth, dragging his shadow of darkness and anarchy with him. Dennis and Thomas, two Warriors of the White who helped to halt Flagg's machinations in Delain, were unable to stop Farson in Gilead. Perhaps they failed because it was not their world, or perhaps because their Flagg was as different from Mid-World's enemy as Jake '77 was from Mid-World Jake, though the two boys crossed paths (or one boy crossed his own path) on Second Avenue, New York, at the beginning of *Wolves of the Calla.*

Like the Crimson King, who in the novel *Insomnia* tried to destroy the town of Derry, Maine (twinner of our world's Bangor, Maine), Flagg travels through the multiverse, leaping from earth to earth and from Mid-World to Mid-World, spreading chaos and disaster like a plague or a poison. Yet each world he tries to destroy gives birth to its own heroes, its own Warriors of the White. And whether these warriors fight with sandalwood-handled six-shooters or arrows with sandalwood bolts, their purpose is the same—to champion that ancient, resilient, yet humble force that has redeemed humankind again and again and again. It is the force that begets life and which makes the Beams, and the Tower, stand true.

APPENDIX V:
POLITICAL AND CULTURAL FIGURES (OUR WORLD) MENTIONED IN *WOLVES OF THE CALLA, SONG OF SUSANNAH,* AND *THE DARK TOWER*

ACTORS, DIRECTORS, AND STAGE PERSONALITIES: Abbott and Costello, Fred Astaire, Jack Benny, Humphrey Bogart, Yul Brynner, Horst Buchholz, James Cagney, George Carlin, George Clooney, Tom Cruise, Robert Culp, Olivia de Havilland, James Dean, Cecil B. DeMille, Clint Eastwood, Emilio Estevez, Henry Fonda, Clark Gable, James Garner, John Gielgud, Whoopi Goldberg, Robert Goulet, Ty Hardin, Rondo Hatton, Alfred Hitchcock, Rock Hudson, Nicole Kidman, Akira Kurosawa, Charles Laughton, Sergio Leone, Jerry Lewis, Rich Little, Rob Lowe, George Lucas, Dean Martin, Harpo Marx, Butterfly McQueen, Marilyn Monroe, Paul Newman, Claude Rains, Robert Redford, Cesar Romero, George Romero, Winona Ryder, Mort Sahl, Peter Sellers, John Sturges, Lee Van Cleef, Van Heflin, Clint Walker, John Wayne

> FILMS AND PLAYS: *Armageddon; Blood Work; Child's Play; Death Valley Days; Dopes at Sea; Fail-Safe; Forbidden Planet; Girl, Interrupted; The Invisible Man; The Lost Continent; The Magnificent Seven; Midnight Cowboy; Night of the Living Dead; The Other Side of Midnight; Our American Cousin; Phantasm; Psycho; Rebel without a Cause; Return to the O.K. Corral; The Seven Samurai; The Snake Pit;* spaghetti westerns; *Stalag 17; Star Wars; The Ten Commandments; Top Hat; War of the Zombies; White Heat; Yankee Doodle Dandy*

BIBLICAL FIGURES AND RELIGIOUS FIGURES FROM AROUND THE WORLD: Adam and Eve, Buddha, Cain, David and Goliath, Devil, Druids, Good Samaritan, Jacob, Jesus, Joseph, Moses, Muhammad, Noah, Saint Peter, Pontius Pilate, the Pope, Samson

CULTURAL AND HISTORICAL FIGURES: Black Panthers, Daniel Boone, John Wilkes Booth, Ted Bundy, Bull Connor, John Dillinger, Albert Einstein, The Elks, Sigmund Freud, Bill Gates, Donald Grant, Ulysses S. Grant, Howard

Hughes, I.B.M., Jim Jones and the People's Temple, Jackie Kennedy, John Kennedy Jr., Elisabeth Kübler-Ross, The Luddites, "Dougout" Doug MacArthur, Manhattan Project, Christa McAuliffe, Microsoft, Mother Teresa, Lee Harvey Oswald, Punxsutawney Phil *(he's a groundhog but I thought I would include him anyway)*, Queen Elizabeth II, Anna Sage, Albert Schweitzer, Alan Shepard, The Shriners, Socrates, Donald Trump

CIVIL RIGHTS ACTIVISTS: James Chaney, Freedom Riders, Andrew Goodman, Coretta Scott King, Martin Luther King, NAACP, Michael Schwerner

MAGAZINES AND NEWSPAPERS: *Fantasy and Science Fiction, Lewiston Sun, Look,* Marvel Comics, *New York Post, New York Sun, New York Times, Newsweek, Playboy, Portland* (Maine) *Press Herald, Publishers Weekly*

MUSICIANS AND BANDS: Andrews Sisters, Joan Baez, The Beatles, Big Bopper (Jay Perry Richardson), Perry Como, Creedence Clearwater Revival, Reverend Gary Davis, Irene Day, Del-Vikings, Bob Dylan, The Four Seasons, Andy Gibb, Merle Haggard, George Harrison, Buddy Holly, Michael Jackson, Wanda Jackson, The Jackson Five, Mungo Jerry, Elton John, John Lennon, Little Richard, Lovin' Spoonful, Madonna, The McCoys, Olivia Newton-John, Phil Ochs, Ozzy Ozbourne, Elvis Presley, Joey Ramone, Lou Reed, Martha Reeves and the Vandellas, The Rivieras, Rolling Stones, Steely Dan, Troy Shondell, Ralph Stanley, The Tokens, Jethro Tull, Richie Valens, Dave Van Ronk, Charlie Watts, Stevie Wonder, ZZ Top

SONGS: "Amazing Grace," "Blowin' in the Wind," "Born to Run," "Bridge over Troubled Water," "Buy Me Another Round You Booger You," "California Sun," "Careless Love," "Come Go with Me," "Crazy Train," "Drive My Car," "Gangsta Dream 19," "Hang On Sloopy," "A Hard Rain's a-Gonna Fall," "Heat Wave," "Hesitation Blues," "Hey Jude," "Hey Nineteen," "Honky Tonk Woman," "I Ain't Marchin' Anymore," "I Left My Heart in San Francisco," "I Shall Be Released," "In the Summertime," "John Henry," "The Lion Sleeps Tonight," "Maid of Constant Sorrow," "Moonlight Becomes You," "Night and Day," "Nineteenth Nervous Breakdown," "Ninety-nine Bottles of Beer on the Wall," "Paint It Black," "She Loves You," "Silent Night," "Someone Saved My Life Tonight," "Stardust," "Stormy Weather," "Streets of Campara," "Sugar Shack," "That's Amore," "This Time," "Velcro Fly," "Visions of Johanna," "Walk on the Wild Side," "What Child Is This?"

NOVEL, CARTOON, FILM, TV, FOLKTALE, AND MYTHICAL CHARACTERS: Ali Baba, Alice (of Wonderland), Archie, King Arthur, Frodo Baggins, Beowulf, James Bond, Edith Bunker, C3PO, Captain America, Carrie, Pa Cartwright (Adam, Hoss, and Little Joe), Hopalong Cassidy, Misery Chastain,

Mr. Chips, Chucky, George M. Cohan, Barnabas Collins, Creature from the Black Lagoon, Croesus, Cujo, Daisy Mae, Marshal Dillon, Doctor Doom, Dorothy (of Oz) and Aunt Em, Dracula, Excalibur, Falstaff, The Fantastic Four, Faust, Huck Finn (Miss Watson and Widow Douglas), Foghorn Leghorn, Frankenstein, Samwise Gamgee, Goldilocks and the Three Bears, Flash Gordon, Prince Hal, Hamlet, Hansel and Gretel, Mina Harker, Sherlock Holmes, Howdy Doody, The Incredible Hulk, Jughead, Keebler Elves, Little Nell, Little Red Riding Hood, Jacob Marley, Silas Marner, Miss Marple, Harpo Marx, Perry Mason, Maturin, Travis McGee, Minotaur, Mordred, Mork, Morlocks, Mickey Mouse, Minnie Mouse, Mutt and Jeff, Mr. Mxyzptlk, Annie Oakley, Olive Oyl, Professor Peabody, Pied Piper, Hercule Poirot, Popeye, Porky Pig, Harry Potter, Sergeant Preston and his dog King, Rastus "Coon," Regulators, Ratso Rizzo, Robbie the Robot, Santa Claus, Ebenezer Scrooge, The Shadow, Shardik, Sheena Queen of the Jungle, Paul Sheldon, Luke Skywalker, Spider-Man, Greg Stillson, Superman, Sylvester the Cat, Tinker Bell, Tony the Tiger, Trampas, Toto, Tweedledee and Tweedledum, Tweety Bird, Darth Vader, Vulcans, Lucy Westenra, White Rabbit, Annie Wilkes, Wimpy, Witch Hazel, Wizard of Oz, Yogi Bear, Yorick

POLITICAL FIGURES (PAST AND PRESENT): Jimmy Carter, CIA, Bill Clinton, Diem brothers (Ngo Dinh Nhu, Ngo Dinh Diem), Papa Doc Duvalier, Herman Goering, Al Gore, Ulysses S. Grant, Alexander Hamilton, Adolf Hitler, Andrew Jackson, Lyndon Johnson, John F. Kennedy, Robert Kennedy, Ed Koch, Abraham Lincoln, Henry Cabot Lodge, Nazi Party, Richard Nixon, Ytzhak Rabin, Ronald Reagan, Nelson Rockefeller, United Nations, George Washington.

RADIO, TELEVISION, AND SPORTS PERSONALITIES: Muhammad Ali, David Brinkley, Bill Buckner, Roger Clemens, Howard Cosell, Walter Cronkite, Bill Cullen, Joe DiMaggio, Bobby Doerr, Dwight Evans, Alan Freed, Dave Garroway, Lefty Grove, Howdy Doody, Chet Huntley, Michael Jordan, Frank Malzone, Frank McGee, Mets, Joe Namath, Don Pardo, Mel Parnell, John Pesky, Red Sox, Jackie Robinson, Babe Ruth, Buffalo Bob Smith, Ed Sullivan, Texas Rangers, Ted Williams, Yankees, Carl Yastrzemski

TV PROGRAMS: *Bonanza, Cheyenne, Concentration, Danger UXB, Dark Shadows, The Ed Sullivan Show, Flash Gordon, General Hospital, The Guiding Light, Howdy Doody, The Huntley-Brinkley Report, Kingdom Hospital, Maverick, Million Dollar Movie, Mork & Mindy, The Price Is Right, Rose Red, Roseanne, Sergeant Preston of the Yukon, Star Search, Star Trek, Sugarfoot, Warner Brothers Cartoons, Yogi Bear*

WRITERS, POETS, PLAYWRIGHTS, AND ARTISTS: Ansel Adams, Richard Adams, Charles Addams, Poul Anderson, Clark Ashton-Smith, Isaac Asimov, W. H. Auden, L. Frank Baum, Thomas Hart Benton, Hieronymus Bosch, Ray

Bradbury, Max Brand, Elizabeth Barrett Browning, Robert Browning, Thomas Carlyle, Lewis Carroll, Miguel de Cervantes, Raymond Chandler, Agatha Christie, Lee Brown Coye, Stephen Crane, Rodney Crowell, Charles Dickens, Emily Dickinson, Gordon Dickson, Allen Drury, T. S. Eliot, Harlan Ellison, Ralph Ellison, William Faulkner, F. Scott Fitzgerald, John Fowles, Robert Frost, Zane Grey, Thomas Hardy, Nathaniel Hawthorne, Shirley Hazzard, Robert Heinlein, Ernest Hemingway, William Hope Hodgson, Ray Hogan, Robert E. Howard, Aldous Huxley, John Irving, James Joyce, Stephen King, Murray Leinster, Elmore Leonard, C. S. Lewis, Jack London, H. P. Lovecraft, John D. MacDonald, Archibald MacLeish, Norman Mailer, Henri Matisse, Ed McBain, Mary McCarthy, Grace Metalious, Michelangelo, Patrick O'Brian, Frank O'Hara, Wayne D. Overholser, Charles Palliser, Maxwell Perkins, Edgar Allan Poe, David Rabe, Rembrandt, William Shakespeare, Irwin Shaw, John Steinbeck, Rex Stout, Algernon Swinburne, Henry David Thoreau, James Thurber, J. R. R. Tolkien, Mark Twain, John Updike, Vincent van Gogh, H. G. Wells, Owen Wister, Thomas Wolfe, Virginia Woolf, Herman Wouk, W. B. Yeats

BOOKS, STORIES, POEMS, AND PAINTINGS: *Alice's Adventures in Wonderland; The Bachman Books;* Bible; *The Caine Mutiny; Canterbury Tales; Carrie;* "The Charge of the Light Brigade"; *A Christmas Carol; The Collector; Complete Poetical Works of Robert Browning; The Dead Zone; Desperation; The Door into Summer; Dracula;* "Epistle to Be Left in the Earth"; "Fall of the House of Usher"; *Fahrenheit 451;* "Fra Lippo Lippi"; *The Garden of Earthly Delights* (painting); *Gormenghast; Hearts in Atlantis; How the Grinch Stole Christmas; Huckleberry Finn; Insomnia; Invisible Man; The Island of Dr. Moreau; It;* "The Lady or the Tiger"; *The Lion, the Witch and the Wardrobe; The Lord of the Rings; The Magus; Marjorie Morningstar;* "Masque of the Red Death"; *Misery; Moby-Dick; The Mystery of Edwin Drood; On Writing; Pet Sematary; Peter Pan; The Quincunx; Roads to Everywhere; 'Salem's Lot;* "The Second Coming"; *Seven Steps to Positive Thinking; Shardik; The Shining; Sign of the Four; The Stand; A Study in Scarlet; Tess of the D'Urbervilles; The Troubled Air;* "Tyger"; *Ulysses; The Virginian;* "The Waste Land"; *Watership Down; We Have Always Lived in the Castle; The Wizard of Oz;* "The Wreck of the Hesperus"; *Yankee Highways*

APPENDIX VI:
MAPS OF MID-WORLD,
END-WORLD, AND OUR WORLD

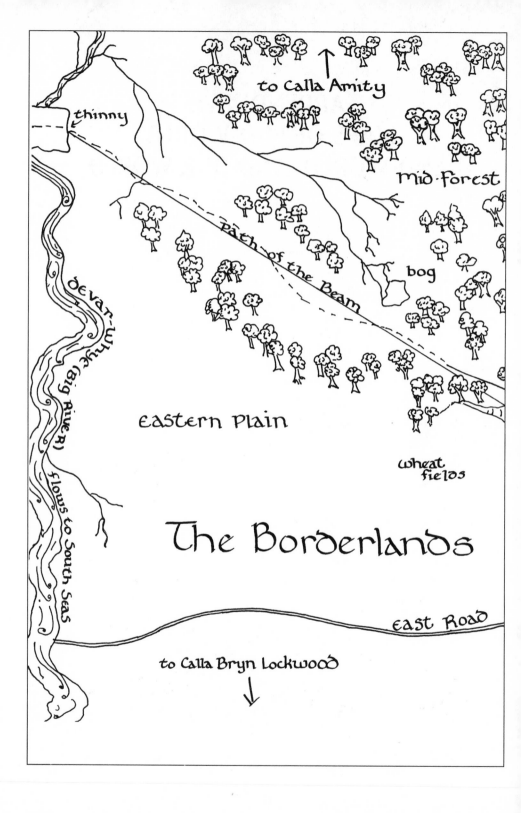

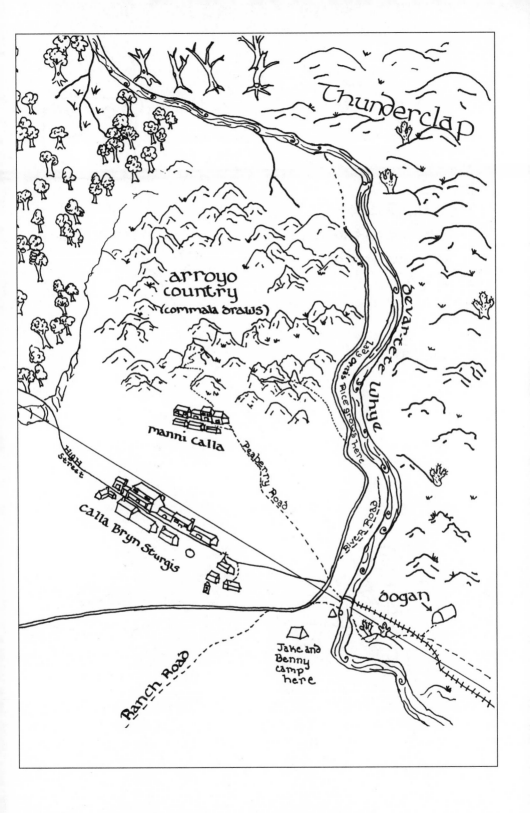

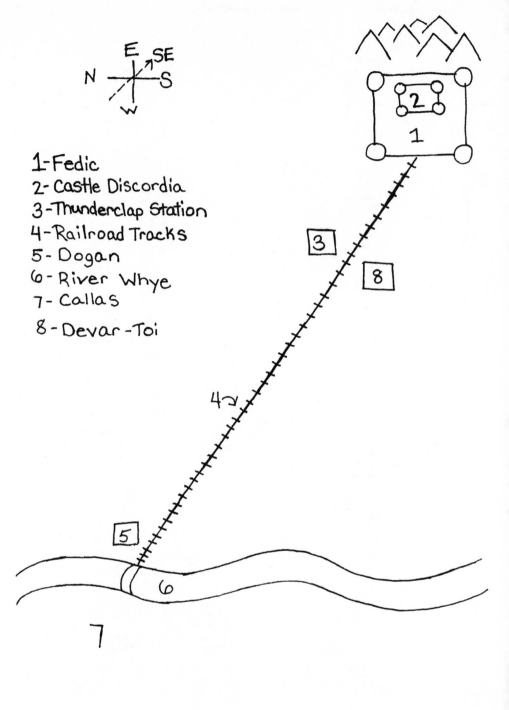

N E SE S W

1-Fedic
2- Castle Discordia
3-Thunderclap Station
4-Railroad Tracks
5- Dogan
6- River Whye
7- Callas
8- Devar-Toi

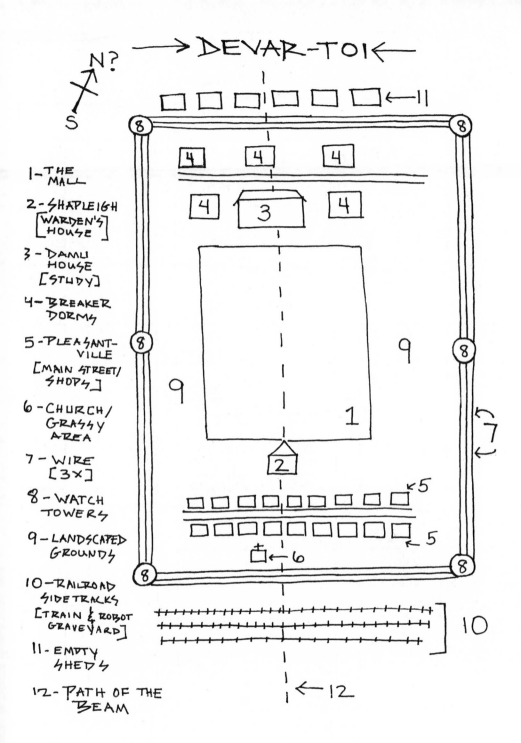

DEVAR-TOI →←

N?

S

1 — THE MALL

2 — SHAPLEIGH [WARDEN'S HOUSE]

3 — DAMLI HOUSE [STUDY]

4 — BREAKER DORMS

5 — PLEASANTVILLE [MAIN STREET/ SHOPS]

6 — CHURCH/ GRASSY AREA

7 — WIRE [3X]

8 — WATCH TOWERS

9 — LANDSCAPED GROUNDS

10 — RAILROAD SIDETRACKS [TRAIN & ROBOT GRAVEYARD]

11 — EMPTY SHEDS

12 — PATH OF THE BEAM

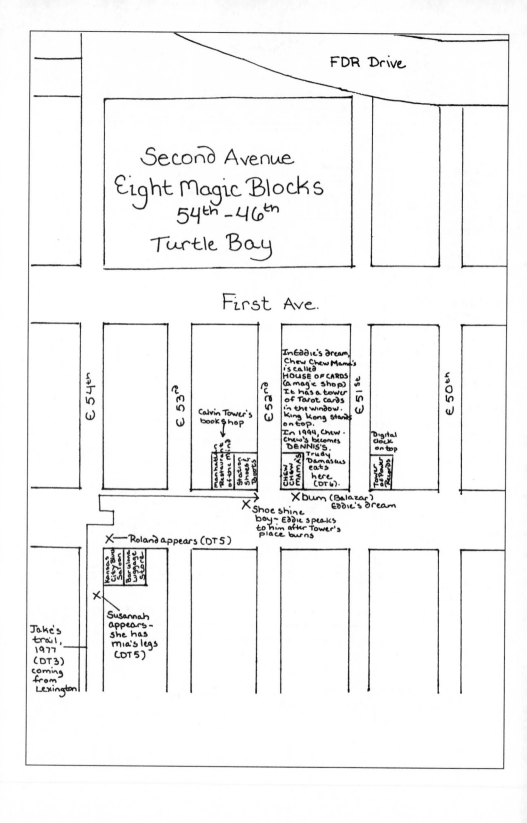

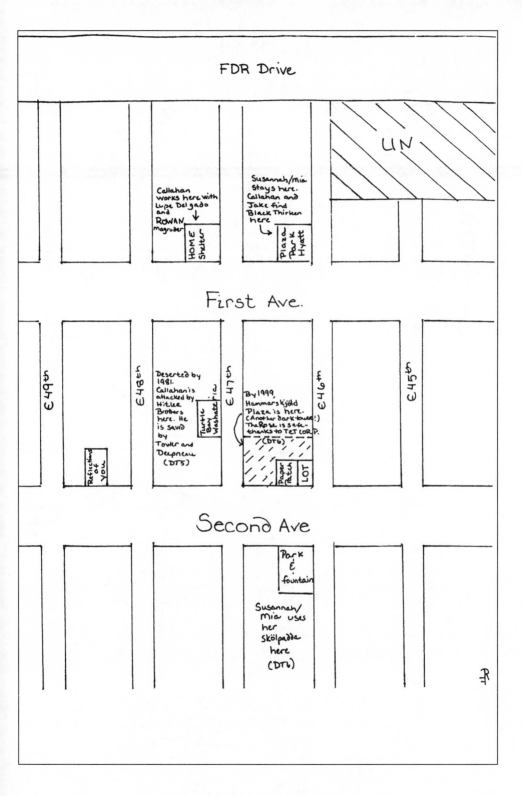

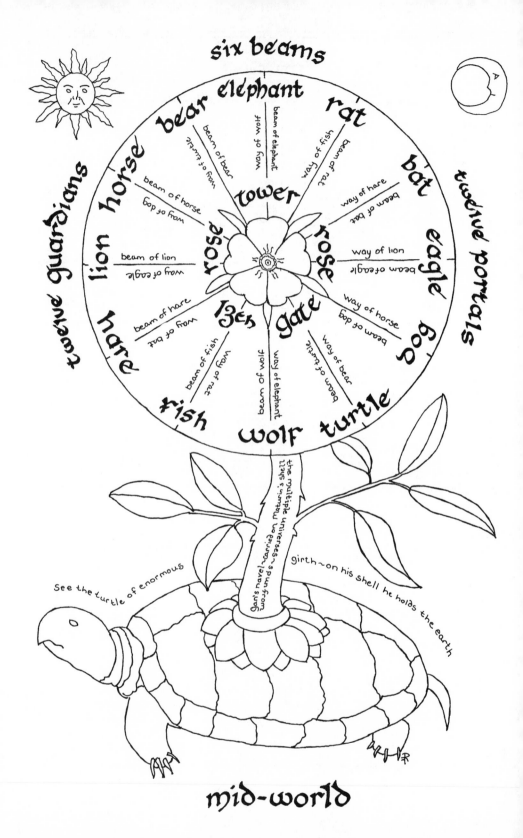

APPENDIX VII:
READING GROUP GUIDES

The Dark Tower I: The Gunslinger, Revised Edition, 2003

1. Who is Roland of Gilead? What is his ancestry? How does his personal history reflect the history of his land?
2. In many ways, Roland reminds us of the semimythical gunslingers of the late-nineteenth-century American West. Like them, he is simultaneously part lawman and part outlaw. Are there any figures from folklore, history, or film that remind you of Roland? How is he similar to them and how is he different? Would you call Roland a hero or an antihero?
3. Why does the term *man in black* have such emotional impact? What images do we automatically associate with such a figure? Do you believe that Walter is actually human? Is he demonic? What role does the demonic play in Roland's world?
4. One of Roland's favorite phrases is "the world has moved on." What does this mean? What do you think Roland's world was like before it moved on?
5. Throughout *The Gunslinger,* we are struck by the number of similarities between our world and Roland's world. The townsfolk of Tull know the words to the Beatles' song "Hey Jude," and they use *bocks* (bucks, or dollars) as their currency. Jake's description of New York (recounted while he is under hypnosis) reminds Roland of the mythical city of Lud, and the tunnels beneath the Cyclopean Mountains contain the ruins of a subway system that remind Jake of home. How do you explain these similarities? What is the relationship between Roland's world and our world?
6. Although Sylvia Pittston claims to be a woman of God, she is actually one of the most actively destructive characters found in *The Gunslinger.* As Roland's lover Allie says, Pittston's religion is poison. What role does Pittston play in the novel? Have you come across Pittston-like characters in any of King's other fiction? How do you explain the discrepancy between Pittston's professed role as a preacher and her actual allegiance to the man in black and the Crimson King? What are the divisions between good and evil in Roland's world?
7. Nort, the weed-eater Roland meets in Tull, suffers a terrible fate. After being poisoned by the addictive devil grass, he is resurrected by the sinister Man in Black, only to be later crucified by Sylvia Pittston and her followers. The terms *resurrection* and *crucifixion* automatically make us reflect upon the biblical account of Jesus' crucifixion and resurrection, and the belief that, come Judgment Day, the dead will rise and be held accountable for the good and evil

of their lives. Why do you think King includes these references? Why do you think Nort is crucified *after* being resurrected, a direct reversal of the biblical events?

8. Nort is not the only sacrificial figure found in *The Gunslinger*. Why does the Man in Black call Jake Roland's "Isaac"? What does this tell us about Roland, about his relationship to the man in black, and his relationship to the Dark Tower?

9. When do the characters of *The Gunslinger* use High Speech? Would it be justified to call this a sacred language? What languages, in our world, are associated with religious ceremonies, ritual, and magic? What makes them special? Can these same attributes be said to belong to High Speech?

10. In literature, settings often serve a symbolic purpose. Throughout *The Gunslinger,* the landscapes Roland traverses are described as hostile, dry "purgatorial wastes." Even relatively lush environments, such as the willow jungle, are full of dangerous forces, both mortal and demonic. In terms of its history, why is Roland's land so dangerous and desolate? What is the symbolic significance of this harshness?

11. Although the setting of the Dark Tower series reminds us of a cowboy western, King's Tower novels draw from many other literary genres, including gothic fiction, science fiction, horror, and medieval Romance. Can you identify these elements in *The Gunslinger*?

12. One of Stephen King's central inspirations for writing *The Gunslinger* was Robert Browning's poem "Childe Roland to the Dark Tower Came." The Victorians who first read "Childe Roland" saw it as a story of heroism and duty. For them, it was a Romance in which a brave knight attempted to make a pilgrimage even though all before him had failed. More recent critics, however, have read the poem in much more psychological terms. They interpret the landscape that Browning's Roland traverses as a reflection of the character's fears, terrors, and preoccupations—in other words, as a reflection of his internal state. In this interpretation, the knight's search for the Dark Tower ultimately leads him to the center of himself, and to the truth of self-awareness. Do you think that either of these interpretations can be applied to *The Gunslinger,* in all or in part? Is Roland's story a heroic tale of a knight on a quest, or can Roland's travails be read as an allegory for the decisions, strivings, successes, failures, and personal betrayals we all face?

13. Ancient warrior cultures developed strict codes of honor and duty, which we now refer to as *heroic codes*. Great heroes were expected to be courageous, fearless, and headstrong. They had little or no regard for personal safety and in fact often acted rashly. What a warrior's peers thought of him mattered above all else, and he thought little or nothing about personal conscience (in the modern sense) or the well-being of the soul. The warrior did not aim to enter Heaven, but to become legendary. Personal honor, family honor, and/or loyalty to the king or chieftain were what made a man worthwhile. Did the gunslingers of Gilead obey a Christian code or a heroic code? What about Roland? Is there a shift between these two codes as the novel progresses?

14. Judeo-Christian culture is primarily a guilt-based culture. In other words, people believe that God alone has the right to judge sins, and that He knows our guilt or our innocence, no matter what the world thinks of us. If an individ-

ual is innocent, he (in theory at least) can hold his head high, even though his reputation has been ruined. What matters is personal conscience. Hence, by the same token, if an individual believes he has committed a crime, he will be consumed by guilt, even if no one else ever discovers what has been done. Warrior cultures, on the other hand, were often shame-based cultures. In shame-based cultures, an individual must avoid "losing face," since the disgrace he or she accrues reflects not only on the individual, but upon the family and the lineage. What a person thinks of himself matters less than what society thinks of him. Did Cort train apprentice gunslingers using guilt or shame? What does this tell us about gunslinger culture? At his hanging, does Hax show either guilt or shame? Why? What kind of culture does he seem to reflect? Does Roland primarily experience guilt or shame? Does this change over the course of the novel? Why, in terms of Roland's personal development (or lack of it), might this happen?

15. Take a look at the tarot reading Walter does for Roland in the golgotha. How many of these cards are from the traditional tarot deck? Are there any others that seem to be versions of traditional cards? Which cards did King create anew? Which ones actually come from other sources? (Hint: Take a look at T. S. Eliot's poem *The Waste Land*.) What is your interpretation of this reading? Why do you think Walter burns the card of Life?

16. At the front of the revised edition of *The Gunslinger* (2003), King adds a quote from Thomas Wolfe's novel *Look Homeward, Angel*. (This quote did not appear at the front of the previous edition.) What emotions does this quote arouse in us? Why do you think King added it? Does it affect your interpretation of the novel?

The Dark Tower II: The Drawing of the Three

1. How does King's writing style change between *The Gunslinger* and *The Drawing of the Three*? What about his storytelling process? What are the strengths of each approach?

2. In the prologue of *The Drawing of the Three*, Roland has a dream in which he becomes the human embodiment of Walter's tarot card the Sailor. Why does he consider this a good dream? What is actually happening to him, and with what results? Do you believe that this is an existential punishment for his previous actions, a violent joke played upon him by the Man in Black, or simply a chance event?

3. What is ka, and how does it affect Roland's life? Does it seem to imply predestination? Are human beings trapped by ka, or do we retain free will?

4. Describe the three magic doors. How do they work? Does ka have anything to do with their existence?

5. What disembodied voices echo inside Roland's mind? What part do they play in Roland's internal monologue/dialogue? Are they forces for good or for ill? In turn, how does Roland *become* a voice in the minds of other people? Does this affect your interpretation of the voices inside Roland's consciousness?

6. Unlike the action of *The Gunslinger*, which takes place in Roland's world, much of the action of *The Drawing of the Three* takes place in our world. In fact, many of Eddie's problems, and most of Detta/Odetta's problems, have

their roots in U.S. culture and U.S. history. What social, economic, and cultural problems of 1980s America touched Eddie Dean's life? What long-range effect did the Vietnam War have upon Henry Dean and, in turn, upon Eddie? How did racial hatred, segregation, and then the Civil Rights Movement affect Odetta Holmes's life? What about Detta Walker's?

7. Why is Eddie Dean willing to put his life at risk for his brother, Henry? Does Henry deserve this kind of loyalty?

8. What, in Roland's treatment of Eddie, shows that Roland comes from a warrior culture, not our culture? What part does patriarchal lineage play in gunslinger culture? Why would this be especially alien to Eddie?

9. Some warriors cultivate battle frenzy, using this altered state of consciousness to achieve feats that would otherwise be almost impossible. A famous historical example of this phenomenon can be found in the Norse berserkers. What is Roland's battle frenzy like? What about Eddie's? Is *frenzy* the right word?

10. Why did Odetta's father refuse to tell her about his past? What metaphor does King use to describe Dan Holmes's protective silence? How does Dan Holmes's treatment of his past contribute to Odetta's fragmentation?

11. How does Roland help to cure Odetta? Why is his timing so significant?

12. Were Jack Mort's attacks upon Odetta racially motivated?

13. How does Roland assess the people of our world—both those he sees on the plane and those he deals with while controlling Jack Mort's body? What does this say about the difference between a world that has "moved on" and one that has not?

14. The second section of *The Drawing of the Three* (the one immediately following "The Prisoner") is entitled "Shuffle." One of the images that King is conjuring is that of a cardsharp, shuffling a deck of cards. Why does King use this image? What kind of deck is being shuffled? What event, from *The Gunslinger,* does this remind us of? Why is the final section of the book entitled "Final Shuffle"?

15. The verb *to draw* has many meanings and can be used in many contexts. Roland, Eddie, and Detta all draw guns. Roland draws his two companions into his world. However, the verb *to draw* can also be used to describe the action of drawing poison from a wound so that the wound can heal. What role does this kind of drawing play in *The Drawing of the Three*?

16. What role does Jake play in this novel? Why is this so significant in terms of Roland's development?

The Dark Tower III: The Waste Lands

1. Between the end of *The Drawing of the Three* and the beginning of *The Waste Lands,* the relationships among Roland, Susannah, and Eddie shift. Describe these changes. What causes them? Does Eddie now trust Roland? Does Susannah?

2. What is the gunslinger litany? What worldview does it imply—from what a gunslinger should honor to how he/she should attack his/her enemies?

3. In what ways are Roland's new friends much like his deadly old friends? What happened to those old friends? Do you think the same fate awaits Roland's new friends?

4. What is ka-tet? How do the forces of ka-tet bind individuals together, and how do they ultimately bind a society together?

5. Describe the metaphysical map that Roland draws at the beginning of the novel. What is its linchpin? What sits upon its circumference? What forces hold the world together? What part did the Great Old Ones play in the devising of this map? Do you think that the forces described there predate them? Why or why not? Does this map describe the actual origins of the world or of the linked worlds? What role did North Central Positronics play in the making of this world, or in the remaking of it?

6. What are the Drawers? Are they objective places—places that you could find on a map—or is their existence more subjective? Have you encountered any such places in your life? If so, what are they? Do you have a special term for such places?

7. What paradox tears Roland's mind apart at the outset of the novel? What causes it? What eases his suffering? Why is this significant?

8. What voices does Jake hear in the Vacant Lot, just before he sees the Rose? What happens to him when he actually sees this flower? How does Jake's vision of the Rose differ from Eddie's vision of the Tower amid its sea of roses?

9. What is the White?

10. While contemplating the rose, Jake sees that it grows out of alien purple grass. Roland sees the same purple grass during his vision in the golgotha, at the end of *The Gunslinger*. Why does King seem to want us to compare these otherwise dissimilar visions? What is he telling us about the nature of the Rose?

11. What is the difference between Jake's door, labeled *The Boy,* and the beach doors?

12. The scene in which Roland and his new ka-tet cross the bridge into Lud eerily echoes the passage in *The Gunslinger* where Jake falls to his death. Compare these two scenes. What do they tell us about the changes happening within Roland?

13. The third book of the Dark Tower series takes its title from T. S. Eliot's long poem "The Waste Land." Two themes that thread through Eliot's poem are fragmentation and alienation—the fragmentation of modern culture and its inevitable loss of meaning, and the sense of alienation that individuals experience in reaction to this. (It must be remembered that "The Waste Land" was written in the aftermath of World War I, when Europe was still in shock over the death and destruction caused by modern weaponry.) How does King's novel reflect these themes? How does this fragmentation extend to the psyches of the characters themselves, and even to the computerized personalities of machines?

14. In his notes on "The Waste Land," T. S. Eliot stated that he was extremely influenced by the Grail legend. What is the legend of the Grail? Do you think it influenced Stephen King when he wrote *The Waste Lands*?

15. Eleven dimensions, worlds made out of vibrating strings, parallel universes that contain alternative versions of you . . . Sounds like another Dark Tower book? It's not, but it does seem as though the scientific community is finally taking Jake Chambers seriously. There *are* other worlds than these. For a fascinating description of string theory (and as a way to begin discussing the sim-

ilarities between contemporary physics and the multiple worlds of the Dark Tower series), visit the following Web sites: www.pbs.org/nova/elegant (a terrific introduction) www.bbc.co.uk/science/horizon/2001/parallelunitrans.shtml (another great introduction) http://superstringtheory.com (for brave folks who are used to technical language) www.scientificamerican.com (in the "search" section, type *Parallel Universes*)

The Dark Tower IV: Wizard and Glass

1. Why, do you think, did the Great Old Ones build Blaine? What purpose did he serve in their world? What do you imagine the Old Ones' world was like?

2. While riding in Blaine, Eddie thinks to himself, *Not all is silent in the halls of the dead and the rooms of ruin. Even now some of the stuff the Old Ones left behind still works. Ant that's really the horror of it, wouldn't you say? Yes. The exact horror of it.* How does Eddie's statement prefigure the coming action? Does his observation hold true for the first three novels of the series?

3. What is a thinny? What effect does it have on those near it? Is it alive? How does the image of the thinny help to bridge the two parts of *Wizard and Glass*—the section that takes place in Topeka and the one that takes place in Hambry?

4. Why does Roland say that in Hambry "the waters on top and the waters down below seemed to run in different directions"?

5. Ka is a wheel; its one purpose is to turn and (inevitably) repeat. In what ways have we seen the wheel of ka turn so far in the series?

6. What is the story of Lord Perth, which we learned about in *The Waste Lands*? How did that myth play out in the novel? How does it continue to resonate throughout *Wizard and Glass*? Do you think the theme of the Lord Perth tale is also one of the themes of the Dark Tower series?

7. Who is Rhea of the Cöos? What role does she play in the novel? How does she compare to Roland's other major enemies—the Man in Black and Sylvia Pittston? If Rhea had been a male character, would she have been as convincing or as formidable? Why or why not?

8. What is the Wizard's Rainbow? What do we know about it? How many of the balls are still in existence, and why are they said to be alive and hungry? What is the relationship between the White, which Roland and the other gunslingers serve, and the spectrum of colors that make up the Wizard's Rainbow?

9. The imagery surrounding Maerlyn's Grapefruit is often sexual; even its color is described as "labial pink." Why does King use this imagery? What is the relationship between the Grapefruit and emotions such as desire, jealousy, and vengeance? How do these emotions drive the action of Roland's Hambry adventure? How did they begin his journey into manhood, even down to the early winning of his guns?

10. How is Roland's experience of Maerlyn's Grapefruit different from those of the other people who have it in their possession? Why do you think this is so? What visions does Roland have while the ball is in his possession? How does the ball lead to his downfall?

11. The tale of Hambry begins under a Kissing Moon and ends under a Demon

Moon. Why is this significant? How does the transition from one of these moons to the other reflect the darkening of the novel's atmosphere?

12. At the beginning of the Hambry portion of *Wizard and Glass,* Susan Delgado must "prove" her honesty. What does this mean? In what other ways does Susan continue to prove her honesty throughout the book? What other characters prove themselves to be honest? Which characters prove to be dishonest?

13. *For if it is ka, it'll come like a wind, and your plans will stand before it no more than a barn before a cyclone.* In what ways have we seen Pat Delgado's description of ka hold true, both in this novel and in the three preceding ones?

14. How would you describe Cuthbert Allgood? What does Roland love about him? What about him angers Roland? In what ways is he like Eddie? Is this similarity also ka?

15. What do you think the relationship is between Walter (also known as the Man in Black), Marten, Flagg, Fannin, and Maerlyn? What part do these nasty characters play in this novel?

16. In what ways does gunslinger culture actually inflame the rebellion led by Farson?

17. When Roland first meets Susan Delgado, King tells us, "Roland was far from the relentless creature he would eventually become, but the seeds of that relentlessness were there—small, stony things that would, in their time, grow to trees with deep roots . . . and bitter fruit." Why does King tell us this? Do you agree with this assessment of Roland's character?

18. Where do we see the sigul of the open, staring eye? Why is it so sinister? How does it connect Hambry, Topeka, and the Green Palace? What does it tell us about Roland's world?

The Dark Tower V: Wolves of the Calla

1. In his author's note, Stephen King acknowledges the influence that several films and film directors have had upon the Dark Tower series. Most notably, he mentions Sergio Leone's spaghetti westerns staring Clint Eastwood (*A Fistful of Dollars; For a Few Dollars More; The Good, the Bad, and the Ugly*), and Akira Kurosawa's classic *The Seven Samurai.* He also gives credit to John Sturges's 1960 western (a remake of the Kurosawa film), *The Magnificent Seven.* Can you describe the influence that any or all of these films have had upon the Dark Tower series as a whole and upon *Wolves of the Calla* in particular?

2. At the beginning of Chapter I of *Wolves of the Calla,* Eddie Dean reflects upon the old Mejis saying *Time is a face on the water.* Do his theories explain why time passes differently in our world and in the borderlands? Why or why not? Do his observations hold true for you, personally? Have you ever experienced such time-dilation or time-contraction?

3. Why are Eddie, Jake, Susannah, and Roland so wary of Andy when they first meet him? Why is this significant, both in terms of our ka-tet's history and in terms of the history of Roland's world?

4. What is happening to Susannah Dean's personality? How did this come to

pass? Do you think this process is part of her ka? Given her condition, what do you think will happen to our ka-tet in the final two books of the series?

5. Who are the roonts? How did they become roont? Do you think that the roonts understand what has happened to them? What, from the text, makes you say this?

6. What power do the Wolves ultimately serve? Why are the people of the Calla so afraid to fight them? Can you understand their fear?

7. What mythical event do the Sisters of Oriza honor? What purpose do they serve in terms of plot? Do you think that King is trying to make us reexamine traditional ideas about men and women?

8. Describe Black Thirteen. What is its history? What role does it play in the book? How does it compare to Maerlyn's Grapefruit, which figured prominently in *Wizard and Glass*?

9. What is todash? Why is it dangerous to travel todash? Who are the Manni? Why do they believe that todash is "the holiest of rites and most exalted of states"?

10. What role does the number 19 play in *Wolves of the Calla*? Where have we seen it before? (Hint: You'll need a 2003 edition of *The Gunslinger* to answer the second part of this question.)

11. Describe the Cave of Voices (also known as Doorway Cave). What is its function? Is it magical or mechanical? What voices do the various characters hear when they are inside the cave? In what way does the "demon" or "mechanism" of this cave expose unconscious fear or guilt? If you were suddenly transported to the Cave of Voices, who would come to speak to you?

12. What is the meaning of the term *commala*? Why would the Commala Song be so important in a rice-growing community? Does the Commala Song—and its accompanying dance—remind you of any ceremonies from our world?

13. Compare the tale of Lady Oriza to the story of Lord Perth, which we learned about in *The Waste Lands*. What do they have in common? How do they differ? What themes do they share with the Dark Tower series as a whole?

14. Where, in King's fiction, have we met Father Callahan before? Why do you think King decided to link a non–Dark Tower book so closely to the Dark Tower series?

15. As we all know from experience, few people are completely good or completely evil. Even the most annoying individual can surprise us with a selfless act, and an otherwise admirable person can sometimes shock us with an angry word or an unfair judgment. The same goes for well-drawn, believable characters. Make a list of the most important characters we meet in Calla Bryn Sturgis. Who is "good"? Who is "bad"? Who would you say is "brave" and whom would you call "cowardly"? Now take a look at any scenes where these characters exhibit unexpected, opposite tendencies. How does the author make us sympathize with the wicked or feel disappointment with the opinions and actions of the "good"? How does King let us see both the savory and unsavory traits of each character?

16. Roland's world contains both machinery and magic. Most of the machinery we've encountered so far has been hostile, but the magic is more ambiguous. In *Wolves of the Calla*, the most potent magical objects are the Rose and

Black Thirteen. Is one completely good and the other completely evil? Why or why not? What greater forces do these objects represent? Do you think that they symbolize a struggle found in our world as well?

17. Both fans and reviewers often refer to King's large body of work as "the Stephen King Universe" or "the Stephen King Multiverse." How do you interpret these terms? What part does the Dark Tower play in this universe? What part does our world play in this universe? Do you think that Stephen King's realistic fiction should also be classed as part of the "Stephen King Universe"?

18. Human beings have always craved magical, supernatural tales. In fact, many of the earliest and greatest of our stories—*The Epic of Gilgamesh, Beowulf,* and *The Odyssey,* to name just a few—tell about man's interaction with the unseen worlds. Although "official" culture denies that telepathy, spirit worlds, and magic exist, such ideas still thrive as part of modern folklore. Why do you think that magical and supernatural tales are still popular? Do you think their appeal has grown over the past few years? Why? Do these kinds of tales serve a particular purpose, either socially or personally? Do you think the appeal of the Dark Tower series lies in the way it successfully weaves together both technology and magic?

The Dark Tower VI: Song of Susannah

1. Stephen King placed two unusual facing pages at the beginning of *Song of Susannah*. At the center of the left-hand page (which is otherwise blank) is the word *REPRODUCTION*. At the center of the right-hand page is one large number—*19*. However, in the bottom left-hand corner of the right-hand page is the tiny number *99*. What effect is King striving for? What effect do these pages have upon you as a reader?

2. How does King shift our mood from one of elation, when the Wolves are defeated near the end of *Wolves of the Calla,* to one of anxiety at the beginning of *Song of Susannah*? What series of tragedies—and inexplicable events—takes place?

3. What is a Beamquake? What effect does it have on the borderlands? What is its significance, as far as our characters' quest is concerned?

4. Who, or what, is Mia? How does her appearance (and disappearance) drive the action of *Song of Susannah*? In what ways does her history intertwine with Roland's?

5. When the Manni help Roland, Eddie, Jake, and Callahan open the Unfound Door, they all expect that it will open onto New York City in 1999, and then onto Stoneham, Maine, in 1977. Eddie and Roland are supposed to follow Susannah into the Big Apple, and Jake and Callahan are supposed to pursue Calvin Tower in Maine. What goes wrong? What series of unexpected events takes place? In your opinion, who or what is behind this change of plan?

6. What is Susannah's can-tah? How do you think it came to Susannah? With what force is it aligned? Have you ever encountered a similar type of object in any of King's other fiction? (Hint: Take a look at the novel *Desperation.*) If so, how does it differ from Susannah's can-tah? What does this say about the forces of the White and the Outer Dark in the Stephen King universe?

7. What is Susannah's Dogan? What part does it play in *Song of Susannah*?

How does it link this novel with *Wolves of the Calla*? Is Susannah's Dogan completely imaginary? Is the machinery within it completely under Susannah's control? Why or why not?

8. What are Demon Elementals? What role do they play in our tet's adventures? Why do you think that King waited until *Song of Susannah* to tell us about them? How do they affect your view of the Guardians? How do they affect your vision of Roland's world?

9. What role does John Cullum play in *Song of Susannah*? Do you think that his appearance is linked to ka? If so, what part does ka play in the battle between the White and the Outer Dark? Does it always play the same role?

10. Unlike most novels, *Song of Susannah* is divided not into chapters but into stanzas, a term we usually associate with songs and poems. Does this name change affect how we read the novel? Does it affect our expectations? At the end of each chapter/stanza, King includes a short rhymed section containing a stave and a response. What do these terms mean, both in and of themselves and in the context of the novel?

11. What is the significance of Susannah's dream at the beginning of the tenth stanza? What visions does she have? What future do they foretell? Can this future be altered, even though the visions show future events in the Keystone World?

12. In stanza eleven, Roland says that Stephen King is the twin of the Rose. Earlier in the Dark Tower series, we were told that the Rose is the twin of the Dark Tower. How do you explain the relationship between King, the Rose, and the Tower?

13. What is the nature of the black shadow that Eddie Dean sees hovering around sai King? What is its possible significance, both in terms of King's life and our tet's quest?

14. Why—according to sai King—did he stop writing the Dark Tower series? What about Roland, in particular, disturbed him? Do you agree or disagree with his assessment of our gunslinger? In your opinion, has Roland changed since King first started writing about him? Were there any other forces that contributed to King's ceasing work on the Dark Tower series?

15. In stanza eleven, King describes his writing process. Does this description surprise you? Why or why not?

16. At the end of *Song of Susannah*, Stephen King includes a section entitled "Coda: Pages from a Writer's Journal." According to the *Oxford English Reference Dictionary*, a coda is a concluding event or series of events. More specifically, it tends to refer to the concluding passage of a piece of music (or of a movement within a piece of music), usually one that acts as an addition to the basic structure. In ballet, the term *coda* refers to the concluding section of a dance. Why do you think King chose to call this section a coda? What does this say about the structure of *Song of Susannah*? What specific event in *Wolves of the Calla* is King consciously echoing?

The Dark Tower VII: The Dark Tower

1. Of all the books in the Dark Tower series, *The Dark Tower* is probably the most action-packed. What are the major crisis points within the novel?

How does King create this dramatic tension? How do you think King goes about planning such a plot? Does the story line just evolve naturally from the characters he imagines?

2. What do Jake and Callahan find in the Dixie Pig? In what ways do the forces of the Outer Dark mock the White? Since the Crimson King is also descended from Arthur Eld, is there some hidden significance in this mockery? If so, what does this say about the nature of the White? What about the nature of the Tower?

3. How does Pere Callahan's death, at the beginning of *The Dark Tower,* refer back to his experiences in *'Salem's Lot*? What does this say about Callahan's ka?

4. What is an aven kal? How is it similar to, or different from, todash?

5. What kind of "walk-in" do Eddie and Roland meet along Route 7 in Lovell? How did this creature enter our world? What connection does King make between walk-ins, the Prim, and the creative imagination?

6. What is the difference between a magical door, which links worlds, and a mechanical one? Where do the different types come from? Is one aligned with the White and one with the Outer Dark? Can such simple labels be put on them? Why?

7. The Breaker prison in Thunderclap is known as the Devar-Toi to the prisoners and Algul Siento to the can-toi and taheen guards. How do these two names express different perspectives on the duties being performed there?

8. The three Breakers who initially aid Roland, Eddie, Susannah, and Jake all come from other places in King's fiction—either from earlier parts of the Dark Tower series or from other stories or novels. Where do these characters come from? Why does King choose these characters? What does this say about the Dark Tower itself, and about the interconnectedness of the "Stephen King Universe"?

9. To describe Pimli Prentiss, Master of the Devar-Toi, Stephen King compares him to Jim Jones, the leader of the People's Temple in Guyana, who convinced his followers to commit mass suicide. What effect does this have upon us? Is King making a wider social statement when he draws this comparison?

10. What is ka-shume? How does this force manifest in the ka of our ka-tet? Can a person escape ka-shume?

11. Although it has its own stark beauty, Roland's world has been devastated by mutations, plagues, and ruinous technology. Now that you've finished the series, how do you think Mid-World relates to our world? Does the company North Central Positronics have any symbolic significance? Is King commenting on contemporary culture? If so, what is he saying? Is his vision completely positive, completely negative, or something in between?

12. In the final two books of the Dark Tower series, King enters the tale directly. In fact, at one point King calls himself the deus ex machina, or the "god out of a machine." What is your reaction to King's appearance in the Dark Tower series? What place does the fictional Stephen King have in the Dark Tower universe? What about the real Stephen King?

13. According to the people of the Tet Corporation, there is a direct link between the Dark Tower series and King's other fiction. What is it? Do you view King's various novels as pieces of a giant jigsaw puzzle, with the Dark Tower nov-

els at the center? Why or why not? If you don't see King's fiction in this way (or if you haven't read many of King's other books), think about any King films you've seen, or any episodes of his various TV series. Are there any themes that seem to repeat?

14. What are the can-toi? What are the taheen? How are they the same and how are they different? King compares the taheen to the monstrous figures found in Hieronymus Bosch's famous triptych, *The Garden of Earthly Delights,* painted circa AD 1500. Take a look at this painting. (It's fairly easy to find. Just type *Hieronymus Bosch,* and *Garden of Earthly Delights,* into your search engine.) As you will see, when the triptych is closed, its outer shutters depict the creation of the world. When the triptych is open, the left panel depicts Adam and Eve and the earthly paradise, the center panel illustrates the world engaged in sinful pleasures, and the right panel (where our taheenlike creatures appear) represents Hell. How are King's creations similar to these painted figures? By drawing this comparison, what other, unspoken comments is King making about End-World, the Devar-Toi, and the Crimson King?

15. At the beginning of *The Dark Tower,* Jake reflects upon one of Roland's sayings. According to our gunslinger, "You needn't die happy when your day comes, but you must die satisfied, for you have lived your life from beginning to end and ka is always served." What does this statement mean? Do you agree or disagree with the philosophy it expresses? Take a look at each member of Roland's ka-tet: Eddie, Susannah, Jake, Oy, Callahan, and even Roland himself. Do any or all of them remain true to this vision?

16. At the beginning of *Wolves of the Calla,* Stephen King includes a section entitled "The Final Argument." According to this introductory piece, each of the seven novels of the Dark Tower series has a subtitle. Moving, in order, from *The Gunslinger* to *Song of Susannah,* these subtitles are "Resumption," "Renewal," "Redemption," "Regard," "Resistance," and "Reproduction." In terms of Roland's quest, what is the meaning of each of these subtitles?

17. Although each of the first six novels of the Dark Tower series has a single-word subtitle, *The Dark Tower* (the final book of the series) has a four-word subtitle. It is "Reproduction, Revelation, Redemption, Resumption." How does this subtitle reflect the action of the novel? How does it interact with the subtitles of the previous novels? If you sit and contemplate the meaning of each of the words in *The Dark Tower*'s subtitle, does it affect your interpretation of the novel's ending? How does it affect your interpretation of Roland's quest?